Karin Sla...

INDELIBLE

FAITHLESS

C

Century · London

This edition published by Century in 2007

Indelible first published in the United Kingdom in 2004 by Century
Faithless first published in the United Kingdom in 2005 by Century

The Random House Group Limited
20 Vauxhall Bridge Road, London, SW1V 2SA

Random House Australia (Pty) Limited
20 Alfred Street, Milsons Point, Sydney
New South Wales 2061, Australia

Random House New Zealand Limited
18 Poland Road, Glenfield, Auckland 10, New Zealand

Random House (Pty) Limited
Isle of Houghton, Corner of Boundary Road & Carse O'Gowrie,
Houghton 2198, South Africa

The Random House Group Limited Reg. No. 954009

www.randomhouse.co.uk

A CIP catalogue record for this book
is available from the British Library

Mixed Sources
Product group from well-managed
forests and other controlled sources
www.fsc.org   Cert no. TT-COC-2139
© 1996 Forest Stewardship Council
FSC

The Random House Group Limited supports The Forest Stewardship Council (FSC),
the leading international forest certification organisation. All our titles that are
printed on Greenpeace approved FSC certified paper carry the FSC logo.
Our paper procurement policy can be found at
www.rbooks.co.uk/environment

Printed and bound in Great Britain by
Clays Ltd, St Ives plc

ISBN 9780099524984

Karin Slaughter grew up in a small south Georgia town and has been writing short stories and novels since she was a child. She is the author of the bestselling novels *Blindsighted*, *Kisscut* and *A Faint Cold Fear* and is currently working on *Faithless*, the fifth novel in the Grant County series.

PRAISE FOR KARIN SLAUGHTER

'Don't read this alone. Don't read this after dark. But do read it'
Mirror

'Karin Slaughter deserves all the praise she gets for her razor-sharp plotting and forensic detail . . . This is crime fiction at its finest'
Michael Connelly, author of *Last Light*

'Another brilliantly chilling tale from Slaughter'
heat

'With *Blindsighted*, Karin Slaughter left a great many mystery writers looking anxiously over their shoulders. With *Kisscut*, she leaves most of them behind'
John Connolly, author of *The Killing Kind*

'A fast-paced and unsettling story . . . A compelling and fluid read'
Daily Telegraph

'Slaughter . . . brings the story to a shattering climax'

Sunday Telegraph

'Pacy and intriguing . . . Karin Slaughter builds up the urgency to fever pitch'

Punch

'Wildly readable . . . deftly crafted, damnably suspenseful and, in the end, deadly serious. Slaughter's plotting is brilliant, her suspense relentless'

Washington Post

'*Blindsighted* is a debut novel of rare quality that grips like a vice from the first page. It's hard to believe this is Karin Slaughter's first outing, so mature is the prose, so taut the suspense, so extreme the engagement with the reader. Against the backdrop of a small Southern town, a terrible drama is played out that will affect Slaughter's readers as much as it affects her characters. A lot of writers are going to read this and weep'

Val McDermid, author of *The Distant Echo*

'Unsparing, exciting, genuinely alarming . . . excellent handling of densely woven plot, rich in interactions, well characterised and as subtle as it is shrewd . . . A formidable debut'

Literary Review

INDELIBLE

FOR D.A.
river deep, mountain high

CHAPTER ONE

Well, look what the cat dragged in," Marla Simms bellowed, giving Sara a pointed look over her silver-rimmed bifocals. The secretary for the police station held a magazine in her arthritic hands, but she set it aside, indicating she had plenty of time to talk.

Sara forced some cheer into her voice, though she had purposefully timed her visit for Marla's coffee break. "Hey, Marla. How're you doing?"

The old woman stared for a beat, a tinge of disapproval putting a crease in her naturally down-turned lips. Sara forced herself not to squirm. Marla had taught the children's Sunday school class at the Primitive Baptist from the day they opened the front doors, and she could still put the fear of God into anyone in town who'd been born after 1952.

She kept her eyes locked on Sara. "Haven't seen you around here in a while."

"Hm," Sara offered, glancing over Marla's shoulder, trying to see into Jeffrey's office. His door was open but he was not behind his desk. The squad room was empty, which meant he was probably in the back. Sara knew she should just walk behind the counter and find him herself—she had done it hundreds of times before—but survivor's instinct kept her from crossing that bridge without first paying the troll.

Marla sat back in her chair, her arms folded. "Nice day out," she said, her tone still casual.

Sara glanced out the door at Main Street, where heat made the asphalt look wavy. The air this morning was humid enough to open every pore on her body. "Sure is."

"And don't you look pretty this morning," Marla continued, indicating the linen dress Sara had chosen after going through nearly every item of clothing in her closet. "What's the occasion?"

"Nothing special," Sara lied. Before she knew what she was doing, she started to fidget with her briefcase, shifting from one foot to the other like she was four instead of nearly forty.

A glimmer of victory flashed in the older woman's eyes. She drew out the silence a bit more before asking, "How's your mama and them?"

"Good," Sara answered, trying not to sound too circumspect. She wasn't naive enough to believe that her private life was no one else's business—in a county as small as Grant, Sara could barely sneeze without the phone ringing from up the street with a helpful "Bless you"—but she would be damned if she'd make it easy for them to gather their information.

"And your sister?"

Sara was about to respond when Brad Stephens saved her by tripping through the front door. The young patrolman caught himself before he fell flat on his face, but the momentum popped his hat off his head and onto the floor at Sara's feet. His gun belt and nightstick flopped under his arms like extra appendages. Behind him, a gaggle of prepubescent children squawked with laughter at his less-than-graceful entrance.

"Oh," Brad said, looking at Sara, then back to the kids, then at Sara again. He picked up his hat, brushing it off with more care than was warranted. She imagined he could not decide which was more embarrassing: eight 10-year-olds laughing at his clumsiness or his former pediatrician fighting an obvious smile of amusement.

Apparently, the latter was worse. He turned back to the group, his voice deeper than usual as if to assert some authority. "This, of course, is the station house, where we do business. Police business. Uh, and we're in the lobby now." Brad glanced at Sara. To call the area where they stood a lobby was a bit of a stretch. The room was barely ten feet by eight, with a cement block wall opposite the glass door at the entrance. A row of photographs showing various squads in the Grant County police force lined the wall to Sara's right, a large portrait in the center showing Mac Anders, the only police officer in the history of the force who had been killed in the line of duty.

Across from the portrait gallery, Marla stood sentry behind a tall beige laminate counter that separated visitors from the squad room. She was not a naturally short woman, but age had made her so by crooking her body into a nearly perfect question mark. Her glasses were usually halfway down the bridge of her nose, and Sara, who wore glasses to read, was always tempted to push them back up. Not that Sara would ever do such a thing. For all Marla knew about everybody and their neighbor—and their dog—in town, not much was known about her. She was a widow with no children. Her husband had died in the Second World War. She had always lived on Hemlock, which was two streets over from Sara's parents. She knitted and she taught Sunday school and worked full-time at the station answering phones and trying to make sense of the mountains of paperwork. These facts hardly offered great insight into Marla Simms. Still, Sara always thought there had to be more to the life of a woman who had lived some eighty-odd years, even if she'd lived all of them in the same house where she had been born.

Brad continued his tour of the station, pointing to the large, open room behind Marla. "Back there's where the detectives and patrol officers like myself conduct their business . . . calls and whatnot. Talking to witnesses, writing reports, typing stuff into the computer, and, uh . . ." His voice trailed off as he finally noticed he was losing his audience. Most of the children could barely see over the counter. Even if they could, thirty empty desks spread out in rows of five with various sizes of filing cabinets between them were hardly attention

3

grabbing. Sara imagined the kids were wishing they had stayed in school today.

Brad tried, "In a few minutes, I'll show y'all the jail where we arrest people. Well, not arrest them," he gave Sara a nervous glance, lest she point out his mistake. "I mean, this is where we take them after we arrest them. Not here, but back in the jail."

Silence fell like a hammer, only to be interrupted by an infectious giggle that started in the back of the group. Sara, who knew most of the children from her practice at the children's clinic, hushed a few with a sharp look. Marla took care of the rest, her swivel chair groaning with relief as she raised herself above the counter. The giggling shut off like a faucet.

Maggie Burgess, a child whose parents gave more credence to her opinion than any child of that age ought to be given, dared to say, "Hey, Dr. Linton," in a grating, singsong voice.

Sara gave a curt nod. "Maggie."

"Uh," Brad began, a deep blush still souring his milk-white complexion. Sara was keenly aware of his gaze lingering a little too long on her bare legs. "Ya'll . . . uh . . . y'all know Dr. Linton."

Maggie rolled her eyes. "Well, *yeah,*" she said, her sarcastic tone reviving a few giggles.

Brad pushed on. "Dr. Linton is also the medical examiner in town, in addition to being a pediatrician." He spoke in an instructional tone, though surely the children already knew this. It was a subject of great humor on the bathroom walls at the elementary school. "I imagine she's here on county business. Dr. Linton?"

"Yes," Sara answered, trying to sound like Brad's peer rather than someone who could remember him bursting into tears at the mere mention of a shot. "I'm here to talk to the Chief of Police about a case we're working on."

Maggie opened her mouth again, probably to repeat something horrible she had heard her mother say about Sara and Jeffrey's relationship, but Marla's chair squeaked and the child remained silent. Sara vowed she would go to church next Sunday just to thank the woman.

Marla's voice was only slightly less condescending than Maggie's when she told Sara, "I'll go check-see if Chief Tolliver is available."

"Thank you," Sara answered, promptly changing her mind about church.

"Well, uh . . ." Brad began, brushing off his hat again. "Why don't we go on back now?" He opened one of the swinging doors in the counter to allow the children through, telling Sara, "Ma'am," giving her a polite nod before following them.

Sara walked over to the photographs on the wall, looking at all the familiar faces. Except for her time at college and working at Grady Hospital in Atlanta, Sara had always lived in Grant County. Most of the men on the wall had played poker with her father at one time or another. The rest of them had been deacons at the church when Sara was a child or had policed football games back when she was a teenager and was desperately infatuated with Steve Mann, the captain of the Chess Club. Before Sara moved away to Atlanta, Mac Anders had caught Sara and Steve making out behind the House of Chilidogs. A few weeks later, his squad car rolled six times during a high-speed chase and Mac was dead.

Sara shuddered, a superstitious fear creeping along her skin like the legs of a spider. She moved on to the next picture, which showed the force when Jeffrey first took over the job as police chief. He had just come from Birmingham and everyone had been skeptical about the outsider, especially when he hired Lena Adams, Grant County's first female cop. Sara studied Lena in the group photograph. Her chin was tilted up in defiance and there was a glint of challenge in her eye. There were more than a dozen women patrolling now, but Lena would always be the first. The pressure must have been enormous, though Sara had never thought of Lena as a role model. As a matter of fact, there were several things about the other woman's personality that Sara found abhorrent.

"He said come on back." Marla stood at the swinging doors. "It's sad, isn't it?" she asked, indicating the picture of Mac Anders.

"I was at school when it happened."

"I won't even tell you what they did to that animal that chased him off the road." There was a note of approval in Marla's voice. Sara knew the suspect had been beaten so severely he'd lost an eye. Ben Walker, the police chief at the time, was a very different cop from Jeffrey.

Marla held open the doors for her. "He's back in interrogation doing some paperwork."

"Thank you," Sara said, taking one more look at Mac before walking through.

The station house had been built in the mid-1930s when the cities of Heartsdale, Madison, and Avondale had consolidated their police and fire service into the county. The building had been a feed store co-op, but the city bought it cheap when the last of the local farms went bust. All the character had been drained from the building during the renovation, and not much had been done to help the decor in the decades that followed. The squad room was nothing more than a long rectangle, with Jeffrey's office on one side and the bathroom on the other. Dark fake paneling still reeked of nicotine from before the county's antismoking policy. The drop ceiling looked dingy no matter how many times the inserts were replaced. The tile floor was made of asbestos and Sara always held her breath when she walked over the cracked portion by the bathroom. Even without the tile, she would have held her breath near the bathroom. Nowhere was it more evident that the Grant County police force was still predominantly male than in the squad room's unisex bathroom.

She muscled open the heavy fire door that separated the squad room from the rest of the building. A newer section had been built onto the back of the station fifteen years ago when the mayor had realized they could make some money holding prisoners for nearby overburdened counties. A thirty-cell jail block, a conference room, and the interrogation room had seemed luxurious at the time, but age had done its work and despite a recent fresh coat of paint, the newer areas looked just as worn-down as the old ones.

Sara's heels clicked across the floor as she walked down the long hallway, then stopped outside the interrogation room to straighten her dress and buy herself some time. She had not been this nervous around her ex-husband in a long while, and she hoped it did not show as she entered the room.

Jeffrey sat at a long table, stacks of papers spread over the surface as he took notes on a legal pad. His coat was off, his sleeves rolled up. He did not glance up when she came in, but he must have been watching, because when Sara started to close the door, he said, "Don't."

She put her briefcase on the table and waited for him to look up. He didn't, and she was torn between throwing her briefcase at his head and throwing herself at his feet. While these two conflicting emotions had been par for the course throughout the nearly fifteen years they had known each other, it was usually Jeffrey prostrating himself in front of Sara, not the other way around. After four years of divorce, they had finally fallen back into a relationship. Three months ago, he had asked her to marry him again, and his ego could not abide her rejection, no matter how many times she explained her reasons. They had not seen each other outside of work since, and Sara was running out of ideas.

Withholding an exasperated sigh, she said, "Jeffrey?"

"Just leave the report there," he said, nodding toward an empty corner on the table as he underlined something on the legal pad.

"I thought you might want to go over it."

"Was there anything unusual?" he asked, picking up another stack of papers, still not looking at her.

"I found a map in her lower bowel that leads to buried treasure."

He did not take the bait. "Did you put that in the report?"

"Of course not," she teased. "I'm not splitting that kind of money with the county."

Jeffrey gave her a sharp look that said he didn't appreciate her humor. "That's not very respectful to the deceased."

Sara felt a flash of shame but she tried not to show it.

"What's the verdict?"

"Natural causes," Sara told him. "The blood and urine came back clean. There were no remarkable findings during the physical exam. She was ninety-eight years old. She died peacefully in her sleep."

"Good."

Sara watched him write, waiting for him to realize she was not going to leave. He had a beautiful, flowing script, the kind you would never expect from an ex-jock and especially from a cop. Part of her had fallen in love with him the first time she had seen his hand-writing.

She shifted from one foot to the other, waiting.

"Sit down," he finally relented, holding out his hand for the re-port. Sara did as she was told, giving him the slim file.

He scanned her notes. "Pretty straightforward."

"I've already talked to her kids," Sara told him, though "kids" hardly seemed appropriate considering that the woman's youngest child was nearly thirty years older than Sara. "They know they were grasping at straws."

"Good," he repeated, signing off on the last page. He tossed it onto the corner of the table and capped his pen. "Is that all?"

"Mama says hey."

He seemed reluctant when he asked, "How's Tess?"

Sara shrugged, because she wasn't exactly sure how to answer. Her relationship with her sister seemed to be deteriorating as rapidly as her one with Jeffrey. Instead, she asked, "How long are you going to keep this up?"

He purposefully misunderstood her, indicating the paperwork as he spoke. "I've got to have it all done before we go to trial next month."

"That's not what I was talking about and you know it."

"I don't think you have a right to use that tone with me." He sat back in the chair. She could see that he was tired, and his usual easy smile was nowhere to be seen.

She asked, "Are you sleeping okay?"

"Big case," he said, and she wondered if that was really what was keeping him up at night. "What do you want?"

"Can't we just talk?"

"About what?" He rocked his chair back. When she did not an-swer, he prompted, "Well?"

"I just want to—"

"What?" he interrupted, his jaw set. "We've talked this through a hundred times. There's not a whole lot more to say."

"I want to see you."

"I told you I'm buried in this case."

"So, when it's over . . . ?"

"Sara."

"Jeffrey," she countered. "If you don't want to see me, just say it. Don't use a case as an excuse. We've both been buried deeper than this before and still managed to spend time with each other. As I recall, it's what makes this crap"—she indicated the mounds of paperwork—"bearable."

He dropped his chair with a thud. "I don't see the point."

She gave humor another stab. "Well, the sex, for one."

"I can get that anywhere."

Sara raised an eyebrow, but suppressed the obvious comment. The fact that Jeffrey could and sometimes did get sex anywhere was the reason she had divorced him in the first place.

He picked up his pen to resume writing, but Sara snatched it from his hand. She tried to keep the desperation out of her voice as she asked, "Why do we have to get married again for this to work?"

He looked off to the side, clearly annoyed.

She reminded him, "We were married before and it practically ruined us."

"Yeah," he said. "I remember."

She played her trump card. "You could rent out your house to someone from the college."

He paused a second before asking, "Why would I do that?"

"So you could move in with me."

"And live in sin?"

She laughed. "Since when did you become religious?"

"Since your father put the fear of God into me," he shot back, his tone completely devoid of humor. "I want a wife, Sara, not a fuck-buddy."

She felt the cut of his words. "Is that what you think I am?"

"I don't know," he told her, his tone something of an apology. "I'm tired of being tied to that string you just yank when you feel lonely."

She opened her mouth but could not speak.

He shook his head, apologizing. "I didn't mean that."

"You think I'm here making a fool of myself because I'm lonely?"

"I don't know anything right now, except that I've got a lot of work to do." He held out his hand. "Can I have my pen back?"

She gripped it tightly. "I want to be with you."

"You're with me now," he said, reaching over to retrieve his pen.

She put her other hand around his, holding him there. "I miss you," she said. "I miss being with you."

He gave a halfhearted shrug, but did not pull away.

She pressed her lips to his fingers, smelling ink and the oatmeal lotion he used when he thought no one was looking. "I miss your hands."

He kept staring.

She brushed his thumb with her lips. "Don't you miss me?"

He tilted his head to the side, giving another indefinite shrug.

"I want to *be* with you. I want to . . ." She looked over her shoulder again, making certain no one was there. She lowered her voice to barely more than a whisper and offered to do something with him that any self-respecting prostitute would charge double for.

Jeffrey's lips parted, shock registering in his eyes. His hand tightened around hers. "You stopped doing that when we got married."

"Well . . ." She smiled. "We're not married anymore, are we?"

He seemed to be thinking it over when a loud knock came at the open door. It might as well have been a gunshot from Jeffrey's reaction. He jerked his hand back and stood up.

Frank Wallace, Jeffrey's second in command, said, "Sorry."

Jeffrey let his irritation show, though Sara could not guess if it was for her or Frank's benefit. "What is it?"

Frank glanced at the phone on the wall and stated the obvious. "Your extension's off the hook."

Jeffrey waited.

"Marla told me to tell you there's some kid in the lobby asking for you." He took out his handkerchief and wiped his forehead. "Hey, Sara."

She started to return the greeting but stopped at the sight of him. He looked dead on his feet. "Are you all right?"

Frank put his hand to his stomach, a sour look on his face. "Bad Chinese."

She stood, putting her hand to his cheek. His skin was clammy. "You're probably dehydrated," she told him, putting her fingers to his wrist to check his pulse. "Are you getting enough fluids?"

He shrugged.

She stared at the second hand on her watch. "Throwing up? Diarrhea?"

He shifted uncomfortably over her last question. "I'm okay," he said, but he obviously wasn't. "You look real nice today."

"I'm glad somebody noticed," Sara said, giving Jeffrey a sideways glance.

Jeffrey tapped his fingers on the table, still annoyed. "Go on home, Frank. You look like shit."

Frank's relief was obvious.

Sara added, "If this isn't better tomorrow, call me."

He nodded again, telling Jeffrey, "Don't forget about the kid in the lobby."

"Who is it?"

"Something Smith. I didn't catch . . ." He put a hand to his stomach and made a sick sound. He turned to leave, managing a garbled "Sorry."

Jeffrey waited until Frank was out of earshot to say, "I have to do everything around here."

"He's obviously not well."

"It's Lena's first day back," Jeffrey said, referring to Frank's ex-partner. "She's supposed to be in at ten."

"And?"

"You run into Matt yet? He tried to call in sick, too, but I told him to get his sorry ass in here."

11

"You think two senior detectives gave themselves food poisoning so they wouldn't have to see Lena?"

Jeffrey walked over to the phone and put the receiver back in the cradle. "I've been here over fifteen years and never seen Matt Hogan eat Chinese."

He had a point, but Sara wanted to give both men the benefit of the doubt. No matter what he said about her, Frank obviously cared for Lena. They had worked together for nearly a decade. Sara knew from personal experience that you could not spend that kind of time with someone and just walk away.

Jeffrey pressed the speaker button, then dialed in an extension. "Marla?"

There was a series of clicking noises as she picked up the receiver. "Yessir?"

"Has Matt shown up yet?"

"Not yet. I'm a little worried what with him being sick and all."

"Tell him I'm looking for him as soon as he walks in the door," Jeffrey ordered. "Is there someone waiting for me?"

She lowered her voice. "Yes. He's kind of impatient."

"I'll be there in a second." He turned the speaker off, mumbling, "I don't have time for this."

"Jeff—"

"I need to see who this is," he said, walking out of the room.

Sara followed him down the hallway, practically running to keep up. "If I break my ankle in these heels . . ."

He glanced down at her shoes. "Did you think you could just waltz in here whoring yourself out and I'd beg you to come back?"

Embarrassment ignited her temper. "Why is it you call it whoring myself out when I *want* to do it, but when I don't want to and I do anyway, all of a sudden it's sexy?"

He stopped at the fire door, resting his hand on the long handle. "That's not fair."

"You think so, too, Dr. Freud?"

"I'm not playing around here, Sara."

"Do you think I am?"

"I don't know what you're doing," he said, and there was a hardness around his eyes that sent a cold chill through her. "I can't keep living like this."

She put her hand on his arm, saying, "Wait." When he stopped, she forced herself to say, "I love you."

He gave her a flippant "Thanks."

"Please," she whispered. "We don't need a piece of paper to tell us how we feel."

"The thing you keep missing," he told her, yanking open the door, "is that I do."

She started to follow him into the squad room, but pride kept her feet rooted to the floor. A handful of patrolmen and detectives were starting their shifts, sitting at their desks as they wrote up reports or made calls. She could see Brad and his group of kids congregating around the coffeemaker, where he was probably regaling them with the brand of filter they used or the number of scoops it took to make a pot.

There were two young men in the lobby, one of them leaning against the back wall, the other standing in front of Marla. Sara took the standing one to be Jeffrey's visitor. Smith was young, probably Brad's age, and dressed in a quilted black jacket that was zipped closed despite the late August heat. His head was shaved and from what she could make of his body under the heavy coat, he was fit and well muscled. He kept scanning the room, his eyes furiously darting around, never resting his gaze on one person for long. He added the front door to his rotation every second time, checking the street. There was definitely something military in his bearing, and for some reason, his general demeanor put Sara on edge.

She looked around the room, taking in what Smith was seeing. Jeffrey had stopped at one of the desks to help a patrolman. He slid his paddle holster to his back as he sat on the edge of the desk and typed something into the computer. Brad was still talking over by the coffeemaker, his hand resting on the top of the mace spray in his belt. She counted five more cops, all of them busy writing reports or entering information into their computers. A sense of danger coursed through

Sara's body like a bolt of lightning. Everything in her line of vision became too sharply focused.

The front door made a sucking sound as it opened and Matt Hogan walked in. Marla said, "There you are. We've been waiting for you."

The young man put his hand inside his coat, and Sara screamed, "Jeffrey!"

They all turned to look at her, but Sara was watching Smith. In one fluid motion he pulled out a sawed-off shotgun, pointed it at Matt's face, and squeezed both triggers.

Blood and brain sprayed onto the front door as if from a high-pressure hose. Matt fell back against the glass, the pane cracking straight up the center but not breaking, his face completely blown away. Children started to scream and Brad fell on them en masse, pushing them down to the ground. Gunfire went wild and one of the patrolmen collapsed in front of Sara, a large hole in his chest. His gun discharged on impact, skidding across the floor. Around her, glass flew as family photographs and personal items shot off desks. Computers popped, sending up the acrid smell of burning plastic. Papers floated through the air in a flurry, and the sound of weapons firing was so intense that Sara's ears felt as if they were bleeding.

"Get out!" Jeffrey screamed, just as Sara felt a sharp sting on her face. She put her hand to her cheek where a piece of shrapnel had grazed the flesh. She was kneeling on the floor but could not remember how she had gotten there. She darted behind a filing cabinet, her throat feeling as if she had swallowed acid.

"Go!" Jeffrey was crouched behind a desk, the muzzle of his gun a constant burst of white as he tried to give her cover. A large boom shook the front of the building, then another.

From behind the fire door, Frank screamed, "This way!" pointing his gun around the jamb, shooting blindly toward the front lobby. A patrolman slammed open the door, exposing Frank as he ran to safety. On the other side of the room, a second cop was shot trying to reach the group of children, his face a mask of pain as he slumped against a filing cabinet. Smoke and the smell of gunpowder filled the air, and still more firepower came from the front lobby. Fear seized Sara as she recognized the snare-drum *tat-tat-tat* of an automatic weapon. The killers had come prepared for a shoot-out.

"Dr. Linton!" someone screamed. Seconds later, Sara felt a pair of small hands clinging to her neck. Maggie Burgess had managed to break loose, and instinctively, Sara wrapped her own body around the girl's. Jeffrey saw this, and he took out his ankle holster, giving Sara the signal to run as soon as he started firing. She slipped off her high heels, waiting for what seemed like hours until Jeffrey raised his head above the desk he was hiding behind and started shooting with both guns. Sara bolted toward the fire door and threw the child to Frank. Floor tiles splintered and exploded in front of her as bullets sprayed, and she backed up on her hands and feet until she was safely behind the filing cabinet again.

Sara's hands moved wildly as she checked to see if she had been shot. There was blood all over her, but she knew it was not her own. Frank cracked open the door again. Bullets popped off the heavy-gauge steel and he returned fire, sticking his hand around the edge and shooting.

"Get out!" Jeffrey repeated, preparing to give her cover, but Sara could see one of her kids from the clinic hiding behind a row of fallen chairs. Ron Carver looked as terrified as she felt, and Sara held up her hands to stop the child from running before a signal from Jeffrey. Without warning, the boy took off toward her, his chin tucked into his chest and his arms pumping as the air exploded around him. Jeffrey started rapid-firing to draw the shooter away, but a stray bullet zinged through the air, practically severing the child's foot. Ron barely broke stride, using the pulp that was left of his ankle to propel himself forward.

He collapsed into Sara's arms, and she could feel his heart flutter-ing in his chest like the wings of a small bird as she ripped off his cot-ton shirt. She tore the material length-wise and used the sleeve to wrap a tight tourniquet. She used the other half of the shirt to tie his foot on, hoping it could be saved.

"Don't make me go out there," the child begged. "Dr. Linton, please don't make me."

Sara made her tone stern. "Ronny, we have to go."

"Please don't make me!" he wailed.

Jeffrey screamed, "Sara!"

Sara scooped the boy close to her body and waited for Jeffrey's signal. It came, and she held Ron tight as she ran in a crouch toward the door.

Halfway there, the boy started to kick and scratch at her in wild panic, shrieking, "No! Don't make me!" at the top of his lungs.

She clamped her hand over his mouth and forced herself toward the door, barely registering the pain as his teeth cut into the flesh of her palm. Frank reached out, snatching Ron by his shirt and yanking him to safety. He tried to grab Sara, too, but she ran back to the filing cabinet, looking for more children. Another bullet whizzed past her, and without thinking, she went farther into the room.

She tried twice to see how many children were with Brad, but with the bullets and chaos all around her, she lost count each time. She searched frantically for Jeffrey. He was about fifteen feet away reloading his gun. Their eyes locked just before his shoulder jerked back, throwing him against the desks. A plant fell to the floor, the pot breaking into a thousand pieces. His body convulsed, his legs gave a violent twitch, and then he was still. With Jeffrey down, everything seemed to stop. Sara darted under the nearest desk, her ears ringing from the gunfire. The room went quiet but for Marla's screaming, her voice trilling up and down like a siren.

"Oh, God," Sara whispered, looking frantically under the desk. Just over the front counter, she saw Smith standing with a gun in each hand, scanning the room for movement. The other young man was beside him, pointing an assault rifle toward the front door. Smith was wearing a Kevlar vest under the jacket, and she could see two more guns holstered to his chest. The shotgun lay on the counter. Both gunmen were out in the open, but no one fired on them. Sara tried to remember who else was in the room but again could not keep count.

Movement came to her far left. Another shot was fired and there was the ping of a ricochet followed by a low groan. A child's scream was stifled. Sara flattened herself to the floor, trying to see under the other desks. In the far corner, Brad had his arms spread open, keeping the kids down on the floor. They were huddled together, sobbing as one.

The officer who had fallen against the filing cabinets moaned, trying to raise his gun. Sara recognized the man as Barry Fordham, a patrol cop she had danced with at the last policeman's ball.

"Put it down!" Smith screamed. "Put it down!"

Barry tried to raise his gun, but he couldn't control his wrist. His gun flopped wildly in the air. The man with the assault rifle turned slowly toward Barry and fired one shot into the cop's head with frightening precision. The back of Barry's skull banged into the metal cabinet and stuck there. When Sara looked at the second gunman, he had returned to guarding the front door as if nothing had happened.

"Who else?" Smith demanded. "Identify yourself!"

Sara heard someone scramble behind her. She saw a blur of colors as one of the detectives ran into Jeffrey's office. A spray of bullets followed him. Seconds later, the window was broken out.

"Stay where you are!" Smith ordered. "Everyone stay where you are!"

A child's scream came from Jeffrey's office, followed by more shattered glass. Remarkably, the window between the office and the squad room had not been broken. Smith broke it now with a single shot.

Sara cringed as the huge shards of glass splintered against the floor.

"Who else is here?" Smith demanded, and she heard the shotgun being cracked and loaded. "Show your face or I'll kill this old lady, too!"

Marla's scream was cut off by a slap.

Sara finally found Jeffrey near the center of the room. She could only see his right shoulder and arm. He was lying on his back. His body was motionless. Blood pooled around him and his hand held his gun at his side, the grip relaxed. He was five desks away on the diagonal, but she could still see the band of his Auburn class ring on his finger.

A hushed "Sara" came from her right. Frank was crouched behind the steel fire door, his weapon drawn. He motioned for her to
crawl back toward him, but Sara shook her head. His voice was an
angry hiss as he repeated, "Sara."

She looked at Jeffrey again, willing him to move, to show some
signs of life. The remaining children were still huddled with Brad,
their sobs slowly stifled by fear. She could not leave any of them and
she told this to Frank with another sharp shake of her head. She ignored his angry snort of breath.

"Who's left?" Smith demanded. "Show yourself or I'm gonna
shoot this old bitch!" Marla screamed, but Smith screamed louder.
"Who's fucking back there?"

Sara was about to respond when Brad said, "Over here."

Before she could let herself think, Sara ran in a crouch toward the
closest desk, hoping Smith was looking at Brad. She held her breath,
waiting to be shot.

"Where're those kids?" Smith demanded.

Brad's voice was amazingly calm. "We're over here. Don't shoot.
It's just me and three little girls left. We're not gonna do anything."

"Stand up."

"I can't, man. I gotta take care of these kids."

Marla cried, "Please don't—" and her words were cut off by another slap.

Sara closed her eyes for a second, thinking about her family, about
all that had been left unsaid between them. Then she pushed them out
of her mind and instead thought about the children left in the room.
She stared at the gun in Jeffrey's hand, pinning everything on the
weapon. If she could get to Jeffrey's gun, maybe they would have a
chance. Four more desks. Jeffrey was only four more desks away. She
let herself look at him again. His body was still, his hand unmoving.

Smith was still focused on Brad. "Where's your gun?"

"It's here," Brad said, and Sara darted toward the next desk, over-
shooting it but managing to stop short behind a lateral filing cabinet.
"I gotta bunch of little girls here, man. I'm not going to draw on you.
I haven't touched my gun."

"Throw it over here."

Sara held her breath and waited until she heard Brad's gun sliding across the floor before she ran to the next desk.

"Don't move!" Smith screamed as Sara skidded to a stop behind the desk. Her feet were sweating, and she saw her own bloody footprints tracing her route across the floor. She stumbled, but caught herself before she fell into the open.

Marla wailed, "Please!"

There was the loud retort of flesh against flesh. Marla's chair gave a god-awful groan, as if it had snapped in two. Sara watched under the desk as Marla's body slammed into the ground. Saliva spurted from her mouth and her teeth slid across the tiles.

"I told you not to move!" Smith repeated, giving Marla's chair a vicious kick that sent it spinning into the wall.

Sara tried to control her breathing as she moved closer to Jeffrey. One desk stood between them, but it was turned the wrong way, blocking her path. She would be in Smith's line of fire if she ran. She was almost directly across from the children. They were three desks away. She could get the gun and . . . Sara felt her heart stop. What could she do with the gun? What could she accomplish that nearly ten cops could not?

Surprise, Sara thought. She had surprise. Smith and his accomplice did not know that she was in the room. She would surprise them.

"Where's your backup?" Smith demanded.

"I'm patrol. I don't carry a second—"

"Don't lie to me!" He fired in Brad's direction and instead of the screams Sara expected, there was silence. She looked back under the desks, trying to see if anyone had been shot. Three sets of glassy eyes stared back. Shock had taken over. The girls were too afraid to scream.

Silence filled the room like a poisonous gas. Sara counted to thirty-one before Smith asked, "You still there, man?"

She put her hand to her chest, scared her heart was beating too loudly. From what she could see of Brad, he was not moving. Her mind flashed on an image of him sitting there, his arms still around the children, his head gone. She squeezed her eyes shut, trying to force the image from her brain.

She chanced another look at Smith, who was standing where Marla had greeted her less than ten minutes ago. He had a nine-millimeter in one hand and the shotgun in another. His jacket was open and Sara could see two empty holsters along with extra shells for the shotgun strapped to his chest. Another pistol was tucked into the front of his jeans and at his feet was a long black duffel bag that probably contained more ammunition. The second gunman was behind the counter, his weapon still pointing toward the front door. His body was tensed, his finger resting to the side of the trigger on his rifle. He was chewing gum, and Sara found his silent gum-chewing more unnerving than Smith's threats.

Smith repeated, "You there, man?" He paused before trying again. "You there?"

Finally, Brad said, "I'm here."

Sara let out a slow breath, relief weakening her muscles. She flattened herself to the floor, knowing the best way to get to Jeffrey would be to slide past a row of overturned filing cabinets. Slowly, she made her way along the cold tiles, reaching her hand out toward his. The tips of her fingers finally grazed the cuff of his jacket. She closed her eyes, inching closer.

The gun in his hand was spent, though Sara could have guessed as much if she had let herself think about it. Jeffrey had been reloading when he was shot, and the magazine had dropped to the floor, splitting on impact. Bullets were everywhere—useless, unused bullets. She shouldn't be surprised by that, just like she shouldn't be surprised to feel the coldness of his skin or, when her fingers finally rested upon his wrist, the absence of his pulse.

CHAPTER TWO

9:22 A.M.

Ethan," Lena said, cradling the phone with her shoulder as she tied the laces on her new black high-top sneakers. "I've got to go."

"Why?"

"You *know* why," she snapped. "I can't be late for work my first day back."

"I don't want you to do this."

"Really? Because it wasn't clear the eighteen million other times you said it."

"You know what?" he said, his tone still controlled because he was actually stupid enough to think he could talk her out of this. "You can be such a bitch sometimes."

"It took you long enough to figure that out."

He embarked on one of his little tirades, but Lena only half listened as she stared at herself in the mirror on the back of the door. She looked good today. Her hair was tied up and the suit she had bought on sale last week was cut just right for her build. She slid back the jacket, resting her hand on her holstered police-issue nine. The metal felt reassuring under her hand.

"Are you listening to me?" Ethan demanded.

"No," she said. "I'm a cop, Ethan. A detective. It's who I am."

"We both know who you are," he told her, his tone sharper. "And we both know what you're capable of." He waited a beat, and she bit her tongue, forcing herself not to respond to the challenge.

He changed tactics. "Does your boss know you're seeing me again?"

"It's not like we're sneaking around."

He had heard the defensiveness in her tone, and pounced. "That'd make things real good for you at work, don't you think? It'll take less than a week for it to get around that you're being nailed by an ex-con."

She dropped her hand from the gun, swearing under her breath.

"What'd you say?" he demanded.

"I said it's already gotten around, you idiot. Everybody at the station already knows."

"They don't know everything," he reminded her in a low, threatening tone.

Lena glanced at the clock by her bed. She could not be late her first day back. Things were going to be tense enough without her breezing in five minutes behind. Frank would use it as another reason she was not ready to return to the force, and Matt, his cohort, would agree. Today would be a harder test for Lena than her first day in uniform. Just like then, everyone would be looking at her to fail. The difference was that now they would feel sorry for her if she fucked up, whereas before they would have cheered. If she was honest with herself, Lena would rather have their cheers than their pity. If this did not work out today, she did not know what she would do. Move, probably. Maybe they were hiring in Alaska.

She told Ethan, "I'll probably have to work late tonight."

"I don't mind," he told her, relaxed by the implication that she would see him later. "Why don't you come over?"

"Because your dorm smells like puke and piss."

"I could come over there."

"Yeah, that'd be great. With my dead sister's gay lover in the next room? No thanks."

"Come on, baby. I want to see you."

"I don't know how late I'll be," she told him. "I'll probably be tired."

"Then we can just sleep," he offered. "I don't care. I want to see you."

His voice was soothing now, but Lena knew if she kept resisting he would turn nasty. Ethan was only twenty-three, almost ten years younger than Lena, and he had yet to figure out that a night spent apart was not the end of their relationship. Though, sometimes, Lena wished it could be that easy to make the break from him. Maybe now that she had a job again, something more demanding to occupy her brain than the daytime TV schedule, she could finally get away.

"Lena?" Ethan said, as if a sixth sense told him she was thinking about leaving. "I love you so much, baby." His voice grew even softer. "Come see me tonight. I'll make us dinner, maybe get some wine . . . ?"

"I missed my period last month."

He sucked in air and her only regret was that she could not see his expression.

"That's not funny."

"You think I'm joking?" she asked. "I'm three weeks late."

Finally, he came up with "Stress can do that, right?"

"So can sperm."

He was quiet, his breathing the only noise on the line.

She forced something that sounded like a laugh. "Still love me, baby?"

His voice was tight and controlled. "Don't be like that."

"Lookit," she said, wishing that she had never even mentioned it to him. "Don't worry, okay? I'll take care of it."

"What does that mean?"

"It means what it means, Ethan. If I'm . . ." She couldn't even say the word. "If something's happened, I'll take care of it."

"You can't—"

The phone beeped, and Lena had never been so thankful for call-waiting in her life. "I've got to get this. I'll see you around." She

clicked the phone to the other call before Ethan could say anything else.

"Lee?" a raspy voice said. Lena suppressed a groan, thinking she
would have been better off sticking with Ethan.

"Hey, Hank."

"Happy birthday, girl!"

She smiled before she caught herself.

"Didja get my card?"

"Yeah," she told her uncle. "Thanks."

"You get yourself something nice?"

"Yeah," Lena repeated, tugging the jacket back into place. Hank's
two hundred dollars could have been better spent on groceries or her
car payment, but Lena had splurged for once. Today was an important
day. She was a cop again.

Her cell phone rang, and she saw from the caller ID that it was
Ethan, calling on his cell phone. He was still holding on call-waiting.

Hank said, "You need to get that?"

"No," she told him, turning off the phone mid-ring and tucking
it into her jacket pocket. She opened the bedroom door and walked
into the hallway as Hank started his usual birthday story about how
the day Lena and her twin sister, Sibyl, came to live with him was the
happiest day of his life. She stopped in the bathroom, checking herself in the mirror again. She had dark circles under her eyes, but the
tinted foundation she'd used helped take care of the problem. Nothing could be done about the deep purple gash on her bottom lip where
she had bitten down too hard and split it.

A picture of Sibyl was tucked into the frame of the mirror. It had
been taken a month or so before she was killed, and though Lena
wanted to remove the photograph, this wasn't her house. As she did
almost every morning, Lena compared the picture of her twin to her
own reflection in the mirror, not liking what she saw. When Sibyl
died, they had appeared almost completely identical. Now Lena's
cheeks were hollow and her dark hair wasn't as thick or shiny. She
looked a hell of a lot older than thirty-three, but it was the hardness
in her eyes more than anything else that gave her that appearance.

Her skin didn't glow like it used to, but Lena was hoping to get that back. She was running every day and doing free weights at the gym with Ethan almost every night.

Call-waiting beeped again, and Lena gritted her teeth, wishing she hadn't said anything to Ethan about her period. She had never been regular, but neither had she ever been this late. Maybe it was because she was working out so much, training to get ready for the job again. The last six weeks had been like preparing for a marathon. And then, Ethan was right about stress. She was under a lot of stress lately. She had been under a lot of stress for the last two years.

Lena pressed her hand to her eyes. She wasn't going to think about it. Last year, a pretty good shrink had told her that sometimes denial could be a good thing. Today was definitely a good day to pull a Scarlett O'Hara. She would think about it tomorrow. Shit, maybe she wouldn't think about it until next week.

She interrupted Hank's story, which had left out some important details, like the fact that he'd been a speed freak and an alcoholic when social services had dropped Sibyl and Lena on his lap—and that was the happy part of the story. "How'd this weekend go?"

"Better than I thought," Hank said, sounding pleased. He had turned The Hut, his dilapidated bar on the outskirts of the shithole town where Lena had grown up, into a weekend karaoke bar. Considering Hank's regular clientele, this was somewhat of a gamble, but Hank's success proved Lena's long-held theory that a drunk redneck would do anything when the lights were turned down low.

"Baby," Hank began, his tone turning serious. "I know today's a big day and all. . . ."

"It's no big deal," she said. "Really."

"You don't have to talk all tough with me," he said, his temper flaring. Sometimes, he was so like her that Lena felt a flicker of shock when he spoke.

"Anyway," Hank said, "I just want you to know if you need anything—"

"I'm fine," she interrupted, not wanting to have this conversation again.

"Just let me damn finish," he snapped. "I'm trying to say that if you need anything, I'm here. Not just money and all, but you know you've got that if you need it."

"I'm fine," she repeated, thinking hell would freeze over before she went to her uncle Hank for help with anything.

The phone beeped, and Lena ignored it again. She walked into the kitchen and would have turned back around if Nan hadn't grabbed her arm.

"Happy birthday!" Nan said, clapping her hands with sheer joy. She took a box of matches from her apron, and Lena watched as she lit the single candle on top of a white-frosted yellow cupcake. There was another cupcake on the counter with a similar candle, but Nan left that one alone.

Nan began to sing, "Happy birthday to you," and Lena told Hank, "I've got to go."

"Happy birthday!" he repeated, nearly in time with Nan.

Lena ended the call. The phone began ringing almost immediately, and she turned it on then quickly off again as Nan finished the song.

"Thanks." Lena blew out the candle, hoping to God Nan didn't expect her to eat anything. Her stomach felt like she had swallowed a rock.

"Did you make a wish?"

"Yeah," Lena said, thinking it best not to tell her what.

"I know you're too nervous to eat it," Nan said, peeling the paper away from the little round cake. She smiled, taking a bite. Sometimes Nan was so damn intuitive it made Lena uncomfortable; it was like they were an old married couple.

Nan asked, "Is there anything I can do?"

"No, thanks," Lena said, pouring herself a cup of coffee. The coffeemaker was one of the few things Lena kept in the shared parts of the house. Most of the time, she stayed confined to her room, reading or watching the small black-and-white television she had gotten free from the bank when she opened a new checking account.

Lena had moved in with Nan out of dire necessity, but no matter what Nan did to try to make her feel comfortable here, Lena had a strong sense of not belonging. Nan was the perfect roommate, if you could tolerate that kind of perfection, but Lena had finally gotten to the place where she wanted her own house with her own things. She wanted a mirror she could look at in the morning without having the last two years thrown back in her face. She wanted Ethan out of her life. She wanted the rock in her gut to go away. For the first time in her life, she wanted her period.

The phone rang again. Lena pressed the buttons in rapid succession, hanging up the call.

Nan took another bite of cupcake, watching Lena over the mound of frosting. She chewed slowly, then swallowed. "It's such a shame you have to wear makeup now. You've got great skin."

The phone rang again, and Lena clicked it off. "Thanks."

"You know," Nan said, sitting down at the kitchen table, "I don't mind if Ethan stays over sometimes." She indicated the house with a wave of her hand. "This is your place, too."

Lena tried to return the smile. "You have frosting on your lip."

Nan patted her mouth with a napkin. She would never use the back of her hand or lick it away. Nan Thomas was the only person Lena had ever met who actually kept napkins in a dispenser on the table. Lena was a neat person herself and God knows she liked to have things orderly, but it was disconcerting the way Nan couldn't just put something in its place. She had to have a crocheted cover for it, preferably with tassels or a teddy bear.

Nan finished the cupcake, using the napkin to clean crumbs off the table. She stared at Lena in the ensuing silence. The phone rang again.

"So," Nan said. "Big day today. First day back."

Lena clicked the phone on, then off. "Yep."

"Think they'll have some sort of party?"

Lena snorted a laugh. Frank and Matt had both made it more than clear that Lena didn't belong back on the force. Most days, Lena wasn't sure she disagreed with them, but this morning when she had put on her holster and clipped her cuffs onto the back of her belt, Lena had felt like she was falling back into the natural pattern of her life.

The phone rang, and Lena thumbed the keys again. She looked at Nan to gauge her reaction, but Nan was busy folding the paper from her cupcake into a tiny, neat square, as if this was just an ordinary moment in her ordinary life. If Nan Thomas ever decided to be a cop, she'd have criminals lining up to confess. If she chose a life of crime, there was no way she would ever get caught.

"Anyway," Nan resumed. "You don't have to move out. I'm fine having you around."

Lena looked at the lone cupcake on the counter. Nan had bought two: one for Lena and one for Sibyl.

"They had a two-for-one special at the bakery," Nan said, but then amended, "Actually, I'm lying. Sibyl loved cupcakes. It was the only sugar she would ever eat. I paid full price."

"I guessed."

"I'm sorry."

"You don't have to apologize."

"Oh, I know." Nan walked over to the trash can, which was decorated with green and yellow bunny rabbits to match her apron. "I did go to the bakery for you, though. I wanted to get you something to celebrate. Just because she's dead—"

"I know, Nan. Thanks. I really appreciate it."

"I'm glad."

"Good," Lena said, making herself meet Nan's steady gaze. As much of a neat freak as the woman was, she never cleaned her glasses. Lena could see the fingerprints from six feet away. Still, behind the lenses, Nan's owl-like eyes were piercing, and Lena clamped her mouth shut, fighting the urge to confess.

Nan said, "It's just hard without her. You know that. You know what it's like."

Lena nodded, a lump rising in her throat. She tried to chase it down with a swallow of coffee, but ended up scorching the roof of her mouth instead.

"The thing is, it's nice having you here."

"I appreciate you letting me stay this long."

"Honestly, Lee, you can stay forever. I don't care."

"Yeah," Lena managed over her coffee. How would Nan feel about a kid? Lena gave a mental groan. Nan would probably love a kid, would probably crochet booties for it and dress it up in something stupid every Halloween. She would switch to part-time work at the library and help raise it, and they would be a happy little married couple until Lena was so old her teeth fell out and she needed a walker to get around.

As if to remind her of Ethan's part in this, the phone rang. Lena silenced it.

Nan continued, "Sibyl would like you living here. She always wanted to protect you."

Lena cleared her throat, feeling a sweat break out over her body. Had Nan guessed?

"Protect you from things maybe you think you can handle, only you can't."

The phone rang. Lena turned it on and off without looking at the keypad.

"It's nice for me to have someone around who knew Sibyl," Nan continued. "Someone who loved her and—" she paused as the phone rang and Lena turned it off "—cared about her. Someone who knows how hard it is to have her gone." She paused again, but this time not for the phone. "You don't even look like her anymore."

Lena looked down at her hands. "I know."

"She would have hated that, Lee. She would have hated that more than anything else."

They both started to tear up for their own reasons, and when the phone rang for the hundredth time, Lena answered it just to break the spell.

"Lena," Frank Wallace barked. "Where the fuck have you been?"

She looked at the clock over the stove. She wasn't due at the station for another half hour.

Frank didn't wait for her response. "We've got a hostage situation at the station. Get your ass down here right now."

The phone slammed down in her ear.

Nan asked, "What?"

"There's a hostage situation," Lena said, putting the phone down on the table, fighting the urge to put her hand to her chest, where her heart was thumping so hard that she felt it in her neck. "At the station."

"Oh, God." Nan gasped. "I can't believe it. Was anyone hurt?"

"He didn't say." Lena gulped down the rest of the coffee, though her adrenaline did not need the boost. She looked on the counter for her keys, her nerves on edge.

Nan asked, "Remember when that happened in Ludowici?"

"I'd rather not," Lena said, feeling her heart stop. Six years ago in a nearby county, some prisoners had managed to grab one of the cops walking through the cells. They had pistol-whipped him with his own gun and used his keys to free themselves. The stand-off had lasted three days and fifteen prisoners had been wounded or killed. Four officers had died. In her mind, Lena ran through all the cops she knew at the station, wondering if any of them had been injured.

Lena checked her pockets, though she knew she hadn't seen her keys all morning.

The phone rang again.

Lena said, "Where are my—"

Nan pointed to a duck-shaped hook by the back door. The phone rang a second time and she picked it up without answering. "What should I tell him?"

Lena grabbed her keys off the duck's bill. She avoided Nan's gaze as she opened the door, saying, "Tell him I left for work."

Lena drove her Celica down Main Street, surprised to find the town deserted. Heartsdale wasn't exactly a thriving metropolis, but even on a Monday morning you would usually find a few people walking down the sidewalks or students tearing through on their bikes. There was a four-way stop at the mouth of the street, and Lena rolled through, looking around for signs of civilization. The hardware store's neon OPEN sign was darkened, and the dress shop had a piece of paper taped to the window with a hastily scribbled CLOSED. Two Grant County cruisers blocked the road twenty feet ahead, and she pulled her car into one of the vacant spots in front of the diner. Lena got out, thinking it was like being in a ghost town. The air was still and quiet, almost expectant. She glanced past her reflection into the darkened diner as she walked by. Chairs had been upended onto tables and the dollar menu had fallen off its suction cup in the window. That was nothing new. The diner had been closed over a year now.

Up the road, she could see two unmarked cop cars in front of Burgess's Cleaners, directly across from the police station. More cop cars were in the children's clinic parking lot, and three cruisers were parked on a diagonal in front of the police station. The main entrance to the college was blocked off by a campus security Chevy, but the rent-a-cop who should have been with the car was nowhere to be seen.

Lena stood on the sidewalk, looking up the street, half expecting some tumbleweeds to roll by. The windows to the cleaners were tinted nearly black, and even at close range they were hard to see into. She imagined that was where Jeffrey had set up the command post. There was nothing but a long parking lot behind the jail, and the prisoners had probably already barricaded the doors. The cleaners was the only position that made sense.

She said, "Hey," to the Uniform standing by the cruisers. He was looking up the street, the wrong way for his post.

He turned, his hand on his gun. Tension radiated from him like a bad odor.

She held out her hands. "I'm on the job. Chill out."

His voice shook. "You're Detective Adams?"

She did not recognize the man, but even if she had, Lena doubted she could say much to calm him. His face was ashen, and if he did manage to pull his gun, he'd probably shoot himself in the foot before he managed to aim it at anyone.

"What's going on?" she asked.

He clicked his shoulder mic on. "Detective Adams is here."

Frank's response came almost immediately. "Send her around the back."

"Go through the five-and-dime," the Uniform said. "The back door to the cleaners is open."

"What's going on?"

He shook his head, and she could see his Adam's apple bob as he swallowed.

Lena did as she was told, walking through the front entrance of the Shop-o-rama. There was a cowbell over the door, and the loud banging set her teeth on edge. She reached up and stilled the bell before entering the empty store. A half-filled shopping basket sat in the middle of the center aisle as if a shopper had abandoned it in place. Someone had been putting up a neon green sign advertising a special on suntan lotion, but it had been left hanging by one corner from a thin wire. All the lights were on, the neon pharmacy sign brightly lit, but the place was deserted. Even the yellow-haired freak who was always at the desk in the back office was nowhere to be seen.

The doors to the stockroom made a sucking sound as she pushed them open. Rows of marked bins lined the walls from floor to ceiling: toothpaste, toilet tissue, magazines. Lena was surprised some enterprising kid from the college had not figured out the shops were wide open and unguarded. She had worked at Grant Tech for a few months and knew from experience that the bastards spent more time stealing from each other than they did actually studying.

The back door stood wide open, and Lena blinked at the unrelenting sunlight. Sweat dripped down the back of her neck, but she was not sure if that was from the heat or her own apprehension. Her shoes crunched the gravel as she walked toward the cleaners, where two uniformed cops stood guard. One of them was a shortish, attractive woman who would have probably had Lena's job if Lena had not come back. The other was a young man who looked more skittish than the guy by the cruisers.

Lena pulled out her badge and identified herself, though she knew the woman. "Detective Adams."

"Hemming," the cop said, resting her hand on her gun belt. She stared openly at Lena, managing to convey her distaste despite the circumstances. She did not introduce her partner.

Lena asked, "What's going on?"

Hemming jabbed her thumb toward the cleaners. "They're in there."

Inside, the cool air almost immediately dried the sweat on her neck. Lena pushed past the rows of laundry that were waiting to be picked up. The smell of chemicals was overwhelming, and she coughed as she passed the starching area. The industrial ironers were still turned on, heat coming off them like an open flame. Old man Burgess was nowhere to be found, and it seemed odd that he would just leave things like this. Lena turned off the dials on the ironers as she passed, watching a group of men fifteen feet away. She stopped at the last machine when she recognized the tan pants and dark blue shirts of the Georgia Bureau of Investigation. They had gotten here fast. Nick Shelton, Grant County's GBI field agent, was standing with his back to Lena, but she knew him from his cowboy boots and mullet haircut.

She scanned the room for other Grant County cops. Pat Morris, a detective who had been recently promoted from patrol, sat on top of a dorm-size refrigerator holding a bag of ice to his ear. His carrot red hair was plastered to his head. Thin red lines of blood cut across his face, and Molly, the nurse from the children's clinic, was poking at them with a cotton swab. Aside from a Uniform over by the folding table, Frank was the only other cop from the county.

"Lena," Frank said, waving her over. Blood streaked down his shirt, but from what Lena could tell, it wasn't his. He looked sick as hell, and Lena didn't know how he was standing up on his own, let alone trying to run this thing with Nick.

On the table in front of them was a rough map of what had to be the station. Red and black X's riddled the areas by the coffee machine and the fire door, each of them with a set of initials to identify a person. She guessed the oblong rectangles and lopsided squares were desks and filing cabinets. If the map was accurate, the room had been pretty much torn apart.

"Jesus," she said, wondering how the prisoners had managed to take the squad room.

Nick motioned her closer as he finished drawing a long rectangle for the filing cabinets under the window to Jeffrey's office. "We were just about to start." He indicated the map, asking Pat, "This look right, buddy?"

Pat nodded.

"All right." Nick dropped the marker on the table and indicated Frank should begin.

"The gunman was waiting here with his accomplice here." Frank pointed to two spots in the front lobby. "Around nine A.M., Matt came in. He was shot in the head at point-blank range."

Lena put her hand on the table to steady herself. She looked across the street at the station. The front door was propped open a few inches, but she did not know with what.

Frank pointed to a desk by the fire door. "Sara Linton was here."

"Sara?" she asked, unable to follow. How had this happened? Who would want to shoot Matt Hogan? She had assumed the prisoners had rioted, not that someone from the outside had come in to kill in cold blood.

Frank continued, "We got two kids out." He pointed to other red X's near the door. "Burrows, Robinson, and Morgan were taken down in the first minute." He nodded at Pat. "Morris managed to break the window in Jeffrey's office and drag out three more of the kids. Keith Anderson jumped over me through the fire door. He was shot in the back. He's in surgery right now."

When she could speak, Lena asked, "There were kids?"

Nick provided, "Brad was giving them a tour of the station."

Lena swallowed, trying to get enough spit in her mouth to talk. "How many are left?"

"Three," Nick said, indicating the three small black X's by a larger one. "This is Brad Stephens." He pointed to the others. "Sara Linton, Marla Simms, Barry Fordham." His finger rested on a black X by a filing cabinet that indicated Fordham. There was a question mark beside it. Lena knew Barry was a beat cop, eight years on the job, with a wife and kid at home.

Nick said, "Barry was injured, we don't know how bad. There was another shot fired about fifteen minutes ago; we think it was from an assault rifle. Two more officers are unaccounted for. We don't think anyone else is in there." He amended, "Anyone else alive."

Frank coughed into his handkerchief, his chest rattling like a chain. He wiped his mouth before he continued. "Two cruisers came in right at the beginning of it." He indicated the cars on the map. Lena saw them still parked outside along with a third that she recognized as Brad's pulled into his usual space. She had not noticed them in the street, but from this vantage point she could see four cops crouched behind the cruisers, their guns drawn on the building.

Frank continued, "Old man Burgess came out with his shotgun." He meant the old guy who owned the cleaners. Burgess had a difficult enough time hefting her laundry. She could not picture him with a shotgun. "His granddaughter was over there," Frank said. "She was the first one Sara got out." He paused, and Lena could see the pain it caused him to remember what happened. "Burgess tried to shoot through the glass, but—"

"It's bulletproof," Lena remembered.

"It held," Frank told her. "But a ricochet hit Steve Mann in the leg down by the hardware store. Everybody backed off after that."

Nick said, "Between Burgess and the patrols, they pretty much boxed the shooters inside." He pointed behind the front counter, where Marla always sat. "From what we can tell, the second shooter is standing here behind the counter guarding the front door while the other one keeps the hostages in line."

Lena looked back into the street. The windows to the station were tinted, but not as dark as the cleaners'. There were white blast marks and spiderwebs where the buckshot hadn't been able to break the glass. She guessed the splotches from the inside were Matt's blood.

There was a darker, solid mass at the bottom; a headless image from the back. The door was being held partially open by the weight of Matt's body.

She made herself turn away, asking, "Have you found their car?"

"We're checking right now," Nick told her. "They probably parked on campus and walked to the station."

"Which would mean they've been here before," Lena surmised. She asked Frank and Pat, "Did y'all recognize either one of them?"

They both shook their heads.

She looked at the map again. "Jesus."

"The first guy has at least three weapons. He used the sawed-off on Matt, probably a Wingmaster." Nick paused respectfully. "The second shooter has the assault rifle."

"It'll pierce the glass with the right cartridges," Lena said, thinking the gunmen had done more than a casual reconnaissance of the station.

"Right," Nick confirmed. "He hasn't used it on anyone in the street."

Frank added, "Yet."

"We're trying to establish contact, but they won't pick up the phone." Nick indicated one of his guys standing with the phone to his ear. "Meanwhile, we've got the negotiator on the way from Atlanta. Helicopter should have a team here in under an hour."

Lena studied the street, wondering how the hell all of this had started. Heartsdale was supposed to be a small, sleepy town. People came here to get away from this kind of violence. Jeffrey had told her a long time ago that the reason he had moved here from Birmingham was because he couldn't take the big-city horrors anymore. From what Lena could see, it had followed him.

She felt a shudder, like somebody had walked over her grave. There was a red X in the center of the map with two initials beside it. Lena's eyes blurred and she could not read it. When she looked back up, everyone was staring at her. She shook her head, smiling like this was all a really bad joke. "No," she said, seeing the initials stamped on her retinas, reading them clearly now even though she was no longer looking at the map. "No."

Frank turned his back to her, coughing into his handkerchief.

Lena grabbed the black marker. "You made a mistake," she said, yanking off the top. "He should be in black." She started to draw over the red, but her hand was shaking too much.

Nick took the marker from her hand. "He's dead, Lena." He put his hand on her shoulder. "Jeffrey's dead."

CHAPTER THREE

1991
Sunday

Tessa flounced back on the bed, her feet flopping into the air. "I can't believe you're going to Florida without me."

Sara responded with an absent "Hm" as she folded a T-shirt.

"When's the last time you went on a vacation?"

"Don't remember," she said, but she did. The summer Sara graduated from high school, Eddie Linton had dragged his wife and two reluctant daughters on their last family vacation to Sea World. Sara had spent every summer since then either in classes or working in the hospital lab for credits so she could graduate early. Except for an occasional long weekend spent at her parents' house, she had not gone on an actual vacation in what seemed like forever.

"But this is a *real* vacation," Tessa said. "With a *man.*"

"Hm," Sara repeated, folding a pair of shorts.

"I hear he's pretty hot."

"Who said that?"

"Jill-June at the Shop-o-rama."

"She's still working there?"

"She's the manager now." Tessa snickered. "She's dyed her hair this awful yellow."

"On purpose?"

"Well, you wouldn't think so, but it's not like she doesn't have access to two damn aisles of hair-care products."

Sara threw a pair of pants at her sister. "Help me fold some of these."

"I will if you tell me about Jeffrey."

"What'd Jill-June say?"

"That he's sex on a stick."

Sara smiled at the understatement.

"And that he's dated every woman in town worth dating." Tessa paused, mid-fold. "There's an obvious joke in there, but I'm gonna let it go because you're my sister."

"Such a price to pay." Sara threw a sock back into the laundry basket, recalling from the last time she'd washed clothes that it didn't have a mate. She tried to change the subject, asking, "Why is it that you never lose the socks you want to lose?"

"Is he good in bed?"

"Tess!"

"Do you want your underwear folded or not?"

Sara smoothed out a shirt, not answering.

"Y'all've been seeing each other for two months."

"Three."

Tessa tried again. "You have to be sleeping with him or he wouldn't have invited you to the beach."

Sara shrugged off a response. The truth was that she had slept with Jeffrey on their first date. They hadn't even made it out of her kitchen. Sara had been so ashamed the next morning that she sneaked out of her own house before the sun came up. If not for a robbery-homicide that forced them to work together three days later, she probably would never have spoken to Jeffrey Tolliver again.

Tessa turned serious. "Was he your first time since . . . ?"

Sara gave her sister a sharp look, making it clear that topic was off-limits. "Tell me what else Jill-June said."

"Uh . . ." Tessa dragged it out, giving a sly smile. "That's he's got a great body."

"He's a runner."

"Mmm," Tessa approved. "That he's tall."

"He's three inches taller than me."

"Look at that grin," Tessa laughed. "All right, all right, you don't have to give me the speech about how horrible it was being six feet tall in the third grade."

"Five eleven." Sara threw a dishrag at her sister's head. "And it was ninth grade."

Tessa folded the rag, sighing. "He has dreamy blue eyes."

"Yes."

"He's incredibly charming and has very nice manners."

"Both true."

"Extremely good sense of humor."

"Also true."

"He always pays with correct change."

Sara laughed as she pushed more clothes toward her sister. "Talk and fold."

Tessa picked the lint off a pair of black slacks. "She says he used to be a football player."

"Really?" Sara asked, because Jeffrey had never told her this. As a matter of fact, he had told her very little about himself. His general dislike of talking about the past was one of the things she enjoyed about him.

"I hope he's worth it," Tessa said. "Is Daddy talking to you yet?"

"Nope," she answered, trying to sound as if she did not care. Though her parents had never met Jeffrey, like everyone else in town they had already formed their own opinions.

Tessa pressed on. "Tell me some more. What do you know about him that Jill-June doesn't?"

"Not much," Sara admitted.

"Come on." Tessa obviously thought she was teasing. "Just tell me what he's like."

From the hallway, Cathy Linton said, "Too old for her, for a start."

Tessa rolled her eyes as their mother walked into the room.

Sara said, "You'd never guess this was my house."

"You don't want people walking in, don't leave your front door unlocked." Cathy kissed Sara's cheek as she handed her a green Tupperware bowl and a grease-stained paper bag. "I brought this over for your drive down."

"Biscuits!" Tessa reached for the bag but Sara slapped her away.

"Your father made cornbread, but he wouldn't let me bring it." Cathy gave her a pointed look. "Said he didn't slave over a hot stove just to feed your fancy man."

Her words hung in the air like a black cloud, and even Tessa knew better than to laugh. Sara picked up a pair of jeans to fold.

"Give me those." Cathy snatched the jeans away from her. "Like this," she said, tucking the cuffs under her chin and magically working the jeans into a perfect square, all in under two seconds. She surveyed the mountain of laundry on Sara's bed. "Did you just wash this today?"

"I haven't had—"

"There's no excuse for not doing laundry when you live alone."

"I have two jobs."

"Well, I had two children and a plumber and I managed to get things done."

Sara looked to Tessa for help, but her sister was matching up a pair of socks with the kind of focus that could split an atom.

Cathy continued, "You just put your dirty clothes right in the washer, then every other day or so you run a load, and you don't ever have to deal with this again." She snapped open one of the shirts Sara had already folded. Her mouth turned down in disapproval. "Why didn't you use a fabric softener? I left you that coupon on the counter last week."

Sara gave up, kneeling down on the floor in front of a stack of books, trying to figure out which ones to take to the beach.

"From what I've heard," Tessa volunteered helpfully, "you won't have much time for reading."

Sara was hoping the same thing, but she didn't want it announced in front of her mother.

"A man like that . . ." Cathy said. She took her time before adding, "Sara, I know you don't want to hear this, but you are in *way* over your head."

Sara turned around. "Thanks for the vote of confidence, Mother."

Cathy's frown deepened. "Are you planning on wearing a bra with that shirt? I can see both your—"

"All right." Sara untucked her shirt as she stood.

Her mother added, "And those shorts don't fit. Have you lost weight?"

Sara looked at herself in the mirror. She had spent nearly an hour choosing an outfit that looked both flattering and like she had not spent an hour picking it out. "They're supposed to be baggy," she said, tugging at the seat. "It's the style."

"Oh, Lord's sake, Sara. Have you seen your ass lately? I sure haven't." Tessa cackled, and Cathy moderated her tone if not her words. "Honey, there's just your shoulder blades and the backs of your calves. 'Baggy' wasn't meant for women like you."

Sara took a deep breath, bracing herself against the dresser. "Excuse me," she said as politely as possible, and went into the bathroom, taking great pains not to slam the door behind her. She closed the toilet lid and sat down, dropping her head into her hands. She could hear her mother outside complaining about static cling, and asking again why she bothered to leave coupons if Sara wasn't going to use them.

Sara slid back her hands to cover her ears, and her mother's complaining subsided to a tolerable hum, slightly less annoying than a hot needle in her ear. From the moment Sara had started dating Jeffrey, Cathy had been riding her about one thing or another. There was nothing Sara could do right, from her posture at the dinner table to the way she parked her car in the driveway. Part of Sara wanted to confront Cathy on her hypercriticism, but another part—the more compassionate part—understood that this was the way her mother coped with her fears.

Sara looked at her watch, praying that Jeffrey would show up on time and take her away from all of this. He was seldom late, which was one of the many things she liked about him. For all of Cathy's

talk about what a cad Jeffrey Tolliver was, he carried a handkerchief in his back pocket and always opened the door for her. When
Sara got up from the table at a restaurant, he stood, too. He helped
her with her coat and carried her briefcase when they walked down
the street. As if all of this was not enough, he was so good in bed that
their first time together she had nearly cracked her back molars
clamping her teeth together so that she would not scream his name.

"Sara?" Cathy knocked on the door, her voice filled with concern.
"Are you okay, honey?"

Sara flushed the toilet and ran water in the sink. She opened the
door to find her sister and mother both staring at her with the same
worried expression.

Cathy held up a red blouse. "I don't think this is a good color
for you."

"Thanks." Sara took the shirt and tossed it into the laundry basket. She knelt back down by the books, wondering if she should take
the literary authors to impress Jeffrey or the more commercial ones
that she knew she would enjoy.

"I don't even know why you're going to the beach," Cathy said.
"All you've ever done is burn. Do you have enough sunscreen?"

Without turning around, Sara held up the neon green bottle of
Tropical Sunblock.

"You know how easily you freckle. And your legs are so white. I
don't know that I'd wear shorts with legs like that."

Tessa chuckled. "What was that girl's name in *Gidget* who wore
the big hat on the beach?"

Sara gave her sister a "you're not helping" look. Tessa pointed to
the bag of biscuits, then to her mouth, indicating her silence could be
bought.

"Larue," Sara told her, moving the bag farther away.

"Tessie," Cathy said. "Run fetch me the ironing board." She asked
Sara, "You *do* have an iron?"

Sara felt the heat from her mother's stare. "In the pantry."

Cathy clicked her tongue as Tessa left. She asked Sara, "When did
you wash these?"

"Yesterday."

"If you'd ironed them then—"

"Yes, and if I didn't wear clothes at all, I'd never have to worry about it."

"That's the same thing you told me when you were six."

Sara waited.

"If I'd left it up to you, you'd've gone to school naked."

Sara absently thumbed through a book, not seeing the pages. Behind her, she could hear her mother snapping out shirts and refolding them.

Cathy said, "If this was Tessa, I wouldn't be worried at all. As a matter of fact," she gave a low laugh, smoothing out another shirt, "I'd be worried about Jeffrey."

Sara put a paperback with a bloody knife slash down the cover in the "take" pile.

"Jeffrey Tolliver is the sort of man who has had a lot of experience. A lot more than you, and I see that smile on your lips, young lady. You'd best realize I'm not just talking about the stuff going on between the sheets."

Sara picked up another paperback. "I really don't want to have this conversation with my mother."

"Your mother is probably the only woman on earth who will tell you this," Cathy said. She sat on the bed and waited for Sara to turn around. "Men like Jeffrey only want one thing." Sara opened her mouth, but her mother wasn't finished. "It's okay if you give them that thing as long as you get something back out of it."

"Mother."

"Some women can have sex without being in love."

"I know that."

"I'm serious, baby. Listen to me. You're not that kind of woman." She tucked back Sara's hair. "You're not the kind of girl who has flings. You've never been that kind of girl."

"You don't know that."

"You've only had two boyfriends your whole life. How many girlfriends has Jeffrey had? How many women has he slept with?"

"I would guess quite a few."

"And you're just another one on his list. That's why your father is mad about—"

"Don't y'all think it would be nice to actually bother to meet him before you jump to all these conclusions?" Sara asked, too late remembering that Jeffrey was on his way here now. She chanced a look at her alarm clock. In about ten minutes, her mother would be able to see for herself that she was exactly right. If Jill-June Mallard could pick up on it, Cathy Linton would know it the moment Jeffrey entered the room.

Cathy persisted. "You're just not a 'fling' kind of girl, honey."

"Maybe I am now. Maybe I became that sort of person in Atlanta."

"Well." Cathy picked up a pair of underwear to fold, her brows furrowed. "These are too delicate for the machine," she chastised. "If you wash them by hand and dry them on the line, they won't get torn like this."

Sara gave her a tight smile. "They're not torn."

Cathy raised an eyebrow, showing a spark of appreciation. Still, she asked, "How many men have you been with?"

Sara looked at her watch, whispering, "Please."

Cathy ignored her. "I know about Steve Mann. Good Lord, the whole town knew after Mac Anders caught you two behind the Chili-dog."

Sara stared at the floor, willing herself not to spontaneously combust from embarrassment.

Cathy continued. "Mason James."

"Mama."

"That's two men."

"You're forgetting the last one," Sara reminded her, feeling a tinge of regret as she saw her mother's expression darken.

Cathy folded Sara's pajama bottoms. She asked very softly, "Does Jeffrey know you were raped?"

Sara moderated her tone, trying to be gentle. "It hasn't exactly come up in our conversations."

"What did you tell him when he asked why you left Atlanta?"

45

"Nothing," she said, leaving out the fact that Jeffrey had not pressed for details.

Cathy smoothed the pajamas. She turned around for something else to put to order, but she had already folded or refolded everything on the bed. "You should never be ashamed about what happened to you, Sara."

Sara shrugged noncommittally as she stood to get her suitcase. She wasn't ashamed, exactly, just sick to death of people treating her differently because of it—especially her mother. Sara could take the concerned looks and the awkward pauses from the handful of people who knew why she had really moved back to Grant County, but her strained relationship with her mother was almost too much to bear.

Sara opened the case and started to pack. "I'll tell him when it's time. If it's ever time." She shrugged again. "Maybe it'll never be time."

"You can't expect to have a solid relationship if it's founded on secrets."

"It's not a secret," she countered. "It's just private. It's something that happened to me, and I'm tired of . . ." She did not finish the sentence, because talking about the rape with her mother was not a conversation she was ready to have. "Can you hand me that cotton top?"

Cathy gave the shirt a look of disapproval before handing it over. "I've seen too many women fight to get to where you are and give it all up in a minute for some man that ends up leaving them in a couple of years anyway."

"I'm not going to give up my career for Jeffrey." She gave a rueful laugh. "And it's not like I can get pregnant and stay home raising babies."

Cathy absorbed the remark with little more than a frown. "It's not that, Sara."

"Then what is it, Mama? What is it you're so worried about? What could any man possibly do to me that's worse than what's already happened?"

Cathy looked down at her hands. She never cried, but she could go silent in a way that broke Sara's heart.

Sara sat on the bed beside her mother. "I'm sorry," she said, thinking that she had never been so sick of having to apologize to people in her life. She felt such guilt for bringing this on her otherwise perfect family that sometimes Sara felt like it would be better for her to just go away and leave them to heal on their own.

Cathy said, "I don't want you to give up your *self*."

Sara held her breath. Her mother had never come this close to voicing her true fears. Sara knew better than anyone how easy it would be to just give in. After the rape, all Sara had been able to do was lie in bed and cry. She had not wanted to be a doctor, a sister, or even a daughter. Two months passed, and Cathy had pleaded and cajoled, then physically pushed Sara out of bed. As she had done a hundred times when Sara was a child, Cathy had driven her to the children's clinic, where this time Dr. Barney had made things better by giving Sara a job. A year later, Sara had taken a second job as county coroner in order to buy out Dr. Barney's practice. For the last two and a half years, she had struggled to rebuild her life in Grant, and Cathy was terrified Sara would lose all of that for Jeffrey.

Sara stood up and walked to her dresser. "Mama . . ."

"I worry about you."

"I'm better now," Sara said, though she did not think she would ever be fully whole again. There would always be the before and after, no matter how many years distanced her from what had happened. "I don't need you to look after me, or try to toughen me up. I'm stronger now. I'm ready for this."

Cathy threw her hands up. "He's just having fun. That's all this is to him—fun."

Sara opened several drawers, looking for her swimsuit. She said, "Maybe that's all it is for me, too. Maybe I'm just having a good time."

"I wish I could believe you."

"I wish you could, too," Sara told her. "Because it's true."

"I don't know, baby. You have such a gentle heart."

"It's not that gentle anymore."

"What happened to you in Atlanta doesn't change who you are."

Sara shrugged, tucking her swimsuit into the case. It was how other people had changed that made what happened even more horrible. Sara was angry as hell that she had been raped, and livid that the animal who had attacked her could, and probably would, get out of jail in a few years with good behavior. She was pissed off that her whole life had been turned upside down, that she'd had to resign her internship at Grady Hospital, the job she had worked toward her entire life, because everyone in the ER treated her like broken china. The attending who had worked on Sara could no longer look her in the eye, and her fellow students wouldn't joke with her for fear of saying the wrong thing. Even the nurses treated her with kid gloves, as if being raped made Sara some sort of martyr.

Cathy said, "Is that all I get? That look from you that says you don't want to talk about it?"

"I *don't* want to talk about it," Sara told her, exasperated. "I don't want to talk about anything serious. I'm tired of being serious." She tugged at the zipper on the suitcase. "I'm tired of being the smartest girl in the class. I'm tired of being too tall for the cute boys. I'm tired of dating men who are worried about my feelings and wanna take it slow and be gentle and *process* what we're doing and *plan* our future together and treat me like I'm some delicate flower and—"

"Mason James is a very sweet boy."

"That's the point, Mama. He's a boy. I'm sick of boys. I'm sick of people walking on eggshells around me, trying to protect my feelings. I want somebody to shake things up. I want to have fun." Without thinking, she said, "I want to fuck around."

Cathy gasped—not because she had never heard the word before, but because she had never heard it from Sara. Sara could think of only a few occasions when she had used the expletive, but never in front of her mother.

All Cathy said was, "Language, please."

"You don't mind when Tessa says it."

Cathy wrinkled her nose at the logic. "Tessa says it like she means it, not like she's trying to shock her mother."

"I say it all the time," Sara lied.

"Do your cheeks always get that red when you do?"

Sara felt her cheeks go redder.

"From here," Cathy coached, pressing her hand below her diaphragm. She gestured broadly with her other hand, singing an operatic "Fuck."

"Mother!"

"If you're going to say it, say it with gusto."

"I don't need you to tell me how to say it," Sara snapped, and when Cathy laughed in her face, she added a mumbled "Or how to do it."

Cathy laughed harder. "I suppose you know all about it now?"

Sara jerked the suitcase off her bed. "Let's just say some of that expertise rubbed off."

"Oh-ho-ho," Cathy chuckled appreciatively.

Sara tucked her hands into her hips. "We do it all the time."

"Is that a fact?"

"Night and day."

"And day?" Cathy laughed again, sitting back on the bed. "Scandalous!"

"It's not like I'm seeing him for the scintillating conversation," Sara bragged. "I don't even know if he went to college."

From the doorway, Tessa said, "Sara?"

"As a matter of fact," Sara continued, wanting more than anything to take the smug look off her mother's face, "I'm fairly certain he's not even that smart."

Cathy smiled like she knew better. "That so?"

Tessa tried again. "Sara?"

"Yes, that's so, and you know what? I don't even care. He's probably stupid as a box of hair and I don't give a rat's ass. It's not like I'm dating him for his mind."

Tessa said, "For chrissake, Sara. Just shut up and turn around."

She did as she was told, regret taking hold like a fever.

Jeffrey was leaning against the door, his arms crossed over his chest. There was a half-smile on his lips that did not quite reach his eyes as he nodded toward her suitcase. "Ready to go?"

A gentle mist of rain met them as they drove out of Grant County, and Sara watched the wipers sluice water off the windshield at steady intervals, trying to think of something to say. With each pass, she told herself she was going to break the silence, but the next thing she knew, the wipers were swiping across the glass again and nothing had been said. She stared out the side window, counting cows, then goats, then billboards. The closer they got to Macon, the higher the number got, so that by the time they took the bypass, Sara had reached triple digits.

Jeffrey shifted gears, passing an eighteen-wheeler. He had not spoken since they left Grant, and he chose to break the ice with "Car handles well."

"Yes," Sara agreed, so glad he was talking to her that she could have cried. Thank God they had taken her car instead of his truck or there was no telling how long the silence would have lasted. To keep the conversation going, she said, "German engineering."

"I guess it's true what they say about doctors driving BMWs."

"My dad bought it for me when I got into medical school."

"Nice dad," he said, pausing before he added, "Your mom seems nice, too."

Sara cleared her throat, unable to recall any of the apologies she had been rehearsing in her mind for the last hour. "I would have preferred for you to meet her under different circumstances."

"I never expected to meet her at all."

"Oh, right," she said, flustered. "I didn't mean—"

"I'm glad we got to meet."

Sara nodded, thinking that the fewer times she opened her mouth, the less likely she was to put her foot in it.

"Your sister's cute."

"Yes," she agreed, knowing a lesser person would hate her sister by now. Sara had been hearing the same thing all her life. Tessa was the cute one, the funny one, the cheerleader, the one everyone wanted to be friends with. Sara was the tall one. On a good day, she was the tall redheaded one.

Before Sara could phrase something more elegant, she blurted out, "I'm so sorry about what I said."

"That's okay," he told her, but she could tell from his tone that it was not. Why he had still wanted her to go to Florida with him was anyone's guess. If Sara had any self-respect, she would have let him leave without her. The forced smile he had kept on his face as he loaded her bags into the trunk could have cut glass.

"I was just trying to . . ." She shook her head. "I don't know what I was trying to do. Make an idiot of myself?"

"You did a good job."

"It's part of my personality to want to excel in everything I do."

He did not smile.

She tried again. "I don't think you're stupid."

"As a box of hair."

"What?"

"You said 'stupid as a box of hair.'"

"Oh. Well." She laughed once, like a seal's bark. "That doesn't even make sense."

"But it's good to know you don't really think that." He glanced behind him and passed a church van. Sara stared at his hand on the shift, watching the tendons work as he passed the cars. His fingers gripped the shaft, his thumb tapping lightly on the knob.

"By the way," he told her. "I *did* go to college."

"Really?" she asked, unable to check her surprised tone. She made it worse by saying, "Well, good. Good for you."

Jeffrey gave her a sharp glance.

"I mean, that's good as in . . . well . . . because it's . . ." She laughed at her own ineptitude, putting her hand over her mouth as she mumbled, "Oh, God, Sara, shut up. Shut up."

She thought he smiled, but wasn't certain. She dared to ask, "Exactly how much did you hear?"

"Something about me rubbing off on you?"

She tried, "I meant it in the good way."

"Uh-huh," he said. "Just FYI, I've heard you say that word before." This time, he showed his teeth when he smiled. "Well, not say it. More like scream it."

Sara bit the tip of her tongue, watching the passing scenery.

He said, "It's good your mama worries about you."

"Sometimes."

"Y'all are pretty close, right?"

"I suppose," Sara answered, knowing there was more to it than that.

He asked, "Did you tell her I passed the test?"

"Of course not," Sara answered, surprised he had even asked. "That's private."

He nodded his approval, keeping his eyes on the road.

Their second date had ended with a kiss at the door and Sara asking Jeffrey to get tested for HIV. Granted, the request was a little late in coming—their frenzied first time hadn't exactly stopped for a frank discussion about the prevention of sexually transmitted diseases—but Sara had picked up on Jeffrey's reputation well before the news had hit the Shop-o-rama. For his part, Jeffrey had seemed only slightly insulted when she asked him for a blood sample.

She said, "I saw so many cases at Grady. So many women my age who never thought it could happen to them."

"You don't have to explain it to me."

"Hare's lover died of AIDS last year."

His foot slipped off the gas pedal. "Your cousin's gay?"

"Of course."

"You're kidding?" he asked, giving her an uneasy look.

"He wasn't born with that falsetto."

"I thought he was just joking around."

"He was," Sara said. "Is. I mean, he just does that to annoy me. Everyone. He likes to annoy people."

"He played football in high school."

"Only straight people can play football?"

"Well . . . no," he said, but he did not seem certain.

They both stared at the road again. Sara could think of nothing to say. She knew hardly anything about the man beside her. In the three months they had dated, she had heard nothing about Jeffrey's family or his past. She knew he had been born in Alabama, but he was vague with the details. When they weren't in bed, Jeffrey mostly talked about cases he had worked in Birmingham or things that were happening in Grant. Now that she thought about it, when they were together it was Sara who did most of the talking. He seldom volunteered any personal information about himself, and if she pushed him too far with questions, his response was to either shut down completely or run his hand up and down her thigh until she forgot what she was saying.

She chanced a look at him. His dark hair was getting long in the back, which was a little dangerous considering the Grant County school system routinely sent boys home from class if their hair touched the back of their collars. As usual, his face was clean-shaven and smooth. He was wearing a pair of worn jeans and a black Harley Davidson T-shirt. His tennis shoes looked high-tech, with extra padding in the sole and black waffle treads for running. The muscles in his legs were well defined under the denim, and though his shirt was not tight enough to show the firm abs underneath, Sara was more than familiar with them.

Sara stared down at her legs, wishing she had worn something different. She had changed into an ocean blue wraparound skirt, but her white calves were the color of fat on uncooked bacon against the dark floor mat. Despite the air conditioning, she was sweating under the cotton shirt she wore, and if Sara could have waved a magic wand to stop time, she would have stripped off her constricting bra and thrown it out the window.

"So," Jeffrey said.

"So," she returned, trying to think of something to restart the conversation. All she could come up with was, "You're a universal donor."

"Huh?"

"A universal donor," she repeated. "You can donate blood to anyone." Grasping another straw, she added, "Of course, you can't accept from anyone. You can only accept from other O negatives."

He gave her a strange look. "I'll keep that in mind."

"Your blood has antigens that—"

"I'll donate some as soon as we get back."

The conversation was lagging again, and she asked, "Do you want some chicken?"

"Is that what I keep smelling?"

Sara leaned over the backseat and rummaged around for the plastic bowl her mother had packed. "I think there's some biscuits if Tess didn't steal them."

"That'd be nice," he said, tickling the back of her thigh. "Too bad we don't have some tea."

She tried to ignore his hand. "We could stop for some."

"Maybe."

He pinched her leg and she slapped at his hand, saying, "Hey."

He laughed good-naturedly at the rebuke. "Do you mind if we take a detour?"

"Sure," she said, finding the Tupperware under a pillow. She dropped back into the seat as he passed a Winnebago. "Where to?"

"Sylacauga."

Sara stopped in the middle of removing the plastic lid. "Sill-a-what?"

"Sylacauga," he repeated. "My hometown."

CHAPTER FOUR

"**M**att?" Someone said, more like a stutter. "M-a-a-a-a-att."

His ears held on to the echo, stretching the "a" even more.

"M-a-a-a-a-a-a-att."

He tried to move but his muscles would not respond. Inexplicably, his fingers ached. They were cold. Everything was cold.

"Matt," Sara said, her voice suddenly sharp as a tack. "Matt, wake up." She put her hands on either side of his face. "Matt."

He forced open his eyes, his vision blurring, then doubling. He saw two Saras looming over him. Two Marlas. Two kids he had never met before in his life. They were all huge, like giant versions of themselves. The ceiling tiles above their heads were even larger, like flying saucers with mammoth fluorescent lights.

He tried to sit up.

"Matt, no," Sara stopped him. "Don't."

He put his hand to his head, feeling like his brain was in a vise. His right shoulder burned as if someone was grinding a hot poker into the flesh. His moved his left hand to touch it, but Sara stopped him.

"Matt," she said. "Don't."

He felt around his mouth with his tongue, trying to find the blood he could taste in the back of his throat.

She pushed back his hair and he saw a glint of gold on her finger. She was wearing his Auburn football ring. Why was she wearing his ring?

"Matt?"

He blinked, hearing a distant ringing in his ears. Jeffrey squeezed his eyes shut, trying to orient himself. The ringing came from the phone on Marla's desk. The blood he tasted was from a cut somewhere on his head.

"Matt?" Sara repeated. "Can you hear me?"

He said, "Why are you—"

She put a bottle of water to his lips. "Drink this. You need water."

Jeffrey drank, feeling the cool liquid opening up his parched throat. Water pooled down his neck as Sara tilted the bottle too far to keep up with his swallowing.

"Okay," he said, pushing away her hand.

He squeezed his eyes shut again, trying to clear them. When he opened them, the two Marlas melded into one. Her cheeks were sunken, her eye bruised and bleeding. There was actually a pair of kids, but their expressions were identical. A third was leaning against Sara, the young girl's breathing more like gasps as she tried to control her fear.

Jeffrey turned back to Sara. He had never seen her so frightened. She met his gaze pupil to pupil, staring a hole into him like she was trying to force a thought into his brain. Slowly, he nodded his understanding. He was supposed to be Matt.

She still asked, "Okay?"

"Yeah." He looked around, trying to figure out what was going on. They were on the floor in the back of the squad room, the area cleared out around them. Brad was stacking filing cabinets in front of the fire door. Jeffrey's office window and door were similarly barricaded. Bodies were scattered around with the debris. Burrows, Robinson, Morgan. Morgan had five kids at home. Burrows was an avid animal lover fostering a pair of rescued greyhounds. Robinson . . . Robinson was new. Jeffrey could not even remember the man's first name, though he had hired him less than a week ago.

Jeffrey's vision blurred and he closed his eyes as the vertigo brought on a wave of nausea.

"Breathe," Sara coaxed, smoothing back his hair. His head was in her lap and, judging by the blood on her skirt, had been for a while. He tried to move, but found that his feet were tied together with his own belt.

Suddenly, a man stood over them, pointing a shotgun at Marla while keeping a military-issue Sig Sauer trained on Brad. He had two more guns holstered to his chest along with a full complement of ammunition.

Smith. Jeffrey remembered he had given his name as Smith. He remembered it all now: Sara screaming his name, Matt's head exploding against the front door, the ensuing gun battle, the deaths. Sam. The new patrolman's first name was Sam.

The killer gave Jeffrey a cold look of appraisal. "Sit up."

Sara said, "He needs to go to the hospital." She did not wait for a response. "The children are in shock. They all need to go to the hospital."

Smith cocked his head like he had heard something. He turned toward the lobby, where another man rested an assault rifle on the front counter, pointing it toward the front entrance. He was similarly dressed with a dark coat and Kevlar vest. A black ball cap was pulled low on his head, casting his face in shadow. The man did not look Smith's way, but he gave a curt nod.

Sara took advantage of the brief exchange, whispering something to Jeffrey that sounded like "Stall it."

Smith turned back to Jeffrey. "Sit up." He kicked Jeffrey's feet, and the movement jarred his shoulder enough to make him yell from the pain.

"He needs to go to the hospital," Sara repeated.

"Hey," Brad said, like a child trying to get between his arguing parents. "I need a hand over here with this one."

Smith pointed the shotgun in Sara's face. "Help him."

Sara stayed where she was. "Matt needs medical attention," she said, keeping her hand on Jeffrey's good shoulder. Her words came out in a rushed panic. "The pulse in his arm is thready. The bullet probably nicked the artery. He lost consciousness for God knows how long. His head wound needs to be assessed."

"You don't seem too worried about me," Smith said, indicating a piece of white cloth tied tightly around his left arm. A circle of dark blood spotted the center.

"You both seem capable of taking care of yourself," she told him, then looked past his shoulder to his partner in the front lobby.

"Damn right," Smith said, bouncing on the balls of his feet. Jeffrey tried to get a good look at the second man's face, but the overhead light was so bright that he could not keep his eyes open.

Brad stumbled and dropped a filing cabinet. With lightning speed, Smith and the second gunman turned around, both ready to shoot.

Brad held up his hands. "Sorry," he said. "I just—"

The second shooter turned back to the front door as Smith walked over to Brad. Sara kept her eyes on the second man as she slipped her hand under Jeffrey's back. Wallet. She had said "Wallet."

He raised himself up to help her, biting through the pain in his shoulder, and she took out his wallet just as Smith swung around on them. He stared, his eyes darting to each person in the group, some sort of sixth sense igniting his suspicion. The children were so frightened that they were hardly moving, and Marla seemed to be in her own world as she stared blindly at the floor.

Brad said, "Maybe you can—"

Smith held out his hand, cutting him off. The room was silent, but the gunman could obviously hear something they could not. Or maybe, Jeffrey reasoned, he was just a paranoid fuck hopped up on cocaine or meth. Why the hell would someone do something like this? What could they possibly gain?

Smith walked backward, both guns trained on Brad. He stopped in front of the bathroom door, looking at his partner and getting a quick nod in return. The two men worked together like a precision instrument. Even without the military gear, it was obvious that they had either trained or been in combat together.

The bathroom door opened soundlessly as Smith went in, gun

raised. Jeffrey counted off the seconds, staring at the door as it slowly closed. Suddenly, they heard a woman's scream and a single gunshot. Less than minute later, Smith came out of the bathroom holding up a police-issue gun belt like it was a trophy.

Smith told his partner. "She was hiding under the sink."

The second man shrugged, like it was none of his concern, and Jeffrey felt his heart sink at the thought of another one of his officers shot dead by these animals. She must have been hiding under the sink cabinet all this time, hoping to God they would not find her.

Smith threw the gun belt toward the lobby before going back to Jeffrey. "Sit up," he said, and when Jeffrey did not move fast enough, he grabbed him up by his collar.

Jeffrey felt his stomach pitch as his brain tried to adjust to the sudden change. Sara sat up too, putting her hand on the back of his neck, coaching, "Breathe through it. Don't get sick."

He tried to do as he was told, but the grits he'd had for breakfast would not obey. They came up in a hot rush of bile.

"Jesus fuck," Smith stepped back quickly to avoid the splatter. "What'd you have for breakfast, man?"

Jeffrey gave him another clue, throwing up the rest of the grits. He felt Sara's hand at the back of his neck, the metal of his Auburn class ring pressing into his skin. Why had she taken his ring?

Smith said, "Give me your wallet."

Jeffrey wiped his mouth with the back of his hand. "It's in my coat," he said, saying a small prayer of thanks that he had been too pissed at Sara in the interrogation room to stop and put his jacket back on.

"Where is it?" Smith challenged. "Where's your coat?"

Jeffrey inhaled deeply, trying to quell the squall building in his stomach.

Smith kicked Jeffrey's feet. "Where's your coat?" he repeated.

"In my car."

Smith grabbed Jeffrey's collar and jerked him up to standing. Jeffrey screamed from the pain, fireworks detonating behind his eyelids. He pressed his face to the wall as he tried not to slide back to the floor. The muscles in his shoulder were throbbing with every beat of his heart, and his knees were so weak they started to buckle.

"You're okay," Sara told him, gripping him under his arm. Her strength was surprising, and he loved her more in that moment than he had in his entire life. "Keep breathing," she told him, rubbing his back in a soothing, circular motion. "You're okay."

"Move." Smith pushed her away. He tucked the shotgun into his belt and gave Jeffrey an expert pat-down. The man knew the correct way to frisk a suspect, and he did not go lightly near Jeffrey's shoulder.

"All right." Smith backed up and Jeffrey struggled to face him, leaning against the wall so he would not collapse. The phone started ringing again, the metallic clang grating on every nerve in his body.

"Y'okay, Matt?" Smith hit the *t*'s hard, like he was testing them. Jeffrey did not know if it was paranoia or panic, but he got the feeling Smith knew exactly who he was looking at, and that it was not Matt Hogan.

"He's not," Sara said. "The bullet's probably pressed against the artery. If you keep pushing him, it might dislodge. He could bleed to death."

"My heart's breaking," Smith said, glancing over at Brad to check his work.

The phone continued to ring in the background, and Sara said, "Why don't you pick that up and tell them you're sending out the children?"

Smith cocked his head to the side as if he was considering her suggestion. "Why don't you wrap your lips around my dick and suck it?"

Sara ignored the remark, telling him, "You need to show them good faith by letting the children go."

"I don't *need* to do anything."

Brad added, "She's right. You're not a baby killer."

"No," Smith said, taking the shotgun out of his belt and pointing it at Brad's chest. "I'm just a cop killer."

He let this sink in, the phone's insistent ringing punctuating the tension.

Sara told him, "The sooner you make your demands, the sooner we can all get out of here."

"Maybe I don't want to get out of here, Dr. Linton."

Jeffrey clenched his jaw, thinking there was something too familiar about the way the man had said Sara's name.

Smith noticed his reaction. "You don't like that, boy?" he asked, standing a few inches from Jeffrey's face. "Dr. Linton and me, we go way back. Don't we, Sara?"

Sara stared at the young man, looking unsure of herself. "How long has it been?"

Smith gave her a crooked smile. "A while, don't you think?"

Sara tried to hide her uncertainty, but to Jeffrey it was clear as day that she had no idea who the boy was. "You tell me."

They held each other's gaze, tension held between them like a tight wire. Smith gave a suggestive flick with his tongue and Sara looked away. Had Jeffrey been able, he would have jumped the man and beaten him dead.

Again, Smith picked up on this. He asked Jeffrey, "Are you gonna be a problem for me, Matt?"

Jeffrey stood as straight as he could with his ankles belted together. He shot the other man a look of pure hatred. Smith returned it in kind.

Brad spoke up, breaking the tension. "Keep me," he volunteered.

Smith kept his face turned toward Jeffrey, though his gaze slid slowly toward Brad.

Brad said, "Let them go and keep me."

Smith laughed at the suggestion, and in the lobby his partner joined in.

"Then keep me," Sara said, and they both stopped laughing.

Jeffrey told her, "No."

She ignored him, addressing Smith. "You've already killed Jeffrey." Her voice caught on his name, but she said the rest clearly enough. "You don't want Brad or Matt. You certainly don't want an old woman and three 10-year-olds. Let them go. Let them all go and keep me."

CHAPTER FIVE

The drive to Sylacauga turned out to be a longer detour than Jeffrey had promised. He said they would stay the night at his mother's, but at the rate they were going, Sara thought it would be more like morning. Closer to Talladega, the highway started to back up with traffic for the race at the NASCAR super speedway, but Jeffrey took this more like a challenge than an obstacle. After weaving in and out of cars, trucks, and RVs at such a close distance that Sara put on her seatbelt, Jeffrey finally exited. She was relieved until she realized that the last vehicle to use the road was probably a horse and buggy.

The deeper they drove into Alabama, the more relaxed Jeffrey seemed, and the long stretches of silence became companionable instead of unbearable. He found a good Southern-rock station and they listened to the likes of Lynyrd Skynyrd and The Allman Brothers as they drove through backwoods country. Along the way, he pointed out different attractions, such as three recently closed cotton mills and a tire factory that had been shut down after an industrial accident. The Helen Keller Center for the Blind was an impressive set of buildings, but hardly much to look at going ninety miles per hour.

Jeffrey patted her knee as they passed yet another country jail. He smiled and said, "Almost there," but there was an odd expression on his face, like he regretted asking her to come.

They took a last-minute turn onto another ill-used roadway, and Sara was contemplating how to ask him if he was lost when a large sign loomed in the distance. She read aloud, "Welcome to Sylacauga, birthplace of Jim Nabors."

"We're a proud people," Jeffrey told her, downshifting as the road curved. "Ah," he said fondly. "There's a point of local interest." He indicated a run-down-looking country store. "Yonders Blossom."

The sign was faded, but Sara could still read that it was, in fact, called Yonders Blossom. Various items one would expect to find in front of a country store were strategically placed around the yard, from a radiator with a fern growing out of it to a couple of rubber tires that had been painted white and turned into flower planters. To the side of the building was a large Coca-Cola freezer.

Jeffrey told her, "I lost my virginity behind the cooler there."

"Is that so?"

"Yep," he said, a crooked grin on his face. "The day of my twelfth birthday."

Sara tried to hide her shock. "How old was she?"

He gave a self-satisfied chuckle. "Not too old to be taken over her mama's knee when Blossom got thirsty and happened upon us."

"You seem to have that effect on mothers."

He laughed again, putting his hand on her leg. "Not all of them, honey."

"Honey?" she repeated, thinking from his tone that he might as well have called her his favorite side of beef.

He laughed at her reaction, though she had never been more serious. "You're not going to turn into a feminist on me?"

She looked at his hand on her leg, sending a clear message that it should be removed now. "Right before your very eyes."

He squeezed her leg in response, flashing that same grin that had probably gotten him out of trouble a thousand times before. Sara was not so much angry as feeling he had paid her back for calling him stupid in front of her mother. Against her better judgment, she let it slide.

They drove slowly through downtown, which was similar to Heartsdale's but half the size. He showed her other "points of interest" from his childhood along the way. Sara got the distinct impression from his lopsided smiles that there were different girls attached to each of these spots, but she decided she would rather not know the details.

"There's where I went to high school." He pointed to a long, flat building with several trailers outside. "Ah, Mrs. Kelley."

"Another one of your conquests?"

He gave a low growl. "I wish. Good God, she's probably eighty now, but back then . . ."

"I get the picture."

"You jealous?"

"Of an eighty-year-old?"

"Here we go," he said, taking a left. They were on Main Street, which again looked very much like Heartsdale's. He asked, "Look familiar?"

"Your Piggly Wiggly's closer in town," she said, watching a woman come out of the grocery store with three bags in her hands and a small child on either side. Sara stared at the children as they held on to their mother's dress, wondering what it would be like to have that kind of life. Sara had always thought that once she got her practice going, she would get married and have a few children of her own. An ectopic pregnancy subsequent to the rape had removed that possibility forever.

She felt a lump rise in her throat as she was reminded yet again of how much had been taken from her.

Jeffrey pointed to a large building on their right. "There's the hospital," he said. "I was born there back when it was just two stories and a gravel parking lot."

She stared at the building, trying to regain her composure.

He handed her his handkerchief. "You okay?"

Sara took the cloth. She had been tearing up before, and for some reason his gesture made her want to really cry. Instead, she wiped her nose and said, "Must be the pollen."

"Here," he said, leaning over to roll up the window. "Damn dog-woods."

She put her hand on the back of his neck, brushing her fingers through his hair. She was always surprised by how soft it was, almost like a child's.

He looked up at the road, then back to her. He gave her one of his half-smiles, saying, "God, you're so beautiful."

She blew her nose to defray the compliment.

He sat up, slowing the car more. "You're beautiful," he repeated, kissing her just below the ear. The car slowed more, and he kissed her again.

"You're going to block traffic," she warned, but theirs was the only car on the road.

He kissed her again, this time on the lips. She was torn between enjoying the sensation and the odd feeling that half the hospital was looking out the blinds at the spectacle they were making.

She gently pushed him away, saying, "I don't want to end up being one of the 'local points of interest' for the next girl you bring here."

He asked, "You think I bring other girls here?" and she could not tell if he was serious or not.

A car horn beeped behind them and he resumed the posted thirty-five-mile-an-hour speed limit. Sara knew better than to point out that this was the first time he had driven the speed limit since they had gotten into the car. Something had shifted, but she was not quite sure what. Before she could think of a way to frame the question, he turned onto a side street by the hospital and pulled into a driveway behind a dark blue pickup truck. A pink child's bike was propped against the front porch and a tire swing hung from the tall oak in the yard. She asked, "This is your mother's house?"

"Last detour." He gave her a smile that seemed forced. "I'll be right back," he said, and got out of the car before she could ask him who lived here.

Sara watched Jeffrey walk up to the front door and knock. He tucked his hands into his pockets and turned back around. She waved, but then realized he probably couldn't see her because of the glare.

Jeffrey knocked again, but there was still no answer. He turned back toward the car, shielding the sun out of his eyes and holding up his finger to her, indicating he would just be another minute. She opened the car door to get out as he ran around the back of the house.

Sara surveyed the neighborhood as she waited for him. The street was fairly similar to those in Avondale, which was not exactly the nicest part of Grant County. The houses looked to have been hastily built to accommodate the soldiers who returned from World War II, ready to start their families and put the war behind them. During the mid-1940s, the area must have been nice, but now it looked run-down. There were a couple of cars on blocks, and a fair number of the yards needed to be trimmed. The paint was peeling on most of the houses, and weeds grew out of the sidewalks. Some of the owners had not yet given up the fight, though, and their immaculate yards and vinyl-sided houses showed meticulous care. The one Jeffrey had parked in front of fell into this second category, with its carefully manicured lawn and well-raked gravel driveway.

Sara went up the drive, passing the truck. A large orange stripe went down the side, with the words "Auburn Tigers" painted in blue. There was an orange flag with a blue paw print on it swaying by the front door. She noticed the mailbox was painted orange and blue, too. Apparently, someone in the house was a college football fan.

Without warning, a small dog ran up the sidewalk and jumped at her, putting his dirty paws on Sara's skirt. She told him, "No," to no avail, then finally knelt down to pet the overly excited animal so he would stop jumping.

The dog barked, and Sara tried not to gag at his breath. She stroked back the fur on its head, thinking she had never seen an uglier animal in her life. Halfway down his back, he had curly hair like a poodle, but the fur on his legs was wiry like a terrier's. The coloring was an ungodly mixture of black, gray, and tan. His eyes bugged out as if someone were squeezing his testicles, even though a quick check proved he didn't have any. The check also revealed he was a she.

Sara stood, trying to brush the paw prints off her skirt. Georgia clay didn't have a thing on Alabama dirt, and nothing short of a long soak would take the stains out.

"Zaftig!" a man called from the driveway, and Sara felt herself blush crimson until she realized the man was not talking to her.

He held a shopping bag in one hand and patted his leg with the other. "Tig! Come're, girl." The dog did not leave Sara's side, and the man laughed good-naturedly as he walked across the front yard. He stopped in front of Sara, giving a low whistle as he looked her up and down. "Darlin', if you're one a them Jehova's Witnesses, I'm ready to convert."

The front door banged open, and a dark-haired woman around Sara's age walked outside. "Don't listen to that fool," she told Sara, giving her the once-over with considerably less appreciation than the man had showed. "Sara, right?"

"Uh," Sara stammered. "Right."

"I'm Darnell, but everybody calls me Nell. This'n's my husband, Jerry."

"Call me Possum," he said, tipping his orange and blue baseball cap.

Confused, Sara told them, "Nice to meet you both."

"Ma'am." Possum tipped his hat again before heading into the house.

Nell let the dog in, but not Sara. "So," she said, leaning against the doorjamb. "You're Jeffrey's new thing?"

Sara could not tell if she was joking, but she had had enough of this sort of treatment in Grant. She crossed her arms, resigned. "I suppose so."

Nell twisted her lips to the side, still not finished. "Are you a stewardess or a stripper?"

Sara barked a laugh, but stopped when Nell didn't join in. She squared her shoulders, choosing "Stripper" because it sounded more exotic.

The woman narrowed her eyes. "Jeffrey said you work with children."

Sara tried to think of something witty, but could only come up with "I use balloon animals in my act."

"Right." Nell finally stepped aside. "They're all in the back."

Sara walked into the living room of the modest home, which contained more Auburn paraphernalia than was probably legal. Pompoms and pennant flags draped the fireplace, and a framed jersey with the number seventeen hung over the mantel. Under a glass dome on the coffee table was a small village that must have resembled the university campus. A rack held several college football magazines, and even the lampshade had an orange and blue AU logo painted on it.

Nell led her down a hall toward the back door, but Sara stopped in front of a framed magazine cover. Underneath the *SEC Monthly* banner was a picture of Jeffrey standing at the fifty-yard line. His hair was longer and his mustache dated the picture by about fifteen years. He was wearing a blue jersey and rested his sneaker on a football. The type at the bottom said, "The Next Big Thing for the Tigers?"

Before she could stop herself, Sara asked, "He played for Auburn?"

Darnell finally laughed. "He got you into bed without showing you his Sugar Bowl ring?" she asked, managing to make Sara sound stupid and loose at the same time.

"Hey," Jeffrey said, coming in a little too late for Sara's liking. He was holding a bottle of beer in his hand. "I see y'all met."

Nell said, "You didn't tell me she was a stripper, Slick."

"Only weekends," he said, handing Nell the beer. "Just until she gets on full-time with the airline."

Sara tried to catch his eye to tell him she wanted to get the hell out of here, but either Jeffrey had not learned to read her signs in the last few months or he was fully aware of the treatment she was getting and did not mind a bit. His shit-eating grin told her the truth of the matter.

Jeffrey threw his arm around her, dragging her close and kissing her head. It felt more like he was telling her to be a good sport than anything else, and Sara pinched the fire out of the back of his arm to let him know she was not up for that kind of play.

He winced, rubbing his arm. "Nell, can you give us a minute?"

Nell walked down the hall and went into what was probably the kitchen. Outside the open back door, Sara could see a pool in the yard with another couple sitting around in beach chairs. In the distance, a dog was barking. Possum stood behind a grill with a long fork in his hand, and he waved at them both through the screen door.

Sara said, "This detour seems a little planned to me."

"Sorry?"

She kept her voice low, mindful that Nell was probably listening. "Is this part of the indoctrination for all your new things?"

"My what?"

She indicated the kitchen. "That's what your friend called me."

To his credit, he looked annoyed. "She's just—"

"Thinking I'm one of your sluts?" Sara finished, her throat straining even as she whispered. "Because that's what she pretty much said, that I'm one of your sluts."

He tried his smile again. "Sara, honey—"

"Don't you *dare* call me that, you asshole."

"I didn't—"

She fought to keep her tone low. "I don't know who the hell you think you are, dragging me all the way down here below the damn Gnat Line just to embarrass me, but I don't appreciate it and you've got about two seconds to say goodbye to these people, because I'm driving back to Grant right now and I don't give a damn whether you're in the car or not."

About three seconds passed before he burst into laughter. "My God," he said. "That's more than you've said to me the entire trip."

Sara was so furious that she punched him in the shoulder as hard as she could.

"Ow," he said, rubbing the spot.

"Mr. Big Football Player can't take a hit?" She punched him again. "Why didn't you tell me you played football?"

"I thought everybody knew."

"How would I know that?" she demanded. "Rhonda at the bank?" He grabbed her hand before she could punch him again.

"That slut at the sign shop?" She tried to get her hand back but he held her too tightly.

"Honey—" He stopped himself with a grin that said he was humoring her. "Sara."

"You think I don't know you've screwed practically every woman in town?"

He took on a wounded look. "They were just place-holders while I waited for you."

"You are so full of shit."

He stepped toward her, reaching out to put his hands on her waist. "Do you kiss your mama with that mouth?"

She tried to push him away, but he backed her toward the wall. Sara felt the familiar weight of his body press into her, but all she could think about was the fact that his friends were right outside the door watching. She expected him to give her a passionate kiss or make some other show of his manly prowess, followed by a victory lap around the pool and a high-five from Possum, but all he did was kiss her forehead and say, "I haven't been back here in six years."

She stared at him, mostly because his face was less than two inches away from hers.

Suddenly, the door banged open, and one of the most gorgeous men Sara had seen outside of a fashion magazine sauntered into the house. He was as tall as Jeffrey but with broader shoulders and more swagger.

When he opened his mouth, he spoke with the sexiest Southern drawl Sara had every heard. "You too scared to introduce me to your new girl, Slick?"

"Course not," Jeffrey said, slipping a proprietary arm around Sara's waist. "Honey, this is Spot. He and Possum were my best friends growing up."

"Still waiting on this one to finish," the man said, feigning a punch at Jeffrey. "And it's Robert now."

Possum called from outside, "One 'a y'all fetch me them burgers from the fridge."

Robert said, "Slick, why don't you handle that?" then took Sara by the arm and led her down the hall before Jeffrey could stop them.

Robert opened the screen door for Sara, asking, "How was your trip over?"

"Good," she told him, though that was debatable. She cast about for something positive to say. "My God, what a gorgeous yard."

Possum beamed. "Nell loves being outside."

"It shows," Sara said, meaning it. Lush flowers bloomed all over the place, spilling out of pots on the deck, climbing up the wooden fence. A huge magnolia tree shaded a hammock at the back of the yard, and several holly trees added contrast to the fence line. Except for the barking dogs next door, the yard was an oasis.

"Whoa," Robert said, bumping into her as the dog shot past them.

"Tig!" Possum yelled halfheartedly as the dog dove into the pool. She swam a lap across, climbed out, then rolled around in the grass, kicking her legs in the air.

"Man," Possum said. "What I wouldn't do for that life."

The woman sitting by the pool looked over her shoulder. "She learned everything from Jeffrey." She indicated the chair beside her. "Come sit by me, Sara. I'm not as horrible as Nell."

Sara gladly took the offer.

"Jessie," the woman introduced herself. She indicated Robert with a lazy wave of her hand. "That specimen's my husband." She pronounced the word "huzz-bun," managing with her tone to make it sound slightly pornographic.

Sara offered, "He seems nice."

"They all do at first," she said offhandedly. "How long have you known Slick?"

"Not long," Sara confessed, wondering if everyone here had a nickname. She was getting the distinct impression that Jessie was probably worse than Nell. She was just more polite about it. Judging by the woman's breath, a liberal dose of alcohol was responsible for her mellow tone.

"They're all a tight little group," Jessie commented, leaning over

71

to pick up a glass of wine. "I'm new in town, which means I've only been here twenty years. I moved from LA during my freshman year."

Sara guessed from her accent she meant Lower Alabama.

"Robert's a cop, just like Jeffrey. Isn't that nice? I call 'em Mutt and Jeff, only Jeffrey hates being called Jeff." She took a healthy swallow of wine. "Possum runs the store over by the Tasty Dog. You should meet his and Nell's children, especially the oldest. He's a beautiful little boy. Children are such a joy to have around. Isn't that right, Bob?"

"What's that, sugar?" Robert asked, though Sara was certain he had heard her.

Nell sat down beside Sara, handing her a bottle of beer. "Peace offering," she said.

Sara took it, though beer had always tasted like swill to her. She forced herself to make an effort, saying, "You've got a beautiful yard."

Nell inhaled deeply, then exhaled, "The azaleas bloomed and went away quicker than spit. Neighbor's never home to take care of his dogs so they bark all day. I can't get rid of the fire ants by the hammock and Jared keeps coming in with poison ivy, but for the life of me, I can't figure out where he's getting it." She paused for another breath. "But thank you. I try."

Sara turned to include Jessie in the conversation, but the other woman's eyes were closed.

"She's probably passed out." Nell fanned herself with her hand. "God, I was such a bitch to you."

Sara did not argue.

"I'm not normally so testy. If Jessie was awake, she'd tell you otherwise, but you can't trust a woman who drinks a whole bottle of wine before four in the afternoon, and I'm not just talking on Sundays." She swatted a fly. "She tell you about being new here?"

Sara nodded, trying to keep up.

"You should be glad she passed out. Couple'a more minutes she'd be telling you how she always depends on the kindness of strangers."

Sara took a sip of beer.

"Slick hasn't been back here in forever. Left town like he was running through hell with gasoline britches on." She paused. "I guess I was mad at him and took it out on you." She put her hand on Sara's chair. "What I'm saying is I'm sorry I showed my ass."

"Thank you for apologizing."

"I near about cracked up when you said that about the balloon animals." She laughed. "He told me you were a doctor, but I didn't believe him."

"Pediatrician," Sara confirmed.

Nell sat back in the chair. "You have to be smart to get into medical school, right?"

"Pretty much."

She nodded appreciatively. "Then I'll assume you know what you're doing with Jeffrey."

"Thank you," Sara told her, and meant it. "You're the first person I've met who's said that."

Nell turned serious, looking at Sara with something like pity. "Don't be surprised if I'm the last."

CHAPTER SIX

During the five hours she spent at Nell's, Sara found out more about Jeffrey Tolliver than she had in three months of dating him. Jeffrey's mother was a confirmed alcoholic and his father was serving time in prison for something no one was very specific about. Jeffrey had dropped out of Auburn two classes away from graduating and joined the police force without telling anybody why. He was an excellent dancer and he hated lima beans. He was definitely not the marrying kind, but Sara did not need Nell to tell her this. Jeffrey radiated the words "confirmed bachelor."

Considering Nell had managed to mumble most of these details under her breath during a particularly competitive game of Trivial Pursuit, Sara was only privy to the headlines and none of the details behind them. It was pitch dark by the time they left the group, and as Sara and Jeffrey walked down the street toward his mother's house, she tried to think of a way to find out more.

She settled on "So, what does your mother do?"

"Different things," he said, not offering anything else.

"And your dad?"

He switched her suitcase to his other hand and wrapped his arm around her. "You seem like you had a good time tonight."

"Nell's just full of insight."

"She likes the sound of her own voice." He slid his hand to her hip. "I wouldn't believe everything she says."

"Why is that?"

His hand slid lower as he nuzzled her neck. "You smell good."

She got the message, but did not exactly change the subject. "Are you sure your mother won't mind us staying over?"

"I called her from Nell's a few hours ago," Jeffrey said. "You remember when Nell was telling you my life story?" He gave her a look that said he knew exactly what had been going on with Nell, though Sara had to assume Jeffrey would not have taken her to meet his friends without knowing exactly what would happen.

She decided to call him on it. "This is a pretty cheap way for me to find out all about your life without you having to say a word."

"I told you, I wouldn't believe everything Nell has to say."

"She's known you since you were both six."

"She's not exactly my biggest fan."

Sara finally picked up on the tension between them. "Don't tell me you dated her, too?"

He didn't answer, which she took for an affirmation. "It's right here," he said, indicating a house with a beat-up Chevy Impala parked in the driveway. Even though Jeffrey had called ahead, his mother hadn't bothered to leave on any lights for them. The house was completely dark.

Sara hesitated. "Shouldn't we stay in a hotel?"

He laughed, helping her as her foot caught on some loose gravel. "There aren't any hotels here except the one behind the bar that truck drivers rent by the hour."

"Sounds romantic."

"Maybe for some of them," he suggested, leading her up the front steps. Even in the darkness, Sara could tell the house was one of the ones that had been allowed to fall into disrepair. Jeffrey warned her, "Watch that board," as he slid his hand along the top of the doorframe.

"She locks her door?"

"We were robbed when I was twelve," he explained, jiggling the key in the lock. "She's lived in fear ever since." The door stuck at the bottom and he used his foot to push it open. "Welcome."

The smell of nicotine and alcohol was overwhelming, and Sara was glad the darkness hid her expression. The house was stifling and she could not imagine spending the night, let alone living here.

"It's okay," he said, indicating she should go in.

She lowered her voice, "Shouldn't we be quiet?"

"She can sleep through a hurricane," Jeffrey said, closing the door behind him. He locked it with the key, then, judging from the sound, dropped the key into a glass bowl.

Sara felt his hand on her elbow. "Back this way," he said, walking close behind her. She took about four steps through the front room before she felt the dining room table in front of her. Three more steps and Sara was in a small hallway, where a nightlight revealed a bathroom in front of her and two closed doors on either side. He opened the door on the right and followed her through, closing the door again before he turned on the light.

"Oh," Sara said, blinking at the small room. A twin bed with green sheets and no blanket was pushed into the corner under a window. Posters of half-naked women were taped around the walls, with Farrah Fawcett given a place of prominence over the bed. The closet door was the only departure from the decorating scheme: a poster showed a cherry red convertible Mustang with an exaggerated blonde leaning over the hood—probably because the weight of her enhanced breasts prevented her from standing up straight.

"Lovely," Sara managed, wondering how bad the hotel was.

Jeffrey seemed embarrassed for the first time since she had met him. "My mother hasn't changed things much since I left."

"I can see that," she said. Still, part of Sara was intrigued. As a teenager, her parents had made it clear that boys' rooms were off-limits and Sara had therefore missed the experience. While the Farah Fawcett poster was predictable, there was something else to the room, some sort of essence. The smell of cigarette smoke and bourbon did not exist here. Testosterone and sweat had muscled it out.

Jeffrey put her suitcase flat on the floor and unzipped it for her. "I know it's not what you're used to," he said, still sounding embarrassed. She tried to catch his eye, but he was busy sorting through his duffel bag. She realized from his posture that he was ashamed of the house and what she must be thinking about him for growing up here. The room looked different in light of this, and Sara noticed how neatly everything had been arranged and the fact that the posters were hung equidistant, as if he had used a ruler. His house back in Grant County reflected this need for orderliness. Sara had only been there a few times, but from what she had seen, he kept everything exactly in its place.

"It's fine," she assured him.

"Yeah," he said, though not in agreement. He found his toothbrush. "I'll be right back."

Sara watched him leave, pulling the door shut quietly behind him. She took advantage of the situation and quickly changed into her pajamas, all the while keeping her eye on the door in case his mother walked in. Nell had not sounded exactly complimentary when she had talked about May Tolliver, and Sara did not want to meet the woman with her pants down.

Sara sat on the floor and went through her suitcase, looking for her hairbrush. She found it wrapped up in a pair of shorts and managed to remove her hair clip without tearing out too much of her curly, tangled hair. She looked around the room as she brushed her hair, taking in the posters and the various items Jeffrey had collected throughout his childhood. On the windowsill were several dried bones that had once been in a small animal. The bedside table, which looked homemade, had a small lamp and a green bowl with a handful of loose change. Track ribbons were scattered on a bulletin board, and a milk crate held cassette tapes with song titles typewritten neatly across the labels. Across from where she sat was a makeshift bookshelf of two-by-fours and bricks, stacked end to end with books. Where Sara had been expecting comic books and the occasional Hardy Boys, she found thick tomes with titles such as *Strategic Battles of the Civil War* and *The Socio-Political Ramifications of Reconstruction in the Rural South.*

She put down the brush and picked up the least intimidating-looking textbook. Flipping to the front, she found Jeffrey's name, followed by a date and course information. Thumbing through the pages, she saw where he had taken copious notes in the margins, underlining and highlighting passages that were of interest. Sara was slightly shocked to realize that she was completely unfamiliar with Jeffrey's handwriting. He had never left her notes or written lists in her presence. Contrary to her own cramped printing, he wrote in a beautiful, flowing script, the kind they no longer taught in school. His *w*'s were impeccable, transitioning neatly into adjoining vowels. The loops on his *g*'s were all the same identical pattern, as if he had used a stencil to make them. He even wrote in a straight line, not diagonally like most people did without a baseline to follow.

She traced her finger along his notations, feeling the indentation the pencil had made in the page. The words seemed almost engraved, as if he had gripped the pencil too tightly.

"What are you doing?"

Sara felt a flicker of guilt, as if she had been caught reading his diary instead of a textbook from long ago. "The Civil War?"

He kneeled beside her, taking the book. "I majored in American History."

"You're just full of surprises, Slick."

He winced at the name as he slid the book back into place, lining it up carefully so that it was flush with the others. A thin line of dust marked the exact spot. He pulled out a slim leather-bound volume. Gold letters stamped the cover, saying, simply, LETTERS.

"Soldiers wrote these to their sweethearts back home." Jeffrey said, thumbing through the fragile-looking book, turning to a page he must have known from heart. He cleared his throat and read, " 'My darling. Night comes and I lay awake, wondering at the character of the man I have become. I look at the velvet sky and wonder if you look up on these same stars, and pray that your mind holds on to the image of the man I was to you. I pray that you still see me.' "

Jeffrey stared at the words, a smile at his lips like he shared something secret with the book. He read the way he made love: deliberately, passionately, eloquently. Sara wanted him to continue, to lull her to sleep with the deep cadence of his voice, but he broke the spell with a heavy sigh.

"Anyway." He tucked the book back into place, saying, "I should have sold these back when the classes ended, but I didn't have the heart."

She wanted to ask him to continue, but said, "I kept some of mine, too."

He sat down behind Sara, his legs on either side of her. "I couldn't afford to."

"I wasn't exactly rich," she told him, feeling defensive. "My father's a plumber."

"Who owns half the town."

Sara did not comment, hoping he would drop it. Eddie Linton had invested well in real estate down by the college, which Jeffrey had found out on a couple of landlord calls about soon-to-be-evicted noisy tenants. She supposed by Jeffrey's standards the Linton family was wealthy, but Sara and Tessa had grown up with the impression that they should never spend more money than what they had in their pockets—which was never much.

Jeffrey said, "I guess Nell told you about my dad."

"A little."

His laugh had a harsh edge to it. "Jimmy Tolliver was a small-time crook who thought he was walking into a big score. Two men were shot and killed robbing that bank, and now he's locked up with no chance of parole." Jeffrey picked up the hairbrush. "You talk to any-body in town, they'll tell you I'm just as bad as he is."

"I seriously doubt that," Sara countered. She had worked with Jef-frey for a while now, and knew that he always went out of his way to do the right thing. His integrity was one of the main things that had attracted her to him.

He said, "I got into trouble a lot when I was a kid."

"Most boys do."

"Not with the police," he countered, and she did not know what to say. He couldn't have been that bad or there was no police force in the country that would have accepted him, let alone given him the keys to the station house.

He added, "I imagine Nell gave you an earful about my mother."

Sara did not answer.

He started to brush her hair. "Is that why you sucked at Trivial Pursuit? You were too busy trying to follow what Nell was saying?"

"I've never been good at board games."

"What about other games?"

She closed her eyes, enjoying the stroking bristles. "I beat you at tennis," she reminded him.

"I let you," he said, though she knew he had nearly killed himself trying to win.

Jeffrey pulled back her hair and gently kissed her neck.

"We could have a rematch?" she suggested.

He wrapped his arms around her, pulling her closer. He did something with his tongue that made her sink back into him without thinking.

She tried to sit up but he would not let her. She whispered, "Your mother is in the next room."

"The toilet's in the next room," he told her, slipping his hands under her shirt.

"Jeff—" She gasped as his hand dipped below her pajama bottoms. She stopped him before he could go any farther.

Jeffrey said, "Trust me, she can sleep through anything."

"That's not the point."

"I locked the door."

"Why did you lock it if she can sleep through anything?"

He growled at her much the way he had growled over his high school teacher. "Do you know how many nights I laid awake in this very room when I was a kid, wishing I had a beautiful woman in here with me?"

"I seriously doubt I'm the first woman you've had here."

"Here?" he asked, indicating the floor.

She twisted around so she could see him. "Do you think that's some kind of aphrodisiac, telling me how many women you've had in your bedroom?"

He scooted a few inches across the floor, dragging her with him. "You're the first one I've ever had *here*."

She gave an exaggerated sigh. "Finally, a way to distinguish myself."

"Stop that," he said, suddenly serious.

"Or what?" she teased.

"I'm not playing around."

"According to what I've heard—"

"I mean it, Sara. I'm not having fun."

She stared at him, not following.

"What you said to your mother," he told her, tucking a strand of hair behind her ear. "I'm not just having fun with you." He paused before looking away from her, staring at the bookshelf. "I know that's what you're doing, but I'm not, and I want you to stop saying stuff like that."

Every warning Sara had heard over the last few months came flooding into her brain, and she bit back the raging impulse to throw her arms around him and declare her love. Instinctively, she knew that part of the reason Jeffrey was saying this to her now was because he had no idea how she felt. Sara was not foolish enough to tell him.

Her silence obviously unnerved him. She saw his jaw work, and he stared somewhere over her shoulder.

Sara tried to face him, but he would not look at her. She traced her finger along his lips, smiling as she realized he had shaved for her. His skin was smooth, and she smelled his aftershave along with something like oatmeal.

He said, "Tell me how you feel."

Sara could not trust herself to answer. She kissed his jaw, then his neck. When he did not respond, she kissed the palm of his hand, knowing better than to tell him that was exactly where he held her.

Jeffrey put his hands on either side of her face, his eyes intense and unreadable. He gave her a long, sensual kiss as he pushed her back, and Sara felt herself melt to the floor. He cupped her breasts, using his tongue to bring out chills along her skin. Slowly, he started to work his way down, his breath a feathery kiss across her belly, then lower. He put his tongue inside of her, and Sara felt a momentary weightlessness as everything in her body focused on that one spot. She ran her fingers through his hair, pulling him up toward her, making him stop.

His voice was a hoarse whisper. "What?"

She drew him closer, kissing him, tasting herself in his mouth. Nothing was rushed, but Sara felt the need for urgency as she fumbled with the zip on his jeans. He tried to help, but Sara told him, "No," relishing the weight of him in her hand.

"Inside me," she said, biting his ear until a guttural sound caught in his throat. "I want you inside me."

"Christ," he whispered, his body shaking as he tried to hold himself back. He reached for his pocket, trying to find a condom, but she pulled his attention sharply back to focus, guiding him inside her.

She arched up as he entered her. At first, he moved slowly, almost painfully so, until Sara's entire body was tense as a violin string. The muscles along his back were equally taut, and she could not help digging her nails in as she tried to pull him in deeper. Jeffrey kept the rhythm slow, watching her every move, tuning his body to hers so that several times she was taken to the edge, only to be gently brought back. Finally the rhythm increased, his hips grinding into hers, the weight of his body pressing her to the limit until the release forced her head back, her mouth open. He kissed her, stifling the sounds she made, even as his own body shuddered against hers.

"Sara," he breathed into her ear, finally letting himself go.

She held him inside her, and he started kissing her again, slow and sensual, his hand stroking the side of her face like a cat. Her body pulsed with aftershocks, and she slid her arms around him, holding him close, kissing his lips, his face, his eyelids, until he finally rolled to his side, resting his weight on his elbow.

She let out a short breath, feeling her body slowly come down from the high. Her head was still swimming and she could not keep her eyes open no matter how hard she tried.

He stroked his fingers along her temple, touching her eyelids, her cheeks. "I love the way your skin feels," he said, letting his hand slide down her body.

She rested her hand on his, letting out a content sigh. She could stay like this all night—maybe even for the rest of her life. She felt closer to Jeffrey now than she had ever felt with a man in her life. Sara knew that she should be scared, should try to hold part of herself back, but right now all she could think to do was lie there and let him do whatever he liked.

His fingers found the scar on her left side, and he said, "Tell me about this."

Sara's mind reeled with white-hot panic, and she forced herself not to jerk away from him. "Appendix," she said, though the injury had come from a hunting knife.

He opened his mouth, and she was sure he would ask how she could be a doctor and not know that the appendix was on the right side, but what he said was, "Did it burst?"

She nodded, hoping that would suffice. Lying was not a normal habit of Sara's, and she knew better than to invent a complicated story.

"How old were you?"

She shrugged, watching him watch his finger trace along the scar. The edge was jagged, far from the precision slice of a surgeon's scalpel. A serrated blade had made the cut as the knife was buried nearly to the hilt in her side.

"It's kind of sexy," he told her, leaning down to kiss it.

Sara put her hand to the back of his head, staring up at the ceiling as the enormity of the lie began to sink in. This was just the beginning. If she ever wanted any kind of future with Jeffrey, she should tell him now before it was too late.

He brushed his lips across hers. "I thought we'd get out early tomorrow."

Her mouth opened, but instead of telling him the truth, she said, "You don't want to say goodbye to your friends?"

He shrugged. "We can call them when we get to Florida."

"Crap." Sara sat up, looking for a clock. "What time is it?"

He tried to pull her back but Sara was too fast. She rifled through her suitcase, asking, "Where's my watch?"

He folded his hands behind his head. "Women don't need to wear watches."

"Why is that?"

He gave a smug, deeply satisfied smile. "There's a clock on the stove."

"Very funny," she said, throwing her brush at him. He caught it with one hand. "I told my mother I'd call as soon as we got to Florida."

"So call her tomorrow."

Sara found her watch, cursing under her breath. "It's past midnight. She'll be worried."

"There's a phone in the kitchen."

Her underwear was still wrapped around her ankle from where she had not quite managed to kick it off. Sara tried to look as graceful as possible as she pulled them back on, followed by her pajama bottoms.

"Hey," he said.

She looked up, but he shook his head, indicating he had changed his mind.

She buttoned her shirt as she walked toward the door. Her hand was on the knob before she realized, "It doesn't have a lock."

He feigned surprise. "Is that so?"

Sara walked into the hall and pulled the door to behind her. She felt her way along the wall, stopping when she remembered the dining room table. The nightlight did not illuminate much this far from the bathroom, and Sara used her hands to feel her way toward the kitchen. Outside the room, the smell of nicotine was even stronger than she had remembered. By sheer luck, she found the telephone on the wall by the refrigerator.

She dialed her parents' house collect, whispering her name when the operator asked, hoping she would not wake up Jeffrey's mother. The call was put through and the phone rang once before her father picked up.

"Sara?" Eddie said, his voice like a croak.

She leaned against the counter, relieved to hear him. "Hey, Daddy."

"Where the hell are you?"

"We stopped in Sylacauga."

"What the hell is that?"

She started to explain, but he would not let her.

"It's past midnight," he said, his tone sharp now that he realized she was okay. "What the hell have you been doing? Your mother and I have been worried sick."

She heard Cathy murmur something in the background, and Eddie said, "I don't want to hear that bastard's name. She never used to call late before him."

Sara braced herself for a tirade, but her mother managed to wrestle the phone from her father before he could get another word out.

"Baby?" Cathy sounded equally worried, and Sara felt guilty for how she had spent the last two hours when she could have taken two minutes to call her parents and let them know she was okay.

"I'm sorry I didn't call before," Sara told her. "We stopped in Sylacauga."

"And that is?"

"A town," Sara said, still not sure she was pronouncing it correctly. "It's where Jeffrey grew up."

"Oh," Cathy said. Sara waited for more, but all her mother said was, "Are you okay?"

"Yes," Sara assured her. "We had a nice time with his friends. They all went to school together. It's just like home, only smaller."

"Is that so?"

Sara tried to decipher her tone, but could not. "We're at his mother's now. I haven't met her yet, but I'm sure she's nice, too."

"Well, let us know when you get to Florida tomorrow if you have the time."

"Okay," Sara answered, still unable to read her mother's tone. She wanted to tell her what had happened, what Jeffrey had said, but she did not have the courage. What's more, she did not want to be called a fool.

Cathy seemed to read nothing into Sara's hesitation. She said, "Good night, then."

Sara wished her the same, and hung up the phone before her father could get back on the line. She pressed her head back against the kitchen cabinet, wondering if she should call them again. As much as she hated her mother being in her business, Sara valued Cathy's opinion. Too much was happening right now. She needed to talk to someone about it.

A loud bump came from the dining room as someone fell against the table and a woman's voice growled a curse.

"Hello?" Sara said, trying not to surprise Jeffrey's mother.

"I know you're there," she said, her voice raspy and cold. "Jesus Christ," she mumbled to herself, opening the refrigerator door. In the light, Sara saw a bent-over old woman with salt-and-pepper hair. Her face was wrinkled far beyond her years, and every line in her mouth seemed devoted to smoking a cigarette. She held one there now, ash hanging off the end.

May Tolliver pounded a bottle of gin onto the counter, took a long drag from her cigarette, then turned her attention on Sara. "What do you do?" she asked, then gave a nasty chuckle. "That is, other than fuck my son?"

Sara was so taken aback she began to stutter. "I . . . I . . . d-don't . . ."

"Fancy doctor," she said. "Isn't that right?" The laugh came again, this time even nastier. "He'll bring you down a peg or two. You think you're the first one? You think you're special?"

"I—"

"Don't lie to me," the old woman barked. "I can smell him on your cunt from here."

Seconds later, Sara was in the street. She could not recall finding the key or opening the front door or even leaving the house. The only thing she knew was that she had to put as much distance between herself and Jeffrey's mother as she could. Never in her life had another woman spoken to her that way. Sara's face burned from the shame of it, and when she finally stopped under a street lamp to catch her breath, she found that tears were streaming down her cheeks.

"Shit," she hissed as she turned in a full circle, trying to get her bearings. She had taken a left turn at least, but beyond that, Sara was completely unsure of her surroundings. She could not even recall the name of Jeffrey's street, let alone remember what his house looked like. A dog barked as she passed a yellow house with a white picket fence, and Sara felt a chill as she realized that she did not recognize the dog or the fence. To make matters worse, her feet were burning from the hot asphalt and mosquitoes had come out in force to feast on the idiot who was walking around alone, wearing nothing but a thin pair of cotton pajamas, in the middle of the night. She did not know why she cared about finding the house. Even if she made it back, Sara would sleep in the street before she went back in. Her only hope was to backtrack from Jeffrey's to find Nell and Possum's house. There was a magnetic key safe on the undercarriage of the BMW. Jeffrey could find his own ride to Grant. Sara did not care if she ever saw her clothes or suitcase again.

Suddenly, a bloodcurdling scream cut through the night. Sara stopped mid-stride, tension filling the air like molasses. A car backfire sounded like gunshot, and adrenaline tensed every muscle in her body. In the distance, she could see a tall figure moving quickly toward her, and instinctively Sara turned, running away as fast as she could. Heavy footsteps pounded behind her, and she pumped her arms, her lungs nearly exploding in her chest as she pushed herself to get away.

"Sara," Jeffrey called, his fingertips brushing against her back. She stopped so quickly that he smacked into her, knocking them both down. He managed to cushion the fall with his body, but her elbow was jarred against the pavement.

"What is wrong with you?" he demanded, jerking her up by the arm. He slapped grit off the side of her pajama leg. "Did you scream?"

"Of course not," she snapped, suddenly angrier with him than she had ever imagined herself capable. Why had he brought her here? What did he hope to accomplish?

"Just calm down," he said, reaching out at if to soothe her.

She slapped away his hand. "Don't touch me" was all she could say before the car backfired again. Though this time, Sara knew it was not a car. She had been to the firing range often enough to know the sound of a weapon being discharged.

Jeffrey cocked his head to the side as he tried to figure out from which direction the sound had come. Again, there was a single gunshot, and he turned away from her, saying, "Stay here," as he bolted down the road toward the yellow house with the picket fence.

Sara followed as best she could, going around the fence that Jeffrey had hurdled, using a worn path in someone's garden to get to the backyard of the yellow house. There was a bright flash of light as Jeffrey kicked in the back door, followed by another scream. He ran out seconds later, and all the lights seemed to turn on in the house at once.

"Sara!" Jeffrey yelled, waving her in. "Hurry!"

She jogged toward him, feeling a sharp sting in the arch of her foot as she crossed the grass. There were pine needles and cones in the yard, and she tried to step as carefully as she could without slowing down.

Jeffrey grabbed her arm and pulled her the rest of the way into the house. The layout was similar to Possum's, with a long hallway down the center and the bedrooms on the right.

"Down there," Jeffrey said, pushing her toward the hall. He picked up the kitchen phone, telling her, "I'll call the police."

Shock overcame Sara for a moment as she walked into the master bedroom.

The ceiling fan wobbled out of balance overhead, the blades making an awkward chopping sound. Jessie stood beside an open window, her mouth moving but no noise coming out. A shirtless man lay facedown on the floor by the bed. The right side of his head was blown off. Streaks of blood led to a short-nosed gun that looked as if it had been kicked away from the area near his left hand.

"My God," Sara breathed. Blood sprayed the area by the bed in a fine mist, spattering parts of the ceiling and the light on the fan. A chunk of skull and scalp was hanging from the bedside table; what looked like a section of earlobe was stuck to the front of the drawer.

Despite the horrific scene in front of her, Sara felt her medical training kick in. She went to the man, pressing her fingers against his neck, trying to find a pulse. She checked his carotids and found nothing, her fingers sticking to the skin when she pulled them away. There was a sheen of sweat on the body. The sickly sweet smell of vanilla filled the air.

"Is he dead?"

Sara spun around at the question.

Robert stood behind the bedroom door. He was partially bent over, leaning against the wall for support. His left hand covered a wound in his side, blood seeping out between his fingers. His right hand held a gun that was pointed toward the dead man.

Sara told Jessie, "Get me some towels," but the woman did not move.

"Are you okay?" Sara asked, keeping her distance from Robert. He still held the gun at his side and there was a glassy look to his eyes, like he did not know where he was.

Jeffrey entered, assessing the scene with a quick glance. "Robert?" he said, taking a few steps toward his friend. The other man blinked, then seemed to recognize Jeffrey.

Jeffrey indicated the gun. "Why don't you give me that, man?"

His hand shook as he handed the weapon to Jeffrey muzzle first. Jeffrey engaged the safety and tucked it into the waistband of his jeans.

Sara told Robert, "I need to take off your shirt, okay?"

He looked at her with a puzzled expression. "Is he dead?"

"Why don't you sit down?" she suggested, but he shook his head, leaning back against the wall again. He was a tall man and very muscular. Even in his undershirt and boxer shorts, he looked like someone who was not used to taking orders.

Jeffrey caught Sara's eye before asking, "What happened, Bobby?"

Robert's mouth worked, as if he had difficulty speaking. "He's dead, isn't he?"

Jeffrey stood between his friend and the body. "What happened?"

Jessie spoke in a rush, pointing to the window. "Here," she said. "He came in through here."

Jeffrey walked along the periphery of the room, peering though the open window without touching it. He said, "The screen's off."

Robert hissed with pain as Sara peeled back the shirt. Still, he helped her lift it over his head so she could see the full extent of the damage. He cursed between his teeth, gripping his shirt in his hand as she tentatively pressed the wound. Blood dribbled steadily from the small hole in his side into the waistband of his boxer shorts, but he put his shirt over the area to staunch the blood before Sara could properly examine the wound. She could see an exit wound higher up in his back before he turned his body away from her. The bullet was lodged in the wall directly behind him, red pinpricks of blood forming a circle around the hole.

"Bob," Jeffrey said, his tone sharp. "Come on, man. What happened?"

"I don't know," Robert said, practically grinding his shirt into the wound. "He just . . ."

Jessie interrupted, "He shot Bobby."

"He shot you?" Jeffrey repeated, obviously trying to get the story from Robert. There was a surprising underlayer of anger to his tone as he looked around the room, probably trying to reconstruct the scene in his head.

Jeffrey pointed to a bullet hole in the wall on the far side of the bed. "Is this from his gun or yours?"

"His," Jessie said in a high-pitched voice. From the way she was acting, Sara guessed the other woman was talking loudly to try to hide the fact that she was stoned out of her mind. She swayed back and forth like a pendulum, her pupils wide enough to blind her in direct sunlight.

Jeffrey hushed Jessie with a look. "Robert, tell me what happened."

Robert shook his head, holding his hand tightly to his wounded side.

Jeffrey demanded, "Goddammit, Robert, let's get your story straight before somebody puts it on paper."

Sara tried to help, saying, "Just tell us what happened."

"Bob?" Jeffrey prodded, his anger still palpable.

Sara tried to be gentle, telling Robert, "This would be easier if you sat down."

"It'd be easier if he fucking talked," Jeffrey yelled.

Robert looked at his wife, his mouth a straight line. He shook his head, and Sara thought she saw tears in his eyes. For her part, Jessie just stood there, slightly swaying, her robe pulled around her as if to stop a chill. She probably would not even realize how close they had both come to death until the morning.

"He came in through the window," Robert finally told them. "He put a gun on Jess. A gun to her head."

Jessie's expression as he said this was unreadable. Even from this distance, Sara could see that the other woman was having difficulty following the story. At Jessie's feet were several opened prescription bottles that had probably fallen from the bedside table. Blood splotched the triangular-shaped white pills. Sara could see where her footprints had smeared into the thick pile of the carpet. Jessie had run past the body on the way to the window. Sara wondered what she had been thinking. Was she trying to escape while her husband fought for his life?

Jeffrey asked, "What happened next?"

"Jessie screamed, and I pushed . . ." Robert glanced at the dead man on the floor. "I pushed him back and he fell . . . and then he shot at me—shot me—and I . . ." He stopped, trying to control the emotion that obviously wanted to come.

"There were three shots," Sara remembered. She looked around the room, trying to reconcile what she had heard in the street with the story he told.

Robert stared at the dead man. "Are you sure he's gone?"

"Yes," she told him, knowing that lying would serve no purpose.

"Here?" Jeffrey said, obviously trying to distract Robert from the grim truth. He pointed to the bullet hole by the bed. "He missed the first time?"

Robert made a visible swallow. Sara could see a bead of sweat roll down his neck when he answered, "Yeah."

"He came in through the window," Jeffrey began. "He put a gun to Jessie's head." He looked at Jessie for confirmation, and she nodded quickly. "You pushed him off the bed and he shot at you. You got your gun then. Right?" Robert gave a curt nod, but Jeffrey was not finished. "You keep your piece where? The closet? In the drawer?" He waited, but again Robert was reluctant. "Where do you keep your piece?"

Jessie opened her mouth, but closed it when Robert pointed to the closed armoire opposite the bed, saying, "There," before Jeffrey could repeat himself.

"You got your gun," Jeffrey said, opening the armoire door. A shirt fell out and he replaced it on the pile. Over his shoulder, Sara could see there was a plastic-molded gun safe on the top shelf. "You keep your backup in here, too?"

He shook his head. "The living room."

"All right." Jeffrey rested his hand on the open door. "You went for your gun. He shot you then?"

"Yes," Robert nodded, though he did not sound convinced. His voice was stronger when he added, "And then I shot him."

Jeffrey turned back to the scene, nodding his head as if he was having a conversation with himself, working everything out. He walked over to the window again and looked out. Sara watched him do all of this, shocked. Not only had Jeffrey changed the crime scene, now he was helping Robert concoct a plausible story for how this had all happened.

Jessie cleared her throat, and her voice shook when she asked Sara, "Is he going to be okay?"

Sara took a moment to realize Jessie was talking to her. She was still focused on Jeffrey, wondering what he would do next. He'd had a few minutes alone with Robert and Jessie before he called Sara into the house. What had he done during that time? What had they worked out?

"Sara?" Jessie prompted.

Sara made herself concentrate on what she could control, asking Robert, "Can I look?"

He moved his hand away from the bullet wound and Sara resumed the examination. His shirt had smeared the blood, but she thought she could make out a V-shaped sear pattern just below the opening.

She tried to wipe away the blood, but Robert put his hand back over the wound, saying, "I'm all right."

"I should check—"

He interrupted her. "I'm fine."

Sara tried to hold his gaze, but he looked away. She said, "Maybe you should sit down until the ambulance gets here."

Jeffrey asked, "Is it bad?"

"It's okay," Robert answered for her, leaning back against the wall again. He told Sara, "Thank you."

"Sara?" Jeffrey asked.

She shrugged, not knowing what to say. In the distance, she heard the wail of a siren. Jessie crossed her arms over her chest with a shudder. Sara wanted to see that shirt, wanted to see if the material was burned in the same pattern as Robert's skin, but he held it tightly in his fist, pressing it into the wound.

Sara had been a coroner for only two years, but the type of marking she thought she had seen was textbook quality. Even a rookie cop two days on the job would know what it meant.

The gun had been fired at contact range.

CHAPTER SEVEN

11:45 A.M.

Lena stood in the front of Burgess's Cleaners, looking across Main Street at the police station. The tinted glass door was too dark to see anything inside, but still she stared as if she could see into the building, knew exactly what was happening. Another shot had been fired thirty minutes ago. Of the two cops missing at the start of this, only Mike Dugdale had checked in. Marilyn Edwards was still missing and Frank said he thought the attractive young police officer had been in the squad room at the start of the attack. Everyone from the Grant force was walking around like the living dead. All Lena could think was that if she had gone into work a few minutes earlier, she might have been able to do something. She might have been able to save Jeffrey. Right now, she wanted to be in that building so bad that she could taste it.

She turned around, watching Nick and Frank talking by the map table. The GBI agents were milling around the coffee machine, voices low as they waited for orders. Pat Morris talked with Molly Stoddard, and Lena wondered if Pat had been one of Sara's patients. He was young enough.

"The hell you say," Frank told Nick, his voice loud enough to be heard over the activity. Everyone in the room looked up.

Nick indicated old man Burgess's office. "In here."

They both went into the small, windowless room, shutting the door behind them. The tension they stirred up was still in the room, and a few people went to the back of the cleaners, probably to go outside to smoke and talk about the outburst.

Lena took out her cell phone and waited for it to power up. It chirped twice, indicating she had messages waiting. She debated who to call, Nan or Ethan. Her uncle Hank briefly entered her mind, but considering their conversation that morning during which he practically begged her to lean on his shoulder, calling him now seemed like giving in, and Lena was not about to do that. She hated the thought of needing people almost as much as she hated having to reach out to them. In the end, she turned off the phone and tucked it back into her pocket, wondering why she had turned the damn thing on in the first place.

Frank came up beside her. His breath was sour when he asked, "Tactical's on the roof?"

Lena pointed at the building by the station. "Two up there that I can see," she said, indicating the black-clad men lying on their stomachs with high-powered rifles.

"Twenty more people from Nick's office just showed up," he told her.

"What for?"

"Stand around with their thumbs up their asses, from what I can see."

"Frank," Lena began, feeling a lump rise in her throat. "Are you sure?"

"What?"

"Jeffrey," she said, the word sticking.

"I saw it with my own eyes," Frank said, obviously upset by the memory. He wiped his nose with his hand as he crossed his arms over his chest. "He just went down. Sara crawled over to him and . . ." He shook his head. "Next thing I know, the shooter's putting a gun to her head, telling her to move away."

Lena chewed her lip, feeling a surprising shock of sympathy for Sara Linton.

"Nick seems to know what he's doing," Frank said. "They just cut the power to the whole building."

"Will the phones work without it?"

"There's a straight line to Marla's desk," Frank said. "The Chief put it in when he came here. Never knew why until now."

Lena nodded, trying not to think about it too much. When he had first taken the job as Chief, Jeffrey had done a lot of things that had seemed unusual at the time but ended up making perfect sense.

Frank said, "Phone company's made it so they can't call out unless it's to us."

Lena nodded again, wondering who had known to do all of this. If it was left up to her, they would be storming the building right now, finding the fuckers who had started all of this and finishing it by carrying out their bodies feet-first.

She put her foot on the window ledge, retying her shoe so that Frank would not see the tears welling in her eyes. She hated the fact that she could cry at the drop of a hat now. It made her feel stupid, especially because someone like Frank would take it as a weakness, when the truth was, she was crying because she was a hairsbreadth from full-out rage. How could someone do something like this? How could they come to the station, the last place Lena held as sacred, and do this kind of thing? Jeffrey had been her rudder through all of the shit that had happened to her in the last few years. How could he be taken away from her now, when she was getting her life back?

Frank muttered, "Goddamn media's already trying to get in."

"What?" she asked, hiding a sniff.

"Media," he said. "They're trying to get helicopters down here to film it."

"The station's within the no-fly zone," Lena pointed out, wiping her nose with the back of her hand. Fort Grant had been shut down under Reagan, putting thousands of locals out of their jobs and running the city of Madison into the ground. Still, the military's no-fly zone was in force, and that should keep the news stations from letting their helicopters hover over the area.

Frank said, "The hospital isn't."

"Fuckers," she said, wondering how anybody could do that job. They were vultures, and the people back home who watched it all live were no better than animals themselves.

Frank lowered his voice, saying, "We gotta keep in control here."

"What does that mean?"

"With Jeffrey gone . . ." Frank stared out into the street. "We gotta keep our people in charge."

"You mean you?" Lena asked, but she could read on his face that he hadn't meant it that way. She asked, "What's wrong with you? Are you sick?"

He shrugged, wiping his mouth with a dirty-looking handkerchief. "Me and Matt ate something bad last night." She was startled to see tears in his eyes at the mention of Matt. Lena could not imagine what it had been like for him to watch his friend die right in front of his eyes. Frank had been Matt's supervisor when the younger man first came onto the force. Almost twenty years had passed since then and they had spent just about every working day in each other's company.

Frank said, "We know Nick. We know what kind of guy he is. He needs all the support we can give him."

"Is that what you were talking about in the office?" Lena asked. "It didn't seem like you were so hot on supporting him five minutes ago."

"We have a difference of opinion about how this should go down. I don't want some bureaucrat walking in here and fucking things up."

"This isn't a cowboy movie," Lena countered. "If the negotiator knows what he's doing, then we should follow his lead."

"It's not a guy," Frank said. "It's a woman."

Lena gave him a scathing look. Frank had made it clear from Lena's first day that he did not think women belonged in uniform. It must have burned him up knowing that a woman was coming down from Atlanta to take charge.

Frank said, "It ain't about her being a female."

Lena shook her head, pissed off as hell that he was worried about something as stupid as this. "You don't get into the freaking GBI baking cookies."

"Nick trained with this gal when he first joined up. He knows her."

"What'd he tell you?"

"He won't talk about it," Frank said, "but everybody knows what happened."

Lena bristled. "I don't."

"They were holed up in a restaurant outside of Whitfield. Two idiots with guns looking to score off the lunch crowd." He shook his head. "She hesitated. The whole thing went bad in less than a minute. Six people died." He gave her a knowing look. "We got our people in there praying for a savior," he jabbed a finger at the station, "and she ain't got the balls to do it."

Lena stared across the street. They only had six people left in the squad room.

She looked back at Frank. "We need to find out what's going on in there." There were parents and wives and boyfriends who were left hanging, waiting to find out whether or not their loved one was living or dead. Lena knew what it felt like to lose somebody, but at least she had found out Sibyl was dead fairly fast. She hadn't had to wait like the families were doing now. Jeffrey had told her, then they had gone to the morgue. That was that.

Frank asked, "What is it?"

She had let her thoughts get away from her, remembering all the second chances Jeffrey had given her, including this one today. No matter what stupid thing Lena did, he never stopped believing in her. There was no one else who would ever do that again.

Frank repeated, "What?"

"I was just thinking . . ." she said, but the sight of a helicopter swooping over the college stopped her. Lena and Frank both watched as the big black bird hung in the air over the college, then touched down on the roof of the Grant County Medical Center. The building was little more than two stories of old brick, and Lena half expected it to buckle. It obviously held, because a few seconds later Nick Shelton's phone rang. He opened it, listened for a couple of beats, then shut it.

He said, "Cavalry's here," but there was no relief in his voice. He motioned for Lena and Frank to follow him outside the back of the cleaners, and they all made their way toward the hospital, the heat bearing down like a sauna.

Lena asked Nick, "Is there anything we can do?"

He shook his head, saying, "This's their show now. It's got nothing to do with us."

Lena tried to get confirmation on Frank's story. "You trained with this woman?"

His tone was clipped. "Not long."

"She good?" Lena prodded.

"She's a machine," Nick said, but it did not sound like a compliment.

They were silent as he led them past the shops on Main Street. They reached the hospital in under five minutes, but with the heat and anxiety, it seemed like hours. Lena did not know what she had been expecting when they reached the hospital, but it was not the elegantly dressed woman who threw open the back exit door and walked toward them with a purposeful stride. Behind her were three burly men dressed in the requisite shirts and chinos of the Georgia Bureau of Investigation. They wore huge Glocks on their sides and walked like they had brass balls. The woman leading them was small, around five three with a slight build, but she walked toward Nick with the same swagger.

"Glad you could get here," Nick said, a tone of resignation in his voice. He made introductions, telling Frank and Lena, "This is Dr. Amanda Wagner. She's the GBI's chief negotiator. She's been doing this longer than anybody in the state."

Wagner barely acknowledged them as she shook Nick's hand. She did not bother to introduce the three men she'd brought with her, and none of them seemed too upset about it. Up close, she was older than Lena had first thought, probably in her fifties. She had clear polish on her fingernails and little makeup. A simple diamond ring was all the jewelry she wore, and her hair was cut in one of those flyaway styles that took forever to fix. There was something calming about her presence, though, and Lena thought that whatever had gone on between the negotiator and Nick must have been personal. Despite what

Frank had said, there was nothing hesitant about Amanda Wagner. She seemed more than ready to jump into the fray.

Wagner spoke in a cultured drawl, asking Nick, "We've got two adult male shooters, heavily armed, with six hostages, three of them children?"

"That's correct," Nick said. "Phones and utilities are controlled. We're monitoring for cell transmissions, but nothing's come out yet."

"This way?" she asked. Nick nodded and they walked back toward the cleaners as she questioned him. "Car been found?"

"We're working on it."

"Entrances and exits?"

"Secured."

"Sharpshooters?"

"Standard six-point formation."

"Minicams?"

"We'll need them from you."

She glanced behind her, and one of the men got on his cell phone. She continued, "The jail population?"

"Evacuated to Macon."

Overhead, the helicopter that had brought them here took off. Wagner waited for the roar of the blades to die down before asking, "Have you established contact?"

"I got one of my men on the phone. They haven't picked up yet."

"Is he trained in negotiation?" Wagner asked, though surely she knew the answer. Nick shook his head, and she said, "Let's hope they don't answer, Nicky. The first contact is generally the primary negotiator throughout the entire siege. I thought you'd learned that lesson." She paused a moment, but when Nick did not respond, she suggested, "Perhaps you could stop him and get me the number?"

Nick took his radio off his belt. He walked ahead of them, relaying the order. When he called out the station's phone number, one of the men from Wagner's team dialed it into a cell phone and held it to his ear.

"Who've we got inside?" she asked as they started walking again. "Run it down for me one more time."

Nick recited like a good student, numbering people off on his fingers. "Marla Simms, station secretary. She's elderly. She won't be much help. Brad Stephens, foot patrol. He's got six years on the job."

Wagner asked Frank, "Can we count on him?"

Frank seemed surprised she had addressed the question to him. "He's a solid beat cop."

Lena felt the need to add, "He's kind of shaky under stress."

They all turned to look at her. Frank seemed angry, but Lena did not regret warning the negotiator about Brad. "I rode in a squad car with him last year. He's not steady under pressure."

Wagner gave her a look of appraisal. "You've been a detective for how long?"

Lena felt a lump in her throat, and all her resolve disappeared with that one question. "I took some time off this year for personal—"

"How lovely for you," Wagner said, turning back to Nick. "Who else?"

Nick continued walking and they followed. "Sara Linton, town pediatrician and coroner."

Her lip curled in a smile. "That's novel."

"She was married to our Chief of Police," Nick said. "Jeffrey Tolliver."

"Just give me the names of the living."

He stopped at the open cleaners' door, where Hemming and her fellow patrolman still stood guard. "There's three kids in there, around ten years old and freaked the fuck out."

"The pediatrician's probably helping. How many children were killed?"

"None," Nick answered. "One of them's in the hospital, might lose his foot. School's in the process of tracking down parents. A lot of them commute to Macon for work, but we've identified all the kids." He paused to regroup. "There's another officer inside. Barry Fordham. He was shot pretty bad from what Frank could see."

"We have to assume he's dead," Wagner said matter-of-factly as she walked into the cleaners. Inside, the crowd of officers and agents cleared a path for her. Wagner glanced around the room, her gaze assessing everyone from the four GBI agents Nick had brought to Molly Stoddard, Sara's nurse. She finally turned her sights back on Lena, saying, "Would you get me some coffee, dear? Black, two sugars."

Lena felt a flicker of anger, but she walked over to the coffeemaker to do as she was told. Pat Morris tried to catch her eye, but she ignored him.

Wagner leaned against the edge of the folding table, addressing the group. "First is the initial assault. You've got—what—five bodies in there?"

Lena bit back her pride and provided, "There's another patrol cop missing," as she dumped two packs of sugar into a paper cup.

"Six bodies, then," Wagner said. "The whole town's lit up with this. There's only one reason he's not checking in."

"Marilyn," Nick corrected. "The missing cop is a woman."

"That's the two extra shots you heard. They're going to take out the ones most likely to resist. The uniforms will be big bull's-eyes. Perhaps your shaky one"—she walked over to Lena and poured the coffee herself—"doesn't seem threatening enough. That's saved your Brad his life. For now."

Wagner checked her watch before asking, "Do we have a ventilation plan for the station?"

Frank said, "All the plans are at the town hall. We've already got two people searching."

"That's our priority." Wagner told one of her men, "James, be so kind as to go with Nicky to help speed the search along." Before they could leave, she added, "Let's see about cutting the water while you're at it."

Frank asked, "What's the next step?"

Wagner sipped her coffee before answering. "They'll secure the area. Put all the prisoners in one place so they can control them. Step three, they make sure no one can get in. They'll barricade the doors, and since the shooter who is obviously in charge was smart enough to bring a friend, one will always stay on point to make sure no surprises come through the front door."

She took another sip of coffee as she seemed to calculate variables in her head. "They've had ample time to do all of this, which means they'll soon be moving on to step four, which is to make their demands. That's where the negotiations come in. First, they're going to want the water and power back, then food. What *we* want is a chance to get inside that place." She saw Lena open her mouth to volunteer and Wagner held up a finger, saying, "We'll get to that when we come to it."

Frank said, "We got parents want to talk to their kids."

"That won't happen," Wagner told him. "The goal from our end is to keep as much emotion out of this as possible. We're not going to have crying parents pleading for their children's lives. Our shooters already know how valuable the hostages are without us reinforcing the fact."

"What else?" Lena asked. "What happens next?"

"They'll get hungry or want to see themselves on TV. Eventually, we'll get to the point where we've traded everything we can and they'll want out of there. We need to anticipate what they'll want at that point besides money. They always want money—unmarked and small denominations." She paused. "We need to find their car. They didn't sprout wings and fly here, and they're certainly not planning on leaving that way."

Lena said, "There's a lake behind the college."

"Private?"

"Semi," she said. "It's hard to get a boat in without people seeing, but you can if you want to badly enough."

Wagner picked out one of Nick's people. "That'll be you, okay? Take a couple of men and search the shore for boats. We're talking walking distance from the scene. They didn't plan a leisurely hike as part of their getaway." She asked Frank, "I suppose any reports filed on missing boats in the last week are inside the station?"

"Yeah."

"You've rerouted 9-1-1 calls?"

"Yeah," Frank repeated. "To the fire station up the street."

"Could you please see if anyone reported a missing boat this morning?"

Frank picked up one of the telephones on the counter to make the call.

Wagner looked at the two remaining men on her team. "We'll get the children out first for food and water." She asked Lena, "Is there a water cooler in there?"

"In the back by the jails."

"How many toilets?"

Lena did not understand the question, but she answered, "One."

She saw Lena's confusion and explained, "Drinking water. There's around a gallon and a half of water in the tank. They'll use that between themselves."

Frank hung up the phone. "No missing boats," he said. "I put out a feeler on the radio to see if anyone remembers taking a report."

"Good man," Wagner said. Then, to her team, "We'll try to get the old woman or the patrolman out after the children. They won't care about hanging onto them; the cop is still iffy and they'll see the old woman as dead weight. My guess is they'll want to keep the pediatrician." She asked Frank and Lena, "She's attractive?"

Lena began, "I wouldn't say—" just as Frank answered, "Yes."

"I imagine she's fairly confident," Wagner said. "Women don't get through medical school being demure." She frowned. "They won't like that."

Molly said, "I'm her nurse at the clinic. Sara's the most levelheaded person I know. She wouldn't do anything to compromise the situation, especially with children there."

Wagner looked at her crew. "What do you think, boys?"

The one who held the cell phone to his ear said, "No doubt they'll have a problem with her."

The other added, "They'll need to get rid of that adrenaline soon." He started to nod. "I'll go with them keeping the woman."

"I concur," Wagner said, and Lena felt her blood run cold.

Molly said, "You don't think they'll . . ."

Wagner's incredulous tone was sharp as a tack. "They've killed four police officers and shot at children, severely wounding one of them. Do you think they'll draw the line at sexual assault?" She turned her attention toward Frank. "You were in there, Detective. What did they come for? What else will they want?"

He shrugged, and Lena could feel his anger and confusion. "I don't know."

Wagner started to interrogate him. "What's the first thing they did?"

"They shot Matt. They shot up the station."

"Would you say that their primary goal was to shoot Detective Hogan?"

Even though Lena had heard Nick giving someone details over the phone, she was surprised the woman knew Matt's name.

Wagner prompted, "Detective Wallace?"

Frank shrugged again. "I don't know."

"You know more than we do, Detective. You were there. What did they say?"

"I don't know. They were yelling. Well, one of them was yelling. He started slapping Marla around. I went to the back of the station to call Nick."

Lena chewed the tip of her tongue. She had never liked Marla, but there was something horrific about beating up an old lady. Considering all they had done, Lena should not have been surprised, but still, hearing about Marla took her anger up yet another notch.

"Wait a minute," Frank said. Judging by his look, a lightbulb had gone off in his head. "He asked for the Chief. The one who said his name was Smith. He told Marla he wanted to see the Chief. She told me, and I found Jeffrey and . . ." He had spoken in a rush until he got to Jeffrey's name.

Somehow, Wagner made sense of what he was trying to say. "They asked for Chief Tolliver but they shot Detective Hogan?"

"I . . ." Frank shrugged. "I guess."

She looked around the room, finding Pat Morris over by Lena. "You're Morris?"

He nodded, obviously uncomfortable with being singled out. "Yes, ma'am."

She gave him a disarming smile, as if they were old friends. "You were there from the beginning?"

"Yes, ma'am."

"And what did you see?"

"Same as Frank."

Her smile thinned slightly. "Which was?"

"I was at my desk typing up a report," Morris began. "The Chief came into the room and I asked him a question about how to get to the D-15 screen. I'm not that great with computers."

"That's fine," Wagner soothed. "And then?"

Lena could see Morris swallow hard. "And then Matt came in the front door. Marla said something to him, like 'There you are,' then Dr. Linton screamed."

"Just screamed?"

"No, ma'am. She said, 'Jeffrey,' like she was warning him."

Wagner took a breath, then let it go. She pressed her lips together and Lena noticed her lipstick had smeared a bit. "So, we could have a case of mistaken identity."

Frank said, "How's that?"

"The shooter thought Detective Hogan was your Chief." Wagner looked around the room. "I know this is a silly question, but is there a particular perp your Chief put away who might be capable of doing something like this?"

Lena racked her brain for cases, wondering why she had not done this before. There were plenty of people she could think of who were angry enough to want to kill Jeffrey, but none of them had the balls to do it. Besides, it was never the big talkers who acted on their threats. It was the quiet ones, the ones who let their anger burn in the pit of their stomachs until it exploded, who actually showed up with a gun.

"It was worth a shot." Wagner addressed the group again. "Either way, mission accomplished for our two shooters. They came to kill Tolliver and as far as they know that was done in the first two minutes. Their escape was blocked by our helpful dry cleaner here, who ran into the street with his shotgun. I would guess their primary goal right now would be to get out of the building without being killed."

"Amanda?" Nick said. He walked through the room holding a rolled-up blueprint in his hand. "Ventilation plan."

"Good," she told him, spreading the schematic out on the table. She studied the layout of the ventilation system for a moment, tracing a shaft along a section of the back wall. "This looks like the best spot," she decided. "We can go through the drop ceiling in the conference room to access the duct and slide a Minicam through to get a bird's-eye of what's going on."

Frank said, "Why can't we just go through the ceiling?"

"The tiles break too easily. We don't want dust falling down and alerting them to—"

"No," he interrupted her, his voice excited. "The drop ceiling goes the whole length of the station. You could just climb over that back wall and drop down and—"

"End up killing everyone in there," Wagner finished. "We're far from last resorts at this point, Detective Wallace. What we want now is video and sound coming out of that room. Our first step toward controlling the situation is knowing what they're up to."

Wagner motioned her team closer, and they bent over the map, planning their point of entry. Lena watched them for a few minutes, trying to follow their jargon as they ran down the supplies they would need. She noticed Nick standing to the side, a hard look on his face. How he had left this kind of action was beyond her. There had to be more to the story of the Whitfield hostage situation than Frank knew. There was always a darker truth behind those sorts of rumors. God knows what kind of shit people had made up about Lena when she left the force.

Beside her, Pat Morris shifted against the table holding the coffee machine. He whispered to Lena, "You following anything they're saying?"

She shook her head.

"They seem to know what they're doing," Morris told her, and though Lena agreed, she did not comment.

"It's so weird," Morris continued, his voice still low. "The shooters, they can't be much older than my little brother, and he's still in high school."

She turned to him, warning bells going off in her head. "You're serious?" she asked. "How young? How young did they look?"

He shrugged. "They gotta be older, but they looked eighteen at the most."

"Why do they have to be older?" Lena asked. She noticed that Wagner and her team had grown quiet, but she didn't care. "Slight builds? Androgynous?"

Morris shifted uncomfortably under the pressure. "I don't know, Lena. It happened so fast."

Wagner broke in. "What are you thinking, Detective Adams?"

"The last case I worked on before I left," Lena said, the lump rising in her throat making it hard for her to speak.

Nick slammed his fist into the table, saying, "Goddammit," and Lena imagined the horror on his face mirrored her own. He had worked the case, too, and seen the damage firsthand.

"Oh, no," Molly said. "You don't think . . ."

Wagner's tone said her patience was running low. "Let's cut the suspense, folks."

"Jennings," Lena finally said, the name bringing the taste of bile to the back of her throat. "A pedophile who's good at getting young men to do all the dirty work."

CHAPTER EIGHT

Jeffrey helped the paramedics carry Robert down the front steps. He was still refusing to get onto a stretcher for his own hardheaded reasons, and every time Jeffrey tried to talk to him, Robert just shook his head, as if he could not speak.

Jeffrey offered, "I'll be by the hospital as soon as Hoss gets here."

Robert shook his head for the hundredth time. "No, man. I'm okay. Just make sure Jessie gets to her mama's."

Jeffrey patted his shoulder. "We'll talk tomorrow when you're more up to it."

"I'm okay," Robert insisted. Even when they loaded him into the back of the ambulance, he only said, "Make sure you look after Jess."

Jeffrey walked back to the house, but he did not go in. Instead, he sat on the front steps, waiting for Hoss to show up. Clayton Hollister was the town's sheriff—had been as long as Jeffrey could remember—and when he'd called about the shooting, Jeffrey had learned that the old man had literally gone fishing. Hoss was heading back from Lake Martin, which was about half an hour's drive away. When Jeffrey had offered to go ahead and help process the scene, his old mentor had told him to hold up. "He'll still be dead when I get there."

Two sheriff's deputies stood outside talking to Robert's neighbors, both of them knowing better than to go inside the house until the boss arrived. Hoss ran his force with an iron fist, a management style Jeffrey had never taken to. Jeffrey knew the old man would be doubly attentive on this one; Robert and Jeffrey would likely be career criminals right now except for Hoss's early intervention. He had ridden them hard when they were teenagers, hawking their every move. Even when Hoss wasn't around, his deputies knew that the two boys were his special project, and they were just as vigilant as the sheriff, maybe even more so.

At the time, Jeffrey had resented the man's prying—he already had a father, even if Jimmy Tolliver spent more time in jail than he did at home—but now that he was a cop himself, Jeffrey understood the favor Hoss had done him as a kid. There was a reason both Jeffrey and Robert had chosen law enforcement as their careers. In his own way, Hoss had led by example. Though who knew what the hell Robert was up to now.

Sitting on the front porch watching the deputies, Jeffrey kept running back over Robert's story, trying to make sense of what he and Jessie had said. Something wasn't adding up, but that shouldn't have been surprising, considering Jeffrey was back in Sylacauga. He hated this Podunk town, hated the way every second that passed here seemed to be sucking the life out of him. He had been an idiot for coming back, and even more stupid for dragging Sara along with him. Nothing here had changed in the last six years. Possum and Bobby were still spending every Sunday together, waxing nostalgic by the pool while Jessie got drunk off her ass and Nell added her bitter quips to the mix. Sara being here had made things worse than he could have imagined.

Despite his idiotic admission last night, Jeffrey could not decide exactly how he felt about Sara. She had managed somehow to get under his skin, and part of him had asked her to go to Florida in the hopes that he would be able to fuck her out of his system once and for all. Normally, the women he dated bent over backward to please him, which generally got old after a few months and became a good justification for moving on to the next one in line. Sara was not like that.

On the surface, she was the kind of woman he always thought he would end up settling down with: a perfect combination of sexuality and self-confidence that made it impossible for him to get bored. It was a case of being careful what you wished for, though, because underneath it all, she was a lot of work. She had her own opinions about things and her mind was not easily changed. To make matters worse, her mother obviously thought he was the Devil incarnate and her sister had pegged him instantly for the kind of player he'd been all his life. She had actually laughed in his face when she opened the door to Sara's house yesterday, giving him a knowing up-and-down look, telling Jeffrey his reputation preceded him.

His gut reaction was to prove them all wrong. Maybe that was the problem—and the root to his attraction. Jeffrey wanted their approval. He wanted people to think he was a good guy, the kind of guy who came from a nice middle-class, God-fearing family that stood on the right side of the law. That seemed like a lost cause now. Sara was looking at him the same way everyone else in Sylacauga did, like he was just as bad as his father.

"Hey," Sara said, sitting down beside him on the steps.

He moved away from her. "How's Jessie?"

"Passed out on the couch," Sara told him, folding her arms around her knees. Her tone was reserved, like they were strangers.

"Is she on something?"

"I think her adrenaline gave out and whatever she took earlier finally caught up with her." She stared at him, seemed to be studying him.

"What?"

"We need to talk."

Dread washed over Jeffrey, but of the thousand things that came to his mind, what she actually said was more shocking than any of them.

"You changed the crime scene."

"What?" He stood up, putting himself between Sara and the crowd on the street. He knew he had done nothing wrong, but still he felt defensive. "What the hell are you talking about?"

"You left the door open."

"The back door? How else were you supposed to get in?"

Sara tucked her chin into her chest, the way she did when she was trying to keep her calm. "The armoire," she said. "You opened the door. You put the shirt back in."

He remembered now, and for the life of him he could not understand his own actions. "I just—" He couldn't find an answer. "I don't know what I was doing. I was upset. It doesn't mean anything."

Sara spoke matter-of-factly. "A man holds a gun to his wife's head, shoots at him, and Robert runs to the armoire, grabs his gun, and shuts the door?"

Jeffrey tried to think of a logical explanation. "He probably shut it without thinking." Even as he spoke, Jeffrey knew he was grasping at straws. The timing didn't work.

Sara stood up, brushing dirt off the back of her pajamas. "I'm not going to be an accomplice to this," she told him, and it sounded like a warning.

"An accomplice?" he repeated, thinking he had heard wrong.

"Changing the crime scene."

"That's ridiculous," he said, heading back inside.

She followed him like she did not trust him alone in the house. "Where are you going?"

"I'll close it back," he answered, walking into the bedroom. He stopped in front of the armoire. The door was already closed.

When he looked at Sara for an explanation, she said, "I didn't close it."

Jeffrey opened the door again and stood back. He took another step back and as they both watched, it closed. He laughed with relief. "See?" He duplicated his actions with the same result. "The floor must be uneven," he explained, testing the floorboards. "When you step back here, it closes."

A flicker of doubt crossed Sara's eyes. "Okay," she said, like she still was not sure.

"What?"

"Was the safe locked?"

He opened the door again, finding a black gun safe on the top shelf. "Combination lock," he said. "He could have left it open. They don't have kids."

She was staring at the dead man on the floor. "I want to sit in on the autopsy."

Jeffrey had somehow forgotten about the body in the room. He turned now, and looked at the corpse. The man's blond hair was matted with blood, partially concealing his face. His bare back was riddled with blood and brain, the laces of his untied tennis shoes stringing across the floor. Jeffrey never understood how people could think a dead person was just sleeping. Death changed the air, charged it with something thick and unsettling. Even with his half-opened eye and slackened jaw, there was no mistaking that the man was dead.

Jeffrey said, "Let's get out of here," leaving the room.

Sara stopped him in the hallway. "Did you hear me?" she said. "I want to sit in—"

"Why don't you do it yourself?" he interrupted, thinking this would be the only way to shut her up. "They don't have a coroner here. The guy who runs the funeral home does it for a hundred bucks a pop."

"All right," she said, but the guarded look on her face was far from reassuring. Jeffrey knew if she found anything out of place, from a pattern wound to an ingrown toenail, she'd throw it back at him that she was right.

"What do you think you're going to find?" he demanded, then remembering Jessie was in the next room, he lowered his voice. "You think my best friend's a murderer?"

"He already admitted to shooting that man."

Jeffrey walked toward the front door, wanting to get out of the house and away from Sara. Typically, she followed him, unable to let it go.

She put her hands on her hips, her tone the same she probably used to talk to her patients. "Think about their story, Jeffrey."

"I don't have to think about it," he said, but the more Sara talked, the more he did, and he did not like the conclusions his mind was drawing. He finally asked, "Why are you doing this?"

"The time frame doesn't jibe with what we heard in the street."

Jeffrey shut the front door, not wanting their conversation to be overheard. Through the narrow window, he could see the deputies talking to the ambulance driver who had just pulled up.

Sara said, "There was a lag between the scream and the first shot."

He tried to remember the sequence, but could not. Still, he said, "That's not how it happened."

"The shot was a few beats later."

"What's a few beats?"

"Maybe five seconds."

"Do you know how long five seconds is?"

"Do you?"

He saw Hoss's cruiser pull into the street. It was the same damn car he had driven when Jeffrey was a teenager, right down to the peeling sheriff's star on the side. Jeffrey and Robert had washed that car every weekend their junior year as penance for duct-taping a hapless freshman to the water fountain at school.

"All right," Jeffrey told Sara, wanting to get this the hell over with. "Five seconds. That goes with what they said—she screamed, Robert pushed him back, he fired. That could take five seconds."

Sara stared at him, and he did not know if she was going to call him an idiot or a liar. She surprised him by saying, "I honestly can't remember what they said, whether she screamed first or he pushed the guy first." Then, probably just to be a bitch, she added, "You might want to help Robert get that straight before he makes his statement."

Jeffrey watched Hoss talking to his deputies. He was wearing his fishing vest and a beat-up old hat with lures pinned to it. Jeffrey felt a sense of dread overwhelm him.

He said, "We didn't hear the second shot until I caught up with you. That's, what, another ten seconds?"

"I don't know. It wasn't immediate."

"Robert could have been looking for his gun."

She surprised him again by conceding, "True."

"Then the next shot was a few seconds later, right?" When she did not respond, he said, "Maybe two or three seconds later?"

"About."

"It could fit," he insisted. "The guy shoots at him, Robert goes to get his gun. It's dark, he can't find it at first. While he's looking for it, he's shot. He's surprised that he's shot, but he still manages to shoot back."

She nodded, but did not seem convinced. Jeffrey knew in his gut there was something else she was holding back, and he was running out of time.

"What?" he said, wanting to shake it out of her. "What aren't you telling me?"

"Just forget it."

"I mean it, Sara. There's something you're not saying. What is it?"

She stared out the window, not answering.

Hoss was still standing at the end of the walk. The ambulance made a low beeping noise as it backed into the driveway. Each beep seemed to heighten Jeffrey's frustration, so that when Sara started to leave the house, Jeffrey grabbed her arm and would not let her go.

She gave a surprised "What are you—"

"Not one word to him," he warned, feeling like the sky was falling down and there was nothing he could do to stop it. If he could just keep Sara quiet for a few more hours, maybe he could get to the bottom of it.

Sara tried to jerk her arm back, a look of shock on her face. "Let go of me."

"Just promise me."

"Let go," she repeated, wrenching her arm away.

Jeffrey felt so angry and helpless that he punched his fist into the wall behind her. Sara flinched, like she thought he meant to hit her. Fear, then sheer hatred flashed in her eyes.

"Sara," he said, taking a step back, holding up his hands. "I didn't . . ."

Her mouth tightened into a thin line. When she spoke, her tone was deep, like she was fighting to keep from raising her voice. He had never seen her really angry before, and there was something about her stillness that was more threatening than if she held a gun to his head.

"You listen to me, you asshole," she hissed through clenched teeth. "I will not be intimidated by you."

He tried to calm her. "I wasn't—"

She jerked away from him. "If you ever touch me again, I'll rip your throat open with my bare hands."

Jeffrey could feel his heart stop in his chest. The way she was looking at him now made him feel dirty and mean, like a bully. No wonder his father always got loaded to the gills after punching up his mother. The hatred must have felt like it was eating him alive.

Outside, Jeffrey could see Hoss and the deputies starting toward the house. He swallowed the bitter taste in his mouth, trying to reason with Sara.

"All we have are questions," he told her. "I'll get you into the autopsy, okay? We'll talk to Bobby and Jess tomorrow, okay? Just give me some time to figure out what the hell is going on here before you help send my best friend to the goddamn electric chair."

She would not even look at him, but he could feel her anger ringing in his ears clear as a bell.

"Sara—"

Hoss knocked on the front door and Jeffrey put his hand on the knob, as if he could keep him out. The old man gave him a look through the window that cut right into Jeffrey, and he felt like he was fifteen years old again, caught red-handed right outside the Ben Franklin with a transistor radio he had not paid for.

Sara reached for the knob and Jeffrey opened the door.

"Hey there." Hoss held out his hand and Jeffrey shook it, surprised by the grip. The man's hair had gone completely gray and the lines on his face were deeper, but other than that, he looked exactly the same.

Hoss said, "Damn shame to see you again under these circumstances, Slick." He tipped his hat to Sara. "Ma'am."

Sara opened her mouth to speak but Jeffrey interrupted her, saying, "Hoss, this is Sara Linton. Sara, this is Sheriff Hollister."

Hoss gave her one of his rare smiles. "I hear you doctored Robert for us. Thank you for taking care of my boy."

Sara nodded, and Jeffrey could tell she was waiting for the right moment to have her say. She was still so angry that her whole body seemed to vibrate with it.

Hoss told her, "We can get your statement tomorrow morning. I know it's been a hard night for you."

Jeffrey held his breath, waiting for her to explode.

Sara cleared her throat, like she had trouble finding her voice. She surprised him by saying, "Tomorrow will be fine." With barely more than a glance at Jeffrey, she asked him, "Do you think Nell would mind if I stayed on her couch tonight?"

Jeffrey looked at the ground, letting out a slow breath of relief. "No."

Hoss volunteered one of his deputies, saying, "Why don't you drive the lady over to Possum's?"

Jeffrey recognized the man from church back when May Tolliver was capable of staying sober enough on Sundays to force her son to get some religion. He said, "Thanks, Paul."

Paul tipped his hat, giving Jeffrey a suspicious look—the same suspicious look Jeffrey had been getting since he was old enough to walk. To make matters worse, Sara gave it to him, too, walking out of the house without saying another word.

Hoss watched her go, not bothering to hide an appreciative look. Even in a pair of faded striped pajamas, Sara was an attractive woman. "Tall drink of water."

Jeffrey said, "She's upset," knowing exactly how Hoss would take his words.

"Not the kind of thing a woman should see," he agreed. "Jessie okay?"

"She's on the couch," Jeffrey said, then added, "Sleeping," feeling like he was ten years old again and lying for his mother.

Hoss nodded, and Jeffrey knew he understood that Jessie's sleep was induced by something other than exhaustion. "I called her mama to come over and fetch her to the house. You know Faith's the only person who can calm that girl."

He turned back to his other deputy, who had a camera around his neck and a bright red toolbox in his hand. The man looked about twelve years old and was probably what passed for a crime scene tech around here. Jeffrey suppressed a wince of recognition as Hoss told the deputy, "Reggie, hang out around here for Jessie's mama. We'll be right back."

Reggie put down his toolbox, giving a respectful "Yes, sir."

Hoss stepped into the house, glancing around the front room. There were photos on the walls, most of them of Jeffrey, Possum, and Robert back during high school. Nell and Jessie were in some, but for the most part, it was the three men. A group photo showed Jeffrey and Robert's high school football team with a huge banner behind it announcing "State Champs." Sitting poolside yesterday, Possum had told Sara about their final winning game against Comer High, embellishing in a way that made Jeffrey embarrassed and sad. Possum had always been the ultimate spectator.

Hoss asked, "What the hell happened here tonight?"

"Let me take you back to the room," Jeffrey told him, not exactly answering the question. "Sara and I were in the street when we heard Jessie scream." He chewed the inside of his mouth as they walked down the hallway, lies of omission eating a hole in his stomach.

As usual, Hoss saw right through him. "Something wrong, son?"

"No, sir," he answered. "It's just been a long night."

Hoss slapped Jeffrey hard enough on the back to make him cough; it was his way of showing other men affection. "You're tough. You'll get through this." He stopped outside the door of the bedroom. "Christ a'mighty," he muttered. "What a mess."

"Yeah," Jeffrey answered, trying to see the scene the way Hoss was, for the first time. The ceiling fan overhead was still whirring, but he could tell it had been off when the man was shot; the blades had interrupted the blood spray pattern on the ceiling. There was a streak of blood where the switch for the fan had been turned on, probably by Robert. That made sense. He would have turned on the lights to see how badly he was wounded after the gunplay. It also made sense that there would be a lag between the last two shots. Robert had been handling guns since he was eight. He knew better than to fire into the dark. He had probably let his eyes adjust, tried to tell where Jessie was. Knowing her, she was standing helpless in the corner. It would be just like Robert to take his time.

Hoss looked out the window, saying, "Screen's been knocked out." Jeffrey didn't know if he meant from the inside or the outside, but Jesus Himself could not drag him back into the room. Jeffrey would look around outside when Hoss was gone.

Hoss asked, "What'd Robert say?"

Jeffrey tried to think of how to answer, but Hoss waved him off. "I'll get it from the horse." Jeffrey's expression must have registered his surprise, because he added, "You can give your statement tomorrow when you bring your girl in."

From the way Sara was looking at Jeffrey when she left the house, he was not sure whether or not he would have a girl tomorrow, but he did not volunteer that information. Instead, he watched Hoss walk around the room, felt his gut constricting every time he thought about what he was keeping back. This was the main reason Jeffrey had never seriously pursued a life of crime. Unlike Jimmy Tolliver, guilt could and did keep Jeffrey up at night. He hated lying—maybe because his childhood had been riddled with lies. His mother would not admit his father was ever guilty of the crimes that put him in jail, and his father denied his mother had a problem with her drinking. Meanwhile, Jeffrey had told some whoppers of his own to anybody who would listen. He had left Sylacauga so he could stop being that person. The minute he got back, he had returned to his old ways. It was like slipping back into a pair of familiar shoes.

"Son?" Hoss said. He was still by the window. Jeffrey noticed he was standing on one of Jessie's bloody footprints. A few of her little white pills had been crushed under his heel.

"Sir?" Jeffrey said, thinking Hoss must have been as distraught as he was. Everybody showed it in different ways.

"I said it looks pretty straightforward to me," Hoss said. He nudged the dead man's foot with the toe of his boot, and Jeffrey felt like he had been kicked in the gut seeing the casual way Hoss was dealing with this man's death. That was how it had always been for Hoss, though. There were good guys and bad guys, and to protect one, you did what you had to do to the other. He had always been hard on Robert and Jeffrey, but he was the only man in town allowed to say anything bad about them.

Hoss squatted down, looking at the corpse. Greasy blond shoulder-length hair covered most of the face. Still, Hoss asked, "Recognize him?"

"No, sir," Jeffrey said, kneeling down for a better look. He was still in the doorway, and down close to the carpet, he could see back-splatter fanning from the body. The edges of the fan led to where Jeffrey knelt. Robert must have been trying to find the light when he was shot.

"Luke Swan." Hoss stood, looping his thumb in his belt.

The name was familiar to Jeffrey if not the face. "We went to school with him."

"He dropped out before y'all graduated," Hoss said. "Remember?"

Jeffrey nodded, though he didn't. His high school life had been spent in an insulated clique of football players and cheerleaders. Luke Swan was hardly the athletic type. He looked like he weighed ninety pounds wet.

"Been in and out of trouble ever since," Hoss said, a sad note to his voice. "Drugs, alcohol. He's slept off more than a couple of good times at the station."

"Did Robert ever arrest him?"

Hoss shrugged off the question. "Hell, Slick, we only got eight deputies on the street any given shift. All of us have seen the boy one time or another."

"He ever do anything like this before?" Jeffrey asked. When Hoss shook his head, he added, "Armed B&E is a big step up from just getting in and out of trouble."

He crossed his arms. "You saying something? Should I be concerned?"

Jeffrey looked at the body. He still could not see all of the man's face, but the thin blue lips and small build gave him a youthful quality. "No, sir."

Hoss came toward him, not bothering to look where he was walking. He told Jeffrey, "That lady of yours seemed like she had something to say."

"She's a coroner in our town."

He gave a low whistle, impressed, but not for the obvious reason. "Y'all can afford a full-time coroner?"

"She's part-time," Jeffrey told him.

"She charge much?"

Jeffrey shook his head, though he had no idea what Sara made. Judging by her house and her car, she made a hell of a lot more money than he did. Of course, it was a lot easier to make money when you came from it. Jeffrey had seen the truth of that his entire life.

Hoss tilted his head toward the body. "Think she'd do this one for us?"

Jeffrey felt his chest tighten again. "I'll ask her."

"Good." He turned back around, looking at the room. He said, "I want to get this mess cleared up and Robert back on the street as soon as possible."

Then, as if to put an end to any further discussion, he reached over and turned off the light.

CHAPTER NINE

Sara woke in a sweat, her head spinning as she sat up too fast. She looked frantically around the room, trying to remember where she was. The Auburn memorabilia was almost comforting. Even the orange and blue blanket Nell had given her last night was a welcome sight. She sat back on the couch, tucking the blanket up around her neck as she adjusted to the quiet sounds of the neighborhood. Coffee was brewing in the kitchen, and somewhere, a car horn beeped.

Sara pulled her legs up, resting her chin on the top of her knees. She had not dreamed about Atlanta in a long time, but seconds ago, she had been back there—back in that bathroom at Grady Hospital where she had been raped. Her attacker had handcuffed her arms behind her and defiled Sara in ways she could still feel if she let her mind stay there long enough. Then he had stabbed her in the side and left her to bleed to death.

At the memory, her throat constricted again, and Sara closed her eyes, trying to breathe through her emotions.

"You okay?" Nell asked. She stood in the doorway with a cup of coffee in her hand.

Sara nodded, trying to find her voice.

"Possum's gone to open the store. Jeffrey went to check on Jessie.

He's a fool if he thinks she'll be out of bed before noon." She paused when Sara did not respond. "He said to tell you to be ready to go at eight-thirty."

Sara looked at the clock on the mantel. It was half past seven.

Nell said, "Coffee's ready when you are," and left Sara alone in the room.

Sara sat up, hitting her toe on her suitcase. Jeffrey had put it there a few hours ago while she pretended to sleep. He had sneaked in like a thief, and she had watched him go, wondering exactly what she had gotten herself into. Jeffrey Tolliver was not the man she thought he was. Even Cathy Linton would have been surprised by his behavior last night. Sara had felt threatened, and at one point she had been frightened enough to think that he would actually hit her. She could not let herself get involved with someone like that. There was no denying that she had feelings for Jeffrey, maybe she was even in love with him, but that did not mean she had to put herself in a situation where she was afraid of what might happen next.

Sara pressed her lips together, looking at the framed magazine cover of Jeffrey on the wall. Maybe being back home had altered him in some way. The man Sara had seen last night was nothing like the Jeffrey Tolliver she had grown to know over the last few months.

She found herself trying to reason out his behavior. Prior to this, there had been nothing in his personality that would have pointed to last night's outburst. He was frustrated. He had punched the wall, not her. Maybe she was overreacting. Maybe the circumstances had brought him to the edge, and she had done nothing but help push him over. He had grabbed her arm, but he had also let it go. He had warned her not to talk, but when the sheriff came, he had done nothing to stop her. In the light of day, Sara could understand his anger and frustration. Jeffrey was right about one thing: Alabama was a death-penalty state, and not just a death-penalty state, but almost as gung-ho about it as Texas and Florida. If Robert was found guilty, he could be looking at the electric chair.

Though she was punch-drunk from lack of sleep, Sara tried to go over in her mind again what she had seen in Robert's bedroom last night. She was no longer certain about what she had heard in the street, nor was she sure about the sear pattern she had seen when Robert had removed his hand. He had been fast about it, and had done a very good job of smearing blood around the wound. What it came down to was that Sara had to ask herself why he had gone to such great lengths to cover the entrance wound if there was nothing to hide.

If she was correct, the muzzle of the gun that shot Robert had been placed at an upward angle against the skin. The hot metal had seared a V-shaped impression of the muzzle into the flesh. Either the person who shot him had been in an inferior position, squatting or kneeling, or Robert had held the gun to his own side and pulled the trigger. The second theory would explain why so little damage was done. The abdomen contained seven major organs and around thirty feet of intestines. The bullet had managed to miss them all.

Sara would have voiced her suspicions to the sheriff last night, but after taking one look at the man, she knew that, like Jeffrey, he was going to do everything he could to give Robert the benefit of the doubt. Clayton "Hoss" Hollister screamed good ol' boy, from his nickname to his cowboy boots. Sara knew exactly how his kind operated. Her father certainly wasn't part of Grant's network of powerful old men—he hated doing favors because he *had* to—but Eddie Linton played cards with most of them. Sara had learned how they worked her first week as coroner, when the mayor explained to her that the county had an exclusive contract to order all their medical supplies through his brother-in-law's company, no matter how much he charged.

Today, Sara wanted to see Robert's wound again, and even if Jeffrey wouldn't—or couldn't—keep his promise to let her do the autopsy, she wanted to watch while whoever was in charge examined the slain man—or victim, depending on how you looked at it. After that, all she wanted to do was get the hell out of Sylacauga and away from Jeffrey. She needed time and some distance so she could get her head together and figure out exactly how she felt about him in light of last night's explosion.

Sara tested her weight on her feet. Her soles were bruised from the impromptu run last night, and something sharp had taken a chunk of skin out of her heel. She would stop to buy Band-Aids once she got on the interstate.

Nell offered a faint smile when Sara limped into the kitchen. "Kids won't be up for another hour."

Sara tried to be polite. "How old are they?"

"Jared's ten, Jennifer's ten months younger."

Sara raised an eyebrow.

"Trust me, I got my tubes tied the second she was out." Nell took a coffee cup out of the cabinet. "You like it black?" Sara nodded. "Jen's the smart one. Don't tell Jared I said that, but Jen's a full grade ahead of him in school. It's his own damn fault—he's not stupid, he's just more interested in sports than books. Boys that age just can't sit still for anything. You probably know all about that with your job." She put the cup down in front of Sara and poured coffee as she spoke. "I guess you want a houseful of kids when you settle down."

Sara watched steam rise from the cup. "I can't actually have children."

"Oh," Nell said. "There's my foot in my mouth again. You'd think I loved the taste of leather."

"It's okay."

Nell sat down across from Sara with a heavy sigh. "God, but I'm nosey. It's the only thing my mother says about me that's true."

Sara forced a smile. "Really, it's okay."

"I won't press you for details," Nell said, but her tone of voice implied she would be more than open to hearing them.

"Ectopic pregnancy," Sara provided, though she went no further.

"Does Jeffrey know?"

She shook her head.

"You could always adopt."

"That's what my mother keeps saying," Sara said, and for the first time she voiced the reason why she couldn't bear the thought of adoption. "I know this sounds horrible, but I take care of other people's children all day. When I get home . . ."

"You don't have to tell me," Nell said. She reached over and squeezed Sara's hand. "Jeffrey won't mind."

Sara gave her a tight smile and Nell breathed out a heavy sigh, saying, "Well, shit. Can't say I didn't see that coming, but I was hoping it would last a little longer."

"I'm sorry."

"Forget about it." Nell slapped her thighs as she stood. "Nothing bad between you and me. Jeffrey's loss is my gain. First damn time that's ever happened, I can tell you."

Sara stared down at her coffee again.

"You want pancakes?"

"I'm not that hungry," Sara told her, even as her stomach grumbled.

"Me neither." Nell took out the griddle. "Three or four?"

"Four."

Nell put the griddle on the stove and went about preparing the batter. Sara watched, thinking she had seen her mother do this same thing thousands of times. There was something so comforting about being in a kitchen, and Sara felt the nightmares from the night before start to fade.

"Stupid neighbor," Nell said, tossing a cheery wave at someone outside the window over the sink. A car door slammed, followed by an engine starting. "He's gone every weekend with some whore he met in Birmingham. Watch it," she said, tossing Sara a look over her shoulder to make sure she was paying attention. "Soon as he pulls out of the driveway, those dogs will start barking and they won't shut up till he comes back around ten tonight." She stood on the tips of her toes and craned her head to see into the neighbor's yard. "I've talked with him ten times about getting those poor things some shelter. Possum even offered to build him something. God, they howl when it rains."

The dogs started barking on cue. Just to keep her talking, Sara asked, "They don't have a doghouse?"

She shook her head. "Nope. He kept having to come home because they jumped the fence, so he put them on chains. So, of course every morning like clockwork they knock their water bowls over and

I have to trudge over there and fill 'em back up." She handed Sara a carton of eggs and a bowl, saying, "Make yourself useful," before continuing, "Boxers are so damn ugly. They're not even the cute kind of ugly. And Lord, do they slobber. It's like taking a spit bath every time I go over there."

Sara broke the eggs into the bowl, not listening to Nell's words so much as the cadence of her voice. She was thinking about Jeffrey and trying to put logic to what had happened last night. Sara knew that both her biggest strength and her biggest weakness was that she saw things clearly in black and white, but right now, for the first time in her life, she was seeing the gray. She had been tired last night, and upset by everything that had happened. Had she really seen the sear mark? The more she thought about it, the more she convinced herself that she had not. But her gut still told her to go with what she had first thought. And why would Robert keep covering the wound unless he really had something to hide?

"Sara?" Nell said. She had obviously asked a question.

"I'm sorry," Sara apologized. "What?"

"I asked did Robert recognize the man?"

Sara shook her head. "I guess not or he would've said something."

"It hasn't made the papers yet—we only get a weekly here and it's not due until next Sunday—but I heard on my walk this morning that it's Luke Swan. The name won't mean anything to you, but we all went to school with him. He used to live a couple of houses over." She pointed toward the backyard. "Possum was born here and I grew up across the street—did I tell you?" Sara shook her head. "We moved in after his mama died. I couldn't stand the woman—" she knocked three times on the wooden cabinet under the sink, "but it was nice of her to leave the house to us. I thought Possum's brother would make a stink, but it all worked out." She paused for breath. "Where was I?"

"Luke."

"Right." She turned back to the stove. "He lived here a few years before his father lost his job, then they moved over by the school. He didn't exactly run with our crowd."

Sara could guess she meant the popular crowd. The same groups had been at her own school, and though Sara had been far from popular, she was lucky enough not to have been picked on for it.

Nell continued, "I heard he's a troublemaker, but who knows? People say all kinds of things after somebody's dead. You should hear Possum talk about his mama like she was Mary Poppins, and that woman was never happy a day of her life. She was a lot like Jessie that way." Nell poured four pancakes onto the griddle. "I heard Jessie's at her mama's."

"Yes," Sara confirmed.

"Good Lord," Nell mumbled, taking the bowl of eggs from Sara. She beat them with a fork, then dumped them into a frying pan. Even though Sara had graduated in the top ten percent of her class at one of the toughest medical schools in the country, she always felt inadequate around women who could cook. The one meal she had prepared for her last boyfriend had resulted in the throwing away of two pots and a perfectly good garbage can.

Nell said, "I ebb and flow with that woman. Maybe it's because Robert and Possum throw us together all the time and expect us to make happy. Sometimes I think she's not that bad and sometimes I just want to pop her upside the head to knock some sense into her." She tapped the fork on the edge of the pan before setting it on a napkin. "Right now I just feel sorry for her."

"It's an awful thing to have happen."

Nell flipped the pancakes with a spatula. "Bobby's a real doll but you never know what they're like until you get them home and take them out of their packages. Maybe he sucks his teeth. Possum started doing that a few years ago until I threatened to beat him with a bat." She put the pancakes and some of the eggs onto a plate and handed it to Sara. "Bacon?"

"No thank you."

Nell took three strips of bacon out from under a napkin and put them on Sara's plate. "I was hating her something awful until a few months ago. She had a miscarriage. I was over at her house every day making sure she didn't do something stupid. Liked to tore the both of them up. She's wanted a kid ever since I met her. We're talking back in junior high school. Never been able to have one, though."

Sara poured syrup onto the pancakes. They were all perfectly round and the same thickness. "What stupid thing did you think Jessie would do?"

"Take too many pills," Nell said, flipping the pancakes one by one. "She's done it before. If you ask me, it was just to get attention. Not that Robert seems all that inattentive, but you just never know, do you?"

"No," Sara agreed around a mouthful of bacon. Until last night, she never would have guessed that Jeffrey was capable of threatening her. She could still feel the breeze from his fist passing just a few inches from her head as he punched the wall. "Would she ever cheat on him?"

"Ha," Nell laughed, filling up her plate. She sat down across from Sara, pouring a liberal amount of syrup over the pancakes as she talked. "If she did, it'd have to be with somebody up in Alaska. Robert knows everything that goes on in this town. He'll probably take over for the sheriff if the old fart ever retires. Hoss has held the office since before dirt. I think the only way he'll leave is feet-first. Hell, knowing this town, people'd still vote for him, even if he was dead."

"You don't have a police force, it's only the sheriff's office?"

Nell took a bite of egg. "You know how small this town is? If we had both, there wouldn't be anybody left to work at the gas station." She stood up. "Juice?"

"I'm fine."

Nell got two glasses out of the cabinet and put them on the table. "Mind you, if Jeffrey was around, Hoss would have retired years ago."

"Why is that?"

She poured the juice. "Heir apparent. Robert's father was half useless, but better half useless than being stuck with Jimmy Tolliver. That man was a monster. Jeffrey won't talk about it, but that scar under his shoulder came from his daddy."

Sara had seen the scar, but not wanting to open a conversation about scars, she had never asked about it. Now she asked, "How?"

Nell sat back down. "I was standing right there," she said, taking a bite of pancake. Sara waited while she chewed, wishing for once that Nell would get on with it. Finally, she swallowed. "May said something smart-ass and Jimmy just laid into her. I mean like a fury. I've never seen anything like it. Never hope to see it again, knock wood." She rapped her knuckles on the table.

Sara swallowed, though she had nothing in her mouth. "He hit her?"

"Oh, hon, he hit her all the time. It was like she was his own private punching bag. Jeffrey, too, when he was home. Not that he was home much. He spent most of his time out by the quarry, trying to get away from it. He'd just sit out there and read until the sun went down. Sometimes he'd sleep out there unless Hoss found him, then he'd make Jeffrey sleep at the station." She drank some juice. "Anyway, this one time I was there, they were hauling off on each other and Jeffrey tried to step in between them. Jimmy backhanded the shit out of him and Jeffrey went flying—and I do mean flying—across the room. Cut his back open on the stovetop. This was back when they had those knobs with the sharp metal edges, not like now where it's all just buttons and dials."

After a while, Sara said, "I didn't know." She tried to imagine what it must have been like for Jeffrey growing up in that kind of environment and could not. Like most pediatricians, she had seen her share of abused children. Nothing made her more angry than a cowardly adult who took out his or her frustrations on a child. As far as Sara was concerned, they should all be left to rot in jail.

"Takes a hell of a lot to get Jeffrey angry," Nell continued. "I guess that's a good thing, though maybe not. You've got to wonder about him holding that in all the time. He hates to argue. Always has. You know he had an academic scholarship to Auburn?"

"Jeffrey?" Sara asked, trying to absorb this new information.

"Part of it was football, but they don't give you a full ride to warm the bench." She gave a surprised laugh, as if she could not believe what had just come from her mouth. "Don't ever tell Possum I said that, but it's the God's truth. The minute Jeffrey got to Auburn, he hated football. He would have quit the team if Hoss'd let him."

"What did Hoss have to do with it?"

Nell put down her fork. "You know why Jeffrey's called Slick?"

"I can take a wild guess."

She snorted a laugh. "Yeah, he's slick, I'll give him that, but the name came because no matter what kind of trouble he got into, he was real slick at getting out."

"What kind of trouble?"

"Oh, not anything big when you consider what kids get up to today. Stealing things from the five-and-dime, borrowing his mama's car while she was passed out on the couch. The same kinds of things his daddy probably did when he was that age. We're talking ten or twelve. You gonna finish that?" Sara shook her head and Nell reached over with her fork and took the last bite of pancake. "Jeffrey'd probably be where his daddy is if Hoss hadn't come along."

"What did Hoss do?"

"Made him cut the grass at the jail instead of spending a couple of nights locked up in it. Sometimes, he'd take Jeffrey back in the cells and make him talk to some of the guys who were hard cases. Basically, he scared the shit out of him. Robert, too, but he didn't need as much scaring. He's always been more of a follower, and with Jeffrey straightened out, you got Robert, too."

"It's a good thing Hoss came along."

"Sometimes I wonder," Nell said, sitting back with her coffee. "Jeffrey's got a tender heart. I guess you noticed."

Sara did not answer, though she wondered if Nell had an accurate picture of him. A lot could happen in six years. A lot could happen in one night.

"I always saw him ending up teaching, maybe coaching football at the high school. After Jimmy went up for life, he changed. Maybe Jeffrey thought joining the force and being a cop would make up for the fact that his daddy was a criminal. Maybe he thought it'd make Hoss happy."

"Did it?"

Nell pushed away her plate. "Like you wouldn't believe."

Sara saw Jeffrey walk by the kitchen window and she stood from the table, telling Nell, "I should get dressed."

Jeffrey opened the back door. He seemed surprised to find Nell and Sara eating breakfast.

Sara said, "I was just going to get changed."

He gave her a quick glance, saying, "You look fine," even though she was still in the pajamas she had been wearing when she ran out of his mother's house last night.

Nell asked, "How's Jessie and them?"

"Like you'd think." He indicated their cleaned plates. "That smells good."

"I didn't marry Possum to cook for you," she said, standing up. "There's plenty of batter left in the bowl and the eggs shouldn't be too cold. I've gotta go check-see if those stupid dogs have knocked over their water bowls yet."

Nell took all the conversation with her when she left the room. Not knowing what else to do, Sara sat back down at the table. She felt like the pancakes she had eaten were expanding in her stomach. The coffee left in her cup was lukewarm, but she managed to swallow it.

Jeffrey chewed a piece of bacon as he poured himself a cup of coffee. He put the pot on the warmer, then took it out again, holding it up to see if Sara wanted more. She shook her head no, and he put it back, eating another piece of bacon as he stared at the kitchen faucet.

Sara took up her fork and traced it around the syrup in her plate, wondering what, if anything, to say. Really, the burden to speak was on him. She put down the fork and crossed her arms, staring at Jeffrey, waiting.

He cleared his throat before asking, "What are you going to say today?"

"What do you want me to say?" she asked. "Or are you going to threaten me again?"

"I shouldn't have done that."

"No, you shouldn't have," she told him, her anger coming back in sharp focus. "I'll tell you this right now, between the way your mother talked to me last night and your threats, I could leave right now and never look back."

He looked down at the floor, and she could feel his shame without seeing it. His voice caught as he tried to speak, and he cleared his throat before he could manage, "I've never hit a woman in my life."

Sara waited.

"I'd cut off my own hands before I did anything like that," he told her, his jaw working as he obviously tried to fight the emotions welling up inside. "I watched my daddy beat my mama every day of my life. Sometimes she pissed him off, sometimes he did it just because he could." He kept his face turned away from her. "I know you don't have any reason to believe me, but I would never hurt you."

When Sara did not answer, he asked, "What did my mother say to you last night?"

Sara was too embarrassed to repeat it. "It doesn't matter."

"It does," he said. "I'm sorry. I'm sorry I brought you here to this . . . this place." He chanced a look at her, and she could see his eyes were bloodshot. "I just wanted you to see . . ." He stopped. "Hell, I don't know what I wanted you to see. Who I really am, I guess. Maybe you're seeing that now. Maybe this is who I really am."

She felt sorry for him, and then she felt stupid for doing so.

He pulled out the chair Nell had vacated, dragging it a few feet from the table before he sat. "Bobby wouldn't talk to me this morning."

Sara waited for the rest.

"I walked in the room and he was getting dressed to go home." Jeffrey paused, and she sensed rather than saw his feelings of helplessness. "I told him we needed to talk and he just said no. Just like that, 'No,' like he has something to hide."

"Maybe he does."

He tapped his fingers on the table.

"Was Jessie with him?"

"No. She wasn't even awake yet when I dropped by the house to check on her."

Sara chewed her lip, debating whether or not to tell him what she had seen.

"Go ahead," he said. "Go ahead and say whatever it is that I'm not seeing." He slammed his palm against the table, frustrated. "Jesus, I'm not doing this on purpose, Sara. No matter how many years have passed, he's still my best friend. It's not exactly easy for me to be a cop right now."

Sara took a deep, calming breath. She had flinched when he hit the table, and her first response had been to get up and leave. Just because he came from a violent family did not mean Jeffrey was a violent man, but she could not help but see him differently now. His broad shoulders and well-muscled body, which she had once found so attractive, only served to remind her of how much stronger than her he was.

He must have sensed this, because he moderated his tone. "Please don't look at me like that."

"I just—"

When she said nothing, he prompted, "What?"

Sara tucked her chin into her chest, not ready to have this conversation. She directed him back toward the problem at hand, saying, "I want to see Robert's gunshot wound again."

"Why?"

"I'm not sure, but . . ." she began, but even as she said it, she *was* sure. "There was a sear mark at the bottom of the wound."

"You're not sure?"

"I don't want to be, but I am."

He gave a humorless laugh. "He kept covering it with his hand."

"He used the shirt to stanch the blood."

"Did he let you see the shirt?"

She shook her head. If the gun had been held at contact range, the sear mark as well as soot would be on the shirt.

He said, "They probably threw it away at the hospital."

"Or he did."

"Or he did," Jeffrey conceded. He shook his head again. "If he'd talk to me, try to explain what'd happened . . ."

"What are we going to do?"

He kept shaking his head. "Why won't he talk to me?"

Sara did not volunteer the obvious answer.

He said, "Luke Swan could have been going for him. His body was only a few feet away."

"Probably three or four feet."

"Robert pushed him," Jeffrey said. "Swan would have been crouched or on his knees."

"Could have been."

She could hear the strain in his voice as he tried to explain it all away. "Swan could have heard Robert getting his gun. He moved toward him. Maybe he held his gun up and in front of him." Jeffrey illustrated, holding out his hand, his fingers in the shape of a gun. "He shot Robert, then Robert shot him."

Sara tried to see the holes in his theory. "It's possible."

His relief was palpable. "Let's see what the autopsy says, okay? We'll just keep this to ourselves until then. The autopsy will show what happened."

"Did you ask if I could sit in?"

"Hoss wants you to do the exam."

"All right."

"Sara . . ."

"I'm already packed," she said, standing. "As soon as it's finished, I want to leave." Then, to make herself clear, she said, "I want to go home."

CHAPTER TEN

The ringing telephone grated like nails on a blackboard. Sara's hearing started to play tricks on her, the ringing fading in and out like a retreating police car. To pass the time, she would count the seconds between rings, sometimes losing count, sometimes sure that it had stopped, only to hear the startling bell again. And it was a bell, not the usual computer-generated bleep from the digital phones. The black telephone was so old Sara was surprised that it did not have a rotary dial. It didn't have any sleek lines or shiny buttons. Between cell phones and cordless phones and the digitization of noise, she had almost forgotten what a real telephone sounded like.

She used the back of her hand to wipe sweat off her lip. The heat from outside had started encroaching on the poorly ventilated squad room from the moment the power was cut. Now, over an hour later, the air was heavy, almost suffocating. To make matters worse, the bodies scattered around the room were starting to smell.

Brad's uniform shirt and pants were off, stuffed into the air-conditioning grates by Smith, probably to block prying eyes on the part of the police. Brad sat in his white boxer shorts and black socks, his embarrassment long past. Smith trusted Brad for some reason and he was the only one of them allowed any sort of freedom. Sara had sneaked him Jeffrey's wallet while he was taking the girls to the bathroom. She had no idea where he had hidden it. Her only hope was that he had done it well.

Stress had finally drained two of the remaining little girls, and they both slept with their heads in Brad's lap. Marla sat at a distance from the group, her mouth open, staring blankly at the floor. Sara was terrified the older woman would have another fit and tell Smith Jeffrey's true identity. She realized with cold clarity that if a choice had to be made, she would do whatever she needed to do to protect Jeffrey.

She leaned her head against the wall, allowing herself to look at Smith. He was pacing again, muttering under his breath. He had taken off his coat and she could see that every inch of his body was built, the muscles of his arms and shoulders bulging under his short-sleeved T-shirt. A huge blue tattoo of an eagle covered his right bicep, and on every second pass he took across the room Sara tried to decipher the words underneath to no avail.

Like his accomplice, he wore thick nighttime camouflage pants with his combat boots. The Kevlar vest must have felt like a straitjacket in this heat, but he kept it strapped tightly to his chest. Animal aggression sweated from Smith's every pore, but it was the second shooter, the quiet one, who scared Sara most. He was the one who followed orders, who did whatever he was told to do, whether it was to shoot at small children or blow a hole through a police officer's head. This personality type was hardly uncommon among young men—the military actively recruited for it—but adding Smith to the mixture made him even more volatile. If something happened to Smith, the second shooter was a wild card. Cut off the head of the scorpion and the tail could still sting.

Jeffrey stirred in Sara's lap, and she put her hand on his good shoulder to still him, saying, "It's all right."

He rubbed his eyes like a sleepy child. A fold in the material of her dress had creased his face, and she wanted nothing more than to kiss the line away.

"What time is it?"

She looked at her watch. "Half past one," she told him, stroking his hair off his forehead. "Do you remember where we are?"

He took a deep breath, then let it go. "I was dreaming about the first time I really made love to my wife."

Sara pressed her lips together. She wanted so much to be back in that place that tears came to her eyes.

He continued, "We were in the house where I grew up, on the floor in my room . . ."

"Shh," she shushed, not wanting him to say too much.

He understood, but he closed his eyes for a moment like he did not want to let the memory go. When he opened his eyes again, Sara could tell how much pain he was in. Still, he did not complain about his wounds. Instead, he told her, "Goddamn phone is driving me crazy."

"I know," she said, illogically wishing they would just unplug it if they were not going to answer. She waited for the next ring to finish before asking, "Are you in much pain?"

He shook his head no, but she knew he was lying. Sweat poured off his body, and not just from the heat. The wound had clotted, but the blood could be pooling on the inside. His arm was cold to the touch, the pulse still thready. She guessed the bullet was between a torn artery and a nerve. Whenever Jeffrey moved, the nerve pinched, causing shooting pains that must be unbearable. Any movement also brought the risk of dislodging the bullet. Because the wound was so high up, she could not apply a tourniquet. The only thing keeping him from bleeding out was the pressure from the bullet. If he didn't get help soon, Sara did not know how much longer he could hold on.

"I was thinking," she said, her voice barely more than a whisper, "how much you . . ." She looked at Smith, but he was talking to his accomplice. "How much has changed," she said. He was so different from the man she had first fallen in love with, yet so much about him was the same. Time had done nothing but smooth his character, polishing it like a stone.

"Where are they?" he asked, trying to sit up.

She pressed gently on his shoulder and he stayed where he was.

The fact that he had so little fight in him was alarming. "They're in the front," she said. "They have Allison."

"Ruth Lippman's daughter?" he asked, managing to raise his head. She let him see the girl before gently pushing him back down. Allison sat on the front counter, her legs dangling in the air. There was a long gash down the front of her shin where she'd slid down the sidewalk after attempting a particularly silly stunt on her bicycle last week. Sara had put in two sutures and extracted a promise in exchange for a lollipop that the little girl would be more careful the next time.

Smith had stopped pacing and was standing beside Allison, his shotgun in the crook of his arm. On the other side of the girl stood the second shooter, his rifle resting on the counter, still pointing toward the front door. Smith watched them carefully, and Sara knew that he could hear everything they said.

She told Jeffrey, "I'm worried about your arm."

"It's okay," he said, trying to sit up again.

"Don't," she told him, then, "Please. You shouldn't move any more than you have to."

Jeffrey must have heard the concern in her voice because he stopped struggling.

He asked, "Have they said what they want?"

She shook her head, trying not to make eye contact with Smith. Sara had worked in pediatrics most of her life. Even though Smith was not a child, he had all the markings of a twenty-something-year-old who had not quite grown up. She knew how aggressive young men could behave when they were challenged, especially if there was someone around to impress. She did not want to get shot in a case of one-up between Smith and his friend.

Jeffrey shifted to get more comfortable, and she prayed he wouldn't do any more damage to his arm. He lowered his voice, asking, "One of them seemed to know you. Do you recognize him?"

She shook her head again, wishing to God she could tell him she knew exactly who the two shooters were and why they were here. She had moved back to Grant from Atlanta almost fifteen years ago, and would surely remember Smith if he had been a patient. Then, if Smith was a patient she could not recall, why was he here to kill Jeffrey? Or was he here on orders from his friend? Sara craned her neck, trying to get a better look at the second man. His ball cap was pulled low to hide his face, but the flash of sunlight coming in from the partially open front door showed Sara his eyes. They were empty, like a stagnant pool of water.

Sara realized Smith was watching her stare at his buddy, and she forced herself to smile at Allison. The little girl was slumped against the back of the counter with her skirt bunched up around her knees. Tears streamed down her face. Ruth Lippman had been Sara's tenth-grade English teacher. The woman was a perfect combination of tough and challenging, and Sara had loved her for it.

"He doesn't have much of an accent," Jeffrey said, and he was right. There was a definite Southern twang when Smith let his temper get out of control, but for the most part, he spoke in the flat, unaccented English of a military brat. Or, maybe Sara was just making that fit the mold. For all she knew, he could be a wanna-be, someone whose father had been career military, but whose own criminal record or psychological profile had washed him out of the military before he even made it to his first week of boot camp.

Jeffrey closed his eyes.

"Why don't you try to sleep?"

"I shouldn't," he said, but his eyelids fluttered and stilled.

Sara looked up at Smith, who had taken all this in with a watchful eye. She tried to keep her voice strong, but couldn't suppress the tremor in her voice. "He needs medical attention. Please let him leave."

Smith twisted his lips to the side as if he was actually considering her request. Beside him, the second shooter shifted. He said something under his breath and Smith walked over to the phone and picked it up mid-ring.

He said, "We'll trade the old lady for sandwiches and bottled water. None of it better be fucked with. We can test it." He listened to the response, his head to the side. "No, I don't think so." There was another pause, and Smith turned around, facing Allison. He held the phone in front of her face and Sara sensed he was smiling at her. She willed the girl not to trust him, but she saw Allison smile back just before Smith pinched her leg. Allison screamed, and Smith put the phone back to his ear.

He gave a steely laugh. "That's right, lady. We're gonna hold on to the kids." He turned back around, his eyes scanning the remaining hostages. "We want some beer, too."

His partner's head jerked around, and Sara got the impression that Smith had deviated from the script. So, she thought, maybe Smith wasn't completely in charge of this after all.

Smarting from the reprimand, Smith took his anger out on the person at the other end of the phone. "One hour, bitch. You take any longer than that, the body count's gonna get a lot higher."

CHAPTER ELEVEN

Sara drove to the funeral home, Jeffrey giving her directions from the passenger seat. Normally, she liked to have time alone before an autopsy to get a sense of the task in front of her, but there was no time for that luxury. She had called her mother before they left Nell's and told Cathy she would be back home in Grant that evening.

"Here," Jeffrey said, indicating a long U-shaped building on the side of the highway. Nothing else was around except a small flower shop across the road. Eighteen-wheelers stirred the hot air as Sara got out of the car. In the distance, there was a grumble of thunder, which perfectly reflected her mood.

She winced as she stepped onto the asphalt, a loose rock digging through the thin sole of her sandals.

Jeffrey asked, "You okay?" and she nodded, walking toward the entrance.

Paul, the deputy who had taken her to Nell's last night, stood at the doorway smoking a cigarette. He stubbed it on the side of the trash can and left it in the sand on top.

"Ma'am," he said, opening the door for Sara.

"Thank you," Sara answered, noticing the suspicious look the deputy gave Jeffrey.

Jeffrey asked, "Where are they?"

When he answered, he looked at Sara instead of Jeffrey. "They're down that hall in the back."

The deputy walked between them as they headed toward the back of the building, and Sara could hear his keys jangling and the leather of his gun belt squeaking with every step. The funeral home was almost institutional, with painted cinder-block walls and fluorescent lighting giving a yellow cast to everything. Sara could smell embalming fluid and some sort of air freshener that might have been pleasant in a living room or office but here was almost sickening.

Paul indicated, "Through here," reaching ahead of her to open the door at the end of the hall. She chanced a look at Jeffrey, but he was staring past her into the room, his jaw set. Embalming equipment surrounded a concave metal table where the body had been placed. Covering the dead man was a clean white sheet, the edges blowing gently in the breeze generated by a loud window air-conditioning unit. The air was so cold it was stifling.

"Hey there," Hoss said, holding out his hand to Sara. She went to shake it, too late realizing he meant to put his hand on her elbow and guide her into the room. Sara knew that men of Hoss's generation generally did not shake hands with women unless it was in jest. Her grandfather Earnshaw, whom she dearly loved, was the same way.

Hoss introduced her to the men in the room. "This is Deacon White, the funeral director." A rotund, dour man with a receding hairline gave Sara a curt nod. "That's Reggie Ray." Hoss indicated the second deputy who had been at Robert's house last night. The young man still had a camera around his neck, and Sara wondered if he slept with it.

"Slick," Hoss said, addressing Jeffrey. "Don't think I mentioned this last night—Reggie's Marty Ray's boy."

"That so?" Jeffrey said, without much interest. Still, he offered the other man his hand. Reggie seemed reluctant to take it, and Sara wondered again why the deputies were so cagey around him.

Hoss said, "Got Robert's statement this morning," and Sara saw the surprised look on Jeffrey's face. "Neighbors pretty much backed up his story."

Sara waited for Jeffrey to ask what Robert had said, but he stared at the floor instead.

After a few moments of awkward silence, Deacon White indicated a door behind Sara. "We keep our protective clothing in the storage room. You're welcome to anything we have."

"Thank you," Sara told him, getting a solemn nod in return. She wondered if the man was annoyed she was taking over. Grant County's funeral director had been a childhood friend of Sara's and more than happy to relinquish the responsibility of town coroner, but Deacon White was a lot harder to read.

She walked over to the storage room, which was little more than a glorified closet. Still, she shut the door. The moment she did, the men started talking. She could hear Hoss's deep baritone mixing with Paul's. From what she could gather, they were discussing a recent basketball game at the high school.

Sara opened a surgical gown and slipped it on, feeling foolish as she spun like a dog chasing its tail trying to tie the back. The gown was huge on her, obviously meant for Deacon White's pronounced midsection. By the time she had slipped on a pair of paper shoes and a hair protector, Sara felt like a clown.

She put her hand on the door, but did not open it. Closing her eyes, she tried to block out all that had happened in the last twenty-four hours. Focusing on her belief that Robert's wound was self-inflicted might shadow her findings during the autopsy, and Sara wanted to make certain she only went with known facts. She was not a detective. Her task now was to give her professional opinion to the police and let them decide how to proceed. The only thing she could control was how well she performed her job.

The men grew quiet as she walked back into the room. She thought she saw a smile on Paul's face, but he looked back down at his notebook, writing something with a well-chewed nub of pencil. Deacon White stood by the body, and Jeffrey and Hoss both leaned against the wall with their arms crossed over their chests. Reggie was by the sink, his camera gleaming in the light. An air of expectancy filled the room, but despite this, Sara got the distinct impression that this was merely a case of going through the motions.

Still, she asked, "Where are the X rays?"

Deacon exchanged a look with Hoss before saying, "We don't normally do X rays."

Sara tried to cover her shock, knowing how it would look to come into their backyard and start treating them like a bunch of yokels. X rays were standard procedure for an autopsy, but they were especially important when dealing with a head wound. The bullet punched out bone as it entered the skull, and X rays of bone chips would provide conclusive evidence of the path the bullet had taken. Excising the wound could distort the path or even create false tracks.

She asked, "Have you found the bullet?"

"From his head?" Reggie asked, sounding surprised. "I got two twenty-twos out of the walls. I didn't find anything near his head except for . . . head."

"The bullet could still be in there," Sara told him.

Hoss cleared his throat politely before saying, "Maybe ol' Reg here missed it on his sweep through the room. I'm sure we'll find it when we look again."

Reggie seem to bristle a bit at this, but he had regained his composure by the time Hoss looked his way. He gave the sheriff a slight shrug as if to say it could happen.

Sara tried to phrase her words carefully. "Sometimes, brain tissue can slow a bullet down enough so that it has insufficient velocity to exit the skull."

Hoss pointed out, "The right side of his head has been blown out."

"That could be from a fracture." Knowing the policeman's ammunition of choice, she made an educated guess, asking Reggie, "We're talking a nine-millimeter hollow-point, I would assume?"

He flipped back through his notebook, reading, "The Beretta had twenty-two long rifle, the Glock had hollow-point."

Sara said, "That could exert enough force to fracture the bone out through the scalp." She did not add that an X ray would easily show this.

Hoss said, "All right."

She waited for him to say more, but when he did not, Sara pulled back the sheet. She should not have been surprised to find the body faceup, and hoped she managed to hide her irritation. Livor mortis had shifted to the back of the head, which meant blood could have seeped into the soft tissue of the scalp. Any evidence of confluent bruising would be difficult to tell from antemortem bruising. Unless there was a laceration or some sort of pronounced abrasion in the scalp, it would be almost impossible for Sara to tell whether the bruises came from the man's own pooling blood or from someone hitting him in the head.

Rigor mortis had set in, fixing the body in a casketing position. Swan's hair was plastered to most of his face with sweat and blood. Still, she could see his mouth and eyes were slightly open, and there was a purple-blue cast to the side of his face where it had rested on the carpet. His chest was narrow, his ribs pronounced. His hands had not been bagged to preserve evidence from the scene, such as gunpowder residue or any fibers he might have clutched in his hand—and "clutched" was the right word in this case; Swan's right hand was in a tight fist.

Reggie said, "I tried, but I couldn't get his hand open."

"That's fine," Sara said, thinking that if she was able to find gunshot residue, there would be no proving whether or not it came from Reggie's or the dead man's hands. "Do you have photographs of the scene yet?"

He shook his head no. "I've got my drawings here," he said, taking a folded mailing envelope out of his pocket. Inside were three sheets of paper with crude diagrams of the crime scene. He seemed apologetic when he showed them to Sara. "I was gonna do 'em up better this morning."

"That's fine," she repeated, smoothing out the papers on a table by the sink. The bed and armoire were two lopsided rectangles across from each other. Luke Swan had been reduced to a stick figure with two X's for eyes. His right hand was under his body, the other out to his side. She asked, "He was lying on his right hand?"

Reggie nodded again. "Yeah. It was stuck like that when we turned him over."

Deacon added, "Rigor mortis was extremely pronounced."

"What time did you get there?"

"About two hours after the accident," he said, and Sara tried not to dwell on the fact that the man who would have performed the autopsy was already calling it an accident.

"Did you have trouble moving him?"

"We had to break the rigor to get him on the gurney."

"Arms and legs?" she asked, and he nodded yes. Rigor mortis generally started in the jaw and worked its way out to the extremities. The body would take anywhere between six and twelve hours before it became fixed.

Jeffrey spoke for the first time, saying, "Maybe he panicked. Maybe he was high on something that got his heart rate going."

"We'll do a tox screen."

Hoss broke in with strained politeness, "Wanna explain that for those of us who didn't go to college?"

Sara told him, "Rigor mortis can be brought on more quickly by strenuous exercise before death. A depletion of adenosine triphosphate, or ATP, would cause the muscles to stiffen more quickly."

The sheriff nodded, though she could tell from his expression that he had not absorbed the information.

Sara opened her mouth to explain again, but something about Hoss's posture told her it would do no good. He was so much like her grandfather Earnshaw that she caught herself smiling.

Reggie said, "These're the casings from the bullets," indicating a line he had drawn near the door. Two more were marked beside the victim. "The twenty-twos were here and here. The nine-mil is here by the door."

Jeffrey cleared his throat, seemingly reluctant to speak. "Did you fingerprint the casings?"

Reggie let his rancor show this time. "Of course I did." He added,

"And the guns. We traced the Glock back to Robert. It's his service weapon. The Beretta had the serial number shaved off."

Hoss nodded, tucking his hands into his pockets.

Sara asked Deacon, "Gloves?" and he took a box down from the cabinet by the sink. All the men watched Sara as she pulled on two pairs of surgical gloves, one over the other. Deacon rolled over a mayo tray, and she glanced down at the instruments, relieved to find a breadloafing knife, scissors, scalpels, and the other requisite tools for autopsy.

Deacon said, "I'll help you with this," and together he and Sara folded back the sheet covering the lower half of Luke Swan's body. His jeans and underwear had already been removed, which meant she could only guess by the lack of blood spatter from the head wound as to where the pants had been on the body.

Swan was a small man, probably no more than five seven and around a hundred sixty pounds, his body containing none of the grace his last name implied. Though he kept his blond hair long to the shoulder, he was far from hirsute, with a sparse patch of pubic hair around his groin. His penis was slightly tumescent, the swollen testicles showing signs of petechiae. His legs were spindly, and a large scar ran down the side of his left thigh. Sara guessed the wound had come during childhood. At the time it must have been a significant injury. For some reason, she thought of the scar on Jeffrey's back, and wondered what had been going through Jeffrey's mind when his father had hit him.

She asked Paul, "Do you mind taking notes for me?"

"No, ma'am," he said, turning to a fresh page in his notebook.

"He's how old?"

Paul said, "Thirty-four."

She nodded, thinking that fit the man in front of her. She called out her findings so far, pausing to give Paul time to write. Back in Grant, she used a Dictaphone for her reports, and she was not used to having to pause the natural cadence of the exam.

"Skin is slightly dry, probably due to lack of nourishment," she said, running her hand down his arm. "Track marks, probably a few years old, along the right arm." On a hunch, she examined the area between his toes, saying, "Fresh needle marks."

"What's that?" Hoss interrupted.

Jeffrey explained, "He was using the area between his toes to shoot up to try to hide the fact that he was using." To Sara, he said, "That would explain the ATP."

"Depending on what he was using, it might." She asked Deacon, "Have you taken blood and urine?"

The man nodded. "It'll take a week or two to get it back, though."

Sara held her tongue, but Jeffrey said, "Can we get a rush on that?"

Hoss said, "It'll cost."

Jeffrey shrugged, and Hoss gave a slight nod to Deacon, indicating it was okay.

Sara examined the surface of the body, finding nothing remarkable other than a star-shaped scar below the right ankle.

She asked Deacon, "Can you help me open his hand?"

He put on a pair of gloves, and as they all watched, Deacon tried to pry open the fingers. The hand would not give, and he adjusted his footing, giving himself a wide stance as he tried to press his thumb into the small opening between Swan's thumb and index finger. When he put his shoulder into it, the finger broke open. The next was easier, and one by one he broke back the fingers and thumb. The snaps sounded like twigs breaking.

"Nothing," Deacon said. He was leaning over the hand, and he moved out of the way so that Sara could see. Fingernail grooves cut into the meaty flesh of Swan's palm, but it appeared empty.

Deacon asked, "Death spasm?"

"Those are very rare," Sara answered, looking back at the chest where the fist had been. "He was lying on his fist. The weight of his body could have closed the fingers and the rigor fixed it in place." She looked around, finding a rolling lamp in the corner. "Do you mind getting that so I can take a closer look?"

He did as he was asked, unwrapping the cord and getting Paul to plug it into the wall socket. The bulb flickered a few times but easily illuminated the empty palm.

Using the sharp edge of the tweezers, she scraped under his fingernails, removing dry skin as well as some larger, unidentifiable flakes. She put them in a specimen bottle, along with some nail clippings, and watched Paul seal them with a strip of bright green tape.

While Reggie took photographs, Sara held a ruler next to the scars and other identifying marks she had found. They progressed to the head, and she used her fingers to pick out pieces of skull and gray matter before pushing the hair back off Swan's face and exposing the entrance wound on the left side of his head.

Jeffrey had been quiet through all of this, and when he said, "Powder tattooing," his voice was so low Sara was not sure if he had spoken the words or she had heard them in her own head.

He was right. There was a scatter-shot of reddish brown lesions surrounding the entrance wound where hot powder grains from the gun had burned the skin. Sara held the ruler as Reggie took photographs. She lightly combed her fingers through the hair and checked the surrounding skin for telltale markings. Finally, she said, "There's no soot that I can see."

"Did he bleed it off?" Jeffrey asked, standing beside her.

"Not from this side," she told him, feeling slightly relieved. The head was a mess, but she could see it clearly under the light now. Powder tattooing with the absence of soot most likely indicated an intermediate-range wound, meaning Robert was standing at least eighteen to twenty-four inches from the man when Swan was shot.

Jeffrey asked, "What'd he have in the Glock again?"

Paul was thumbing back through his notes. "Federal, one-fifteen grain."

"Ball powder," Jeffrey said, with palpable relief. He told Hoss, "Ball powder travels faster. That puts Robert anywhere from two to four feet away."

"Goes with what he said this morning," Hoss told them. "Had a hangfire when he pulled the trigger."

"Hangfire?" Sara repeated, though not because she did not understand the word. A hangfire meant there was a delay between Robert pulling the trigger and the bullet being fired from the gun.

Jeffrey asked, "Did he say how long it took?"

"He wasn't sure," Hoss answered. "Maybe half a second or so."

Jeffrey looked at Sara, and she wondered if her own expression of disbelief mirrored his. There was no scientific way to prove or disprove how the gun had fired or when. Bullets did not come with a time stamp, and whether or not the gun had in fact had a hangfire was impossible to prove with any scientific accuracy.

Sara turned her focus back to the head, combing through the hair for debris and setting it aside on the tray for collection. She tried to keep her mind on the task, but all she could think was how quickly excuses were being made for every question the evidence raised. If the situation had been reversed and Robert was lying on the table in front of her, she knew that all the men here would track down Luke Swan like a rabid dog.

As if he knew what she was thinking, Jeffrey asked Hoss, "Where's Robert now?"

"He's with Jessie at her mama's," Hoss provided. "Why?"

"I thought I'd check in on him. See how he's doing."

"He's fine," Hoss said, looking at his watch. "This is running a little later than I thought it would. I need to step out for a meeting."

Jeffrey asked, "Do you want Paul to take our statements?"

Hoss seemed to have forgotten about this, but he answered, "No, I'll do that. Let's meet back at the station around three."

Jeffrey told him, "We were planning on leaving before then."

"That's fine," Hoss told them, giving Jeffrey a hard pat on the back. "Y'all drop by the station on your way out of town. I'm sure it won't take long."

Paul waited for his boss to leave before saying, "I need to get back to some paperwork myself." He gave Sara a polite nod, then left the room. Deacon White was next, making an excuse about a lunch appointment. Sara wondered if he noticed the clock in the room read ten.

Reggie put down his camera and leaned against the sink, his

expression plainly stating he had nowhere to go and even if he did, he did not trust Jeffrey alone in the room with the corpse.

Jeffrey made it worse by asking Reggie, "What did Robert's statement say?"

Reggie shrugged. "Why are you so curious?"

Jeffrey returned the shrug.

Sara did not know how Reggie would handle this, but still, she told Jeffrey, "I don't want to dig around for the bullet. We need X rays first or I'll destroy any evidence."

Reggie said, "There wasn't another bullet in the room. I checked. It was just the two twenty-two LRs in the walls and casings on the floor like I drew."

Jeffrey seemed cautious, like he was feeling Reggie out. "What did Robert carry for backup?"

Reggie stared without answering.

Sara added, "A twenty-two would have less velocity than a nine-mil. It would be more likely to stay in the skull."

Reggie's chin dropped slightly. His eyes went from Jeffrey to Sara. "I think we should find that bullet."

Jeffrey nodded his agreement, saying, "Yeah."

Sara changed into a fresh pair of gloves, thinking she hardly had the authority to do this, but also knowing that this was the only way to find the truth. Carefully, she probed around the exit wound in the skull with her fingers, not wanting to use the forceps because they could scratch or change the markings on the metal.

"Nothing," she finally said. "It could be deeper in."

Reggie told her, "Hoss won't let us take him back for X rays."

"Luke," Jeffrey said. "His name's Luke Swan. You ever have him in your cruiser?"

"Hell," Reggie snorted. "About a million times."

"For what?"

"Mostly breaking and entering, but he always made sure the houses were empty. Usually, he picked when he thought folks were at church."

"Last night was Sunday."

"Church is over by eight. Even if he was stoned, he would've seen the cars in the driveway and known."

"You ever find a weapon on him?"

"Not once."

"He ever do anything violent?"

"No." Reggie paused as if to think it over. "He was small-time, usually just taking what he could carry out in a pillowcase." He added, "But you never know, do you? I bet the people said the same thing about your daddy before he hooked up with them fellas who shot my uncle Dave."

Sara saw Jeffrey's throat work as he swallowed.

Reggie continued, "You never know what some people are capable of. One minute they're stealing lawn mowers, the next minute they're murdering a sheriff's deputy in cold blood."

Sara felt the need to say something, though she could not think what. Jeffrey's fists were clenched like he wanted nothing more than to beat Reggie to a pulp. Making things worse, Reggie tilted his chin up, practically begging Jeffrey to take a swing.

Sara asked, "Reggie, would you mind taking notes?"

Reggie took his time breaking eye contact with Jeffrey. "No, ma'am," he said, taking out his notebook. He glanced back at Jeffrey. "Anything to help."

While he wrote, Sara went back through her findings, not wanting to track down Paul for his earlier notes and delay leaving this god-awful town a minute longer than necessary. Out of the corner of her eye, she caught Jeffrey staring at Luke Swan and wondered what he was thinking. He had not told her that the shooting his father was involved in resulted in the death of a cop. Reggie's words had obviously hit their mark, and she could feel Jeffrey's anger melt into a sadness that felt almost like a fourth presence in the room.

The rest of the autopsy was as routine as was possible with any gunshot victim. There were no remarkable findings and no clues that pointed to anything other than what Robert had told them last night. Long-term drug use was obvious, as was a fatty diet that left deposits of calcium in Swan's heart. His liver was larger than expected, but considering Sara found alcohol in the man's stomach, it made sense. As for the missing bullet, maybe Reggie had overlooked it at the house or maybe it was buried deeper in the brain. Sara had not opened Swan's head, wanting to leave the option of X rays open should Hoss later be persuaded to actually investigate the case.

Sara was closing the Y-incision with the usual baseball stitch when she remembered to ask about clothing.

Reggie supplied, "They're in a bag at the station."

"They're not here?" Sara asked, thinking that was odd.

"Hoss took them for evidence this morning," Reggie said, flipping back through his notes. "Pair of twenty-nine–thirty Levis, pair of Nike sneakers and white socks, wallet with six bucks in it and a license."

"No underwear?" Sara asked.

He reread the notes. "Guess not."

"Car keys?"

"He never drove himself anywhere. Lost his license on a DUI coupla three years back."

"DUI doesn't mean he stopped driving," Jeffrey pointed out.

Reggie shrugged. "Never caught him on the street. Car belonged to his grandma, anyway. She's crazy as a loon. Hoss caught her driving the wrong way a couple of times, then she ran through that stop sign over on Henderson and tore off the front end. Even if he wanted to drive after that, the car wouldn't start."

Sara took off her gloves. "Is there somewhere I can sit to write out my report?"

"I'll go fetch Deacon," Reggie offered. "I'm sure he won't mind you using his office."

Sara went to the sink to wash her hands, feeling Jeffrey watch her every move. She tried to catch his eye again, but Deacon came into the room and he looked away.

"Well," Deacon said, shuffling through some papers. "I guess these are probably what you're used to."

Sara glanced down at the autopsy forms. "Yes, thanks."

"I usually fill them out in here," Deacon added, rolling a chair over to the counter by the sink.

"That's fine."

Jeffrey said, "I'll be out by the car when you're ready," and left the room.

Deacon said, "I'll leave you to it."

Sara pulled up the chair and Reggie walked over, looking over her shoulder as she wrote in her name and the various details the state required. She recorded Luke Swan's address and home phone number, then the various weights and measurements of organs and other landmarks she found on the body. She was writing her conclusion when Reggie cleared his throat. Sara looked up, waiting for him to speak.

For some reason, she anticipated a treatise against Jeffrey. What she got was, "This look pretty straightforward to you?"

Sara tried to measure her words, not knowing whether or not to trust the man. "I don't think any shooting is straightforward."

"That's true," he agreed, his tone just as cautious as hers. "How long you known Jeffrey Tolliver?"

For some reason, Sara felt the need to take up for Jeffrey. "A while. Why?"

"Just asking," he said.

"Was there something else?"

He shook his head no and she went back to the report.

A few minutes later, Reggie cleared his throat again, and she looked up, expectant.

He said, "The Beretta takes seven rounds in the magazine."

"Then you should have found five bullets in the magazine."

"Six if he had one in the chamber."

Sara waited, thinking this was like pulling teeth. "How many did you find?"

"Six."

She put down the pen. "Reggie, are you trying to tell me something?"

His jaw worked just like Jeffrey's did when he was angry. Sara was getting tired of drawing out information from reluctant men.

She said, "If you've got something to say, then say it."

Instantly, she knew she had pushed him in the wrong direction, but Sara was no longer worried about stepping on people's feelings. "Reggie, if you think there's something suspicious about this shooting, then you need to speak up. All I can do is fill in these forms. I'm not a cop and I'm not your mama."

"Lady," Reggie began, his voice shaking with anger, "you don't know what you're getting yourself into here."

"That sounds an awful lot like a threat."

"It's a warning," he said. "You seem like a nice enough person, but I don't trust the company you keep."

"You've made that abundantly clear."

"You might want to think about why people keep warning you off him." He tipped his hat to Sara as he headed toward the door. "Ma'am."

CHAPTER TWELVE

The heat slammed into Sara like a brick as soon as she opened the door to leave the funeral home. Overhead, she could tell a storm was coming, but the rolling clouds did nothing to cool the air. Her skin seemed to contract for a few seconds before it adjusted, and by the time she got to Jeffrey standing by the car, she could feel sweat dripping down her back. Despite this, she told him, "Let's go for a walk."

He did not ask questions as they made their way through the cemetery behind the building. There was no breeze as they climbed a sloping hill, and Sara felt slightly dizzy from the heat. Still, she kept going, absently reading markers as they walked toward the wooded area at the rear of the cemetery. There was a gate in the fence, and Jeffrey held it open for her.

The sky darkened even more as they walked into the forest, and Sara did not know if it was from the canopy of trees overhead or the impending thunderstorm. Either way, the temperature seemed to drop about ten degrees in the shade, and for that she was thankful.

They walked along a narrow path, Jeffrey ahead of her pushing back branches and kicking debris out of the way. Birds called overhead, and she heard a buzzing sound that could belong to a cricket or a snake, depending on how much she let her imagination get away from her.

Finally, she broke the silence. "I know this is a crazy question considering we're in Alabama, but has anyone thought to ask why Luke Swan wasn't wearing a shirt?"

Jeffrey pulled a twig off a low-hanging branch. "I don't think anybody's asking much of anything." He glanced at her over his shoulder. "There weren't any footprints outside the window." Seemingly as an afterthought, he added, "Of course, the ground was dry. You could make the argument that nothing would leave footprints."

"It seems to me arguments are being made to dismiss a lot of things," she said, flinching as a tree root dug into her heel.

He stopped, facing her. "I couldn't tell if the screen was pulled off from the outside or pushed from the inside."

"What are you going to do?"

"Hell," he said, throwing the twig into the woods. "I don't know." He knelt down and started to untie his shoes.

"What are you doing?"

"You might as well be walking barefoot in those sandals." He slipped off his tennis shoe and handed it to her.

Sara hesitated, and he added, "I've had my mouth on every part of your body, Sara. You think I haven't noticed your feet are the same size as mine?"

"They're not that big," she mumbled, putting her hand on his shoulder to steady herself as she slipped her foot into his shoe. To her embarrassment, the fit was nearly perfect.

She looked down to see if he had noticed, and he smiled up at her. "I love the way you blush."

"I'm not blushing," she said, though she could feel it in her cheeks.

He helped her into the other sneaker. She started to kneel down to tie the laces, but Jeffrey did it for her, saying, "I keep waiting for somebody to say something. There's no way they're all buying this story."

"I think Reggie has some questions," she said, watching him double-knot the laces. He had such large hands, but they were soft, and his touch was always so gentle. For some reason, the anger Sara had felt toward him this morning had dissipated, and all she could think was that twenty-four hours ago she had been on the verge of falling in love with this man. As much as she wanted to change her mind, she could not alter how she felt about him.

"There." He stood, holding her sandals in one hand. "Okay?"

She took a step, lying, "They're a little loose."

"Yeah, right." He continued, walking in his socks. "Did Reggie mention I dated his sister?"

"I just assumed you'd dated every woman in town."

He gave her a look.

"Sorry," she said, and she really was. They walked for a few more minutes before she asked, "Why is everyone so against you?"

"My dad wasn't exactly in the Rotary Club."

"It goes back further than that," she said, wondering what he was hiding. She had her own secrets, though, and she was hardly in a position to fault him for being reticent.

He stopped, facing her again. "I want to stay in town another day."

"Okay."

"And I want you to stay with me."

"I don't—"

"You're the only person here who doesn't think I'm some kind of criminal."

"Hoss doesn't."

"He will after I give my statement."

"What are you going to say?" she asked, wary of his answer.

"Exactly what you'll say: the truth." He resumed walking and she followed. "Maybe it'd be different if Robert was talking." He stopped, pointing behind Sara. She turned, looking at the mountains on the horizon.

"That's Herd's Gap," he said. "All the rich people live there. Jessie's family included."

Sara shaded her eyes, taking in the view.

"I know it doesn't look like much, but it's right at the foot of the Appalachian Mountains. You can't see them from here, but up that

159

way," he indicated the space to their left, "are the Cheaha Mountains." He started walking again. "And underneath us, there's thirty-two miles of the hardest, whitest marble in the world. It goes about four hundred feet down."

Sara watched his back, wondering why he was telling her this. "Is that so?"

"Sylacauga marble is in the Washington Monument and the Supreme Court building," he continued. "I remember when I was a kid the windows would shake from all the blasting." He stepped over a fallen tree and held out his hand to help Sara over. She could see his socks were getting filthy, but he did not seem to care.

He said, "There's an underground river that cuts through the city. Between the river and the blasting in the quarry, there are sinkholes all over town. A few years ago one of them opened up at the Baptist church and the back half of the building dropped about ten feet underground."

"Jeffrey—"

He stopped again. "That's what I feel like, Sara. I feel like this whole town is sinking, and I'm going right down with it." He gave a harsh laugh. "They say you can't get any lower than the ground, but this is the one place you can."

She took a deep breath, and breathed out, "I can't have children."

He did not speak for what seemed like an eternity, then he gave her a neutral "Okay."

"I gather we're supposed to pretend you didn't say what you said last night before . . ." she threw a hand into the air, ". . . before all hell broke lose."

"No," he stopped her. She believed him when he told her, "I meant what I said."

"Then tell me," she asked. "Tell me why Reggie doesn't trust you."

Droplets of rain splattered against the leaves overhead, and Sara looked up at the sky just as the bottom dropped out. In seconds, they were both soaked. The rain was so dense she reached out to take Jeffrey's hand for fear she would lose him.

"This way," he yelled over the downpour. He walked fast, then started jogging when a bolt of lightning cracked the sky. The tall trees all around them that had been so beautiful before were nothing more than lightning rods now, and Sara picked up the pace along with him, wanting to find shelter before the storm got worse.

The sky grew darker, and Sara looked up just as Jeffrey pulled her down into a squatting position. Carefully, he pushed back a clump of hanging vines and rotted old boards before leading her through a four-foot-wide opening into a cave. Inside, the air turned almost cold, and she put her hand against the rough rock of the ceiling, trying to get her bearings. Even with her knees bent, Sara could not stand up straight. She curved at the waist, reaching out with her hands, trying to feel her surroundings as Jeffrey pulled her farther into the cave. There was nothing but empty space to her left and right, but overhead the ceiling sloped up so that she could straighten a bit more. Still, she had to keep her head and shoulders down so she would not scrape against the ceiling.

In the distance, she could hear the muffled rain as well as a constant dripping. Just enough light came in through the vines and cracked boards at the entrance to keep them from total darkness, but somehow that was no comfort. Even as her vision adjusted, she could not see the back of the cave.

"You okay?" Jeffrey asked.

"Fine." Sara shuddered, but not from the cold. She kept her hand against the ceiling, feeling claustrophobia overwhelm her.

"Jesus, it smells in here." He passed by her again, doing something at the entrance of the cave. More light came in as he kicked out the boards, but it was still too dark for comfort.

Sara blinked a few times, making out a long bench seat like the kind they used to put in cars. Stuffing and springs jutted out of the vinyl upholstery. In front of the seat was an old coffee table with hemp rope around the edges, scuffs showing where people had sat with their feet propped up. Jeffrey brushed something out of his hair as he walked over to the seat. He searched under the bench, and over the steady hush of the rain she heard him laugh.

"They're still here," he said, sounding pleased.

She stepped closer to him, unsettled by the darkness. A musty odor was in the air, and underneath that the scent of decay. She wondered if there were any animals in here, or perhaps an animal was on his way back home, looking to get out of the storm.

Jeffrey struck a match, and the cave was briefly illuminated before the flame flickered out. Like her, he was standing with his shoulders hunched against the ceiling. Unlike her, he seemed perfectly at ease. She felt embarrassed for being so frightened. Sara had never been afraid of the dark before, but the closed space had a feel to it that she could not quite name.

He struck another match. The fire burned down just as quickly as it had with the first, casting the cave back into darkness. He said, "I guess they got wet."

Sara spoke before she could stop herself. "I don't like it in here."

"The storm will pass soon," he told her, taking Sara's arm and leading her to the seat. "It's okay," he soothed. "We used to come here after school."

"Why?" she asked, thinking this was as close to being buried alive as she ever wanted to come. Even sitting down, she could feel the cave looming over her. She reached out, grabbing Jeffrey's hand.

"It's okay," he repeated, finally sensing her fear. He put his arm around her and kissed the side of her head.

Sara leaned into him, asking, "How did you find this place?"

"It's near the quarry," he told her. "Robert came across it one day while we were out looking for arrowheads."

"Arrowheads?"

"This area was filled with Indians. Creek at first, then Shawnee warriors. They called it Chalakagay. DeSoto's records mention the town in the early 1500s." He paused. "Of course, the government came in around 1836 and moved them all out west." He stopped again. "Sara, I don't want kids."

The sound of rain filled the cave, sounding like a thousand brooms sweeping across the rock.

"I didn't exactly have the best role models growing up, and who knows what the hell my genes will pass on."

She put her fingers to his lips. "Tell me more about the Indians."

He kissed her fingers, then asked, "Why, you want something to help you sleep?"

Sara laughed, and she realized with a start that she could stay here forever as long as he kept talking. She repeated, "Tell me more."

He paused, probably trying to think of what to say. "You can't see it, but there's a lot of marble in here. Not enough to get the quarry folks interested, but you can see the veins along the back wall. That's why the air is so cool. Are you cold?"

"No, just soaking wet."

He pulled her closer and she put her head in the crook of his neck, thinking that everything would be okay if they could just stay this way until the storm passed.

He continued, "We stole this bench seat from an old car out in the junkyard. Possum's probably still got the scars on his ass from the dog we had to wrestle for it. The coffee table was out by the road for trash pickup. We carried it two miles up the highway to get it here." He laughed good-naturedly. "We thought we had it made."

"I bet you brought girls here all the time."

"Are you kidding? They were afraid of spiders."

"Spiders?" She stiffened.

"Don't tell me you're suddenly afraid of spiders."

"I'm just afraid of things crawling on me that I can't see." He stood up, and she asked, "Where are you going?"

"Hold on," he told her, and she could hear his hand feeling along the wall of the cave. "We used to keep a coffee can . . ." He stopped, and she heard the jangle of metal against metal. "Aha. More matches. Possum got them out of the back of a comic book. They're supposed to be waterproof."

Sara tucked her feet underneath her, keeping her back flat to the seat. Crazy as it was, she had the unnatural fear that something—or someone—would reach out and touch her shoulder.

"Here we go," he said, striking a match. She could see his face in the light as he held the flame to a small utility candle. There was a flicker, and she held her breath, not breathing until the wick caught.

"I can't believe it still works after all this time."

In the flickering light, Sara saw a form behind him. Her heart jumped into her throat and she gasped so loudly that Jeffrey startled, banging his head against the ceiling.

He looked behind him, shouting, "Jesus Christ!" In his haste to get away, he tripped against the coffee table, unable to catch himself before he hit the ground.

Sara panicked, reaching out for the candle. Hot wax burned her hand, but she managed to keep the flame from blowing out. Her heart was pounding so hard that her ribs ached.

"Christ," Jeffrey said, brushing dirt off his jeans. "What the fuck is that?"

Sara forced herself to stand, and walked over to the skeleton that had scared her so much seconds before.

The remains were laid on a rock that jutted out like a seat. Though the bones looked yellowed with age, sinew remained in a few areas, probably because of the coolness of the cave. Part of the left leg down to the foot was missing, as well as some fingers on the right hand. Even in the dim candlelight, Sara could see the teeth marks where some kind of rodent had gnawed skin from the bone. She held the candle up to the head, which had tilted sideways and become lodged in a crevice between two rocks. The skull was fractured on the right side, the bone collapsed into the braincase from the force of what must have been a very heavy object.

She looked back at Jeffrey just in time to see him slip something into his pocket.

His tone was defensive. "What?"

Sara turned back to the skeleton. "I think this person was murdered."

CHAPTER THIRTEEN

Lena was gritting her teeth so hard her jaw hurt. Wagner wasn't saying much into the phone, but Lena and probably everyone in the cleaners could hear the shooter screaming on the other end.

Wagner said, "Why don't you tell me your name?" Only to be answered with a barked laugh. When she asked about the children, the only response she got was a little girl yelling into the phone. The sound echoed in the room, and Lena fought the urge to cover her ears.

Wagner remained calm. "I take it that means you're holding on to the children?"

The answer was mumbled, but the shooter's last demand was loud and clear, especially since Wagner held the phone a few inches from her ear to deflect the sound. "One hour, bitch. You take any longer than that, the body count's gonna get a lot higher."

Despite the threat, Wagner smiled as she closed her cell phone. "Well," she said. "They want beer."

Lena opened her mouth to restate her offer to volunteer, but Wagner held up a finger for silence, saying, to Frank and Nick, "Gentlemen, if I could have a moment of your time?"

The two men followed her into Bill Burgess's office. Wagner smiled at Lena before shutting the door. It was a cat's smile, and Lena could not tell if the woman was being polite or warning her off. Either way, Lena would fight tooth and nail to be the one to go into the station. She had to do her part. Jeffrey had allowed her back on the force despite what everyone in town was saying. The worst crime was that he was lying dead right now and Lena was alive.

Molly Stoddard had been leaning against the folding table, but she stood up and knocked on the door to Burgess's office. She entered without waiting for a reply, closing the door behind her.

Lena watched Wagner's guys for a reaction, but they seemed un-interested. One of them was talking so low on his cell phone she wondered if he was just moving his lips, and the other two were leaned over a map of the station, pointing to different areas like they were hatching a plan. They had not been able to get a camera into the air-conditioning vent because the shooters had blocked them with clothing.

She walked over to see what they were planning. The guy on the cell phone ended the call. He told her, "Jennings was killed in a six-car pile-up outside Friendswood, Texas, last year."

"You're kidding," she said, feeling like all the wind had been knocked out of her.

The guy added, "There were two kids in the back. One of them walked away from the accident. That's good, right?"

"Yeah," Lena said, though she doubted the kid felt lucky. She had seen the kind of damage Jennings was capable of firsthand. That the animal had died in such a seemingly normal way was just wrong.

The office door opened and Amanda Wagner came out followed by Frank. Nick and Molly were still inside, and Lena could see that Molly was using the phone on old man Burgess's desk. Her head was bent down and she had her hand wrapped around the back of her neck like she wanted to keep the conversation private.

Wagner's man repeated the information about Jennings. His boss said, "Well, it was a long shot anyway." She motioned Lena toward the office. "Follow me."

Nick waited until they were all inside before shutting the door.

Molly looked up at Lena, a flash of irritation in her eyes. Into the phone, she said, "Baby, Mama has to go now, okay?" She waited a beat. "I love you, too."

Lena had not given Sara's nurse much thought beyond noticing her around the clinic, and it had never occurred to Lena that the woman was a mother. She was probably a good one, too—always calm, always there for her kids. She did not seem to have a selfish bone in her body. Some people were just made for that kind of life.

"Detective Adams," Wagner began. "We've selected you to go into the building."

Nick said, "I want to repeat that I'm against this."

Lena went on the defensive. "I know what I—"

"Not you," Nick interrupted. "Her."

"Wait a minute," Lena said, finally understanding what Molly had done. "She's going, too?"

Wagner provided, "We'll send you in as paramedics under the guise of offering medical assistance."

"You said Barry was probably dead."

Molly looked at Nick as she spoke. "Some of the kids could be hurt. Sara could need me."

Nick's mouth went into a straight line, and Lena wondered why he was so vehement. His objection seemed more personal than professional.

"Just for the record," Wagner began, "I'm a little hesitant to send you in, Detective, but Nicky assures me you're up to the challenge."

Lena bit back the defensive remark that wanted to come. Instead, she swallowed her pride and said, "If you're not certain . . ." She tried to find the words, struggling with her emotions. "If you think someone else is more qualified, then I'll step down."

"That's just it," Wagner answered. "There isn't anyone more qualified. If I send in one of my boys, the shooters will know immediately what's going on. I think our best plan of action is to send in both of you. They'll be more comfortable with women."

"Or they'll take you both hostage," Nick added. "Or just shoot you."

"He's right," Wagner said. "There's nothing to keep them from doing either or both." She crossed her arms. "Are you still so eager to get into that building?"

Lena did not hesitate. "Yes."

They all looked at Molly.

"Ms. Stoddard?" Wagner asked.

Molly exchanged a look with Nick. "Yes."

Wagner said, "Your resolve seems to have slipped a little."

"No." Molly stood. "I'm ready."

2:15 P.M.

Lena washed her hands in the bathroom sink of the Grant Medical Center. Her hands shook slightly, but that was nothing new. Her hands had been shaking off and on for the last two years, ever since she was abducted. Sometimes, Lena thought the shaking was because of the scars in her hands that her attacker had made, but her doctors assured her there was no nerve damage.

"You okay?" Molly Stoddard asked. She was watching Lena's hands like they told a story.

"I'm fine," Lena told her, snatching a paper towel off the roll.

"It's okay to be nervous," Molly said. "As a matter of fact, I'd feel better if you did."

"Right," Lena answered. She took the EMT uniform off the counter and went into a stall to change.

"*I'm* nervous," Molly said. She was obviously waiting for Lena to speak, but when she did not, Molly drew out an "O-okay."

Lena took off her jacket and hung it on the hook on the back of the stall door. She was unbuttoning her shirt when a knock came at the bathroom door.

Nick Shelton asked, "Y'all decent?"

Molly said yes as Lena said no.

"Sorry," Molly apologized, but Lena could already hear Nick in the room. She sat on the toilet, not wanting to be undressed with him in the room, even though there was a locked stall door between them.

"I wanted to say," Nick began, his voice sounding hesitant. "I just . . ."

"We'll be fine," Molly said, as if she knew exactly what was bothering him. Lena peered through the crack in the door and she saw that Molly had her hand on Nick's face.

Molly whispered again, "I'll be fine."

"You don't have to do this," Nick said.

"If I was in there and Sara—"

"Sara doesn't have two kids at home, and that's exactly what she'd be telling you now if she was here."

Molly looked Lena's way, and Lena stood to continue changing so they would not think she had been watching. Her pants dropped to the floor and she heard a muffled clank as the knife she always kept in her back pocket hit the tile. Lena looked out the crack to make sure Molly and Nick had not seen. They were still whispering, as if the fact that she was three feet away meant nothing. Nick clearly did not want Molly to go into the station. Lena couldn't blame him. There was no guarantee the shooters weren't looking for more hostages.

Lena opened her pocketknife and ran her finger along the sharp blade. The knife was little more than three inches long, but she could do some damage with it. The only question was where she could hide it in case the shooters frisked her.

Nick raised his voice to include Lena. "They capitulated too easily," he said. "Usually, hostage takers are unstable. They're emotional. You have to deal with them for a while, get their trust, before they make concessions. They're sending Marla out too soon."

Lena slipped on the pants for the paramedic's uniform. They were about one size too big, which was a better fit than she had hoped. She suggested, "Maybe they're hungry."

"There's something not right here," Nick insisted. "They obviously know what we're doing. They wouldn't have blocked the vents just for the hell of it. They knew we would have cameras and that standard operating procedure is to try the vents first. This could be a trap to get more hostages."

Lena slid off her sneaker and dropped in the pocketknife. She stepped back into the shoe, wiggling the knife around until it was snug against the arch of her foot.

"Lena?" Nick prompted.

"I know the dangers, Nick," Lena snapped, thinking he was treating her like a ten-year-old instead of a seasoned cop. She put on the white paramedic's shirt, which was tight across her chest. The badge over the pocket read MARTIN, and she wondered if Martin was a skinny guy or a flat-chested woman.

When she opened the door, Molly moved away from Nick as if they had been caught. Lena checked herself in the mirror, thinking that with the buttons stretched across her chest she looked like some slut out of a porn movie. Considering some of the Grant paramedics she had seen around town, she fit right in.

She told Nick, "I know you don't trust Wagner."

"Do you know why?" Nick asked, but he did not let her answer. "I know the rumor, but let me set it straight. I'm the one who hesitated. She didn't hesitate. She never hesitates. She's ice. And I'll tell you another thing." He gave Molly a meaningful look. "She doesn't like women."

Lena blew air out through her lips.

"It's true," Nick said. "She doesn't mind using them as bait. That's exactly what she's doing here, no matter what you think. That's what happened in Ludowici. She sent in a female cop and the shooters kept the woman. She was dead ten minutes later."

"Because *you* hesitated?" Lena asked. She could see the guilt flash in his eyes and she regretted her words—not because she didn't mean them, but because the situation was stressful enough without having Molly Stoddard pissed off with her, too.

Nick said, "This won't go down like you think. You've been on the job long enough to know something isn't right here. You feel it in your gut. You know that, Lena."

"I'll be outside," Lena told him, thinking it would be best to leave them alone. She walked out of the bathroom and ran into one of Wagner's men. He was built like a brick wall, and he grabbed her in surprise. His hands stayed on her body a little too long, and she pushed him back, trying not to show her anger. She walked toward Wagner, who was standing at the end of the hallway with a cell phone to her ear. She ended the call as Lena reached her.

Wagner said, "What's in your shoe?"

"It's just tight," Lena said. "Kind of like this shirt."

"Better too tight than too big," Wagner countered. "What happened to your lip?"

Lena put her hand to her mouth, a second later realizing she had given herself away. "Accident," she said, but the lie sounded weak even to her.

Wagner seemed to be taking all of this in, but she did not challenge Lena. "I don't quite trust you, Detective Adams, but I'm letting you go in there because you're familiar with the layout and because they'll see you as less threatening."

"Thanks for the vote of confidence."

"You don't need any more confidence from me, Detective," Wagner shot back. "Listen closely: you're to deliver the food and get Marla Simms out of there as quickly as possible."

"All right."

"I don't need heroics, and I certainly don't need you exchanging yourself for any hostages."

Lena looked down, trying to hide her expression. That had been exactly what she was planning.

"It might seem like a good idea, but you're more useful to me out here than you are in there. You're trained to appraise dangerous situations. I need your expert opinion."

She seemed like a frank person, so Lena decided to say what was on her mind. "That sounds like you're blowing smoke up my ass."

Wagner's lip curled up in a smile, and she got a look in her eyes that Lena had seen several times before in other people; the woman realized she had underestimated Lena. "Maybe a little of it's smoke, but you worked with Brad Stephens. Maybe he can communicate something to you. I know partners pick up on each other's codes."

"He wasn't my partner."

"I don't have time for your ego," Wagner reprimanded. "What I want from you when you come out of that place is a detailed drawing of where everyone is. I need to know how many desks and filing cabinets are against the doors and I need to know exactly how they're armed. What are they using, Sig, S&W, Glock? Detective Wallace thinks the shotgun is a Wingmaster. Did they bring extra ammo? What caliber? Are they still wearing Kevlar? How are they getting along? Is one getting a little too big for his britches? Maybe the other one can be turned or distracted. I need to know every weakness in their armor, and I can't get that from you if you stay inside."

Lena nodded. All of that would be useful, and there was no way Molly Stoddard would even begin to know how to tell the difference between a twenty-two and a nine-mil, let alone give an accurate assessment of available firepower.

Lena asked, "Should I try to pass them anything?"

"No," Wagner said. "Not at this point. We need to establish some trust. They're going to pat you down head to toe." She glanced at Lena's shoe. "If they find anything, they're going to be angry, and they're going to take it out on someone. This someone might not be you, so before you take any risks, you need to ask yourself if it's worth jeopardizing the lives of the people around you."

"Okay," Lena said, shifting her weight. "I'm ready."

Wagner stared at her for a beat. She smiled ruefully. "Sweetheart, you can piss on my face, but don't tell me it's raining."

Lena was caught out, but she tried not to show it.

Wagner glanced down at Lena's shoe again. All she said was, "Be careful."

CHAPTER FOURTEEN

Jeffrey trudged back through the woods, his socks bunching from the wet earth. He stopped by a tree, using it to lean on while he peeled them off. The rain was barely more than a memory, and the air was filled with mist as the sun evaporated it up to the clouds. Jeffrey wiped sweat off his forehead with the back of his hand as he walked into the cemetery. The sun was sharper in the open grave-yard, and the sloping hill with its jutting white markers seemed like teeth in the big mouth that was trying to swallow him.

Reggie was sitting in his cruiser with the door open, a cigarette hanging from his lips. He stayed where he was, making Jeffrey come to him. The asphalt was blistering against Jeffrey's bare feet, but he was damned if he'd show it.

Reggie gave a leisurely glance down at the wet athletic socks Jeffrey held in his hand. His lip curled up in a sarcastic sneer, but Jeffrey didn't let him get out whatever shitty thing he wanted to say.

"Take me to the station," Jeffrey ordered, climbing into the passenger seat of the cruiser.

Reggie took one last suck on his cigarette before closing the door. He cranked the engine and let it idle for a few minutes. "Where's your girl?"

"She's fine," Jeffrey told him. Despite the fact that she had been scared out of her mind seconds before finding the bones, Sara had insisted on staying with them while Jeffrey went to get help.

Reggie rested his hand on the shift for a moment before putting the car in gear. He took his time merging onto the interstate and drove the posted speed limit into town, waving at folks out the window like he hadn't a care in the world. Jeffrey tried not to show his irritation, knowing Reggie was doing all this on purpose, but as they crawled past the high school at twenty miles per hour, he had to let off some steam or he would explode.

"Is there a reason you're going this slow?"

"Just to piss you off, Slick."

Jeffrey stared out the window, wondering how much worse this day could get.

Reggie said, "You wanna tell me what's going on here?"

"No."

"That's your prerogative."

Jeffrey gave a low whistle. "Big word."

"I thought you might be impressed."

"Your sister teach you that?"

"You shut up about my sister."

"How's Paula doing?"

"I said shut up, you fucker," Reggie said, his voice a low warning. "Why don't you ask me how my cousins are doing? How they're getting by without their father? How it feels for all of us when we get together and my uncle Dave's not there?"

Jeffrey felt all the guilt his words could bring and more. Still, he said, "I'm not my father's keeper."

"Yeah," Reggie said, making a sharp turn into the sheriff's station parking lot. "That's real convenient for you. I'll tell that to my cousin Jo when she graduates this fall and her daddy's not around to congratulate her. I'm sure it'll be a real comfort."

Jeffrey grabbed his wet socks off the floorboard and got out of the car before Reggie cut the engine. He walked into the building, ignoring the secretary and the deputy who was leaning over her desk as he went back to Hoss's office, opening the door without knocking.

Hoss looked over the newspaper he was reading when Jeffrey closed the door. "What is it, son?"

Jeffrey wanted to sit down, but something stopped him. Instead, he leaned against the wall for support, the weight of his fears catching up with him. He looked at Hoss's office. Like the man, nothing had changed in the last decade. The fishing trophies and photographs of Hoss on his boat were still around, and the folded American flag that had been on his brother's coffin when they brought his body back from Vietnam was still given a place of prominence on the shelf by the window. After his brother had died, Hoss had tried to join up, but his flat feet had kept him out. He always joked that the Army's loss was Sylacauga's gain, but Jeffrey knew he did not like to talk about it, as if having flat feet made him less of a man.

Hoss prompted, "Jeffrey?"

"We found some bones."

"Bones?" Hoss asked, creasing his newspaper in a tight fold.

"In the old cave me and the boys used to use when we were in junior high."

"Out on the edge of the quarry?" Hoss asked in a careful tone. "Probably just a bear or something."

"Sara's a doctor, Hoss. She knows what human bones look like. Hell, even if she didn't, the damn thing was laying out on the rocks like she was taking a nap."

"She?" Hoss asked, and all the air went out of the room.

A knock came at the door.

"What is it?" Hoss demanded.

Reggie opened the door. "I was just—"

"Give us a minute," Hoss barked, his tone inviting no dissension.

Jeffrey heard the click of the door, but his eyes were on Hoss. The old man seemed to have aged about a hundred years in the past few seconds.

Jeffrey reached into his pocket and pulled out the chain he had found in the cave. He held it up, letting the gold heart-shaped locket twirl in the light.

"It doesn't prove anything," Hoss said. "She went to the cave a couple dozen times. Everybody knows that. Hell, she told them herself."

"Sara won't let this go."

"I thought y'all were leaving this afternoon?"

"I talked her into staying another day before all this happened," Jeffrey told him. "Even without that, she'll want to see this through."

"I don't see giving her a choice."

Jeffrey felt the heat of his remark and the underlying warning. "I don't have anything to hide," he said, hearing the false bravado in his own voice.

"It's not a matter of hiding anything, Slick. It's about burying the past and getting on with your life. You and Robert both."

"No matter how much of a bitch Lane Kendall is, she deserves to know this."

"Know what?" Hoss asked. He stood from his chair and walked to the window. Like Jeffrey's, his office had a stellar view of the parking lot. "We don't know anything right now."

"Sara will find out soon enough."

"Find out what?"

"Her head was bashed in," Jeffrey said. "Someone killed her."

"Maybe she fell," Hoss suggested. His posture was ramrod straight, his back to Jeffrey. "You ever think of that?"

Jeffrey said, "Then we should let Sara figure it out."

"Could be it's not even her," Hoss tried. He turned back around and seemed to have collected himself. He reached out to Jeffrey, asking for the necklace.

Jeffrey handed it over, saying, "She wore it all the time. Everybody saw it."

"Yep," Hoss agreed. He took out his pocketknife and pried open the heart-shaped locket. He palmed the charm and held it out for Jeffrey to see. Baby pictures had been crudely cut into the shape of the heart and glued into either side. A strand of blond hair curled around the photograph on the left, a small piece of twine holding the ends together.

"Two different babies," Jeffrey said. One photo was in color and the other in black and white, but it was still easy to tell that the child on the right had a shock of dark black hair, while the one on the left was fair.

Hoss turned the necklace around to look at the photos. He gave a heavy sigh and closed the locket before handing it back to Jeffrey, saying, "Hold on to this."

Jeffrey did not want to, but he took the necklace and tucked it back into his pocket.

Hoss said, "I told Reggie to wait for you back at the funeral home."

"Why's that?"

"You need to go talk to Robert."

"He didn't seem too interested in talking to me this morning."

"He is now," Hoss said. "He called the station looking for you."

"Sara's waiting back at the cave with the body."

"I'll run go fetch her."

"She won't give up on this," Jeffrey repeated.

"On what?" Hoss asked. "Could be some bum walked into the cave and forgot to come out. Could be somebody fell and hit their head. Could be a lot of things, right?" When Jeffrey did not answer, he reminded him, "You've got nothing to hide."

Jeffrey remained silent. They both knew that he did. Things were going downhill faster than he could keep up with.

Hoss gave him a hard pat on the shoulder. "I ever let anything bad happen to you, son?"

Jeffrey shook his head, thinking that the words were no great comfort. Hoss had proven more than a few times that he was not above bending the law to keep Jeffrey and Robert out of trouble.

Hoss flashed one of his rare smiles. "It'll be fine." He opened the door and waved in Reggie as he asked Jeffrey, "What happened to your shoes?"

Jeffrey looked down at his bare feet. They should be digging in the sands of Florida by now. He should be rubbing suntan lotion on Sara's back and front and every other part of her body while she laughed at his jokes and looked at him like he was the second coming.

Hoss asked, "What size are you?"

"Ten."

"I'm an eleven and a half." He asked Reggie, "What size shoe do you wear?"

Reggie looked embarrassed, as if his answer would be the punch line to a joke. Still, he said, "Nine."

"You're stuck with mine, then." Hoss took a set of keys out of his pocket and handed them to Reggie. "Run go fetch my boots out of the back of my truck."

CHAPTER FIFTEEN

Hoss's boots smelled like he had worn them ankle-deep in fish guts. Considering the dried scales stuck to the soles, Jeffrey guessed that was exactly what he had been doing in them. Steel-toed with leather uppers, they were hot as hell and heavy as lead. Jeffrey did not even have to look at them to hate them. If he could have gotten away with not wearing anything, he would have gladly gone barefoot.

Growing up, Jeffrey had always been forced to wear hand-me-downs or used shoes and clothing bought cheap from the Baptist church's quarterly yard sale. He hated wearing other people's stuff, and when he was old enough, most of his shoplifting was done at the Belk's in Opelika. Sometimes when the shoe department got busy, the clerks were not able to keep up with who got what, and Jeffrey's first pair of new shoes that actually fit had been part of his most brazen shoplifting stunt ever: he had walked out of the shoe department bold as God, a pair of gleaming new fifteen-dollar black loafers hugging his feet, the soles so new he nearly slipped on the polished marble floor. His heart had been beating like a snare drum the whole time, but showing up at school the next day looking and feeling like a million bucks had made it all worthwhile.

In Hoss's shoes, Jeffrey felt like he was wearing two blocks of cement. Loose blocks, since they were a size and a half too big. There was already a blister working on his heel, and the arch of his foot felt like it had a piece of grit stuck in it, probably something from a fish.

Reggie drove the car through town just as slowly as before, managing an irritating crawl as they got stuck behind a tractor for what seemed like a hundred miles. He kept his scanner turned down low as he listened to country music on the radio, one hand on the wheel, one hand on the center console, lightly tapping along with Hank Williams.

Jeffrey chanced a look at the other man as they headed up Herd's Gap toward Jessie's mother's house. Reggie Ray was of average height, but he was a little on the scrawny side. He could not have been more than twenty-five or -six, but his dirty brown hair was already receding at the temples. A spot in the back looked a little fluffier than it should have been, and Jeffrey guessed he was combing over to hide a thinning area. Reggie would probably be bald by the time he reached his mid-thirties.

Jeffrey ran his hand through his own hair, thinking the only good thing his father had ever given him was a full head of hair. Even at close to sixty, Jimmy Tolliver still had the same thick, wavy hair he'd sported in high school. He still kept it in the same style that was popular at the time: a slicked-back variation of a pompadour. In his prison stripes, he looked like an extra from an Elvis movie.

Reggie said, "What's so funny?"

Jeffrey realized he had been smiling at the memory of his old man, but he was not about to share that with Reggie, especially considering the mark Jimmy had left on the Ray family.

He said, "Nothing."

"Those boots smell like shit," Reggie said, rolling down the window. Hot air sucked into the cab like a furnace. "What happened to your shoes?"

"I left them with Sara," he said, offering no further explanation.

"She seems like a real nice woman."

"Yeah," Jeffrey said. Then, to beat him to the punch, he added, "Don't know what the hell she's doing with me."

"Amen," Reggie agreed. He tilted his hat back as they crested a hill. In the distance, Jeffrey could see people standing out on the golf course at the Sylacauga Country Club. Jeffrey had caddied a few times for some of the players, but he had quickly grown irritated by the condescending way the rich men treated him. Besides that, he had never understood the lure of golf. If he was going to spend a few hours outside, Jeffrey would rather be running and using his muscles for something other than chasing a little white ball around in a tiny clown car.

Reggie cleared his throat, and Jeffrey could tell it took something out of him to ask, "What's going on?"

"What do you mean?"

"Why's Robert wanna talk to you?"

Jeffrey was honest but only because he knew Reggie would not believe the truth. "I don't know."

"Right," Reggie said, skeptical. "Why'd Hoss want me to drive you out instead of him?"

That was a good question, one Jeffrey had not considered when Hoss had volunteered to help Sara back at the cave. That was more the type of scut work Hoss usually gave to his deputies. Hoss would normally be more likely to drive out to see Robert with Jeffrey than trek through the forest looking for Sara. Maybe he thought he would be able to distract her somehow. Jeffrey wished him luck, but he knew Hoss was bound to fail.

"Slick?" Reggie prompted.

"I wish you wouldn't call me that," Jeffrey told him, knowing even as he said it that Reggie would now call him Slick until the day he died. "Hoss went back to find Sara."

"She lost?"

"No." Jeffrey did not debate long on whether or not to tell Reggie what was going on. The deputy would find out soon enough. "She found something. We found something. There's this cave near the quarry—"

"The one with the boards over it," Reggie said. He must have noticed Jeffrey's surprised look, because he added, "Paula told me about it."

"How'd she find out?" Jeffrey asked, knowing he had never taken Reggie's sister to the cave. It was an unwritten rule between him, Robert, and Possum that no girls were allowed. Except for that one time, he knew that they had all kept to it.

Reggie shrugged, not giving an answer. "What'd you find?"

"Bones," Jeffrey said, trying to gauge the other man's reaction. "A skeleton."

"Well." His jaw relaxed, and he glanced over at Jeffrey. "This ain't your week, is it, Slick?" He gave a raspy chuckle that turned into a full-on laugh. "Oh, me," he managed through laughter. He even slapped his thigh.

"That's real professional of you, Reggie," Jeffrey said, relief washing over him as they turned onto Elton Drive. Jessie's mother was out in the yard watering some flowering plants. Behind her was a two-story white house with large columns holding up a second-story balcony. Jasper Clemmons was probably retired by now, but he had worked in senior management at the local mill and his home reflected his position. The first time Jeffrey had seen the place, he had been reminded of something out of *Gone With the Wind*. Now he thought it looked more like a low-rent Tara. The place had been kept up, but to Jeffrey's more seasoned eye, he understood that the house was trying too hard. Considering Jessie's family, it was a perfect fit.

Faith Clemmons had never liked Jeffrey. Despite popular opinion, Jeffrey had not dated every woman in town, and Faith seemed to take it personally that Jeffrey had passed on her daughter. There was no denying Jessie had been gorgeous—hell, even now she was still a beautiful woman—but there was something about her that was too desperate for Jeffrey's liking. He did not like clingy women, and even as a teenager, he had recognized Jessie for what she was: a bottomless pit of need.

At first, Jeffrey had been worried when Jessie set her sights on Robert, but now he knew that they were a perfect couple—if you could call two people who needed each other more than they loved each other a perfect couple. Robert liked rescuing people. He liked being the good guy and feeling like he was doing the right thing.

Jessie, a constant damsel in distress, was the perfect excuse for him to get on his white horse and come to the rescue. Some men liked that kind of thing, but the thought of it made Jeffrey feel like he had a noose around his neck.

"Hey, Faith."

"Jeffrey," she said, spraying water on the plant bed between them. "Robert's inside."

"Thanks," he answered, but she had already turned her back to him.

Reggie gave a tight grin, murmuring, "Another one of your fans."

Jeffrey ignored him as they walked to the house. The blister on his heel was starting to throb, but Jeffrey would be damned if he limped around Reggie.

To take his mind off the pain, Jeffrey thought about Sara back at the cave. Hoss had probably shown up by now. What was he telling her? What story was he weaving to try to protect Jeffrey? Sara would get sick of this, he knew. She wasn't the type of woman who put up with being lied to, and last night's business had nearly chased her away forever. Soon, she would probably start to realize that there was some truth to what everyone was saying. The part that hurt most was that it was Jeffrey's own damn fault. Bringing her here had been like swallowing a live grenade. Jeffrey was just waiting for it to explode.

Through the screen door, Jeffrey could see the long hallway that ran to the back of the house. The place had been built back when mansions were the real thing: something for the elite to own and not just big empty boxes that echoed when you walked into them. Jeffrey had only been to Jessie's house a handful of times, but he remembered there was a formal parlor as well as a sitting room, on either side of the front hall, with a dining room, kitchen, and huge family room at the back. He raised his hand to knock on the door just as Jessie came out of the kitchen. She had a glass in her hand and he guessed from the color of the liquid and the clinking ice as she walked that she was drinking straight scotch.

Reggie noticed, too. He made a show of looking at his watch. "Barely past noon."

Jeffrey started to make an excuse for her, but stopped himself at the last minute.

"Hey, boys," Jessie said. She was a good drunk in that she never slurred her words or turned sloppy. As a matter of fact, drinking did nothing but sharpen her edges. Underneath Jessie's flawless skin and perfect figure was a bitter woman who saw only the bad in things. Alcohol brought the acid to the surface.

Jeffrey asked, "Is Robert here?"

"Not like we could go home," Jessie said, pushing open the door. She stepped to the side but still blocked the doorway enough so that Jeffrey had to brush past her to get into the house. Reggie was denied the same treatment. She cut him off at the door, saying, "Y'all can wait in the parlor. I'll go get Robert."

Jeffrey watched her go. She was teetering on heels so high that it did not seem possible she could walk in them. How she managed to accomplish the balancing act three sheets to the wind was beyond the laws of science.

Reggie cleared his throat. He had his arms crossed over his chest like a disapproving schoolmaster. Of course he had taken Jeffrey's appraisal of Jessie the wrong way. "She's your best friend's wife."

Jeffrey ignored him as he walked into the front parlor. Like the rest of the house, nothing had changed much here. Two long couches covered in burgundy-and-white-striped silk faced each other, a spindly coffee table between them. Wingback chairs framed a large picture window at the front of the room, facing a massive fireplace you could roast a small man in. All of the furniture looked delicate enough to fall over with a sneeze, but Jeffrey knew better. He sank into one of the couches to wait for Robert while Reggie stood at the door with the same snide look on his face.

Jeffrey stared at the white carpet, which looked like it had been vacuumed to within an inch of its life. He could see his footprints making a pattern toward the couch, and wondered if the odor in the air was from the dead fish on Hoss's boots or the bowl of potpourri on the coffee table. He thought again of Sara and what she was doing now. He wanted to be with her, to try to control what she was thinking, to make her believe he wasn't a monster. If only it was within his power, he would snap his fingers and they would magically be somewhere, anywhere, other than here.

Reggie asked, "You got a thing with the mother, too?"

"What?" Jeffrey realized his gaze had ventured out the window to where Faith Clemmons was watering her azaleas. "Jesus Christ, Reggie. Lay off it, okay?"

He crossed his arms over his chest. "Or what?"

Footsteps slowly padded down the stairs, and Jeffrey felt all the steam go out of him as Robert entered the room. He had looked bad this morning, but now he looked as if he had been hit by a truck. His shoulders were stooped and he kept one hand to his side, much the same way he had the night before.

Jeffrey stood, not knowing what to say. He settled on "Why don't you sit down?"

"I'm okay," Robert said. "Reggie, can you give us a minute?"

"Sure," Reggie answered, his tone slightly guarded. Still, he tipped his hat before leaving the room.

Robert waited until the screen door had shut before he spoke. "You found her body in the cave."

Jeffrey was stunned by Robert's certainty. He had not asked a question; rather, he had made a statement. Her body had been found.

"Hoss called me," Robert said, carefully sinking into one of the wingback chairs. "He thinks it might be some bum or something— fell and hit his head. You know it's Julia Kendall."

The name brought a heaviness to the room. Jeffrey felt sweat break out on his brow despite the air conditioning. He dug around in his pocket and pulled out the necklace with the heart-shaped charm. "I found this by the bench seat."

Robert reached out for the necklace and Jeffrey gave it to him. Using the nail on his thumb, Robert pried the locket open and looked at the photographs. "Jesus. Julia."

Jeffrey looked out the window to where Faith had turned off the hose and was talking to Reggie. They were probably having a good time comparing notes on what an asshole Jeffrey was. Reggie might even be telling her about Julia. News would be around town before Jeffrey even had a chance to tell Sara. She would get the story from somebody else, somebody who would get it all wrong. He slumped back into the couch, thinking he could not take it if she looked at him again the same way she had last night.

Robert asked, "What did you tell Sara?"

"Nothing," Jeffrey said, feeling remorse wash over him. That would have been the time to tell her, in the cave. He wasn't sure if she had seen him find the necklace and put it into his pocket. He should have said something right then and there instead of acting like he was guilty of something.

Jeffrey said, "I hid the necklace from her."

"Why?"

"Because I've got enough people in town telling her I'm some kind of animal without proving it."

"What does this prove?" Robert asked, handing the necklace back to Jeffrey. No one wanted to keep the damn thing, and Jeffrey was irritated that it kept coming back to him.

Jeffrey said, "It's going to stir up all that shit all over again. Jesus, I hate this fucking place."

Robert stared at his hands. "Everyone said she just ran away."

"I know."

They were both quiet, each of them probably thinking the same thing. For Jeffrey's part, he had a sick feeling in his gut like his life was about to turn upside down and there was nothing he could do to stop it.

Robert said, "You know what they do to cops in jail?"

Jeffrey felt his throat close. "We're not going to jail," he managed. "Even if they found something . . . some way to connect us to this . . . it was such a long time ago—"

"No," Robert said. "I'm asking you. I have no idea except what I've seen on television, and that's enough to make your blood turn. What do they do to cops in jail?"

"Robert—"

"I'm serious, Jeffrey. What do they do to them? What should I expect?"

Jeffrey looked at his friend maybe for the first time since the other man had entered the room. Except for a few lines around his eyes, Robert looked the same way he had in high school. He was still fit and a little lanky, but the way he slouched into the chair and bounced the heel of his shoe up and down was new. On the football field, Jeffrey had known every thought going through the other man's mind, but now he had no idea what Robert was thinking.

Jeffrey finally asked, "What are you trying to say, Bobby?"

"I'm not trying, I'm telling. I shot Luke. I shot him in cold blood."

Jeffrey was sure he had heard wrong.

"He was having an affair with Jessie."

Shock stopped Jeffrey for another moment. "What are you—"

Robert's tone was matter-of-fact, like he was talking about killing ants in his garden instead the death of another human being. "I went to the store to pick up some things, then I came home and found them together. He was . . . shit, I guess you know what he was doing with her."

It was too much; Jeffrey couldn't handle anything else today. "Robert, why are you saying this? It's not true."

"I got out my gun and shot him." He shook his head. "Not like that. I saw them first, then I went back to get my gun. I came back into the room and Jessie screamed. I asked them what the hell they were doing. He tried to make excuses and I just pulled the trigger."

Jeffrey stood up. "Don't say anything else to me."

"His head . . . it just exploded."

"Robert, shut the fuck up. You need a lawyer."

"I don't need a lawyer," he said. "I need something to wipe this out of my mind. I need something that'll help me forget what it was like seeing his head just—"

"Robert," Jeffrey interrupted, making his voice firm. "You don't need to tell me this."

"Yeah," he said. "I do. I'm confessing. There wasn't a break-in.

The second piece is my backup. I used it to shoot myself. Sara knows, she saw where I held the gun. Jesus, that was stupid, but I did it. I wasn't thinking. I didn't have a lot of time. The lights were already turning on next door. You get called out on these things as a cop and you think, 'Christ, what a fucking idiot,' but the truth is when it happens to you, you don't have time to think. Maybe it's shock or fear or some kind of stupid thing that just kicks in, but you make mistakes. You don't *want* to get caught, but you can't think how not to." He indicated the chair. "Sit down, Jeffrey. You're making me nervous."

Jeffrey sat. "Why are you doing this?"

"Because it's not right," he answered. "I talked to Hoss this morning, gave him my statement just like I told you last night. It's like back when we were in school. Any old story we reel out, he bites."

"He doesn't know any of this?"

"No, I wanted to tell you first. I owed you that much."

"Robert," Jeffrey said, thinking the man had done him no great favor. Despite the sense it made, Jeffrey could not believe the story. He had grown up with this man, spent countless hours listening to records with him, talking about girls, planning the cars they were going to buy when they turned sixteen.

Robert said, "I've got to take responsibility for my actions. That man is dead because of me, because I couldn't control myself—all my anger and hatred and . . . everything. It just came up to the surface and the next thing I knew, he was dead on the floor." He started to tear up. "I killed him. He's dead. He was screwing my wife and I killed him."

Jeffrey pressed his fingers into his temples, not knowing what to say.

"Did you know Jessie had a miscarriage a few months ago?"

Jeffrey tried to talk past the lump in his throat. "No."

"Would've been a boy. How do you like that? It's the one thing that would have finally made her happy, and God just wouldn't let it happen."

Jeffrey doubted seriously anything could make Jessie happy, but he still said, "I'm sorry."

"It was my fault," Robert said. "Something about me ... I don't know, Slick. Something about me never works for her. I'm just poison."

"That's not true."

"I'm not a good man. I'm not a good husband." He gave a heavy sigh. "I've never been a good husband. People stray for all kinds of reasons, I guess, but in the end ..." He looked up. "I haven't been much of a friend to you."

"That's not true," Jeffrey repeated.

Robert just stared at Jeffrey, a kind of despair on his face. He slumped back farther in the chair as if he did not have the strength to sit up. He kept staring at Jeffrey, his eyes moving back and forth like he was reading a book.

"It was me," Robert finally said. "It was all me. I killed Swan and I killed Julia, too."

Jeffrey felt like all the breath had been sucked from his lungs.

"All that other stuff—I did that, too.

"No, you didn't," Jeffrey insisted. What the hell was he talking about? There was no way Robert had killed anybody.

"I used a rock to hit her in the head," Robert told him. "It was pretty quick."

"You didn't do that," Jeffrey said, either anger or fear making his voice waver. This was just too much. "Everyone thought she ran away. You said it yourself less than five minutes ago."

"I lied," he countered. "I'm telling you the truth now. I threw the rock in the abandoned quarry. You'll never be able to find it, but my confession should be good enough."

"Why are you saying this?"

He stood up, wincing from the pain in his side. "Go get Reggie."

"I won't. Not until you tell me why you're lying."

Robert knocked on the window and motioned Reggie inside. "I want Reg to take me in."

"That's not—"

"It's better this way, Slick. Simpler. Now we've got everything tied up all neat. It's finally over and done with." Robert wiped his eyes. "Look at me crying like a girl." He gave a humorless laugh. "Reggie sees me like this he'll think I'm some kind of pansy."

"Fuck Reggie," Jeffrey said, just as the deputy walked in. Reggie's eyebrow shot up, but for once, he kept his mouth shut.

Robert held out his hands to the deputy. "You need to cuff me."

Reggie looked back and forth between the two men. "This some kind of stupid joke?"

"I killed Luke Swan last night," Robert said, putting his hand in his front pocket. For some reason, Jeffrey's first thought was that he was going to pull out some type of weapon. Instead, Robert showed them a spent bullet.

Reggie examined the casing. "Federal," he noticed, just like the bullets Robert had in his Glock.

Robert told him, "It was just sticking out from his head." He put his index finger to the area beneath his ear. "Just the tip of it, right here. You wouldn't think a bullet would be like that, just peeking out like someone put it there, but it slid right out. I didn't even have to pull much."

Reggie still wouldn't buy it. He handed the bullet back to Robert, but Robert wouldn't take it. "Y'all are shitting me, right?" He snorted a laugh. "This one of your practical jokes, Bubba? You trying to get me in trouble with Hoss again?"

"Stop dicking around, boy," Robert demanded, his tone harder than Jeffrey had ever heard it. Robert was Reggie's superior, and he was giving him an order when he said, "Cuff me and read me my rights. Do it by the book."

Jessie came in, her drink topped off to the rim. "Y'all want something to . . ." Her voice trailed off as for once she noticed that she was not the center of some drama. Her eyes locked onto Robert's, and in the split second before she managed to control herself, she looked terrified. She recovered quickly, but still put her hand to the doorjamb like she needed something to keep her from falling over. "What did you tell them?"

Robert's eyes watered again, and his voice was full of regret as he said, "The truth, baby. I told them the truth." Again, he held out his hands to Reggie. "Luke Swan was having an affair with my wife. I came home and found them together, and I shot him." He shook his hands. "Come on, Reggie. Get it over with."

Jessie murmured, "Oh, Jesus."

Robert said, "Cuff me."

Reggie put his hand to the back of his belt, but he did not get his handcuffs. "I'm not cuffing you," he said. "I'll take you to the station to talk to Hoss, but no way I'm putting handcuffs on you."

"Reggie, I'm ordering you."

"No fucking way," Reggie said. "Not that I wouldn't love to see you riding in the back of my car, but I ain't gonna have Hoss come down on me for something you did." He added, "Not this time, anyway."

"You need to do this by the book," Robert told him.

Reggie would not relent. "I'll go crank up the car, let it cool down a little. You come out when you're ready."

"I'm ready now," Robert said. When Jeffrey moved to follow them, he held up his hand. "No, Jeffrey. Let me do this alone."

Jessie was still in the doorway, and Robert had to pass his wife to leave. Jeffrey watched as Robert kissed her cheek, saw the way Jessie flinched away from his touch, try as she might to pretend she wasn't. Jeffrey wanted to grab her and shake her, to throw her to the ground and throttle the life out of her, for treating Robert this way. There was no way he had killed a man. Jeffrey did not buy it. Something was not right here.

Still, when Robert asked Jeffrey, "Look after Jess for me, will you?" Jeffrey nodded.

He told Robert, "I'll be up at the station later."

"Jess," Robert said. "Give him the keys to my truck." He managed a sad smile. "I don't guess I'll be needing it for a while."

"Don't say anything to them, not even Hoss," Jeffrey coached. "We need to find you a lawyer."

Robert left the room without responding. Seconds later, the screen door popped shut.

"Well," Jessie said, then took a long drink. The glass had been nearly full when she started and she had left little more than the ice cubes. Jeffrey watched her throat work as she drank it all down, wondering how she could appear to be so calm with her husband on the way to being charged with murder.

Jessie sucked an ice cube into her mouth before dropping it back into the glass. "This must be the best day of that old hick's life." She waited for Jeffrey to say something, but he did not oblige. "Reggie's been waiting like a hawk lo these many years, looking for the day Robert stumbled. I'm sure he's planning on swooping in tomorrow and getting that promotion that has so long eluded him."

"Doesn't sound like Robert's the one who stumbled to me," Jeffrey told her, letting all the bile he felt rise out in his tone. This was her fault. She had brought this down on Robert. She had brought this down on all of them.

"Oh, that's just perfect, Slick. So damn typical. He shoots and kills a man and somehow you manage to paint me in the black."

"Why'd you cheat on him?" Jeffrey demanded. "Why?"

She shrugged like it was a casual thing. There was something nervous about her, almost twitchy.

"He was good to you."

"Now, don't go getting on your high horse, Jeffrey Tolliver. You're forgetting who you're talking to."

"I never cheated on anybody," he said, disgusted by the knowing look she gave him. Jeffrey might have done his share of fucking around, but he made certain the women he was involved with knew exactly what they were—or were not—getting into.

He said, "When I make a promise to someone, I keep it. I sure as shit wouldn't run around on my wife."

"Easy to say now," Jessie said, sucking the liquor off another ice cube. She smacked her lips. "You're the worst kind of cheat because you think you're too good to let it happen."

"Don't you even care that he's going to jail? This is a death-penalty state, Jessie. He could end up getting a needle in his arm."

She looked down at her glass, swirling the ice around.

"How'd it start?" Jeffrey demanded. "Were you buying drugs from him?"

"Drugs?" She looked startled. "Robert?"

"Luke Swan," he said. "He was using. Is that how it went down?" He grabbed her arm, looking for needle marks. "You two shot up together and it went from there?"

"You're hurting me."

He pushed up her sleeve, checked the crease of her elbow and under her arm.

"Stop it!"

He checked her other arm, spilling ice onto the floor. "What made you do it, Jessie? What?"

"Goddammit, Slick," she screamed, pushing him away. "Where the hell do you get off?"

"I don't have time for this," Jeffrey said, thinking if he did not get away from Jessie right now he'd really hurt her. With Sara last night, the thought repulsed him, but now he wanted nothing more than to smack some sense into Jessie.

He said, "Give me Robert's keys."

She held his gaze for a second longer, then said, "They're in my purse in the kitchen." She waited a beat, like she wanted to make sure he knew she was making a choice. "I'll go get them."

Jeffrey paced in the doorway as he waited for her. He was sick of this crap. It was one thing for Reggie to break his balls, but he sure as shit wasn't going to take it from Robert's cheating wife.

"Here go," Jessie said, coming back from the kitchen with a full drink in one hand and the keys in the other.

"You're some piece of work," he said, holding out his hand for the keys.

She gave him a strange look that he could not quite read. "I should have married you."

"I don't recall asking."

She laughed like what he had said was the funniest thing she'd heard all day. "You watch, Slick."

"Watch what?"

"That Sara of yours sure seems to have you tied around her little finger."

"Leave her out of this."

"Why, because she's better than me?"

It was true, but Jeffrey didn't want to get into it. He had learned the hard way that you could not reason with a drunk. "Give me the damn keys."

"You're gonna marry her, and then you're gonna fuck around on her."

"Jessie, I'm only going to tell you one more time."

"There's gonna come a day when you realize you're not the center of her world anymore, and then you're gonna run out sniffing around for something new. Mark my word."

Jeffrey kept his hand out, forcing himself not to speak.

She held the keys over the palm of his hand and dropped them as she said, "Come see me in a couple of years."

"I'd rather watch my dick rot off."

She smiled, holding up her glass in a toast. "Until then."

Robert's truck was the same piece-of-shit '68 Chevy he had been driving since high school. The gears were temperamental, and the whole truck groaned each time Jeffrey tried to shift. There had to be some art to making the truck move, but that knowledge was lost on Jeffrey. At each stop sign, he lurched like a sixteen-year-old kid just learning to drive, the engine cutting out more often than not as he tried to get the damn thing into first.

Once he drove out of Herd's Gap, he did not know where to go. Sara was probably at the funeral home going over the bones. Hoss was at the station booking Robert. Jeffrey could go home, but his mother would be there for lunch and the last thing he needed was to watch his mother fortifying herself with cheap vodka before she started her second shift at the hospital. Dealing with one alcoholic a day was enough. He was heading toward Nell's, thinking she'd probably already know about Robert's arrest by now, when he remembered Possum.

That was the way it had always been with Possum: he was an afterthought. Unlike Robert, who was on the football team with Jeffrey and could carry his own socially, Possum was a third wheel, someone who tagged along as a buffer between his two ultracompetitive friends. He laughed at their jokes and kept score between them. Not that Possum was completely altruistic. Sometimes he got lucky and managed to snag some of Jeffrey's and Robert's castoffs.

Nell was definitely one of Jeffrey's castoffs, and one he had been glad to get rid of. Even as a teenager, she had known exactly what she wanted and was not afraid to speak her mind. That her mind was usually focused on what she saw as Jeffrey's many faults was the biggest problem he had with her. She was very outspoken and could be downright nasty when it came to giving her opinion on his latest transgressions. If not for the fact that she was one of the few respectable girls in school who still put out, he would have dropped her after their first date.

Jeffrey would be the first to admit that he liked a challenge, but Nell was the sort of person you could never win with. In the end, he had to admit that Possum was a better fit for her—he didn't mind being told what to do and gladly accepted any sort of criticism at face value—though Jeffrey had been surprised to learn the month after he left for Auburn University that they had gotten married. It made him wonder what had been going on behind his back. Nine months later, he realized exactly what had been going on. If he let himself think about it, it still stuck in his craw, but in all fairness, he had told Nell they should date other people when he moved away. The problem was, he had imagined her pining away for him, not jumping into the sack with his best friend.

Jeffrey forced the truck into second as he turned into the parking lot of Possum's store. The place was still run-down and depressing, with faded Auburn flags banking either side of the door. Signs in the windows advertised cold beer and live bait; two things essential to any small-town country store.

The bell over the door clanked loudly as Jeffrey entered the building. Wooden floors that had been installed back during the Depression squeaked underfoot, dirt from sixty years of wing tips and work boots and now sneakers filling the grooves.

Jeffrey walked straight to the back and pulled out a six-pack of Bud from the walk-in cooler. Before the door closed, he pulled out a second six-pack and walked to the front of the store.

"Hello?" Jeffrey called, putting the beer on the front counter. The cash register was the older kind that didn't take much to get into, and there was a coin dispenser with around a hundred dollars in change ready for the taking. Typical Possum to rely on other people's honesty.

"Possum?" Jeffrey said, taking one of the beers out of the cardboard pack. He used the Coca-Cola opener on the side of the counter to open the bottle. The beer was bitter, and Jeffrey tossed it back, trying to bypass his taste buds. He walked around the counter, looking at the photographs Possum had taped up around the cigarette displays. Like Robert, he had a lot of pictures from their high school days. Unlike Robert, there were photos of kids at various stages in life. Jennifer went from a red face in a bundle of blankets to a precocious girl. Jared grew from a little baby to a tall and rangy-looking kid. Jeffrey guessed he was about nine now, and felt genuine empathy for the kid; at that age, Jeffrey had been all hands and feet, like a colt just learning how to walk. Jared had dark hair like Nell and the same haughty tilt to his chin. There was nothing about Possum in the kid, but Jennifer was very much her father's daughter. She had his eyes, and her shoulders were hunched in that good-natured, nonthreatening way that had saved Possum from getting his ass kicked on more than one occasion.

Jeffrey took a healthy swig of beer, his tongue anesthetized to the taste by now. He thought about Robert, and what hell he must have gone through when Jessie lost their kid. Marriages were perplexing animals, always changing, sometimes gentle, sometimes vicious. When Jeffrey was a beat cop, he had hated domestic disturbance calls because there was always something, some indefinable connection that attached a husband to a wife and turned them from wanting to kill each other to wanting to kill whoever was interfering, in this case the cops. One minute they could be wailing on each other, calling each other every name in the book, the next minute they could be throwing themselves in front of the squad car to keep their spouse from going to jail.

Children always made things worse, and as a patrolman, Jeffrey had done his best to keep them out of the fray. This was always difficult because most kids thought they could help take some of the heat off their parents by getting in the middle of things. Jeffrey had done this often enough with his own parents, and he knew what drove kids to get involved. He also knew how futile it was. There was nothing more horrible than getting a domestic call and going out to find some kid whimpering in the corner with a black eye or a busted lip. On more than one occasion, Jeffrey had set a father straight. He knew he was channeling some of his own fury when he took on an abusive parent, and up until a few years ago, Jeffrey had considered that to be one of the perks of being a cop.

Jeffrey dropped his empty into the trash and got out another bottle of beer. He used the edge of the counter to pop open the top and gathered from the scratch it made in the wood that Possum used the counter for the same thing.

He leaned his head back, taking a long swig of beer. His stomach grumbled in protest, and Jeffrey realized he had not eaten anything since the bacon he'd had at Nell's that morning. At this point, Jeffrey did not care. He was halfway through the bottle when he heard a toilet flush in the back.

"Hey, Slick." Possum came out of the bathroom, buttoning up his pants. He saw the beer. "Go on and help yourself."

"Good thing I didn't," Jeffrey said, hitting the No Sale button on the cash register. The drawer popped open, showing neat rows of cash. "There's at least two hundred dollars in here."

"Two fifty-three eighty-one," Possum said, taking one of the beers. He popped the top off on the counter and took a pull.

Jeffrey finished his beer and took another. Possum glanced at the two empties but held his tongue.

Jeffrey said, "Guess you heard about Robert?"

"What's that?"

Jeffrey felt a sinking in his gut. He took a healthy drink, trying to push his brain to a point where none of this mattered anymore. "He turned himself in."

Possum coughed as beer went down the wrong way. "What?"

"I was just at Jessie's mama's. He said he did it."

"Did what?"

"Shot that man."

"Luke Swan," Possum whispered. "Jesus wept."

"Jessie was cheating on him."

Possum shook his head. "I don't believe that."

"You don't have to believe me. Talk to Robert. He said he walked in on the guy banging her."

"Why would she cheat on him?"

"Because she's a slut."

"There's no need to talk like that."

"Talk like what, Possum? The truth?" Jeffrey took another swig of beer, then another. "Jesus, you haven't changed a damn bit."

"Come on, now."

"Possum," Jeffrey said. "That's what you are, playing dead until it all passes over and then coming out like nothing's wrong." He finished his beer, waiting for that buzz in his head that took away some of the pain. "He said he killed Julia, too."

Possum leaned against the counter, his mouth slightly open. "That's just crazy talk."

"Yeah, it's crazy. This whole damn town is crazy."

"Do you believe him?"

Jeffrey was surprised by the question, mostly because Possum never questioned anything. "No," he said. "Hell, I don't know."

"Damn," Possum said.

Jeffrey reached for another beer. Possum's hand caught his, and he told Jeffrey, "Maybe you oughtta pace yourself."

"I've already got a mama."

"She's as good a reason as any to slow down a bit."

Before he could stop himself, Jeffrey punched Possum in the jaw. His aim was off, but the power behind his fist was enough for Possum to lose his balance and fall back against the store safe.

"Ow!" Possum said, more surprised than outraged. He put his hand to his mouth and looked at the blood. "Jesus, Slick, you near about broke my tooth."

Jeffrey raised his fist to hit him again, but the look in Possum's eye stopped him. Possum wouldn't hit back. He never hit back. He never got angry and he never thought anything Jeffrey did was wrong.

Jeffrey reached into his pocket and took out a couple of tens for the beer.

"No," Possum said, pushing the money away even as blood dribbled down his chin. "Forget about it."

"I pay my own way," Jeffrey said, throwing the money on the counter. He picked up the remaining bottles and the other six-pack.

"Listen, Slick, lemme give you a ride—"

"Fuck off," Jeffrey said, pushing him away.

Still, Possum followed him to the door, saying, "You don't need to be driving like this."

"Like what?" Jeffrey asked, opening the passenger door to Robert's truck. He put the beer in and walked around to the driver's side, his foot catching on a loose bit of pavement. He grabbed the hood ornament, keeping himself up.

Possum said, "Jeffrey, come on."

Jeffrey climbed in behind the wheel, feeling his eyes blur as the world turned upside down. The truck turned over with a rewarding purr, and he pulled out of the parking lot, jerking the wheel at the last minute so he would not take out the gas pumps.

CHAPTER SIXTEEN

Molly climbed into the passenger's seat of the ambulance, looking Lena up and down. "They didn't have a tighter shirt?"

"Guess not," Lena said, knowing the other woman was trying to lighten things up but unable to play along. Her hands were sweating and her nerve, usually as strong as steel, was failing her. Things would be okay once she got inside the station. Lena was the type of person who faced her fears head-on. Jitters were understandable, but once the show was on, she would be ready to perform.

Molly took a deep breath. When she let it go, her shoulders dropped like a deflating balloon. Her stethoscope was wrapped around her neck, and she grabbed either end in her fists and said, "All right, I'm ready."

Lena tried to put the key in the ignition, but she could not keep her hand steady enough. After a couple of tries, Molly leaned over, saying, "Here."

"It's from the scars," Lena said as the ignition caught. "Nerve damage."

"Does it bother you much?"

Lena gassed the engine, feeling the vibrations through the floor. "No," she said, then, "Sometimes."

"Did they have you do physical therapy?"

Lena did not understand why they were having this stupid conversation, but she kept it up as she put the ambulance in gear, liking the chatter. "About three months," she said. "Paraffin soaks, playing with a tennis ball, putting pegs in holes."

"For dexterity," Molly said, staring straight ahead at the street.

"Yeah," Lena said. The Grant Medical Center was less than three hundred yards from the police station, but the closer they got, the farther away it seemed. Lena felt like they were following a tunnel into a black hole.

"I had to do PT for my knee a while back," Molly said. "Hurt it running up the stairs after my youngest."

"You have two kids?"

"Two boys," she said, a note of pride to her voice.

Lena steered the van over a steel plate covering a hole in the road, the heavy ambulance barely registering the rough terrain. She wondered if there was a baby growing inside of her, and whether it was a boy or a girl. What would happen if she had a kid? If she married Ethan, she would never be able to get away from him.

Molly said, "Twins."

"Shit," Lena said, though not for the reason Molly was probably thinking. Twins. Twice as much responsibility. Twice as much danger. Twice as much pain.

"You okay?" Molly asked again.

"It's my birthday today," Lena said, not really paying attention to where she was going.

"That so?"

"Yep."

Molly said, "Here should be a good spot," and Lena realized she had nearly passed the station. Nick had said not to block the door, but they had figured the best place to park would be closer to the dress shop, not the college.

Lena considered backing up, but it was too late. "Guess it'll have to do."

"Right," Molly said, rubbing her hands on her thighs. "Well, this should be routine, right? Just go in with the food and get out with Marla, yes?"

"Yes," Lena agreed, her hand slipping on the gearshift as she put the van in park. She cursed under her breath, trying to psych herself into doing this. She was never afraid of things. Lena had seen more horror in the last few years than anyone should see in a lifetime. What did she have to be afraid of? What was waiting in that building that could be worse than what had happened to her two years ago?

"Listen," Molly began, a tinge of hesitancy to her voice. "Nick told me not to tell you this. . . ."

Lena waited.

"Standard procedure is to have a time limit. If we don't come out, they come in."

"Why didn't he want me to know?"

"Because he was afraid they would find out," she said, meaning the gunmen.

"Right," Lena said, understanding. Nick didn't trust her to be in there. He had said as much to Amanda Wagner. He thought she was going to do something stupid, something that would get them all killed. Maybe she would. Maybe without even thinking, Lena would screw this up like she had screwed up everything else in her life. Maybe this was it. The end of everything.

"We'll be okay," Molly said, reaching over and taking Lena's hand.

For lack of anything better to do, Lena looked at her watch.

Molly followed suit, saying, "We synchronized mine to his," as she showed Lena the large Snoopy watch she wore. Lena adjusted her digital watch to Molly's, wondering if this would come to anything.

"They'll come in exactly forty minutes after we walk through the door." She checked her watch again. "I guess that'll be 3:32."

Lena said, "Okay."

Molly put her hand on the door handle. "We'll get you back in time for your party."

"Party?" Lena asked, wondering what the hell she meant.

"For your birthday," Molly reminded her. She opened the door a few inches. "Ready?"

Lena nodded, not trusting herself to speak. They both got out of the van and met at the back, where Wagner's men had loaded boxes of cold water and prewrapped sandwiches they had gotten from one of the gas stations on the outskirts of town. As they walked toward the station, Lena concentrated on the sandwiches. She read the labels, wondering who would actually pay money for a ham salad sandwich on white bread. The expiration date on the pack read three months from now. There were probably enough preservatives in one bite to pickle a horse.

"Here we go," Molly said, just as the door was pushed open from the inside.

Lena suppressed a gag as Matt's body flopped back onto the ground. What was left of his head made a splattering sound as it hit the concrete, blood and brain spilling out onto the sidewalk. Most of his face was gone, his left eye dangling from a nerve like a fake Halloween mask. The bottom part of his jaw was exposed, and she could see everything—his teeth, his lolling tongue, the way the tendons and muscles held the whole thing in place.

"Slow," said the man standing just inside the doorway. He was wearing a black knit ski mask that had almond-shaped slits for the eyes and mouth but no nose. He reminded Lena of something out of a horror movie, and she felt a cold shock of fear that nearly paralyzed her. Frank had not mentioned masks. The men had put them on specifically to hide their identity from the paramedics. What that meant for the hostages who had already seen them, Lena did not know.

"Nice and easy," he said, motioning them in. In one hand he held a shotgun—the Wingmaster Frank had seen—and in the other was a Sig Sauer. His Kevlar vest was tight to his chest, and she could see another pistol sticking out of the waistband of his fatigues.

Lena realized she had stopped walking when Molly whispered, "Lena!"

By sheer force of will, Lena managed to get her feet moving. She tried to step over Matt without actually looking at him, her stomach in such a knot the whole time that she felt the urge to double over. Her sneakers left tracks in his blood.

Inside, the temperature of the station was at least twenty degrees hotter than on the street. There was a second shooter standing behind the counter, an AK-47 resting on the surface in front of him. He wore a ski mask, too, but his had more of an hourglass shape to it, leaving ample room to breathe. His eyes were flat, almost lifeless, and he barely glanced at Lena and Molly as they entered the lobby.

The first one, probably Smith, tried to shut the door but Matt was in the way. He slammed the door into the body, but it would not move. "Fuck," he mumbled, viciously kicking Matt in the side. His boots were steel-toe military issue, and Lena heard something break, probably Matt's ribs. They snapped like twigs.

Smith said, "Come move this fucker."

Lena stood there, the box of sandwiches in her hands, frozen to the floor. Molly gave her a panicked look before setting down the box of bottled water. She walked over to Matt and grabbed his ankles to pull him back into the station.

"No," Smith said. "Outside. Get this fucker outside." He wiped at his mouth with the back of his arm. "Fucker stinks." As Molly walked toward the head, Smith gave Matt another solid kick to the chest. "Fucking prick," he said, an edge to his voice that stopped Molly in her tracks. He raised his foot again, kicking Matt in the groin. The dead weight did not resist, and the sound of boot hitting flesh reminded Lena of the noise Nan made when she would hang the rugs from the house on the laundry line and beat them with the broom.

Smith's anger was spent fairly quickly, and with one final kick, he told Molly, "What the fuck are you waiting for? Move the fucker."

Molly looked like she did not know where to touch him. Matt was wearing his usual short-sleeved white shirt with a tie that had gone out of style when Jimmy Carter left the White House. Blood from his head wound saturated his shirt, and there were fresh rents along his arms where Smith had kicked him. These newer wounds were a strange purple color, and they did not bleed.

Smith pushed Molly with his boot. It was not a threatening gesture in and of itself, but considering his earlier display, Molly seemed to take it for the threat it was. She tried to pull Matt by his shirt, but it just came untucked, the buttons popping off and tapping against the floor like hail, his white fish-belly rounding over his pants. Finally, she grabbed him under his arms and pulled.

The body would not move, and Smith was about to give it another kick when Molly said, "No."

Smith was incredulous. "What did you say?"

"I'm sorry," Molly said, looking down. The front of her uniform was covered in black blood. She looked at Lena. "For God's sake, give me a hand."

Lena looked around, like she did not know where to put the box she was holding. She did not want to touch him. She could not touch his dead body.

Smith leveled the Wingmaster on her. "Do it."

Lena put down the box, feeling her lungs shake in her chest as she tried to breathe. She clamped her jaw shut, trying to keep her teeth from chattering. She had never been so scared in her life. Why was she afraid? There had been times in the past when she had welcomed death, even begged it to come to her door, but now she was terrified by the thought of being killed.

Somehow, she managed to kneel at Matt's feet. She stared at his cheap black loafers, the frayed cuffs of his worn pants, the white athletic socks that had a dirty brown cast to them. Molly counted to three, and they lifted him. The pant cuff slid up on his left leg, and Lena saw his ankle jutting out, the pasty white, hairless skin around the bone wrinkling as the foot flexed flat against Lena's abdomen. She thought of the baby inside her, wondered if he knew how close he was to a dead man. Wondered, too, if it was catching.

They set him out on the sidewalk away from the front door, Smith watching their every move. His mouth was twisted into an expression of deep satisfaction as he watched them, and Lena fought the urge to run as she followed Molly back into the station. She did not realize what had happened until they were back inside. Smith had the food and water. He could have shut them out right then and there. He could have shot them in the face or told them to fuck off, but he hadn't.

"That's better," Smith said. "Tolliver was stinking up the room."

Molly's head jerked around, her mouth open.

"What?" Smith asked, pointing the Sig at Molly's forehead. "You want to say something else, bitch? You want to mouth off?"

"No," Lena answered for her, surprised she was capable of saying the word.

Smith's smile behind the mask was horrifying. She saw his eyes crawl up and down her body, paying specific attention to her breasts; the glint told her he liked what he was seeing. He pushed the muzzle of his gun into Molly's head one last time before turning his attention to Lena. "That's what I thought." He motioned for her to turn around. "Hands against the wall."

The phone started ringing, a shrill bell that cut through the air like a knife.

Smith repeated, "Turn around."

Lena pressed her palms between two framed photographs from the 1970s Grant County police force. They were all men, all in blues, all with shaggy mustaches. Ben Walker, then the Chief of Police, was the only one who looked out of place with his military crew cut and clean-shaven face. Farther down was a photograph with Lena in it. She held her breath, hoping to God Smith did not notice.

"You hiding anything?" Smith's hands were like a sledgehammer as he patted her down. He pushed her flat to the wall, pressing himself against her. "You hiding anything?" he repeated, deftly unbuttoning her blouse with one hand.

She was silent, her heart pounding in her chest. She tried not to look at the photograph less than two feet from her nose. She had been so young then, so open to her future and what it held. Being a cop like her old man had been Lena's life plan for as long as she could remember. The day that photograph had been taken was one of the best days of her life, and now it might end up killing her.

Smith slipped his hand into her open shirt, his palm cupping her breasts. "You got something good in here?" he asked. "Heart sure is beating fast."

She stood as still as she could, eyes squeezed shut as his hand moved to her other breast. His breath was heavy, his pleasure evident.

Lena should have been terrified, but she was not. Something was eerily familiar about the threat of his body pressed into hers. Smith was a small man, compactly built. Muscles rippled along his arms and chest, and if Lena let herself consider it, he reminded her of Ethan. She knew how to handle Ethan, how to keep him walking that tight line between anger and control. Seeing how far she could push her lover was almost a game by now. The problem was that sometimes she lost. Lena had the split lip to prove it.

Smith whispered, "You got something good?" his breath hot in her ear. She could feel him pressing harder into her, making his intentions obvious. Lena felt herself floating somehow, like her soul was in another place while her body remained at the station.

Then there was another voice that Lena did not recognize. The second shooter had said, "Stop that," with little authority, but Smith still backed away, his hand lingering for as long as it could.

Smith ordered Lena, "Take off your shoes." Then told Molly, "You next. Up against the wall."

Molly's trepidation was obvious, but she followed suit, leaning her hands against the wall between the photographs. Lena buttoned her shirt as she watched Smith give Molly a solid pat-down without copping any feels. She moved away from the photographs and sat on the floor to untie her shoes. She had taped the knife to the indentation just behind her ankle bone, underneath her sock. The tendon throbbed, and she tried not to show her nervousness as she handed Smith her shoes. The high tops had covered her ankle when he frisked her. If he did not frisk her again or ask her to remove her socks, she would be okay.

Smith turned her shoes upside down, looking at the soles and peering inside. He did the same with Molly's shoes, then dropped them both back on the floor. Molly went to put on hers, but Smith stopped her.

He rummaged through the boxes, looking for contraband, then said, "Pick these up and tote 'em in the back."

Lena knelt down and picked up the box, covering her chest in the process. She waited for Molly to pick up the drinks before pushing open the swinging doors to the squad room. Lena had managed to slip her sneakers on but had not tied them. Her feet were sweating, but she could feel the surgical tape holding the knife. How could she pass it along? How could she leave it where it would do anyone any good?

She concentrated on the things that she could control, checking out the room. The station was turned upside down, but Lena was glad to find that the map Frank and Pat had drawn was pretty accurate. Clothes had been shoved into the air vents, and the filing cabinets and desks were shoved against the doors. Brad stood in the center of the room wearing his boxer shorts and a white undershirt, his hairless white legs looking like matchsticks poking out of his black socks and regulation shoes. Beside him, the three girls were on the floor tucked under Marla's arms like a flock of chickadees. At the rear of the room, Sara sat with her back to the wall. A man lay with his head in her lap, the bottom soles of his shoes facing Lena. She stumbled, dropping the box. The man was Jeffrey.

"Here," Brad said, picking up sandwiches and putting them back in the box. His eyes were open wider than usual, and he spoke in a deep baritone. "Matt was shot in the shoulder," he said.

"What?"

"Matt," Brad said, his eyes going to Jeffrey. "He was shot in the shoulder."

Her mouth said, "Oh," as if she understood, but Lena could feel her brain stretching to make the connection.

Sara's voice was a hoarse whisper, her concern obvious. "He's in and out. I don't know how much longer he can hold on."

Molly asked, "Can we do anything to help him?"

Sara had trouble speaking. She cleared her throat, then said, "You could get him out of here."

"That ain't gonna happen," Smith said, rifling through the sandwiches, reading the labels. "Man, this is ass." He seemed to be showing off, and Lena guessed it was for her benefit. She was becoming one of those women she hated seeing as a cop. She would go to their houses when their boyfriends got out of hand, and they would beg and cry to keep the bastard out of jail. There was something about them, something about the way they held themselves and looked at the world like they were waiting for one more punch. They gave off some kind of scent or something that invited the kind of guy who liked to hit women.

Sara said, "He needs medical attention."

Molly took her stethoscope and headed toward the back.

Smith said, "You going somewhere?"

"I was going to—"

"That's okay," Smith stepped aside with a slight bow. He saw Lena watching and gave her a wink.

Lena knew what was expected of her, and she said, "Thank you," without giving it another thought.

She started unpacking the sandwiches, handing them to the children and asking them each in turn if they were okay. Still, she felt that same disconnection, as if someone else was in the room handing out sandwiches and Lena as floating overhead, watching the scene.

The phone was still ringing, and Smith walked over, picked up the receiver and slammed it back down.

One of the girls jumped at the noise. She cried, "I want my daddy."

Lena soothed, "I know. It won't be long."

The girl started crying in earnest and Lena gave her a bottle of water, feeling helpless and angry at the same time. "Don't cry," she said, sounding more like she was pleading. Lena had always been horrible with kids. Still, she tried, "It's going to be okay."

Marla gave a low moan, her eyes glassy as she stared at Lena.

Lena tried to get the old woman's attention, saying, "Are you all right?" She tried to act like a paramedic, putting her hand on Marla's shoulder, asking, "Are you okay?"

Smith was over near Molly and Sara. He obviously did not like what he was hearing, because he finally said, "That's enough. Get out of here. Take the old bitch."

Molly said, "He needs help."

"What about me?" Smith asked, indicating a small strip of white cloth wrapped around his arm. Blood spread out from the center, nearly saturating it.

The phone started ringing again. Wagner had probably freaked when they carried Matt outside.

"There are supplies in the ambulance," Molly said. "Let Matt go and I'll stay here and suture you."

"Got a couple of heroes here," Smith said to his partner, and Lena realized he meant her as well.

Lena was kneeling by Marla, and Smith practically swaggered as he walked toward them. Without a word, he jerked up one of the girls by her wrist and yanked her toward the front of the room. She yelled, but he must have twisted her arm enough to shut her up. He took the crying child with him and talked to his partner. Lena was still on her knees, and she turned to watch them, putting her feet behind her. Slowly, she moved her hand to her ankle, feeling the pocketknife. She felt someone's hand over her's, but dared not turn around. Brad was to her right, so she knew it wasn't him. The children were too frightened to move. Marla. It must have been Marla whose fingers worked so deftly with the tape and removed the pocketknife.

Smith said, "We got a doctor, couple of paramedics. Why not?"

His partner gave a wary shake of his head, but seemed resigned to whatever Smith had planned.

Smith walked back to Lena, dragging the girl. "Go get your case out of the ambulance."

"What?" she said, not understanding.

He looked at his watch, which was the kind she had seen in magazines, advertising the fact that Navy SEALs used the same brand. He said, "Get your case and get back here." He pressed the Sig to the little girl's head. "You've got thirty seconds."

"I don't—"

"Twenty-nine."

"Fuck," Lena cursed. She scrambled to stand and bolted toward the door, her heart lurching in her chest. At the ambulance, she threw open the back doors, looking for anything that resembled a case.

"Officer?" a man called. She knew it was one of the cops by the cruisers but she did not have time. "Officer?"

"It's okay!" she yelled, panic filling her voice. "It's okay!" There was a long plastic case strapped into the side of the ambulance. She had been on accident scenes enough to know this was the first thing the EMTs brought with them. Her fingers fumbled with the buckle and she said, "Fuck-fuck-fuck," trying to remember how long she had been out of the building.

The man kept pushing. "Do you need help?"

"Shut up!" she screamed, throwing open the case. There were all kinds of drugs and boxes. She hoped it had everything they would need. At the last minute, she grabbed another bag and the defibrillator.

She ran through the front door, startling the second shooter. He reared up but did not pull the trigger on her. Lena rushed to the back, where Smith still had the gun pressed to the little girl's head. He was looking at his watch, smiling, and she felt such seething hatred for him that she dropped the gear and reached for the little girl, snatching her away.

The muzzle of Smith's gun caught Lena in the forehead, stunning her for a moment. She dropped to her knees and he kicked her in the chest. She fell back just as Brad tried to come to her aid. Smith trained the Sig on Brad and pressed his foot into Lena's sternum.

He said, "I knew you would try to be a hero."

"No," Lena said, the pressure from his boot pushing the life out of her.

Smith pressed harder. "You want to be a hero?"

"No," she said. "Please." She tried to pry up his boot but that just made him press harder. "Please," she repeated, thinking about the child inside her, wondering what this was doing.

Smith exhaled sharply, like he was disappointed. "All right," he said, removing his foot. "Let that be a lesson."

Brad helped Lena stand. She found that her knees were weak and she felt sick all over. Had the pressure done something? Had Smith broken her inside?

Smith used his foot to push the plastic case toward Sara. "This should be enough to do it," he said. "Field surgery, just like on TV."

Sara shook her head. "It's too dangerous. There's no way—"

"Sure there's a way."

"He should be in an operating room."

"This'll have to do."

"He could die."

Smith indicated his gun. "He might die anyway."

"What do you have against . . ." Sara stopped, obviously trying to control her emotions. They seemed to get the better of her, though, and she demanded, "What do you have against us? What did we do to you?"

"It's not you," Smith told her. He picked up the phone, shouting, "What the fuck do you want?"

"Then Jeffrey," Sara said, her voice catching again. Smith would not look at her, so she addressed her words to the second gunman. "What did Jeffrey ever do to you?"

The second shooter turned toward Sara, his rifle still aimed at the door.

"Shut the fuck up," Smith barked into the phone. "We're just gonna perform a little field surgery here. That's why you sent the medics, right?"

Sara would not let go. "What?" she demanded. "What's the point? Why are you doing this?" she begged, sounding desperate. "Why?"

The second shooter kept staring at her, and Smith put the phone to his chest, waiting to see if his partner would answer. The young man had a quiet voice, but it carried when he answered, "Because Jeffrey's his father."

Sara looked as if she had seen a ghost. Her lips trembled when she asked, "Jared?"

CHAPTER SEVENTEEN

Sara counted off the rings on the phone, waiting for her parents' answering machine to pick up. Eddie hated answering machines, but he had gotten one when Sara came back from Atlanta just to help her feel safer. After the sixth ring, the machine whirred on, her father's voice gruff as he asked the caller to leave a message.

Sara waited for the beep, then said, "Mama, it's me—"

"Sara?" Cathy said. "Hold on." Sara waited while her mother went to turn off the machine, which was upstairs in her parents' bedroom. There were only two telephones in the house: the one in the kitchen that had a fifty-foot cord and the one in the master bedroom that had become off-limits to Sara and Tessa as soon as they had reached dating age.

Sara let her gaze fall to the skeleton on the table where just this morning Luke Swan had lain. Hoss had brought three cardboard boxes to transport the bones, and though Sara had been shocked by his lackadaisical attitude, she was not in a position to question the man's methods. She had painstakingly put the skeleton together, trying to find clues that would help identify her. The whole process had taken hours, but she was finally certain about one thing: the girl had, in fact, been murdered.

Cathy came back on the line. "You okay?" she asked. "Is something wrong? Where are you?"

"I'm fine, Mama."

"I was out buying sprinkles for cupcakes."

Sara felt a tinge of guilt. Her mother only made cupcakes when she was trying to cheer Sara up.

Cathy continued, "Your daddy got called away to the Chorskes' again. Little Jack flushed a handful of crayons down the toilet."

"Again?"

"Again," she echoed. "You wanna come on over and help me with the frosting?"

"I'm sorry," Sara told her. "I'm still in Sylacauga."

"Oh." The word managed to convey disappointment as well as disapproval.

"There was a problem," Sara began, wondering whether or not to tell her mother what had happened. This morning, she had told Cathy about Robert and the shooting, but left out her suspicions about who had pulled the trigger. Now Sara realized as she talked that she could not hold back, and told her mother everything, from the sear mark to Reggie's warning to her worries about whatever Jeffrey had put in his pocket.

"Was it a bracelet or something?" Cathy asked.

"I don't know," Sara said. "It looked like a gold chain."

"Why would he do that?"

"Good question," Sara said. "I've been looking at the bones all day."

"And?"

"Her cranial sutures haven't fully closed." Sara leaned against the table, looking at the girl, wondering what had brought her short life to such a tragic end. "The knobbed ends of her long bones haven't completely fused, either."

"Which means?"

"She was probably in her late teens or early twenties."

Cathy was silent, then, "Her poor mother."

"I put in a call to the sheriff to ask if there are any open missing persons."

"And?"

"I haven't heard back from him. I haven't heard from anyone all day, as a matter of fact." Even Deacon White had barely spoken to her when she had returned with the skeleton. Sara added, "In a town this small, I don't imagine there's a long list of missing people."

"Do you think it's recent?"

"Recent as in ten, maybe fifteen years," Sara guessed. "I've been working on putting the skeleton together for the last five hours. I think I know what happened to her."

"Did she suffer?"

"No," Sara lied, hoping she sounded convincing. "I don't know what's going to happen next. I'm not sure we'll be able to come home tomorrow."

"You're going to stay with Jeffrey, then?"

Sara bit her bottom lip. She had gotten this far and decided that she might as well continue. "It seems like the more people say bad things about him, the more I want to . . ."

"Take care of him?"

"I wouldn't say that."

"Defend him?"

"Mama . . ." Sara began, her voice trailing off. "I don't know," she said, and that was the truth. "It bothers me that you're so set against us." She paused, thinking of her father. "It bothers me that Daddy hates him so much."

"I remember," Cathy said, "back when you were four or five."

Sara pressed her lips together, waiting for the lecture.

"We were all down at the Gulf, and your father took you fishing just to get away, the two of you. Do you remember?"

"No," Sara said, though she had seen the pictures often enough to think she did.

"You were fishing with rubber worms, but the crabs kept coming along and clamping onto them, thinking it was food." She laughed. "I heard your daddy screaming and cussing up a storm, yelling at the crabs to let go, that they were just holding on to worthless nothing." She waited a beat, probably to make sure Sara understood. "He tried everything to get them to let go. He even beat them with a hammer, but their claws just kept clamped down on the line no matter what he did. He finally ended up cutting bait and letting them go."

Sara let out a slow breath. "Am I the stubborn crab or the worthless bait?"

"You're our little girl," Cathy said. "And your father will come around. Eventually, he'll cut bait and let you go."

"What about you?"

She laughed. "I'm the hammer."

Sara knew this all too well. She told her mother, "I just know what my gut tells me."

"What's it saying?"

"That I . . ." She was about to say that she loved Jeffrey, but Sara could not bring herself to do it.

Cathy picked up on it anyway. "So much for your fucking around."

She could not put into words exactly what had happened in the cave, but she tried, "I don't know why, but even with all that's happened, I trust him. I feel safe with him."

"That's no small thing."

"Yes," Sara agreed. "I suppose you know me better than I think."

"I do," Cathy said, giving a resigned sigh. "But I should trust you more."

Sara said nothing.

"I can't protect you from everything in the world."

"I don't need you to," Sara told her. "I may *want* you to, but I don't need you to." To soften her words, she added, "But I love you for being there."

"I love you, too, baby."

Sara let out her own sigh, feeling everything catch up with her. Usually, when things got bad she wanted nothing more than to sit in her mother's kitchen and listen to her talk. Cathy had been her touchstone for as long as Sara could remember. Now all she wanted to do was to fall asleep with her head on Jeffrey's shoulder. The transition was startling. She had never felt this way about a man in her life. Even with Steve Mann, back when she was a teenager and everything was so emotional and desperate, Sara had not felt this same burning need to be with him. Jeffrey was like some drug that she could not get enough of. Sara was caught, and there was nothing she could do but wait it out and see what happened next.

Sara said, "I need to go, Mama. I'll call you tomorrow, okay?"

"Take care," Cathy said. "I'll save some cupcakes for you."

Sara waited until her mother had hung up the phone. She went to do the same, but there was a noise on the line—someone breathing—then a second click.

Someone had been listening in on the conversation.

Sara went to the door and looked out the window into the hallway. The lights had been turned off hours ago when Deacon White had gone home. She knew there was an intern named Harold who lived in an apartment over the garage, but she was told that after hours he pretty much kept to himself unless he was called to transport a body.

She picked up the phone again and pressed the button marked "Apt."

There were six rings before the man picked up with a bleary-sounding "Hello?"

"Harold?"

"Uhn," he grunted, and she heard him moving around. Obviously she had awakened him. He repeated, "Hello?"

"Were you just on the phone?"

"What?"

Sara tried again. "This is Sara Linton. I'm in the building."

"Oh . . . right . . ." he managed. "Mr. White said you were staying late." He paused and she guessed from the sound he was yawning. "I'm sorry," he said, then under his breath, "Jeesh."

Sara stretched the phone cord so she could see through the window again. A car turned into the parking lot and a pair of headlights lit up the hallway. She shielded her eyes, trying to see who it was. The car had pulled into the handicap space next to her BMW, lights on high beams.

Harold sounded irritated. "Hello?"

"I'm sorry," Sara apologized. "I wanted to leave and—"

"Oh, right," he said. "I'll come lock you out."

"No, I—" she tried, but he had already hung up.

Sara looked into the hallway again, narrowing her eyes past the bright headlights, trying to see if anyone came to the door. A few minutes passed before a figure cut the glare. Harold stood in the middle of the hall, shielding his eyes as Sara had done. He was dressed in his pajamas and had his mouth open in a wide yawn when Sara joined him.

"Who the heck is that?" Harold asked, walking to the front door.

"I was—" She stopped. The car was a truck, and she could see Jeffrey climbing out of the driver's seat. He had the radio blaring with some country music station, and she suppressed a curse, telling the intern, "Thank you for letting me out."

"Yeah," he said, giving another yawn that was so wide Sara could see his back molars. He twisted the lock and opened the door.

Sara started to leave, but could not help but ask the intern, "Is there anyone else in the building?"

Harold looked over his shoulder. "Nobody breathing." He yawned again, one yawn too many, and Sara wondered if he had really been sleeping when she called.

She opened her mouth to question him, but he tossed her a wave as he locked the glass door, giving another yawn for her benefit.

Sara could smell Jeffrey from ten feet away; it was like walking past a brewery. Even without the overwhelming stench of beer, he was weaving as he walked toward her. Sara was slightly taken aback. She had not considered Jeffrey a teetotaler, but neither had she ever seen him drink more than a glass of wine or an occasional beer. Knowing what she did about his mother, this made sense, and the fact that he had chosen tonight to get drunk sent up warning signals Sara did not quite know how to read.

She gave a cautious "Hey."

He had a silly grin on his face, and he held his finger in the air for silence as Elvis Presley's "Wise Men Say" came on the radio.

"Jeffrey . . ."

He put his arm around her waist and pulled her toward him, making sloppy work of leading her in a dance.

She looked at the truck, which was probably older than she was. A long bench seat like the kind she had seen in the cave stretched from door to door, a single gearshift sticking up from the floorboard.

She asked, "Did you drive here?"

"Shh," he said, the smell of beer on his breath so overpowering that she turned her head away.

"How much have you had to drink?"

He hummed with the song, picking up the line "Falling in love . . . with . . . you . . ."

"Jeff."

"I love you, Sara."

"That's nice," she said, gently pushing him away. "Let's get you home, all right?"

"I can't go to Possum's."

She put her hands on his shoulders, aware that she was literally keeping him upright. "Yes, you can."

"They arrested Robert."

Sara absorbed this information, but did not offer an opinion. "We'll talk about it when you're sober."

"I'm sober now."

"Sure you are," she said, glancing back to see if Harold was watching.

"Let's go somewhere," Jeffrey said, trying to climb into the truck headfirst.

"Hold on," Sara said, catching him when he fell back. She braced her hands against his butt and pushed him in.

He slurred his words, saying, "Shh-ure been a long day."

"I can't believe you drove like this."

"Who's gonna arrest me?" he asked. "Hoss wouldn't've arrested Robert if it wasn't for me." He put his hands on the wheel. "Jesus, I'm bad luck. Whole town goes to hell when I show up."

"Scoot over," she said, giving him a nudge.

"Men don't let women drive."

Sara laughed, giving him more of a push than a nudge. "Come on, big boy. You'll still be a man in the morning."

Beer bottles clanged onto the floor as he slid onto the passenger's side. He leaned down, rummaging through the bottles. "Shit," he said. "We need more beer."

"We'll get some," she told him, climbing into the truck and closing the door. The metallic clang echoed in the cab. She reached down to crank the engine, but the keys were gone.

"He'll probably get the needle," Jeffrey said, and she could hear the pain in his voice. "Oh, Jesus," he said, putting his hand to his eyes.

Sara stared at the front entrance of the funeral home, not knowing what to say. Thanks to her stint at Grady Hospital's emergency room, she had dealt with more than her share of drunks. There was no use trying to reason with them when logic was the last thing on their mind.

She asked, "Where are the keys?"

Jeffrey leaned his head back against the window and closed his eyes. "In my pocket."

Sara stared at him, feeling torn between wanting to slap him and wanting to tell him everything was going to be okay. She settled on saying, "Scooch down on the seat a little." When he did, she put her hand into his front pocket.

He smiled, and moved her hand a little closer to center. Considering his lack of sobriety, she was surprised to find his libido none diminished.

"Hey," he protested when she found the keys and removed her hand.

"Sorry," she said, her tone contrary to the word as she looked for the ignition key.

"How about a blow job?"

Sara laughed as she found the clunky key. "You're the one who's drunk, remember? Not me." She cranked the engine, relieved when it caught on the first try. "Put on your seatbelt."

"There aren't any seatbelts," he said, sliding closer to her.

Sara engaged the clutch and put the truck into reverse. Jeffrey had positioned himself so that he was straddling the shift. She asked, "How much have you had to drink?"

"Too much," he admitted, rubbing his eyes.

The sign on top of the building lit up the cab as she backed up, and Sara saw at least eight empty beer bottles rolling around on the floorboard. Jeffrey was wearing black boots she hadn't seen before, and one of the legs of his jeans was pulled up, showing his hairy calf.

She waited until they were on the highway to ask, "When did they arrest Robert?"

"A little while after I left you," he said, his head bumping back against the glass. "He wanted me to come see him. I was just glad he was talking to me."

He went quiet, and she prompted, "What did he say?"

"That he did it," Jeffrey said, throwing his hand into the air as if in resignation. "I was standing right there in their goddamn stupid front parlor and he looked me in the eye and said he did it."

Sara was having a hard time following him, but she said, "I'm sorry."

"Came back from the store and just shot him. No questions asked."

Sara could only repeat, "I'm sorry."

"You were right."

"I didn't want to be."

"Is that true?"

She chanced a look at him. He seemed to be getting back to himself, but his breath was enough to make her turn her head back toward the road. "Of course it's true." She put her hand on his leg. "I'm sorry it happened this way. I know you did everything you could."

"You won't believe me," he said. "I know you said Robert was lying before, and I said you were wrong, but now I think you're right. I mean—I think he's lying now."

Sara stared at the road ahead.

"You're thinking it's because he's my friend, but it's not. I know it adds up. I know his story makes sense, but he's a cop. He's had time to think about it and get it right so that it all matches up." He tapped his finger to his head, missing a few times. "I know it here. I've been a cop too long to not know when people are lying."

"We'll talk about it tomorrow," she told him, knowing this was useless.

He rested his head on her shoulder. "I love you, Sara."

She had ignored him the first time, but now she felt the need to comment. "You've just had too much to drink."

"No," he disagreed, his breath hot on her neck. "You don't know how it is."

She squeezed his leg before shifting into fourth. "Try to sleep."

"I don't want to sleep," he said. "I want to talk to you."

"We'll talk tomorrow." She slowed at an intersection, trying to remember which way to turn. A billboard pointing to a bank looked familiar, and she took a left.

She asked, "Is this the right way?"

"People only say what they mean when they're drunk," he told her. "I mean, being drunk doesn't make you say things you don't mean."

"I don't know about that," she said, glad to recognize a gas station from this morning. The store was dark and, like everything else in town, had probably closed hours ago.

"I love you."

Sara laughed because that was all she could do.

"Turn here," he said. When she didn't turn quickly enough, he grabbed the steering wheel.

"Jeffrey!" she said, her heart jumping into her throat. He had turned them onto a gravel road.

"Just keep going straight," he told her, pointing ahead.

Sara slowed the truck. "Where are we?"

"Just a little farther."

She leaned closer to the steering wheel, trying to make out the road ahead of her. When she saw a fallen tree in the distance, she stopped. "The road's blocked."

"Little more," he said.

Sara put the truck in neutral and stepped on the parking brake before turning to him. "Jeffrey, it's late, and I'm tired, and you're dru—"

He kissed her, but not the way she was used to. He was rushed and sloppy, his hands clumsy on the buttons of her jeans.

"Hold on—"

"I want you so much."

She could tell, he was like a piece of steel against her thigh, but even though Sara could feel her body reacting to his, sex was the last thing on her mind.

"Sara," he sighed, and kissed her so deeply that she could not breathe.

She managed to soften the kiss, and when his lips moved to her neck, she said, "Slow down."

"I want to be inside you," he said. "I want it like last night."

"We're parked in the middle of nowhere."

"Let's pretend," he said. "Let's pretend we're at the beach." He scooped his hands under her bottom and she gave what could only be called a yelp as she suddenly went horizontal, her feet splayed out against one door and her head bumped into the other. Sara had not been flat on her back in a parked truck since the tenth grade.

Jeffrey tried to move down on her, but considering they were both two grown adults of above average height stuck in a space that was barely five feet long, his attempt was far from successful.

"Sweetheart," she said, trying to reason with him. She forced his head up to look at her, surprised to see the raw need in his eyes.

"I love you," he said, leaning up to kiss her again.

Sara returned the kiss, trying again to slow him down. He took the hint, and his kiss was not as probing. When he came up for breath, he moaned, "I love you."

"I know," she said, stroking the back of his neck.

He looked up at her again, and she watched as his eyes seemed to focus on her for the first time since she had walked out of the funeral home. He looked forlorn, like the world had abandoned him and Sara was his only hope. "Is this okay?"

She nodded, not knowing what else to say.

He repeated, "Is it okay?"

"Yes," she said, helping him slide down her jeans.

Even though her body was ready for him, Sara braced herself when Jeffrey entered her. She put her hand behind her, trying to keep her head from bumping into the armrest as he moved inside of her. Overhead, she could see an index card tucked into the sun visor. A woman's hand had hastily scribbled a grocery list on the card, and Sara read the items silently to herself between thrusts. *Eggs . . . milk . . . juice . . . toilet paper . . .*

She turned slightly, trying to keep the gearshift from stabbing her thigh. That was all Jeffrey needed to finish the job, and he collapsed like dead weight on top of her.

Sara dropped her hand to her forehead, wondering how she had gotten herself into this. She said, "Well, that was romantic."

Jeffrey did not respond, and when she put her hand on his back he turned his head and let out a heavy breath.

He was asleep.

Sara woke up with a pounding headache that started at the back of her neck and worked up her head like a vise. She could not begin to imagine what Jeffrey felt like this morning, but part of her hoped he was in agony. God knew that she'd had some bad sex in her life, but last night ranked right at the top of what was, thankfully, a rather short list.

She felt for her shoes as she rose from the couch, wondering what time it was. Sunlight was streaming in through the windows and Sara guessed it was almost ten. The clock told another story: it was nearly noon.

"Crap," Sara mumbled, stretching her arms up to the ceiling. Her back felt as if all the muscles were knotted into bows, and her spine probably resembled a hook from the way she had slept on the couch.

She continued to stretch her back and shoulders as she walked through the house, looking for Nell. The kitchen was empty, pots and pans drying in the sink. She looked outside and saw Nell standing in the neighbor's yard with an ax raised over her head. As Sara watched, Nell brought down the ax on the chain that staked the dogs to a tree.

"What was that?" a voice behind Sara asked. She spun around and saw a young, dark-haired boy standing in the doorway. He was dressed in shorts with no shirt, his skinny chest concave in the center.

"Jared?"

"Yes, ma'am," he said, looking around the room. "Where's my mama?"

"She's outside," Sara told him, wondering if Nell would want her son to know what she was up to. Truth be told, Sara was a little curious herself.

Jared walked to the back door, his sneakers shuffling across the floor. Sara was more than familiar with this curious phenomenon that plagued young boys—most of them did not learn to pick up their feet when they walked until they reached their twenties.

Sara trailed him outside, keeping well back to avoid the dust his shoes were stirring up. He reminded her of Pigpen in the Peanuts comics.

Nell was on the back porch at the neighbor's, putting leashes on the dogs. She saw Jared and said, "What are you doing out of bed?"

"I'm bored."

"You should've thought about that before you said you were too sick to go to day camp." Nell smiled at Sara. "Did you introduce yourself to Dr. Linton?"

"Doctor?" he asked, a hint of fear in his voice.

Nell said, "You best get back in that bed before I make her take your temperature."

There was something so familiar about his reaction—the set to his mouth, the annoyance that flashed in his eyes—that Sara caught herself staring at the boy, her mouth open.

"What?" Jared asked, giving her another familiar look.

Sara shook her head, not trusting herself to speak. His resemblance to Jeffrey was startling.

Nell saw the look on her face, and shooed Jared away. "Go on, now. Take Mama's ax."

He shuffled back to the house, dragging the ax behind him, and Sara pressed her lips together, biting back the obvious question.

Nell clicked her tongue and tugged on the leashes. The dogs stood at attention. "You look like you've got something to say."

"It's none of my business."

"That's never stopped me." Nell led the dogs around to the front of the house as she told Sara, "Jeffrey doesn't know."

Sara nodded, acknowledging that she had heard her but still not trusting herself to comment.

At the front of the neighbor's house, Nell sat on the porch with a sigh. "Possum and I got married a few weeks after Jeffrey moved away to Auburn."

"You didn't tell him?"

"So he'd come back and marry me?" she asked, petting one of the dogs. "Not much point in that; we would've both killed each other the first week. I got on his nerves because I was always telling him he was wrong, and he got on mine because he wouldn't admit that I was right."

Sara could only stare.

"He would've done the right thing," Nell said. "And I didn't want anybody to marry me because it was the right thing." The dog rolled on its back, and Nell scratched his stomach. "I love Possum. I liked him at first, but then he stepped in when Jeffrey was gone and we had Jared and Jen came later—not much later." She gave a private smile. "But we have a family now, a life together. Possum is a good man. He works less than five minutes away and he still calls if he's gonna be late. He doesn't mind picking up Motrin or tampons for me at the Piggly Wiggly and he's never said anything makes me look fat, even when I wore overalls for three years straight after I had Jen. I know where he is every second of the day, and I know if I fart in church he's gonna take the rap." She gave Sara a pointed look. "I like my life exactly how it is."

"You don't think Jeffrey has a right to know?"

"To what end?" she asked, and she had a point. "Possum's Jared's father. He changed that boy's diapers and walked the floor with him while I was passed out from exhaustion. He signs his report cards and coaches the Little League. There's nothing either of them wants for, and no reason to rock the boat."

"I understand."

"Do you?"

"I won't tell him," she said, wondering how she could keep such a secret.

"It's not good for Jeffrey being back here right now," Nell said. "God knows I was mad at him for staying away so long, but there's too much history here. Too much has happened." She slipped off her flip-flop and scratched the other dog with her toes. "Jeffrey's turned out all right. He really has. There's something about him inside that's good, just like with Possum, only you have to scratch the surface to get to it. I don't know what you'd call it, but he's grown into the person I always thought he could be if he just got away from . . ." She indicated the street. "From this place where everybody thinks they know your story and they don't give a never-you-mind about filling everybody else in on what they think about it."

"Reggie Ray gave me an earful."

"Don't listen to that old redneck," she chastised. "He's the worst of the lot. Keeps saying he was born again. He needs a couple of more rebirths before he turns into a decent human being."

"He seemed all right."

"Then you weren't looking close enough," Nell said, an edge of warning to her tone. "There's two things you need to know about this town, Sara: the Rays think their shit don't stink and the Kendalls are pure white trash." She indicated her own front yard. "Not that I can say much with all that crap Possum put in the yard, but at least my kids show up to school in clean clothes."

"Who are the Kendalls?"

"They run the fruit stand outside of town," she said. "Mean bastards, every one of them." She added, "Don't get me wrong, there's nothing wrong with being poor—me and Possum's brought it to an art form—but that doesn't mean you can send your kids out with dirt on their faces and muck under their fingernails. You see them at the store and you have to hold your breath, they're so filthy." Nell paused, shaking her head in disapproval. "A few years ago, one of them showed up to school with lice. Infected the entire ninth grade."

"Has anyone called children's services?"

Nell snorted. "Hoss has been trying to run the whole family out of town for years. The old man was horrible. Beat his wife, beat his kids, beat his dogs. Best thing he ever did was drop dead of a heart attack mowing the grass back behind the seed store." She shook her head again. "Still left his wife with one in the oven, and that one's the worst of all. Thank God he's not in Jared's grade. He gets thrown out of school every other day for fighting or stealing or God knows what. Punched a girl last week. Little bastard's just like his father."

Sara said, "Sounds horrible," but still, she could not help but feel sorry for the child. She often wondered if kids like that could straighten themselves out with the right parent around. She had never completely bought the "bad seed" theory, though Nell's appraisal that the apple had not fallen far from the tree was probably shared by everyone in town.

Nell changed the subject, saying, "Y'all got in late last night."

"I hope we didn't wake you up."

"I was already up with Possum," she said. "Fool man slammed his chin against the counter at work. Don't ask me how he did it, but it gave him a toothache all night long. Tossing and turning till I about strangled him."

A car with a woman and a young boy coasted by the house, the woman holding a sheet of paper in her hands like she was trying to read directions.

Sara said, "Jeffrey had a little too much to drink."

Nell's surprise was obvious. "I've never seen him drink much."

"I don't think it's a habit."

Nell studied her, like she was trying to figure Sara out. "Was it about Julia?"

"Who's Julia?"

Nell looked out into the street, where the car that had coasted by earlier had backed up and was parking in front of the driveway.

"Who's Julia?" Sara repeated. "Nell?"

Nell stood up. "You need to talk to Jeffrey about that."

"About what?"

She waved to the woman getting out of the car, saying, "You found it."

The woman smiled as her son ran up to the dogs and threw his arms around them. "They look just like the pictures."

"This one's Henry," Nell said, indicating one of the dogs. "This is Lucinda. Truth be told, she only comes to Lucy." She held out the leashes to the boy, who gladly took hold.

The woman opened her mouth, looking like she was about to protest, but Nell reached into her pocket and pulled out a wad of cash. "This should cover the cost for having them fixed. My husband and I never got around to it."

"Thank you," the woman said, the cash obviously helping to make up her mind. "Is there any particular food they like?"

"Anything," Nell said. "They just love to eat and they love kids."

The boy said, "They're great!" with that enthusiastic tone children use when they're trying to convince their parents they will become future astronauts or presidents if only they get the thing they are asking for.

"Anyway." Nell looked at Sara then back to the woman. "I should be going. We've got to finish packing up the house. Movers will be here at two."

The woman smiled. "It's a shame you can't keep them in the city."

"Landlord won't allow it," Nell told her, holding out her hand. "Thank you kindly."

"Thank you," the woman said, shaking her hand. She shook Sara's, too, then told the child, "Honey, say 'Thank you.' "

The boy mumbled a "Thank you," but his attention was squarely set on the dogs. Sara watched them bound toward the car, the boy jogging to keep up with the rambunctious animals.

Sara waited until the woman was in the car, but Nell held up a hand to keep her from speaking. "Put an ad in the paper," she said. "No sense letting those dogs waste away out back when there's people who know how to care for them."

"What are you going to tell your neighbor when he gets home from work?"

"I guess they broke their chains," Nell shrugged. "I'd better go check on Jared."

"Nell—"

"Don't ask me questions, Sara. I know I talk too much, but there's some things you need to hear from Jeffrey."

"He doesn't seem interested in telling me much of anything."

"He's over at his mama's," Nell said. "Don't worry, she won't be home for another few hours. She grabs lunch at the hospital on Tuesdays."

"Nell—"

Nell held up her hand, walking away.

After walking up and down the street twice, Sara realized she could always look at the mailboxes instead of trying to remember what Jeffrey's mother's house looked like. She found the one marked "Tolliver" five houses down from Nell's and hoped to God no one had been watching her make a fool of herself. She felt especially stupid when she recognized Robert's truck parked in the driveway.

In the daylight, the house looked more run-down than Sara had thought the first time she had seen it. Several coats of paint had been added over the years, giving the siding a rippled effect. The lawn was a depressing brown and the spindly tree in the front yard looked like it was about to fall over.

The front door was wide open, the screen door unlocked, but still she knocked, saying, "Jeffrey?"

There was no response, and Sara walked into the house just as she heard a door slam in the back.

She repeated, "Jeffrey?"

"Sara?" he asked, coming into the family room. He had a hand-held propane torch in one hand and an adjustable wrench in the other.

"Nell said you were here."

"Yeah," he said, not exactly looking at her. He held up the torch. "The pipe in the kitchen burst about two years ago. She's been washing dishes in the bathroom ever since." She did not respond, and he motioned her back to the kitchen. "I'm gonna finish up with this, then go over to the jail and check on Robert. I just don't buy what he said yesterday. I know there's something he's not telling me."

"Lot of that going around," Sara mumbled.

"What?"

She shrugged, looking at the mess on the floor. He had taken apart the entire faucet just to replace the pipe. She asked, "Did you turn off the water?"

"That's what I was doing outside," he told her, sitting on the floor. He took some sand cloth and sanded an end piece of copper pipe with the methodic precision of an amateur.

Sara sat across from him, trying not to be critical of the work he had already performed. Had her father been here, he would have called Jeffrey a girl.

There was a note of pride in Jeffrey's voice when he said, "I went ahead and replaced everything."

"Hm," she mumbled. "Need help?"

He cut his eyes at her, and she gathered this was something like driving in that only men did it. Considering her father had taught both Sara and Tessa safety procedures for using propane and acetylene torches before they could comfortably say the words, this was more than slightly insulting.

Still, she let it pass, saying, "I didn't tell you last night—"

"About that," he interrupted. "I'm really sorry. I promise you, I don't usually drink like that."

"I didn't think you did."

"As for the other . . ." His voice trailed off, and Sara picked up the can of flux, needing to do something with her hands.

She said, "Don't worry, I'm not going to hold you to it."

"Hold me to what?"

She shrugged. "What you said."

"What did I say?" he asked, his tone of voice wary.

"Nothing," she told him, trying to open the can.

"I was talking about what we did," he said, then corrected, "I mean, what *I* did."

"It's okay."

"It's not," he said, taking the flux and opening it for her. "I'm not . . ." He paused, as if searching for a word. "I'm not usually that selfish."

"Forget about it," she told him, but somehow his half-ass apology made her feel better. She dipped the brush into the flux and daubed it onto one of the elbows he had already sanded. "I want to talk to you about the skeleton."

His attitude changed completely, and she could see his defenses go up. "What about it?"

"It's a woman. A young woman."

He gave her a careful look. "Are you sure?"

"The shape of the head is obvious. Men usually have larger skulls." She took the measuring tape and measured the distance from the sink to the cutoff valve at the floor. "Men's skulls are heavier, too. Usually with a bony ridge above the eyes." She measured a length of pipe and clamped the cutter at the correct spot. "Men have longer canine teeth and wider vertebrae," she continued, spinning the cutter until the pipe broke. "Then there's the pelvis. Women's are wider for childbearing." She lightly sanded the pipe. "Plus, there's the sub-pubic angle. If it measures less than ninety degrees, then it's male, more than ninety, it's female."

He put flux on the pipe as Sara slipped on a pair of safety glasses. His face remained blank as he shoved the elbow onto the pipe, and he waited until Sara had used the flint striker to light the torch before asking, "How do you know she was young?"

Sara adjusted the torch before waving the flame over the pipe, heating it enough to make the flux boil. "The pelvis tells the story. The public bones meet in the front of the pelvis. If the bone surface has bumps or ridges, that means it belongs to a young person. Older people have smoother bones."

She turned off the torch and threaded out the solder, watching it melt into the joint. She continued, "There's also a depression area in the public bone. If a woman has given birth, there's a notch where the bones separated in order to allow room for the baby's head."

Jeffrey seemed to be holding his breath. When Sara did not continue, he asked, "Did she have a baby?"

"Yes," she told him. "She did."

Jeffrey put the pipe down in front of him.

"Who's Julia?"

He exhaled slowly. "Didn't Nell tell you?"

"She said to ask you."

Jeffrey sat back against the cabinet, leaning his hands on his knees. He would not look at her. "It was a long time ago."

"How long?"

"Ten years, I guess. Maybe more."

"And?"

"And she was . . . I don't know, it sounds bad now, but she was kind of like the town slut." He wiped his mouth. "She did things. You know, touched you." He glanced at her, then looked away. "Rumor was she'd give a blow job if you bought her something. Clothes or lunch or whatever. She didn't have much, so . . ."

"How old was she?"

"Our age," he said. "She was in the same class as me and Robert."

Sara saw where he was going with this. "Did you ever buy her anything?"

He looked offended. "No," he said. "I didn't have to pay for that kind of stuff."

"Of course not."

"Do you want to hear this or not?"

"I want you to tell me what happened."

"She just left one day," he said with a forced shrug. "She was there one day and gone the next."

"There's more to it than that."

"I can't . . ." He let his voice trail off. "I found this yesterday in the cave," he said, taking something out of his pocket. Sara saw a necklace with a charm on it.

"Why didn't you tell me then?"

He opened the locket and looked inside. "I don't know. I just—" He stopped. "I just didn't want you to know one more bad thing about me."

"What bad thing?"

"Talk," he said, meeting her eyes. "It's just talk, Sara. The same old bullshit that's been following me around since I got here. You get to a point where you're guilty of one thing and people think you're guilty of another."

"What do they think you're guilty of?"

Jeffrey held out the chain. "I showed it to Hoss. He didn't want anything to do with it."

Sara looked at the cheap gold heart and the pictures inside. The children were still infants, probably only a few weeks out of the hospital.

Jeffrey said, "She wore it all the time. Everybody saw her with it, not just me." He gave a harsh laugh. "The thing was, nobody knew what she had done to get it. No one would cop to it, you know? She'd show up in a new dress at school one day and we'd start talking shit about who bought it for her, what she did to get it. This"—he indicated the necklace—"she showed it to everybody. She didn't know any better. She thought it was expensive. It's not even solid gold, it's plate." His shoulders dropped. "There's no telling what she did for it."

"It looks old to me," Sara told him. "Not an antique, but old."

He shrugged.

"What about the photographs?"

He took back the locket and looked at the pictures inside. "I've got no idea."

"So, yesterday in the cave, you knew it was her?" Sara asked, wondering why he had not said anything at the time.

"I didn't want to think it was her," Jeffrey said. "I've been feeling

guilty all my life for things I didn't do. Things I had no control over."
He gave a long, sad sigh. "My parents, the house I lived in, the clothes
I wore. I always felt so ashamed of everything, wanted to show people
a better part of me than my circumstances." He looked around the
kitchen. "That's why I left here, why I was so anxious to get away and
never come back. I was sick of being Jimmy Tolliver's son. I was sick
of walking down the street and feeling everybody's eyes on me, waiting for me to mess up."

Sara waited.

"You see the better part of me."

She nodded, because she could not deny this, despite what reason
would dictate.

"Why?" he asked, and he seemed like he really wanted to know.

"I don't . . ." She let her voice trail off, giving a shrug. "I wish I
could say. My brain keeps telling me all these things. . . ." She did not
elaborate. "I just feel it in here," she said, tapping her fingers to her
chest. "The way you make me feel when you make love to me and
the way you double-knot my shoes so they won't come untied and the
way you listen—you're doing it now, really listening to what I have
to say because you honestly want to know what I'm thinking." She
thought of the soldier's letter he had read to her what seemed like a
lifetime ago, and couldn't explain it any better than, "I guess that you
see me, too."

He put his hand over hers. "This thing with the bones. It's going
to blow wide open."

"How?"

"Julia," he told her, and it seemed to take great effort for him to
say her name. "I need you here, Sara. I need you seeing me the way I
really am."

"Tell me what's going on."

"I can't," he told her. She thought she saw tears in his eyes, but he
looked away. "It's a mess," he said. "I thought maybe Robert had . . ."

"Robert had what?"

She saw his throat work as he swallowed. "Robert says he
killed her."

Sara put her hand to her chest. "What?"

"He told me yesterday."

"Morning?"

"No, after we found the bones." Sara started to tell him that the sequence did not make sense, but Jeffrey continued, "I showed him the necklace and he said he bashed her head in with a rock."

Sara sat back, trying to absorb what he was saying. "Did you tell him that her skull was broken?"

"No."

"Then how did he know?"

"He might have gotten it from Hoss. Why?"

"Because that's not how she died," Sara said. "The skull fracture came at least three weeks before she died."

"Are you sure?"

"Of course I'm sure," Sara told him. "Bone is living tissue. The fracture was already healing when she was killed."

"It looked like she'd been hit in the head."

"That was from something else. Maybe a rock fell in the cave or an animal . . ." She did not want to tell him what the animals could have done. "Absent scalp and tissue, I can't tell you whether or not she was hit in the head immediately before she died, but even with that, her hyoid bone was broken."

"Her what?"

"The hyoid," she said, putting her fingers to her throat. "It's here, a U-shaped bone in the center. It doesn't just break on its own. There has to be significant pressure there, some sort of blunt force or manual strangulation." She watched Jeffrey, trying to gauge his reaction. "It wasn't just fractured, it was broken in two."

He sat up. "Are you sure?"

"I'll show you the bone if you want."

"No," he said, tucking the necklace back into his pocket. "Why would he say he killed her when he didn't?"

"That was my next question."

"Maybe if he's lying about that, he's lying about the other night."

"Why?" Sara asked. "Why would he lie about either?"

"I don't know," Jeffrey told her. "But I've got to find out." He in-dicated the sink. "Can you finish this?"

Sara looked at the mess. "I guess."

He started to leave, then turned around. "I meant it, Sara."

She looked up. "Meant what?"

"What I said last night," he told her. "I do love you."

Despite the horrors of the last few days, she felt a smile on her face. "Go talk to Robert," she told him. "I'll finish this and meet you back at Nell's."

CHAPTER EIGHTEEN

Jeffrey pulled down the visor of Robert's truck, trying to get the sun out of his eyes. He was not exactly hungover, but a small headache was sitting right behind his nose like a hot dime. Like her husband, May Tolliver had passed on one thing to her son for which Jeffrey was grateful: unless he got rip-roaring drunk, he never got hungover. It was a gift as well as a curse. In college, while Jeffrey had been able to drink anyone under the table and still be able to perform at football practice the next day, most of the guys had stopped their heavy drinking by the end of the first quarter for fear of getting kicked off the team. Jeffrey had taken a few years more. After waking up in a hospital outside of Tuscaloosa with his hand in a cast and no memory of how he had gotten there, Jeffrey had decided to bring his drinking days to an end.

Reggie Ray was sitting at the front desk when Jeffrey walked into the sheriff's station. He said, "What are you doing here?"

Jeffrey did not have time for pleasantries. "Fuck off, you little pissant."

Reggie stood so fast his chair fell over. "You wanna say that to my face?"

Jeffrey had walked past the desk, but he turned around. "I thought I already had."

They both waited in that stupid game of chicken that men were supposed to outgrow by this age. Even knowing this, Jeffrey stood his ground. He was sick of being treated this way. No, it went further than that. He was sick of *letting* people treat him this way. Talking to Sara, Jeffrey had finally realized after all these years that the guilt and shame he had experienced had been his own damn doing. Sara did not see him as his father's son. Even now, hearing the worst she could from all kinds of people, she stood by her original view of him. She had known him the least amount of time, yet she seemed to know him better than all of them rolled together, even Nell.

Jeffrey crossed his arms, asking Reggie, "Well?"

"Why is it every time you're in town something bad happens?"

"Luck, I guess."

"I don't like you," Reggie said.

"Is that all you can come up with?" Jeffrey asked. "Well, guess what, you little shit, I don't like you, either. I haven't liked you since you walked in on your sister giving me a blow job in your father's garage."

Reggie took a swing, but Jeffrey caught his fist in the palm of his hand. The impact sounded harder than it was, making a loud smack in the empty room. Jeffrey squeezed Reggie's hand until the other man's knees bent.

"Asshole," Reggie hissed, trying to get his hand back.

Jeffrey jerked the other man forward, banging him against the desk before he let him go. The front door opened and Possum walked in, glancing at Reggie, who was doubled over, before giving Jeffrey a friendly smile as if nothing had happened the day before.

"Possum," Jeffrey began, feeling like a total bastard when he noticed the bruise running along the bottom of Possum's chin.

Possum held his friendly smile, just like always. "No big thing, Slick," he said, patting Jeffrey on the back. "I got your change from yesterday. Don't let me forget to give it to you."

"No," Jeffrey said, thinking he had never felt so bad in his life.

Possum moved on. "You talk to Robert?"

"I was just going to try."

239

"Bail was set this morning," Possum said, taking a thick envelope out of his pocket.

Jeffrey saw a wad of cash in the envelope and took Possum a few feet down the hall. Not that Reggie Ray wasn't listening, but he felt better having some distance from the other man.

He said, "Possum, where'd you get that money?"

"Borrowed it against the store," Possum said. "Nell about had a heart attack, but we can't leave Robert locked up like that."

Jeffrey felt his shame return. He had not even considered the possibility of Robert making bail, let alone helping out. "Jessie's family's got plenty of money," he said. "You should let them do this."

"They already said they won't," Possum told him, and for once he looked angry about something. "I tell you, Slick, it hurts my heart the way she's treating him. No matter what was going on, he's still her husband."

"Did you talk to her?"

"Just came from there." He lowered his voice. "She was drunk as a mop and it's not even noon yet."

"What did she say?"

"Said he could rot in hell for all she cared," Possum told him, his tone as bitter-sounding as possible in such an affable man. "Can you believe that? They've been together longer than dirt, and she just writes him off."

"She *was* having an affair," Jeffrey reminded him.

"How long?" he asked, and Jeffrey thought that was a good question. "It doesn't make sense to me, is the thing. Mean as she could be, how could she tool around town making the nasty and nobody ever finds out and tells Robert?"

"Maybe somebody told him," Jeffrey said, giving Reggie a glance. The deputy was staring at them with open hatred, and Jeffrey wondered if he was about to snap.

Possum must have noticed this, too. He put himself between the men, asking Reggie, "Where do I pay bail?"

"In the back," Reggie said. "I'll take you."

He shifted his gun belt as he walked toward Jeffrey, his hand resting on the butt of his gun like he wanted to remind him he could do something with it. When he bumped his shoulder against Jeffrey, Jeffrey let it go, thinking he had started enough fights lately without getting into it again so soon. When the two men were gone, he knocked on Hoss's office door, not waiting to be asked in.

"Hey," Hoss said, standing up from his desk. Robert was sitting in front of him, hands on his lap, shoulders rolled in like he was waiting for the executioner.

"Possum's here bailing you out," Jeffrey told him.

Robert's shoulders slumped even more. "He shouldn't be doing that."

"He took out money against the store."

"Christ," Robert breathed. "Why'd he do that?"

"He couldn't see you staying here," Jeffrey said, trying to get Hoss's attention. The old man stared out at the parking lot. Jeffrey got the feeling he had interrupted something. "I've gotta say I'm not too crazy about it myself."

Robert said, "I'm okay."

Jeffrey waited for him to turn around, but he would not. "Bobby?"

He gave Jeffrey a quick glance, but that was enough to show that he had a black eye and a split lip. Jeffrey walked around the chair, trying to get a better look at him. Bruises peeked out of the top of his orange jail uniform and his left arm had a large bandage wrapped around it. Jeffrey's fists clenched without thinking about it, and he had trouble asking, "What happened?"

Hoss answered for him. "Got a little rowdy last night."

"Why wasn't he sequestered?" Jeffrey demanded.

"He didn't want special treatment."

"Special treatment?" Jeffrey repeated, not bothering to hide his outrage. "Good God, that's not special treatment, that's common sense."

"Don't question me, boy," Hoss warned, his finger pointed in Jeffrey's direction. "I can't make any man do what they don't want to do."

"That's bullshit!" Jeffrey countered. "He's a fucking inmate. You can make him sleep in his own shit if you want to."

"Well, I wasn't here to do it!" Hoss raged. "Goddammit, I wasn't here." He used the back of his hand to wipe his mouth, and Jeffrey could feel the misery radiating off him like a bad smell. Whatever Jeffrey was feeling at this moment, he knew that Hoss felt worse.

"Who did it?" Jeffrey asked Robert. "Was it Reggie Ray? If he's the one—"

Robert interrupted, "It wasn't Reggie's fault."

"If he—"

"I asked to be put in," Robert said. "I wanted to see what it was like."

Jeffrey still could not find the words to express himself.

Hoss shifted his belt much as Reggie had done. "I'm gonna walk outside and give you time to cool your temper," he told Jeffrey. His tone was even enough, but the way he slammed the door behind him sent a clear message.

Jeffrey went to the source, asking Robert, "What happened?"

Robert shrugged, wincing as it caused him obvious pain. "I was sleeping. They woke me up and moved me into general population."

Jeffrey felt sick at the thought of cops doing this to one of their own. There was a code, and even now Robert was upholding it despite what the bastards had exposed him to.

"Why didn't you call for help?"

"From who?" Robert asked, a sadness in his tone. "They've all been waiting for something like this," he said, indicating the deputies in the station with a nod of his head. "It's the same as when we were kids, Jeffrey. Not a damn thing has changed. Every guy in here was just waiting for me to fuck up so they could throw me to the lions." He gave a sad laugh. And Jeffrey could only imagine how horrible his night had been. The other inmates had probably thought it was Christmas, having a cop to take out all their hostilities on for the night.

Robert continued, "All these years . . . I really thought some of those men were my friends, that I had proven myself." He paused,

242

obviously trying to control his emotions. "I had a wife. I was part of a family. Hell, I even coached Little League. Did you know that? We got to the quad-A championship last year. Liked to won but one of the Thompson boys overthrew to home." He smiled at the memory. "Did you know that? We made it to the big stadium over in Birmingham."

Jeffrey shook his head. He had grown up with this man, spent every day of his boyhood with him, yet he knew nothing about his life as an adult.

"You just never know what people think about you, do you?" Robert asked. "You go to ballgames and picnics and watch their kids grow up and hear about their divorces and affairs and it doesn't mean shit. They smile to your face while they're stabbing you in the back."

"You should've called Hoss last night," Jeffrey said. "He would've come down and straightened all of this out."

"It'd just make things worse the next time."

"Worse?" Jeffrey said. "What's worse than getting the shit beat out of you?" His mind answered his own question, and he sunk down in the chair beside Robert before his knees gave out. "They didn't . . . ?"

Robert's voice sounded like it was coming out of a dead man. "No."

Jeffrey put his hand to his stomach, a hot sickness churning in his belly. "Jesus . . ." he whispered, as close to a prayer as he had come in twenty years.

Robert's hands started to tremor, and Jeffrey noticed the handcuffs keeping them together. His fingers were as beaten up as his face, deep gashes on his knuckles where his fists had met something hard. He looked as if he had fought for his life last night.

Jeffrey asked, "Why are you cuffed?"

"I'm a dangerous criminal," Robert reminded him. "I've killed two people."

"You didn't," Jeffrey said. "Robert, I know you didn't do this. Why are you lying?"

"I can't do this," Robert said. "I thought I was strong enough, but I'm not."

Jeffrey put his hand on Robert's shoulder, but pulled it away when the other man flinched. He wondered if Robert was telling him the truth about last night, though if he really thought about it, Jeffrey did not want to know a damn thing.

Jeffrey said, "We'll get you a lawyer."

"I don't have any money," he said. "Jessie's family wouldn't piss on me if I was on fire."

"I'll pay for it," Jeffrey told him, even as he racked his brain to think of where he could find that kind of money. "I don't have enough equity in my house, but I've got a retirement plan I can cash out. It's not much, but it'll be a retainer. Between me and Possum, we can find a way to do this. I'll work security, get another job if I have to." He cast about for something concrete. "I can move back to Birmingham and drive down on the weekends."

"I can't let you do that."

"You don't have a choice," Jeffrey told him. "You can't spend another night in jail."

Robert shook his head, an overwhelming sadness filling the room. "I've never had much of a choice about anything, Jeffrey. I'm so sick of living this life. Just plain dog tired of everyone and everything in it." He closed his eyes. "Jessie's finished with me. She was finished with me a long time ago."

"Is this because of the miscarriage?" Jeffrey asked, thinking that was enough to put a strain on any relationship. There had to be a reason Jessie went out on her husband. People did not cheat for no reason.

"It goes back further than that," Robert said. "It goes back to that day Julia came to school, saying I raped her. She never trusted me. Not after that."

Jeffrey felt all of his senses strain. "Did you tell Jessie what happened?"

"She never asked," Robert said. "There's things she knows in her head, but she never asks the question. Why don't people ask the question?"

"Maybe they don't want to know the answers," Jeffrey told him, thinking he was just as bad as Jessie. Still, he said, "Jessie didn't believe those rumors. Nobody who really knew you believed it was true."

"They believed it about you," Robert said. He looked up at Jeffrey, his eyes watering. "I let them think that all this time."

"Think what?"

"That you raped Julia," he said, his eyes shifting around, like he wanted to take in every part of Jeffrey's reaction. "I let them think it was you in the woods. I let them think you raped her."

Jeffrey felt all the saliva in his mouth go dry.

"I was just protecting myself," Robert said. "You went away, but I had to stay here, had to live with them all bearing down on me, thinking they knew my nature." He looked away. "Every Sunday at church, I could feel Lane Kendall staring a hole into me, like she could see what was going on, like she knew what happened that day."

"What happened, Robert?" Jeffrey waited, but he did not answer. "Tell me what happened," he repeated. "I've never asked you before because I believed you were innocent. If you're saying you're guilty now, then tell me what happened."

Robert cleared his throat a few times, then reached out with both hands to get a cup of water off the desk. He took a sip of water and winced as it went down, his Adam's apple jerking in his throat. Jeffrey saw the bruises around his neck and knew that someone had tried to strangle him. Or had they put their hands around his neck to keep him from calling out? The bruises darkened as they wrapped around the front of his neck. Had someone stood behind him, squeezing his throat shut? What were they doing that was so bad they needed to make sure Robert could not call out?

"Robert," Jeffrey whispered, trying to find his voice. "Tell me what happened."

He shook his head. "Go home, Slick."

"I'm not leaving you."

"Go back to Grant County and marry Sara. Start a life. Have some kids."

"I'm not gonna do that, Robert. I'm not gonna leave you a second time."

"You didn't leave me the first time," Robert said, anger flashing in his eyes. "Look, I raped her. That's just what I'm going to tell them:

I took her to the cave and I raped her, and she started screaming, say-ing she was going to tell everybody. I panicked, just like I panicked the other night. I took a rock and smashed the side of her head in." He gave Jeffrey a hard look. "Does that satisfy you?"

"Which side?" Jeffrey asked. "Which side of her head did you hit her on?"

"Hell, I don't know. Look at her damn skull. It's the side that's broken."

"You didn't kill her," Jeffrey said. "She was strangled, she wasn't beaten."

"Oh." Robert could not hide his surprise, but he recovered quickly. "Yeah, I strangled her, too."

"You didn't."

"I did," he insisted. "I strangled her just like this," he said, the cuffs clinking as he wrapped his hands around an imaginary neck.

"You didn't," Jeffrey countered.

Robert dropped his hands, though he would not admit defeat.

"I was just talking to her at first, trying to be nice," he said, his voice getting smaller. His eyes glazed over as he went somewhere else, and he spoke so softly that Jeffrey had to strain to listen "When she looked away, I hit her in the head, and when she fell over, I got on top of her, behind her. She screamed, and I started choking her to shut her up." He used his hands again to illustrate. "She wouldn't stop screaming, and it got me mad just hearing her, and it got me excited, too—excited like I don't know. I kept one hand on the back of her neck." He put his hand palm down, like he was there. "I knew she was scared—terrified. I was scared, too. I thought somebody would come, somebody would see me like that, like some animal. And I couldn't stop. I couldn't get anybody to help me. My throat . . ." He put his hand to his neck. "My throat felt like I swallowed a handful of tacks. I just couldn't breathe. I couldn't even make a sound more than a whimper, but in my mind, I could hear them laughing about it, egging me on, like it was some kind of game to see how far I could go before I broke." He let his hands drop to his lap, his breath coming in sharp rasps. Jeffrey did not know if he was talking about Julia anymore or what had happened to him last night. "I just wanted to go somewhere in my head, somewhere safe where I was okay, but it was all so horrible that I couldn't do anything but bite down on my tongue and pray to God it would be over soon." His lips trembled, but there were no tears.

"Robert," Jeffrey said, reaching out again to touch him.

Robert pulled away as if Jeffrey had slapped him. He curled into himself as much as he could. "Don't touch me," he whispered. "Please don't touch me."

"Robert," Jeffrey repeated, trying to keep his voice controlled. If he had a gun, he'd go back to the jail right now and kill every one of those fucking bastards. He'd start with Reggie and work his way up the food chain until—what?—until he put the gun to his own head and pulled the trigger? He was just as guilty in all of this as the others were.

Still, he had to know, "Why are you lying to me about Julia?"

"I'm not lying," Robert said, anger flaring up again. "I raped her." He gave Jeffrey a steady look. "I raped her and then I killed her."

"You didn't kill Julia," Jeffrey insisted. "Stop saying you did. You didn't even know how she died."

"What does it matter?" Robert said. "I'm going to get the needle anyway."

"You're not," Jeffrey said. "Not if you cop to manslaughter. You can be out in seven years. You can still have a life."

"What kind of life?"

"I'll help make a life for you," Jeffrey said, and in that moment, he was certain he could make it work. "You can come to Grant with me. Work on the force."

"Not with a felony rap."

"We'll find something else, then," Jeffrey told him. "We'll get you the fuck out of this town. You can start over, have a new life."

"What kind of life?" Robert repeated. He raised his hands, indicating the station. "What kind of life can I have after this?"

"We'll get to that when the time comes," Jeffrey said. "Just stop talking to people, okay? Don't talk to anybody but the lawyer—not even Hoss. We'll get the best guy we can. We'll go to Atlanta if we have to."

"I don't want a lawyer," Robert said. "I just want some peace."

"You're not going to find peace in a prison uniform, Robert. You have to know that by now."

"I don't care anymore," he said. "I really don't."

"That's just for right now," Jeffrey told him. "That's just because of last night."

"Nothing happened last night," Robert said. "We got into a scuffle, but that was it. They knew better after I got finished with them."

Jeffrey sat back in the chair.

"I beat the shit out of them," Robert said, his teeth showing in what he probably wanted to be a smile but looked like more of a snarl. "Three on one, and I beat the ever-loving shit out of them."

"That's good," Jeffrey said, knowing he could not disagree. Three on one. Robert hadn't had a chance.

Robert's false bravado continued. "I punched one of 'em so hard he was begging for his mama."

"There you go," Jeffrey said, his heart breaking even as he said the words. "You showed 'em, Bobby. You showed 'em all."

Robert took a deep breath, sitting up straighter, squaring his shoulders. "All right," he said, like he was bracing himself. "It's all right. I can do this."

"You don't have to do it alone," Jeffrey told him. "I'm here. Possum's here."

"No," Robert said, like his mind was made up. "I'm going to do this, Jeffrey. It's the least I can do."

"Least you can do for what?"

"For you," he said, giving Jeffrey a knowing look. "I know what really happened."

Jeffrey felt as if he had been threatened, but he did not know why. "What do you mean?" he asked.

"I saw you in the woods with Julia that day. I saw you both going to the cave."

Jeffrey shook his head. They had been alone that day. He had checked.

"I'm willing to take the rap for everything," Robert said, tears welling back into his eyes. When he spoke, his voice shook from the effort. "I'll say I did it, take the blame for all of it and let you walk away. Just tell me, Slick. Tell me the truth. Did you kill her?"

CHAPTER NINETEEN

Sara was sitting in a chair on Nell's front porch as Jeffrey pulled into the driveway. He had exchanged Robert's truck for her BMW, and she was glad to see it back in one piece. She walked toward him as he got out of the car, but something about his expression stopped her.

"What's wrong?" she asked.

"Nothing," he told her, though he was obviously lying. "Let's go to Robert's house again."

"Okay," she agreed. "Let me go tell Nell where I'm going."

He grabbed her hand, pulling her back toward the street. "She'll figure it out."

"Okay," she repeated, wondering what was going on. He held on to her hand as they walked down the street. There was a slight breeze in the air, which made the day more bearable, but it was still hot on the black asphalt, and Sara could not help thinking back to two short nights ago when she had run down the street trying to get away from Jeffrey. Maybe he was thinking about the same thing, because he squeezed her hand.

She asked, "Are you okay?"

He shook his head, but did not elaborate.

"Why do you want to look at the house again?"

"Something's not right," he said. "It doesn't add up."

"What did Robert say?"

"Nothing new," Jeffrey told her. "He's still taking the rap for it. Taking the rap for everything." His jaw tightened, and he was quiet a beat. "He's lying about Julia. It makes me wonder what else he was lying about."

"Like what?" Sara said, thinking that it was pretty clear what had happened in the bedroom that night. "All the evidence backs what he's saying."

"I just want to look at it again," he said. "I want see for myself that it works out."

"What specifically do you think doesn't add up?"

He let go of her hand as they approached Robert's house, not answering her question. The yellow clapboard looked freshly painted and the white picket fence gave the place a surreal effect, like it was a Hollywood version of what a home should be.

There was a bright yellow strip of police tape on the door. Jeffrey took out his Swiss Army pocketknife, prying up the blade with his fingernail. "He was attacked last night."

"In the jail?"

He nodded.

"By whom?"

Jeffrey sliced through the police tape. "He won't say."

"How could Hoss let that happen?"

"It wasn't Hoss," Jeffrey told her, closing the knife. "Robert won't say who put him in general population, but I have a feeling it was Reggie."

"Why didn't he just paint a target on his back?"

"If I see that stupid redneck fuck again, I'm going to rip his head off."

Sara had a hard time reconciling Reggie with these actions, but Nell had said he was not to be trusted.

She asked, "Is Robert all right?"

Jeffrey opened the door and stepped back, letting Sara enter the house first. "I tried to get him to talk to me, to tell me what went down, but he wouldn't."

"Was he badly beaten?"

"It's not that I'm worried about," Jeffrey said, and she read everything on his expression in a moment.

"Oh, no," she said, putting her hand to her chest. "Is he okay?"

He closed the door behind them. "He says he's fine."

"Jeffrey," she said, wrapping her hand around his shoulder. He looked down the hallway, not at her, and she could tell he was struggling to maintain his composure.

"Possum was down there this morning to bail him out," he said. "I didn't even think about doing that."

"How could he make bail?"

"Hoss must have pulled some strings," Jeffrey told her. "It's not like he's a flight risk. Where would he go?"

"I'm so sorry," she told him, feeling his sadness wash over her.

He put his arms around her, and she held him, trying to offer comfort when she knew there was little else she could do.

"Oh, Sara," he breathed, burying his face in her neck. His whole body relaxed, and despite all that had happened, she felt an overwhelming sense of happiness knowing that just by holding him she could bring him such peace.

He said, "I just want to get away with you."

"I know," she told him, stroking the nape of his neck.

"I want to take you dancing," he said, and she laughed because they both knew she had the coordination of a just-born colt. "I want to walk on the beach with you and drink piña coladas out of your belly button."

She laughed again, pulling away, but he would not let her. Sara kissed his neck, letting her lips linger on his skin. He tasted salty, like the ocean, and she could smell the musky odor of his aftershave. "I'm here," she said.

"I know," he told her, finally breaking the embrace. He gave a heavy sigh, indicating the house with a toss of his hand. "Let's just get this over with."

"What are we looking for?" she asked, following him into the living room.

"I don't know," he said, opening one of the drawers in the coffee table. He rummaged around inside, then closed it. "Where did he keep his backup gun?"

"I think he said the living room?" Sara said, more of a question because she could not remember.

"There should be a safe," he said. "If he was telling the truth about where he kept it."

Sara was not sure if anything Robert said could be trusted, but she opened the doors on the television cabinet. Except for a large TV and a bunch of videotapes, she saw nothing. She bent down to go through the drawers, saying, "They don't have kids in the house. He could've just kept it in a drawer."

"Robert knows better than that," Jeffrey said, getting on his hands and knees to look under the couch. "Hoss taught us both that you always secure your weapon." He sat back on his heels, a sad look in his eyes. "Robert coached Little League," he said. "He probably had kids in here all the time. He wouldn't have left a gun laying around."

"Jessie had an episode," Sara told him. "Nell told me around the miscarriage she took too many pills."

"Another reason for him to keep it hidden," Jeffrey pointed out.

Sara rummaged through a stack of instruction sheets for every piece of electronic equipment in the house. She found several old remote controls, a few spent batteries, and a fingernail file, but no gun safe. She asked, "Where do you keep your backup?"

"By my bed," he answered. "When I'm home, my service piece is in the kitchen."

"Why there?"

"I've never thought about it," he said, running his hand under the coffee table. "Just seemed logical. One upstairs, one downstairs."

"Where in the kitchen?" Sara asked, walking toward the back of the house.

"Cabinet over the stove," he called, then, "Shit."

"What?"

"Got a splinter."

"Try to be a little more careful," she advised him, walking down the hall. The bedroom was directly across from the kitchen, but she did not let herself look. The stench of dried blood was overpowering, and Sara knew that it would linger in the house long after Robert and Jessie found someone who could clean it. She could not imagine how Jessie could go on living here after what had happened.

Sara opened the cabinet over the stove, finding a stack of Tupperware bowls with their lids neatly piled beside them. She stood on the tips of her toes, peering all the way to the back, but there was nothing even resembling a gun. She went around the room, opening and closing all the cabinets, with the same results. She even checked the refrigerator, which had a full gallon of milk, juice, and the usual staples, but no gun.

"Find anything?" Jeffrey asked. He stood in the doorway with one hand cradling the other.

"Does it hurt?" Sara asked.

"Not much," he said, holding out his hand. She turned on the light and saw a thick splinter in the palm of his hand.

"They must have some tweezers," she said, opening the drawers. A quick search found nothing but common kitchen utensils. "I'll check the bathroom."

She headed toward the master bathroom but stopped when she caught sight of a sewing basket sitting on the highboy beside the dining room table.

She told Jeffrey, "Come in here, the light's better," as she searched the basket. "These will work," she said, finding a pair of straight-edged tweezers among the pins and needles.

"You want me to open these?" Jeffrey asked, but he was already twisting the rod to open the blinds. He looked out into the backyard, saying, "It's nice here, huh?"

"Yes," she said, taking his hand in hers. She wore glasses sometimes at work, but she had been too vain to bring them along on the trip. "This might hurt."

"I can take it," he said, then, "Ow, shit." He jerked back his hand.

"Sorry," she said, trying not to smile at his reaction. She held his hand closer to the window, taking advantage of the light. "Just think about something else."

"That won't be hard," he told her sarcastically, wincing as the tweezers grew near.

"I haven't even touched it," she said.

"Are you this mean to your kids?"

"Usually they're a little braver."

"That's nice."

"Come on," she teased him. "I'll give you a lollipop if you're good."

"I'd rather give *you* something to suck on."

She raised an eyebrow, but did not respond. Slowly, she worked at the splinter, trying to get it to come out in one piece.

Jeffrey asked, "Did you notice something weird about Swan?"

"Weird how?" She groaned as the splinter broke.

"Like . . ." He made a hissing sound as she dug into the skin. "He's the exact opposite of Robert."

She shrugged. "Maybe that was the point. She wanted something different. A change."

"Am I different from the guys you usually date?"

Sara worked on the splinter, trying to come up with a good answer. "I can't say that I've given it much thought." She smiled as the splinter came out. "There."

He put his hand to his mouth, something Sara saw kids do at the clinic, as if some genetic imperative convinced them that their mouth could cleanse a wound.

"Let's look in the bedroom," Jeffrey said.

"You think he was lying about keeping a backup in the living room?"

"I don't know."

"He could have kept it in his truck."

"Maybe."

"What else is bothering you?" She decided not to let him brush it off. "I'm not stupid, Jeffrey. Something's bothering you. Either tell me or not, but don't keep denying it."

He put his hand on the windowsill. "Yes, something is bothering me. I just can't talk about it."

"Okay," she agreed, glad that she had at least gotten him to admit it. "Let's finish in here. Maybe then we can go back to Nell's and try to make some sense of all this."

The bedroom door was slightly ajar, and the hinges squeaked when she opened it. Light was streaming in through the windows, and Sara was surprised to find that her memory of what the room had looked like the night Swan had been shot was completely skewed. Somehow, her mind had exaggerated everything so that whenever she tried to imagine the room, she saw blood everywhere. In actuality, except for the splatter fanning out to the door and ceiling and the pool of blood and matter where Swan had lain, the room was clean.

Jeffrey opened the armoire and searched the shelves as Sara went to the bedside table opposite the side Swan had been shot. Everything in the room had been dusted for prints, black powder showing specks of dirt and ridges on every available surface. She assumed Reggie had lifted whatever evidence he needed, but still Sara tried not to touch the black powder on the cabinet door, knowing from experience how difficult it was to wash off. She opened the door from the top, stepping back as a baby-blue vibrator fell out onto the floor.

Jeffrey was looking over her shoulder. "That explains a lot," he said in a knowing tone.

"What does it explain?" Sara asked him, taking a tissue to use as she returned the machine to its resting place. "Every woman I know has one of these."

He seemed surprised. "Do you?"

"Of course not, honey," she joked. "You're more than man enough for me."

"I'm serious, Sara."

"What?" she asked, glancing in the cabinet before shutting the door. There was a small tube of personal lubricant, but she thought better than to tell Jeffrey. She said, "It doesn't mean anything. Sometimes couples use them. What sort of smoking gun are you looking for here?"

"I don't know," he said, sounding defeated. "He's not telling me the truth. We've got to either prove he's lying or prove he's not." He shrugged his shoulders. "Either way, I'm going to support him through this."

Sara told him, "Sometimes when people lie, they sprinkle in the truth so that it sounds believable."

"Meaning?"

"Robert might have told us a bit of information that we're just not hearing." Sara suggested, "Let's take it from the beginning and go over what Robert and Jessie said happened the first time."

"You mean what they told us when Luke was shot?"

She nodded.

"All right," he said, looking around the room. "Let's take it from the top. We were in the street. I heard the shots and ran through the backyard to here." He stood in the doorway. "I saw what had happened, or at least saw the dead guy. Robert groaned and I turned around. He was here," Jeffrey pointed behind the door. "Jessie was over here," he said, indicating the area by the window.

"Then what?"

"I asked Robert if he was okay, then I went to get you."

"All right," Sara began, taking up the narration. "I came in and you went to call the police. I checked Swan's pulse, then I went to help Robert."

"He wouldn't let you look at the wound," Jeffrey provided. "Jessie kept interrupting while I tried to get the story."

"Which was," Sara took over, "they were in bed. Swan came in through the window."

Jeffrey walked over to the window. He looked out into the backyard. "Someone could have sneaked in through here."

"Did Robert ever say he knocked the screen out?" She clarified, "As part of his new story where he says he did it. Did he say that he knocked out the screen?"

"No."

Sara glanced around the room, trying to remember how things had looked that night.

"So, Swan has a gun," Jeffrey said, picking back up on Robert's first explanation. "He crawls to the bed. Jessie wakes up and screams. Robert stirs and Swan shoots at him."

"He misses," Sara provided. "Robert runs to the armoire and gets his gun." She stood in front of the armoire. "He shoots at Swan, but the gun hangs."

Jeffrey finished, "Swan shoots him, then Robert's gun goes off and shoots Swan in the head."

Sara looked down at where she was standing. The blood-spray pattern did not point to the armoire.

She said, "He would've had to have been here," walking to the door and lining herself up with the pattern. "Look at this," she said, indicating blood in the carpet where Swan had fallen. "Robert had to have been standing here."

"Why?"

"He shoots," she said, holding out her hand with her thumb and index finger forming the shape of a gun. "The bullet hits Swan in the head, and there's backsplatter from the bullet. It's basic science: for every action, there's an equal and opposite reaction. The bullet goes in, the blood sprays back. Look at the pattern of the blood."

Jeffrey stood beside her, looking at the carpet. "Okay," he said. "I see it. He was standing here."

"Hold on," she told him, leaving the room before he could ask why. She got the sewing basket and came back, saying, "This isn't exactly scientific."

"What are you doing?"

She found a spool of yellow thread, thinking that would show up best. "Blood's subject to gravity, just like anything else."

"So?"

"So," she said, opening a box of straight pins. "You can tell from the shape of the drop which way the blood fell. If it was splattered, if it fell straight down." She pointed to the bullet hole behind the door.

"See?" she told him. "You can tell from the pattern that Robert was standing near the wall when the bullet exited his body. The blood drops are almost perfectly round except at the top, where you can see they've got a slight teardrop shape to them. That means the bullet was on an upward trajectory."

"But it looks scattered," Jeffrey said, pointing to the hairline ribbons of red radiating from the circular drops.

"The blood hit the wall straight on, but it still splattered back." She used a straight pin to point this out. "This is where the bulk of the impact took place."

"All right," he agreed, though she could tell he still did not buy it. "What can the rest of this tell us?"

"Watch," she told him, picking at the end of the thread. She pulled it out a few yards, then bent to the carpet to match it to the blood. "I'm just guessing at the angle, and of course I'll have to adjust it— probably up—for the parabolic, but I—"

"What are you talking about?"

"Basic trigonometry," she answered, thinking it was obvious. "I really don't have the right equipment, so this is just a hunch, but the formula goes something like, the ratio of width and length of the bloodstain equals the angle of impact. . . ." She had lost him again, so she said, "Go find some tape."

"Masking? Duct? Scotch?"

"Anything sticky."

While Jeffrey searched the house for tape, Sara went about lining up the thread. She used the pins to attach the ends to the carpet and spun out the thread in lengths of ten to twelve feet.

"Will this work?" Jeffrey asked, handing her a roll of electrical tape.

"It should," Sara said, peeling off strips of tape and sticking them to her arm. She found the major splatters on the bedside table, careful not to touch the chunks of flesh that remained. She wished she had put on a pair of gloves before starting this, but it was too late now.

She told Jeffrey, "Stand here," pointing to the foot of the bed.

"What are you going to do?"

"There's nothing to attach the thread to on this end," she said. "I need to use you."

"Okay," he agreed, and she went back to each piece of thread, probably thirty in all, and judging the angle as best she could without the proper instruments, she followed the angle of the splatter, pinning the ends of the thread to Jeffrey's clothing. She used the black tape to highlight where the yellow threads crossed. By the time she had finished, Sara had worked up quite a sweat in the closed room, but it was well worth the effort.

"His head was here," Jeffrey said, indicating the point at which all the string converged. The black electrical tape represented the area of impact, like some sort of forensic spider on a web, showing the exact spot where the bullet exploded out blood, bone, and brain.

Sara had already gotten her jeans dirty crawling around on the bloody carpet, but she was hesitant to put herself where Swan had been kneeling when he was shot. He must have been a few feet from the bed when the bullet hit. She said, "He was a little shorter than I am, so his head must have been about here, give or take a few inches because of miscalculations on my part."

"Jessie was in bed," Jeffrey said, not moving because of the string. "Swan must have been on his knees in front of her."

Sara saw what could have been an outline of a handprint. "Here," she said. "Do you see this?"

"Yeah," he nodded. "Swan must have had his hand there. Maybe he was leaning against the bed, using it for balance."

"He was facing this way," Sara said, indicating the bed. "The bullet entered the side of his head, here," she put her fingers to the space above her ear. "It came out low on the other side." She indicated the glob of flesh still stuck to the bedside table. "This is his earlobe."

"So it fits," Jeffrey said. "Robert was standing over here about where I am and Swan was kneeling beside the bed, doing whatever."

"He was facing Jessie."

Jeffrey's shoulders slumped, and the string went with him. "What he said was right, then. He didn't even give him a warning. He just shot him in cold blood."

"Let's get these off," Sara said, meaning the pins. "This doesn't tell us why."

"The why is clear enough," he said, helping her with the pins. "He saw another man fucking his wife. I'd feel the same way."

"You wouldn't shoot someone."

"I don't know what I'd do," Jeffrey said. "If I saw you with some-body else . . ."

"Robert saw them first," Sara said, still trying to think it through. "He wasn't carrying his gun when he walked in the first time."

"No," Jeffrey agreed. "He must have gone back out into the room or his truck or wherever the fuck it is he keeps his gun."

"Then he came back," Sara continued. "That's premeditation."

"I know," Jeffrey said, dropping some pins into the plastic box.

She wound up the string, wondering what they were going to do now. Robert had already confessed. Their purpose here had been to try in some way to break his story. They had done nothing more than proven he had shot the man with premeditation. It was the difference between ten years with early release and death row.

Car tires screeched outside, and Jeffrey said, "I wonder what—" just as a door slammed. They both walked to the front of house to see who was there. Jeffrey threw open the door just as a woman was raising her fist to bang on it.

"You!" she screamed, her voice reminding Sara of a gravel truck. "You fucking bastard, I knew you'd be here!"

Jeffrey tried to close the door but the woman inserted herself in the house. The smell of her hit Sara first, the metallic tinge of men-strual blood, though the woman was well past that time in her life. She was enormous, probably a hundred pounds overweight, with a face that was a mask of sheer rage.

"You fucking pig!" the woman screamed, punching her hand into Jeffrey's chest.

"Lane—" he began, holding up his hands to stop her.

"You killed my daughter, you murdering bastard!" she bellowed. "You and your fucking friends aren't going to get away with this!"

Jeffrey tried to push her out the door, but she was able to keep it open by sheer force of weight. She punched her hands into Jeffrey's chest again, this time hard enough to knock him back into the house. The door flew open as he fell to the floor.

Sara went to him, telling the woman, "Stop!" before she could help herself.

She turned on Sara, giving her the kind of up-and-down appraisal that she would probably give a leper. "I heard about you," she said. "You fucking slut. You don't even know what kind of trash you're with."

Jeffrey had managed to stand, but he was breathing hard, and Sara wondered if the force of the punch had broken one of his ribs.

Sara hissed, "Who is this?"

"Eric!" the woman called back into the yard. "Get in here. You, too, Sonny."

Jeffrey leaned hard against the wall, like he needed help to stay up. Sara was about to ask him what was going on when she saw two young boys walking up the porch stairs. They were pitiful creatures, undernourished and filthy. Sara was reminded of two baby birds who had fallen out of their nest and been abandoned by their mother, and she felt angry just looking at them. What sort of person could allow such neglect? Who could treat two children this way?

The woman grabbed one of the boys by the back of his neck and thrust him toward Jeffrey. "Say hello to your father, you little bastard."

Sara caught the boy before he fell. Under his dirty gray shirt she could feel his ribs poking through.

The woman said, "This is the asshole who raped your mama."

Sara felt as if her throat had closed. She looked at Jeffrey but he would not meet her gaze.

"Rape?" Sara managed, the word echoing in her head like a bell.

"You pig," the woman told Jeffrey. "Be a fucking man and take some responsibility for once in your pathetic life."

"Please," Sara said to the woman, trying to concentrate on the things she could control. "Don't do this in front of the children."

"Don't do what?" the woman demanded. "Boy needs to know his

262

father. Ain't that right, Eric? Don't you wanna meet the man who raped and killed your mama?"

Eric looked up at Jeffrey, curious, but Jeffrey's face was stone, and he did not even glance at the child.

"Are you okay?" Sara asked the boy, using her fingers to push his dirty hair out of his eyes. He was tall enough to be Jared's age, but there was something sickly about him. She could see odd-looking bruises on his arms and legs. She asked, "Are you sick?"

The woman answered for him. "He's got bad blood," she said. "Just like his piece-of-shit father."

"Get out of here," Jeffrey growled, his voice a warning. "You don't belong here."

"You're gonna let Robert pay for this," she said. "You fucking coward."

"You don't know anything about it."

"I know I got medical bills out the ass," she yelled back. "Nobody on my side of the family's ever had this kind of shit." She gave the boy a look of pure hatred, like she could not stand being near him. "You think I'm made of money? You think I can afford to rush this'un up to the hospital for a transfusion every time he falls down?"

Jeffrey warned, "Get the fuck out of here before I call Hoss."

She stood her ground. "Bring him on! Bring him on right now and we'll settle this once and for all."

"There's nothing to settle," Jeffrey shot back. "Nothing's changed, Lane. You can't do anything now."

"The hell you say," she told him. "Everybody knows you raped her."

"The statute of limitations on that ran out three years ago," he told her, and the fact that he knew this sent a cold shiver through Sara's spine. "Even if you had something, they couldn't touch me."

The woman shoved her fat finger into Jeffrey's face. "I'll fucking kill you myself, you goddamn bastard."

"Ma'am," Sara tried, keeping her hands on Eric, not wanting to let him go. He seemed a million miles away, as if he was used to adults behaving this way. The boy who remained in the yard was playing with a plastic toy truck, his lips making engine noises. Still, Sara said, "Let's not do this in front of the children."

"Who the fuck are you?" she laughed. "Just who the fuck do you think you are?"

Sara stood up, anger compelling her to speak. "I know that this child is sick. He's filthy. How can you let him get like this?" She indicated the other boy. "Him, too. I should call child services on you."

"Go ahead and call them," she said. "You think I give a shit? Two less mouths to feed." Still, even as she said this she reached out her hand, indicating Eric should come to her. The boy followed the command, and Sara reached to stop him, her fingers brushing his arm. She could feel raised welts where the black and blue marks riddled his skin.

The woman told Sara, "Your boyfriend here raped my daughter."

Sara felt light-headed. She put her hand out to the wall to keep herself steady.

"He raped her and got her pregnant, and when she asked him for help, he killed her, and left me to raise his little bastard of a son." The woman shoved her finger back in Jeffrey's face. "This isn't over."

"Yes," he said. "It is."

"You tell that fucking buddy of yours if I see him in the street, he's a dead man."

"Why don't I tell Hoss and he can run you in for making threats?"

"You fucking coward," she said, her lips twisting into a sneer as she coughed in the back of her throat. Before Jeffrey could move away, she spit on his face.

"This isn't over," she repeated, grabbing Eric by the wrist. He already had bruises up and down his arm, but the child did not protest. The other boy in the yard trotted back to the car, looking for all the world as if his mother had told him they were going for ice cream.

Jeffrey took out his handkerchief and carefully unfolded it. He patted his face, wiping off the spit.

Sara took several minutes to find her voice. She kept hearing the woman's accusation over and over in her head. Finally, she managed, "Do you want to tell me what that was about?"

"No."

She threw her hands into the air, feeling angry and vulnerable. "Jeffrey, she said you raped her daughter."

"Do you believe her?" he asked, looking her right in the eye. "Do you believe I raped somebody? That I killed somebody?"

She had been too shocked to let her mind fully consider the possibility. The accusation had hit her like a hammer, knocking her senseless.

"Sara?"

"I don't . . ." She shook her head. "I don't know what I believe anymore."

"Then we don't have much to say to each other," he told her, walking away.

"Wait," she told him, following him down the driveway. "Jeffrey." He did not turn around, and she had to run to catch up with him. "Talk to me."

"Looks like you've already made up your mind."

"Why won't you tell me what happened?"

He stopped, turning to face her. "Why won't you let it be, Sara? Why can't you just trust me?"

"It's not a matter of trust," Sara told him. "My God, that woman says you raped her daughter. She says you have a son."

"That's bullshit," he snapped. "You think I could have a kid and not know it? There's no way."

Sara remembered Jared, and bit back the urge to throw Nell's secret in his face.

"What?" he demanded, mistaking her reticence for something more sinister. "You know what? Fuck this." He continued to walk down the street, obviously exasperated. "I thought you were different. I thought you were somebody I could trust."

"It's not an issue of trust."

" 'Issue,' " he repeated. "Fuck that."

"Oh, that's really mature," she said, mocking him. " 'Fuck that.' "

She tried to grab his shoulder to stop him but he jerked away, advising, "You wanna leave me alone right now."

"Why?" she asked. "Are you going to rape me, too? Strangle me?"

He had been angry before, livid, but she read his hurt like an open book, immediately regretting her words.

Sara tried to take it back, but he shook his head like he did not trust himself to talk. He held up his finger to her, as if to make a point, but still he said nothing. Finally, he shook his head again and continued down the street, walking toward his mother's house.

"Shit," Sara whispered, tucking her hands into her hips. Why did everything have to be so difficult between them? The minute things were going well, something—usually someone—came along and ruined it. Rape. She could handle anything they said about him but this. Why had he not told her before? Why hadn't he trusted her? Probably for the same reasons she did not completely trust him.

Nell was sitting on the front steps when Sara walked up to the house, and she stood, holding her hand out to Sara, saying, "I saw Lane Kendall's car up at Robert's. What did that old cow say to you?"

Sara opened her mouth and to her surprise burst into tears.

"Oh, honey," Nell said, leading her into the house. "Come here." She pulled Sara toward the couch. "Sit down."

Sara sat, and Nell hugged her. She felt ridiculous and grateful at the same time, and her words came in jagged murmurs between sobs as she let everything out that she had wanted to tell Jeffrey. "Those poor children."

"I know."

"They looked so dirty, so hungry."

Nell shook her head, tsking.

"I don't want to feel this way."

"Oh, now," Nell said, stroking her hair. "Shh . . ."

"What happened?" she begged. "Please just tell me what happened."

"Come on," Nell soothed, taking a Kleenex out of the box. She held the tissue to Sara's nose and said, "Blow."

Sara did as she was instructed, feeling silly for her outburst. She sat up, wiping her eyes with another tissue. "Oh, God, I'm so sorry."

"It's a wonder you haven't broken down before this," Nell said, taking another tissue to wipe her own eyes.

"Those children . . ." Sara murmured. "Those poor boys."

"I know. It makes my stomach ache every time I see them."

"Why can't anyone *do* something?"

"Don't ask me," she said. "I'd put an ad in the paper if I thought someone would take them."

Sara tried to laugh, but she could not. "What about children's services?"

"You wanna know something funny?"

Sara waited.

"She used to work for them."

"No," Sara said. She could not believe it.

"She did," Nell confirmed. "About fifteen years ago she was a caseworker at the Department of Family and Children's Services. Then she got into a car accident on the way to do a house visit and sued the county and the state and anybody else she could get her hands on. Between her disability and whatever she got from the settlement, she's not hurting for money."

"Where does she spend it?"

"Not on any of her kids," Nell answered ruefully. "The upshot is, she knows all the rules. She knows how to get around having those kids taken away. D-FACS is scared of her. If it wasn't for Hoss making drop-bys every now and then, she'd probably put those two boys in a closet and throw away the key."

"What's wrong with the youngest?"

"Some blood thing," Nell said. "He's always having to get transfusions."

"Hemophilia?" she asked, thinking Nell probably meant infusions. Even in a town as small as Sylacauga, the doctors would know better.

"No, something else like that, but not hemophilia," Nell told her. "State pays all the bills, I'm sure."

Sara sank back into the sofa, feeling an overwhelming exhaustion. The two women sat there in silence, and for some reason Sara told her, "I was raped."

For once, Nell did not respond.

"I've never said that out loud," she said. "I mean, the actual words. I always say I was attacked or I was hurt. . . ." She pressed her lips together. "I was raped."

Nell let her take her time.

"It was when I worked in Atlanta," Sara said, adding, "Jeffrey doesn't know." She picked at a piece of string on the cushion.

Nell gave Sara a moment before saying, "I guess we've each got our secrets from him."

"I've never felt like this with a man," Sara said. "Not about anybody." She tried to find a way to articulate it. "I feel totally out of control, like no matter what my brain tells me, there's this little thing in the back of my head saying, 'No, don't listen to them. You can't live without him.' "

Nell repeated, "He has that effect on women."

"I just want . . ." She threw her hands into the air. "I don't know what I want." She picked at the string again. "I can't even tell him to his face that I love him, but every time I see him or even think about him . . ."

Nell took another tissue and handed it to Sara. "I never believed it," she told her. "What they said about him and Julia."

"What exactly did they say?"

"That Jeffrey and Robert raped her in the woods."

Sara bit her bottom lip. Nell had said the words matter-of-factly, but they still had power. The word "rape" in and of itself was the most obscene sort of profanity.

"She was a slut," Nell said. "Not that that's any excuse. Hell, my sister Marinell was a bigger slut, but she knew better than to brag about it."

"Tell me everything," Sara said. "Jeffrey won't."

Nell shrugged. "She did things with boys. I don't know, it sounds like no big deal today, but back then, you just didn't put out." She amended, "Well, you did it, but you sure as shit didn't let everybody know about it."

"I remember," Sara said. Fear had kept her from giving in to Steve

Mann, and shame had kept her from really enjoying it when she finally did.

"Julia wasn't pretty," Nell said. "She wasn't plain, either, but there's a quality girls like that have that makes them ugly. I guess it's some sort of desperation, where they grab onto anybody they think can make them feel better about themselves." She stared at the pictures of her family that lined the wall. "I look at Jen and it just makes me cringe sometimes because I see this need in her. She's not even a teenager yet and she's got this unquenchable thirst for approval."

"Most girls are like that."

"Are they?"

"Yes," Sara said. "Some are better at hiding it."

"I try to tell her she's pretty. Possum's just crazy about her. Went to the father-daughter dance with her at the end of school last year. My God, but that man can carry off a baby-blue tux like nobody you've ever seen."

Sara laughed, imagining Possum in the tuxedo.

"She's doing sports now," Nell said. "Basketball, softball. It's making a difference."

Sara nodded. Girls who participated in sports had more self-confidence; it was a proven fact. She said, "I look back and thank God I had my mother." Sara laughed at herself. "Not that I ever believed a word she said, but she was always telling me I could do anything I wanted to do."

"Obviously, part of you was listening," Nell pointed out. "You don't get to be a doctor just because you're pretty."

Sara felt a tinge of a blush at the compliment.

"Anyway," Nell said, folding and unfolding the tissue. "Julia was kind of loose. She didn't make a secret of it, either. She thought it meant something that the boys would go with her, like they thought she was special or they loved her. Like blowing them behind the gym after school made her some kind of special. She actually bragged about it."

"Did she ever go with Jeffrey?"

"The truth?" Nell asked.

Sara could only nod.

"The truth is, I can't tell you. I don't see why he would. I was giving it to him pretty regular then." She laughed at herself. "You never know with boys that age, though. A sixteen-year-old boy is gonna pass up on getting laid? Hell, most grown men wouldn't pass that up. Sex is sex, and they'll do just about anything to get it."

"Did you ever ask him about what happened?"

"I didn't have the guts," Nell said. "I wouldn't have a problem now, but you know how it is when you're young. You're scared to say something that might piss him off and make him leave you for the next hot thing."

"Who was the next hot thing?"

"Jessie, I thought, but in retrospect I know that he never would have done that to Robert." Nell tucked her feet under her legs. "I don't think he did, if you want my gut reaction. Even then, Jeffrey had this thing about him, this sort of guide that let him know the difference between right and wrong."

"I thought he was in trouble all the time."

"Oh, he was," Nell said. "But he knew he was wrong. That's what I kept after him about. He just knew better than to do the crap he did. He had to get to that point where he made the decision to listen to his gut." She added, "Your gut's a lot smarter than you think."

Sara thought of her conversation with her mother yesterday. "My gut tells me to trust him."

"Mine, too," Nell said. "I remember when Julia came to school the next day after she said she was raped. It was horrible. She told anybody who would listen. The details just filtered through so that by lunchtime we were all thinking she was bruised and battered." She paused. "Then I saw her in the hall, and she didn't look that upset to me. She seemed to be enjoying the attention." Nell gave another shrug. "The thing was, she lied all the time. Lied for attention, lied for pity. No one believed her. She probably didn't even believe herself."

"What did she say exactly?"

"That Robert took her to the cave, gave her some beer, loosened her up."

"Where does Jeffrey come in?"

"Later," Nell answered. "The story took on a life of its own, just like these things always do. He swore up and down he was with Robert when it happened, and she said sweet as you please that, by the way, Jeffrey was there, too. Said they both took turns on her."

"She changed her story?"

"From what I heard, but gossip goes both ways. She could have been saying they were both involved from the beginning and I just heard it wrong. It was a mess. By the end of the day there were rumors she'd been gang-raped by a group of boys from Comer. Some of the football team was talking about going after them. People just go crazy with that kind of thing."

"Were the police—" Sara stopped. "Hoss."

"Oh, yeah. Hoss was called. Some teacher at the school overheard Julia crying about it and they called in Hoss."

"What did he do?"

"He interviewed her, I guess. God knows he knew where she lived. Right before her father died, Hoss was there every weekend breaking up a fight between him and Lane."

"Did he interview Jeffrey and Robert?"

"Probably," Nell said, not sounding certain. "Julia backed off the story real quick after Hoss was called in. Stopped talking about it at school, stopped acting like the injured party. People tried to get her to say something—not because they were concerned but because it was a good scandal—but she wouldn't talk. Wouldn't say a thing. She was gone a month or so later."

"Gone where?"

"To have that baby, I'd guess," Nell said. "Fat as Lane is, no one made a connection when she told everybody she was pregnant again. Her husband had just died and we all felt sorry for her." Nell paused. "Now, there was a blessing, that old man dying. He was a terror, worse than Lane ever thought to be. Worse than Jeffrey's dad, I'd say. Just a mean, nasty piece of work."

"How many children did she have?"

"Last count, six."

"Is the one I saw today—Sonny—her youngest one?"

"He's a cousin. I don't know why she took him on. Probably for the extra money the state gives her."

"That's unbelievable," Sara said, wondering how anyone could allow that woman to raise a child, let alone two.

"Julia came back nine or ten months later and there was Eric, her new brother."

"No one said anything about the timing?"

"What were they going to say?" Nell asked. "And then a few more weeks later, she was gone again. It was just easier to say that Lane was the mother and Julia had run off somewhere. Dan Phillips, one of the boys who'd been on the football team, ran off around that time. There were all kinds of rumors, but they died off pretty quick. It made it easier for everybody, I guess."

Nell sat up on the couch and took a photo album out from under the coffee table. She thumbed through some of the pages until she found what she was looking for. "That's her, there in back."

Sara saw a photograph of Possum, Robert, and Jeffrey standing in the bleachers of a football stadium. They were all wearing their letterman jackets with their last names stitched on the front above their football jersey numbers. Jeffrey had his arm around Nell, and she leaned into him like a love-struck young girl. Inexplicably, Sara felt a stab of jealousy.

"Bastard never would give me his jacket," Nell said, and Sara laughed, but felt secretly relieved for some reason. In high school, wearing a boy's letterman jacket was right up there with wearing his class ring. It was not so much a symbol of the boy's love, but a way for the girl to make the rest of her friends jealous.

As if reading her mind, Nell asked, "Whose ring did you wear?"

Sara felt herself blush, but more from shame than anything else. Steve Mann's class ring had been a hulking chunk of gold with a hideous chess knight on the side—nothing like the football and basketball rings the athletes wore. Sara had hated wearing it and took it off as soon as she moved to Atlanta. Three months passed before she got up the nerve to mail it back to him along with a note explaining that she wanted to break up. To her credit, she had apologized to him years later, but Sara wondered if she would have given it a second thought had she not been forced to move back to Grant after what happened in Atlanta.

Nell took her silence for something else, probably assuming someone like Sara had not dated much in high school. She said, "Well, it's stupid anyway. Jeffrey didn't have a class ring—couldn't afford it—but all the other girls wore theirs like a damn wedding ring." She laughed. "The only way they could get them to fit was by wrapping half a roll of tape around the band."

Sara allowed a smile. She had done the same thing.

Nell returned to the photo album, saying "There" as she put her finger beside a blurry image of a young girl standing behind a picture of Possum and Robert. "That's Julia."

Sara had been expecting something horrible from Nell's description, but Julia looked like any other teenage girl from that time period. Her hair was straight to her waist and she was wearing a simple dress with a floral pattern. She looked sad more than anything else, and as sudden as her previous stab of jealousy, Sara felt a sharp sense of sympathy for the teenager.

Nell leaned over to look. "Now that I'm seeing her again, she wasn't that bad. You really can't judge personality in a picture, can you?"

"No," Sara agreed, thinking the girl was fairly attractive. Yet, that had not been enough to help her transcend the circumstances of her family life. She asked, "Was her father abusive?"

"He beat the crap out of them."

"No," Sara said. "The other way."

"Oh, you mean . . ." Nell seemed to think about it. "I have no idea, but it'd make sense."

"Do you know who the father of her child might have been?"

"No telling," Nell said. "If you wanted a list of everybody she'd been with, it'd end up being half the town." She gave Sara a pointed look. "Reggie Ray included."

"He was younger than her."

"So?"

Sara conceded the point, then said, "From what Lane said, it sounds like Eric has to go to the hospital a lot to get treatments. So he has to have some sort of clotting problem with his blood." She tried to think of other possibilities. "There has to be an autosomal recessive or dominant transmission." She saw Nell's perplexed expression and said, "Sorry, it means that the disorder is genetic. It has to do with one of the two proteins that make up clotting factors."

"Is that supposed to make sense?"

"Bleeding disorders are passed from parent to child."

"Ah."

"Do you know if Julia had anything like that?"

"I wouldn't think so," Nell said. "I remember one time during home ec, she sliced her finger open pretty bad with a pair of scissors. Whether or not it was an accident, I don't know, but she didn't seem to bleed any longer than a normal person would."

"If she had something like von Willebrand's disease, then having a child without proper medical supervision would have been life-threatening," Sara said. "There would also be other people in her family who were affected, and Lane pretty much said that wasn't the case."

"So you're saying it had to come from the father?" Nell asked. "I can't think of anyone in town with that kind of problem." She added, "Not Robert, especially. He got pretty banged up on the football field and never seemed the worse for it."

"Jeffrey, too," Sara said. She remembered drawing his blood sample. The puncture had bled no longer than usual. Even as she considered this, Sara felt ashamed. She had never genuinely thought Jeffrey could be guilty of either crime, but some part of her was glad that there was irrefutable proof.

"I could ask around," Nell offered.

"It comes in degrees," Sara said. "Some people have it and don't even know it. It's not as easy for women because of their menstrual cycles. Generally, they know there's a problem. My bet would be it came from the father."

"A needle in a haystack," Nell pointed out. "Who knows, maybe Dan Phillips has it." She reminded Sara, "The one who ran off about the same time Julia did." She reached over and paged through the album. "Here," she said, indicating a young man standing in the back row of the football team photo.

"He doesn't look like a football player," Sara said. Phillips was on the thin side and his dark hair was combed straight back off his head. He looked healthy enough, though one photo could not give the full story.

"He mostly played tackle dummy," Nell said. "Just being on the team and wearing the letterman jacket was all most of these guys wanted. Go down to the hardware store on game day and you can still hear them talking about it like they were in the damn Super Bowl."

"Glory days," Sara said. It was the same in Grant. She turned the page, looking at the other pictures. There was a black-and-white snapshot of Jared from a few years back, and she said, "He's growing up to be a handsome boy."

"You're not going to tell Jeffrey, are you?" Nell tried to smile. "Don't answer that." She put the album back under the table. "You still leaving town?"

"I don't know."

"Stick around." Nell patted her leg. "I'm making cornbread tonight."

"Where's Robert?"

"Possum took him to the store to buy him some clothes," she said. "Robert didn't want to go back to the house and God only knows what Jessie did with the stuff at her mama's."

"What about Robert?"

"He'll be okay."

"No," Sara said. "Robert. We've only been talking about Jeffrey. Did you ever think he was involved in what happened to Julia?"

Nell took her time answering. "He was always secretive."

"About what?"

"Maybe 'secretive' is the wrong word. Makes him sound shifty. He's just private. Doesn't talk about his feelings much."

"Jeffrey doesn't, either."

"No, not like that. Like he doesn't want anyone to get too close to him." She sat back on the couch, her back slumped into a C. "Everybody thought it was Possum who was on the outside, but I think it was Robert. He never seemed to fit in. Not that Jeffrey treated him that way, but it's that same thing we were talking about earlier. He always waited to see what Jeffrey did before he acted."

"That's not uncommon for teenagers."

"It was more than that," Nell said. "If Jeffrey got into trouble, Robert would take the blame. He was like Jeffrey's safety net and Jeffrey let him do it." She looked at Sara. "The minute Jeffrey left, Robert did the same thing with Hoss. He'd take a bullet for either one of them, and I'm not exaggerating."

Sara debated before telling her, "Robert is saying that he killed Julia."

Something in Nell's face shifted, though Sara could not pin down what. Her voice had changed, too. "I don't know about that."

"No," Sara said. "Me neither."

CHAPTER TWENTY

Jeffrey found his mother's Impala parked in her usual space in front of the hospital. She could have easily walked to work and back, but May Tolliver would never add more minutes to the time it took for her to get that first drink after her shift in the hospital cafeteria ended.

As usual, she had left the windows down to keep the car from turning into an oven. Jeffrey smelled stale cigarette smoke wafting through the air as he opened the door. She always kept a spare key in the glove compartment, and he found it underneath a bunch of religious tracts and brightly colored pamphlets that must have been stuck under the windshield wiper of the car at some point. She might have been a chain-smoking drunk, but May never littered.

The engine turned over after he pumped the gas several times, and Jeffrey brushed cigarette ash off the gear console as he shifted the car into drive. The windows were foggy from nicotine, and he took out his handkerchief, wiping the windshield as he drove out of the parking lot. If his mother left the hospital before he got back with the car, she would easily put two and two together and realize that with Jeffrey in town he had probably borrowed her car. He had "borrowed" it often enough as a teenager, and May had never mentioned it to a soul. The two times Jeffrey had been pulled over by sheriff's deputies, May had insisted she had loaned the car to her son.

Jeffrey drove aimlessly through downtown, not heading in any particular direction. He felt sick in his gut, like someone had died. Maybe someone had. He was sinking back into that old feeling that his life was totally out of control. He was the eye of a storm that caused nothing but destruction.

He could not get over the fact that all these years Robert had even for a minute entertained the thought that Jeffrey had killed Julia Kendall. Back in Hoss's office, when Robert had asked the question, Jeffrey had been too shocked to show anything but anger. Even when he denied it, tried to tell Robert what had really happened, the other man had simply shaken his head, like he did not want to hear whatever yarn Jeffrey had concocted to explain his actions.

"It doesn't matter," Robert had kept saying. "I'll take the rap."

Jeffrey realized he was close to the funeral home, and he took a last-minute turn across the highway, pulling into the lot. He parked in the back, hoping Deacon White would not have the car towed. Jeffrey was sick of borrowing people's cars and shoes and whatever else he'd taken these last few days. He wanted to be in his own home in his own bed. He wanted to be alone. The cave was the closest thing he could think of that might bring him some peace.

No one came out of the building to warn him off, so Jeffrey got out of the car and walked the back way to the cemetery. He had a grandfather buried somewhere on the hill, but Jimmy Tolliver had never mentioned the man's name. Knowing how these things worked, Jeffrey guessed that Jimmy's old man had taught him everything about parenting that he knew; which was to say, not a lot. Jeffrey had never felt that genetic urge that some men feel, like they had to get a woman pregnant and pass on their heritage. Maybe nature was correcting an error. Some people were not meant to pass on their blood.

As he walked into the woods, Jeffrey could not help but think of Sara and the way she had talked to him. She obviously believed everything Lane Kendall had said, no matter the fact that the woman was lying trash. Jeffrey still felt the burn of shame Lane had brought him

all those years ago, the way she had talked around town, letting everyone know that she was sure Jeffrey had raped her daughter, even
though Julia's story had changed so many times even she could not
keep up with it.

But what was rape? People always thought of it as something violent and vicious, some deranged psychopath forcing a woman to
spread her legs under threat of harm. Julia had been with plenty of
boys, and Jeffrey was certain she had not wanted any of them. She had
been looking for love and acceptance, and seen sex as a way to get that.
Probably most of the guys who went with her knew that, but at that
age, it was hard to care. If a girl was more than half willing, you were
halfway there. Being sweet to Julia before she lifted her skirt or holding her for a few minutes afterward was the price you paid to get laid.
Some of the boys even joked about it, trying to guess who had done
what to get in her pants. The jokes had flown the day Julia had shown
up with that damn necklace, acting like she had finally convinced
someone to love her. The poor fuck who'd given it to her had probably been shitting in his pants when she started showing that thing off.

Maybe some guy had felt guilty for taking advantage of her, figured out after coming in her mouth that maybe she wasn't exactly enjoying it. Of course, what man hadn't had sex with a woman who
wasn't exactly into it? Drunk as he was the other night, Jeffrey had
known Sara wasn't in the mood, but he had somehow managed to get
her to say yes. He had been so desperate for that release, for that moment when everything seemed okay, that he had ignored the fact that
she was doing him a favor.

Julia Kendall had called it doing a guy a favor. Jeffrey could still
remember the way she looked at him, twirling that stupid cheap necklace around her finger, saying, "Hey, Slick, you want me to do you a
favor?"

In the forest, Jeffrey stopped at the mouth of the cave. The boards
had been broken away, probably where Hoss had come in to get the
bones. Julia's bones. Jeffrey hesitated before going in, thinking this
was a grave, no longer his boyhood hideout. Still, he went in, thinking
there was no better place for him to be right now.

He sat on the bench, his mind again going back to Sara. She thought he was guilty, and why not? The things people had been telling her were horrible—and some of it was true. God only knew what Nell was putting into her head right now. Back when Julia disappeared, Nell had started acting differently around him. She had started to pull away, like she did not quite trust him anymore. Three weeks before graduation, she had broken up with him in the gymnasium, yelling at him like he was a dog. God, she had hated him that day, and Jeffrey still did not know what he had done.

He had left the gym and run into Julia. She was back from wherever she had run off to, come home to help her mother with the new baby. Lane Kendall's husband was dead and she needed all the help she could get. Even with the false charges Julia had made against Jeffrey and Robert, when he ran into her—and he had literally run into her, she had been standing right outside the gym doors—and she asked if he wanted her to do him a favor, he had said, "Sure."

The rape allegations had died down when Julia left town the first time. No one really believed her, anyway. She had slept around too much for people to think she was not a willing participant, and why the hell would a man rape her when she was giving it up easily enough?

"I'm sorry about what I said," Julia had told him, following him through the woods, the back way to the cave. "I didn't mean to get y'all in trouble."

"You didn't get us in trouble."

She laughed. "I bet not," she said. "That old Hoss can't abide anybody doing you wrong."

Jeffrey had not responded. They had reached the cave, and he held back the vines.

"It's dark in there."

"You gonna do this or not?" he said, giving her a push toward the cave. At seventeen, Jeffrey had not yet learned the fine art of seduction. Hell, he hadn't even learned how to keep his brain working when all the blood in his body rushed to that one place. Standing outside the cave, knowing that in a few minutes Julia was going to be doing the one thing Nell refused to do, his pants had been so tight across the front that he could barely move.

"You still mad at me?" she asked, a curious smile at her lips as she glanced down at his crotch. "Maybe I shouldn't go in there."

"Suit yourself," he said, going into the cave ahead of her, his erection so painful he was surprised he could speak.

Jeffrey looked around the cave now, trying to remember what it felt like to have Sara in here. Certainly, better than when Julia was there. She had finally followed him inside and within minutes she had started crying, telling him she had made a mess of her life, apologizing for what she had said about Robert and Jeffrey. He had gotten angry because all he wanted was a blow job, not her fucking life story.

Julia had wanted him to kiss her, but Jeffrey had refused. There was something ugly about the shape of her mouth, and all he could think about was how many other guys had been there. In the end, he had told her to go away. When she would not go, he left the cave. The next time he saw Julia Kendall, Sara was there and Julia was nothing but a skeleton, laid out on the rocks as if she had gone to sleep that day, waiting for Jeffrey to come back.

The question was, did Robert really kill her? God knew he hated the girl for spreading that rumor that they had raped her. Unlike Jeffrey, who just chalked it up to Julia trying to get attention, Robert had seethed with the kind of hatred that burns you from the inside. Maybe it was because Jeffrey knew that he would be going away to Auburn in the fall, or maybe it was because he knew how baseless the allegations were, but he had not taken Julia's charges to heart the way Robert had. In retrospect, Robert could have been angry because he felt guilty. Someone had made that baby.

Jeffrey took a deep breath and slowly let it go. Robert could not have killed her. He did not even know how she had died. Someone out there did, though. Someone had been in this cave with Julia. An argument had sparked or maybe whoever did it had just had enough of her. Jeffrey had seen this kind of thing all the time when he was a cop in Birmingham. It was depressing when you heard firsthand the stupid excuses people could come up with to try to justify the fact that they took another life. Was there a man out there right now, going to church on Sundays, playing ball in the yard with his kids after work, telling himself he was still a good guy because Julia Kendall had asked for it? The thought made him sick.

He rested his foot on the coffee table and looked around the dank cave. The first time they had found this spot, he had thought it was the best place in the world. Now it just looked like a damp hole in the ground. More than that, it was a tomb.

He stood as best he could and walked out into the sunlight. Slowly, he made his way back toward the funeral home, trying to think about what to do next. He wanted answers to all of this, wanted it solved once and for all. Robert was not going to help him with anything, but being a cop, Jeffrey was used to noncooperation from the chief suspect. Maybe that's what Jeffrey needed to do now, think about this case like a cop instead of as Robert's friend. Looking at it that way, he had forgotten an important step: talking to the victim's family.

A few years before he moved to Grant County, Jeffrey had spent two weeks driving around the South, looking at all the historic homes he could only read about when he was growing up. The trip was born of impulse and the need to get out of Birmingham while a certain assistant district attorney he had been dating cooled her heels over Jeffrey telling her there was no way in hell they were going to get married. Looking back, it had been one of the best times of his life.

Among other sights on the trip, he saw the Biltmore House, Belle Monte, and Jefferson's Monticello. He toured battleships and historic battlefields and walked the same path Grant took to Atlanta. Wandering through downtown after viewing The Dump, an old apartment building that really was a dump yet held the distinction of being where Margaret Mitchell had written most of *Gone with the Wind,* he happened upon a classically designed mansion called the Swan House.

Like everyone else of any rank in Georgia, the Inman family had got its money from cotton and decided to build a house that celebrated their wealth. They had hired a local architect named Philip

Trammell Shutze to design their mansion, and he had come up with nothing short of a masterpiece. The Swan House had some of the most beautiful rooms Jeffrey had ever seen, including a bathroom with floor-to-ceiling pink marble that had been painted over to look like white marble; the lady of the house had not liked the original color. Long after the tour had ended, he had managed to sneak into the opulent library and just stare at the old books on the shelves. Jeffrey had never stood in such a room in his life, and he felt at once in awe and humbled.

In great contrast, Luke Swan's house was the kind of shack even Jeffrey had looked down on when he was a kid. As a matter of fact, the house was so bad that somewhere along the way the Swan family had simply abandoned it and moved into a trailer home parked in the driveway. Stacks of newspapers and magazines stood on the porch, just waiting for a stray cigarette or match to bring the whole place down. It stank of poverty and hopelessness, and Jeffrey thought not for the first time that there were still large chunks of the rural South that had not yet fully recovered from Reconstruction.

As Jeffrey parked on the dirt road in front of the house, six or seven dogs ran out to the car—the standard redneck house alarm. A majestic-looking mailbox stood at least four feet high in front of the driveway, fancy script giving the street numbers. Just to be certain, Jeffrey checked the numbers against the page he had ripped out of the phone book he had found dangling from a wire by the pay phones outside Yonders Blossom. The book was at least ten years old, but people in Sylacauga did not tend to move around much. There were only two Swans listed in town, and Jeffrey had taken the wild guess that Luke was not associated with the ones who lived near the country club.

"Git back!" a woman yelled at the dogs as Jeffrey got out of the car. The animals scattered and the old woman stood on the cinder block porch outside the trailer, leaning heavily on a wooden cane. Her cheeks were sunken in, and Jeffrey guessed she had left her teeth in a glass somewhere inside the trailer.

She asked, "You come about the cable?"

"Uh . . ." He looked back at his mother's car, wondering what she must have been thinking. "No, ma'am. I came to talk to you about Luke."

She clasped her housedress together with a gnarled old hand. He walked closer and he could see her rheumy eyes were having trouble focusing.

As if she knew what he was thinking, she said, "I got the cataracts."

Her accent was so heavy that he had trouble understanding her. "I'm sorry."

"Not your fault, is it?" she asked, no menace in her tone. "Come on in," she said. "Mind that first step. My grandson was gonna fix it for me, but then, well, I guess you know what happened."

"Yes, ma'am," Jeffrey said, testing the bottom step. The cinder block shifted, and he could see where rain runoff from the trailer had eroded the soil underneath. He kicked some dirt and stones under it, making it a bit more level, before following her into the trailer.

"Not much," the old woman said, the understatement of the century. The place was a pigsty, the narrow design making it seem like the walls were closing in. More newspapers and magazines were piled around the room, and Jeffrey wondered what she was doing holding on to all this stuff.

"My late husband was quite the reader." She indicated the piles of magazines. "Couldn't bear to part with his things when he passed." She added, "The emphysema got him. Don't smoke, do you?"

"No, ma'am," he said, trying to follow her into the main room, a combination kitchen/dining room/living room that was little more than ten feet square. The trailer smelled of chicken fat and sweat, with a slightly medicinal undertone that older people got when they stopped taking care of themselves.

"That's good," she said, putting her hands out in front of her to feel her way toward her chair. "Smoking's horrible. Kills you something bad in the end."

Beside him, Jeffrey saw a stack of *Guns & Ammo* along with magazines of a considerably more adult nature. He glanced at the old woman, wondering if she was aware that a copy of the 1978 Christmas edition of *Penthouse* sat less than three feet from where she stood.

She said, "Go on and sit if you can find a place. Just move that stuff aside. My Luke used to sit there and read to me." She put her hand behind her, feeling for the chair. Jeffrey took her elbow and helped her sit. "I like the *National Geographic,* but the *Reader's Digest* is getting a little too liberal for my liking."

He asked, "Do you have someone who comes in to take care of you?"

"It was just Luke," she told him. "His mama done run off with a door-to-door salesman. His daddy, that was my youngest boy, Ernest, well, he never amounted to much. Died in the penitentiary."

"I'm sorry," Jeffrey said, walking across the sticky carpet. He considered the chair, but remained standing.

"You sure do apologize a lot for things that ain't got nothing to do with you," the woman said, feeling around on the table beside her. He saw a plate of crackers, and wondered how she chewed them. She put one in her mouth and he saw that she didn't chew them so much as let them melt on her tongue while she talked.

She told him amidst a spray of crumbs, "Cable's been out for two days now. I liked to had a fit when it went off—right in the middle of my program."

Jeffrey started to say he was sorry again, but he caught himself. "Can you tell me about your grandson?"

"Oh, he was a good boy," she said, her whiskered mouth trembling for a moment. "They got him down at the funeral home still?"

"I don't know. I guess."

"I don't know where I'm gonna get the money to bury him. All I got is my social security and the little bit I get from the mill."

"You worked there?"

"Up until I couldn't see no more," she said, smacking her lips. She paused a beat as she swallowed the soggy cracker in her mouth. "That was four, five years ago, I'd say."

She looked about a hundred, but she could not be that old if she was able to work in the mill that recently.

"Luke wanted me to get that surgery," she told him, indicating her eyes. "I don't trust doctors. I've never been to a hospital. Wasn't even born in one," she said proudly. "I say take the burdens God gives you and go on."

"That's a good attitude," Jeffrey said, though he wondered at choosing blindness for the rest of your life.

"He took care of me, that boy," the old woman said. She reached for another cracker, and Jeffrey looked back at the small strip of a kitchen, wondering if that was all the food she had.

He asked, "Was Luke into anything bad that you know about? maybe hanging out with the wrong kind of people?"

"He made money cleaning people's gutters and washing their windows. Nothing wrong with an honest day's work."

She had said "win-ders" for windows, and Jeffrey smiled, thinking he hadn't heard that word in a while. "No, ma'am."

"He had some trouble with the law, but what boy around here hasn't? Always something he was into, but the sheriff was real good about being fair. Let him make restitution to folks." She put the cracker in her mouth. "I just wished Luke'd found him a good woman to settle down with. That's all he needed was somebody to look after him."

Jeffrey thought that Luke Swan had needed a hell of a lot more than that, but he kept this opinion to himself.

"I hear he was going with that deputy's wife."

"That's what they say."

"He always did have a way with the women." She found this hilarious for some reason. She patted her knee as she laughed, and Jeffrey saw her bare gums as well as bits of cracker in her open mouth.

When she had finished, he asked, "Did he live here with you?"

"Back in the back. I slept here on the couch or in my chair sometimes. Don't take much to get me to sleep. I used to sleep out there in that tree when I was a little girl. My daddy'd come out sometimes and holler, 'Girl, you git down from that tree,' but I'd sleep right through it." She smacked her lips again. "You wanna see his room? That's what the other deputy wanted."

"Which deputy?"

"Reggie Ray," she said. "Now, there's a good man. He sings in the choir at church sometimes. I swear, that man has a voice like an angel."

Again, Jeffrey held back his opinion, though he wondered why Reggie did not mention before that he had been to Luke Swan's house. Considering Reggie was a deputy, the visit was routine, but still, Jeffrey wondered.

He asked, "Did Reggie find anything?"

"Not that I know of," she said. "You're welcome to go back and look around."

"I appreciate it," Jeffrey told her, patting her shoulder before heading back into the trailer.

He had to close the bifold door to the bathroom to get down the hall, but before he did, Jeffrey saw the filthiest toilet he had ever seen in his life. The walls were molded plastic shaped to look like tiles, and there were splatters of God knew what all around the tiny room. Only a blowtorch could have cleaned it off.

The old woman called, "You see anything?"

"Not yet," Jeffrey said, trying to breathe through his mouth. He pushed back another bifold door, thinking nothing could be worse than the smell in the hallway. He was wrong. Luke Swan's room was a stinking mess. The sheets were pulled back and there was a stiff-looking patch at the center of the twin bed. A single bare lightbulb dangled over the bed, suspended from a wire looped across the ceiling. He could not believe Jessie could be interested in anyone who lived in a place like this. She was too damn picky. He hated to admit it, but Jessie had a little more class.

Two plastic storage boxes by the bed seemed to hold the bulk of Luke Swan's clothes. The plastic was clear, and Jeffrey was thankful he did not have to touch anything to see inside. Spiderwebs and the kind of dirt that took years to accumulate were under the bed, but except for a filthy-looking white sock, there was nothing else there.

The closet had a locker shoved into it, the same kind you would find in a school. Stained underwear and socks were thrown onto the top shelf, shirts and jeans on the bottom. Jeffrey strained to see into the back, not wanting to put his hand into the locker. Just looking at Luke Swan's room made him feel like he had something crawling on him. Finally, he gave up and brushed the clothes out, hoping nothing bit him. Other than a pair of Speedos with a tear in the crotch, he found nothing.

Jeffrey turned around, looking back at the room. He was not about to touch the mattress, even if there was a letter explaining everything that had happened tucked underneath. Reggie would have done that, anyway. If he had found something incriminating, he sure as shit would have thrown it in Robert's face a long time ago.

Using his foot, Jeffrey kicked Swan's clothes back into the closet. After he had shoved everything back in, he changed his mind and pulled it back out. Hoping he did not get some sort of disease, Jeffrey put his hands on either side of the locker and pulled it out from the closet.

The metal made a horrible groaning noise, shaking the whole room, and the old woman called, "You okay in there?"

"Yes, ma'am," he told her, but then, looking behind the locker, seeing what was hidden in the back of the closet, he suddenly was not okay at all.

"How . . ." he began, but could not ask the question. He could only sit on the nasty bed and stare, his mind reeling for a moment, trying to come up with some kind of explanation or story—something that would help put Robert in the clear instead of pointing the finger right back at him. He kept coming back to the same conclusion, though, and he wanted a drink, several drinks, so bad he could taste the alcohol burning its way down to his belly.

"No," he said, like saying it out loud would make it true. "No," he repeated, but he still could not stop himself from asking, "Robert, what have you done?"

CHAPTER TWENTY-ONE

3:09 P.M.

"Jared?" Smith said, slamming down the phone. "Who's Jared?"

Sara looked panicked, and Lena tried to distract him, saying, "You said you'd let Marla go."

"Shut up," he told her, sauntering toward Sara. "Who's Jared?" he repeated. "Who is he?"

Sara kept her mouth closed, like she was wondering how far she could push him.

Smith placed the shotgun against her ear. "I'm'a ask you one more time," he said, his accent thicker as his voice dropped a few octaves. "Who's Jared?"

Jeffrey spoke, his voice thick with pain. "Jeffrey's son," he said, but even Lena could hear his uncertainty. He wasn't confirming it, he was asking Sara a question.

"He didn't know," Sara told Smith, her hand pressing to Jeffrey's good shoulder. "Jared has a father who raised him."

Smith pulled the gun away, resting it on his shoulder. "Fucker," he spat, turning around to his accomplice. "You hear that, Sonny? He's got another kid."

Lena was watching Sara, and the other woman's face went slack as if she was having a small seizure. She knew, Lena thought. She knew who they were.

Sonny was pissed that he had been given away, and he snapped. "Thanks a lot, *Eric*."

Smith ran over to his partner, and they spoke in harsh whispers to each other. Lena strained to hear them, but they were being too careful. She chanced a look back at Marla, and the old lady had a glint in her eye. Lena realized she had been playing the part all along. She glanced down at Marla's hands, trying to see where she had hidden the knife.

"Fuck off!" Smith screamed, and Sonny pushed him hard enough so that Smith stumbled and fell.

Glass and debris scattered as Smith scrambled to get up. He ripped off his mask, which sent a sharp fear through Lena, as if someone had reached into her chest and grabbed her heart. Smith got back in Sonny's face, screaming obscenities, and all Lena could think was that they were all going to die now. He had shown his face. He did not care who saw him, which meant he did not think anyone would be alive to make an ID.

Sara screamed, "Look down! Don't look at him."

Molly did as she was told, but Lena was too late. Smith reeled around, his heavy boots crunching glass. They made eye contact, and Lena thought she had never seen anyone so dead in her life. Smith ran toward the back of the room, gun raised. She tried to grab him but he shrugged her off like a blanket.

"Don't look at his face," Sara repeated, just as Smith slapped her hard enough to knock her over. Still, she told Molly, "Don't look at him. Close your eyes."

Smith kicked Sara's shin, cutting a gash. He demanded, "What are you doing?"

"She hasn't seen you!" Sara screamed back, scrambling to sit up. "Molly hasn't seen you! Close your eyes!" She reached out to Molly, touching her leg before Smith pushed them apart.

"She has two children," Sara said, panic making her voice shrill. "Two boys at home. Let her go. She hasn't seen you."

Molly sat where she had been since this all started. She held Jeffrey's hand in her own, her eyes tightly closed. She might have been praying.

"She hasn't seen you," Sara repeated, her voice shaking. "She hasn't seen you. Let her go."

Smith stared at them, his eyes moving back and forth, and Lena could see him struggling to think this through. He glanced over his shoulder at his partner, but did not invite his opinion.

Lena said, "You could let her go. Let her take Marla."

Smith seemed to consider this, too. "What about my arm?" he asked. He turned back to Molly, who still had her eyes closed. "You said you'd suture it."

"I need the lidocaine," she said. "I need . . ." She turned and looked at Lena oddly. "Give me thirty-three cc's of the two percent lidocaine." Her tone was sharp, her tongue carving each letter like a razor as she repeated herself, "Thirty-three cc's of two percent."

Sara's confusion came too quickly to hide. Lena saw her brow knit, but Smith obviously knew enough to say, "You trying to put me out?" He pushed her with the toe of his boot. "Huh?"

"No," Molly answered. Still keeping her eyes averted from Smith, she managed to glance at the clock on the wall, reminding Lena that they would come at 3:32. Lena gave a tight nod, letting her know she understood. Twenty minutes to go.

Smith pushed the shotgun into Molly's face, even jumpier now. "Get out of here," he said. "I don't trust you. Take the old lady, too."

Molly stood, Sara with her.

"What are you doing?" Smith asked.

"She's my friend," Sara told him, embracing the nurse. "Tell my family . . ." Sara began, but obviously could not finish.

Molly went to Marla and tried to help her stand, but the old woman was too afraid to do anything.

"It's okay," Lena told her, reaching under Marla's arm to assist her. Marla's hand brushed across her ass, and Lena was confused until she realized that Marla had tucked the pocketknife into her back pocket.

Lena hazarded a look at Smith, but he had not seen anything. Likewise, Sonny seemed unaware.

"All right," Smith said, indicating the door. "Move it." He waved his gun at Marla. "Come on, get going before I change my mind."

Molly kept her head down as she walked with Marla toward the front door. Lena could see her whole body was practically vibrating with fear, and she knew that Molly had realized that her back was a target until she was safely across the street.

Smith strolled after them, his gait still casual. He whispered something as he passed Lena that she was glad she could not hear. She kept her expression neutral, wondering how she could get the knife out of her pocket and drive it deep into Smith's heart.

"Psst," Brad said. She lifted her chin, letting him know she was listening.

"What did she mean?"

Lena kept her voice as low as she could. "Time."

Brad thought for a moment. "Three thirty-two?" he whispered, and she nodded. "On your signal."

"Get ready," Smith told his partner, and Sonny leaned over the counter, lining up his rifle for a shot. "Now!"

Lena saw what they were doing and lunged toward the front of the room, screaming, "No!" just as the gun went off.

She had been several feet away, and Smith had ample time to ward off her blow. He looked annoyed, and pushed her away like he had done before, like he was swatting a fly. Lena stood quickly, but not to challenge him. She looked out the front windows, seeing Molly kneeling over Marla. The old woman had been shot in the back. SWAT swarmed, giving them both cover as they were dragged to the cleaners.

"Marla," Lena said, still looking out the window. "They got Marla." She turned on Smith, her fists raised. "You fucking bastard!" she yelled, pounding into him. It was just like with Ethan—he was nothing but a wall of muscle.

"Whoa," Smith said, stepping back, taking her with him. He

caught her hands easily, laughing at her anger. "You're a feisty one," he said, wrapping his hand around her ass and pulling Lena into him. "You like that, lady? You like that big cock?"

Lena clenched her jaw shut. "You killed her," she hissed, digging her fingernails into his arms. "You killed that old lady."

He put his lips close to her ear. "I might kill you, too, honey, but don't worry, we'll have a little fun first."

She jerked away, her hand catching on the bandage he had tied around his bicep. She threw the bloody cloth on the ground, then wiped her hands down her legs as if she could get the filth off herself. "You bastard," she said. "You murdering bastard."

He had his hand to his arm, and she could see the blood pooling through his fingers. "That's not good," he said.

Sonny put down his gun and took a bandana out of his pants pocket. He said, "Here," and Smith took the cloth.

"Wrap this around my arm," Smith ordered, holding it out to Lena.

"Fuck off," she said, and he gave her an open-palmed slap that sent her to the floor.

"Do it," he told her, handing her the bandana again.

Lena stood and took the cloth. His arm was bleeding profusely, though from what she could tell, the wound was not deep. Still, she tied a tourniquet around his upper arm, pulling it tight, wishing she was squeezing it around his neck.

"What are you looking at?" Smith asked Sara, pushing Lena away as he walked to the back of the room. Sonny had his gun raised again, and he gave Lena a look of warning before turning back to the door.

Smith repeated, "What are you looking at?"

"Nothing," Sara told him, kneeling by Jeffrey again. She put her hand to his face, and Lena saw he stirred, but did not wake. "He needs to be in a hospital."

"We're gonna take care of him right here," he said, using his foot to push over the case from the ambulance. He told Lena, "Grab that other shit."

She got the defibrillator and the IV kit, casting a look over her shoulder for Sonny's benefit. Brad had moved closer to the other man, but not enough to crowd him.

"I'm not a vascular surgeon," Sara said.

"You'll do," Smith told her, taking the bag from Lena.

Sara kept trying. "The axillary artery has been hit. I won't be able to see anything."

"Doesn't bother me," he said, kneeling down beside Jeffrey.

"I can't do a block under these circumstances," she told him. "I'm not an anesthesiologist."

"You keep making excuses, I'm gonna think you don't want to do this." Smith dumped the IV kit onto the floor.

"What are you doing?"

"Might as well give him a fighting chance," Smith said, unbuttoning Jeffrey's shirt cuff.

"I can do that," Sara told him, but Smith waved her off.

Sara demanded, "Why are you doing this?"

"Why not?" he shrugged as he rolled up Jeffery's sleeve. "Nothing better to do." Still, he gave Lena a look over his shoulder, and she wondered again if he was showing off for her benefit or if he just liked playing these games. Maybe it was a little of both.

"You should insert the cannula . . ." Sara began, but Smith shot her a look of warning.

Lena watched as he wrapped the rubber tourniquet around Jeffrey's upper arm. He was by no means an expert, but he managed to get the needle inserted into the vein on the third try.

Smith laughed at his failed attempts. "Good thing he's passed out."

"You've seen this done before," Sara said. "How often do you need infusions?"

He looked up at her, and Lena could see his crystal blue eyes registering first alarm, then something that looked like joy. They both stared at each other for a few beats, before Smith laughed.

He said, "Took you long enough."

"You've got it wrong," she told him, and Lena wished to God she knew what Sara was talking about. "You've got it all wrong."

"Maybe," he said, glancing at his accomplice. The other man was staring out the front window as if he had no concern about what was going on in the rest of the room. Lena knew that he was watching them, though. Sonny, or whatever his name was, had eyes in the back of his head.

Smith connected the IV, then called Lena over. "Hold this," he said, meaning the drip bag. "Make yourself useful."

Lena sat down, her back against the wall. She kept one hand tucked behind her as the other held the IV. Smith was less than a foot away from her, but Lena had no idea what she could do.

Smith opened the medical case. "Tell me what to give you."

Sara said, "I can't do this."

"Lady," Smith told her, "you don't have a choice."

She sat back, shaking her head. "I refuse."

"I'll kill a kid for every minute that you don't do this," he said. When she did not respond, he took the gun out of his waistband, held it up, and aimed the muzzle toward one of the girls.

Brad moved in front of the child, and Smith said, "I'll shoot you, too."

"And then what?" Sara asked. "You shoot them all, and it's just me left?"

He nodded toward Lena without looking at her. "I can think of some other things to do," he said. "What do you think about that, Doctor? You wanna watch that, too?"

"You wouldn't," Sara said, though surely she knew he would.

He asked her, "You think that kind of thing runs in families?"

Sara looked down, something like shame passing across her face.

Lena could not keep herself from asking, "What are you talking about?"

"Don't you know?" Smith responded. "Of course you don't know. It's not like he's gonna advertise he's a fucking rapist, is it?"

"Who?" Lena said, just as Sara told Smith, "No."

"Don't like that, do you?" Smith asked. He kept the gun pointed toward Brad, saying, "How about you, Skippy? You like hearing that?"

Brad shook his head. "It's not true."

"What's not true?" Lena asked.

Smith looked back at Sara. "Tell them, Doc. Tell them why we're all here."

"No," Sara insisted. "You've got it all wrong."

Smith's lips peeled back in an awful smile as he told Lena, "Your boss? Big Chief Tolliver lying out there with his head blown off? He raped my mother, and I'm the bastard that paid for it."

CHAPTER TWENTY-TWO

Sara woke from a hard sleep, no dreams to frighten her this time. She was in Jared's small bed, tooking at a life-size rubber eagle, one of Auburn University's mascots, suspended by piano wire over her head. How the boy managed to sleep with that thing hovering, as if it was going to pounce at any moment, was a mystery. Little boys were strange creatures, as evidenced by the bug-eyed iguana hungrily staring at her from its glass cage.

She sat up, rubbing the sleep out of her eyes. The air conditioning was on, but she was hot from the afternoon nap. Sara had never liked sleeping in the middle of the day, and as if to remind her of this, her right temple throbbed with a dull pain.

In the kitchen, she found a Coke and some aspirin. Between the caffeine and the drugs, she hoped to chase away what was beginning to feel like a migraine headache. Maybe the cotton mill or the quarry spat toxic fumes into the air. Sara had been nursing a headache from the moment she got to Sylacauga.

She padded to the back of the house, feeling a bit like the walking dead. Naps were supposed to be replenishing, but she felt like she hadn't slept a wink. Maybe she had dreamed and just could not remember. If it was bad enough to make her body feel this way, Sara was glad she had forgotten whatever nightmare her mind had come up with.

Nell had warned her not to use the children's bathroom, and after a quick glance, Sara saw why. Towels and clothes were strewn about and there was a suspicious number of toys in the bathtub, considering Jen's and Jared's ages.

She walked through the master bedroom, thinking Nell had surprisingly good taste when given a palate that did not include orange and blue. A huge sleigh bed with a homemade quilt was angled out from the corner, giving a great view of the sunny backyard. An antique rocker was in the corner, and a large chest of drawers had a television on top.

Like the bedroom, the bathroom was neat and tidy. The towels matched the quilt on the bed, and the throw rugs on the floor complimented everything. Sara put the Coke bottle on the edge of the tub as she used the toilet, covering a large yawn with the back of her hand. She was trying to peel off a piece of toilet tissue from the roll when she heard someone in the house. Like some sort of barn animal, Sara had left the bathroom door open, and she rushed to wipe and pull up her pants just as a loud crash came from the front room. Without thinking, she opened her mouth to ask if anyone needed help, but stopped when she heard a suspicious-sounding noise.

Carefully, she walked into the bedroom as another loud crash echoed through the house. Whoever it was had made it to the kitchen. Doors slammed closed one after the other as someone searched the cabinets, just as Sara had done in Jessie's kitchen the day before.

She glanced around, realizing she was trapped in the back of the house. The bathroom led to the bedroom, and other than the window, the only way out was through the hall. Footsteps padded down the hallway as she considered this, and Sara ran back to the bathroom and jumped into the tub, hiding behind the curtain just as the intruder walked into the bedroom.

Whoever was here was looking for something—that much was obvious. The closet door was opened and stuff was shoved off the shelves and onto the floor. Sara felt a bead of sweat roll down her back as the intruder entered the bathroom.

She could see the shadow of a large man standing by the toilet, a few inches from where she hid. The light cast him in shadow, and even though Sara knew he could not see her, she felt exposed, as if any minute she would be found. The man reached down and took something off the edge of the tub. The Coke bottle. He would see that there was condensation, feel the refrigerated drink inside.

He said, "Who's there?"

Sara put her hand to the back of the shower, feeling the cool tiles. Her mind flashed back to that bathroom in Atlanta, where her attacker had left her handcuffed to the stall. She could not forget the sensation of the cold tiles pressing into her bare knees. She had stared at those tiles for what seemed like hours as she waited to be found. Her mouth had been taped shut to keep her from screaming, and there was nothing she could do but watch her life bleed out onto the floor.

The curtain screeched back on the rod, and she jumped, pressing her back to the wall.

Robert stood there with the Coke in his hand. He was obviously angry to see her. "What are you doing here?"

Sara put her hand to her chest, relief washing over her like a flood. She lost it quickly, though, as she realized that she was not the one who did not belong in the house. Why was Robert here? What was he looking for?

She tried, "I was . . ."

Robert looked around, as if an excuse were hidden somewhere in the bathroom. "Get out of there, Sara."

She wanted to do as he said, but her feet would not move.

"What do you want?" he asked her. When she did not answer, he put the bottle down on the counter and started rooting through the bathroom cabinet.

"Nell should be back soon," Sara told him as he threw towels and boxes onto the floor.

He glanced at her over his shoulder. "Possum took them all to see the dollar movie and out to eat."

Sara finally managed to move. Robert would not hurt her; he was Jeffrey's friend. She lifted her foot over the edge of the tub, saying, "Jeffrey should—"

"He won't be back for a while," Robert said, then, "Don't go anywhere, Sara."

Still, she kept moving, heading toward the door. "I'm just—"

"Don't move!" he ordered, the sound of his voice echoing off the walls. There was a wild look to his eyes, and she slowly realized how desperate he was.

She fought back the panic welling inside of her. "I have to go."

He stood, blocking her way. "Go where?"

"Jeffrey's waiting on me."

"Where?"

"At the station."

He stared a hole right through her. "You're lying, Sara. Why are you lying to me?" When she did not answer immediately, he yelled, "Why are you here, goddammit? You're not supposed to—"

"I-I . . ." she stammered, looking for the right words. She had never felt scared of Robert before, but like a lead weight, it fell on her that he was wanted for murder. Looking at him now, she wondered if Jeffrey was wrong. Maybe if he was backed into a corner, Robert *was* capable of killing.

"Come with me," he said, grabbing her by the arm, not giving her a choice. He threw Sara toward the rocking chair, ordering, "Sit down."

Sara tried to refuse, but her knees gave out and she sank into the rocker.

Robert went to the large chest of drawers under the window, close enough to stop her if she tried to move. The television had tinfoil-wrapped clothes hangers bent awkwardly to form antennae. Robert opened the top drawer and the tinfoil made a dry, scritchy noise.

"What are you looking for?" she asked. "Money? Do you need money? I can give you—"

He was on her in a flash, his hands grasping the arms of the rocker, his face less than an inch from hers. "I don't want your fucking money! Do you think money's gonna solve this? Is that what you think?"

"I—"

"Dammit!" He pushed away from her, the chair rocking violently. In a flash, his calm returned, and he went back to the chest of drawers. Sara watched as he opened the bottom drawer and pulled out a small black box that she instantly recognized as a gun safe.

She jumped out of the chair, but stopped when he turned on her, the same angry expression on his face. She pressed into the wall, trying to edge her way to the door as he dialed the combination on the safe. She should move faster. Why wasn't she running? Why couldn't she move?

He seemed calmer now that he had found what he was looking for. "Where're you going?"

"Why do you need a gun?"

"I'm leaving town," he said, using his thumb to dial in the combination. The safe popped open, and he took out the gun. "Six–thirteen, the final score for the last game we played against Comer."

"I should—"

He pointed the gun at her. "Don't go, Sara."

Again, her mind flashed back to the terror she had endured in the bathroom at Grady Hospital, bleeding from everywhere, unable to move her arms or legs, unable to get help. She would not—could not—be trapped like that again. There would be no surviving after that.

He ordered, "Sit down," indicating the chair.

She wanted to be calm, but her heart would not obey. "I won't tell anyone," she told him, realizing that she was begging.

"I can't trust you to do that," he said, using the gun to wave her back to the chair. "Come over here and sit down." He waited for her to comply. When she didn't, he added, "I'm sorry about before. I shouldn't have yelled at you."

She stared at the gun, willing her words to be true. "It's not loaded."

He pulled back the slide with a sharp, metallic click. "It is now."

She stayed where she was. "What are you going to do?"

"Nothing," he told her, then, "Tie you up."

Sara's heart jumped into her throat. She could not be tied up. She would go crazy if she was confined like that. She tried to take a breath, but realized that was the problem. She was breathing too much, too hard.

"I need a head start," he told her, though she had not asked. He pointed the gun at her again. "Get away from the door, Sara. I *will* shoot you."

"Why?" she asked, praying that logic would kick in, but also wondering if this was the last thing Luke Swan saw before his head was blown apart.

"I don't want to hurt you," he said, as if that would reassure her despite the fact that he was pointing a gun at her chest. "But you'd tell Jeffrey and he'd find me."

Sara felt her hands start to tremble. She would hyperventilate soon if she did not get her breathing under control. "I don't know where Jeffrey is."

"He'll be back here soon enough," Robert told her, going through the closet again, still keeping the gun trained on her. He kicked out a small toolbox. "He can't leave you alone. I've never seen anything like it."

Sara gauged the distance to the hallway. Robert was still an athlete. He could make a dash as quickly as she could. A bullet would be even faster, but she had to take the chance. She took a small, almost imperceptible step, closing her distance to the door.

Robert snapped open the toolbox with one hand. He kept his eyes on Sara even as he pulled out a roll of silver duct tape.

Her mouth opened, but she could not take a breath. Her attacker had used the same kind of tape to keep Sara quiet while he raped her. She had been unable to scream as he assaulted her.

"I wish there was something else I could use," Robert said. "This is going to hurt when it comes off."

"Please," she said, her voice shaking. "Lock me in the closet."

"You'll still yell."

"I won't," she promised him, her legs shaking so badly she thought her knees might give out. "I swear I won't yell," she repeated, tears streaming down her face at the thought of the tape touching her skin. Somehow, she managed to take another step toward the door. She held out her hands to him, saying, "I promise I'll be quiet. I won't say a word."

The fact that she was on the verge of being out of control seemed to make him even more calm, and he spoke to her in what sounded like a reasonable voice. "I can't trust you to do that."

She barked a sob. "Oh, please, Robert. Please don't do this. Please . . ."

"Don't—"

Sara bolted toward the door, heading into the hallway. Robert went from a crouch to a dead run, and she felt his fingertips brush against her arm as she passed by. Sara dared not look over her shoulder as she rounded into the living room. She was almost to the front door when hands clamped around her waist, slamming her into the coffee table as Robert tackled her from behind. Possum's Auburn memorabilia fell to the ground and shattered, the thick glass top of the table cracking it neatly in two underneath their combined weight. The wind was knocked out of Sara, and she felt her lungs lurch in her chest.

"Goddammit," Robert said, jerking her up by the waist. Sara's arms flew up, and her feet scattered glass all over the room as he dragged her back toward the bedroom.

"Please—" she begged, digging her fingernails into the back of his hand. She clawed for anything to stop him, hanging onto the wall, knocking down pictures and plants. She grabbed onto the doorjamb as he tried to force her into the bedroom and she felt her fingernails tear as he finally managed to shove her inside.

"Jesus," Robert yelled, dropping Sara onto the floor as she raked a chunk of skin off his arm. She scrambled to get up, screaming in her head but unable to make any noises come out of her mouth. Her hands were bleeding, but she would fight him more if she had to.

"Stop it!" he warned, kicking her feet out from under her. She crawled on her hands and knees toward the door and he picked her up by the middle again.

Sara finally managed to yell, "Let me go!" just as Robert threw her back on the floor. Her head banged against the wood and she felt her stomach roll, her eyelids flutter.

"Sara," he said, helping her sit up. He cradled her head in his lap, saying, "Stop this. I don't want to hurt you."

"Robert, please . . ." she begged, fighting not to be sick. She tried to get up but there was no strength left in her body. All of her muscles felt useless and she could not make her eyes focus on anything.

Robert rested her head back onto the floor and dragged the rocking chair from the other side of the room. "I didn't want to hurt you," he said, gently picking her up off the floor. Her arms and legs flapped like a rag doll's as he placed her in the chair. She tasted vomit in the back of her throat, and without warning, the room began to pitch again.

"Don't pass out," he told her, though she wondered how he could stop her. Sara had never passed out in her life, but her head was reeling so much that she thought she might be concussed.

She took deep breaths even though her ribs ached from the effort. Robert stared at her, watching her every move. After what seemed like several minutes, Sara's vision cleared, and her stomach stopped feeling so tight.

"Just got the wind knocked out of you," Robert said, obviously relieved. Still, he kept his hand on her chest for a minute, making sure she could sit up on her own. He kept a careful eye on her as he stretched out a strip of tape. He pulled down her sock, then wrapped the tape around her ankle and the leg of the chair.

Sara watched, incapable of doing anything to stop him.

"I can't go to prison," he said. "I thought I could, but I just can't. I can't have another night like last night."

He taped her other leg to the chair, which began to rock. Sara felt her stomach turn, but he stopped the rocking, then sat back on his heels, looking at her. "I want you to tell Possum I'll send him money when I get settled. He's worked his ass off to get that store, and I'm not going to have him lose it because I jumped bail."

Sara strained her legs against the tape, feeling her circulation being cut off. "Robert, please don't do this."

He fed out another strip of tape. "Put your hand on the arm of the chair."

Sara did not move, and he lifted her arm by the wrist and put it on the chair for her.

"I can't do this," she said, feeling like the life was seeping out of her. "I can't do it."

He stared at her with curiosity, as if she was overreacting. He offered, "I won't tape your mouth if you promise not to yell for help."

She broke into tears again, so grateful for this small concession that she would have done anything for him.

"Please don't cry," he said, taking out his handkerchief to wipe her tears. She thought of Jeffrey and his handkerchief, and how gentle he was with her. Sara started to cry even harder.

"Jesus," he whispered, as if Sara was punishing him. "It won't be long," he said. "Don't be like this, Sara. I won't hurt you." He looked startled for a moment, saying, "You cut your eye."

She blinked, just now noticing the blood clouding her vision.

"Damn, I'm so sorry," he said, wiping the blood. "I didn't mean for this to happen. I didn't mean for anybody to get hurt."

She swallowed, feeling some of her strength come back. Maybe she could reason with him. Maybe she could talk him into stopping now. She would promise not to yell, not to call anyone, if he would just leave her arm free.

Robert folded the handkerchief into a neat square. She tried to think of a way to get to him, to make him see that she was not a threat. "I'll tell Possum about the money," she said. "Who else? Who else do you want me to talk to? What about Jessie?"

He tucked his handkerchief back into his pocket and picked up the tape. "I tried to write a letter, but I've never been much good at that kind of thing."

"She'll want to know," Sara insisted. "Tell me, and I'll tell her."

"Jessie doesn't care about me."

"She does," Sara pressed. "I know she does."

He exhaled slowly, using his teeth to cut off a strip of tape.

Sara bit her lip hard enough to draw blood.

"I tried to make things work," he told her, taking her wrist. Sara tried to jerk away, but he forced her hand down to the arm of the chair.

She stared at his fingers as he taped her arm, feeling such deep despair that it almost took her breath away.

He sat back on his heels again. "That's not so bad." He reached out his hand to touch her mouth. "You bit your lip," he told her. Sara jerked away without thinking, and a look of hurt flashed in his eyes, as if he had not been the one responsible for all of this.

"I'm not what you think," he said. "I really did love her."

"Please let me go," she begged.

He rubbed his hands on his thighs. The gun was on the floor beside him, but Sara was hardly in a position to reach down and grab it. He had taped her tightly to the chair.

He repeated, almost to himself, "I really did love her."

Sara stared at the gun as if she could will it into her hand. She tried to fight the tremor in her voice when she said, "You say that like you don't anymore."

"I don't know what went wrong." He gave a weak smile. "What tells you in your heart that you love Jeffrey?"

"I don't know," Sara answered, unable to take her eyes off the gun. Finally, she forced herself to look at him, saying, "Robert, please. Don't leave me like this. I can't do it. I can't take it."

"You'll be okay."

"Not like this," she said. "Please. I'm begging you."

"Tell me what it is that makes you love Jeffrey," Robert asked, as if striking some sort of bargain. "What is it that makes you know?"

"I don't know."

"Come on," he said, and she realized that he was trying to help her calm down so that it would be easier for him to do what he needed to do.

"I don't know," she repeated. "Robert—"

"Has to be something," he said, giving her a forced smile, as if they were a couple of good people brought together under bad circumstances. "Don't tell me it's his sense of humor and great personality."

Sara racked her brain for something to tell him. There had to be a right answer, an answer that would make him free her from the chair and let her go, but she could think of nothing to say.

"You don't know?"

She told him the only thing she could think of. "It's the little things. That's what Nell says it is with Possum—the little things."

"Yeah?"

"Yeah," she echoed, trying to keep her panic down, trying to remember what Nell had said. Sara's voice sounded muted in her ears, as if she was talking underwater. "He's always home when he says he'll be and he doesn't mind going to the grocery store for her."

Robert gave a sad smile as he stood. "Maybe I should've gone to the grocery store for Jessie."

Sara felt her brain trying to make a connection but she could not understand why. Still, her mouth kept talking. "I'm sure you did sometimes."

He spooled out an extra-long strip of tape, using his teeth to tear it, letting the roll drop to the floor. "Never did," he told her, wrapping the tape around her chest and upper arms, fixing her back flat to the chair. "She said she liked doing that stuff. Made her feel like she was taking care of me."

"You never went to the grocery store?" Sara asked. Something Jeffrey had told her the night before clicked into place, and she felt an eerie sort of calmness spread over her.

He looked around for the tape. "Damn," he said, wincing as he knelt down in front of the bed. He put his hand to his stomach where he had been shot. "Rolled under the bed," he told her, bracing his hand against the mattress as he bent to retrieve the tape.

"You never went to the store for her?" Sara repeated, watching him kneel in front of the bed. His hand was still on the mattress, and in her mind she saw the bloody outline around Luke Swan's hand on the bed.

"Never went to the store," he assured her, sitting back up, breathing heavily. "Shit, that hurt."

Despite the fact that she could not move, Sara suddenly felt herself gaining some control over the situation. "Did she drive your truck much?"

"That's a funny question," he said, but still answered, "Yeah. She hated to, but if I parked behind her in the driveway, it was easier than backing them both out."

Sara strained her wrist against the tape, trying to see if there was any give, saying, "It wasn't you who went out to the store that night, was it, Robert? It was Jessie. She went in your truck."

He stretched out another long piece of tape. He would not look at her, and instinctively she knew that he wanted her to continue.

"The night Luke was shot," she said, almost dreading his answer. "Sunday. Was Jessie in your truck on Sunday?"

The strip was too long and the tape had folded on itself. He tried to pick it apart. "I don't know what you're talking about."

"Jessie was in your truck," Sara told him, more sure of herself now. "*She* went to the grocery store that night. There was milk and juice in your refrigerator. I saw the grocery list in your truck."

He continued to pick at the tape as if it could be saved.

"If it was Jessie who went to the store, then it was Jessie who came home. You told the truth, but you swapped things around. It was Jessie who came home, and it was you—" She stopped, astonished. "It was you in the bedroom," she said. "You were with Luke Swan, not Jessie."

Robert gave a forced laugh, giving up on the strip of tape and wadding it into a ball.

Sara continued to press, still certain of what had happened. "You were on the floor, kneeling in front of the bed."

"Maybe one will be enough," he said, picking up the roll of tape.

"Was Luke behind you when he was shot?"

308

He tore off a four-inch strip. "I'm going to have to cover your mouth."

She fought back her fear, needing to know the truth. "Just tell me what happened, Robert. You didn't kill him. I know you didn't kill him. Was it Jessie? Did she find you? Robert, you have to tell someone. You can't just leave it like this."

He started to put the tape over her mouth, but stopped at the last minute. Sara stared at him as he tried again, but something would not let Robert cover her mouth.

He walked back a few steps, sitting on the bed with obvious discomfort. He held the tape in his hands, cradling it like he was afraid it would explode.

Sara forced herself to speak gently, not knowing how far she could push him. She asked, "You were with Luke that night, weren't you?"

Robert stared at his hands, his silence enough of an answer to keep her going.

"Did Jessie know before that night?" She paused, then asked, "Robert?"

He slowly shook his head. "I tried so hard with her," he finally said. "She was the only woman in the world I thought I could be a husband to." He looked out the window into the backyard. Sara wondered if he was thinking of family barbecues and picnics, playing catch with the son he could never have. "She was supposed to be gone for a while," Robert continued. "Said she was going to her mama's, then to the grocery store, like she did every Sunday night."

"What happened?"

"She got into a fight with her mama." He let out a weary sigh. "She came home early, had time enough to put up all the groceries. Some kind of cop I am, huh? Didn't even hear her in the kitchen."

"Did she walk in on you?"

"She thought I was still over at Possum's watching the game."

"Did she walk in on you?" Sara repeated.

"I kept it hidden," he said, still not answering her question. "I kept it hidden for all these years." He rubbed his eyes with his fingers. "I made a deal with God. I promised Him I wouldn't do it anymore if He would give Jessie a baby." He dropped his hand. "That's all we needed, see, was to be a family. I would've been a good father."

Obviously, he expected some sort of confirmation, because he looked away when Sara would not give it. "God just knew better than to let it happen. Maybe He knew I couldn't hold up my end of the bargain."

"God doesn't make those kinds of deals."

"No," he said. "Not for men like me."

"Being gay doesn't make you a bad person."

He winced at the word.

Sara strained her leg against the tape, trying to see if there was any chance of escape.

"Everything I did with her turned to poison," he said. Inexplicably, a genuine smile came to his lips. "You know what it's like to be in love for the first time in your life?"

Sara did not answer.

"Dan Phillips," he said. "Damn, but he was beautiful. I know you wouldn't think a boy could be that way, but he had these baby-blue eyes that . . ." He put his hand to his mouth, then dropped it. "Does that make you sick to hear?"

"No."

"It made *me* sick," he said. "Julia caught us behind the gym. Hell, I never took any of her favors. Dan, neither. We didn't know that was where she met boys." He gave a harsh laugh. "It was our first time. First and last."

"What did she do?"

"Screamed to high fucking hell," he said. "I've never felt so ashamed in my life. Threw up for the next week, just thinking about how she looked at us. Like we were filth. Hell, we *were* filth. Dan ran off. Just left town. Couldn't take seeing my face anymore."

"Is that why you killed her?"

He looked wounded, as if she had insulted him. "If that's what you want to think, go ahead."

"I want to know the truth."

He stared at her for a beat. "No." he said. "I didn't kill her. For a while, I thought Jeffrey might have, but . . ." He shook his head. "Jeffrey didn't do it. There's probably a long list of men in this town who hated her for one reason or another, but he's not like that."

"You didn't rape her, either."

"No. That was just her way of torturing me, spreading that damn rumor. She thought I'd say what I was, try to defend myself by letting everybody know." His face turned into a scowl. "Like I'd do that. I'd rather die than let anybody know."

Sara had to ask. "And Jeffrey?"

"She thought I'd take up for him. Some friend I was, huh? Let people think Jeffrey raped her just to hide my secret." He paused, making sure she was listening. "I told you, Sara. I would rather die than have it get out."

He looked her in the eye when he said this, and Sara understood the threat.

She had to keep him talking. "Is that why you took the blame for shooting Luke?"

Robert stared at her, silent. "It was the same thing all over again."

"What was?"

"He knew," he said. "Takes one to know one, I guess."

"Luke?"

"I had him in the back of my car one night. Picked him up on a loitering charge down by the bowling alley." Robert looked out the window again. "He was cold, so I gave him my jacket. One thing led to another. I don't even really remember how it happened . . . just that it felt so good, and then the next day, it felt so horrible."

Sara could see the anguish on his face, and despite the situation, she found herself feeling sorry for him.

"I don't know how, but he kept my letterman jacket. Maybe he stole it out of the car when I wasn't looking. Doesn't matter how he got it, but my name's on it big as day. He called me at the station the next morning. Said he was going to wear it around town, tell everybody he was my *girlfriend*." He snorted in disgust at the word. "He kept following me around, flirting with me like a damn girl." His jaw worked, and he stared down at his hands.

"You could have just told him to go away," Sara pointed out. "No one would have believed him over you."

"That's not how it works here," he said, and part of her knew that Robert was right. Gossip was currency in a small town. Even a rumor that seemed improbable had more value than the boring truth of an everyday, normal life.

She asked, "What happened, Robert?"

He took his time answering, the truth more horrible to him than the lie he had been telling for the last few days. "I was weak. I just wanted somebody to comfort me, to feel right with." He looked back up at Sara, as if he expected her to any moment voice some kind of re-vulsion. "I called him up, told him to come over. Told him I wanted him to fuck me. You like hearing that? You know what we were doing, don't you? Fucking up the ass like two fairies."

Sara was unfazed. "Were you in love with him?"

"I hated him," he said, and she could tell by Robert's tone of voice that he really did. "He was like holding up a mirror, looking at my-self. All the ugly things about me." Under his breath, he added, "Fucking fairy. Faggot."

"Is that why you killed him?"

A car pulled up outside and they both waited as a door was closed. Seconds later, they heard Nell's next-door neighbor go into his house and slam the door. If he noticed the dogs were missing, he did not seem to care.

Sara prompted, "Robert?"

Again Robert paused before answering. "Jessie came in on us," he finally said. "She heard us. The noises we were making." He looked back at Sara as if to gauge her reaction. "She got my gun because she thought somebody had broken into the house. Didn't even bother to call the police." He jumped to a tangent. "That was what the fight with Faith was about. That's why she was home early."

Sara waited, not understanding.

"The fight with her mama. They were arguing because Jessie showed up stoned out of her mind. Drunk on something, taking pills, whatever. Her mama always blamed me for that even though Faith's drunk most days, out there swigging out of a flask when she's supposed to be watering the garden. That's how Jessie got through her life with me. That's how she dealt with my failures. She took pills to keep the pain back."

Sara heard the next-door neighbor slam his front door again. Sara waited, hoping he would come over to ask about his dogs, but the car started and she heard him reverse down the driveway.

"Jessie meant to shoot me," Robert told Sara, looking out the window, probably watching the neighbor head down the street. "She pulled the trigger because she was so shocked. She didn't exactly think it through, but she meant to shoot me, not him. At least that's what she told me later. Said she was so drunk that first she thought there were two of me and I'd finally managed to go fuck myself." He ran his tongue along his top teeth. "I didn't even know she was there. I hear Luke saying in my ear, 'Hey, how about it? You wanna join the party?' I didn't know what the hell he was talking about. Later, I figured he was talking to her. Provoking her, even though he had to see she had a gun in her hand. That's what he did with people, just pushed and pushed until they were over the edge."

"She shot him."

"I was wearing my T-shirt, but . . ." His voice trailed off, and he swallowed hard before continuing. "I felt this spray on my back, like this kind of mist. I didn't hear the sound until later, like two or three seconds later. It must have been faster than that, but my brain just kind of slowed it down. You know how it does that?"

Sara nodded. She knew from her own experience that trauma slowed things down, as if pain was something to be savored rather than endured.

"There was this kind of pop, like a balloon or something." He took a deep breath. "Then he slumped against me, and I felt this wet . . ." He shook his head at the memory. "He slid down my back."

Sara remembered how Robert had kept his back to the wall that night, gripping his shirt tightly in his hand. He must have been covered in blood.

"It was so fast afterward. Slow as it was when it happened, the rest was so fast."

"What happened?"

"Jessie shot at me."

"She missed," Sara said, remembering the bullet hole in the wall.

"I grabbed my backup out of the armoire. The safe wasn't even locked. After we lost the baby . . ." He shook his head, obviously not wanting to talk about that. "I wasn't even really thinking, other than maybe wishing the bullet hadn't missed when she fired." Robert paused. "She stopped, like she couldn't shoot me, even though she'd seen what I was. I just stood there for maybe a second, and I could suddenly see it all—everyone finding out what had happened, finding out who I am, and I put the gun to my belly and pulled the trigger."

"You were lucky it didn't do more damage."

"It was so fast," he repeated. "I couldn't even think. It was like . . ." He snapped his fingers.

Sara was quiet, hearing the snap echo like gunfire.

"It didn't hurt much," he added. "I thought it would hurt, but it wasn't until later that I felt the pain."

"Was it Jessie's idea to say you'd done it?"

"Hell no," he said, and she wondered if he was telling the truth. "She went over and grabbed a handful of pills. Spilled most of them on the floor. I just looked around, thinking, 'Fuck, what can I do?' "

"What did you do?"

"I guess I must've known what I was going to do when I pulled the trigger, but it took a while before my brain kicked in. I picked up the gun and the casings and wiped them off. A couple'a three seconds later, I heard somebody kick open the back door. I tossed everything on the floor, put the gun by his hand. Jeffrey came in, screaming, 'What the hell happened?' He went out to get you and I told Jessie to open the window and push out the screen. First time in her life she ever did something I told her to do without asking why."

"What about the bullet?" Sara asked. Robert had given the bullet to Reggie when he had confessed.

"Jessie got it out later. I don't know when, but she gave it to me. She told me exactly where she had found it in his head. Said it was my souvenir."

Sara knew there was only one time Jessie was alone with the body, and that was when Jeffrey and Sara were on the porch outside, waiting for Hoss. She must have sneaked in while they were arguing.

"Jessie's a lot smarter than folks think," Robert continued. "When y'all got there, she just played along, acted like she was too high to follow what was going on. Me, I was freaking out. I saw all the words coming out of my mouth, making up the story, not even thinking about the parts that didn't make sense. She let me do it, just stood there, letting me feed out enough rope to hang myself."

"Why?" Sara asked, still not understanding. "Why did you lie?"

"Because I'd rather be a cold-blooded murderer than a faggot."

The finality of his words hung heavy in the air, and Sara had never felt more sorry for anyone in her life.

"I'm just not right, Sara." He paused, as if he needed time to collect himself. "If I could get a knife and cut it out of me, I would. I'd cut out my fucking heart to be normal."

"You *are* normal," she insisted. "There's nothing wrong with you."

"It's too late."

"You can stop this," she said. "You can stop this right now. You don't have to leave. You're innocent, Robert. You didn't do any of this. None of it's your fault."

"All of it's my fault," he insisted. "I've sinned, Sara. I've sinned against God. I've broken my vows. I've been with another man. I wished him dead so many times. Jessie pulled the trigger, but I put him there. I brought him into our house. There's no going back now."

"You are who you are," she told him, even as she saw there was no reasoning with him. "You have no reason to be ashamed."

"Yes," he said, picking up the gun. "I do."

"Oh, God—"

He pointed the gun directly at her head, his hand steady. Sara closed her eyes, thinking of all the things she had never done in her life, wondering how her parents would get through this. Tessa still needed her, and Jeffrey . . . there was so much that Sara had left unsaid. She would give anything right now to be with him, feel his arms around her.

"You're not a murderer," she told him, her throat straining from the effort.

"I'm so sorry," Robert said, standing close enough for her to smell the sweat on him. Sara felt the cold metal of the gun press into her forehead, and she cried in earnest now, her eyes shut against everything else in the room. She heard the safety disengage, and another murmured apology.

"Please," she whispered. "Please don't. Please." She said the only thing that she thought might get through to him. "I'm pregnant."

The gun stayed where it was a few long seconds before it dropped, and Robert cursed under his breath.

She opened her eyes to find his back to her. His shoulders shook, and she thought he was crying until he turned around. Terror struck through her as she realized that he was laughing.

"Pregnant?" he repeated, as if she had just told the punch line to a really good joke.

"Robert—"

"Everything comes so goddamn easy to him."

Instantly, Sara realized her mistake. "I didn't—"

"Jesus," he hissed, pointing the gun back at her head. His hand shook this time, and he faltered, cursing again. "Fuck."

"Jeffrey doesn't know," she said, desperate to find the right thing to say. "He doesn't know!"

Robert kept the gun steady. "He never will."

"He will!" she screamed. "At the autopsy!" Robert's jaw set, and she kept talking as fast as she could. "Is that how you want him to find out? Do you want him to find out when I'm dead? He'll find out, Robert. That's how he'll find out."

"Stop," he ordered, pressing the gun to her skull. "Just shut up."

"It's a boy!" she screamed, almost hysterical with fear. "It's a boy, Robert. His son. Jeffrey's son."

He dropped the gun to his side again, not laughing this time.

"You know what it's like to lose a child," she told him, her body shaking so badly the chair began to rock. "You know what it's like."

He ignored her, nodding his head slowly, as if he was having some sort of conversation with himself. Sara saw his lips moving, but no words came out. He engaged the safety before tucking the gun back into his pants, then picked up the roll of tape again.

Sara watched him work the tape, knowing that he was going to tape her mouth shut so he could shoot her.

"He loves me," Sara gripped the arms of the chair with her hands, trying to break free.

Robert tore off a strip of tape.

"You're going to take that away from him," she said, the words rushing out of her mouth. "You're going to take away his child, Robert. His unborn child." Sara's voice caught on the words, mostly because she knew that there was no other time in the world when she would be able to say them. "*Our* child," she said, loving the way the words felt in her mouth. "*Our* baby."

Robert obviously heard the passion in her voice, because he stopped what he was doing.

"I'm carrying his child," Sara repeated, feeling herself letting go. She was at peace with this and whatever happened next. There was no explaining the logic behind her calm; it was simply the way she felt. "Our baby."

"He's gonna hurt you," Robert said. "Anybody who loves him always ends up getting hurt."

"When you love somebody," Sara told him, "that's the risk you take."

He put his fingers to her bottom lip, tracing the broken skin. Before she knew what was happening, Robert leaned down and brushed his lips across hers. It was the softest kiss Sara had ever received, and she was too shocked to pull away.

He said, "I'm sorry," then taped her mouth shut before she could answer. He stood in front of her, arms crossed over his chest. "I'm sorry for hurting you," he said. "I've hurt enough people in my life already." A sour look crossed his face, as if he'd had a thought that did not agree with him. "Jeffrey's gonna think I was into him," he said. "You tell him that's not true, all right? I never thought about him that way—not ever."

Sara nodded because that was all she could do.

"Tell him he's gonna be a great father, and that I would never take that from him." Robert's voice caught. "Tell him he was the best friend I ever had, and that there was nothing else to it."

Sara nodded her head again, trying to understand what had changed.

"I'm sorry about taping up your mouth. I know I promised."

Sara watched him go, helpless to do anything. Seconds later, she heard a car door slam and an engine start. She recognized the shoddy muffler of Robert's truck as he backed out of the driveway.

He was gone.

Sara began to cry again, this time from relief. She could not remember shedding so many tears in her life. Her nose began to run, and she sniffed, choking because of the tape. Her elation was quickly replaced by panic as she labored to get air into her lungs. Several seconds passed before the claustrophobia that threatened to overwhelm her started to recede. She had to get out of this chair. She could not just sit there waiting for Nell or Possum or Jeffrey to rush in and rescue her. She could not let any of them—especially Jeffrey—find her like this; helpless, afraid. No one was ever going to see her that way again.

Sara scanned the room, trying to find something that would help her get out of the chair. Rocking forward would land her face-first on the floor, so she rocked the chair side to side until she managed to tip it over. Her head whacked into the hardwood floor with a firm thud and she felt the same dizziness from before as her eardrum vibrated from the impact. A sharp pain ran up her shoulder where she had landed on it, but the arm of the chair had loosened from the fall, too. She jerked the wood back and forth several times, trying to dislodge the dowels, but the arm held firm. The chair was probably older than all of them, something Nell's ancestors had built to last a lifetime.

Sara took a breath, trying to think what to do next. The rockers on the bottom of the chair kept her from uprighting it and crawling to the door. Robert had taped her wrists, but not her fingers. Even if she could not manage to get free of the chair, she could try to take the tape off her mouth. If she could get the tape off her mouth, she could scream. If she could scream—even if no one could hear her—she would be okay.

Using all her strength, Sara pulled her arm up toward her mouth. After several minutes, perspiration on her arm helped the tape fold into a tight line that cut into her flesh, but she still forced up her arm, stretching the tape to its limit. When the tape had given as much as it would, Sara slid her arm back and forth, rubbing a nasty burn from the friction. The adhesive balled up in black dots, and Sara managed to force her arm a few inches forward. She tried to move it back, but the tape pinched up her skin, blood seeping out from underneath.

She considered the situation like a math problem, calculating the variables, adding in her pain threshold before attempting anything else. She arched her back as much as the tape around her chest and upper arms allowed, contorting her body until her shoulder screamed from the pain. Still, she kept pushing herself, stretching the tape around her chest until her mouth was inches from her hand. Her fingers had turned almost completely white from the lack of circulation, but Sara managed to touch the edge of the tape with her middle finger.

She gave herself a break, counting to sixty, letting the minute pass as the throbbing in her arm and shoulder leveled off to a dull ache. Her fingers had touched the tape. That was enough to keep her trying. Sara stretched again, trying to reach the tape covering her mouth. Sweat from her skin and blood and saliva from her mouth had worked on the adhesive, so that when she gave one final effort, she managed to grab the edge of the tape between her thumb and index finger and pull.

Though not enough to pull off the tape.

Sara's breathing was labored and she felt the room closing in on her again, but she coached herself not to quit, knowing she could not give up this close to the goal. Her body ached from the effort, but still, she managed to contract her muscles enough to make another grab. This time, the tape came off, and she opened her mouth, panting like a dog with its head out the window.

"Ha!" she screamed to the empty room, feeling as if she had vanquished some great foe. Maybe she had. Maybe she had vanquished her fear. Still, she was taped to the chair, lying pretty much facedown on the floor with few options and nothing but time.

"Well," Sara told herself. "No reason to give up now." This same kind of thinking had gotten her through medical school, and she was not about to abandon it now.

She focused on her arm, wondering if she could reach the tape with her teeth. The tape around her chest was already cutting into her breasts. She could not imagine what the bruises would look like, but Sara knew that bruises eventually faded.

Suddenly, she heard a noise in the front of the house. She opened her mouth to call for help but stopped herself. Had Robert changed his mind? Had he returned to finish the job?

Footsteps crunched across the glass from the broken coffee table, but no one called out. Whoever had entered the house was taking their time, going from room to room. She heard movement in the kitchen, and waited to see where they would go next. Had Robert forgotten something? When Sara surprised him, had he been looking for something other than Possum's gun? If it was someone who belonged in the house, they would have surely called out by now.

Sara clenched her teeth, fighting the pain as she tried to stretch toward her hand. She twisted and turned as much as she could in the chair, scratching Nell's good wood floors, pushing her mouth toward the tape.

"Sara?" Jeffrey stood in the doorway, Nell's ax in his hands. "Jesus Christ," he said, looking around the room, obviously searching for the person who had ransacked the house.

"He's gone," Sara told him, still straining toward her hand.

Jeffrey dropped the ax on the floor as he rushed toward her. "Are you okay?" He put his hand to her eye. "You're bleeding." He looked around the room. "Who did this? Who would—"

"Get me loose," Sara told him, thinking if she spent one more second in the chair, she would start screaming and not ever be able to stop.

Jeffrey must have understood, because he took out his pocketknife and sliced through the tape without asking any more questions.

"Oh, God," Sara groaned as she rolled out of the chair, unable to do anything but lie on her back. Her shoulder was killing her and her body felt bruised and battered.

"You're okay," Jeffrey told her, rubbing the circulation back into her hands.

"Robert—"

Jeffrey did not seem surprised to learn his friend had done this. "Did he hurt you?" His expression darkened. "He didn't—"

Sara thought about everything that had happened, what had brought Robert to this point, and said, "He just scared me."

Jeffrey put his hand to her face, checking the cut over her eye and her split lip. He kissed her forehead, her eyelids, her neck, as if his kiss could make everything better. Somehow, it did, and without thinking, Sara felt herself giving in to him, holding on to him as tightly as she could.

"You're okay," he told her, rubbing her back. "You're okay," he kept saying.

"I'm okay," she told him, and with a calming clarity, she knew he was right.

CHAPTER TWENTY-THREE

Smith kept smiling at her, waiting to see her reaction. "He raped my mother," he repeated. "Then he killed her to shut her up."

Lena felt neither shocked nor appalled. "No, he didn't," she said, never more sure of anything in her life. "I know the type of man who can do that sort of thing, and Jeffrey's not like that."

"What do you know about it?" Smith asked.

"I know enough," was all she said.

Smith clicked his tongue once. "You don't know shit," he said, petulant. He told Sara, "Let's get this started."

"I can't do a block," she said. "The brachial plexus is too complicated."

"You don't need to do a block," Smith told her. "He's passed out."

"Don't be stupid."

"Watch it, lady," he warned. He rummaged through the case Lena had brought from the ambulance. "Use this," he said, holding up a vial of lidocaine. He took out a flashlight and shone it in his face with a smile. "Now you can see."

Sara did not move.

"Do it," he ordered, his face made more horrific by the flashlight.

Sara seemed about to refuse, but something made her give in.

Maybe Jeffrey's condition was too serious to let it go on for much longer. Maybe she was trying to buy some time. Either way, she did not look confident that what she was about to do would work.

She took a pair of gloves out of the box and snapped them on. Even Lena could see that she was scared, and she wondered how in the hell Sara thought she could remove a bullet from Jeffrey's arm with her confidence so shaken.

Sara's hands steadied as she used a pair of scissors to cut away Jeffrey's shirt. If he was awake, he wasn't moving, and Lena was glad he could not see what was going on.

"Lena," Sara said. "I need to know if this is really lidocaine."

Lena felt the weight of her question. "I have no idea," she said.

"Why did Molly make such a big deal about it?"

"I don't know," Lena answered, wishing there was some way to tell Sara the truth. "Maybe she thought she could knock him out," she said, meaning Smith.

Sara took the bottle of medicine and snapped off the protective cap. She picked up a syringe and drew back the plunger.

To Smith, she said, "Pour all the Betadine on the wound."

Smith did not protest the order, and he even used a swab to wipe down Jeffrey's arm. With the blood washed away, Lena saw what looked like a small puncture wound in the front part of Jeffrey's armpit.

Sara took the syringe, holding it above the site. She said to Lena, "You're sure?"

"I don't know," Lena repeated, trying to convey with her eyes that it was all right. Smith was staring a hole into her, though, and Lena looked down at Jeffrey, hoping Smith did not see her certainty.

Sara put the needle right into the wound, and Lena sucked air through her teeth without even thinking about it. She forced herself to look away, feeling a phantom pain in her own arm. She saw Brad had moved closer to Sonny. He licked his lips, looking somewhere over her head. She guessed he was looking at the station clock, and a current of panic went up her spine as she realized that it might be fast.

Smith held up the flashlight so that Sara could see, giving Lena a perfect view of his Navy SEAL watch. There were all sorts of buttons and dials on it, and she remembered from the ad that the time was synchronized with the atomic clock in Colorado, which was accurate to within a millisecond or something impossible like that. The watch was huge, like a chunk of metal on his wrist. In the middle of the round black face was a digital readout showing the time to the seconds.

3:19:12.

Twelve minutes. But did his watch have the same time as hers? As Molly's and Nick's? Lena did not dare check her own watch or look at the clock behind her. Smith would know immediately what was going on and they would all be dead.

"Scalpel," Sara said, holding out her hand.

Smith slapped the scalpel into her palm, and Sara cut the skin, dissecting the flesh as she followed the path of the bullet. She used the remaining medicine in the syringe as she went, finally squirting the bulk of it into the open wound. Lena tried not to watch, but she found herself mesmerized by the inner workings of Jeffrey's arm. Sara obviously knew what she was doing, but Lena had no idea how she managed to remain calm. It was like she had become a different person.

"I need more light," Sara told Smith, and he leaned closer with the flashlight as she probed the arm. "Closer," she said, but Smith did not move. Sara cursed under her breath, using the back of her arm to wipe the sweat off her forehead. She leaned closer to better see what she was doing, her body an awkward arch.

Jeffrey gave a low moan, though he did not appear to be awake.

Sara told Lena, "Watch his breathing."

She put her fingers to Jeffrey's chest, feeling the gentle up and down as he took in air. Slowly, she turned her wrist, trying to check her watch. The room was hot, and sweat dripped down her arm. The metal band had slipped around to the inside of her wrist and there was no way to see the time.

Sara jerked back as blood squirted straight up into her face. She wiped it off with the back of her hand and kept going, telling Smith, "Forceps."

He rooted around for the instrument with one hand, holding the light with the other. Sara used some gauze to wipe away blood, saying, "I can't see it."

"Hate that for you," Smith said, sounding as if he was enjoying the drama.

"I can't get it if I can't see it."

"Calm down," Smith said, handing her the forceps, which looked like giant tweezers. "Here," he said, shaking them in the air.

Sara took the forceps, but she did nothing.

"You're taking all the fun out of this," Smith said, patting gauze around the incision. "You can find it," he coaxed. "I have faith in you."

"I could kill him."

"Now you know how I feel," he said, flashing a nasty grin. "Go on."

For a second, Sara looked as if she was going to refuse, but she put her thumb and fingers through the handle of the forceps and inserted them into the wound. More blood squirted up, and she said, "Clamp." When Smith did not move fast enough, she said, "Now! Give me the clamp!"

Smith held out the instrument and Sara dropped the forceps on the floor. They clattered, a crushed bullet pinging against the tiles. She reached in with the clamp even as blood pumped all around her. Then suddenly, the blood stopped.

Lena looked at Smith's watch again.

3:30:58.

"That wasn't so bad," Smith said, obviously pleased. He used the flashlight to see inside the wound, a big smile plastered on his face, as if he was a child who had won a game against an adult.

"He has about twenty minutes," Sara said, packing gauze into the open incision. "If he doesn't get to a hospital, he'll lose his arm."

"He's got more problems to worry about than that," Smith said. He put the flashlight on the floor, but kept his hand on his leg, affording Lena a clear view of his watch.

3:31:01.

3:31:02.

"Like what?" Sara asked, and out of the corner of her eye, Lena saw Brad moving closer to the second gunman. He looked at the clock again, and she knew that he was thinking the same thing: they couldn't coordinate if they weren't looking at synchronized clocks. What if she moved too soon? What if she signaled Brad at the wrong moment, and they both ended up dead before the SWAT team arrived?

"No," Lena whispered, too late realizing she had said the word aloud.

Smith gave her a toothy smile. "She's figured it out," he said. "Ain't that right, darlin'?"

Lena gave a quick shake of her head, her hand moving behind her, feeling the outline of the knife in her pocket. She was overthinking this. What mattered was working in tandem with Brad. What mattered was the element of surprise.

Smith told Sara, "See, some folks here don't think I'm as stupid as you do."

"I don't think you're stupid," Sara said.

Lena glanced down at Smith's watch again. Thirty seconds left. Brad had moved closer to Sonny, started pacing back and forth across the front of the room like the stress was getting to him. Maybe it was. Maybe he couldn't do this.

"I know what you think about me," Smith told Sara.

Lena moved as slowly as possible, her fingers dipping into her back pocket. Her heart shook in her chest. Brad's footsteps echoed against the tile as he paced back and forth at the front of the room.

"I think you're a very troubled young man," Sara told him. "I think you need help."

"You thought I was trash from the moment you laid eyes on me."

"That's not true."

"You did everything you could to try to destroy my life."

"I wanted to help you," Sara said. "I really did."

"You could've taken me in," Smith said. "I wrote you letters. I wrote him letters."

He had indicated Jeffrey, but Sara seemed not to notice. "We never got them," she replied, but Lena could barely hear her past the sound of blood rushing through her ears. Smith had indicated Jeffrey. He knew who Jeffrey was.

Lena gripped the knife, using her thumb to pry up the blade. She pressed the edge of the metal into her heel and heard the click as the blade popped into place.

She held her breath, waiting for Smith to notice, but he was too focused on Sara. How long had he known about Jeffrey? When had he figured out that it wasn't Matt lying on the floor in front of him, but the man he had sworn to kill?

Smith said, "I kept waiting for y'all to come. I kept waiting for y'all to take me away from her." His voice was like a child's. "Do you know the kinds of things she did to me? Do you know how she hurt me?"

In her head, Lena was screaming, "He knows it's Jeffrey," but she kept the words from coming out of her mouth. Whatever sick game Smith was playing had to go on just a little while longer. Just a few more seconds and it would be over.

Lena trained her eyes on his watch.

3:31:43.

"We couldn't help you," Sara told him. "Eric, Jeffrey is not your father."

Lena looked at Brad. He raised his eyebrows, as if to say, "Ready when you are."

Smith said, "You're a fucking liar."

"I'm not lying," Sara said, a certainty to her voice. "I'll tell you who your father is, but you have to let them go."

"Let them go?" Smith asked, taking the Sig Sauer out of his belt, still keeping his other hand resting on his thigh.

3:31:51.

Lena swallowed, though she had no spit left in her mouth. In her peripheral vision, she saw Brad nearing Sonny.

"Let who go?" Smith asked, taking his time, obviously enjoying the drama. He smiled down at Jeffrey. "You mean him? Matt?" He hit the *t*'s hard, spit coming out of his mouth.

Sara hesitated a beat too long. "Yes."

"That's not Matt," Smith said, cocking the hammer. "That's Jeffrey."

"Now!" Lena screamed, lunging for Smith. She slammed the knife into his throat, feeling her fingers slide down the blade, sharp metal slicing open her skin.

Sara had jumped seconds after Lena, and she wrested the Sig away from Smith even as a gun went off at the front of the room. The three little girls started screaming as the glass entrance door exploded.

GBI agents swarmed into the station. Brad stood over Sonny, pointing the rifle at the young man's face as he pressed his foot into his chest.

"Get up," Sara told Lena, pushing her off Smith. Lena slipped in the blood as Sara turned him over onto his back.

"Get an ambulance," Sara said, putting both her hands to Smith's neck, trying to stop the blood. She was fighting a losing battle. Blood was everywhere, flooding out of Smith's carotid like a broken dam. Lena had never seen so much bleeding in her life. It was as if nothing could stop it.

"Help me," Smith said, an improbable request considering all he had done.

"You'll be okay," Sara soothed. "Just hold on."

"He killed people," Lena told her, thinking she must be crazy. "He tried to kill Jeffrey."

"Get an ambulance," Sara repeated. "Please," she begged, her fingers pressing into the gaping wound. "Please. He just needs somebody to help him."

CHAPTER TWENTY-FOUR

Tuesday

Jeffrey slumped into the row of chairs opposite Hoss's office at the sheriff's station. After the last few days, he understood what people meant when they said they felt as if they had the weight of the world on their shoulders. Jeffrey felt like he had two worlds, and neither one of them was a particularly civilized.

Sara sat down beside him, saying, "It'll be good to get back home after this."

"Yeah."

He had wanted to leave this town from the moment he got here, but now Jeffrey thought that everything he needed was right here with him. As always, Sara knew what he was thinking, and when she put her hand on his leg, he laced his fingers through hers, wondering how his life could be so fucked up yet feel so good as long as she was holding his hand.

"Did he say how long he would be?" Sara asked, meaning Hoss.

"I think part of him is still waiting for me to say this is some kind of joke."

"It'll be fine," she said, squeezing his hand.

Jeffrey glanced down the unlit corridor toward the jail, hoping that his emotions did not get the best of him. Sara was so good at being logical that it scared him sometimes. He had never met anyone so completely capable of taking care of anything that came along, and he wondered what kind of place he could have in her life.

Sara interrupted his thoughts, asking a question he had not yet let himself consider. "You think it changes anything because he's gay?"

He shrugged.

"Jeff?"

Jeffrey kissed her fingers, trying to change the subject. "You can't imagine how I felt when I saw you in that chair. The things that went through my mind."

She waited for his answer.

"I don't know how I feel about that," he said. "I want to kick his ass for what he did to you," he said, feeling livid all over again. "That kind of thing . . ." He shook his head, trying not to let it get to him. "I swear to God, if I ever see him again, there's going to be a reckoning for that."

"He was desperate," she said, though Jeffrey did not understand how she could make excuses for him. "Which is worse," she asked, "what he did to me or the fact that he's gay?"

He did not know how to answer the question. "All I know is that he lied to me all these years."

"Would you have wanted to have anything to do with him otherwise?"

"We'll never have a chance to find out, will we?"

Sara let his words hang in the air.

"When I saw Robert's jacket in Swan's closet . . ." He sat back in the chair, letting go of her hand as he crossed his arms over his chest. Jeffrey kept his own jacket in the back of his closet at home, and though he never wore it, he could not bring himself to donate it to charity or throw it away. He was worse than the Monday-morning quarterbacks at the hardware store, holding on to that jacket like he could hold on to his youth.

He told Sara, "I don't know. I saw his jacket, and it popped into my head that maybe there was a connection between him and Swan. Just a split second, and then I thought, 'No way. No way Robert's a . . . ' "

Jeffrey gave a heavy sigh, thinking he'd never be able to use the word again. He probably should not have been using it in the first place. "I came here to the station looking for Hoss, but he was out."

Jeffrey did not tell her that the first thing he'd wanted to do after leaving Swan's was to find Sara, but he had taken the detour to the station to prove to himself that he did not need her. Had he not been so stubborn, Jeffrey could have stopped Robert before things escalated. He could have protected her.

Oblivious to this, she kept pressing, "Does it bother you that he's gay?"

"I can't separate it out, Sara, and that's the truth. I'm mad at him for what he did to you. I'm mad at him for not turning Jessie in, for letting all this shit stir up and not doing anything about it. I'm mad at him for jumping bail and leaving Possum to sweat it out."

"He said he'd send money."

"Yeah, well, I'm calling the state as soon as we get back to see how much I can pull out of retirement." He thought of Possum's bruised jaw, and the way the other man had waved off Jeffrey's apology for hitting him. Jeffrey would not make Possum take all of the financial burden for this. It just wasn't right.

"What else?" she asked. "What else are you mad at him about?"

He stood, needing to pace. "For not telling me." He glanced down the hallway as an inmate in the jail yelled an obscenity. "If you hadn't been in that house, the last thing we'd know is that he jumped bail for killing a man and was on the run. We wouldn't know about Jessie or his relationship, or whatever you want to call it, with Swan. All we'd know is that he was a fugitive." Jeffrey stopped pacing and turned to Sara. "He should have trusted me."

She had a circumspect look on her face, like she wanted to make sure she said the right thing. "My cousin Hare had a hard time at college," she began. "One minute, he was the most popular guy on campus, the next, he was getting death threats."

He had forgotten about her cousin in all this, and now Jeffrey wondered if she was taking up for Robert because she wanted to take up for Hare. "What happened?"

"People just figured it out," she said. "He had this friend, his dorm mate. They were inseparable. When people started to talk, Hare didn't try to hide anything. He was surprised that anyone cared."

"That's pretty naive."

"That's Hare," she told him. "I guess we both grew up in a fairly insulated world. Our parents never let us think that anything was wrong with being gay or straight or black or anything else under the sun. Hare was shocked when his so-called friends turned on him."

Jeffrey could imagine what happened, but still, he wanted to hear it. "What did they do?"

"This was at the end of his junior year at UGA, so there was summer in between for everyone to cool off." She paused, and he could tell she was still upset by the memory. Above anything else, Sara cherished her family, and for one of them to be hurt was just about the only thing in the world she did not seem able to tolerate.

She continued, "We all hoped it would die down during the break, but of course it didn't. His first day back, they tried to beat him up, but he was always a good fighter and he broke a few noses. I heard him tell you he quit football because he hurt his knee, but that wasn't it. He was told to leave."

Jeffrey sat down again. "I can't say I wouldn't have done the same thing to Robert if I had found out back then."

"What about now?"

"Now . . ." He shook his head. "Hell, I just want him to be safe. I can't imagine living like that, people thinking I was something I wasn't."

"Sounds like how you lived the first part of your life."

He laughed, because he had never looked at it that way. "Yeah."

"What did Hoss say when you told him all this on the phone?"

"Nothing," he told her, then added, "He didn't sound surprised."

"Do you think he knew?"

"Maybe he suspected. There's no telling." He gave her a meaningful look. "Trust me, you don't see that kind of thing unless you're looking."

"What's going to happen now?"

"Jessie will be arrested." He hissed air out between his teeth. "That's gonna be fun. I'm sure Reggie Ray will get a big kick out of all this."

"You can't worry about that."

"If he walked through that door right now, I'd have him leaving on a stretcher."

"What about Julia Kendall?"

"What about her?"

"I need to tell you something," she began, taking his hand again. "I need to talk to you about what Lane Kendall said."

"She's a—"

"No," Sara interrupted. "Not that. I need to tell you why I reacted the way I did when she accused you of . . . of raping Julia."

"I didn't," he told her, feeling defensive. "I swear to you, Sara, that kid isn't mine."

"I know that," she responded, but her expression was so peculiar that he did not believe her.

He stood again. "I'm telling you I didn't do it. I didn't have anything to do with it."

"I know you didn't," she repeated.

"You don't look like you believe me."

"I'm sorry you feel that way," she said, and he could see her shutting him out.

He paced again, feeling cornered and guilty even though he knew he had done nothing. All he could think was that they had finally gotten to her. Sara had finally started doubting him the way everyone else did. There was no going back from here.

"Jeff," Sara said, angry. "Stop pacing."

He did, even though his body felt like a live current was going through it. "We can't get past this point," he told her. "Either you trust me or you don't, but I'm not going to—"

"Stop," she interrupted him.

"You think I'm capable of doing that?" he asked. "You think I'd actually . . ." He could not find the words to finish. "Jesus, Sara, if you think I'm capable of raping somebody, what the hell are you doing here with me?"

"I *don't* think you did it, Jeffrey. That's what I'm trying to tell you." She seemed exasperated, and her tone took on an even sharper edge. "Even if I thought you did it—which I don't—medically, there's no way that Eric Kendall is your child."

He stood silent, waiting for her to spell it out.

"You don't have a bleeding disorder in your family?" she asked, like she was talking to a three-year-old.

"I don't even know what you're talking about."

"A bleeding disorder," she said, as if repeating the words would make him understand. "Lane Kendall said that Eric had a bleeding disorder."

Jeffrey wondered where she was going with this. He had tried his best to block out the episode with Lane Kendall and did not relish going back over it.

She said, "I haven't examined him, but from what Nell told me, it sounds more like von Willebrand's disease."

He waited for her to continue.

"Blood won't clot."

"Like hemophilia?"

"Sort of," she answered. "It can be pretty mild. Some people have it and don't even know it. They just think they're easy bleeders. Eric's bruises were raised, like bumps. That's also a sign."

Jeffrey felt all the hairs on the back of his neck stand up.

His expression must have given him away, because Sara asked, "What?"

He shook his head, thinking that this whole ordeal with Robert had made him too suspicious. "It couldn't have come from Lane's family? Or Julia's father?"

"It could," she answered, though her tone said she did not think it was likely. "Generally, women know when they have it. Their menstrual cycles are extremely heavy. A lot of women end up getting hysterectomies when they don't really need them. It's not an easy diagnosis, not many doctors think to look for it." She added, "As many children as Lane has had, she would know if she had it. Pregnancies can be very high risk for anyone with a bleeding disorder."

Jeffrey could only stare at her, his mind making conclusions that turned a knife in his gut. "What if someone gets nosebleeds a lot?"

She wrinkled her brow. "Who are you thinking about?"

"Just answer, Sara. Please just answer."

"It could be," she said. "Nosebleeds, bleeding gums. Cuts that won't stop bleeding."

"You're sure it's genetic?"

"Yes."

"Shit," he whispered, thinking that as bad as everything seemed a few minutes before, it had just gotten worse than he could have ever imagined.

"What are you—"

They both looked up as the door opened.

"I'm sorry it took me so long to get here," Hoss told them, taking his keys out of his pocket as he walked toward his office.

Jeffrey could not move.

Hoss looked at Sara, obviously taking in her cuts and bruises. "I would've never thought Robert was capable of hurting a woman," he told her. "But I guess he wasn't nearly the man I thought he was."

"I'm fine," Sara answered, a tight smile on her face.

"That's good," Hoss said, unlocking his office door. He went in, turning on the lights as he walked to his desk and rummaged through some papers. "Come on in so we can get this over with."

Sara gave Jeffrey an inquisitive look, and he returned the question with an affirmative nod.

Hoss noticed Jeffrey still standing in the doorway. "Slick? There a problem?"

Sara put her hand on Jeffrey's shoulder. She asked him, "Do you want me to wait outside?"

"That's okay," Hoss said, obviously thinking she was talking to him.

"I'll wait outside." She squeezed Jeffrey's shoulder again, and somehow, her confidence that he would do the right thing gave him the strength to walk into the office.

The door clicked shut behind him as he sat in the chair opposite Hoss.

"Guess she's had a hard time of it," Hoss said, obviously thinking Sara was in a delicate state. He picked up a report and scanned it as he talked. "I sent Reggie out to pick up Jessie. Jesus, what a mess. I'm sure she'll fight him hammer and claw."

"We still don't know about Julia."

"Robert confessed."

"He confessed to a lot of things he didn't do."

"Don't know that I can trust his word after what we know about him."

"You're saying because he's gay, that makes him capable of murder?"

"Makes him capable of anything in my book," Hoss said, turning the page over to read the back. "Might open a few of his cases and see what he was really up to."

This more than anything else sparked Jeffrey's anger. "Robert was a good cop."

"He was a fucking queer," Hoss said, still staring at the report. He picked up his pen and signed the bottom. "No telling what else he was doing. We had a missing boy here a few years back. Robert worked the case like it was his own son."

Jeffrey managed to speak through clenched teeth. "You're saying he's a pedophile now?"

He picked up another report. "Goes hand in hand."

Jeffrey could only stare at him.

"He coached the Little League," Hoss said. "I've already called some parents."

"That's bullshit," Jeffrey spat. "Robert loved kids."

"Yeah," Hoss agreed. "They all *love* kids."

Jeffrey tried to sum it up for him, to show Hoss how wrong his thinking was. "So, he's a pedophile, has a thing for boys, but he killed Julia when they were both teenagers?"

"No telling what a sick mind like that will do," Hoss said. "Choke an innocent girl, kill a man for banging his wife . . ."

Hoss's words echoed in Jeffrey's head, and finally he saw it all laid out like a puzzle. "I don't remember telling you she was strangled," he said quietly.

Hoss shot him a startled look. "Your lady told me."

"Did she?" Jeffrey asked, making to get up out of the chair. "You want me to go ask her when?"

Hoss faltered. "Maybe I heard it in town."

Jeffrey couldn't believe how silent the room suddenly was. Everything fell into place. "You know he didn't do it."

Hoss looked at Jeffrey over the report. "I do?"

"Eric Kendall has a bleeding disorder."

He looked back down, eyes moving as he scanned the page. "That right?"

"He's your kid, isn't he?"

Hoss did not answer, but Jeffrey saw a slight tremor in the report he held.

"You told me once how you tried to join the Army after your brother died, but they wouldn't take you on medical grounds."

"So?"

"Why wouldn't they take you?"

Hoss shrugged. "Flat feet. Everybody knows that."

"You sure it wasn't something else? Something that would keep you off the force if it got out?"

"You're just talking crazy now, boy," he said in a tone that ordered this conversation to be ended.

Jeffrey did not obey. "You get nosebleeds all the time. Your gums bleed for no reason. I saw you get a paper cut once and it bled for two days."

He gave a weak smile. "That don't mean—"

"Don't lie to me," Jeffrey demanded, anger boiling to the surface.

"You can say anything you want right now and it stays in this room, but don't you *dare* lie to me."

Hoss shrugged, like it was nothing. "She was loose. You know that."

"She was only sixteen years old."

"Seventeen," Hoss corrected. "I wasn't breaking any laws."

Jeffrey felt disgusted, and it must have read in his face, because Hoss tried a different tack.

"Look," he said. "Times were different. That girl needed someone to look after her."

Jeffrey felt sickened by his words. As a cop, he had heard that same excuse a thousand times from dirty old men, and to hear it now from Hoss was like a slap in the face. "Looking after her doesn't mean screwing her."

"Watch your tone," Hoss warned, as if he still deserved Jeffrey's respect. "Come on, Slick. I took care of her."

"How?"

"Kept her daddy off her, for one," Hoss answered. "Plus, you think her mama paid for her to go off and have that baby?"

"*Your* baby."

He shrugged. "Who knew? Coulda been mine, coulda been yours."

"The hell you say."

"Coulda been anybody's, is what I'm getting at. She went with half the damn town." He took a wad of tissue out of his pocket and blotted at his nose. "Coulda been her daddy's, for all I know."

Jeffrey could only stare at the telltale trickle of blood coming from Hoss's nose. He had always seemed so tough, but thinking back on it, every time the old man got stressed, his nose bled.

Jeffrey said, "You gave her that locket, didn't you?"

Hoss looked at the tissue before putting it back to his nose. "It was my mama's. I guess I was feeling generous that day."

Jeffrey wondered how Hoss had really felt about the girl. If you were using someone to get laid, you didn't give the woman gifts, especially something that had belonged to your mother. He pressed, "Why didn't you marry her?"

Hoss laughed at the suggestion, a tiny spray of blood escaping around the tissue. "Wake up, Slick. You don't marry something like that." He pointed toward the door, toward Sara. "That's the kind of woman you marry." He dropped his hand. "Somebody like Julia, that's the kind of woman you fuck and hope to God she don't give you something you need a shot of penicillin to get rid of."

"How can you talk about her that way? She's the mother of your child."

"Pretty ballsy coming from you."

"What do you mean by that?"

"Nothing," he answered, though Jeffrey was certain he was holding back. "Look, we just had a good time."

"She was too young to know what a good time was." Jeffrey stood up, thinking he had sat idly by long enough. "Did you kill her?"

"I can't believe you're asking me that."

Jeffrey kept silent. He had seen the answer in Hoss's eyes. Everything was turning upside down. The man he thought was good and decent was actually the kind of punk that made Jeffrey glad he was a cop who could put them away. If he had Hoss back in Grant County, shut in the interrogation room, he would be doing everything he could not to haul off and hit the fucker.

"You don't know how it was," Hoss tried. "I've done good by this town for over thirty years."

"You murdered a seventeen-year-old girl," Jeffrey said, fighting the emotions the words brought. "Or are you going to tell me it was okay because she was eighteen by then?"

Hoss threw down the tissue as he stood. "I was trying to protect Robert."

"Robert?" Jeffrey demanded, incredulous. "What did Robert have to do with any of that?"

He put his hands on the desk, leaning over toward Jeffrey. "She said he raped her. I couldn't let that tramp ruin his life."

"That blew over in a week," Jeffrey countered. "Less than a week."

Hoss looked down at his desk. "People still talk. That's all this town is made up of, people talking, telling lies on each other, thinking they know what's right, when the fact is, they don't know shit." He wiped his nose with the back of his hand, a thin streak of blood smearing across the skin. "I've got a reputation to uphold. People in this town need me. They need to know who's in charge. I was doing it for their sake."

"You fool," Jeffrey said. "You selfish old fool."

His head snapped back up. "You've got no right—"

"What'd she do?" Jeffrey asked. "You sent her away to have that baby, but she came back. Did you think she wouldn't come back?"

Hoss waved him off, walking over to the window so that his back was to Jeffrey.

"You think you're untouchable. You think hiding behind that badge is going to protect you."

Hoss did not respond.

"She came back and what, Hoss? What'd she want? Money?"

Hoss rested his hand on top of his brother's flag case. "She thought I'd marry her. Some piece of work, huh? Thought I'd marry her." He laughed. "Shit."

"So you killed her?"

"It wasn't like that." Hoss finally looked contrite, though Jeffrey knew it was because he had been caught, not because he felt any remorse. "It was an accident."

"Yeah, people get strangled by accident all the time."

Hoss's voice took on a high, unnatural pitch. "She was threatening to tell," he said. "Came back from having that baby like she was the damn Virgin Mary. Said she wanted me to make an honest woman of her. Can you beat that? Me marrying her, buying a pie every man in town's done stuck his finger in for a taste? I'd be a laughingstock if I married a whore like that."

"Don't call her that," Jeffrey warned. "You've got no right."

"I got plenty of right," Hoss shot back. "She was nothing but trouble. She accused you of raping her. How did you like that?"

"So," Jeffrey said, seeing where this was going. "Let me get this right, you killed her for me?"

"And for Robert," he added.

Jeffrey tried to quell his astonishment long enough to get the story out of him. "What happened?"

"She came to the office." He indicated the room, indignant at the memory. "Here, to my office."

"And?"

Hoss turned back to the flag, tracing the wooden case with his fingers. "It was late, kind of like now. Not many people here." He paused. "She got kind of frisky with me like she does, and then just stopped. Little prick tease is what she was."

Jeffrey waited for him to continue.

"So," Hoss continued, "we had a conversation about that."

"Did you rape her?"

"She was willing," Hoss said. "She was always willing."

Jeffrey felt sick, but still, he asked, "So, then what?"

"She said she wanted me to marry her. She didn't want her mama raising Eric."

Jeffrey looked at the flag case. He had seen the brass plaque screwed to the top a thousand times, but never made the connection. JOHN ERIC HOLLISTER. Julia had been pushing him, but she had no idea that she had pushed too hard.

"You got into a fight?" Jeffrey prompted.

"Yeah," Hoss nodded. "I offered her some money. She threw it back in my face. Said she would have it all when we were married, anyway." He gave a harsh laugh. "Can you believe how stupid she was, thinking I'd do that? Thinking she was good for anything other than a fuck and suck?"

Jeffrey felt his jaw start to ache from clenching his teeth together. Every time Hoss opened his mouth, he had to fight the urge not to throttle him.

"She kept goading me. Kept threatening me. Nobody threat-
ens me."

"So you killed her?"

"It wasn't like that," Hoss said. "I was trying to reason with her.
Trying to get her to see logic." Hoss turned around, an awkward smile
on his face, as if he expected Jeffrey's approval. "I tried to get her out
of the office. Kind of roughed her toward the door. Next thing I
know, she jumped on my back. How do you like that? Jumped right
on my back, kicking and screaming and clawing. I knew somebody
would hear. I knew somebody would come and want to know what
the hell was going on."

Jeffrey nodded, like he understood.

"Next thing I know, my hands are around her neck," Hoss said,
holding his hands out in front of him. Robert had done the same thing
when he confessed to killing Julia, but Hoss reenacted the scene with
the passion of a man who had been there. He was facing his demons
head-on, trying to strangle the life out of the memory. A steady trickle
of blood came from his nose, but he did not seem to care.

Hoss said, "I was just trying to get her to shut up. I didn't want to
hurt her, just make her stop screaming. And she finally did." He
stared at a point over Jeffrey's shoulder. "I tried to help her. Gave her
mouth-to-mouth. Pushed on her chest. She was gone. Her head just
kind of . . . lolled . . . I guess I broke her neck or something."

Jeffrey let his words hang in the air for a few seconds, trying to understand what had really happened. A few years ago, he would have
taken Hoss's words at face value. He probably would have even
helped cover his tracks. Now he saw the story for what it was: a lie
bent around the truth so that the old man could still get to sleep at
night.

Jeffrey narrowed the space between them. "You strangled her."

"I didn't mean to."

"How long did it take?" Jeffrey asked, taking another step closer.
He knew from a case last year that manual strangulation was not as
easy as it seemed, especially when someone was fighting tooth and
nail, as Julia must have done. "How long before she passed out?"

"I don't know. It wasn't long."

"Why'd you take her to the cave?"

"Wasn't thinking," he said, but there was a flash of unmistakable guilt in his eyes.

"Everybody knew that's where we went," Jeffrey told him. "If she was ever found, people would make the connection that it was me or Robert. Or both of us."

"That's not what—"

"She said we raped her," Jeffrey interrupted. "She said it less than a year before. It'd make sense, wouldn't it? We were just getting her back for telling."

"Hold on," Hoss said, finally looking him in the eye. It took effort, that much was obvious. "You think I was trying to frame you and Robert?"

Jeffrey did not hesitate. "Yes."

He finally lost control. "I said it was an accident!"

"You tell that to the town," Jeffrey countered, and Hoss's face went pale. "You tell that to Deacon White and Thelma down at the bank and Reggie Ray when he gets back with Jessie."

Panic flashed in the old man's eyes. "You wouldn't."

"I wouldn't?" Jeffrey asked. "I don't know about you, but that badge I wear means more to me than free breakfasts down at the diner."

"I taught you to respect that badge."

"You didn't teach me a damn thing."

Hoss jammed his finger in Jeffrey's face. "You'd be down at the prison right now mopping floors with your daddy if it wasn't for me, boy!"

"Makes no difference," Jeffrey said. "I'm still standing in the same room with a murderer."

"Somebody had to protect you," Hoss said, his voice shaky. "That's all I was doing was looking after you and that pansy friend of yours."

Jeffrey recoiled at the word and Hoss picked up on this.

"That's right," Hoss said. "How'd you like it if I let it out that you and Robert were more than friends?"

Jeffrey snorted a laugh.

"For all I know," Hoss continued, "maybe you were."

"Right."

"You two fuckbuddies?" Hoss goaded, desperation pouring off him. "You want everybody in town to hear that? You want your mama to find out? Maybe somebody'll tell your daddy down at the prison?"

"You can tell my daddy yourself when you see him, you pathetic old fuck."

"You watch that mouth."

"Or what?"

"I protected you!" Hoss yelled. "You think your father would have done that? You think that worthless bastard would've helped you?"

Jeffrey slammed his fist into the desk. "I didn't want your help!"

"You sure as shit needed it!" Hoss screamed back. Blood dripped from his nose, but he kept screaming, his face turning red with anger. "I raised you, boy! I made you the man you are today!"

Jeffrey jabbed his thumb at his chest. "*I* made me the man I am today. I made myself despite you." He felt dirty being this close to him. "I thought you were a god. You were everything I wanted to be."

Hoss's lip quivered, as if he wanted to take Jeffrey's words as a compliment.

Jeffrey made himself clear. "You molested a teenage girl. You took a mother from her child."

"I didn't—"

"You make me sick," Jeffrey said, walking toward the door.

Hoss put his hand on his desk as if he needed the support. "Don't leave like this, Slick. Come on." His tone took an edge of desperation. "What are you gonna say? What are you gonna tell people?"

"The truth," Jeffrey said, feeling his calm return. What he saw before him was no longer his mentor, his surrogate father, but a criminal, a lying old man who had destroyed the people he was meant to protect.

"Come on, now," Hoss said, begging. "You can't do this. You'll ruin me. You know what'll happen if you go out there and . . . please,

Slick. Don't do this." He took a step forward as if to stop Jeffrey. "You might as well put a gun to my head." He tried a weak smile. "Come on, son. Don't look at me that way."

"Look at you?" Jeffrey asked, putting his hand on the doorknob. "I can't even stand to see your face."

He did not slam the door behind him, but in his mind, Jeffrey heard a resounding crash. Sara stood up, wringing her hands.

He did not know what to tell her. There would never be the right words to describe how he felt. Rudderless, that was a good one to start with. He had lost the thing that gave him direction.

"Are you okay?" she asked, and the concern in her voice was better than anything she had ever done for him.

"He came to see me after Dad was arrested," Jeffrey told her.

"Hoss?"

"I was at Auburn, just about to graduate. I remember everything about it," he paused, picturing the multicolored leaves on the trees that beautiful fall day. Jeffrey was sitting in his dorm room, trying to figure out how he would pay for his doctorate if Auburn accepted him into the program. He wanted to be a teacher, something respectable with a steady paycheck. He wanted to give something back.

"He knocked on the door," Jeffrey continued. "Nobody knocked. They usually just came in. I thought somebody was playing a joke." He leaned against the wall. "He kept knocking, and I finally opened the door and there he was with this look on his face. Told me Dad had taken a plea. Turned on his friends so he wouldn't get the death penalty. You know what he said?"

Sara shook her head.

" 'Some kind of coward,' " Jeffrey finished. "He told me I had to be a man now, that playtime was over. Playtime, like that's all I had been doing in college, just having fun. He handed me this application. It was already filled out."

"The police academy?"

"Yeah," he nodded. "I just took it and signed it and that was it." For the first time in his life, Jeffrey found himself wondering what would have become of his life if he had told Hoss no. He would not have met Sara, for one. He would probably still be living here in Syla-cauga, dealing with the same snide remarks and secretive looks that had chased Robert away.

He said, "I don't know how I'm going to do this."

"I'll be here as long as you need me."

"I can't even think about it," he told her, and that was the truth. How could he do this? How could he repeat what Hoss had told him?

"It'll be fine," she said, just as a gun exploded in Hoss's office.

Sara must have opened the door. Jeffrey did not feel like he could move. Yet, somehow, he managed to turn around. Somehow, he was facing Hoss's office.

The old man sat in his chair, one hand on the flag from his brother's coffin, the other holding his revolver. He had put the muzzle of the gun flat to his head and pulled the trigger. There was no question in Jeffrey's mind that Hoss was dead, but still, when Sara went around the desk and pressed her fingers to his neck, he managed to form the question with his eyes.

"I'm sorry," she told him. "He's dead."

CHAPTER TWENTY-FIVE

3:50 P.M.

Shit," Lena hissed, trying not to jerk her hand back as Molly stuck a needle into the cut.

"I'm sorry," Molly apologized, but she was looking over her shoulder at Sara and Jeffrey, not Lena.

Lena watched as Jeffrey was loaded into the ambulance. "Will he be okay?"

Molly nodded, though she said, "I hope so."

"What about Marla?"

"They've got her in surgery. She's old, but she's strong." She looked back at Lena's hand. "This is going to sting."

"No shit," Lena answered. The knife slicing open her skin had not hurt as much as the freaking needle.

"It'll block the pain so I can suture you."

"Just hurry," Lena said, biting her lip. She tasted blood and remembered her split lip. Molly jabbed in the needle again. "Christ, that hurts."

"Just a little more."

"Christ," she repeated, looking away from the needle. She saw Wagner talking to Nick, both of them staring at Lena and Molly as they sat in the back room of the cleaners.

"There," Molly said. "It should start numbing up in a few minutes."

"It'd better," Lena told her, feeling phantom pains from the needle. She looked through the front windows again, seeing the mess in the street. There were at least fifty GBI agents swarming around, none of them knowing what the hell they were doing. Smith was dead and Sonny was locked in the back of a squad car on his way to Macon, where he would probably have the shit beaten out of him. There was a special place in hell for cop-killers.

Lena watched Molly open the suture kit she had taken from the ambulance. "Where are the kids?"

"Back with their parents," Molly said, laying out the kit. "I can't imagine what it was like for them. The parents, I mean. My God, when I think about it, my blood runs cold."

Lena realized she had been clenching every muscle in her body, and she relaxed as her hand started to numb.

"Better?" Molly asked.

"Yeah," Lena allowed. "Thanks for doing this here. I hate going to the hospital."

"That's understandable," Molly said, using a syringe to wash out the gash. "You only need three or four sutures. Sara's a lot better at this than I am."

"She's tougher than I thought."

"I think we all are," Molly pointed out. "You had me fooled when we went into the station."

"Yeah," Lena said, though the compliment rang false. She had been terrified.

Molly used a pair of long tweezers to pick up a curved needle. She dug it into Lena's skin, and Lena watched, thinking how odd it was to see her flesh being pierced and feel nothing but a dull tugging as the thread went through.

"How long have you been dating Nick?"

"Not long," Molly said, tying off the thread. "He kept asking Sara out. I guess I was the door prize."

Lena laughed as she tried to imagine Nick and Sara together. "Sara's about ten feet taller than he is."

"She's also in love with Jeffrey," Molly reminded her, as if that was not obvious. "Oh, God, I remember the first time I saw them together." She tied the suture. Lena felt the same dull tug as she punctured the skin again. "I've never seen her so giddy."

"Giddy?" Lena echoed, thinking she had heard wrong. Sara was one of the most serious people she had ever met.

"Giddy," Molly confirmed. "Like a schoolgirl." She tied off the second thread, making a neat knot. "One more, I think."

"I've never thought about him that way."

"Jeffrey?" Molly asked, as if it surprised her. "He's gorgeous."

"I guess," Lena shrugged. "That'd be kind of like dating your father, though."

"Maybe for you," Molly said in a suggestive tone. She dug into the skin one more time and tied off the third suture. "There you go," she said, cutting the thread just above the knot. "All set."

"Thank you."

"The scar shouldn't be bad."

"I'm not worried about that," Lena said, flexing her hand. The fingers moved, but she could not feel them.

"Take some Tylenol when it starts to hurt. I can have Sara call in something for you if you like."

"That's okay," Lena said. "She's got more important things to worry about."

"She wouldn't mind," Molly offered.

"No," Lena assured her. "Thanks."

"All right," Molly said, wrapping the suturing kit. She gave a groan as she stood. "Now, I think I am going home to a large glass of wine and my children."

"That sounds nice," Lena said.

"My mother has kept them away from the news. I don't know how I'm going to tell them about this."

"You'll think of something," Lena told her.

Molly smiled. "Take care."

"Thanks," Lena answered, sliding off the table.

Nick passed her as she walked toward the front of the cleaners. He said, "We'll need to debrief you tomorrow."

"You know how to find me."

Wagner was leaning against the front counter, her cell phone plastered to her ear. When she saw Lena, she said, "Wait a minute," into the phone, then told Lena, "Good work, Detective."

"Thanks," Lena said.

"You ever want to run with the big dogs," Wagner offered, "give me a call."

Lena looked out into the street, watching the local agents strutting around like they had saved the day. She thought about Jeffrey, and how he had given her a second chance. Being honest, it was more like a fifth or sixth chance.

She gave Wagner a smile. "No thanks. I think I'll stay where I am."

Wagner shrugged, like it was no skin off her back. She went back to her call, saying, "We'll obviously need to interrogate him tonight. I don't want him talking to the other inmates and figuring out he needs a lawyer."

Lena pushed open the door with her good hand, nodding to some of the men in the street. She belonged here. She was a part of them. She was Frank's partner again. She was a cop. Hell, maybe she was more than that.

She walked toward the college. Now that the standoff was over, the rent-a-cop from campus security was standing sentry at his car. He tipped his hat to her as she walked by, and Lena, feeling generous, nodded back.

There was a welcome breeze in the air as she walked up the main drive to the student dorms. Lena touched her fingers to her belly. She wondered what was in there, what kind of parent she could be. After today, she was beginning to think that not everything was impossible.

The campus was pretty empty, most of the kids probably glued to their televisions or sacked out on their beds, thankful for a day without classes. Downtown was still blocked off, but Lena figured in a few hours they would start to file out, rubbernecking, trying to absorb some of the drama that had unfolded today. They would call their parents and cry about how horrible it was. The dean would be handling more calls from angry parents, like this kind of thing could be controlled by anybody.

Ethan's dorm this year was quieter than the one he had lived in when Lena had first met him. All-night parties and weekend binges were not exactly his style, and he had managed to befriend the professor in charge of assigning dorm space and gotten placed in a quieter hall.

She climbed the three steps up to the concrete porch, passing a few students as they left the dorm. Ethan's room had been a closet at some point, and even though the university had no qualms about stacking students in dorms like sides of beef, they had not had the gall to make him share. He had measured the space once while Lena watched, surprised that at eight feet by eleven it was bigger than they both had thought.

She knocked on the door before opening it. Ethan was sitting in bed with a book on his lap. The little television on the bookcase showed the news, the sound turned off.

He asked, "What are you doing here?"

"You wanted me to come by after work."

"Wanted," he said. "Past tense. Not anymore."

Lena leaned against the door. "Do you know what kind of day I've had?"

"Do you know what kind of day *I've* had?" he shot back, slamming the book closed.

"Ethan—"

" 'I'll take care of it,' " he interrupted. "That's what you said. 'I'll take care of it.' "

"I didn't mean—"

"Are you pregnant?"

She stared at him, feeling an ache in the pit of her stomach. For the first time since she had met him, Lena did not want to be alone, even if it meant being here on Ethan's terms.

"Are you going to answer me?"

She finally said, "No."

"You're lying."

"I'm not," she insisted, making things up as she went along. "I started my period after we talked. It must have been the stress."

"You said you were going to take care of it if you were."

"But I'm not."

He got off the bed and walked toward her. She felt herself relax until she saw his clenched fist coming up and slamming into her stomach. Lena doubled over from the pain, and he put his hand on her back, keeping her down, whispering, "If you ever 'take care of' anything that's mine, I'll kill you."

"Oh," she cried, trying to breathe.

"Get out of here," he said, shoving her back into the hall. He slammed the door so hard that the bulletin board he kept outside crashed to the ground.

Lena reached out for the wall, trying to straighten herself. Pain shot through her gut, and she felt tears well into her eyes.

Two students were at the front of the hall by the doorway, and she walked past them, trying to keep her spine as straight as possible. She maintained her composure until she was behind the dorm, hidden in the woods where no one could see her.

She leaned against a tree, letting herself sink to the ground. The dirt was wet underneath her, but she did not care.

Her cell phone chirped as it powered up. She waited for the signal, then dialed in a number. Tears streamed down her face as she listened to the ringing on the other end.

"Hello?"

Lena opened her mouth to speak, but she could only cry.

"Hello?" Hank said, then because probably no one else called her uncle in the middle of the afternoon balling like a child, he said, "Lee? Honey, is that you?"

Lena choked back a sob. "Hank," she finally managed. "I need you."

EPILOGUE

Sara sat on the hood of her car, looking out at the cemetery. Nothing had changed about Deacon White's funeral home in the last decade, despite the fact that a large conglomerate had bought them out. Even the rolling green hills looked the same, the white gravestones sticking up like broken teeth.

Still, Sara thought if she never saw another grave again it would be too soon. She had attended funerals all week, mourning the men and women who had been victimized by Sonny and Eric Kendall's rampage. Marilyn Edwards had somehow survived being shot in the bathroom of the station, and it looked like she would pull through. She was strong, but she was a minority. Most of the other victims had died.

"The town looks different," Jeffrey said, and maybe to him it did. He was such a different person from the man who had brought her here the last time.

"You sure you don't want to call Possum and Nell?"

He shook his head. "I don't think I'm ready for that." He paused, probably thinking about his son, wondering yet again what he could do about Jarod. "I wonder if Robert knows."

"I figured it out," she reminded him.

"Robert wasn't sleeping with me," he pointed out. "Man, I wonder what he's up to."

"You could try to find out."

"If he wanted me to know where he is, he'd tell me," Jeffrey said. "I hope wherever he ended up, he's found some peace."

Sara tried to comfort him. "You did everything you could."

"I wonder if he ever talks to Jessie?"

"She's probably been out of prison a while now," Sara said. Much as she had predicted, Jessie had served only a handful of years in jail for killing a defenseless man. Her addiction to drugs and alcohol had been a mitigating factor, but Nell's opinion had been that Robert's sexuality was the evidence that most swayed the jury. Sara hoped that things would be different if the same crime happened today, but you could never tell with small towns.

"She's back at Herd's Gap," he provided. "I got a Christmas card from her the year she got out."

"Why didn't you tell me?"

"We weren't exactly speaking then," he explained, and she guessed this had happened sometime around their divorce.

He said, "Lane Kendall died three days before they came after me."

"How did you find out?" Sara asked. Sonny Kendall had refused to talk about anything to do with his family.

"The sheriff told me."

"Since when did Reggie Ray start volunteering information to you?"

He turned around, giving her a half-smile. "You didn't hear about his oldest son, Rick?"

"What?"

"He's the drama teacher over at Comer High School."

Sara laughed so hard that she had to put her hand over her mouth. Even if Rick had a wife and twelve kids, Reggie would embrace the stereotype the same as if his son was a cross-dressing hairdresser.

"Just goes to show . . ." Jeffrey said, giving a half-shrug that she could tell hurt his shoulder. He was not used to wearing a sling and she practically had to force him into it every morning.

He said, "I wonder what happened to the letters Eric said he sent me?"

"Maybe she didn't mail them," Sara suggested.

"Sounds like something she'd do."

"Sonny won't even talk about that?"

"No," Jeffrey said. "The military wants him when the courts are through. He was AWOL since Lane died. They probably would have overlooked it if he hadn't . . .".

Sara stared at the cemetery. "I forgot all about them," she confessed. "As upset as I was when we left town, I haven't given them a thought in all these years."

"Maybe I should have told Lane the truth," he said. "God, she hated me."

"She wouldn't have believed you," Sara pointed out, the same conclusion they had come to all those years ago.

Lane Kendall's life was fueled by hatred and mistrust. Nothing Jeffrey said would have changed that. Still, at the time, Sara had not completely agreed that Hoss should be allowed to take his secrets to his grave. Jeffrey's arguments had been persuasive. Sitting down with Reggie Ray and talking through Hoss's confession would have been like rolling a boulder up the mountain. Absent any hard evidence, no one would take Jeffrey at his word, especially since Robert was not there to back him up.

Sara had always believed that the real reason Jeffrey kept silent was because he could not bring himself to speak against Hoss when the other man was not around to defend himself. In the end, it was easier for him to continue to take the blame than to stir up more trouble with the truth. Jeffrey did not live in Sylacauga anymore, and there was no need to fight that battle. The people who mattered to him knew what had really happened, and the people who didn't went about living their lives much the same as before. Reggie Ray's report said that the sheriff had been cleaning his gun when it went off, and no one had questioned him. Julia Kendall's murder was still listed as unsolved.

Jeffrey tugged at the sling. "Damn, I hate this thing."

"You need to wear it," she said, making her voice stern.

"It doesn't hurt."

She brushed her fingers along the nape of his neck. "I need you to be able to use that arm."

"That right?" he said, giving her a shadow of his usual sly smile.

She wanted him okay so much that she tried to keep up the teasing. "That hand."

"You like that hand?"

"I like them both," she said.

"Do you remember," he began, "the first time you told me you loved me?"

"Umm . . ." She pretended to think, but she knew.

"When we got back to Grant after being here," he said. "Remember?"

"I was unpacking all my beach stuff," she said, "and I looked around and you weren't there."

"Right."

"And when you came back I asked you what you were doing, and you said—"

"Your trash smelled like something died in it."

"And I told you I loved you."

"I guess you hadn't had that many men take out the trash before."

"No," she admitted. "And you're the only one I've wanted to take out my trash ever since." He gave her a real smile, and she felt her heart lift. "I want to love you so much."

His smile faltered. "What's stopping you?"

"No," she told him, trying to clarify herself. "I've been fighting it for so long. From the moment I met you, I didn't want to be in love with you. I didn't want to feel so desperate for you."

"What's changed?"

Her answer was simple. "You."

"You haven't," he told her. "Changed, I mean."

"Is that so?" she asked, wondering how he managed to make it sound like a compliment.

"You didn't need to," he said. "You were perfect already."

She laughed out loud. "Tell that to my mother."

He waited for her to stop laughing. "Thank you."

"For what?"

"Waiting for me to grow up."

She put her fingers to his cheek. "Patience has always been my strong suit."

"No kidding."

"You were worth the wait."

"Tell me that in another ten years."

"I will," she promised him. "I will."

He looked down at his injured arm, and she tried to stop him, thinking he was going to take off the sling. What he did instead was take her hand and look at his Auburn class ring on her finger. When all hell had broken loose at the station, she had taken the ring, knowing it would help identify Jeffrey to the shooters. At the hospital, while Jeffrey was in surgery, she had nearly worn a blister on her finger, rubbing the blue stone in the ring like a talisman, as if she could somehow make everything okay.

She asked, "Do you want it back?"

He kept his expression neutral. "Do you want to give it back?"

Sara looked at the ring, and thought about everything that had brought them to this place. As silly as it was, she knew what her wearing the ring would mean to Jeffrey, and to everyone else in Grant County.

She said, "I'll never take it off."

He smiled, and for the first time in what seemed like forever, Sara felt like things might eventually be okay.

Jeffrey must have felt this, too, because he tried to tease, "Maybe you should take it off if you're working in the yard."

"Hm," she answered. "Good point."

He rubbed her finger with his thumb. "Or helping out your dad."

"I could wrap some masking tape around the band so it fits better."

He smiled, tugging the ring, pointing out that it was hardly in danger of falling off. "You know what they say about big hands . . ." he began. When she did not answer, he finished, "Big feet."

"Ha-ha," she said, cupping his face in her hand. Before she knew what was happening, Sara had her arms around his neck, holding on to him as if her life depended on it. Whenever she let herself think about how close she had come to losing him, Sara felt a sort of desperation that made her chest ache.

"It's okay," he told her, though he seemed to be saying this more to himself. She could tell he was thinking about the thing that had brought them here in the first place.

She forced herself to let go of him, asking, "Are you ready?"

He glanced back at the cemetery, squaring his shoulders as best as he could.

Sara slid off the hood of the car, but he told her, "No, I need to do this alone."

"You sure?"

He nodded again, heading off toward the cemetery.

Sara got into the car, leaving the door open so she would not suffocate in the heat. She looked at the ring, turning her hand so she could see the football on the side. Like all class rings, it was huge and hideous, yet right now she thought it was one of the most beautiful things she had ever seen.

She looked up, watching Jeffrey make his way up the hill. He picked at the sling around his neck before taking it off and shoving it into his pocket.

"Jeffrey," she admonished, though of course he could not hear her. He did not hate the sling so much as the appearance of infirmity.

He stopped at the corner of the cemetery where a small marble marker stood. She knew Jeffrey well enough to know he was thinking about Sylacauga marble and underground streams, cotton mills and sinkholes. She also knew that the thing he took from his pocket was a small gold locket.

As she watched, Jeffrey used his bad hand to open the heart, taking one last look at the picture of Eric inside before leaving the keepsake on top of Julia's gravestone and walking back down the hill to Sara.

ACKNOWLEDGMENTS

Sylacauga is a lovely small town located in central Alabama near the Cheaha Mountains. They have a full-time sheriff and police force and a population of around 12,000 folks who will probably read this book and wonder if I've ever been to the place. I assure you that I have, but please keep in mind that this is a work of fiction and I have taken great license with streets, buildings, and local landmarks just to make it easier on myself. Like many small towns, Sylacauga is a peculiar blend of friendly, good folks and a smattering of bad. You can find out more at Sylacauga.net. While you're on the web, you can also look up the name Billy Jack Gaither to see the darker side of small town life.

This book has been a long time coming for me. When I first wrote BLINDSIGHTED, I knew that one day I would delve into Jeffrey and Sara's past, so in subsequent books, I left some clues for folks as a little reward for those who were paying attention. My sincere thanks to y'all for being there from the start and making it possible for me to keep doing what I love most: being a writer. I hear from a lot of readers through my website, KarinSlaughter.com, and try to answer all the mail I get as quickly as possible. Thank you all for your patience and support.

There is a long list of people to thank this time around, but I have to narrow it down because sixty pages of acknowledgments would be a little too indulgent even for me. My agent Victoria Sanders, is a great friend and champion of my work. Meaghan Dowling and Kate Elton are the best editors a girl could ask for. Ron Beard, Richard Cable, Michael Dugdale, Jane Friedman, Brian Grogan, Cathy Hemming, Gail Rebuck, and Susan Sandon are my heroes. Faye Brewster, Elspeth Dougall, Rina Gill, Georgina Hawtrey-Woore, Vanessa Kerr, Mark "Wolfie" McCallum, Richard Ogle, Tiffany Stansfield, Rob Waddington and Kate Watkins have my thanks for their generous support. Marilyn Edwards is one of my favorite writers and a certain C.R. has my undying gratitude for you know what. Speaking of initials, thanks to CF, LM, AL and KB. There are plenty more people to name, from the ladies in Scranton to the guys who drive the trucks, but space being what it is, please know you all have my sincere gratitude for the wonderful job you do.

Dan Holod reviewed gun stuff so hopefully I won't get any letters this time. Yet again David Harper, M.D. came to the rescue, making Sara really sound like a doctor. Patricia Hawkins, Amy Place, and Debbie Hartsfield provided some interesting facts about Sylacauga, where they grew up, and I hope I managed to at least capture the flavor of the town through them. I toured a lot while writing this book, from London to Holland to France and back again. Thanks to my publishers The Busy Bee, Century and Grasset. Actually, thanks to all my foreign publishers. I had the great pleasure of meeting most of them during the London Bookfair, and I can honestly say I have some of the nicest publishers in the world.

Fellow authors helped me keep my chin up. I won't name them here, but you can find most of them in LIKE A CHARM, the serial novel I worked on while writing INDELIBLE. Markus Wilhelm deserves special thanks, as does Harlan Coben, who is the only person on earth allowed to call me number two.

Lastly, I've had Sara drive a BMW in every one of these books in the hopes that the nice folks over in Munich will thank me with a shiny new 330ci. No luck yet, but I'll keep trying. Likewise, Tom Jones and Shelby Lynne. Y'all don't call . . . y'all don't write . . .

FAITHLESS

For Susan and Richard

SUNDAY

CHAPTER ONE

Sara Linton stood at the front door of her parents' house holding so many plastic grocery bags in her hands that she couldn't feel her fingers. Using her elbow, she tried to open the door but ended up smacking her shoulder into the glass pane. She edged back and pressed her foot against the handle, but the door still would not budge. Finally, she gave up and knocked with her forehead.

Through the wavy glass, she watched her father making his way down the hallway. He opened the door with an uncharacteristic scowl on his face.

"Why didn't you make two trips?" Eddie demanded, taking some of the bags from her.

"Why is the door locked?"

"Your car's less than fifteen feet away."

"Dad," Sara countered. "Why is the door locked?"

He was looking over her shoulder. "Your car is filthy." He put the bags down on the floor. "You think you can handle two trips to the kitchen with these?"

Sara opened her mouth to answer, but he was already walking down the front steps. She asked, "Where are you going?"

"To wash your car."

"It's fifty degrees out."

He turned and gave her a meaningful look. "Dirt sticks no matter the climate." He sounded like a Shakespearean actor instead of a plumber from rural Georgia.

By the time she had formed a response, he was already inside the garage.

Sara stood on the porch as her father came back out with the requisite supplies to wash her car. He hitched up his sweatpants as he knelt to fill the bucket with water. Sara recognized the pants from high school—her high school, she had worn them for track practice.

"You gonna just stand there letting the cold in?" Cathy asked, pulling Sara inside and closing the door.

Sara bent down so that her mother could kiss her on the cheek. Much to Sara's dismay, she had been a good foot taller than her mother since the fifth grade. While Tessa, Sara's younger sister, had inherited their mother's petite build, blond hair and effortless poise, Sara looked like a neighbor's child who had come for lunch one afternoon and decided to stay.

Cathy bent down to pick up some of the grocery bags, then seemed to think better of it. "Get these, will you?"

Sara scooped all eight bags into her hands, risking her fingers again. "What's wrong?" she asked, thinking her mother looked a little under the weather.

"Isabella," Cathy answered, and Sara suppressed a laugh. Her aunt Bella was the only person Sara knew who traveled with her own stock of liquor.

"Rum?"

Cathy whispered, "Tequila," the same way she might say "Cancer."

Sara cringed in sympathy. "Has she said how long she's staying?"

"Not yet," Cathy replied. Bella hated Grant County and had not visited since Tessa was born. Two days ago, she had shown up with three suitcases in the back of her convertible Mercedes and no explanations.

Normally, Bella would not have been able to get away with any sort of secrecy, but in keeping with the new "Don't ask, don't tell" ethos of the Linton family, no one had pressed her for an explanation. So much had changed since Tessa was attacked last year. They were all still shell-shocked, though no one seemed to want to talk about it. In a split second, Tessa's assailant had altered not just Tessa but the entire family. Sara often wondered if any of them would ever fully recover.

Sara asked, "Why was the door locked?"

"Must've been Tessa," Cathy said, and for just a moment her eyes watered.

"Mama—"

"Go on in," Cathy interrupted, indicating the kitchen. "I'll be there in a minute."

Sara shifted the bags and walked down the hallway, glancing at the pictures that lined the walls. No one could go from the front door to the back without getting a pictorial view of the Linton girls' formative years. Tessa, of course, looked beautiful and slim in most of them. Sara was never so lucky. There was a particularly hideous photo of Sara in summer camp back in the eighth grade that she would have ripped off the wall if her mother let her get away with it. Sara stood in a boat wearing a bathing suit that looked like a piece of black construction paper pinned to her bony shoulders. Freckles had broken out along her nose, giving her skin a less than pleasing orange cast. Her red hair had dried in the sun and looked like a clown Afro.

"Darling!" Bella enthused, throwing her arms wide as Sara entered the kitchen. "Look at you!" she said, as if this was a compliment. Sara knew full well she wasn't at her best. She had rolled out of bed an hour ago and not even bothered to comb her hair. Being her father's daughter, the shirt she wore was the one she had slept in and her sweatpants from the track team in college were only slightly less vintage. Bella, by contrast, was wearing a silky blue dress that had probably cost a fortune. Diamond earrings sparkled in her ears, the many rings she wore on her fingers glinting in the sun streaming through the kitchen windows. As usual, her makeup and hair were perfect, and she looked gorgeous even at eleven o'clock on a Sunday morning.

Sara said, "I'm sorry I haven't been by earlier."

"Feh." Her aunt waved off the apology as she sat down. "Since when do you do your mama's shopping?"

"Since she's been stuck at home entertaining you for the last two days." Sara put the bags on the counter, rubbing her fingers to encourage the circulation to return.

"I'm not that hard to entertain," Bella said. "It's your mother who needs to get out more."

"With tequila?"

Bella smiled mischievously. "She never could hold her liquor. I'm convinced that's the only reason she married your father."

Sara laughed as she put the milk in the refrigerator. Her heart skipped a beat when she saw a plate piled high with chicken, ready for frying.

Bella provided, "We snapped some greens last night."

"Lovely," Sara mumbled, thinking this was the best news she had heard all week. Cathy's green bean casserole was the perfect companion to her fried chicken. "How was church?"

"A little too fire and brimstone for me," Bella confessed, taking an orange out of the bowl on the table. "Tell me about your life. Anything interesting happening?"

"Same old same old," Sara told her, sorting through the cans.

Bella peeled the orange, sounding disappointed when she said, "Well, sometimes routine can be comforting."

Sara made a "hm" sound as she put a can of soup on the shelf above the stove.

"Very comforting."

"Hm," Sara repeated, knowing exactly where this was going.

When Sara was in medical school at Emory University in Atlanta, she had briefly lived with her aunt Bella. The late night parties, the drinking and the constant flow of men had finally caused a split. Sara had to get up at five in the morning to attend classes, not to mention the fact that she needed her nights quiet so that she could study. To her credit, Bella had tried to limit her social life, but in the end they had agreed it was best for Sara to get a place of her own. Things had been cordial until Bella had suggested Sara look into one of the units at the retirement home down on Clairmont Road.

Cathy came back into the kitchen, wiping her hands on her apron. She moved the soup can Sara had shelved, pushing her out of the way in the process. "Did you get everything on the list?"

"Except the cooking sherry," Sara told her, sitting down opposite Bella. "Did you know you can't buy alcohol on Sunday?"

"Yes," Cathy said, making the word sound like an accusation. "That's why I told you to go to the store last night."

"I'm sorry," Sara apologized. She took a slice of orange from her aunt. "I was dealing with an insurance company out west until eight o'clock. It was the only time we could talk."

"You're a doctor," Bella stated the obvious. "Why on earth do you have to talk to insurance companies?"

"Because they don't want to pay for the tests I order."

"Isn't that their job?"

Sara shrugged. She had finally broken down and hired a woman full time to jump through the various hoops the insurance companies demanded, but still, two to three hours of every day Sara spent at the children's clinic were wasted filling out tedious forms or talking to, sometimes yelling at, company supervisors on the phone. She had started going in an hour earlier to try to keep on top of it, but nothing seemed to make a dent.

"Ridiculous," Bella murmured around a slice of orange. She was well into her sixties, but as far as Sara knew, she had never been sick a day in her life. Perhaps there was something to be said for chain-smoking and drinking tequila until dawn after all.

Cathy rummaged through the bags, asking, "Did you get sage?"

"I think so." Sara stood to help her find it but Cathy shooed her away. "Where's Tess?"

"Church," Cathy answered. Sara knew better than to question her mother's disapproving tone. Obviously, Bella knew better, too, though she raised an eyebrow at Sara as she handed her another slice of orange. Tessa had passed on attending the Primitive Baptist, where Cathy had gone since she and Bella were children, choosing instead to visit a smaller church in a neighboring county for her spiritual needs. Under normal circumstances Cathy would have been glad to know at least one of her daughters wasn't a godless heathen, but there was obviously something that bothered her about Tessa's choice. As with so many things lately, no one pushed the issue.

Cathy opened the refrigerator, moving the milk to the other side of the shelf as she asked, "What time did you get home last night?"

"Around nine," Sara said, peeling another orange.

"Don't spoil lunch," Cathy admonished. "Did Jeffrey get everything moved in?"

"Almo—" Sara caught herself at the last minute, her face blushing crimson. She swallowed a few times before she could speak. "When did you hear?"

"Oh, honey," Bella chuckled. "You're living in the wrong town If you want people to stay out of your business. That's the main reason I went abroad as soon as I could afford the ticket."

"More like find a man to pay for it," Cathy wryly added.

Sara cleared her throat again, feeling like her tongue had swollen to twice its size. "Does Daddy know?"

Cathy raised an eyebrow much as her sister had done a few moments ago. "What do you think?"

Sara took a deep breath and hissed it out between her teeth. Suddenly, her father's earlier pronouncement about dirt sticking made sense. "Is he mad?"

"A little mad," Cathy allowed. "Mostly disappointed."

Bella tsked her tongue against her teeth. "Small towns, small minds."

"It's not the town," Cathy defended. "It's Eddie."

Bella sat back as if preparing to tell a story. "I lived in sin with a boy. I was barely out of college, just moved to London. He was a welder, but his hands . . . oh, he had the hands of an artist. Did I ever tell you—"

"Yes, Bella," Cathy said in a bored singsong. Bella had always been ahead of her time, from being a beatnik to a hippie to a vegan. To her constant dismay, she had never been able to scandalize her family. Sara was convinced one of the reasons her aunt had left the country was so she could tell people she was a black sheep. No one bought it in Grant. Granny Earnshaw, who worked for women's suffrage, had been proud of her daughter's brazen attitude and Big Daddy had called Bella his "little firecracker" to anyone who would listen. As a matter of fact, the only time Bella had ever managed to shock any of them was when she had announced she was getting married to a stockbroker named Colt and moving to the suburbs. Thankfully, that had lasted only a year.

Sara could feel the heat of her mother's stare bore into her like a laser. She finally relented, asking, "What?"

"I don't know why you won't just marry him."

Sara twisted the ring around her finger. Jeffrey had been a football player at Auburn University and she had taken to wearing his class ring like a lovesick girl.

Bella pointed out the obvious, as if it was some sort of enticement. "Your father can't stand him."

Cathy crossed her arms over her chest. She repeated her question to Sara. "Why?" She waited a beat. "Why not just marry him? He wants to, doesn't he?"

"Yes."

"Then why not say yes and get it over with?"

"It's complicated," Sara answered, hoping she could leave it at that. Both women knew her history with Jeffrey, from the moment she fell in love with him to their marriage to the night Sara had come home early from work to find him in bed with another woman. She had filed for divorce the next day, but for some reason, Sara was unable to let him go.

In her defense, Jeffrey had changed over the last few years. He had grown into the man she had seen the promise of almost fifteen years ago. The love she had for him was new, in its way more exciting than the first time. Sara didn't feel that giddy, I'm-going-to-die-if-he-doesn't-call-me sort of obsession she had experienced before. She felt comfortable with him. She knew at the end of the day that he would be there for her. She also knew after five years of living on her own that she was miserable without him.

"You're too proud," Cathy said. "If it's your ego—"

"It's not my ego," Sara interrupted, not knowing how to explain herself and more than a little resentful that she felt compelled to. It was just her luck that her relationship with Jeffrey seemed to be the only thing her mother felt comfortable talking about.

Sara went to the sink to wash the orange off her hands. Trying to change the subject, she asked Bella, "How was France?"

"French," Bella answered, but didn't give in that easily. "Do you trust him?"

"Yes," she said, "more than the first time, which is why I don't need a piece of paper telling me how I feel."

Bella was more than a little smug when she said, "I knew you two would get back together." She pointed a finger at Sara. "If you were serious about getting him out of your life the first time, you would've quit your coroner job."

"It's just part-time," Sara said, though she knew Bella had a point. Jeffrey was chief of police for Grant County. Sara was the medical examiner. Every suspicious death in the tri-city area had brought him back into her life.

Cathy returned to the last grocery bag, taking out a liter of Coke. "When were you going to tell us?"

"Today," Sara lied. The look Cathy tossed over her shoulder

proved it wasn't a very good fib. "Eventually," Sara amended, drying her hands on her pants as she sat back at the table. "Are you making roast for tomorrow?"

"Yes," Cathy answered, but wouldn't be sidetracked. "You live less than a mile down the street from us, Sara. Did you think your father wouldn't see Jeffrey's car parked in the driveway every morning?"

"Far as I've heard," Bella said, "it'd be there whether he moved in or not."

Sara watched her mother pour the Coke into a large Tupperware bowl. Cathy would add a few ingredients and soak a rump roast in the mixture overnight, then cook it in the Crock-Pot all day tomorrow. The end result would be the most tender meat that ever crossed a plate, and as easy as it looked, Sara had never been able to duplicate the recipe. The irony was not lost on Sara that she had mastered honors chemistry at one of the toughest medical schools in the country but could not for the life of her make her mother's Coke roast.

Cathy absently added some seasonings to the bowl, repeating her question, "When were you going to tell us?"

"I don't know," Sara answered. "We just wanted to get used to the idea first."

"Don't expect your father to any time soon," Cathy advised. "You know he has firm ideas about that sort of thing."

Bella guffawed. "That man hasn't set foot in a church in nearly forty years."

"It's not a religious objection," Cathy corrected. She told Sara, "We both remember how devastating it was for you when you found out Jeffrey was catting around. It's just hard for your father to see you broken like that and then have Jeffrey waltz back in."

"I'd hardly call it a waltz," Sara said. Nothing about their reconciliation had been easy.

"I can't tell you that your father will ever forgive him."

Bella pointed out, "Eddie forgave you."

Sara watched as all the color drained from her mother's face. Cathy wiped her hands on her apron in tight, controlled movements. In a low voice, she said, "Lunch will be ready in a few hours," and left the kitchen.

Bella lifted her shoulders and gave a heavy sigh. "I tried, pumpkin."

Sara bit her tongue. A few years ago, Cathy had told Sara about what she called an indiscretion in her marriage before Sara had been born. Though her mother said the affair had never been consummated, Eddie and Cathy had nearly divorced over the other man. Sara imagined her mother didn't like being reminded of this dark period in her past, especially not in front of her oldest child. Sara didn't much like the reminder herself.

"Hello?" Jeffrey called from the front hall.

Sara tried to hide her relief. "In here," she yelled.

He walked in with a smile on his face, and Sara assumed her father had been too busy washing her car to give Jeffrey any serious grief.

"Well," he said, looking back and forth between the two women with an appreciative smile. "When I dream about this, we're usually all naked."

"You old dog," Bella chastised, but Sara could see her eyes light up with pleasure. Despite years of living in Europe, she was still every inch the Southern belle.

Jeffrey took her hand and kissed it. "You get better looking every time I see you, Isabella."

"Fine wine, my friend." Bella winked. "Drinking it, I mean."

Jeffrey laughed and Sara waited for a lull before asking, "Did you see Dad?"

Jeffrey shook his head just as the front door slammed closed. Eddie's footsteps were heavy down the hallway.

Sara grabbed Jeffrey's hand. "Let's go for a walk," she said, practically dragging him out the back door. She asked Bella, "Tell Mama we'll be back in time for lunch."

Jeffrey stumbled down the deck steps as she pulled him to the side of the house and out of view from the kitchen windows.

"What's going on?" He rubbed his arm as if it hurt.

"Still tender?" she asked. He had injured his shoulder a while back and despite physical therapy, the joint continued to ache.

He gave a half shrug. "I'm okay."

"Sorry," she said, putting her hand on his good shoulder. She found herself unable to stop there and put her arms around him, burying her face in the crook of his neck. She inhaled deeply, loving the smell of him. "God, you feel so good."

He stroked her hair. "What's going on?"

"I miss you."

"I'm here."

"No," she leaned back so she could see him. "This week." His hair was getting long on the sides and she used her fingers to tuck it behind his ear. "You just come in, drop off some boxes and leave."

"The renters move in Tuesday. I told them I'd have the kitchen ready by then."

She kissed his ear, whispering, "I've forgotten what you look like."

"Work's been busy lately." He pulled away a few inches. "Paperwork and stuff. Between that and the house, I don't have time for myself, let alone seeing you."

"It's not that," she said, wondering at his defensive tone. They both worked too much; she was hardly in a position to throw stones.

He took a couple of steps back, saying, "I know I didn't return a couple of your calls."

"Jeff," she stopped him. "I just assumed you were tied up. It's no big deal."

"What is it, then?"

Sara crossed her arms, suddenly feeling cold. "Dad knows."

He seemed to relax a bit, and she wondered from his relief whether he had been expecting something else.

He said, "You didn't think we could keep it a secret, did you?"

"I don't know," Sara admitted. She could tell something was on his mind but wasn't sure how to draw him out. She suggested, "Let's walk around the lake. Okay?"

He glanced back at the house, then at her. "Yeah."

She led him through the backyard, taking the stone path to the shore that her father had laid before Sara was born. They fell into a companionable silence, holding hands as they navigated the dirt track that cut into the shoreline. She slipped on a wet rock and he caught her elbow, smiling at her clumsiness. Overhead, Sara could hear squirrels chattering and a large buzzard swooped in an arc just above the trees, its wings stiff against the breeze coming off the water.

Lake Grant was a thirty-two-hundred acre man-made lake that

was three hundred feet deep in places. Tops of trees that had been in the valley before the area was flooded still grew out of the water and Sara often thought of the abandoned homes under there, wondering if the fish had set up house. Eddie had a photograph of the area before the lake was made and it looked just like the more rural parts of the county: nice shotgun-style houses with an occasional shack here and there. Underneath were stores and churches and a cotton mill that had survived the Civil War and Reconstruction only to be shut down during the Depression. All of this had been wiped out by the rushing waters of the Ochawahee River so that Grant could have a reliable source of electricity. During the summer, the waterline rose and fell depending on the demand from the dam, and as a child, Sara had made a habit of turning off all the lights in the house, thinking that would help keep the water high enough so that she could ski.

The National Forestry Service owned the best part of the lake, over a thousand acres that wrapped around the water like a cowl. One side touched the residential area where Sara and her parents had houses and the other held back the Grant Institute of Technology. Sixty percent of the lake's eighty-mile shoreline was protected, and Sara's favorite area was smack in the middle. Campers were allowed to stake tents in the forest, but the rocky terrain close to shore was too sharp and steep for anything pleasurable. Mostly, teenagers came here to make out or just to get away from their parents. Sara's house was directly across from a spectacular set of rocks that had probably been used by the Indians before they were forced out, and sometimes at dusk she could see an occasional flash of a match as someone lit a cigarette or who knew what else.

A cold wind came off the water and she shivered. Jeffrey put his arm around her, asking, "Did you really think they wouldn't find out?"

Sara stopped and turned to face him. "I guess I just hoped."

He gave one of his lopsided smiles, and she knew from experience that an apology was coming. "I'm sorry I've been working so much."

"I haven't gotten home before seven all week."

"Did you get the insurance company straightened out?"

She groaned. "I don't want to talk about it."

"Okay," he said, obviously trying to think of something to say. "How's Tess?"

"Not that, either."

"Okay . . ." He smiled again, the sun catching the blue in his irises in a way that made Sara shiver again.

"You wanna head back?" he asked, misinterpreting her response.

"No," she said, cupping her hands around his neck. "I want you to take me behind those trees and ravage me."

He laughed, but stopped when he saw she was not joking. "Out here in the open?"

"Nobody's around."

"You can't be serious."

"It's been two weeks," she said, though she hadn't given it much thought before now. It wasn't like him to let things go this long.

"It's cold."

She put her lips to his ear and whispered, "It's warm in my mouth."

Contrary to his body's reaction, he said, "I'm kind of tired."

She pressed her body closer. "You don't seem tired to me."

"It's gonna start raining any minute now."

The sky was overcast, but Sara knew from the news that rain was a good three hours away. "Come on," she said, leaning in to kiss him. She stopped when he seemed to hesitate. "What's wrong?"

He took a step back and looked out at the lake. "I told you I'm tired."

"You're never tired," she said. "Not tired like that."

He indicated the lake with a toss of his hand. "It's freezing cold out here."

"It's not that cold," she said, feeling suspicion trace a line of dread down her spine. After fifteen years, she knew all of Jeffrey's signs. He picked at his thumbnail when he felt guilty and pulled at his right eyebrow when there was something about a case he was trying to puzzle out. When he'd had a particularly hard day, he tended to slump his shoulders and speak in a monotone until she found a way to help him talk it out. The set he had to his mouth now meant there was something he had to tell her but either did not want to or did not know how.

She crossed her arms, asking, "What's going on?"

"Nothing."

"Nothing?" she repeated, staring at Jeffrey as if she could will the truth out of him. His lips were set in that same firm line and he had his hands clasped in front of him, his right thumb tracing the cuticle of the left. She was getting the distinct feeling that they had been down this road before, and the knowledge of what was happening hit her like a sledgehammer to the gut. "Oh, Christ," she breathed, suddenly understanding. "Oh, God," she said, putting her hand to her stomach, trying to calm the sickness that wanted to come.

"What?"

She walked back down the path, feeling stupid and angry with herself at the same time. She was dizzy from it, her mind reeling.

"Sara—" He put his hand on her arm but she jerked away. He jogged ahead a few steps, blocking her way so she had to look at him. "What's wrong?"

"Who is it?"

"Who's what?"

"Who is *she*?" Sara clarified. "Who is it, Jeffrey? Is it the same one as last time?" She was clenching her teeth so tight that her jaw ached. It all made sense: the distracted look on his face, the defensiveness, the distance between them. He had made excuses every night this week for not staying at her house: packing boxes, working late at the station, needing to finish that damn kitchen that had taken almost a decade to renovate. Every time she let him in, every time she let her guard down and felt comfortable, he found a way to push her away.

Sara came straight out with it. "Who are you screwing this time?"

He took a step back, confusion crossing his face. "You don't think . . ."

She felt tears well into her eyes and covered her face with her hands to hide them. He would think she was hurt when the fact was she was angry enough to rip out his throat with her bare hands. "God," she whispered. "I'm so stupid."

"How could you think that?" he demanded, as if he had been wronged.

She dropped her hands, not caring what he saw. "Do me a favor, okay? Don't lie to me this time. Don't you dare lie to me."

"I'm not lying to you about anything," he insisted, sounding just as livid as she felt. She would find his outraged tone more persuasive if he hadn't used it on her the first time.

"Sara—"

"Just get away from me," she said, walking back toward the lake. "I can't believe this. I can't believe how stupid I am."

"I'm not cheating on you," he said, following her. "Listen to me, okay?" He got in front of her, blocking the way. "I'm not cheating on you."

She stopped, staring at him, wishing she could believe him.

He said, "Don't look at me that way."

"I don't know how else to look at you."

He let out a heavy sigh, as if he had a huge weight on his chest. For someone who insisted he was innocent, he was acting incredibly guilty.

"I'm going back to the house," she told him, but he looked up, and she saw something in his expression that stopped her.

He spoke so softly she had to strain to hear him. "I might be sick."

"Sick?" she repeated, suddenly panicked. "Sick how?"

He walked back and sat down on a rock, his shoulders sagging. It was Sara's turn to follow him.

"Jeff?" she asked, kneeling beside him. "What's wrong?" Tears came into her eyes again, but this time her heart was thumping from fear instead of anger.

Of all the things he could have said, what next came from his mouth shocked her most of all. "Jo called."

Sara sat back on her heels. She folded her hands in her lap and stared at them, her vision tunneling. In high school, Jolene Carter had been everything Sara wasn't: graceful, curvaceous yet thin, the most popular girl in school, with her pick of all the popular boys. She was the prom queen, the head cheerleader, the president of the senior class. She had real blond hair and blue eyes and a little mole, a beauty mark, on her right cheek that gave her otherwise perfect features a worldly, exotic look. Even close to her forties, Jolene Carter still had a perfect body—something Sara knew because five years ago, she had come home to find Jo completely naked with her perfect ass up in the air, straddling Jeffrey in their bed.

Jeffrey said, "She has hepatitis."

Sara would have laughed if she had the energy. As it was, all she could manage was, "Which kind?"

"The bad kind."

"There are a couple of bad kinds," Sara told him, wondering how she had gotten to this place.

"I haven't slept with her since that one time. You know that, Sara."

For a few seconds, she found herself staring at him, torn between wanting to get up and run away and staying to find out the facts. "When did she call you?"

"Last week."

"Last week," she repeated, then took a deep breath before asking, "What day?"

"I don't know. The first part."

"Monday? Tuesday?"

"What does it matter?"

"What does it matter?" she echoed, incredulous. "I'm a pediatrician, Jeffrey. I give kids—little kids—injections all day. I take blood from them. I put my fingers in their scrapes and cuts. There are precautions. There are all sorts of . . ." She let her voice trail off, wondering how many children she had exposed to this, trying to remember every shot, every puncture. Had she been safe? She was always sticking herself with needles. She couldn't even let herself worry about her own health. It was too much.

"I went to Hare yesterday," he said, as if the fact that he had visited a doctor after knowing for a week somehow redeemed him.

She pressed her lips together, trying to form the right questions. She had been worried about her kids, but now the full implications hit her head-on. She could be sick, too. She could have some chronic, maybe deadly, disease that Jeffrey had given her.

Sara swallowed, trying to speak past the tightness in her throat. "Did he put a rush on the test?"

"I don't know."

"You don't know," she confirmed, not a question. Of course he didn't know. Jeffrey suffered from typical male denial about anything relating to his health. He knew more about his car's maintenance history than his own well-being and she could imagine him sitting in Hare's office, a blank look on his face, trying to think of a good excuse to leave as quickly as possible.

Sara stood up. She needed to pace. "Did he examine you?"

"He said I wasn't showing any symptoms."

"I want you to go to another doctor."

"What's wrong with Hare?"

"He . . ." She couldn't find the words. Her brain wouldn't work.

"Just because he's your goofy cousin doesn't mean he's not a good doctor."

"He didn't tell me," she said, feeling betrayed by both of them.

Jeffrey gave her a careful look. "I asked him not to."

"Of course you did," she said, feeling not so much angry as blind-sided. "Why didn't you tell me? Why didn't you take me with you so that I could ask the right questions?"

"This," he said, indicating her pacing. "You've got enough on your mind. I didn't want you to be upset."

"That's crap and you know it." Jeffrey hated giving bad news. As confrontational as he had to be in his job, he was incapable of making waves at home. "Is this why you haven't wanted to have sex?"

"I was being careful."

"Careful," she repeated.

"Hare said I could be a carrier."

"You were too scared to tell me."

"I didn't want to upset you."

"You didn't want me to be upset with *you*," she corrected. "This has nothing to do with sparing my feelings. You didn't want me to be mad at *you*."

"Please don't do this." He reached out to take her hand but she jerked away. "It's not my fault, okay?" He tried again, "It was years ago, Sara. She had to tell me because her doctor said so." As if this made things better, he said, "She's seeing Hare, too. Call him. He's the one who said I had to be informed. It's just a precaution. You're a doctor. You know that."

"Stop," she ordered, holding up her hands. Words were on the tip of her tongue, but she struggled not to say them. "I can't talk about this right now."

"Where are you going?"

"I don't know," she said, walking toward the shore. "Home," she told him. "You can stay at your house tonight."

"See," he said, as if making a point. "This is why I didn't tell you."

"Don't blame me for this," she shot back, her throat clenching around the words. She wanted to be yelling, but she found herself so filled with rage that she was incapable of raising her voice. "I'm not mad at you because you screwed around, Jeffrey. I'm mad at you because you kept this from me. I have a right to know. Even if this didn't affect me and my health and my patients, it affects you."

He jogged to keep up with her. "I'm fine."

She stopped, turning to look at him. "Do you even know what hepatitis is?"

His shoulders rose in a shrug. "I figured I'd deal with that when I had to. If I had to."

"Jesus," Sara whispered, unable to do anything but walk away. She headed toward the road, thinking she should take the long way back to her parents in order to calm down. Her mother would have a field day with this, and rightfully so.

Jeffrey started to follow. "Where are you going?"

"I'll call you in a few days." She did not wait for his answer. "I need some time to think."

He closed the gap between them, his fingers brushing the back of her arm. "We need to talk."

She laughed. "*Now* you want to talk about it."

"Sara—"

"There's nothing more to say," she told him, quickening her pace. Jeffrey kept up, his footsteps heavy behind her. She was starting off into a jog when he slammed into her from behind. Sara fell to the ground with a hollow-sounding thud, knocking the wind out of her. The thud as she hit the ground reverberated in her ears like a distant echo.

She pushed him off, demanding, "What are you—"

"Jesus, I'm sorry. Are you okay?" He knelt in front of her, picking a twig out of her hair. "I didn't mean—"

"You jackass," she snapped. He had scared her more than anything else, and her response was even more anger. "What the hell is wrong with you?"

"I tripped," he said, trying to help her up.

"Don't touch me." She slapped him away and stood on her own.

He brushed the dirt off her pants, repeating, "Are you okay?"

She backed away from him. "I'm fine."

Are you sure?

"I'm not a piece of china." She scowled at her dirt-stained sweatshirt. The sleeve had been torn at the shoulder. "What is wrong with you?"

"I told you I tripped. Do you think I did it on purpose?"

"No," she told him, though the admission did nothing to ease her anger. "God, Jeffrey." She tested her knee, feeling the tendon catch. "That really hurt."

"I'm sorry," he repeated, pulling another twig out of her hair.

She looked at her torn sleeve, more annoyed now than angry. "What happened?"

He turned, scanning the area. "There must have been . . ." He stopped talking.

She followed his gaze and saw a length of metal pipe sticking out of the ground. A rubber band held a piece of wire screen over the top.

All he said was, "Sara," but the dread in his tone sent a jolt through her.

She replayed the scene in her head, the sound as she was slammed into the ground. There should have been a solid thump, not a hollow reverberation. Something was underneath them. Something was buried in the earth.

"Christ," Jeffrey whispered, snatching off the screen. He looked down into the pipe, but Sara knew the half-inch circumference would make it impossible to see.

Still, she asked, "Anything?"

"No." He tried to move the pipe back and forth, but it would not budge. Something underground held it tightly in place.

She dropped to her knees and brushed the leaves and pine needles away from the area, working her way back as she followed the pattern of loose soil. She was about four feet away from Jeffrey when they both seemed to realize what might be below them.

Sara felt her own alarm escalate with Jeffrey's as he started clawing his fingers into the ground. The soil came away easily as if someone had recently dug there. Soon, Sara was on her knees beside him, pulling up clumps of rock and earth, trying not to think about what they might find.

"Fuck!" Jeffrey jerked up his hand, and Sara saw a deep gash along the side of his palm where a sharp stick had gouged out the skin. The cut was bleeding profusely, but he went back to the task in front of him, digging at the ground, throwing dirt to the side.

Sara's fingernails scraped something hard, and she pulled her hand back to find wood underneath. She said, "Jeffrey," but he kept digging. "Jeffrey."

"I know," he told her. He had exposed a section of wood around the pipe. A metal collar surrounded the conduit, holding it tightly in place. Jeffrey took out his pocketknife, and Sara could only stare as he tried to work out the screws. Blood from his cut palm made his hands slide down the handle, and he finally gave up, tossing the knife aside and grabbing the pipe. He put his shoulder into it, wincing from the pain. Still, he kept pushing until there was an ominous groan from the wood, then a splintering as the collar came away.

Sara covered her nose as a stagnant odor drifted out.

The hole was roughly three inches square, sharp splinters cutting into the opening like teeth.

Jeffrey put his eye to the break. He shook his head. "I can't see anything."

Sara kept digging, moving back along the length of the wood, each new section she uncovered making her feel like her heart would explode from her mouth. There were several one-by-twos nailed together, forming the top of what could only be a long, rectangular box. Her breath caught, and despite the breeze she broke out into a cold sweat. Her sweatshirt suddenly felt like a straitjacket, and she pulled it over her head and tossed it aside so she could move more freely. Her mind was reeling with the possibilities of what they might find. Sara seldom prayed, but thinking about what they might discover buried below moved her to ask anyone who was listening to please help.

"Watch out," Jeffrey warned, using the pipe to pry at the wooden slats. Sara sat back on her knees, shielding her eyes as dirt sprayed into the air. The wood splintered, most of it still buried, but Jeffrey kept at it, using his hands to break the thin slats. A low, creaking moan like a dying gasp came as nails yielded against the strain. The odor of fresh decay wafted over Sara like a sour breeze, but she did not look away when Jeffrey laid flat to the ground so that he could reach his arm into the narrow opening.

He looked up at her as he felt around, his jaw clenched tight. "I feel something," he said. "Somebody."

"Breathing?" Sara asked, but he shook his head before she got the word out of her mouth.

Jeffrey worked more slowly, more deliberately, as he pried away another piece of wood. He looked at the underside, then passed it to Sara. She could see scratch marks in the pulp, as if an animal had been trapped. A fingernail about the size of one of her own was embedded in the next piece Jeffrey handed her, and Sara put it faceup on the ground. The next slat was scratched harder, and she put this beside the first, keeping a semblance of the pattern, knowing it was evidence. It could be an animal. A kid's prank. Some old Indian burial ground. Explanations flashed in and out of her mind, but she could only watch as Jeffrey pried the boards away, each slat feeling like a splinter in Sara's heart. There were almost twenty pieces in all, but by the twelfth, they could see what was inside.

Jeffrey stared into the coffin, his Adam's apple moving up and down as he swallowed. Like Sara, he seemed at a loss for words.

The victim was a young woman, probably in her late teens. Her dark hair was long to her waist, blanketing her body. She wore a simple blue dress that fell to mid-calf and white socks but no shoes. Her mouth and eyes were wide open in a panic that Sara could almost taste. One hand reached up, fingers contracted as if the girl was still trying to claw her way out. Tiny dots of petechiae were scattered in the sclera of her eyes, long-dried tears evidenced by the thin red lines breaking through the white. Several empty water bottles were in the box along with a jar that had obviously been used for waste. A flashlight was on her right, a half-eaten piece of bread on her left. Mold grew on the corners, much as mold grew like a fine mustache over the girl's upper lip. The young woman had not been a remarkable beauty, but she had probably been pretty in her own, unassuming way.

Jeffrey exhaled slowly, sitting back on the ground. Like Sara, he was covered in dirt. Like Sara, he did not seem to care.

They both stared at the girl, watched the breeze from the lake ruffle her thick hair and pick at the long sleeves of her dress. Sara noticed a matching blue ribbon tied in the girl's hair and wondered who had put it there. Had her mother or sister tied it for her? Had she sat in her room and looked at the mirror, securing the ribbon herself? And then what had happened? What had brought her here?

Jeffrey wiped his hands on his jeans, bloody fingerprints leaving their mark. "They didn't mean to kill her," he guessed.

"No," Sara agreed, enveloped by an overwhelming sadness. "They just wanted to scare her to death."

CHAPTER TWO

At the clinic, they had asked Lena about the bruises.

"You all right, darlin'?" the older black woman had said, her brows knitted in concern.

Lena had automatically answered yes, waiting for the nurse to leave before she finished getting dressed.

There were bruises that came from being a cop: the rub from where the gun on your hip wore so hard against you that some days it felt like the bone was getting a permanent dent. The thin line of blue like a crayon mark on your forearm from accommodating the lump of steel as you kept your hand as straight to your side as you could, trying not to alert the population at large that you were carrying concealed.

When Lena was a rookie, there were even more problems: back aching, gunbelt chafing, welts from her nightstick slapping her leg as she ran all out to catch up with a perp. Sometimes, by the time she caught them, it felt good to use the stick, let them know what it felt like to chase their sorry ass half a mile in ninety-degree heat with eighty pounds of equipment flogging your body. Then there was the bulletproof vest. Lena had known cops—big, burly men—who had passed out from heat exhaustion. In August, it was so hot that they weighed the odds: get shot in the chest or die from a heatstroke.

Yet, when she finally got her gold detective's shield, gave up her uniform and hat, signed in her portable radio for the last time, she had missed the weight of it all. She missed the heavy reminder that she was a cop. Being a detective meant you worked without props. On the street, you couldn't let your uniform do the talking, your cruiser making traffic slow even if the cars were already going the speed limit. You had to find other ways to intimidate the bad guys. You only had your brain to let you know you were still a cop.

After the nurse had left her sitting in that room in Atlanta, what the clinic called the recovery room, Lena had looked at the familiar bruises, judging them against the new ones. Finger marks wrapped around her arm like a band. Her wrist was swollen from where it had been twisted. She could not see the fist-shaped welt above her left kidney, but she felt it whenever she moved the wrong way.

Her first year wearing the uniform, she had seen it all. Domestic disputes where women threw rocks at your cruiser, thinking that would help talk you out of carting off their abusive husbands to jail. Neighbors knifing each other over a mulberry tree hanging too low or a missing lawn mower that ended up being in the garage somewhere, usually near a little baggie of pot or sometimes something harder. Little kids clinging to their fathers, begging not to be taken away from their homes, then you'd get them to the hospital and the doctors would find signs of vaginal or anal tearing. Sometimes, their throats would be torn down deep, little scratch marks inside where they had choked.

The instructors tried to prepare you for this sort of thing in the academy, but you could never be really prepared. You had to see it, taste it, feel it for yourself. No one explained how terrifying it was to do a traffic stop on some out-of-towner, your heart pounding in your chest as you walked up to the driver's side, hand on your gun, wondering if the guy in the car had his hand on his gun, too. The textbooks had pictures of dead people, and Lena could remember how the guys in class had laughed at some of them. The lady who got drunk and passed out in the bathtub with her panty hose caught around her ankles. The guy who hanged himself getting his nut off, and then you had this moment when you realized the thing he was holding in his hand wasn't a ripe plum. He had probably been a father, a husband, definitely someone's son, but to all the cadets, he was "the Plum-Nut Guy."

None of this got you ready for the sight and smell of the real thing. Your training officer couldn't describe the feel of death, when you walked into a room and the hairs on the back of your neck stood up, telling you something bad had happened, or—worse—was about to happen. Your chief couldn't warn you against the habit of smacking your lips, trying to get the taste out of your mouth. No one told you that no matter how many times you scrubbed your body, only time could wear away the smell of death from your skin. Running three miles a day in the hot sun, working the weights in the gym, the sweat pouring off you like rain coming out of dark clouds until finally you got the smell out—and then you went out on a call—to a gas station, an abandoned car, a neighbor's house where the papers were piled in the driveway and mail was spilling out of the box—and found another grandmother or brother or sister or uncle you had to sweat out of your system again.

No one knew how to help you deal with it when death came into your own life. No one could take away the grief you felt knowing that your own actions had ended a life—no matter how nasty that life was. That was the kicker. As a cop, you learned pretty quickly that there was an "us" and a "them." Lena never thought she'd mourn the loss of a "them," but lately, that was all she could think about. And now there was another life taken, another death on her hands.

She had been feeling death inside out for the last few days, and nothing could rid it from her senses. Her mouth tasted sour, every breath she drew fueling what smelled like decay. Her ears heard a constant shrill siren and there was a clamminess to her skin that made her feel as if she had borrowed it from a graveyard. Her body was not her own, her mind something she could no longer control. From the second she had left the clinic through the night they spent in an Atlanta hotel room to the moment she had walked through the door of her uncle's house, all she could think about was what she had done, the bad decisions that had led her here.

Lying in bed now, Lena looked out the window, staring at the depressing backyard. Hank hadn't changed a thing in the house since Lena was a child. Her bedroom still had the brown water stain in the corner where a branch had punctured the roof during a storm. The paint peeled off the wall where he'd used the wrong kind of primer and the wallpaper had soaked up enough nicotine to give it all the same sickly jaundiced cast.

Lena had grown up here with Sibyl, her twin sister. Their mother had died in childbirth and Calvin Adams, their father, had been shot on a traffic stop a few months before that. Sibyl had been killed three years ago. Another death, another abandonment. Maybe having her sister around had kept Lena rooted in life. Now she was drifting, making even more bad choices and not bothering to rectify them.

She was living with the consequences of her actions. Or maybe barely surviving would be a better way to describe it.

Lena touched her fingers to her stomach, to where the baby had been less than a week ago. Only one person was living with the consequences. Only one person had survived. Would the child have had her dark coloring, the genes of her Mexican-American grandmother surfacing yet again, or would it have inherited the father's steel gray eyes and pale white skin?

She lifted up, sliding her fingers into her back pocket, pulling out a long pocketknife. Carefully, she pried open the blade. The tip was broken off, and embedded in a semicircle of dried blood was Ethan's fingerprint.

She looked at her arm, the deep bruise where Ethan had grabbed her, and wondered how the finger that had made the swirling print in the blade, the hand that had held this knife, the fist that had caused so much pain, could be the same one that gently traced its way down her body.

The cop in her knew she should arrest him. The woman in her knew that he was bad. The realist knew that one day he would kill her. Some unnamed place deep inside of Lena resisted these thoughts, and she found herself being the worst kind of coward. She was the woman throwing rocks at the police cruiser. She was the neighbor with the knife. She was the idiot kid clinging to her abuser. She was the one with tears deep inside her throat, choking on what he made her swallow.

There was a knock on the door. "Lee?"

She folded the blade by the edge, sitting up quickly. When Hank opened the door, she was clutching her stomach, feeling like something had torn.

He went to her side, standing there with his fingers reaching out to her shoulder but not quite touching. "You okay?"

"Sat up too fast."

He dropped his hand, tucking it into his pocket. "You feel like eating anything?"

She nodded, lips slightly parted so she could take a few breaths.

"You need help getting up?"

"It's been a week," she said, as if that answered the question. They had told her she would be able to go back to work two days after the procedure, but Lena didn't know how women managed to do it. She had been on the Grant County force for twelve years and never taken a vacation until now. It'd be funny if this were the sort of thing you could laugh at.

"I got some lunch on the way home," he said, and Lena guessed from his neatly pressed Hawaiian shirt and white jeans that he had been at church all morning. She glanced at the clock; it was after noon. She had slept for fifteen hours.

Hank stood there, hands still in his pockets, like he was waiting for her to say something.

She said, "I'll be there in a minute."

"You need anything?"

"Like what, Hank?"

He pressed together his thin lips, scratching his arms like they itched. The needle tracks scarring his skin were still prominent even after all these years, and she hated the sight of them, hated the way he didn't seem to care that they reminded her of everything that was wrong between them.

He said, "I'll fix you a plate."

"Thanks," she managed, letting her legs hang over the bed. She pressed her feet firmly to the floor, trying to remind herself that she was here in this room. This last week, she had found herself traveling around in her mind, going to places that felt better, safer. Sibyl was still alive. Ethan Green hadn't come into her life yet. Things were easier.

A long, hot bath would have been nice, but Lena wasn't allowed to sit in a tub for at least another week. She wasn't allowed to have sex for twice as long as that, and every time she tried to come up with a lie, some explanation to give Ethan for not being available, all she could think was that it would be easier just to let him do it. Whatever harm came to her would be her own fault. There had to be a day of reckoning for what she had done. There had to be some sort of punishment for the lie that was her life.

She took a quick shower to wake herself up, making sure not to get her hair wet because the thought of holding a hairdryer for however many minutes it took was too tiring to even think about. She was turning lazy through all this, sitting around and staring out the window as if the dirt-packed backyard with its lonesome tire swing and 1959 Cadillac that had been on blocks since before Lena and Sibyl had been born was the beginning and end of her world. It could be. Hank had said more than a few times that she could move back in with him, and the easiness of the offer had swayed her back and forth like the ocean's undertow. If she did not leave soon, she would find herself adrift with no hope of land. She would never feel her feet firmly on the ground again.

Hank had been against taking her to the clinic in Atlanta, but to his credit, he had let her decision stand. Through the years, Hank had done a lot of things for Lena that maybe he didn't believe in—be it for religious reasons or his own damn fool stubbornness—and she was just now realizing what a gift that was. Not that she would ever be able to acknowledge this to his face. As much as Hank Norton had been one of the few constants in her life, Lena was keenly aware that for him, she was the only thing he had left to hold on to. If she were a less selfish person, she'd feel sorry for the old man.

The kitchen was right off the bathroom, and she wrapped herself in her robe before she opened the door. Hank was standing over the sink tearing the skin off a piece of fried chicken. KFC boxes were scattered on the counter beside a paper plate piled with mashed potatoes, coleslaw and a couple of biscuits.

He said, "I didn't know what piece you wanted."

Lena could see the brown gravy congealing on top of the potatoes and the mayonnaise smell from the coleslaw made her stomach clench. Just the thought of food made her want to vomit. Seeing it, smelling it, was enough to push her over the edge.

Hank dropped the chicken leg on the counter, putting his hands out like she might fall, saying, "Sit down."

For once, she did as she was told, taking a wobbly chair from under the kitchen table. There were tons of pamphlets scattered on the top—AA and NA meetings being Hank's most abiding addiction—but he had cleared a small space for her to eat. She put her elbows on the table and rested her head in her hand, not feeling dizzy so much as out of place.

He rubbed her back, his calloused fingers catching on the material of her robe. She gritted her teeth, wishing he wouldn't touch her but not wanting to deal with the hurt look on his face if she pulled away.

He cleared his throat. "You want me to call the doctor?"

"I'm okay."

He pointed out the obvious, "You never had a strong stomach."

"I'm okay," she repeated, feeling like he was trying to remind her of their history, of the fact that he had seen her through just about everything in her life.

He pulled out another chair and sat across from her. Lena could sense him waiting for her to look up, and she took her time obliging. As a kid, she had thought Hank was old, but now that she was thirty-four, the age Hank had been when he took in his dead sister's twin daughters to raise, he looked ancient. The life he'd lived had cut hard lines into his face just as the needles he'd pushed into his veins had left their marks. Ice blue eyes stared back at her, and she could see anger under his concern. Anger had always been a constant companion to Hank, and sometimes when she looked at him, Lena could see her future written out in his cragged features.

The drive to Atlanta, to the clinic, had been a quiet one. Normally, they didn't have much to say to each other, but the heaviness of the silence had been like a weight on Lena's chest. She had told Hank she wanted to go into the clinic alone, but once she got into the building—its bright fluorescent lights almost pulsing with the knowledge of what she was about to do—Lena had longed for his presence.

There was one other woman in the waiting room, an almost pathetically thin mousy blonde who kept fidgeting with her hands, avoiding Lena's gaze almost as keenly as Lena avoided hers. She was a few years younger than Lena, but kept her hair swept up on top of her head in a tight bun like she was an old lady. Lena found herself wondering what had brought the girl there— was she a college student whose carefully planned life had hit a snag? A careless flirt who had gone too far at a party? The victim of some drunken uncle's affection?

Lena didn't ask her—didn't have the nerve and did not want to open herself up to the same question. So they sat for nearly an hour, two prisoners awaiting a death sentence, both consumed by the guilt of their crimes. Lena had almost been relieved when they took her back to the procedure room, doubly relieved to see Hank when they finally wheeled her outside to the parking lot. He must have paced beside his car, chain-smoking the entire time. The pavement was littered with brown butts that he had smoked down to the filters.

Afterward, he had taken her to a hotel on Tenth Street, knowing they should stay in Atlanta in case she had a reaction or needed help. Reese, the town where Hank had raised Lena and Sibyl and where he still lived, was a small town and people didn't have anything better to do than talk about their neighbors. Barring that, neither one of them trusted the local doctor to know what to do if Lena needed help. The man refused to write prescriptions for birth control and was often quoted in the local paper saying that the problem with the town's rowdy youth was that their mothers had jobs instead of staying home to raise their kids like God intended.

The hotel room was nicer than anything Lena had ever stayed in, a sort of mini-suite with a sitting area. Hank had stayed on the couch watching TV with the sound turned down low, ordering room service when he had to, not even going out to smoke. At night, he folded his lanky body onto the couch, his light snores keeping Lena up, but comforting her at the same time.

She had told Ethan she was going to the Georgia Bureau of Investigation's training lab for a course on crime scene processing that Jeffrey wanted her to attend. She had told Nan, her roommate, that she was going to stay with Hank to go through some of Sibyl's things. In retrospect, she knew she should have told them the same lie to make it easier, but for some reason lying to Nan had flustered Lena. Her sister and Nan had been lovers, made a life together. After Sibyl died, Nan had tried to take Lena under her wing, a poor substitute for Sibyl, but at least she had tried. Lena still did not know why she could not bring herself to tell the other woman the real reason for the trip.

Nan was a lesbian, and judging by the mail she got, she was probably some kind of feminist. She would have been an easier person to take to the clinic than Hank, vocalizing her support instead of seething in quiet disdain. Nan would have probably raised her fist at the protesters outside who were yelling "Baby killer" and "Murderer" as the nurse took Lena to the car in a squeaky old wheelchair. Nan probably would have comforted Lena, maybe brought her tea and made her eat something instead of letting her hold on to her hunger like a punishment, relishing the dizziness and the burning pain in her stomach. She certainly wouldn't have let Lena lie around in bed all day staring out the window.

Which was as good a reason as any to keep all of this from her. Nan knew too many bad things about Lena already. There was no need to add another failure to the list.

Hank said, "You need to talk to somebody."

Lena rested her cheek against her palm, staring over his shoulder. She was so tired her eyelids fluttered when she blinked. Five minutes. She would give him five minutes then go back to bed.

"What you did . . ." He let his voice trail off. "I understand why you did it. I really do."

"Thanks," she said, glib.

"I wish I had it in me," he began, clenching his hands. "I'd tear that boy apart and bury him where nobody'd ever think to look."

They'd had this conversation before. Mostly, Hank talked and Lena just stared, waiting for him to realize she was not going to participate. He had gone to too many meetings, seen too many drunks and addicts pouring out their hearts to a bunch of strangers just for a little plastic chip to carry around in their pockets.

"I would'a raised it," he said, not the first time he had offered. "Just like I raised you and your sister."

"Yeah," she said, pulling her robe tighter around her. "You did such a great job."

"You never let me in."

"Into what?" she asked. Sibyl had always been his favorite. As a child she had been more pliable, more eager to please. Lena had been the uncontrollable one, the one who wanted to push the limits.

She realized that she was rubbing her belly and made herself stop. Ethan had punched her square in the stomach when she had told him that no, she really wasn't pregnant, it was a false alarm. He had warned her that if she ever killed a child of theirs, he would kill her, too. He warned her about a lot of things she didn't listen to.

"You're such a strong person," Hank said. "I don't understand why you let that boy control you."

She would have explained it if she knew how. Men didn't get it. They didn't understand that it didn't matter how strong you were, mentally or physically. What mattered was that need you felt in your gut, and how they made the ache go away. Lena used to have such disgust for women who let men knock them around. What was wrong with them? What made them so weak that they didn't care about themselves? They were pathetic, getting exactly what they asked for. Sometimes she had wanted to slap them around herself, tell them to straighten up, stop being a doormat.

From the inside, she saw it differently. As easy as it was to hate Ethan when he wasn't around, when he was there and being sweet, she never wanted him to leave. As bad as her life was, he could make it better or worse, depending on his mood. Giving him that control, that responsibility, was almost a relief, one more thing she didn't have to deal with. And, to be honest, sometimes she hit him back. Sometimes she hit him first.

Every woman who'd ever been slapped around said she had asked for it, set off her boyfriend or husband by making him mad or burning dinner or whatever it was they used to justify having the shit beaten out of them, but Lena knew for a fact that she brought out Ethan's bad side. He had wanted to change. When she first met him, he was trying very hard to be a different person, a good person. If Hank knew this particular fact, he would be shocked if not sickened. It wasn't Ethan who caused the bruises, it was Lena. She was the one who kept pulling him back in. She was the one who kept baiting him and slapping him until he got angry enough to explode, and when he was on top of her, beating her, fucking her, she felt alive. She felt reborn.

There was no way she could have brought a baby into this world. She would not wish her fucked-up life on anyone.

Hank leaned his elbows on his knees. "I just want to understand."

With his history, Hank of all people should understand. Ethan was bad for her. He turned her into the kind of person she loathed, and yet she kept going back for more. He was the worst kind of addiction because no one but Lena could understand the draw.

Musical trilling came from the bedroom, and it took Lena a second to realize the noise was her cell phone.

Hank saw her start to stand and said, "I'll get it," going into the bedroom before she could stop him. She heard him answer the phone, say, "Wait a minute."

He came back into the kitchen with his jaw set. "It's your boss," he said, handing her the phone.

Jeffrey's voice was as dire as Hank's mood. "Lena," he began. "I know you've got one more day on your vacation, but I need you to come in."

She looked at the clock on the wall, tried to think how long it would take to pack and get back to Grant County. For the first time that week, she could feel her heart beating again, adrenaline flooding into her bloodstream and making her feel like she was waking up from a long sleep.

She avoided Hank's gaze, offering, "I can be there in three hours."

"Good," Jeffrey said. "Meet me at the morgue."

CHAPTER THREE

Sara winced as she wrapped a Band-Aid around a broken fingernail. Her hands felt bruised from digging and small scratches gouged into the tips of her fingers like tiny pinpricks. She would have to be extra careful at the clinic this week, making sure the wounds were covered at all times. As she bandaged her thumb, her mind flashed to the piece of fingernail she had found stuck in the strip of wood, and she felt guilty for worrying about her petty problems. Sara could not imagine what the girl's last moments had been like, but she knew that before the day was over, she would have to do just that.

Working in the morgue, Sara had seen the terrible ways that people can die—stabbings, shootings, beatings, strangulations. She tried to look at each case with a clinical eye, but sometimes, a victim would become a living, breathing thing, beseeching Sara to help. Lying dead in that box out in the woods, the girl had called to Sara. The look of fear etched into every line of her face, the hand grasping for some hold on to life—all beseeched someone, anyone, to help. The girl's last moments must have been horrific. Sara could think of nothing more terrifying than being buried alive.

The telephone rang in her office, and Sara jogged across the room to answer before the machine picked up. She was a second too late, and the speaker echoed a screech of feedback as she picked up the phone.

"Sara?" Jeffrey asked.

"Yeah," she told him, switching off the machine. "Sorry."

"We haven't found anything," he said, and she could hear the frustration in his voice.

"No missing persons?"

"There was a girl a few weeks back," he told her. "But, she turned

35

up at her grandmother's yesterday. Hold on." She heard him mumble something, then come back on the line. "I'll call you right back."

The phone clicked before Sara could respond. She sat back in her chair, looking down at her desk, noticing the neat stacks of papers and memos. All of her pens were in a cup and the phone was perfectly aligned with the edge of the metal desk. Carlos, her assistant, worked full-time at the morgue but he had whole days when there was nothing for him to do but twiddle his thumbs and wait for someone to die. He had obviously kept himself busy straightening her office. Sara traced a scratch along the top of the Formica, thinking she had never noticed the faux wood laminate in all the years she had worked here.

She thought about the wood used to build the box that held the girl. The lumber looked new, and the screen mesh covering the pipe had obviously been wrapped around the top in order to keep debris from blocking the air supply. Someone was keeping the girl there, holding her there, for his own sick purposes. Was her abductor somewhere right now thinking about her trapped in the box, getting some sort of sexual thrill from the power he thought he held over her? Had he already gotten his satisfaction, simply leaving her there to die?

Sara startled as the phone rang. She picked it up, asking, "Jeffrey?"

"Just a minute." He covered the phone as he spoke to someone, and Sara waited until he asked her, "How old do you think she is?"

Sara did not like guessing, but she said, "Anywhere from sixteen to nineteen. It's hard to tell at this stage."

He relayed this information to someone in the field, then asked Sara, "You think somebody made her put on those clothes?"

"I don't know," she answered, wondering where he was going with this.

"The bottom of her socks are clean."

"He could have taken away her shoes after she got in the box," Sara suggested. Then, realizing his true concern, she added, "I'll have to get her on the table before I can tell if she was sexually assaulted."

"Maybe he was waiting for that," Jeffrey hypothesized, and they were both quiet for a moment as they considered this. "It's pouring down rain here," he said. "We're trying to dig out the box, see if we can find anything on it."

"The lumber looked new."

"There's mold growing on the side," he told her. "Maybe buried like that, it wouldn't weather as quickly."

"It's pressure treated?"

"Yeah," he said. "The joints are all mitered. Whoever built this didn't just throw it together. It took some skill." He paused a moment, but she didn't hear him talking to anyone. Finally, he said, "She looks like a kid, Sara."

"I know."

"Somebody's missing her," he said. "She didn't just run away."

Sara was silent. She had seen too many secrets revealed during an autopsy to make a snap judgment about the girl. There could be any number of circumstances that had brought her to that dark place in the woods.

"We put out a wire," Jeffrey said. "Statewide."

"You think she was transported?" Sara asked, surprised. For some reason, she had assumed the girl was local.

"It's a public forest," he said. "We get all kinds of people in and out of here."

"That spot, though . . ." Sara let her voice trail off, wondering if there was a night last week when she had looked out her window, darkness obscuring the girl and her abductor as he buried her alive across the lake.

"He would want to check on her," Jeffrey said, echoing Sara's earlier thoughts about the girl's abductor. "We're asking neighbors if they've seen anybody in or out recently who looked like they didn't belong."

"I jog through there all the time," Sara told him. "I've never seen anyone. We wouldn't have even known she was there if you hadn't tripped."

"Brad's trying to get fingerprints off the pipe."

"Maybe you should dust for prints," she said. "Or I will."

"Brad knows what he's doing."

"No," she said. "You cut your hand. Your blood is on that pipe."

Jeffrey paused a second. "He's wearing gloves."

"Goggles, too?" she asked, feeling like a hall monitor but knowing she had to raise the issue. Jeffrey did not respond, so she spelled it out for him. "I don't want to be a pain about this, but we should be careful until we find out. You would never forgive yourself if . . ." She stopped, deciding to let him fill in the rest. When he still did not respond, she asked, "Jeffrey?"

"I'll send it back with Carlos," he said, but she could tell he was irritated.

"I'm sorry," she apologized, though she was not sure why.

He was quiet again, and she could hear the crackling from his cell phone as he changed position, probably wanting to get away from the scene.

He asked, "How do you think she died?"

Sara let out a sigh before answering. She hated speculating. "From the way we found her, I would guess she ran out of air."

"But what about the pipe?"

"Maybe it was too restrictive. Maybe she panicked." Sara paused. "This is why I don't like giving an opinion without all the facts. There could be an underlying cause, something to do with her heart. She could be diabetic. She could be anything. I just won't know until I get her on the table—and then I might not know for certain until all the tests are back, and I might not even know then."

Jeffrey seemed to be considering the options. "You think she panicked?"

"I know I would."

"She had the flashlight," he pointed out. "The batteries were working."

"That's a small consolation."

"I want to get a good photo of her to send out once she's cleaned up. There has to be someone looking for her."

"She had provisions. I can't imagine whoever put her in there was planning on leaving her indefinitely."

"I called Nick," he said, referring to the Georgia Bureau of Investigation's local field agent. "He's going into the office to see if he can pull up any matches on the computer. This could be some kind of kidnapping for ransom."

For some reason, this made Sara feel better than thinking the girl had been snatched from her home for more sadistic purposes.

He said, "Lena should be at the morgue within the hour."

"You want me to call you when she gets here?"

"No," he said. "We're losing daylight. I'll head over as soon as we secure the scene." He hesitated, like there was more he wanted to say.

"What is it?" Sara asked.

"She's just a kid."

"I know."

He cleared his throat. "Someone's looking for her, Sara. We need to find out who she is."

"We will."

He paused again before saying, "I'll be there as soon as I can."

She gently placed the receiver back in the cradle, Jeffrey's words echoing in her mind. A little over a year ago, he had been forced to shoot a young girl in the line of duty. Sara had been there, had watched the scene play out like a nightmare, and she knew that Jeffrey had not had a choice, just like she knew that he would never forgive himself for his part in the girl's death.

Sara walked over to the filing cabinet against the wall, gathering paperwork for the autopsy. Though the cause of death was probably asphyxiation, central blood and urine would have to be collected, labeled and sent to the state lab where it would languish until the Georgia Bureau of Investigation's overburdened staff could get to it. Tissue would have to be processed and stored in the morgue for at least three years. Trace evidence would have to be collected, dated and sealed into paper bags. Depending on what Sara found, a rape kit might have to be performed: fingernails scraped and clipped, vagina, anus and mouth swabbed, DNA collected for processing. Organs would be weighed, arms and legs measured. Hair color, eye color, birthmarks, age, race, gender, number of teeth, scars, bruises, anatomical abnormalities—all of these would be noted on the appropriate form. In the next few hours, Sara would be able to tell Jeffrey everything there was to know about the girl except for the one thing that really mattered to him: her name.

Sara opened her logbook to assign a case number. To the coroner's office, she would be #8472. Presently, there were only two cases of unidentified bodies found in Grant County, so the police would refer to her as Jane Doe number three. Sara felt an overwhelming sadness as she wrote this title in the log. Until a family member was found, the victim would simply be a series of numbers.

Sara pulled out another stack of forms, thumbing through them until she found the US Standard Certificate of Death. By law, Sara had forty-eight hours to submit a death certificate for the girl. The process of changing the victim from a person into a numerical sequence would be amplified at each step. After the autopsy, Sara would find the corresponding code that signified mode of death and put it in the correct box on the form. The form would be sent to the National Center for Health Statistics, which would in turn report the death to the World Health Organization. There, the girl would be catalogued and analyzed, given more codes, more numbers, which would be assimilated into other data from around the country, then around the world. The fact that she had a family, friends, perhaps lovers, would never enter into the equation.

Again, Sara thought about the girl lying in the wooden coffin, the terrified look on her face. She was someone's daughter. When she was born, someone had looked into the infant's face and given her a name. Someone had loved her.

The ancient gears of the elevator whirred into motion, and Sara set the paperwork aside as she stood from her desk. She waited at the elevator doors, listening to the groaning machinery as the car made its way down the shaft. Carlos was incredibly serious, and one of the few jokes Sara had ever heard him make had to do with plummeting to his death inside the ancient contraption.

The floor indicator over the doors was the old-fashioned kind, a clock with three numbers. The needle hovered between one and zero, barely moving. Sara leaned back against the wall, counting the seconds in her head. She was on thirty-eight and about to call building maintenance when a loud ding echoed in the tiled room and the doors slowly slid open.

Carlos stood behind the gurney, his eyes wide. "I thought it was stuck," he murmured in his heavily accented English.

"Let me help," she offered, taking the end of the gurney so that he wouldn't have to angle it out into the room by himself. The girl's arm was still stuck up at a shallow angle where she had tried to claw her way out of the box, and Sara had to lift the gurney into a turn so that it would not catch against the door.

She asked, "Did you get X-rays upstairs?"

"Yes, ma'am."

"Weight?"

"A hundred thirteen pounds," he told her. "Five feet three inches."

Sara made a note of this on the dry erase board bolted to the wall. She capped the marker before saying, "Let's get her on the table."

At the scene, Carlos had placed the girl in a black body bag, and together, they grabbed the corners of the bag and lifted her onto the table. Sara helped him with the zipper, working quietly alongside him as they prepared her for autopsy. After putting on a pair of gloves, Carlos cut through the brown paper bags that had been placed over her hands to preserve any evidence. Her long hair was tangled in places, but still managed to cascade over the side of the table. Sara gloved herself and tucked the hair around the body, aware that she was studiously avoiding the horror-stricken mask of the girl's face. A quick glance at Carlos proved he was doing the same.

As Carlos began undressing the girl, Sara walked over to the metal cabinet by the sinks and took out a surgical gown and goggles. She laid these on a tray by the table, feeling an almost unbearable sadness as Carlos exposed the girl's milk-white flesh to the harsh lights of the morgue. Her small breasts were covered with what looked like a training bra and she was wearing a pair of high-legged cotton briefs that Sara always associated with the elderly; Granny Earnshaw had given Sara and Tessa a ten-pair pack of the same style every year for Christmas, and Tessa had always called them granny panties.

"No label," Carlos said, and Sara went over to see for herself. He had spread the dress on a piece of brown paper to catch any trace evidence. Sara changed her gloves before touching the material, not wanting to cross-contaminate. The dress was cut from a simple pattern, long sleeves with a stiff collar. She guessed the material to be some kind of heavy cotton blend.

Sara checked the stitching, saying, "It doesn't look factory made," thinking this might be a clue in its own right. Aside from an ill-fated home economics course in high school, Sara had never sewn more than a button. Whoever had sewn the dress obviously knew what they were doing.

"Looks pretty clean," Carlos said, placing the underwear and bra on the paper. They were well-worn but spotless, the tags faded from many washings.

"Can you black light them?" she asked, but he was already walking over to the cabinet to get the lamp.

Sara returned to the autopsy table, relieved to see no signs of bruising or trauma on the girl's pubis and upper thighs. She waited as Carlos plugged in the purple light and waved it over the clothes. Nothing glowed, meaning there were no traces of semen or blood on the items. Dragging the extension cord behind him, he walked to the body and handed Sara the light.

She said, "You can do it," and he slowly traced the light up and down the girl's body. His hands were steady as he did this, his gaze intent. Sara often let Carlos do small tasks like this, knowing he must be bored out of his mind waiting around the morgue all day. Yet, the one time she had suggested he look into going back to school, Carlos had shaken his head in disbelief, as if she had proposed he fly to the moon.

"Clean," he said, flashing a rare smile, his teeth purple in the light. He turned off the lamp and started winding the cord to store it back under the counter.

Sara rolled the mayo trays over to the table. Carlos had already arranged the tools for autopsy, and even though he seldom made mistakes, Sara checked through them, making sure everything she needed would be on hand.

Several scalpels were lined up in a row beside various types of surgically sharpened scissors. Different-sized forceps, retractors, probes, wire cutters, a bread-loafing knife and various probes were on the next tray. The Stryker saw and post-mortem hammer/hook were at the foot of the table, the grocer's scales for weighing organs above. Unbreakable jars and test tubes were by the sink awaiting tissue samples. A meter stick and a small ruler were beside the camera, which would be used to document any abnormal findings.

Sara turned back around just as Carlos was resting the girl's shoulders on the rubber block in order to extend her neck. With Sara's help, he unfolded a white sheet and draped it over her body, leaving her bent arm outside the cover. He was gentle with the body, as if she was still alive and could feel everything he did. Not for the first time, Sara was struck by the fact that she had worked with Carlos for over a decade and still knew very little about him.

His watch beeped three times, and he pressed one of the many buttons to turn it off, telling Sara, "The X-rays should be ready."

"I'll take care of the rest," she offered, though there wasn't much left to do.

She waited until she heard his heavy footsteps echoing in the stairwell before she let herself look at the girl's face. Under the overhead spotlight, she looked older than Sara initially had thought. She could even be in her early twenties. She could be married. She could have a child of her own.

Again, Sara heard footsteps on the stairs, but it was Lena Adams, not Carlos, who pushed open the swinging doors and came into the room.

"Hey," Lena said, looking around the morgue, seeming to take in everything. She kept her hands on her hips, her gun sticking out under her arm. Lena had a cop's way of standing, feet wide apart, shoulders squared, and though she was a small woman, her attitude filled the room. Something about the detective had always made Sara uncomfortable, and they were rarely alone together.

"Jeffrey's not here yet," Sara told her, taking out a cassette tape for the Dictaphone. "You can wait in my office if you want."

"That's okay," Lena answered, walking over to the body. She gazed at the girl a moment before giving a low whistle. Sara watched her, thinking something seemed different about Lena. Normally, she projected an air of anger, but today, her defenses felt slightly compromised. There was a red-rimmed tiredness to her eyes, and she had obviously lost weight recently, something that didn't suit her already trim frame.

Sara asked, "Are you okay?"

Instead of answering the question, Lena indicated the girl, saying, "What happened to her?"

Sara dropped the tape into the slot. "She was buried alive in a wooden box out by the lake."

Lena shuddered. "Jesus."

Sara tapped her foot on the pedal under the table, engaging the recorder. She said, "test" a couple of times.

"How do you know she was alive?" Lena asked.

"She clawed at the boards," Sara told her, rewinding the tape. "Someone put her in there to keep her . . . I don't know. He was keeping her for something."

Lena took a deep breath, her shoulders rising with the effort. "Is that why her arm's sticking up? From trying to claw her way out?"

"I would imagine."

"Jesus."

The rewind button on the recorder popped up. They were both quiet as Sara's voice played back, "*Test, test.*"

Lena waited, then asked, "Any idea who she is?"

"None."

"She just ran out of air?"

Sara stopped and explained everything that had happened. Lena took it all in, expressionless. Sara knew the other woman had trained herself not to respond, but it was unnerving the way Lena could distance herself from such a horrific crime.

When Sara had finished, Lena's only response was to whisper, "Shit."

"Yeah," Sara agreed. She glanced at the clock, wondering what was keeping Carlos just as he walked in with Jeffrey.

"Lena," Jeffrey said. "Thanks for coming in."

"No problem," she said, shrugging it off.

Jeffrey gave Lena a second, closer look. "You feeling okay?"

Lena's eyes flashed to Sara's, something like guilt in them. Lena said, "I'm fine." She indicated the dead girl. "You got a name on her yet?"

Jeffrey's jaw tightened. She could not have asked a worse question. "No," he managed.

Sara indicated the sink, telling him, "You need to wash out your hand."

"I already did."

"Do it again," she told him, dragging him over and turning on the tap. "You've still got a lot of dirt in there."

He hissed between his teeth as she put his hand under the hot water. The wound was deep enough for sutures, but too much time had passed to sew it up without risking infection. Sara would have to butterfly it closed and hope for the best. "I'm going to write you a prescription for an antibiotic."

"Great." He shot her a look of annoyance when she put on a pair of gloves. She gave him the same look back as she wrapped his hand, knowing they didn't need to have this discussion with an audience.

"Dr. Linton?" Carlos was standing by the lightbox looking at the girl's X-rays. Sara finished with Jeffrey before joining him. There were several films in place, but her eyes instantly went to the abdominal series.

Carlos said, "I think I need to take these again. This one's kind of blurry."

The X-ray machine was older than Sara, but she knew nothing was wrong with the exposure. "No," she whispered, dread washing over her.

Jeffrey was at her side, already picking at the bandage she had wrapped around his hand. "What is it?"

"She was pregnant."

"Pregnant?" Lena echoed.

Sara studied the film, the task ahead taking shape in her mind. She hated infant autopsies. This would be the youngest victim she had ever had in the morgue.

Jeffrey asked, "Are you sure?"

"You can see the head here," Sara told him, tracing the image. "Legs, arms, trunk . . ."

Lena had walked up for a closer look, and her voice was very quiet when she asked, "How far along was she?"

"I don't know," Sara answered, feeling like a piece of glass was in her chest. She would have to hold the fetus in her hand, dissecting it like she was cutting up a piece of fruit. The skull would be soft, the eyes and mouth simply hinted at by dark lines under paper-thin skin. Cases like this made her hate her job.

"Months? Weeks?" Lena pressed.

Sara could not say. "I'll have to see it."

"Double homicide," Jeffrey said.

"Not necessarily," Sara reminded him. Depending on which side screamed the loudest, politicians were changing the laws governing fetal death practically every day. Thankfully, Sara had never had to look into it. "I'll have to check with the state."

"Why?" Lena asked, her tone so odd that Sara turned to face her. She was staring at the X-ray as if it was the only thing in the room.

"It's no longer based on viability," Sara explained, wondering why Lena was pressing the point. She had never struck Sara as the type who liked children, but Lena was getting older. Maybe her biological clock had finally started ticking.

Lena nodded at the film, her arms crossed tightly over her chest. "Was this viable?"

"Not even close," Sara said, then felt the need to add, "I've read about fetuses being delivered and kept alive at twenty-three weeks, but it's very unusual to—"

"That's the second trimester," Lena interrupted.

"Right."

"Twenty-three weeks?" Lena echoed. She swallowed visibly, and Sara exchanged a look with Jeffrey.

He shrugged, then asked Lena, "You okay?"

"Yeah," she said, and it seemed as if she had to force herself to look away from the X-ray. "Yeah," she repeated. "Let's . . . uh . . . let's just get this started."

Carlos helped Sara into the surgical gown, and together they went over every inch of the girl's body, measuring and photographing what little they found. There were a few fingernail marks around her throat where she had probably scratched herself, a common reaction when someone was having difficulty breathing. Skin was missing from the tips of the index and middle finger of her right hand, and Sara imagined they would find the pieces stuck to the wooden slats that had been above her. Splinters were under her remaining fingernails where she had tried to scrape her way out, but Sara found no tissue or skin lodged under the nails.

The girl's mouth was clean of debris, the soft tissue free from tears and bruising. She had no fillings or dental work, but the beginning of a cavity was on her right rear molar. Her wisdom teeth were intact, two of them already breaking through the skin. A star-shaped birthmark was below the girl's right buttock and a patch of dry skin was on her right forearm. She had been wearing a long-sleeved dress, so Sara assumed this was a bit of recurring eczema. Winter was always harder on the fair-skinned.

Before Jeffrey took Polaroids for identification, Sara tried to press the girl's lips together and close her eyes in order to soften her expression. When she had done all she could, she used a thin blade to scrape the mold from the girl's upper lip. There wasn't much, but she put it in a specimen jar to send to the lab anyway.

Jeffrey leaned over the body, holding the camera close to her face. The flashbulb sparked, sending a loud pop through the room. Sara blinked to clear her vision, the smell of burning plastic from the cheap camera temporarily masking the other odors that filled the morgue.

"One more," Jeffrey said, leaning over the girl again. There was another pop and the camera whirred, spitting out a second photograph.

Lena said, "She doesn't look homeless."

"No," Jeffrey agreed, his tone indicating he was anxious for answers. He waved the Polaroid in the air as if that would make it develop faster.

"Let's take prints," Sara said, testing the tension in the girl's raised arm.

There was not as much resistance as Sara had expected, and her surprise must have been evident, because Jeffrey asked, "How long do you think she's been dead?"

Sara pressed down the arm to the girl's side so that Carlos could ink and print her fingers. She said, "Full rigor would happen anywhere between six to twelve hours after death. From the way it's breaking up, I'd say she's been dead a day, two days, tops." She indicated the lividity on the back of the body, pressing her fingers into the purplish marks. "Liver mortis is set up. She's starting to decompose. It must've been cold in there. The body was well preserved."

"What about the mold around her mouth?"

Sara looked at the card Carlos handed her, checking to make sure he had gotten a good set from what remained of the girl's fingertips. She nodded to him, giving back the card, and told Jeffrey, "There are molds that can grow quickly, especially in that environment. She could have vomited and the mold set up on that." Another thought occurred to her. "Some types of fungus can deplete oxygen in an enclosed space."

"There was stuff growing on the inside of the box," Jeffrey recalled, looking at the picture of the girl. He showed it to Sara. "It's not as bad as I thought."

Sara nodded, though she could not imagine what it would be like to have known the girl in life and see this picture of her now. Even with all Sara had tried to do to the face, there was no mistaking that the death had been an excruciating one.

Jeffrey held the photo out for Lena to see, but she shook her head. He asked, "Do you think she's been molested?"

"We'll do that next," Sara said, realizing she had been postponing the inevitable.

Carlos handed her the speculum and rolled over a portable lamp. Sara felt they were all holding their breath as she did the pelvic exam, and when she told them, "There's no sign of sexual assault," there seemed to be a group exhalation. She did not know why rape made cases like this that much more horrific, but there was no getting around the fact that she was relieved the girl hadn't had to suffer one more degradation before she'd died.

Next, Sara checked the eyes, noting the scattershot broken blood vessels. The girl's lips were blue, her slightly protruding tongue a deep purple. "You don't usually see petechiae in this kind of asphyxiation," she said.

Jeffrey asked, "You think something else could have killed her?"

Sara answered truthfully. "I don't know."

She used an eighteen-gauge needle to pierce the center of the eye, drawing out vitreous humor from the globe. Carlos filled another syringe with saline and she used this to replace what she had taken so that the orb would not collapse.

When Sara had done all she could as far as the external exam, she asked, "Ready?"

Jeffrey and Lena nodded. Sara pressed the pedal under the table, engaging the Dictaphone, and recorded into the tape, "Coroner's case number eighty-four-seventy-two is the unembalmed body of a Caucasian Jane Doe with brown hair and brown eyes. Age is unknown but estimated to be eighteen to twenty years old. Weight, one thirteen; height, sixty-three inches. Skin is cool to the touch and consistent with being buried underground for an unspecified period of time." She tapped off the recorder, telling Carlos, "We need the temperature for the last two weeks."

Carlos made a note on the board as Jeffrey asked, "Do you think she's been out there longer than a week?"

"It got down to freezing on Monday," she reminded him. "There wasn't much waste in the jar, but she could have been restricting her fluid intake in case she ran out. She was also probably dehydrated from shock." She tapped on the Dictaphone and took up a scalpel, saying, "The internal exam is started with the standard Y incision."

The first time Sara had performed an autopsy, her hand had shaken. As a doctor, she had been trained to use a light touch. As a surgeon, she had been taught that every cut made into the body should be calculated and controlled; every movement of her hand working to heal, not harm. The initial cuts made at autopsy—slicing into the body as if it were a piece of raw meat—went against everything she had learned.

She started the scalpel on the right side, anterior to the acromial process. She cut medial to the breasts, the tip of the blade sliding along the ribs, and stopped at the xiphoid process. She did the same on the left side, the skin folding away from the scalpel as she followed the midline down to the pubis and around the umbilicus, yellow abdominal fat rolling up in the sharp blade's wake.

Carlos passed Sara a pair of scissors, and she was using these to cut through the peritoneum when Lena gasped, putting her hand to her mouth.

Sara asked, "Are you—" just as Lena bolted from the room, gagging.

There was no bathroom in the morgue, and Sara assumed Lena was trying to make it upstairs to the hospital. From the retching noise that echoed in the stairwell, she hadn't made it. Lena coughed several times and there was the distinct sound of splatter.

Carlos murmured something under his breath and went to get the mop and bucket.

Jeffrey had a sour look on his face. He had never been good around anyone being sick. "You think she's okay?"

Sara looked down at the body, wondering what had set Lena off. The detective had attended autopsies before and never had a bad reaction. The body hadn't really been dissected yet, just a section of the abdominal viscera was exposed.

Carlos said, "It's the smell."

"What smell?" Sara asked, wondering if she had punctured the bowel.

He furrowed his brow. "Like at the fair."

The door popped open and Lena came back into the room looking embarrassed.

"I'm sorry," she said. "I don't know what—" She stopped about five feet from the table, her hand over her mouth as if she might be sick again. "Jesus, what is that?"

Jeffrey shrugged. "I don't smell anything."

"Carlos?" Sara asked.

He said, "It's . . . like something burning."

"No," Lena countered, taking a step back. "Like it's curdled. Like it makes your jaw ache to smell it."

Sara heard alarms go off in her head. "Does it smell bitter?" she asked. "Like bitter almonds?"

"Yeah," Lena allowed, still keeping her distance. "I guess."

Carlos was nodding, too, and Sara felt herself break out into a cold sweat.

"Christ," Jeffrey exhaled, taking a step away from the body.

"We'll have to finish this at the state lab," Sara told him, throwing a sheet over the corpse. "I don't even have a chemical hood here."

Jeffrey reminded her, "They've got an isolation chamber in Macon. I could call Nick and see if we can use it."

She snapped off her gloves. "It'd be closer, but they'd only let me observe."

"Do you have a problem with that?"

"No," Sara said, slipping on a surgical mask. She suppressed a shudder, thinking about what might have happened. Without prompting, Carlos came over with the body bag.

"Careful," Sara cautioned, handing him a mask. "We're very lucky," she told them, helping Carlos seal up the body. "Only about forty percent of the population can detect the odor."

Jeffrey told Lena, "It's a good thing you came in today."

Lena looked from Sara to Jeffrey and back again. "What are you two talking about?"

"Cyanide." Sara zipped the bag closed. "That's what you were smelling." Lena still didn't seem to be following, so Sara added, "She was poisoned."

MONDAY

CHAPTER FOUR

Jeffrey yawned so hard his jaw popped. He sat back in his chair, staring out at the squad room through his office window, trying to appear focused. Brad Stephens, the youngest patrolman on the Grant County force, gave him a goofy grin. Jeffrey nodded, feeling a shooting pain in his neck. He felt like he had slept on a slab of concrete, which was appropriate as the only thing between him and the floor last night had been a sleeping bag that was so old and musty that Goodwill had politely refused to take it. They had, however, accepted his mattress, a couch that had seen better days and three boxes of kitchen stuff Jeffrey had fought Sara for during the divorce. Since he had not unpacked the boxes in the five years since the papers were signed, he figured it would be suicide to take them back to her place now.

Clearing out his small house over the last few weeks, he had been startled by how little he had accumulated during his bachelorhood. Last night, as a substitute for counting sheep, he had made a mental list of new purchases. Except for ten boxes of books, some nice sheets that had been a gift from a woman he prayed to God Sara would never meet and some suits he had to buy for work over the years, Jeffrey had nothing new to show for the time they had lived apart. His bike, his lawn mower, his tools—except for a cordless drill that had been purchased when he accidentally dropped his old one into a five-gallon bucket of paint—had been in his possession that final day he'd left Sara's house. And now, everything of value he ever owned had already been moved back.

And he was sleeping on the floor.

He took a swig of tepid coffee before returning to the task that had occupied the last thirty minutes of his morning. Jeffrey had never been one of those guys who thought reading directions somehow made you less of a man, but the fact that he had for the fourth time carefully followed every single step in the instruction sheet that came with the cell phone and still couldn't program his own number into the speed dial made him feel like an idiot. He wasn't even sure Sara would take the phone. She hated the damn things, but he didn't want her traveling all the way to Macon without a way of getting in touch with him in case something happened.

He mumbled under his breath, "Step one," as if reading the directions out loud would convince the phone to see logic. Sixteen more steps went by for a fifth time, but when Jeffrey pressed the recall button, nothing happened.

"Shit," he said, pounding his fist into the desk, then "Fuck!" because he had used his injured left hand. He twisted his wrist, watching blood wick into the white bandage Sara had applied last night at the morgue. He threw in a "Jesus" for good measure, thinking the last ten minutes put a fine point on what was proving to be an extremely shitty day.

As if he had been summoned, Brad Stephens stood at the office door. "Need help with that?"

Jeffrey tossed him the phone. "Put my number on speed dial."

Brad pressed some buttons, asking, "Your cell number?"

"Yeah," he said, writing Cathy and Eddie Linton's home number on a yellow Post-it. "This one, too."

"Okey doke," Brad said, reading the number upside down, punching more buttons.

"You need the instructions?"

Brad gave him a sideways look, like Jeffrey might be pulling his leg, and kept programming the phone. Suddenly, Jeffrey felt about six hundred years old.

"Okay," Brad said, staring at the phone, pressing more buttons. "Here. Try this."

Jeffrey hit the phone book icon and the numbers came up. "Thanks."

"If you don't need anything else . . ."

"That's fine," Jeffrey said, standing from his chair. He slipped on his suit jacket, pocketing the phone. "I guess there haven't been any hits on the missing persons report we put out?"

"No, sir," Brad answered. "I'll let you know as soon as I hear."

"I'll be at the clinic, then back here." Jeffrey followed Brad out of
his office. He rolled his shoulder as he walked to the front of the
squad room, trying to loosen up the muscles that were so tight his
arm felt numb. The police station reception area had been open to
the lobby at one time, but now it was walled in with a small banker's
window so visitors could check in. Marla Simms, the station's secretary since before dirt, reached under her desk to buzz the door open
for Jeffrey.

"I'll be at Sara's office if you need me," he told her.

Marla gave him a cat's grin. "You be good, now."

He gave her a wink before heading outside.

Jeffrey had been at the station since five thirty that morning, having given up on sleep sometime around four. He usually ran for
thirty minutes every weekday, but today he had fooled himself into
thinking he wasn't being lazy if he went straight to work instead.
There was a mountain of paperwork to get through, including final-
izing the station's budget so the mayor could veto everything on it
right before going to his annual two-week mayors' conference in
Miami. Jeffrey imagined the mayor's minibar bill could pay for at
least two Kevlar vests, but the politician never saw things that way.

Heartsdale was a college town, and Jeffrey passed several students going to class as he walked down the sidewalk. Underclassmen
had to live in the dorms, and the first thing any sophomore with half
a brain did was move off campus. Jeffrey had rented his house to a
couple of juniors who he hoped were as trustworthy as they looked.
Grant Tech was a school of eggheads, and while there weren't
nonacademic fraternities or football games, some of the kids knew
how to party. Jeffrey had carefully screened prospective tenants,
and he had been a cop long enough to know that there was no way in
hell he would get his house back in one piece if he rented it to a
bunch of young men. Something was wrong with your wiring at that
age, and if it involved beer or sex—or both, if you were lucky—the
brain ceased all higher levels of thinking. The two girls moving in
had both listed reading as their only hobby. The way his luck was
going lately, they were probably planning on turning the place into a
meth lab.

The college was at the mouth of Main Street, and Jeffrey walked
toward the front gates behind a group of students. They were all

girls, all young and pretty, all oblivious to his presence. There had been a time when Jeffrey's ego would have been bothered by a bunch of young women ignoring him, but now he was concerned for other reasons. He could be stalking them, listening to their conversation to find out where they would be later on. He could be anybody.

Behind him, a car horn beeped, and Jeffrey realized he had stepped into the street. He waved to the driver as he crossed the road, recognizing Bill Burgess from the dry cleaners, saying a small prayer of thanks that the old man had managed to see past his cataracts and stop the car in time.

Jeffrey seldom remembered dreams, which was a gift considering how bad some of them could be, but last night he'd kept seeing the girl in the box. Sometimes, her face would change, and he would see instead the girl he had shot and killed a year ago. She had been just a child, little more than thirteen, with more bad stuff going on in her world than most adults experience in a lifetime. The teen had been desperate for someone to help her, threatening to kill another kid in the hopes that it would end her own suffering. Jeffrey had been forced to shoot her in order to save the other kid. Or maybe not. Maybe things could have been different. Maybe she wouldn't have shot the kid. Maybe they would both be alive now and the girl in the box would just be another case instead of a nightmare.

Jeffrey sighed as he walked along the sidewalk. There were more maybes in his life than he knew what to do with.

Sara's clinic was on the opposite side of the street from the station, right by the entrance to Grant Tech. He glanced at his watch as he opened the front door, thinking that at a little after seven she would already be in. The clinic didn't see patients until eight on Mondays, but a young woman was already pacing the front waiting room, jiggling a crying baby as she walked the floor.

Jeffrey said, "Hey."

"Hey, Chief," the mother said, and he saw the dark circles under her eyes. The baby on her hip was at least two, with a set of lungs on him that rattled the windows.

She shifted the kid, lifting her leg for support. She probably weighed ninety pounds soaking wet, and Jeffrey wondered how she managed to hold on to the baby.

She saw him watching and told him, "Dr. Linton should be right out."

Jeffrey said, "Thanks," taking off his suit jacket. The east-facing side of the waiting room was built with glass brick, so even on the coldest winter morning the rising sun could make you feel like you were in a sauna.

"Hot in here," the woman said, resuming her pacing.

"Sure is."

Jeffrey waited for her to say more, but she was concentrating on the child, shushing him, trying to soothe his crying. How mothers managed to keep from falling over into a coma when they had small children was beyond Jeffrey. At times like this, he understood why his own mother had kept a flask in her purse at all times.

He leaned back against the wall, taking in the toys stacked neatly in the corner. There were at least three signs posted around the room that warned, "NO CELL PHONES ALLOWED." Sara figured if a kid was sick enough to go to the doctor, the parents should be paying attention, not yakking on the phone. He smiled, thinking of the first and only time Sara had carried a phone in her car. Somehow, she kept accidentally hitting the speed dial, so that Jeffrey would answer his phone and hear her singing along to the radio for minutes at a time. It had taken three calls before he figured out he was hearing Sara trying to harmonize with Boy George and not some sick freak beating up a cat.

Sara opened the door beside the office and went to the mother. She didn't notice Jeffrey, and he kept quiet, taking her in. Normally, she pulled her long auburn hair back into a ponytail while she worked, but this morning it was loose around her shoulders. She was wearing a white button-down shirt and a black A-line skirt that hit just below the knee. The heel on her shoe wasn't high, but it did something nice to her calf that made him smile. In the outfit, anyone else would look like a waitress from an uptown steakhouse, but on Sara's tall, slim frame, it worked.

The mother shifted the baby, saying, "He's still fussy."

Sara put her hand to the boy's cheek, shushing him. The child calmed as if a spell had been cast, and Jeffrey felt a lump rising in his throat. Sara was so good with children. The fact that she couldn't have any of her own was something they seldom talked about. There were some things that just cut too close.

Jeffrey watched as Sara took a few more seconds with the baby, stroking his thin hair over his ear, a smile of sheer pleasure on her lips. The moment felt private, and Jeffrey cleared his throat, having the strange sensation of being an intruder.

Sara turned around, taken off guard, almost startled. She told Jeffrey, "Just a minute," then turned back to the mother, all business as she handed the woman a white paper bag. "These samples should be enough for a week. If he's not significantly better by Thursday, give me a call."

The woman took the samples with one hand, holding tight to the baby. She had probably had the kid while she was just a teenager. Jeffrey had learned just recently that before going off to college he had fathered a child. Well, not a child anymore — Jared was nearly a grown man.

"Thank you, Dr. Linton," the young mother said. "I don't know how I'm gonna pay you for —"

"Let's just get him better," Sara interrupted. "And get some sleep yourself. You're no good to him if you're exhausted all the time."

The mother took the admonishment with a slight nod of the head, and without even knowing her, Jeffrey understood the advice was falling on deaf ears.

Sara obviously knew this, too. She said, "Just try, okay? You're going to make yourself sick."

The woman hesitated, then agreed, "I'll try."

Sara looked down at her hand, and it seemed to Jeffrey that she had not realized she was holding the baby's foot in her palm. Her thumb rubbed his ankle, and she gave that private smile again.

"Thank you," the mother said. "Thank you for coming in so early."

"It's fine." Sara had never been good at taking praise or appreciation. She walked them to the door, holding it open as she reminded, "Call me if he's not better."

"Yes, ma'am."

Sara pulled the door to after them, taking her time as she walked back across the lobby, not looking at Jeffrey. He opened his mouth to speak, but she beat him to it, asking, "Anything on the Jane Doe?"

"No," he said. "We might get something later on when the West Coast opens for the day."

"She doesn't look like a runaway to me."

"Me, either."

They were both quiet for a beat, and Jeffrey didn't know what to say.

As usual, Sara broke the silence. "I'm glad you're here," she said, walking back toward the exam rooms. He followed her, thinking he was hearing good news until she said, "I want to draw some blood for a hep and liver panel."

"Hare already did all that."

"Yeah, well," she said, leaving it at that. She didn't hold the door for him, and he had to catch it before it popped back in his face. Unfortunately, he used his left hand and the hard surface caught him smack on the open cut. He felt like someone had stuck him with a knife.

He hissed, "Jesus, Sara."

"I'm sorry." Her apology seemed genuine, but there was a flash of something like revenge in her eyes. She reached for his hand and he pulled back on sheer reflex. Her look of irritation at this persuaded him to let her see the bandage.

She asked, "How long has it been bleeding?"

"It's not bleeding," he insisted, knowing she'd probably do something really painful to it if he told her the truth. Still, he followed her down the hall toward the nurses' station like a lamb to the slaughter.

"You didn't get that prescription filled, did you?" She leaned over the counter and riffled through a drawer, grabbing a handful of brightly colored packets. "Take these."

He looked at the pink and green sample packs. There were farm animals printed on the foil. "What are these?"

"Antibiotics."

"Aren't they for kids?"

Her look said she wasn't going to go for the obvious joke. "It's half the dose of the adult formula with a movie tie-in and a higher price," she told him. "Take two in the morning and two at night."

"For how long?"

"Until I tell you to stop," she ordered. "Come in here."

Jeffrey followed her into an exam room, feeling like a child. His mother had worked in the hospital cafeteria when Jeffrey was a kid, so he had missed out on going to a pediatrician's office for various bumps and scrapes. Cal Rodgers, the ER doc, had taken care of him and, Jeffrey suspected, had taken care of his mother as well. The first time he had heard his mother giggle was when Rodgers had told a stupid joke about a paraplegic and a nun.

"Sit," Sara ordered, cupping his elbow as if he needed help getting up on the exam table.

"I've got it," Jeffrey told her, but she was already unwrapping his hand. The wound gaped open like a wet mouth, and he felt a throbbing ache pulse up his arm.

"You broke it open," she admonished, holding a silver basin under his hand as she washed out the wound.

Jeffrey tried not to react to the pain, but the truth was it hurt like hell. He never understood why an injury hurt more during treatment than it did when you first got it. He could barely remember cutting his hand in the woods, but now, every time he moved his fingers, he felt like a bunch of needles were digging into his skin.

"What did you do?" she asked, her tone full of disapproval.

He didn't answer. Instead, he thought about the way Sara had smiled with that baby. He had seen Sara in a lot of moods, but he had never seen that particular smile.

"Jeff?" she prompted.

He shook his head, wanting to touch her face but afraid he'd pull back a bloody stub where his hand used to be.

"I'll wrap it again," she said, "but you need to be careful with this. You don't want an infection."

"Yes, ma'am," he answered, waiting for her to look up and smile.

Instead, she asked, "Where did you sleep last night?"

"Not where I wanted to."

She didn't take the bait, rather she began wrapping his hand again, her lips pressed together in a tight line. She used her teeth to cut through a strip of surgical tape. "You need to be very careful and keep this clean."

"Why don't I drop by later and you can do it?"

"Right . . ." She let her voice trail off as she opened and closed some drawers. She took out a vacuum tube and a syringe. Jeffrey felt a moment of panic that she was going to stick a needle in his hand but then remembered she wanted to draw blood.

She unbuttoned the cuff of his shirt and rolled up the sleeve. He looked up at the ceiling, not wanting to watch, waiting for the sharp sting of the needle. It didn't come—instead he heard her give a heavy sigh.

He asked, "What?"

She tapped his forearm to find a vein. "It's my fault."

"What's your fault?"

She waited before answering, as if she needed to think about how to phrase her response. "When I left Atlanta, I was in the middle of my vaccinations for hep A and B." She wrapped a tourniquet around his biceps, pulling it tight. "You get two injections a few weeks apart, then five months later you get the booster." She paused again, wiping his skin with alcohol. "I got one and two, but when I moved back here, I didn't follow up. I didn't know what I was going to do with my life, let alone whether or not I was going to keep practicing medicine." She paused. "I didn't think to finish the series again until around the time . . ."

"Around what time?"

She used her teeth to uncap the syringe, saying, "The divorce."

"Well that's good then," Jeffrey said, trying not to jump off the table as she slid the needle into his vein. She was being gentle, but Jeffrey hated shots. Sometimes just thinking about them could make him woozy.

"These are baby needles," she told him, more out of sarcasm than consideration. "Why is it good?"

"Because I only slept with her once," he said. "You kicked me out the next day."

"Right." Sara hooked up the vacuum tube and released the tourniquet.

"So, you were finished with the vaccinations by the time we started seeing each other again. You should be immune."

"You've forgotten that one time."

"What one—" He stopped, remembering. The night before the divorce was finalized, Sara had shown up on his doorstep drunk as a mop and in a receptive mood. Desperate to have her back, Jeffrey had taken advantage of the situation, only to have her sneak out of the house before the sun came up the next morning. She hadn't returned his calls the next day and when he had shown up at her house that night, she had slammed the door in his face.

"I was in the middle of the series," she told him. "I hadn't had the booster."

"But you had the first two?"

"It's still a risk." She slid out the needle and topped it. "And there's no vaccination for hepatitis C." She put a cotton ball on his arm and made him bend his elbow to hold it in place. When she looked up at him, he could tell he was about to get a lecture.

"There are five major types of hepatitis, some with different strains," she began, dropping the syringe into the red biohazard box. "A is basically like a bad flu. It lasts a couple of weeks, and once you have it, you develop antibodies. You can't get it again."

"Right." That was the one detail he remembered from his visit to Hare's office. The rest was pretty much a blur. He had tried to listen—really tried—as Sara's cousin explained the differences, the risk factors, but all he could really focus on was how to get out of the office as fast as he could. After a sleepless night, he had formed several questions, but couldn't force himself to call Hare to ask them. In the ensuing days, he had found himself swinging back and forth between denial and cold panic. Jeffrey could remember every detail of a case from fifteen years ago, but couldn't recall a damn thing about what Hare had said.

Sara continued, "Hep B is different. It can come and go, or it can be chronic. About ten percent of the people who are infected with it become carriers. The risk of infecting another person is one in three. AIDS has a risk of about one in three hundred."

Jeffrey certainly didn't have Sara's mathematical abilities, but he could calculate the odds. "You and I have had sex more than three times since Jo."

She tried to hide it, but he saw her flinch at the name. "It's hit-or-miss, Jeffrey."

"I wasn't saying—"

"Hep C is generally passed through blood contact. You could have it and not even know it. You usually don't find out until you start showing symptoms, then it can go downhill from there. Liver fibrosis. Cirrhosis. Cancer."

All he could do was stare at her. He knew where this was going. It was like a train wreck and there was nothing he could do but hang on and wait for the wheels to skid off the rails.

"I'm so angry at you," she said, the most obvious statement that had ever come from her lips. "I'm angry because it's bringing all this up again." She paused as if to calm herself. "I wanted to forget it happened, to start over, and this just throws it back into my face." She blinked, her eyes watering. "And if you're sick . . ."

Jeffrey focused on what he thought he could control. "It's my fault, Sara. I fucked up. I'm the one who ruined things. I know that." He had learned a long time ago not to add the "but," though in his head he went through it. Sara had been distant, spending more time at work and with her family than with Jeffrey. He wasn't the kind of husband who expected dinner on the table every night, but he had thought she would at least make some time for him out of her busy schedule.

Her voice was barely above a whisper. "Did you do things with her that you do with me?"

"Sara—"

"Were you unsafe?"

"I don't even know what that means."

"You know what it means," she told him. It was her turn to stare, and he had one of those rare moments when he could read her mind.

"Jesus," he muttered, wishing like hell he was anywhere but here. It wasn't like they were a couple of perverts, but it was one thing to explore certain acts while you were in bed, quite another to analyze them in the cold light of day.

"If you had a cut in your mouth and she was . . ." Sara obviously couldn't finish. "Even with normal intercourse, people can get tears, microscopic injuries."

"I get what you're saying," he told her, his tone sharp enough to stop her.

Sara picked up the tube of his blood and labeled it with a ballpoint pen. "I'm not asking this because I want the gory details."

He didn't call her out on the lie. She had drilled him before when it happened, asking him pointed questions about every move he made, every kiss, every act, as if she had some sort of voyeuristic obsession.

She stood, opening a drawer and taking out a bright pink Barbie Band-Aid. He had kept his elbow bent this entire time, and his arm felt numb when she straightened it. Peeling back the edges, she pressed the Band-Aid down over the cotton. She didn't speak again until she had thrown the strips into the trash.

"Aren't you going to tell me I need to get over it?" She feigned a dismissive shrug. "It was only once, right? It's not like it meant anything."

Jeffrey bit his tongue, recognizing the trap. The good thing about beating this dead horse for the last five years was he knew when to shut up. Still, he struggled not to argue with her. She didn't want to see his side of things, and maybe she had a point, but that didn't take away the fact that there were reasons he did what he did, and not all of them had to do with him being a total bastard. He knew his part in this was to play the supplicant. Being whipped was a small price to pay for peace.

Sara prompted, "You usually say that I need to get over it. That it was a long time ago, that you're different, that you've changed. That she didn't matter to you."

"If I say that now, will it make any difference?"

"No," Sara said. "I don't suppose anything will."

Jeffrey leaned back against the wall, wishing he could read her mind now. "Where do we go from here?"

"I want to hate you."

"That's nothing new," he said, but she didn't seem to catch the levity in his voice, because she nodded in agreement.

Jeffrey shifted on the table, feeling like an idiot with his legs dangling two feet above the floor. He heard Sara whisper, "Fuck," and his head snapped up in surprise. She seldom cursed, and he did not know whether to take the expletive as a good or bad sign.

"You irritate the hell out of me, Jeffrey."

"I thought you found that endearing."

She gave him a cutting look. "If you ever . . ." She let her voice trail off. "What's the use?" she asked, but he could tell it wasn't a rhetorical question.

"I'm sorry," he told her, and he really meant it this time. "I'm sorry

I brought this on us. I'm sorry I screwed things up. I'm sorry we had to go through that hell—that *you* had to go through that hell—to get us here."

"Where's here?"

"I guess that's up to you."

She sniffed, covering her face with her hands, letting out a long breath of air. When she looked back up at him, he could tell she wanted to cry but wouldn't let herself.

Jeffrey stared down at his hand, picking at the tape on the bandage.

"Don't mess with that," she told him, putting her hand over his. She left it there, and he could feel her warmth penetrating through the bandage. He looked at her long, graceful fingers, the blue veins on the back of her hand making an intricate map underneath her pale white skin. He traced his fingers along hers, wondering how in the world he had ever been stupid enough to take her for granted.

"I kept thinking about that girl," he said. "She looks a lot like—"

"Wendy," she finished. Wendy was the name of the little girl he'd shot and killed.

He laid his other hand flat over hers, wanting to talk about anything but the shooting. "What time are you going to Macon?"

She looked at his watch. "Carlos is going to meet me at the morgue in half an hour."

"It's weird they could both smell the cyanide," Jeffrey said. "Lena's grandmother was from Mexico. Carlos is Mexican. Is there some connection?"

"Not that I know of." She was watching him carefully, reading him like a book.

He slid down off the table, saying, "I'm okay."

"I know." She asked, "What about the baby?"

"There has to be a father out there somewhere." Jeffrey knew that if they ever found the man, they would be taking a hard look at him for the murder.

Sara pointed out, "A pregnant woman is more likely to die as a result of homicide than any other factor." She went to the sink to wash her hands, a troubled look on her face.

He said, "Cyanide isn't just lying around on the shelves at the grocery store. Where would I get it if I wanted to kill somebody?"

"Some over-the-counter products have it." She turned off the tap and dried her hands with a paper towel. "There have been several pediatric fatalities involving nail glue removers."

"That has cyanide in it?"

"Yes," Sara answered, tossing the towel into the trash. "I checked it out in a couple of books when I couldn't sleep last night."

"And?"

She rested her hand on the exam table. "Natural sources are found in most fruits with pits—peaches, apricots, cherries. You'd need a lot of them, so it's not very practical. Different industries use cyanide, some medical labs."

"What kinds of industries?" he asked. "Do you think the college might have some?"

"It's likely," she told him, and he made a note to find out for himself. Grant Tech was primarily an agricultural school, and they performed all sorts of experiments at the behest of the large chemical companies who were looking for the next big thing to make tomatoes grow faster or peas grow greener.

Sara provided, "It's also a case hardener in metal plating. Some laboratories keep it around for controls. Sometimes it's used for fumigation. It's in cigarette smoke. Hydrogen cyanide is created by burning wool or various types of plastics."

"It'd be pretty hard to direct smoke down a pipe."

"He'd have to wear a mask, too, but you're right. There are better ways to do it."

"Like?"

"It needs an acid to activate. Mix cyanide salts with a household vinegar, and you could kill an elephant."

"Isn't that what Hitler used in the camps? Salts?"

"I think so," she said, rubbing her arms with her hands.

"If a gas was used," Jeffrey thought out loud, "then we would've been in danger when we opened the box."

"It could've dissipated. Or been absorbed into the wood and soil."

"Could she have gotten the cyanide through ground contamination?"

"That's a pretty active state park. Joggers go through there all the time. I doubt anyone could've sneaked in a bunch of toxic waste without someone noticing and making a fuss."

"Still?"

"Still," she agreed. "Someone had time to bury her there. Anything's possible."

"How would you do it?"

Sara thought it through. "I would mix the salts in water," she said. "Pour it down the pipe. She would obviously have her mouth close by so that she could get air. As soon as the salts hit her stomach, the acid would activate the poison. She would be dead in minutes."

"There's a metal plater on the edge of town," Jeffrey said. "He does gold leafing, that sort of thing."

Sara supplied, "Dale Stanley."

"Pat Stanley's brother?" Jeffrey asked. Pat was one of his best patrolmen.

"That was his wife you saw coming in."

"What's wrong with her kid?"

"Bacterial infection. Their oldest came in about three months ago with the worst asthma I've seen in a long time. He's been in and out of the hospital with it."

"She looked pretty sick herself."

"I don't see how she's holding up," Sara admitted. "She won't let me treat her."

"You think something's wrong with her?"

"I think she's ready for a nervous breakdown."

Jeffrey let this sink in. "I guess I should pay them a visit."

"It's a horrible death, Jeffrey. Cyanide is a chemical asphyxiant. It takes all of the oxygen from the blood until there's nothing left. She knew what was happening. Her heart must have been pumping ninety miles an hour." Sara shook her head, as if she wanted to clear the image away.

"How long do you think it took her to die?"

"It depends on how she ingested the poison, what form was administered. Anywhere from two to five minutes. I have to think it was fairly quick. She doesn't show any of the classic signs of prolonged cyanide poisoning."

"Which are?"

"Severe diarrhea, vomiting, seizures, syncope. Basically, the body does everything it can to get rid of the poison as quickly as possible."

"Can it? On its own, I mean."

"Usually not. It's extremely toxic. There are about ten different things you can try in the ER, from charcoal to amyl nitrate—poppers—but really, all you can do is treat symptoms as they occur and hope for the best. It's incredibly fast-acting and almost always fatal."

Jeffrey had to ask, "But you think it happened fast?"

"I hope so."

"I want you to take this," he said, reaching into his jacket pocket and pulling out the cell phone.

She wrinkled her nose. "I don't want that thing."

"I like knowing where you are."

"You know where I'm going to be," she told him. "With Carlos, then in Macon, then back here."

"What if they find something during the autopsy?"

"Then I'll pick up one of the ten telephones at the lab and call you."

"What if I forget the words to 'Karma Chameleon'?"

She gave him a nasty look, and he laughed. "I love it when you sing to me."

"That's not why I don't want it."

He put the phone beside her on the table. "I guess asking you to do it for my sake wouldn't change your mind?"

She stared at him for a second, then walked out of the exam room. He was still wondering if he was expected to follow her when she returned with a book in her hand.

She said, "I don't know whether to throw this at your head or give it to you."

"What is it?"

"I ordered it a few months ago," she told him. "It came last week. I was going to give it to you when you finally moved in." She held it up so he could read the title on the maroon slipcase. "Kantor's *Andersonville*," she said, adding, "It's a first edition."

He stared at the book, his mouth opening and closing a few times before words would come out. "It must have cost a fortune."

She gave him a wry look as she handed him the novel. "I thought you were worth it at the time."

He slid the book out of the paper case, feeling like he was holding the Holy Grail. The buckram was blue and white, the pages slightly faded at the edges. Carefully, he opened it to the title page. "It's signed. MacKinlay Kantor signed it."

She half shrugged, acting as if it wasn't a big deal. "I know you like the book, and . . ."

"I can't believe you did this," Jeffrey managed, feeling like he couldn't swallow. "I can't believe it."

When he was a kid, Miss Fleming, one of his English teachers, had given him the book to read during after-school detention. Jeffrey had been a general fuckup until then, pretty much resigned to the fact that his career choices were limited to mechanic or factory worker or worse, a petty thief like his old man, but the story had opened something up inside him, something that wanted to learn. The book had changed his life.

A psychiatrist would probably say there was a connection between Jeffrey's fascination with one of the Confederacy's most notorious Civil War prisons and his being a cop, but Jeffrey liked to think that what *Andersonville* gave him was a sense of empathy that he'd lacked until that point. Before Jeffrey had moved to Grant County and taken the job as police chief, he had gone to Sumter County, Georgia, to see the place for himself. He could still remember the chill he got standing just inside the stockade at Fort Sumter. Over thirteen thousand prisoners had died in the four years the prison was open. He had stood there until the sun went down and there was nothing more to see.

Sara asked, "Do you like it?"

All he could say was, "It's beautiful." He ran his thumb along the gilt spine. Kantor had gotten the Pulitzer for this book. Jeffrey had gotten a life.

"Anyway," Sara said. "I thought you'd like it."

"I do." He tried to think of something profound to tell her that would help convey his gratitude, but instead found himself asking, "Why are you giving it to me now?"

"Because you should have it."

He was only half-kidding when he asked, "As a going-away present?"

She licked her lips, taking her time responding. "Just because you should have it."

From the front of the building, a man's voice called, "Chief?"

"Brad," Sara said. She stepped into the hall, answering, "Back here," before Jeffrey could say anything else.

Brad opened the door, his hat in one hand, a cell phone in the other. He told Jeffrey, "You left your phone at the station."

Jeffrey let his irritation show. "You came all the way over here to tell me that?"

"N-no, sir," he stammered. "I mean, yes, sir, but also, we just got a call in." He paused for a breath. "Missing person. Twenty-one years old, brown hair, brown eyes. Last seen ten days ago."

He heard Sara whisper, "Bingo."

Jeffrey grabbed his coat and the book. He handed the new cell phone to Sara, saying, "Call me as soon as you know something on the autopsy." Before she could object, he asked Brad, "Where's Lena?"

CHAPTER FIVE

Lena wanted to run, but in Atlanta, they had told her to give it a couple of weeks before doing anything jarring. This morning, she had stayed in bed as long as she could, pretending to sleep in until Nan left for work, then slipping out for a walk a few minutes later. She had wanted time to think about what she had seen on the dead girl's X-ray. The baby had been as big as her two fists put together, the same size as the baby they had taken from her womb.

As she walked down the street, Lena found herself wondering about the other woman in the clinic, the furtive looks they had given each other, the guilty way the woman had slumped into her chair, as if she wanted to disappear into nothing. Lena wondered how far along she had been, what had brought her to the clinic. She had heard stories about women who got abortions instead of worrying about birth control, but could not believe that anyone would willingly put themselves through such an ordeal more than once. Even after a week had passed, Lena couldn't close her eyes without her mind's eye conjuring up a twisted image of the fetus. The things she imagined in her head were surely worse than what was actually done.

The one thing she was grateful for was that she didn't have to sit through the autopsy that was going to happen today. She didn't want a concrete image of what her own baby had looked like before. She just wanted to get on with her life, and right now, that meant dealing with Ethan.

Last night, he had tracked her down at home after badgering her whereabouts out of Hank. Lena had told him the truth about her return, that Jeffrey had called her back into town, and laid the foundation for not seeing him much over the next few weeks by saying that she had to devote all of her attention to the case. Ethan was smart,

probably smarter than Lena in a lot of ways, and whenever he sensed
her pulling away, he always said the right thing to make her feel like
she had a choice in the matter. Over the phone, his voice had been as
smooth as silk as he'd told her to do what she had to do, and to call
him when she got the chance. She wondered how far she could press
that, how much slack was in the rope he had around her neck. Why
was she so weak where he was concerned? When did he get all this
power over her? She had to do something to get him out of her life.
There had to be a better way to live than this.

Lena turned down Sanders Street, tucking her hands into her
jacket pockets as a blast of cold air ruffled the leaves. Fifteen years
ago, she had joined the Grant County police force so that she could
be near her sister. Sibyl had worked at the college in the science department, where she'd had a very promising career until her life was
cut short. Lena couldn't say the same for her own job opportunities.
She had taken what was now being politely called a hiatus from the
force several months ago, working at the college for a stretch before
deciding to get her life back on track. Jeffrey had been very generous letting Lena have her old job back, but she knew that some of the
other cops were resentful.

She couldn't blame them. From the outside, it must look like Lena
had it fairly easy. Living it all from the inside, she knew better. Almost three years had passed since she had been raped. Her hands
and feet still had deep scars where her attacker had nailed her to the
floor. The real pain only began after she was released.

Somehow, it was getting easier, though. She could walk into an
empty room now without feeling the hair on the back of her neck
bristle. Staying in the house by herself was no longer a source of
panic. Sometimes, she would wake up and get through half the
morning without remembering what had happened.

She had to admit that Nan Thomas was one of the reasons her life
was getting easier. When Sibyl had first introduced them, Lena had
hated the other woman on sight. It wasn't as if Sibyl hadn't had other
lovers before, but there was something permanent about Nan. Lena
had even stopped talking to her sister for a while after the two
women moved in together. As with so many other things, Lena regretted that now, and Sibyl wasn't around to hear the apology. Lena

supposed she could apologize to Nan, but whenever the thought struck her, the words wouldn't come.

Living with Nan was like trying to learn the lyrics of a familiar song. You started out telling yourself that this was the time you were really going to pay attention, hear every last word, but three lines in you'd forget the plan and just settle into the familiar rhythm of the music. After six months of sharing a house together, Lena knew little more than surface things about the librarian. Nan loved animals despite severe allergies, liked to crochet and spent every Friday and Saturday night reading. She sang in the shower and in the morning before work she drank green tea out of a blue mug that had belonged to Sibyl. Her thick glasses were always smudged with fingerprints but she was incredibly fastidious about her clothes, even if her dresses tended to run to colors better suited to Easter eggs than a grown woman of thirty-six. Like Lena and Sibyl, Nan's father had been a cop. He was still around, but Lena had never met him or even heard him call on the phone. As a matter of fact, the only time the phone rang in the house, it was usually Ethan calling for Lena.

Nan's brown Corolla was parked behind Lena's Celica when she walked up the driveway to the house. Lena glanced at her watch, wondering how long she had been walking. Jeffrey had given her the morning off to make up for yesterday, and she had looked forward to spending some time alone. Nan usually came home for lunch, but it was barely past nine o'clock.

Lena grabbed the *Grant Observer* off the lawn and scanned the headlines as she walked toward the front door. Someone's toaster had caught fire Saturday night and the fire department had been called. Two students at Robert E. Lee High had placed second and fifth at a state math competition. There was no mention of the missing girl found in the woods. Probably the paper had been put to bed before Jeffrey and Sara had stumbled across the burial site. Lena was sure there would be a huge story on the front page tomorrow. Maybe the newspaper could help them find the girl's family.

She opened the door, reading about the toaster fire, wondering why it had taken sixteen volunteer firemen to put it out. Sensing a change in the room, she looked up, shocked to see Nan sitting in a chair across from Greg Mitchell, Lena's old boyfriend. They had lived together for three years before Greg decided he'd had enough of her temper. He had packed all his stuff and left while she was at work—a cowardly yet in retrospect understandable move—leaving a brief note stuck to the fridge. So brief that she could remember every word. "I love you but I can't take it anymore. Greg."

They had talked to each other a total of two times in the almost seven years since then, both conversations taking place on the telephone and both ending with Lena slamming down the receiver before Greg could say anything more than, "It's me."

"Lee," Nan practically screamed, standing up quickly, as if she had been caught.

"Hey," Lena managed, her throat clenching around the word. She had put the newspaper to her chest as if she needed some kind of protection. Maybe she did.

On the couch beside Greg was a woman around Lena's age. She had olive skin and her brown hair was pulled back into a loose pony-tail. On a good day, she might pass for one of Lena's distant cousins—the ugly ones on Hank's side. Today, sitting next to Greg, the girl looked more like a whore. It gave Lena some satisfaction that Greg had settled for a lesser copy, but she still had to swallow a tinge of jealousy when she asked, "What are you doing here?" He appeared taken aback, and she tried to moderate her tone, saying, "Back in town, I mean. What are you doing back in town?"

"I, uh . . ." His face broke into an awkward grin. Maybe he had been expecting her to hit him with the newspaper. She had done it before.

"Shattered my tib-fib," he said, indicating his ankle. She saw a cane tucked into the couch between him and the girl. "I'm back home for a while so my mom can look after me."

Lena knew his mother's house was two streets over. Her heart did an odd kind of tumble in her chest as she wondered how long he had been living there. She racked her brain for something to say, settling on, "How's she doing? Your mom."

"Still cantankerous as ever." His eyes were a crystal clear blue, in-congruous with his jet-black hair. He was wearing it longer now, or maybe he had forgotten to get it cut. Greg was always forgetting that sort of thing, spending hours in front of the computer figuring out a program while the house was falling apart around him. They had argued about it constantly. They had argued about everything constantly. She had never let up, not giving him an inch on anything. He had annoyed the shit out of her and she had hated his guts and he was probably the only man she had ever really loved.

He asked, "And you?"

"What?" she said, still stuck in her thoughts. His fingers tapped on the cane, and she saw his nails had been bitten to the quick.

Greg glanced at the other women, his smile a little more hesitant. "I asked how you were doing."

She shrugged, and there was a long moment of silence where she could only stare at him. Finally, she made herself look down at her hands. She had shredded the corner of the newspaper like a nervous housewife. Jesus, she had never been this uncomfortable in her life. There were lunatics in the asylum with better social skills.

"Lena," Nan said, her voice taking on a nervous pitch. "This is Mindy Bryant."

Mindy reached out her hand, and Lena shook it. She saw Greg looking at the scars on the back of her hand and pulled back self-consciously.

His tone had a quiet sadness. "I heard what happened."

"Yeah," she managed, tucking her hands into her back pockets. "Listen, I've got to get ready for work."

"Oh, right," Greg said. He tried to stand. Mindy and Nan reached out to help, but Lena stood where she was. She had wanted to help, even felt her muscles twitch, but for some reason her feet stayed rooted to the floor.

Greg leaned on his cane, telling Lena, "I just thought I'd drop by and let you guys know I'm back in town." He leaned over and kissed Nan's cheek. Lena remembered how many arguments she'd had with Greg over Sibyl's sexual orientation. He had always been on her sister's side and probably thought it was really rich that Lena and Nan were living together now. Or maybe not. Greg was not the petty type and never held a grudge for long; it was one of the many qualities she hadn't understood about him.

He told Lena, "I'm sorry about Sibyl. Mama didn't tell me until I got back."

"I'm not surprised," Lena said. Lu Mitchell had hated Lena on sight. She was one of those women who thought her son walked on water.

Greg said, "So, I'll get going."

"Yeah," Lena answered, stepping back so he could make his way to the door.

"Don't be a stranger." Nan patted his arm. She was still acting nervous, and Lena noticed that she was blinking a lot. Something was different about her, but Lena couldn't put her finger on it.

Greg said, "You look great, Nan. Really good."

Nan actually blushed, and Lena realized she wasn't wearing her glasses. When had Nan gotten contacts? And for that matter, why? She had never been the type to worry about her appearance, but today she had even forgone her usual pastels and had dressed in jeans and a plain black T-shirt. Lena had never seen her in anything darker than chartreuse.

Mindy had said something, and Lena apologized, saying, "Sorry?"

"I said it was nice meeting you." She had a twang that grated, and Lena hoped the smile she managed didn't betray her aversion.

Greg said, "Nice meeting you, too," and shook Mindy's hand.

Lena opened her mouth to say something, then changed her mind. Greg was at the door, his hand on the knob.

He gave Lena one last look over his shoulder. "I'll see you around."

"Yeah," Lena answered, thinking that was pretty much all she had said for the last five minutes.

The door clicked shut and the three women stood in a circle.

Mindy gave a nervous laugh, and Nan joined in just a tad too loudly. She put her hand to her mouth to stop herself.

Mindy said, "I'd better get back to work." She leaned over to kiss Nan's cheek, but Nan pulled back. At the last minute, she realized what she had done and leaned forward, hitting Mindy in the nose.

Mindy laughed, rubbing her nose. "I'll call you."

"Um, okay," Nan answered, her face the color of a turnip. "I'll be here. Today, I mean. Or at work tomorrow." She looked at everything in the room but Lena. "I mean, I'll be around."

"Okay," Mindy answered, the smile on her face a little tighter. She told Lena, "Nice meeting you."

"Yeah, you, too."

Mindy gave Nan a furtive look. "See you later."

Nan waved, and Lena said, "Bye."

The door closed, and Lena felt like all the air had been sucked from the room. Nan was still blushing, her lips pressed together so tightly they were turning white. Lena decided to break the ice, saying, "She seems nice."

"Yeah," Nan agreed. "I mean, no. Not that she's not nice. I just . . . Oh, dear me." She pressed her fingers to her lips to stop them.

Lena tried to think of something positive to say. "She's pretty."

"You think so?" Nan blushed again. "I mean, not that it matters. I just—"

"It's okay, Nan."

"It's too soon."

Lena didn't know what else to say. She wasn't good at comforting people. She wasn't good at anything emotional, a fact that Greg had cited several times before he'd finally gotten fed up and left.

"Greg just knocked on the door," Nan said, and when Lena looked out the front door, she added, "not now, before. We were sitting around. Mindy and I. We were just talking and he knocked and—" She stopped, taking a deep breath. "Greg looks good."

"Yeah."

"He said he walks in the neighborhood all the time," Nan told her. "For his leg. He's in physical therapy. He didn't want to be rude. You know, if we saw him in the street and wondered what he was doing back in town."

Lena nodded.

"He didn't know you were here. Living here."

"Oh."

Silence took over again.

Nan said, "Well," just as Lena said, "I thought you were at work."

"I took the morning off."

Lena rested her hand on the front door. Nan had obviously wanted to keep her date a secret. Maybe she was ashamed, or maybe she was scared what Lena's reaction might be.

Lena asked, "Did you have coffee with her?"

"It's too soon after Sibyl," Nan told her. "I didn't notice until you got here . . ."

"What?"

"She looks like you. Like Sibyl." She amended, "Not exactly like Sibyl, not as pretty. Not as . . ." Nan rubbed her eyes with her fingers, then whispered, "Shit."

Lena was yet again at a loss for words.

"Stupid contacts," Nan said. She dropped her hand, but Lena could see her eyes were watering.

"It's okay, Nan," Lena told her, feeling an odd sense of responsibility. "It's been three years," she pointed out, though it felt like it had barely been three days. "You deserve a life. She would want you to—"

Nan cut her off with a nod, sniffing loudly. She waved her hands in front of her face. "I'd better go take these stupid things out. I feel like I have needles in my eyes."

She practically ran to the bathroom, slamming the door behind her. Lena contemplated standing outside the door, asking her if she was okay, but that felt like a violation. The thought that Nan might one day date had never occurred to Lena. She had considered her as asexual after a while, existing only in the context of their home life. For the first time, Lena realized that Nan must have been terribly lonely all this time.

Lena was so lost in thought that the phone rang several times before Nan called, "Are you going to get that?"

Lena grabbed the receiver just before the voice mail picked up. "Hello?"

"Lena," Jeffrey said, "I know I gave you the morning off—"

Relief came like a ray of sunshine. "When do you need me?"

"I'm in the driveway."

She walked over to the window and looked out at his white cruiser. "I need a minute to change."

✻ ✻ ✻

Lena sat back in the passenger's seat, watching the scenery go by as Jeffrey drove along a gravel road on the outskirts of town. Grant County was comprised of three cities: Heartsdale, Madison and Avondale. Heartsdale, home to Grant Tech, was the jewel of the county, and with its huge antebellum mansions and gingerbread houses, it certainly looked it. By comparison, Madison was dingy, a lesser version of what a city should be, and Avondale was an outright shithole since the army had closed the base there. It was just Lena and Jeffrey's luck that the call came from Avondale. Every cop she knew dreaded a call from this side of the county, where poverty and hatred made the whole town simmer like a pot about to boil over.

Jeffrey asked, "You ever been out this far on a call?"

"I didn't even know there were houses out here."

"There weren't the last time I checked." Jeffrey handed her a file with a slip of paper containing the directions paper clipped to the outside. "What road are we looking for?"

"Plymouth," she read. At the top of the page was a name. "Ephraim Bennett?"

"The father, apparently." Jeffrey slowed so that they could check a faded road sign. It was the standard green with white letters, but there was something homemade looking about it, as if someone had used a kit from the hardware store.

"Nina Street," she read, wondering when all of these roads had been built. After working patrol for nearly ten years, Lena thought she knew the county better than anyone. Looking around, she felt like they were in foreign territory.

She asked, "Are we still in Grant?"

"We're right on the line," he told her. "Catoogah County is on the left, Grant is on the right."

He slowed for another road sign. "Pinta Street," she told him. "Who got the call first?"

"Ed Pelham," he said, practically spitting out the name. Catoogah County was less than half the size of Grant, warranting no more than a sheriff and four deputies. A year ago, Joe Smith, the kindly old grandfather who had held the post of sheriff for thirty years, had keeled over from a heart attack during the keynote speech at the Rotary Club, kicking off a nasty political race between two of his deputies. The election had been so close that the winner, in keeping with county law, was decided by a coin toss, two out of three. Ed Pelham had entered office with the moniker "Two-Bit" for more reasons than the two quarters that went his way. He was about as lazy as he was lucky, and he had no problem letting other people do his job so long as he got to wear the big hat and collect the paycheck.

Jeffrey said, "The call came in to one of his deputies last night. He didn't follow up on it until this morning, when he realized they're not in his jurisdiction."

"Ed called you?"

"He called the family and told them they'd have to take it up with us."

"Nice," she said. "Did he know about our Jane Doe?"

Jeffrey was more diplomatic than Lena would have been. "That cocksucker wouldn't know if his own ass was on fire."

She snorted a laugh. "Who's Lev?"

"What?"

"The name under here," she said, showing him the directions. "You wrote 'Lev' and underlined it."

"Oh," Jeffrey said, obviously not paying attention to her as he slowed down to read another sign.

"Santa Maria," Lena read, recognizing the names of the ships from her junior high school history class. "What are they, a bunch of pilgrims?"

"The pilgrims came over on the *Mayflower*."

"Oh," Lena said. There was a reason her school counselor had told her college wasn't right for everyone.

"Columbus led the *Nina*, *Pinta* and *Santa Maria*."

"Right." She could feel Jeffrey staring at her, probably wondering if she had a brain in her head. "Columbus."

Thankfully, he changed the subject. "Lev's the one who called this morning," Jeffrey told her, speeding up. The tires kicked back gravel and Lena saw a cloud behind them in the side-view mirror. "He's the uncle. I called back and spoke with the father."

"Uncle, huh?"

"Yeah," Jeffrey said. "We'll take a close look at him." He braked to a stop as the road made a sharp left into a dead end.

"Plymouth," Lena said, pointing to a narrow dirt road on the right.

Jeffrey reversed the car so he could make the turn without going into a ditch. "I ran their names through the computer."

"Any hits?"

"The father got a speeding ticket in Atlanta two days ago."

"Nice alibi."

"Atlanta's not that far away," he pointed out. "Who the hell would live way out here?"

"Not me," Lena answered. She looked out her window at the rolling pastures. There were cows grazing and a couple of horses ran in the distance like something out of a movie. Some people might think this was a slice of heaven, but Lena needed more to do than look at the cows all day.

"When did all this get here?" Jeffrey asked.

Lena looked on his side of the road, seeing a huge farm with row after row of plants. She asked, "Are those peanuts?"

"They look a little tall for that."

"What else grows out here?"

"Republicans and unemployment," he said. "This has to be some kind of corporate farm. Nobody could afford to run a place this size on their own."

"There you go." Lena pointed to a sign at the head of a winding driveway that led to a series of buildings. The words "Holy Grown Soy Cooperative" were written in fancy gold script. Underneath this, in smaller letters, it said "Est. 1984."

Lena asked, "Like hippies?"

"Who knows," Jeffrey said, rolling up the window as the smell of manure came into the car. "I'd hate to have to live across from this place."

She saw a large, modern-looking barn with a group of at least fifty workers milling about outside. They were probably on break. "The soy business must be doing well."

He slowed the car to a stop in the middle of the road. "Is this place even on the map?"

Lena opened the glove compartment and took out the spiral-bound Grant County and surrounding areas street map. She was flipping through the pages, looking for Avondale, when Jeffrey mumbled a curse and turned toward the farm. One thing she liked about her boss was that he wasn't afraid to ask for directions. Greg had been the same way—usually it was Lena saying they should just go a couple more miles and see if they lucked out and found their destination.

The driveway to the barn was more like a two-lane road, both sides rutted deep from tires. They probably had heavy trucks in and out to pick up the soy or whatever it was they grew here. Lena didn't know what soy looked like, but she imagined it would take a lot to fill a box, let alone a whole truck.

"We'll try here," Jeffrey said, slamming the gear into park. She could tell he was irritated, but didn't know if it was because they had gotten lost or because the detour kept the family waiting even longer. She had learned from Jeffrey over the years that it was best to get the bad news out of the way as quickly as possible unless there was something important to be gained from waiting.

They walked around the big red barn and Lena saw a second group of workers standing behind it, a short, wiry looking old man yelling so loud that even from fifty feet away, she could hear him clear as a bell.

"The Lord does not abide laziness!" the man was screaming, his finger inches from a younger man's face. "Your weakness has cost us a full morning's work!"

The man with the finger in his face looked down, contrite. There were two girls in the crowd, and they were both crying.

"Weakness and greed!" the old man proclaimed. Anger edged his tone so that each word sounded like an indictment. He had a Bible in his other hand, and he raised it into the air like a torch, shining the way toward enlightenment. "Your weakness will find you out!" he screamed. "The Lord will test you, and you must be strong!"

"Christ," Jeffrey muttered, then, "Excuse me, sir?"

The man turned around, his scowl slipping into a puzzled look, then a frown. He was wearing a white long-sleeved shirt starched to within an inch of its life. His jeans were likewise stiff, a razor crease ironed into the front of the legs. A Braves ball cap sat on his head, his large ears sticking out on each side like billboards. He used the back of his sleeve to wipe spittle from his mouth. "Is there something I can help you with, sir?" Lena noticed that his voice was hoarse from yelling.

Jeffrey said, "We're looking for Ephraim Bennett."

The man's expression yet again turned on a dime. He smiled brightly, his eyes lighting up. "That's across the road," he said, indicating the way Jeffrey and Lena had come. He directed, "Go back down, take a left, then you'll see it about a quarter mile down on the right."

Despite his cheerful demeanor, tension hung in the air like a heavy cloud. It was hard to reconcile the man who had been screaming a few minutes ago with the kindly old grandfather offering his help to them now.

Lena checked out the crowd of workers—about ten in all. Some looked as if they had one foot in the grave. One girl in particular looked like she was having a hard time standing up, though whether this was from grief or intoxication, Lena wasn't sure. They all looked like a bunch of strung-out hippies.

"Thank you," Jeffrey told the man, but he looked like he didn't want to leave.

"Have a blessed day," the man answered, then turned his back to Jeffrey and Lena, pretty much dismissing them. "Children," he said, holding the Bible aloft, "let's return to the fields."

Lena felt Jeffrey's hesitation, and didn't move until he did. It wasn't like they could push the man to the ground and ask him what the hell was going on, but she could tell they both were thinking the same thing: something strange was happening here.

They were quiet until they got into the car. Jeffrey started the car and reversed it out of the space so he could turn around.

Lena said, "That was weird."

"Weird how?"

She wondered if he was disagreeing with her or just trying to get her take on the situation.

She said, "All that Bible shit."

"He seemed a little wrapped up in it," Jeffrey conceded, "but a lot of folks around here are."

"Still," she said. "Who carries a Bible to work with them?"

"A lot of people out here, I'd guess."

They turned back onto the main road and almost immediately Lena saw a mailbox sticking up on her side of the road. "Three ten," she said. "This is it."

Jeffrey took the turn. "Just because somebody's religious doesn't mean there's something wrong with them."

"I didn't say that," Lena insisted, though maybe she had. From the age of ten, she had hated church and anything that smacked of a man standing in a pulpit, ordering you around. Her uncle Hank was so wrapped up in religion now that it was a worse addiction than the speed he'd shot into his veins for almost thirty years.

Jeffrey said, "Try to keep an open mind."

"Yeah," she answered, wondering if he'd let it slip his mind that she'd been raped a few years ago by a Jesus freak who got off on crucifying women. If Lena was antireligion, she had a damn good reason to be.

Jeffrey drove down a driveway that was so long Lena wondered if they had taken a wrong turn. Passing a leaning barn and what looked like an outhouse gave Lena a feeling of déjà vu. There were places like this all over Reese, where she had grown up. Reaganomics and government deregulation had crippled the farmers to their knees. Families had simply walked away from the land that had belonged to them for generations, leaving it to the bank to figure out what to do. Usually, the bank sold it to some multinational corporation that in turn hired migrant workers on the sly, keeping the payroll down and profits up.

Jeffrey asked, "Do they use cyanide in pesticides these days?"

"Got me." Lena took out her notebook to remind herself to find the answer.

Jeffrey slowed the car as they breached a steep hill. Three goats stood in the drive, and he beeped his horn to get them moving. The bells around their collars jangled as they trotted into what looked like a chicken coop. A teenage girl and a young boy stood outside a pigpen holding a bucket between them. The girl was wearing a simple shift, the boy overalls with no shirt and no shoes. Their eyes followed the car as they drove by, and Lena felt the hairs on her arm stand straight up.

Jeffrey said, "If somebody starts playing a banjo, I'm outta here."

"I'm right behind you," Lena said, relieved to see civilization finally come into view.

The house was an unassuming cottage with two dormers set into a steeply pitched roof. The clapboard looked freshly painted and well tended, and except for the beat-up old truck out front, the house could have easily been a professor's home in Heartsdale. Flowers ringed the front porch and followed a dirt path to the drive. As they got out of the car, Lena saw a woman standing behind the screen door. She had her hands clasped in front of her and Lena guessed from the palpable tension that this was the missing girl's mother.

Jeffrey said, "This isn't going to be easy," and not for the first time she was glad that this sort of thing was his job and not hers.

Lena shut the door, letting her hand rest on the hood as a man came out of the house. She expected the woman to follow, but instead an older man came shuffling out.

"Chief Tolliver?" the younger man asked. He had dark red hair but without the freckles that usually accompanied it. His skin was as pasty as you would expect, and his green eyes were so clear in the morning sunlight that Lena could tell their color from at least ten feet away. He was good-looking if you liked that sort, but the short-sleeved button-down shirt that he wore tightly tucked into his khaki Dockers made him look like a high school math teacher.

Jeffrey looked momentarily startled for some reason, but he recovered quickly, saying, "Mr. Bennett?"

"Lev Ward," he clarified. "This is Ephraim Bennett, Abigail's father."

"Oh," Jeffrey said, and Lena could tell he was surprised. Even wearing a baseball cap and overalls, Ephraim Bennett looked to be about eighty, hardly the age of a man with a twenty-ish daughter. Still, he was wiry-thin with a healthy glint in his eyes. Both his hands trembled noticeably, but she imagined he didn't miss much.

Jeffrey said, "I'm sorry to meet you under these circumstances."

Ephraim gave Jeffrey what looked like a firm handshake despite his obvious palsy. "I appreciate your handling this personally, sir." His voice was strong with the kind of Southern drawl Lena never heard anymore except in Hollywood movies. He tipped his hat to Lena. "Ma'am."

Lena nodded in return, watching Lev, who seemed to be in charge despite the thirty-odd years that separated the two.

Ephraim told Jeffrey, "Thank you for coming out so quickly," even though Lena would hardly characterize their response as quick. The call had come in last night. Had Jeffrey been on the other end of the line instead of Ed Pelham, he would have driven straight out to the Bennett home, not waited until the next day.

Jeffrey apologized, saying, "There was a question of jurisdiction."

Lev said, "That's my fault. The farm is in Catoogah County. I guess I just wasn't thinking."

"None of us were," Ephraim excused.

Lev bowed his head, as if to accept the absolution.

Jeffrey said, "We stopped at the farm across the street for directions. There was a man there, about sixty-five, seventy —"

"Cole," Lev provided. "Our foreman."

Jeffrey paused, probably waiting for more information. When nothing came, he added, "He gave us directions."

"I'm sorry I wasn't more clear about how to get here," Lev told him. Then offered, "Why don't we go inside and talk to Esther?"

"Your sister-in-law?" Jeffrey asked.

"Baby sister," Lev clarified. "I hope you don't mind, but my brother and other sisters are coming by, too. We've been up all night worried about Abby."

Lena asked, "Has she ever run away before?"

"I'm sorry," Lev said, focusing his attention on Lena. "I didn't introduce myself." He held out his hand. Lena had been expecting the dead-fish flop that most men affected, lightly gripping a woman's fingers as if they were afraid of breaking them, but he gave her the same hearty shake he had given Jeffrey, looking her square in the eye. "Leviticus Ward."

"Lena Adams," she told him.

"Detective?" he guessed. "We've been so anxious about this. Forgive my poor manners."

"It's understandable," Lena said, aware that he had managed to sidestep answering her question about Abby.

He stepped back, graciously telling Lena, "After you."

Lena walked toward the house, watching their shadows follow her, wondering at their old-fashioned manners. When they reached the front door, Lev held it open, letting Lena walk in first.

Esther Bennett sat on the couch, her feet crossed at the ankles, hands folded in her lap. Her spine was ramrod straight, and Lena, normally given to slouching, found herself pulling her shoulders back as if she was trying to measure up.

"Chief Tolliver?" Esther Bennett asked. She was much younger than her husband, probably in her forties, her dark hair graying slightly at the temples. Wearing a white cotton dress with a red-checkered apron, she looked like something out of a Betty Crocker cookbook. She kept her hair in a tight bun behind her head, but judging from the wisps that had escaped, it was nearly as long as her daughter's. There was no doubt in Lena's mind that the dead girl was this woman's daughter. They were carbon copies of each other.

"Call me Jeffrey," Jeffrey offered, then, "you've got a beautiful home, Mrs. Bennett." He always said this, even if the place was a dump. In this case, though, the best way to describe the Bennett house was plain. There were no knickknacks on the coffee table and the mantel over the fireplace was clean but for a simple wooden cross hanging on the brick. Two faded but sturdy-looking wingback chairs banked the window looking out into the front yard. The orangish couch was probably a relic from the 1960s, but it was in good shape. There were no drapes or blinds on the windows and the hardwood floor was bare of any carpeting. The ceiling fixture overhead was probably original to the house, which put it at around Ephraim's age. Lena guessed they were standing in the formal parlor, though a quick glance down the hallway proved the rest of the house followed the same minimalist decorating style.

Jeffrey must have been thinking the same thing about the house, because he asked, "Have y'all lived here long?"

Lev answered, "Since before Abby was born."

"Please," Esther said, spreading her hands. "Have a seat." She stood as Jeffrey sat, and he popped back up. "Please," she repeated, motioning him back down.

Lev told him, "The rest of the family should be here soon."

Esther offered, "Would you like something to drink, Chief Tolliver? Some lemonade?"

"That'd be nice," Jeffrey answered, probably because he knew accepting the offer would help put the woman at ease.

"And you, Miss—?"

"Adams," Lena provided. "I'm fine, thank you."

Lev said, "Esther, this woman is a detective."

"Oh," she said, seeming flustered by her mistake. "I'm sorry, Detective Adams."

"It's fine," Lena assured her, wondering why she felt like she should be the one apologizing. There was something strange about this family, and she wondered what secrets they were hiding. Her radar had been on high alert since the old nut at the farm. She didn't imagine he fell far from the tree.

Lev said, "Lemonade would be nice, Esther," and Lena realized how deftly he managed to control the situation. He seemed to be very good at taking charge, something that always made her wary in an investigation.

Esther had regained some of her composure. "Please make your-selves at home. I'll be right back."

She left the room silently, only pausing to rest her hand briefly on her husband's shoulder.

The men stood around as if they were waiting for something. Lena caught Jeffrey's expression and she said, "Why don't I go help her?"

The men seemed relieved, and as she walked down the hallway after Esther, Lena could hear Lev chuckling at something she didn't quite catch. Something told her it had to do with a woman's place being in the kitchen. She got the distinct impression that this family did things the old-fashioned way, with the men taking charge and the women being seen and not heard.

Lena took her time walking to the back of the house, hoping to see something that might explain what was so weird about the inhabi-tants. There were three doors on the right, all closed, that she as-sumed were bedrooms. On the left was what looked like a family room and a large library filled floor to ceiling with books, which was kind of surprising. For some reason, she had always assumed reli-gious fanatics didn't tend to read.

If Esther was as old as she looked, then her brother Lev had to be closer to fifty. He was a smooth talker and had the voice of a Baptist preacher. Lena had never been particularly attracted to pasty men, but there was something almost magnetic about Lev. In appearance, he reminded her a bit of Sara Linton. They both exuded the same confidence, too, but on Sara this came across as off-putting. On Lev, it was calming. If he were a used car salesman, he'd probably be at the top of his trade.

"Oh," Esther said, startled by Lena's sudden appearance in the kitchen. The woman was holding a photograph in her hand, and she seemed hesitant about showing it to Lena. Finally, she made up her mind and offered the picture. It showed a child of about twelve with long brown pigtails.

"Abby?" Lena asked, knowing without a doubt that this was the girl Jeffrey and Sara had found in the woods.

Esther studied Lena, as if trying to read her thoughts. She seemed to decide she didn't want to know, because she returned to her work in the kitchen, turning her back to Lena.

"Abby loves lemonade," she said. "She likes it sweet, but I must say that I don't care for it sweet."

"Me, either," Lena said, not because it was true but because she wanted to seem agreeable. Since stepping into this house, she had felt unsettled. Being a cop, she had learned to trust her first impressions.

Esther cut a lemon in two and twisted it by hand into a metal strainer. She had gone through about six lemons and the bowl underneath the strainer was getting full.

"Can I help?" Lena asked, thinking the only drinks she'd ever made came from a package and usually went into a blender.

"I've got it," Esther said, then, as if she had somehow insulted Lena, added in an apologetic tone, "The pitcher's over the stove."

Lena walked to the cabinet and took out a large crystal glass pitcher. It was heavy and probably an antique. She used both hands to transfer it to the counter.

Trying to find something to say, Lena said, "I like the light in here." There was a large florescent strip overhead, but it wasn't turned on. Three large windows lined the area over the sink and two long skylights over the kitchen table lit the room. Like the rest of the house, it was plain, and she wondered about people choosing to live in such austerity.

Esther looked up at the sun. "Yes, it's nice, isn't it? Ephraim's father built it from the ground up."

"You've been married long?"

"Twenty-two years."

"Abby's your oldest?"

She smiled, taking another lemon out of the bag. "That's right."

"We saw two kids coming in."

"Rebecca and Zeke," Esther said, still smiling proudly. "Becca is mine. Zeke is Lev's by his late wife."

"Two girls," Lena said, thinking she sounded idiotic. "Must be nice."

Esther rolled a lemon around on the cutting board to soften it up. "Yes," she said, but Lena had heard the hesitation.

Lena looked out the kitchen window at the pasture. She could see a group of cows lying down under a tree. "That farm across the street," she began.

"The cooperative," Esther finished. "That's where I met Ephraim.

He came to work there, oh, it must have been right after Papa bought the second phase in the mid-1980s. We got married and moved in here a little after."

"You must have been around Abby's age," Lena guessed.

Esther looked up, as if the thought hadn't occurred to her. "Yes," she said. "You're right. I'd just fallen in love and moved out on my own. I had the whole world at my feet." She pressed another lemon into the strainer.

"The older guy we ran into," Lena began, "Cole?"

Esther smiled. "He's been on the farm forever. Papa met him years ago."

Lena waited for more, but nothing came. Like Lev, Esther didn't seem to want to volunteer much information about Cole, and this only made Lena more curious about the man.

She remembered the question Lev had avoided before, and felt like now was as good a time as any to ask, "Has Abby ever run away before?"

"Oh, no, she's not the type."

"What type is that?" Lena asked, wondering if the mother knew her daughter was pregnant.

"Abby's very devoted to the family. She would never do anything so insensitive."

"Sometimes girls that age do things without thinking about the consequences."

"That's more Becca's thing," Esther said.

"Rebecca's run away?"

The older woman skipped the question, saying instead, "Abby never went through that rebellious phase. She's a lot like me in that regard."

"How's that?"

Esther seemed about to answer, but changed her mind. She took the pitcher and poured in the lemon juice. She walked over to the sink and turned on the water, letting it run so it would cool.

Lena wondered if the woman was naturally reticent or if she felt the need to censor her answers lest her brother find out she had said too much. She tried to think of a way to draw the woman out. "I was the youngest," she said, which was true, though only by a couple of minutes. "I was always getting into trouble."

Esther made an agreeing noise, but offered nothing more.

"It's hard to accept that your parents are real people," Lena said. "You spend most of your time demanding they treat you like an adult, but you're not willing to give them the same courtesy."

Esther looked over her shoulder into the long hallway before allowing, "Rebecca ran away last year. She was back a day later, but it put an awful fright into us."

"Has Abby ever disappeared before?" Lena repeated.

Esther's voice was almost a whisper. "Sometimes she would go over to the farm without telling us."

"Just across the street?"

"Yes, just across the street. It's silly to think we were upset. The farm is an extension of our home. Abby was safe the entire time. We were just worried when supper came and we hadn't heard from her."

Lena realized the woman was referring to a specific time rather than a series of incidences. "Abby spent the night over there?"

"With Lev and Papa. They live there with Mary. My mother passed away when I was three."

"Who's Mary?"

"My oldest sister."

"Older than Lev?"

"Oh, no, Lev's the oldest child. There's Mary next, then Rachel, then Paul, then me."

"That's quite a family," Lena said, thinking their mother must have died from exhaustion.

"Papa grew up an only child. He wanted lots of children around him."

"Your father owns the farm?"

"The family owns most of it along with some other investors," Esther replied, opening one of the cabinets and taking down a three-pound bag of sugar. "Papa started it over twenty years ago."

Lena tried to phrase her question diplomatically. "I thought cooperatives were owned by the workers."

"All the workers have the opportunity to invest after they've been on the farm for two years," she explained, measuring out a cup of sugar.

"Where do these workers come from?"

"Atlanta, mostly." She stirred the lemonade with a wooden spoon to mix the sugar. "Some of them are transients, looking for a few months of solitude. Others want a way of life and decide to stay. We call them 'souls,' because they're very much like lost souls." A wry smile touched her lips. "I'm not naïve. Some of them are downright hiding from the law. We've always been hesitant to involve the police because of this. We want to help them, not hide them, but some are avoiding abusive spouses or parents. We can't protect just the ones we agree with. It has to be all or none."

"Involve the police in what?"

"There've been thefts in the past," Esther said, then added, "I know I've spoken out of turn, but Lev wouldn't likely mention this to you. We're very isolated out here, as you probably noticed, and the local sheriff isn't too keen to drop everything and come running just because a pitchfork has shown up missing."

Pelham wouldn't come running for anything but dinner. "Is that all it's been? Missing pitchforks?"

"Some shovels have been taken, a couple of wheelbarrows."

"Any wood?"

She gave Lena a look of confusion. "Well, I don't know about that. We don't use much wood on the farm. You mean like stakes? Soybean plants don't vine."

"What else has been missing?"

"The petty-cash box was stolen out of the barn about a month ago. There was, I think, around three hundred dollars in it."

"What's petty cash kept for?"

"Running to the hardware store, sometimes buying a pizza if folks have been working late. We process the plants here ourselves, which is a lot of repetitive work. Some of the souls we get aren't highly skilled, but others find themselves bored with it. We move them into other areas of the farm, like deliveries, accounting. Not big accounting, but going through invoices, filing. Our goal is to teach them a useful skill, give them some sense of accomplishment, to take back into their real lives."

It sounded like a cult to Lena, and her attitude got the better of her when she said, "So, you bring them back from Atlanta and all they have to do in return is say their nightly prayers?"

Esther smiled like she was humoring Lena. "We only ask them to go to services on Sunday. It's not mandatory. We have fellowship every evening at eight, and they're welcome then as well. Most of them choose not to attend, and that's perfectly fine. We don't require anything but that they obey the rules and behave respectfully toward us and their peers."

They had gotten way off the point, and Lena tried to steer her back. "Do you work on the farm?"

"Normally, I school the children. Most of the women who come here have kids. I try to help them as much as I can, but again, they're usually not here for long. Structure is all I can give them."

"How many people do you have at a time?"

"Around two hundred would be my guess. You can ask Lev about that. I don't keep up with employment records and such."

Lena made a mental note to get those records, though she couldn't keep her mind from flashing on a bunch of young kids being brainwashed into giving up their worldly possessions and joining this weird family. She wondered if Jeffrey was getting the same impression in the other room. "You still school Abby?"

"We talk about literature, mostly. I'm afraid I can't offer her much beyond the usual high school curriculum. Ephraim and I discussed sending her to a small college, perhaps Tifton or West Georgia, but she wasn't interested. She loves working at the farm, you see. Her gift is helping others."

"Have you always done that?" Lena asked. "Homeschooling, I mean."

"We were all homeschooled. All of us but Lev." She smiled proudly. "Paul had one of the highest SAT scores in the state when he entered UGA."

Lena wasn't interested in Paul's academic career. "That's your only job at the farm? Teaching?"

"Oh, no," she laughed. "Everyone on the farm has to do everything at some time. I started in the fields, just like Becca is doing. Zeke's a little too young now, but he'll start in the next few years. Papa believes you have to know every part of the company if you're going to run it some day. I got stuck in bookkeeping for a while. Unfortunately, I have a talent for numbers. If I had my way, I'd lie around on the couch all day reading. Papa wants us to be ready when something happens to him."

"You'll run the farm eventually?"

She laughed again at the suggestion, as if running a company was something a woman couldn't possibly manage. "Maybe Zeke or one of the boys will. The point is to be ready. It's also important considering our labor force isn't particularly motivated to stay. They're city people, used to a faster way of life. They love it here at first — the quiet, the solitude, the easiness of it compared to their old lives on the street, but then they start to get a little bored, then a lot bored, and before they know it, everything that made them love it here makes them want to run screaming. We try to be selective in our training. You don't want to spend a season teaching someone to do a specialized job when they're going to leave in the middle of it and go back to the city."

"Drugs?" Lena asked.

"Of course," she said. "But we're very careful here. You have to earn trust. We don't allow alcohol or cigarettes on the farm. If you want to go into town, you're welcome to, but no one is going to give you a ride. We have them sign a behavioral contract the minute they step foot on the place. If they break it, they're gone. A lot more people than not appreciate that, and the new ones learn from the old-timers that when we say an infraction gets you sent back to Atlanta, we mean it." Her tone softened. "I know it sounds harsh, but we have to get rid of the bad ones so that the ones who are trying to be good have a chance. Surely, as a law enforcement officer, you understand that."

"How many people come and go?" Lena asked. "Ballpark, I mean."

"Oh, I'd say we have about a seventy percent return rate." Again, she deferred to the men in her family. "You'd have to ask Lev or Paul for an exact percentage. They keep up with the running of things."

"But you've noticed people coming and going?"

"Of course."

"What about Abby?" Lena asked. "Is she happy here?"

Esther smiled. "I would hope so, but we never make people stay here if they don't want to." Lena nodded as if she understood, but Esther felt the need to add, "I know this all may sound odd to you. We're religious people, but we don't believe in forcing religion onto others. When you come to the Lord, it must be of your own volition or it means nothing to Him. I can tell from your questions that you're skeptical about the workings of the farm and my family, but I can assure you we're simply working for the greater good here. We're obviously not invested in material needs." She indicated the house. "What we're invested in is saving souls."

Her placid smile was more off-putting than anything Lena had experienced today. She tried to work with it, asking, "What sort of things does Abby do on the farm?"

"She's even better with numbers than I am," Esther said proudly. "She worked in the office for a while, but she started to get bored, so we all agreed she could start working as a sorter. It's not a highly difficult job, but it brings her into contact with a lot of people. She likes being in a crowd, blending in. I suppose every young girl feels that."

Lena waited a beat, wondering why the woman had yet to ask about her daughter. Either Esther was in denial or she knew exactly where Abby was. "Did Abby know about the thefts?"

"Not many people did," Esther said. "Lev likes to let the church handle church problems."

"The church?" Lena asked, as if she hadn't already figured this out.

"Oh, I'm sorry," she said, and Lena wondered why she started just about every sentence with an apology. "The Church for the Greater Good. I always just assume everyone knows what we're about."

"And what are you about?"

Lena obviously wasn't doing a good job of hiding her cynicism, but Esther still patiently explained, "Holy Grown subsidizes our outreach into Atlanta."

"What kind of outreach?"

"We try to carry on Jesus's work with the poor. We have contacts at several shelters for the homeless and abused women. Some halfway houses keep us on their speed dial. Sometimes we get men and women who have just gotten out of jail and have nowhere to go. It's appalling the way our penal system just chews these people up and spits them out."

"Do you keep any information on them?"

"As much as we can," Esther said, returning to the lemonade. "We have education facilities where they learn manufacturing. The soy business has changed over the last ten years."

"It's in just about everything," Lena said, thinking it would be unwise to mention that the only reason she knew this was because she lived with a tofu-eating health-food nut lesbian.

"Yes," Esther agreed. She took three glasses out of the cabinet.

Lena offered, "I'll get the ice." She opened the freezer and saw a huge block of ice instead of the cubes she'd been expecting.

"Just use your hands," Esther said. "Or I could—"

"I've got it," Lena told her, taking out the block, getting the front of her shirt wet in the process.

"We have an icehouse across the road for cold storage. It seems a shame to waste water here when there's plenty across the street." She indicated Lena should set the block in the sink. "We try to preserve as many of our natural resources as we can," she said, using an ice pick to dislodge some shards. "Papa was the first farmer in the region to use natural irrigation from rainwater. Of course, we have too much land for that now, but we reclaim as much as we can."

Thinking of Jeffrey's earlier question about possible sources of cyanide, Lena asked, "What about pesticides?"

"Oh, no," Esther said, dropping some ice into the glasses. "We don't use those—never have. We use natural fertilizers. You have no idea what phosphates do to the water table. Oh, no." She laughed. "Papa made it clear from the start that we would do it the natural way. We're all a part of this land. We have a responsibility to our neighbors and the people who come to the land after us."

"That sounds very . . ." Lena looked for a positive word. "Responsible."

"Most people think it's a lot of trouble for nothing," Esther said. "It's a difficult situation to be in. Do we poison the environment and make more money that we can use to help the needy, or do we maintain our principles and help fewer people? It's the sort of question Jesus often raised: Help the many or help the few?" She handed Lena one of the glasses. "Does this taste too sweet for you? I'm afraid we don't normally use much sugar around here."

Lena took a sip, feeling her jaw clench into a death grip. "It's a little tart," she managed, trying to suppress the guttural sound welling in her throat.

"Oh." Esther took out the sugar again, spooning more into Lena's glass. "Now?"

Lena tried again, taking a less generous sip. "Good," she said.

"Good," Esther echoed, spooning more into another glass. She left the third alone, and Lena hoped it wasn't meant for Jeffrey.

"Everyone's particular, aren't they?" Esther asked, walking past Lena toward the hall.

Lena followed. "What's that?"

"About tastes," she explained. "Abby loves sweets. Once, when she was a baby, she ate almost a full cup of sugar before I realized she had gotten into the cabinet."

They passed the library, and Lena said, "You have a lot of books."

"Classics, mostly. Some potboilers and westerns of course. Ephraim loves crime fiction. I guess he's attracted to the black and white of it all. The good guys on one side, the bad guys on the other."

"It'd be nice," Lena found herself saying.

"Becca loves romances. Show her a book with a long-haired Adonis on the cover and she'll finish it in two hours."

"You let her read romances?" Lena asked. She had been thinking these people were the same kind of nutballs who got on the news for banning Harry Potter.

"We let the children read anything they like. That's the deal for not having a television in the house. Even if they're reading trash, it's better than watching it on the tube."

Lena nodded, though in her mind she wondered what it would be like to live without television. Watching mindless TV was the only thing that had kept her sane the last three years.

"There you are," Lev said when they entered the room. He took a glass from Esther and handed it to Jeffrey.

"Oh, no," Esther said, taking it back. "This one's yours." She handed the sweeter lemonade to Jeffrey, who, like Ephraim, had stood when they entered the room. "I don't imagine you like it as tart as Lev does."

"No, ma'am," Jeffrey agreed. "Thank you."

The front door opened and a man who looked like the male version of Esther walked in, his hand at the elbow of an older woman who seemed too fragile to walk by herself.

The man said, "Sorry we're late."

Jeffrey moved, taking his lemonade with him, so that the woman could take his chair. Another woman who looked more like Lev entered the house, her reddish-blond hair wound into a bun on the top of her head. To Lena, she looked like the quintessential sturdy farm-woman who could drop a baby in the fields and keep on picking cotton the rest of the day. Hell, the whole family looked strong. The shortest one was Esther, and she had a good six inches on Lena.

"My brother, Paul," Lev said, indicating the man. "This is Rachel." The farmwoman nodded her head in greeting. "And Mary."

From what Esther had said, Mary was younger than Lev, probably in her mid-forties, but she looked and acted like she was twenty years older. She took her time settling into the chair, as if she was afraid she'd fall and break a hip. She even sounded like an old woman when she said, "You'll have to excuse me, I haven't been well," in a tone that invited pity.

"My father couldn't join us," Lev told them, deftly sidestepping his sister. "He's had a stroke. He doesn't get out much these days."

"That's quite all right," Jeffrey told him, then addressed the other family members. "I'm Chief Tolliver. This is Detective Adams. Thank you all for coming."

"Shall we sit?" Rachel suggested, going to the couch. She indicated Esther should sit beside her. Again, Lena felt the division of tasks between the men and women of the family, seating arrangements and kitchen duties on one side, everything else on the other.

Jeffrey tilted his head slightly, motioning Lena to Esther's left as he leaned against the fireplace mantel. Lev waited until Lena was seated before helping Ephraim into the chair beside Jeffrey. He raised his eyebrows slightly, and Lena knew that he had probably gotten quite an earful while she was in the kitchen. She couldn't wait to compare notes.

"So," Jeffrey said, as if the small talk was out of the way and they could finally get down to business. "You say Abby's been missing for ten days?"

"That's my fault," Lev said, and Lena wondered if he was going to confess. "I thought Abby was going on the mission into Atlanta with the family. Ephraim thought she was staying on the farm with us."

Paul said, "We all thought that was the case. I don't think we need to assign blame." Lena studied the man for the first time, thinking he sounded a lot like a lawyer. He was the only one of them wearing what looked like store-bought clothes. His suit was pin-striped, his tie a deep magenta against his white shirt. His hair was professionally cut and styled. Paul Ward looked like the city mouse standing next to his country-mouse brother and sisters.

"Whatever the case, none of us thought anything untoward was happening," Rachel said.

Jeffrey must have gotten the full story about the farm, because his next question was not about the family or the inner workings of Holy Grown. "Was there someone around the farm Abby liked being around? Maybe one of the workers?"

Rachel provided, "We didn't really let her mingle."

"Surely she met other people," Jeffrey said, taking a sip of lemonade. He seemed to be doing everything in his power not to shudder from the tartness as he put the glass on the mantel.

Lev said, "She went to church socials, of course, but the field workers keep to themselves."

Esther added, "We don't like to discriminate, but the field workers are a rougher sort of person. Abby wasn't really introduced to that element of the farm. She was told to stay away from them."

"But she worked some in the fields?" Lena asked, remembering their earlier conversation.

"Yes, but only with other family members. Cousins, mostly," Lev said. "We have a rather large family."

Esther listed, "Rachel has four, Paul has six. Mary's sons live in Wyoming and . . ."

She didn't finish. Jeffrey prompted, "And?"

Rachel cleared her throat, but it was Paul who spoke. "They don't visit often," he said, the tension in his voice echoing what Lena suddenly felt in the room. "They haven't been back in a while."

"Ten years," Mary said, looking up at the ceiling like she wanted to trap her tears. Lena wondered if they had run screaming from the farm. She sure as hell would have.

Mary continued, "They chose a different path. I pray for them every day when I get up and every evening before I go to bed."

Sensing Mary could monopolize things for a while, Lena asked Lev, "You're married?"

"Not anymore." For the first time, his expression appeared unguarded. "My wife passed away in childbirth several years ago." He gave a pained smile. "Our first child, unfortunately, but I have my Ezekiel to comfort me."

Jeffrey waited an appropriate interval before saying, "So, you guys thought Abby was with her parents, her parents thought she was with you. This was, what, ten days ago you went on your mission?"

Esther answered, "That's right."

"And you do these missions about four times a year?"

"Yes."

"You're a registered nurse?" he asked.

Esther nodded, and Lena tried to hide her surprise. The woman seemed to volunteer yards of useless information about herself at the drop of a hat. That she had kept back this one detail seemed suspicious.

Esther supplied, "I was training at Georgia Medical College when Ephraim and I married. Papa thought it'd be handy to have someone with practical first aid experience around the farm, and the other girls can't stand the sight of blood."

"That's the truth," Rachel agreed.

Jeffrey asked, "Do you have many accidents here?"

"Thank goodness, no. A man sliced through his Achilles tendon three years ago. It was a mess. I was able to use my training to control the bleeding, but there was nothing else I could do for him other than basic triage. We really need a doctor around."

"Who do you normally see?" Jeffrey asked. "You have children around here sometimes." As if explaining, he added, "My wife is a pediatrician in town."

Lev interposed, "Sara Linton. Of course." A slight smile of recognition crossed his lips.

"Do you know Sara?"

"We went to Sunday school together a *long* time ago." Lev stretched out the word "long," as if they had many shared secrets.

Lena could tell that Jeffrey was annoyed by the familiarity; whether he was jealous or just being protective, she didn't know.

Being Jeffrey, he didn't let his irritation interfere with the interview, and instead directed them back on track by asking Esther, "Do you normally not telephone to check in?" When Esther seemed confused, he added, "When you're away in Atlanta. You don't call to check in on the children?"

"They're with their family," she said. Her tone was demure but Lena had seen a flash in her eyes, as if she had been insulted.

Rachel continued her sister's theme. "We're very close-knit, Chief Tolliver. In case you hadn't picked up on that."

Jeffrey took the slap on the nose better than Lena would have. He asked Esther, "Can you tell me when it was you realized she was missing?"

"We got back late last night," Esther said. "We went by the farm first to see Papa and pick up Abby and Becca—"

"Becca didn't go with you, either?" Lena asked.

"Oh, of course not," the mother said, as if she had suggested something preposterous. "She's only fourteen."

"Right," Lena said, having no idea what age was appropriate for a tour of the homeless shelters of Atlanta.

"Becca stayed with us at the house," Lev provided. "She likes to spend time with my son, Zeke." He continued, "When Abby didn't show up for supper that first night, Becca just assumed Abby had changed her mind about going to Atlanta. She didn't even bother to bring it up."

"I'd like to talk to her," Jeffrey said.

Lev obviously did not like the request, but he nodded his consent. "All right."

Jeffrey tried again, "There was no one Abby was seeing? A boy she was interested in?"

"I know this is difficult to believe because of her age," Lev replied, "but Abby led a very sheltered life. She was schooled here at home. She didn't know much about life outside the farm. We were trying to prepare her by taking her into Atlanta, but she didn't like it. She preferred a more cloistered life."

"She had been on missions before?"

Esther provided, "Yes. Twice. She didn't like it, didn't like being away."

" 'Cloistered' is an interesting word," Jeffrey observed.

"I know it makes her sound like a nun," Lev told him, "and maybe that's not far off base. She wasn't Catholic, of course, but she was extremely devout. She had a passion for serving our Lord."

Ephraim said, "Amen," under his breath, but it felt cursory to Lena, like saying, "Bless you," after someone sneezed.

Esther supplied, "She was very strong in her faith." Quickly, she put her hand to her mouth, as if she realized her slip. For the first

time, she had spoken about her daughter in the past tense. Beside
her, Rachel took her hand.

Jeffrey continued, "Was there anyone hanging around the farm
who seemed to pay more attention to her than he should have? A
stranger perhaps?"

Lev said, "We have many strangers here, Chief Tolliver. It's the
nature of our work to invite strangers into our homes. Isaiah be-
seeches us to 'bring the poor that are cast out to thy house.' It is our
duty to help them."

"Amen," the family intoned.

Jeffrey asked Esther, "Do you remember what she was wearing
the last time you saw her?"

"Yes, of course," Esther paused a moment, as if the memory might
break a dam of emotions she had been holding back. "We had sewn a
blue dress together. Abby loved to sew. We found the pattern in an
old trunk upstairs that I believe belonged to Ephraim's mother. We
made a few changes to update it. She was wearing it when we said
good-bye."

"This was here at the house?"

"Yes, early that morning. Becca had already gone to the farm."

Mary provided, "Becca was with me."

Jeffrey asked, "Anything else?"

Esther told him, "Abby's very calm. She never got flustered as a
child. She's such a special girl."

Lev spoke up, his voice deadly serious in a way that made his
words sound not like a compliment to his sister, but as a matter of
record. "Abby looks very much like her mother, Chief Tolliver. They
have the same coloring, same almond shape to their eyes. She's a
very attractive girl."

Lena repeated his words in her mind, wondering if he was intimat-
ing another man might want his niece or revealing something deeper
about himself. It was hard to tell with this guy. He seemed pretty
open and honest one minute, but then the next Lena wasn't even
sure if she would believe him if he told her the sky was blue. The
preacher obviously was the head of the church as well as the family,
and she got the distinct feeling that he was probably a lot smarter
than he let on.

Esther touched her own hair, recalling, "I tied a ribbon in her hair.

A blue ribbon. I remember it now. Ephraim had packed the car and we were ready to go, and I found the ribbon in my purse. I had been saving it because I thought I could use it as an embellishment on a dress or something, but it matched her dress so well, I told her to come over, and she bent down while I tied the ribbon in her hair . . ." Her voice trailed off, and Lena saw her throat work. "She has the softest hair . . ."

Rachel squeezed her sister's hand. Esther was staring out the window as if she wanted to be outside and away from this scene. Lena saw this as a coping mechanism that she was more than familiar with. It was so much easier to keep yourself removed from things rather than wearing your emotions out on your sleeve.

Paul said, "Rachel and I live on the farm with our families. Separate houses, of course, but we're within walking distance of the main house. When we couldn't locate Abby last night, we did a thorough search of the grounds. The workers fanned out. We checked the houses, the buildings, from top to bottom. When we couldn't find anything, we called the sheriff."

"I'm sorry it took him so long to get back to you," Jeffrey said. "They've been pretty busy over there."

"I don't imagine," Paul began, "many people in your business get concerned when a twenty-one-year-old girl goes missing."

"Why is that?"

"Girls run off all the time, don't they?" he said. "We're not completely blind to the outside world here."

"I'm not following you."

"I'm the black sheep of the family," Paul said, and from his siblings' reaction, Lena could tell it was an old family joke. "I'm a lawyer. I handle the farm's legal business. Most of my time is spent in Savannah. I spend every other week in the city."

"Were you here last week?" Jeffrey asked.

"I came back last night when I heard about Abby," he said, and the room fell silent.

"We've heard rumors," Rachel said, cutting to the chase. "Horrible rumors."

Ephraim put his hand to his chest. The old man's fingers were trembling. "It's her, isn't it?"

"I think so, sir." Jeffrey reached into his pocket and took out a

Polaroid. Ephraim's hands were shaking too much to take it, so Lev stepped in. Lena watched both men look at the picture. Where Ephraim was composed and quiet, Lev gasped audibly, then closed his eyes, though no tears spilled out. Lena watched his lips move in a silent prayer. Ephraim could only stare at the photograph, his palsy becoming so bad that the chair seemed to vibrate.

Behind him, Paul was looking at the picture, his face impassive. She watched him for signs of guilt, then any sign at all. But for his Adam's apple bobbing when he swallowed, he stood as still as a rock.

Esther cleared her throat. "May I?" she said, asking for the picture. She seemed perfectly composed, but her fear and underlying anguish were obvious.

"Oh, Mother," Ephraim began, his voice cracking from grief. "You may look if you like, but please, trust me, you don't want to see her like this. You don't want this in your memory."

Esther demurred to her husband's wishes, but Rachel reached out for the photograph. Lena watched the older woman's lips press into a rigid line. "Dear Jesus," she whispered. "Why?"

Whether she meant to or not, Esther looked over her sister's shoulder, seeing the picture of her dead child. Her shoulders started shaking, a small tremble that erupted into spasms of grief as she buried her head in her hands, sobbing, "No!"

Mary had been sitting quietly in the chair, but she stood abruptly, her hand to her chest, then ran from the room. Seconds later, they heard the kitchen door slam.

Lev had remained silent as he watched his sister go, and though Lena couldn't read his expression, she got the feeling he was angered by Mary's melodramatic exit.

He cleared his throat before asking, "Chief Tolliver, could you tell us what happened?"

Jeffrey hesitated, and Lena wondered how much he would tell them. "We found her in the woods," he said. "She was buried in the ground."

"Oh, Lord," Esther breathed, doubling over as if in pain. Rachel rubbed her sister's back, her lips trembling, tears streaming down her face.

Jeffrey didn't offer specifics as he continued, "She ran out of air."

"My baby," Esther moaned. "My poor Abigail."

The kids from the pigpen came in, the screen door slamming closed behind them. The adults all jumped as if a gun had been fired.

Ephraim spoke first, obviously struggling to regain his composure. "Zeke, what have you been told about the door?"

Zeke leaned against Lev's leg. He was a spindly kid, not yet showing signs of his father's height. His arms were as thin as toothpicks. "Sorry, Uncle Eph."

"Sorry, Papa," Becca said, though she hadn't been the one to slam the door. She too was stick-thin, and though Lena wasn't good with ages, she wouldn't have put the girl at fourteen. She obviously hadn't hit puberty yet.

Zeke was staring at his aunt, his lips trembling. He obviously sensed something was wrong. Tears sprang into his eyes.

"Come here, child," Rachel said, dragging Zeke into her lap. She put her hand on his leg, petting him, soothing him. She was trying to control her grief, but losing the battle.

Rebecca kept to the door, asking, "What's wrong?"

Lev put his hand on Rebecca's shoulder. "Your sister has passed on to be with the Lord."

The teenager's eyes widened. Her mouth opened and she put her hand to her stomach. She tried to ask a question, but no words came out.

Lev said, "Let's pray together."

Rebecca breathed, "What?" as if the air had been knocked out of her.

No one answered her question. All of them but Rebecca bowed their heads, yet instead of the booming sermon from Lev that Lena expected, they were silent.

Rebecca stood there, hand to her stomach, eyes wide open, while the rest of her family prayed.

Lena shot Jeffrey a questioning look, wondering what they should do now. She felt nervous, out of place. Hank had stopped dragging Lena and Sibyl to church after Lena had torn up another girl's Bible. She wasn't used to being around religious people unless they were down at the police station.

Jeffrey just shrugged, taking a sip of lemonade. His shoulders went up, and she watched him work his jaw to get the sour out.

"I'm sorry," Lev told them. "What can we do?"

Jeffrey spoke as if he was reading from a list. "I want employment records on everyone at the farm. I'd like to talk to anyone who had contact with Abigail at any time over the last year. I want to search her room to see if we can come up with something. I'd like to take the computer you mentioned and see if she's been contacted by anyone through the Internet."

Ephraim said, "She was never alone with the computer."

"Still, Mr. Bennett, we need to check everything."

Lev said, "They're being thorough, Ephraim. Ultimately, it's your decision, but I think we should do everything we can to help, if only to eliminate possibilities."

Jeffrey seized on this. "Would you mind taking a lie detector test?"

Paul almost laughed. "I don't think so."

"Don't speak for me, please," Lev challenged his brother. He told Jeffrey, "We will do everything we can to help you."

Paul countered, "I don't think —"

Esther straightened her shoulders, her face was swollen with grief, her eyes rimmed red. "Please don't argue," she asked her brothers.

"We're not arguing," Paul said, but he sounded like he was spoiling for a fight. Over the years, Lena had seen how grief exposed people's real personalities. She felt the tension between Paul and his older brother and wondered if it was general sibling rivalry or something deeper. Esther's tone implied the pair had argued before.

Lev raised his voice, but he was talking to the children. "Rebecca, why don't you take Zeke into the backyard? Your aunt Mary's there and I'm sure she needs you."

"Hold on," Jeffrey said. "I've got a couple of questions for her."

Paul put his hand on his niece's shoulder and kept it there. "Go ahead," he answered, his tone and posture indicating Jeffrey was on a short leash.

Jeffrey asked, "Rebecca, did you know if your sister was seeing anyone?"

The girl looked up at her uncle, as if asking permission. Her eyes finally settled back on Jeffrey. "You mean a boy?"

"Yes," he answered, and Lena could tell that he saw this as a fruitless exercise. There was no way the girl would be forthcoming in front of her family, especially considering she was a bit rebellious herself. The only way to get the truth out of her was to get her alone, and Lena doubted very seriously that Paul—or any of the men— would allow that.

Again, Rebecca looked at her uncle before answering. "Abby wasn't allowed to date boys."

If Jeffrey noticed that she didn't answer the question, he didn't let on. "Did you think it was strange when she didn't join you at the farm when your parents were away?"

Lena was watching Paul's hand on the girl's shoulder, trying to see if he was exerting pressure. She couldn't tell.

"Rebecca?" Jeffrey prompted.

The girl's chin lifted a little, and she said, "I thought she'd changed her mind." She added, "Is she really . . . ?"

Jeffrey nodded. "I'm afraid she is," he told her. "That's why we need all your help to find out who did this to her."

Tears flooded into her eyes, and Lev's composure seemed to drop a little at his niece's distress. He told Jeffrey, "If you don't mind . . ."

Jeffrey nodded, and Lev told the girl, "Go on and take Zeke out to your aunt Mary, honey. Everything's going to be okay."

Paul waited until they were gone before getting back to business, telling Jeffrey, "I have to remind you that the employment records are spotty. We offer food and shelter in return for an honest day's work."

Lena blurted out, "You don't pay anyone?"

"Of course we do," Paul snapped. He must've been asked this before. "Some take the money, some donate it back to the church. There are several workers who have been here for ten, twenty years and never seen any money in their pocket. What they get in return is a safe place to live, a family and the knowledge that their lives are not wasted." To put a finer point on it, he indicated the room he was standing in, much as his sister had done before in the kitchen. "We all live very modest lives, Detective. Our aim is to help others, not ourselves."

Jeffrey cleared his throat. "Still, we'd like to talk to all of them."

Paul offered, "You can take the computer now. I can arrange for the people who've been in contact with Abby to be brought to the station first thing tomorrow morning."

"The harvest," Lev reminded him, then explained, "We specialize in edamame, younger soy beans. The peak time for picking is from sunrise to nine P.M., then the beans have to be processed and iced. It's a very labor-intensive process, and I'm afraid we don't use much machinery."

Jeffrey glanced out the window. "We can't go over there now?"

"As much as I want to get to the bottom of this," Paul began, "we've got a business to run."

Lev added, "We also have to respect our workers. I'm sure you can imagine that some of them are very nervous around the police. Some have been the victims of police violence, others have been recently incarcerated and are very fearful. We have women and children who have been battered in domestic situations without relief from local law enforcement—"

"Right," Jeffrey said, as if he had gotten this speech before.

"It *is* private property," Paul reminded him, looking and sounding every bit the lawyer.

Lev said, "We can shift people around, get them to cover for the ones who have come into contact with Abby. Would Wednesday morning work?"

"I guess it'll have to," Jeffrey said, his tone indicating his displeasure at the delay.

Esther had her hands clasped in her lap, and Lena felt something like anger coming off the mother. She obviously disagreed with her brothers, just as she obviously would not contradict them. She offered, "I'll show you to her room."

"Thank you," Lena said, and they all stood at the same time. Thankfully, only Jeffrey followed them down the hall.

Esther stopped in front of the last door on the right, pressing her palm into the wood as if she couldn't trust her legs to hold her up.

Lena said, "I know this is hard for you. We'll do everything we can to find out who did this."

"She was a very private person."

"Do you think she kept secrets from you?"

"All daughters keep secrets from their mothers." Esther opened the door and looked into the room, sadness slackening her face as she saw her daughter's things. Lena had done the same thing with

Sibyl's possessions, every item conjuring some memory from the past, some happier time when Sibyl was alive.

Jeffrey asked, "Mrs. Bennett?" She was blocking their entrance.

"Please," she told him, grabbing the sleeve of his jacket. "Find out why this happened. There has to be a reason."

"I'll do everything I can to—"

"It's not enough," she insisted. "Please. I have to know why she's gone. I need to know that for myself, for my peace of mind."

Lena saw Jeffrey's throat work. "I don't want to make empty promises, Mrs. Bennett. I can only promise you that I'll try." He took out one of his cards, glancing over his shoulder to make sure no one saw him. "My home number's on the back. Call me any time."

Esther hesitated before taking the card, then tucked it into the sleeve of her dress. She gave Jeffrey a single nod, as if they had come to an understanding, then backed away, letting them enter her daughter's room. "I'll leave you to it."

Jeffrey and Lena exchanged another glance as Esther returned to her family. Lena could tell he was feeling just as apprehensive as she was. Esther's plea was understandable, but it only served to add more pressure to what was going to be an incredibly difficult case.

Lena had walked into the room to start the search, but Jeffrey stayed outside the doorway, looking toward the kitchen. He looked back to the family room as if to make sure he wasn't being observed, then walked down the hall. Lena was about to follow him when he appeared in the doorway with Rebecca Bennett.

Deftly, Jeffrey led the girl into her sister's bedroom, his hand at her elbow like a concerned uncle. In a low voice, he told her, "It's very important you talk to us about Abby."

Rebecca glanced nervously toward the door.

"You want me to shut it?" Lena offered, putting her hand on the knob.

After a moment's deliberation, Rebecca shook her head. Lena studied her, thinking she was as pretty as her sister was plain. She had taken her dark brown hair out of the braid and there were kinks of waves in the thick strands that cascaded down her shoulders. Esther had said the girl was fourteen, but there was still something womanly about her that probably drew a lot of attention around the farm. Lena found herself wondering how it was Abby instead of Rebecca who had been abducted and buried in the box.

Jeffrey said, "Was Abby seeing anyone?"

Rebecca bit her bottom lip. Jeffrey was good at giving people time, but Lena could tell he was getting antsy about the girl's family coming into the room.

Lena said, "I have an older sister, too," leaving out the fact that she was dead. "I know you don't want to tell on her, but Abby's gone now. You won't get her into trouble by telling us the truth."

The girl kept chewing her lip. "I don't know," she mumbled, tears welling into her eyes. She looked to Jeffrey, and Lena guessed the girl saw him as more of an authority figure than a woman.

Jeffrey picked up on this, urging, "Talk to me, Rebecca."

With great effort, she admitted, "She was gone sometimes during the day."

"Alone?"

She nodded. "She'd say she was going into town, but she'd take too long."

"Like, how long?"

"I don't know."

"It takes around fifteen minutes to get downtown from here," Jeffrey calculated for her. "Say she was going to a store, that'd take another fifteen or twenty minutes, right?" The girl nodded. "So, she should've been gone an hour at most, right?"

Again, the girl nodded. "Only, it was more like two."

"Did anyone ask her about this?"

She shook her head. "I just noticed."

"I bet you notice a lot of things," Jeffrey guessed. "You probably pay more attention to what's going on than the adults do."

Rebecca shrugged, but the compliment had worked. "She was just acting funny."

"How?"

"She was sick in the morning, but she told me not to tell Mama."

The pregnancy, Lena thought.

Jeffrey asked, "Did she tell you why she was sick?"

"She said it was something she ate, but she wasn't eating much."

"Why do you think she didn't want to tell your mother?"

"Mama would worry," Rebecca said. She shrugged. "Abby didn't like people to worry about her."

"Were you worried?"

Lena saw her swallow. "She cried at night sometimes." She tilted her head to the side. "My room's next door. I could hear her."

"Was she crying about something specific?" Jeffrey asked, and Lena could hear him straining to be gentle with the girl. "Maybe someone hurt her feelings?"

"The Bible teaches us to forgive," the girl answered. From anyone else, Lena might have thought she was being dramatic, but the girl seemed to be relaying what she thought of as wise advice rather than a sermon. "If we cannot forgive others, then the Lord cannot forgive us."

"Was there anyone she needed to forgive?"

"If there was," Rebecca began, "then she would pray for help."

"Why do you think she was crying?"

Rebecca looked at the room, taking in her sister's things with a palpable sadness. She was probably thinking about Abby, what the room had felt like when the older girl had been alive. Lena wondered what kind of relationship the sisters had shared. Even though they were twins, Lena and Sibyl had been involved in their share of battles over everything from who got to sit in the front seat of the car to who answered the telephone. Somehow, she couldn't see Abby being that way.

Rebecca finally answered, "I don't know why she was sad. She wouldn't tell me."

Jeffrey asked, "Are you sure, Rebecca?" He gave her a supportive smile. "You can tell us. We won't get mad or judge her. We just want to know the truth so that we can find the person who hurt Abby and punish him."

She nodded, her eyes tearing up again. "I know you want to help."

"We can't help Abby unless you help us," Jeffrey countered. "Anything at all, Rebecca, no matter how silly it seems now. You let us decide whether it's useful or not."

She looked from Lena to Jeffrey, then back again. Lena couldn't tell if the girl was hiding something or if she was just scared of speaking to strangers without her parents' permission. Either way, they needed to get her to answer their questions before someone started to wonder where she was.

Lena tried to keep her voice light. "You want to talk to me alone, honey? We can talk just you and me if you want."

Again, Becca seemed to be thinking about it. At least half a minute passed before she said, "I —" just as the back door slammed shut. The girl jumped as if a bullet had been fired.

From the front room, a man's voice called, "Becca, is that you?"

Zeke plodded up the hallway, and when Rebecca saw her cousin she went to him and grabbed his hand, calling, "It's me, Papa," as she led the boy toward her family.

Lena bit back the curse that came to her lips.

Jeffrey asked, "You think she knows something?"

"Hell if I know."

Jeffrey seemed to agree, and she could feel her frustration echoed in his tone when he told her, "Let's get this over with."

She went to the large chest of drawers by the door. Jeffrey went to the desk opposite. The room was small, probably about ten feet by ten. There was a twin bed pushed up against the windows that faced the barn. There were no posters on the white walls or any signs that this had been a young woman's room. The bed was neatly made, a multi-colored quilt tucked in with sharp precision. A stuffed Snoopy that was probably older than Abby was propped against the pillows, its neck sloped to the side from years of wear.

Neatly folded socks were in one of the top drawers. Lena opened the other, seeing similarly folded underwear. That the girl had taken the time to fold her underwear was something that stuck with Lena. She's obviously been meticulous, concerned with keeping things in order. The lower drawers revealed a precision bordering on obsession.

Everyone had a favorite place to hide things, just like every cop had a favorite place to look. Jeffrey was checking under the bed, between the mattress and boxspring. Lena went to the closet, kneeling to check the shoes. There were three pairs, all of them worn but well-taken care of. The sneakers had been polished white, the Mary Jane's mended at the heel. The third pair was pristine, probably her Sunday shoes.

Lena rapped her knuckles against the boards of the closet floor, checking for a secret compartment. Nothing sounded suspicious and all the boards were nailed firmly in place. Next, she went through the dresses lined up on the closet rod. Lena didn't have a ruler, but she would have sworn each dress was equidistant, no one touching the other. There was a long winter jacket, obviously store bought. The pockets were empty, the hem intact. Nothing was hidden in a torn seam or concealed in a secret pouch.

Lev was at the door, a laptop computer in his hands. "Anything?" he asked.

Lena had startled, but she tried not to show it. Jeffrey straightened, with his hands in his pockets. "Nothing useful," he replied.

Lev handed the computer to Jeffrey, the power cord trailing behind it. She wondered if he had looked at it himself while they were searching the room. She had no doubt Paul would have.

Lev told him, "You can keep this as long as you like. I'd be surprised if you found anything on it."

"Like you said," Jeffrey responded, wrapping the cord around the computer, "We need to eliminate every possibility." He nodded to Lena, and she followed him out of the room. Walking down the hallway, she could hear the family talking, but by the time they reached the living room, everyone was silent.

Jeffrey told Esther, "I'm sorry for your loss."

She looked straight at Jeffrey, her pale green eyes piercing even to Lena. She didn't say a word, but her plea was evident.

Lev opened the front door. "Thank you both," he said. "I'll be there Wednesday morning at nine."

Paul seemed about to say something, but stopped at the last minute. Lena could almost see what was going through his little lawyer brain. It was probably killing him that Lev had volunteered for the polygraph. She imagined Paul would have an earful for his brother when the cops were gone.

Jeffrey told Lev, "We'll have to call in someone to perform the test."

"Of course," Lev agreed. "But I feel the need to reiterate that I can volunteer only myself. Likewise, the people you see tomorrow will be there on a voluntary basis. I don't want to tell you how to do your job, Chief Tolliver, but it's going to be difficult enough getting them there. If you try to force them into taking a lie detector test, they're likely to leave."

"Thank you for the advice," Jeffrey said, his tone disingenuous. "Would you mind sending your foreman as well?"

Paul seemed surprised by the request. "Cole?"

"He's probably had contact with everyone on the farm," Lev said. "That's a good idea."

"While we're on it," Paul said, glancing Jeffrey's way. "The farm is private property. We don't generally have the police there unless it's official business."

"You don't consider this official business?"

"Family business," he said, then held out his hand. "Thank you for all your help."

"Could you tell me," Jeffrey began, "did Abby drive?"

Paul dropped his hand, "Of course. She was certainly old enough."

"Did she have a car?"

"She borrowed Mary's," he answered. "My sister stopped driving some time ago. Abby was using her car to deliver meals, run chores in town."

"She did these things alone?"

"Generally," Paul allowed, wary the way any lawyer is when he gives out information without getting something in return.

Lev added, "Abby loved helping people."

Paul put his hand on his brother's shoulder.

Lev said, "Thank you both."

Lena and Jeffrey stood at the base of the steps, watching Lev walk into the house. He shut the door firmly behind him.

Lena let out a breath, turning back to the car. Jeffrey followed, keeping his thoughts to himself as they got in.

He didn't speak until they were on the main road, passing Holy Grown again. Lena saw the place in a new light, and wondered what they were really up to over there.

Jeffrey said, "Odd family."

"I'll say."

"It won't do us any good to be blinded by our prejudices," he said, giving her a sharp look.

"I think I have a right to my opinion."

"You do," he said, and she could feel his gaze settle onto the scars on the back of her hands. "But how will you feel in a year's time if this case isn't solved because all we could focus on was their religion?"

"What if the fact that they're Bible-thumpers is what breaks this open?"

"People kill for different reasons," he reminded her. "Money, love, lust, vengeance. That's what we need to focus on. Who has a motive? Who has the means?"

He had a point, but Lena knew first-hand that sometimes people did things just because they were fucking nuts. No matter what Jeffrey said, it was too coincidental that this girl had ended up buried in a box out in the middle of the woods and her family was a bunch of backwoods Bible-thumpers.

She asked, "You don't think this is ritualistic?"

"I think the mother's grief was real."

"Yeah," she agreed. "I got that, too." She felt the need to point out, "That doesn't mean the rest of the family isn't into it. They're running a fucking cult out here."

"All religions are cults," he said, and though Lena hated religion herself, she had to disagree.

"I wouldn't call the Baptist church downtown a cult."

"They're like-minded people sharing the same values and religious beliefs. That's a cult."

"Well," she said, still not agreeing but not knowing how to challenge him on it. She doubted the Pope in Rome would say he was running a cult. There was mainstream religion and then there were the freaks who handled snakes and thought electricity provided a conduit straight to the Devil.

"It keeps coming back to the cyanide," he told her. "Where did it come from?"

"Esther said they don't use pesticides."

"There's no way we'll get a warrant to test that out. Even if Ed Pelham cooperated on the Catoogah side, we don't have cause."

"I wish we'd looked around more when we were over there."

"That Cole person needs a harder look."

"You think he'll come Wednesday morning?"

"No telling," he said, then asked, "What are you doing tonight?"

"Why?"

"Wanna go to the Pink Kitty?"

"The titty bar on Highway Sixteen?"

"The strip joint," he corrected, as if she had offended him. Driving with one hand, he rooted around in his pocket and pulled out a book of matches. He tossed them to her and she recognized the Pink Kitty's logo on the front. They had a huge neon sign outside the bar that could be seen for miles.

"Tell me," he said, turning onto the highway, "why a naïve twenty-one year old would take a book of matches from a strip club and shove it up the ass of her favorite stuffed animal."

That was why he had been so interested in the stuffed Snoopy on Abby's bed. She had hidden the matchbook inside. "Good question," she told him, opening the cover. None of the matches had been used.

"I'll pick you up at ten thirty."

CHAPTER SIX

When Tessa opened the front door, Sara was lying on the couch with a wet rag over her face.

"Sissy?" Tessa called. "You home?"

"In here," Sara managed around the cloth.

"Oh, Christ," Tessa said. Sara felt her hovering near the end of the couch. "What did Jeffrey do now?"

"Why are you blaming Jeffrey?"

Tessa turned off the CD player mid-harmony. "You only listen to Dolly Parton when you're upset with him."

Sara slid the rag up to her forehead so she could see her sister. Tessa was reading the back of the CD case. "It's a cover album."

"I guess you skipped the sixth track?" Tessa asked, dropping it into the pile Sara had made as she rummaged for something to listen to. "God, you look horrible."

"I feel horrible," she admitted. Watching the autopsy of Abigail Bennett had been one of the most difficult things Sara had done in recent memory. The girl had not passed gently. Her systems had shut down one by one, until all that remained was her brain. Abby had known what was happening, had felt every single second of the death, right up until the painful end.

Sara had been so upset that she had actually used the cell phone to call Jeffrey. Instead of pouring out her heart to him, she had been drilled for details on the autopsy. Jeffrey had been in such a rush to get off the phone that he hadn't even told her good-bye.

"That's better," Tessa said as Steely Dan whispered through the speakers.

Sara looked out the windows, surprised that the sun had already gone down. "What time is it?"

"Almost seven," Tessa told her, adjusting the volume on the player. "Mama sent y'all something."

Sara sighed as she sat up, letting the rag drop. She saw a brown paper bag at Tessa's feet. "What?"

"Beef roast and chocolate cake."

Sara felt her stomach rumble, hungry for the first time that day. As if on cue, the dogs sauntered in. Sara had rescued the greyhounds several years ago and in return for the favor, they tried to eat her out of house and home.

"Get," Tessa warned Bob, the taller of the two, as he sniffed the bag. Billy went in for his turn, but she shooed him away as she asked Sara, "Do you ever feed them?"

"Sometimes."

Tessa picked up the bag and put it on the kitchen counter beside the bottle of wine Sara had opened as soon as she got home. Sara hadn't even bothered to change her clothes, just poured the wine, drank a healthy swig and wet a washrag before collapsing onto the couch.

"Did Dad drop you off?" Sara asked, wondering why she had not heard a car. Tessa wasn't supposed to drive while she was taking her anti-seizure medication, a rule that seemed destined to be broken.

"I brought my bike," she answered, staring at the bottle of wine as Sara poured herself another glass. "I would kill for some of that."

Sara opened her mouth then closed it. Tessa wasn't supposed to drink alcohol with her medication, but she was an adult, and Sara was not her mother.

"I know," Tessa said, reading Sara's expression. "I can still want things, can't I?" She opened the bag, taking out a stack of mail. "I got this for you," she said. "Do you ever check your mail? There's about a gazillion catalogues in there."

There was something brown on one of the envelopes, and Sara sniffed it suspiciously. She was relieved to find it was gravy.

"Sorry," Tessa apologized, taking out a paper plate covered in tinfoil, sliding it over to Sara. "I guess it leaked."

"Oh, yes." Sara practically moaned as she removed the foil. Cathy Linton made a mean chocolate cake, the recipe going back through three generations of Earnshaws. "This is too much," Sara said, noting the slice was big enough for two.

"Here," Tessa said, taking two more Tupperware containers out of the bag. "You're supposed to share with Jeffrey."

"Right." Sara grabbed a fork from the drawer before sitting on the bar stool under the kitchen island

"You're not going to eat the roast?" Tessa asked.

Sara put a forkful of cake in her mouth and washed it down with some wine. "Mama always said when I could pay to put a roof over my own head I could eat what I wanted for supper."

"I wish I could pay for my own roof," Tessa mumbled, using her finger to scoop some chocolate off of Sara's plate. "I'm so sick of not doing anything."

"You're still working."

"As Dad's tool bitch."

Sara ate another bite of cake. "Depression is a side effect of your medication."

"Let me add that to the list."

"Are you having other problems?"

Tessa shrugged, wiping crumbs off the counter. "I miss Devon," she said, referring to her ex, the father of her dead child. "I miss having a man around."

Sara picked at the cake, wishing not for the first time that she had killed Devon Lockwood when she'd had the chance.

"So," Tessa said, abruptly changing the subject. "Tell me what Jeffrey did this time."

Sara groaned, returning to the cake.

"Tell me."

After letting a few seconds pass, Sara relented. "He might have hepatitis."

"Which kind?"

"Good question."

Tessa furrowed her brows. "Is he showing any symptoms?"

"Other than aggravated stupidity and acute denial?" Sara asked. "No."

"How was he exposed?"

"How do you think?"

"Ah." Tessa pulled out the stool next to Sara and sat. "This was a long time ago, though, right?"

"Does it matter?" She corrected herself, "I mean, yes, it matters. It's from before. That *one time* before."

Tessa pursed her lips. She had not made it a secret that she didn't think there was any way in hell Jeffrey had slept with Jolene just once. Sara thought she was going to renew her theory, but instead Tessa asked, "What are y'all doing about it?"

"Arguing," Sara admitted. "I just can't stop thinking about her. What he did with her." She took another bite of cake, chewing slowly, making herself swallow. "He didn't just . . ." Sara tried to think of a word that summed up her disgust. "He didn't just *screw* her. He wooed her. Called her on the phone. Laughed with her. Maybe sent her flowers." She stared at the chocolate running off the side of the plate. Had he spread chocolate on her thighs and licked it off? How many intimate moments had they shared leading up to that final day? How many came after?

Everything Jeffrey had done to make Sara feel special, to make her think he was the man she wanted to share the rest of her life with, had been a technique easily employed on another woman. Hell, probably more than just one other woman. Jeffrey had a sexual history that would give Hugh Hefner pause. How could the man who could be so kind also be the same bastard who had made her feel like a dog kicked to the curb? Was this some new routine Jeffrey had come up with to win her back? As soon as she was settled, was he going to use it on someone else?

The problem was, Sara knew perfectly well how Jo had managed to snatch him away. It had to have been a game for Jeffrey, a challenge. Jolene was much more experienced at this kind of thing than Sara. She had probably known to play hard to get, balancing just the right amount of flirting and teasing to get him on the line, then reeling him in slowly like a prize fish. Certainly, she had not ended up at the end of their first date with the balls of her feet braced against the edge of the kitchen sink as she writhed in ecstasy on the floor, biting her tongue so that she would not scream his name.

Tessa asked, "Why are you smiling at the sink?"

Sara shook her head, taking a drink of wine. "I just hate this. I hate all of this. And Jimmy Powell is sick again."

"That kid with leukemia?"

Sara nodded. "It doesn't look good. I've got to go see him at the hospital tomorrow."

"How was Macon?"

Unbidden, Sara's mind flashed onto the image of the girl on the table, her body flayed open, the doctor reaching into the womb to extract the fetus. Another child lost. Another family devastated. Sara did not know how many more times she could witness this sort of thing without cracking.

"Sara?" Tessa asked.

"It was as awful as I thought it would be." Sara used her finger to swirl what remained of the chocolate sauce. Somewhere in all of this, she had eaten the entire piece of cake.

Tessa walked to the refrigerator and took out a tub of ice cream, returning to the original subject. "You have to let this go, Sara. Jeffrey did what he did, and nothing's going to change that. Either he's back in your life or he's not, but you can't keep yo-yoing him back and forth." She pried off the top to the ice cream. "You want some?"

"I shouldn't," Sara told her, holding out her plate.

"I've always been the cheater, not the cheatee," Tessa pointed out, taking two spoons from the drawer, closing it with her hip. "Devon just left. He didn't cheat. At least I don't think he cheated." She dropped several spoonfuls of Blue Bell onto Sara's plate. "Maybe he cheated."

Sara held her other hand under the paper plate so that it wouldn't fold from the weight. "I don't think so."

"No," she agreed. "He barely had time for me, let alone another woman. Did I tell you about the time he fell asleep right in the middle of it?" Sara nodded. "Jesus, how do people stay interested in each other for fifty years?"

Sara shrugged. She was hardly an expert.

"God, but he was good in bed when he was awake." Tessa sighed, holding the spoon in her mouth. "That's one thing you have to keep in mind with Jeffrey. Never underestimate the value of sexual chemistry." She scooped more ice cream onto Sara's plate. "Devon was bored with me."

"Don't be silly."

"I mean it," she said. "He was bored. He didn't want to do things anymore."

"Like go out?"

"Like, the only way I could get him to go down on me was put a television on my stomach and wire the remote control to my—"

"Tess!"

She chuckled, taking a big bite of ice cream. Sara could remember the last time they'd eaten ice cream together. The day that Tessa had been attacked, they had gone to the Dairy Queen for milkshakes. Two hours later, Tessa was lying on the ground with her head split open, her child dead inside of her.

Tessa braced her hands on the counter and squeezed her eyes shut. Sara bolted from her chair, alarmed, until Tessa explained, "Ice cream headache."

"I'll get you some water."

"I got it." She put her head under the kitchen faucet and took a swig. She wiped her mouth, asking, "Yeesh, why does that happen?"

"The trigeminal nerve in the—"

Tessa cut her off with a look. "You don't have to answer every question, Sara."

Sara took this as a rebuke, and looked down at her plate.

Tessa took a less generous bite of ice cream before going back to the subject of Devon. "I just miss him."

"I know, sweetie."

There was nothing more to say on the matter. In Sara's opinion, Devon had shown his true colors at the end, slinking out when things got tough. Her sister was well rid of him, though Sara understood that was hard for Tessa to grasp at this point. For Sara's part, the one time she had seen Devon downtown, she had crossed the street so that she would not have to pass him on the sidewalk. Jeffrey had been with her, and she had practically ripped his arm off in order to keep him from going over and saying something to the other man.

Out of the blue, Tessa said, "I'm not going to have sex anymore."

Sara barked out a laugh.

"I'm serious."

"Why?"

"Do you have any Cheetos?"

Sara went to the cabinet to fetch the bag. She tried to tread cautiously when she asked, "Is it this new church?"

"No." Tessa took the bag. "Maybe." She used her teeth to open the package. "It's just that what I've been doing so far isn't working. I'd be pretty stupid to keep on doing it."

"What isn't working?"

Tessa just shook her head. "Everything." She offered the bag of Cheetos to Sara, but she refused, instead tugging open the zipper of her skirt so she could breathe.

Tessa asked, "Has anyone told you why Bella is here?"

"I was hoping you'd know."

"They won't tell me anything. Every time I walk into the room, they stop talking. I'm like a walking mute button."

"Me, too," Sara realized.

"Will you do me a favor?" Tessa asked.

"Of course," Sara offered, noting the change in Tessa's tone.

"Come to church with me Wednesday night."

Sara felt like a fish that had just been thrown from its tank, her mouth gaping open as she tried to think of an excuse.

"It's not even church," Tessa said. "It's more like a fellowship meeting. Just people hanging around, talking. They've even got honey buns."

"Tess . . ."

"I know you don't want to go, but I want you there." Tessa shrugged. "Do it for me."

This had been Cathy's device for guilting her two daughters into attending Easter and Christmas services for the last twenty years.

"Tessie," Sara began. "You know I don't believe—"

"I'm not sure I do, either," Tessa interrupted. "But it feels good to be there."

Sara stood to put the roast in the refrigerator.

"I met Thomas in physical therapy a few months ago."

"Who's Thomas?"

"He's kind of the leader of the church," Tessa answered. "He had a stroke a while back. It was pretty bad. He's really hard to understand, but there's this way he has of talking to you without saying a word."

The dishwasher had clean dishes from several days ago, and Sara started to empty it just to give herself something to do.

"It was weird," Tessa continued. "I was doing my stupid motor exercises, putting the pegs in the right holes, when I felt like someone was staring at me, and I looked up and it was this old guy in a wheelchair. He called me Cathy."

"Cathy?" Sara repeated.

"Yeah, he knows Mama."

"How does he know Mama?" Sara asked, certain that she knew all her mother's friends.

"I don't know."

"Did you ask her?"

"I tried to, but she was busy."

Sara closed the dishwasher and leaned against the counter. "What happened then?"

"He asked if I wanted to come to church." Tessa paused a beat. "Being up there in physical therapy, seeing all these people who are so much worse off than I am . . ." she shrugged. "It really put things into perspective, you know? Like how much I've been wasting my life."

"You haven't been wasting your life."

"I'm thirty-four years old and I still live with my parents."

"Over the garage."

Tessa sighed. "I just think what happened to me shouldn't go to waste."

"It shouldn't have happened at all."

"I was lying in that hospital bed feeling so sorry for myself, so pissed at the world for what happened. And then it hit me. I've been selfish all my life."

"You have not."

"Yes, I have. Even you said that."

Sara had never regretted her words so much in her life. "I was angry with you, Tess."

"You know what? It's like when people are drunk and they say they didn't mean to say something and you should just excuse them and forget it because they'd been drinking." She explained, "Alcohol lowers your inhibitions. It doesn't make you pull lies out of your ass. You got angry with me and said what you were thinking in your head."

"I didn't," Sara tried to assure her, but even to her own ears, the defense fell flat.

"I almost died, and for what? What have I done with my life?" Her hands were clenched in fists. Again, she shifted her focus. "If you died, what's the one thing you would regret not doing?"

Instantly, Sara thought but did not say, "Having a child."

Tessa read her expression. "You could always adopt."

Sara shrugged. She could not answer.

"We never talk about this. It happened almost fifteen years ago and we never talk about it."

"There's a reason."

"Which is?"

Sara refused to get into it. "What's the point, Tessie? Nothing's going to change. There's no miraculous cure."

"You're so good with kids, Sara. You'd be such a good mother."

Sara said the two words that she hated to say more than any others. "I can't." Then, "Tessie, please."

Tessa nodded, though Sara could tell that this was just a temporary retreat. "Well, what I would regret is not leaving my mark. Not doing something to make the world better."

Sara took a tissue to blow her nose. "You do that anyway."

"There's a reason for everything," Tessa insisted. "I know you don't believe that. I know you can't trust anything that doesn't have some scientific theory behind it or a library full of books written about it, but this is what I need in my life. I have to think that things happen for a reason. I have to think that something good will come out of losing . . ." She stopped there, unable to say the name of the child she had lost. There was a tiny marker out at the cemetery with the girl's name, tucked between Cathy's parents and a much-loved uncle who had died in Korea. It pained Sara's heart every time she thought about the cold grave and the lost possibilities.

"You know his son."

Sara furrowed her brow. "Whose son?"

"Tom's. He went to school with you." Tessa took a mouthful of Cheetos before folding the bag closed. She talked while she chewed. "He's got red hair like you."

"He went to school with me?" Sara asked, skeptical. Redheads tended to notice each other, what with sticking out from the general population like a sore thumb. Sara knew for a fact that she had been the only child with red hair her entire tenure at Cady Stanton Elementary School. She had the scars to prove it. "What's his name?"

"Lev Ward."

"There wasn't a Lev Ward at Stanton."

"It was Sunday school," Tessa clarified. "He's got some funny stories about you."

"About me?" Sara repeated, her curiosity getting the better of her.

"And," Tessa added, as if this were more enticement, "he's got the most adorable five-year-old son you've ever seen."

She saw through the ruse. "I meet some pretty adorable five year olds at the clinic."

"Just think about going. You don't have to answer now." Tessa looked at her watch. "I need to get back before it gets dark."

"You want me to drive you?"

"No, thanks." Tessa kissed her cheek. "I'll see you later."

Sara wiped Cheeto dust off her sister's face. "Be careful."

Tessa started to leave, then stopped. "It's not just the sex."

"What?"

"With Jeffrey," she explained. "It's not just the sexual chemistry. When things get bad, y'all always get stronger. You always have." She reached down to scratch Billy, then Bob, behind the ears. "Every time in your life that you've reached out for him, he's been there. A lot of men would just run the other way."

Tessa finished with the dogs and left, pulling the door gently closed behind her.

Sara put up the Cheetos, contemplating finishing the bag even though the open zipper on her skirt was cutting into her flesh. She wanted to call her mother and find out what was wrong. She wanted to call Jeffrey and yell at him, then call him back and tell him to come over and watch an old movie on television with her.

What she did instead was return to the couch with another glass of wine, trying to push everything from her mind. Of course, the more she tried not to think about things, the more they came to the surface. Soon, she was flashing through images of the girl in the woods to leukemia-stricken Jimmy Powell to Jeffrey in the hospital with end-stage liver failure.

Finally, she made herself focus back on the autopsy. She had stood behind a thick glass wall while the procedure was performed, but even that had seemed too close for Sara's comfort. The girl's physical results were unremarkable but for the cyanide salts found in her stomach. Sara shivered again as she thought about the plume of smoke rising from her gut as the state coroner cut into her stomach. The fetus had been unremarkable; a healthy child who would have eventually led a full life.

There was a knock at the front door, tentative at first, then more insistent when Sara didn't answer. Finally, she yelled, "Come in!"

"Sara?" Jeffrey asked. He looked around the room, obviously surprised to see her on the couch. "You okay?"

"Stomachache," she told him, and in fact her stomach was hurting. Maybe her mother had been right about not eating dessert for dinner.

"I'm sorry I couldn't talk earlier."

"It's okay," she told him, though it wasn't really. "What happened?"

"Nothing," he said, his disappointment evident. "I spent the whole fucking afternoon at the college, going from department to department looking for someone who could tell me what poisons they keep around there."

"No cyanide?"

"Everything but," he told her.

"What about the family?"

"They didn't offer much. I sent out a credit check on the farm. It should be back tomorrow. Frank's been calling all the shelters, trying to get the story on what exactly happens on these missions." He shrugged. "We spent the rest of the day going through the laptop computer. It was pretty clean."

"Did you check instant messages?"

"Brad cracked that first off. There were a couple back and forth with the aunt who lives on the farm, but mostly those were about Bible studies, work schedules, what time she was going to come over, who was going to fix chicken one night, who was going to peel carrots the next. It's hard to tell which were from Abby and which were from Rebecca."

"Was there anything during the ten days after the family left?"

"One file was opened the day they went to Atlanta," Jeffrey told her. "Around ten fifteen that morning. The parents would've been gone by then. It was a resume for Abigail Ruth Bennett."

"For a job?"

"Looks like it."

"You think she was trying to leave?"

"The parents wanted her to go to college, but she'd said no."

"Nice to have an option," Sara mumbled. Cathy had practically poked her girls with a stick. "What kind of job was she looking for?"

"No idea," he said. "She mostly listed office and accounting skills. She did a lot of stuff on the farm. I guess it'd look well-rounded to a potential employer."

"She was homeschooled?" Sara asked. She knew this wasn't true everywhere, but in her experience, people tended to homeschool for two reasons: to keep their white children away from minorities or to make sure their kids weren't taught anything other than creationism and abstinence.

"Most of the family are, apparently." Jeffrey loosened his tie. "I've got to change." Then, as if he felt the need for an explanation, he added, "All my jeans are over here."

"Change for what?"

"I'm going to talk to Dale Stanley, then Lena and I are going to the Pink Kitty."

"The titty bar on Sixteen?"

He scowled. "Why is it okay for women to call it that, but men get kicked in the nuts for it?"

"Because women don't have nuts." She sat up, feeling her stomach lurch. Thank God she hadn't eaten any Cheetos. "Why are you going? Or is this your way of punishing me?"

"Punishing you for what?" he asked as she followed him back to the bedroom.

"Just ignore me," she told him, not really sure why she had said that. "I've had a really, really bad day."

"Can I do anything?"

"No."

He opened a box, "We found a book of matches in the girl's room. They're from the Pink Kitty. Why would I punish you?"

Sara sat on the bed, watching him root through boxes to find his jeans. "She didn't strike me as the Pink Kitty type."

"The whole family isn't the type," he told her, finally finding the right box. He looked up at her as he unzipped his pants and kicked them off. "Are you still mad at me?"

"I wish I knew."

He pulled off his socks and threw them in the laundry basket. "I do, too."

Sara looked out the bedroom windows at the lake. She seldom closed the curtains because the view was one of the most beautiful in the city. She often lay in bed at night, watching the moon move across the sky as she drifted off to sleep. How many times last week had she looked out these same windows, not knowing that just across the water lay Abigail Bennett, alone, probably freezing cold, certainly terrified. Had Sara lain in bed, warm and content, while under cover of darkness, Abby's killer had poisoned her?

"Sara?" Jeffrey stood in his underwear, staring at her. "What's going on?"

She didn't want to answer. "Tell me more about Abigail's family."

He hesitated a second before returning to his clothes. "They're really weird."

"Weird how?"

He pulled out a pair of socks and sat on the bed to put them on. "Maybe it's just me. Maybe I've seen too many people using some sick religious justification for their sexual attraction to teenage girls."

"Did they seem shocked when you told them she was dead?"

"They'd heard rumors about what we found. I don't know how since that farm sounds hermetically sealed. One of the uncles gets out a bit. I can't put my finger on it, but there's something about him I don't trust."

"Maybe you've got a thing against uncles."

"Maybe." He rubbed his eyes with his hands. "The mother was pretty upset."

"I can't imagine what it's like to hear that kind of news."

"She really got to me."

"How so?"

"She begged me to find out who did this," he said. "She might not like it when I do."

"You really think her family is involved?"

"I don't know." He stood to finish dressing, all the while giving Sara a more detailed impression of the group. One uncle was overbearing and seemed to have a lot more power over the family than Jeffrey thought was normal. The husband was old enough to be his wife's grandfather. Sara sat with her back against the headboard, arms folded across her chest as she listened. The more he told her, the more warning bells she heard.

"The women are very . . . old-fashioned," he said. "They let the men do all the talking. They defer to the husbands and the brothers."

"That's typical of most conservative religions," Sara pointed out. "In theory, at least, the man is supposed to be in charge of the family." She waited for him to make a wistful comment, but when he didn't, she asked, "Did you get anything from the sister?"

"Rebecca," he supplied. "Nothing, and there's no way they'll let me talk to her again. I have a feeling the uncle would string me up by the short hairs if he knew I talked to her in Abby's room."

"Do you think you'd get anything from her anyway?"

"Who knows?" he asked. "I couldn't tell if she was hiding something or if she was just sad."

"It's a hard thing to go through," Sara said. "She's probably not thinking right now."

"Lena got from the mother that Rebecca has run away before."

"Why?"

"She didn't find out."

"Well, that could be something."

"It could be just that she's a teenage girl," he pointed out, as if Sara needed to be reminded that one out of every seven children ran away at least once before the age of eighteen. "She's pretty young for her age."

"I imagine it's hard to be worldly growing up in that environment." She added, "Not that there's anything wrong with trying to keep your kids away from the world in general." Without thinking, she said, "If it was my kid . . ." She caught herself. "I mean, some of the kids I see at the clinic . . . I can understand why their parents want to keep them as sheltered as they can."

He had stopped dressing, staring at her with his lips slightly parted as if he wanted to say something.

"So," she said, trying to clear the lump in her throat. "The family is pretty wrapped up in the church?"

"Yeah," he said, his pause letting her know he was aware of what she was doing. He continued, "I don't know about the girl, though. I got this sense from her even before Lena told me she'd run away. She seemed kind of rebellious. When I questioned her, she sort of defied her uncle."

"How?"

"He's a lawyer. He didn't want her to answer any questions. She did anyway." He was nodding to himself as if he admired her courage. "I don't guess that kind of independence fits into the family dynamic, especially considering it's coming from a girl."

"Younger children tend to be more assertive," Sara said. "Tessa was always getting into trouble. I don't know if that was because Daddy was harder on her or because she acted up more."

He couldn't hide his appreciative grin. He had always admired Tessa's free spirit. Men often did. "She's a little wild."

"And I'm not," Sara said, trying to keep the regret out of her voice. Tessa had always been the risk-taker while Sara's biggest childhood infractions were usually education-related: staying too late at the library so that she could study, sneaking a flashlight into her bed so that she could read past bedtime.

She asked, "Do you think you'll get anything out of the interviews Wednesday?"

"Doubtful. Maybe Dale Stanley will have something. They're certain it's cyanide salt?"

"Yes."

"I checked around. He's the only metal plater in the area. Something tells me this goes back to the farm. It's too coincidental to me that they've got a bunch of convicts running around on that place and this girl turns up dead. Plus," he looked up at her, "Dale Stanley's house is a brisk hike from the Catoogah line."

"Do you think Dale Stanley put her in the box?"

"I have no idea," Jeffrey told her. "At this point, I'm not trusting anybody."

"Do you think there's a religious connotation? Burying someone in the ground?"

"And poisoning them?" he asked. "That's where I get stuck. Lena's certain there's a religious connection, something to do with the family."

"She's got a good excuse to be against anything that smacks of religion."

"Lena's my best detective," he told her. "I know she's got . . . problems . . ." He seemed to understand this was a gross understatement, but continued anyway. "I don't want her running off in one direction just because it fits with her view of the world."

"She has a narrow way of looking at things."

"Everybody does," he told her, and though Sara agreed, she knew he thought he was an exception. "I'll give her this, that place is weird. There was this guy we ran into early on. He was out there by the barn toting a Bible and preaching the Word."

"Hare's father does the same thing at family reunions," Sara pointed out, though her uncle's two sisters tended to laugh in his face so hard when he began to proselytize that uncle Roderick seldom made it past the first sentence.

"It's still suspicious."

She said, "This is the South, Jeffrey. People hold on to religion down here."

"You're talking to the boy from central Alabama," he reminded her. "And it's not just the South. Go out to the Midwest or California or even upstate New York and you'll find pockets of religious communities. We just get more press for it because we've got better preachers."

Sara didn't argue with him. The farther you got from a major metropolitan city, the more religious people tended to be. Truth be told, it was one of the things she liked about small towns. While Sara wasn't religious herself, she liked the idea of church, the philosophy behind loving your fellow man and turning the other cheek. Unfortunately, she didn't seem to find that dictum being upheld much lately.

Jeffrey said, "So, let's say Lena's instincts are right and the whole family's in on it. They're this evil cult and they buried Abby for whatever reason."

"She was pregnant."

"So, they buried her because she was pregnant. Why poison her? It doesn't make sense."

Sara had to agree. "For that matter, why would they bury her in the first place? Surely they're pro-life?"

"It just doesn't hold up. There has to be some other reason."

"So," Sara said, "it's an outsider. Why would an outsider go to the trouble of burying her alive then killing her?"

"Maybe he comes back and removes the body after she's dead. Maybe we found her before he could finish doing whatever he does."

Sara hadn't considered that, and the thought now sent a cold chill through her.

"I sent samples of the wood to have it analyzed," he said. "If there's some DNA on it, we'll find it." He thought about it, then added, "Eventually."

Sara knew the test results would take weeks if not months to get back. The GBI crime lab was so behind it was a wonder any crimes in the state were ever solved. "Isn't there a way for you to just go out to the farm and start talking to people?"

"Not without cause. That's assuming I don't catch hell from sheriff asshole for being out of my jurisdiction."

"How about social services?" Sara suggested. "From what you said, I've gathered there are children on the farm. Some of them could be runaways, underage."

"Good point," he said, smiling. Jeffrey loved it when he found a way around an obstacle. "I'll have to be careful. Something tells me this Lev guy knows his rights. I bet the farm keeps ten lawyers on retainer."

She sat up. "What?"

"I said he's probably got ten lawyers—"

"No, his name."

"Lev, one of the uncles," Jeffrey said. "It's weird, but he kind of looks like you. Red hair." He slipped on a T-shirt. "Pretty blue eyes."

"My eyes are green," she said, aggravated by his old joke. "How does he look like me?"

"Just like I said," he shrugged, smoothing down his Lynyrd Skynyrd T-shirt. "Do I look like a redneck who belongs in a strip club?"

"Tell me about this guy, this Lev."

"Why are you so curious?"

"I just want to know," she said, then, "Tessa is going to that church."

He gave an incredulous laugh. "You're kidding."

"Why is that so hard to believe?"

"Tessa? In a church? Without your mama standing behind her with a whip?"

"What does that mean?"

"They're just really . . . devout," he said, combing back his hair with his fingers. He sat on the edge of the bed. "They don't seem like Tess's kind of people."

It was one thing for Sara to call Tessa loose, quite another for someone else to do it—even Jeffrey. "What are her kind of people?"

He put his hand on her foot, obviously sensing a trap. "Sara—"

"Just forget it," she said, wondering why she kept trying to pick a fight.

"I don't want to forget it. Sara, what's wrong with you?"

She slid down the bed, curling herself away from him. "I've just had a really bad day."

He rubbed her back. "The autopsy?"

She nodded.

"You called me because you needed to talk about it," he said. "I should've listened."

She swallowed as a lump came into her throat. That he had realized his mistake meant almost as much to her as if he hadn't made it in the first place.

He soothed, "I know it was hard, baby. I'm sorry I couldn't be there."

"It's okay."

"I don't like you going through something like that on your own."

"Carlos was with me."

"That's not the same." He kept rubbing her back, making small circles with his palm. His voice was barely a whisper when he asked, "What's going on?"

"I don't know," she admitted. "Tessa wants me to go to this church with her on Wednesday night."

His hand stopped. "I wish you wouldn't."

She looked at him over her shoulder. "Why?"

"These people," he began, "I don't trust them. I can't tell you why, but something's going on."

"Do you really think they killed Abigail?"

"I don't know what they did," he told her. "All I know is that I don't want you mixed up in this."

"What's to get mixed up in?"

He did not answer. Instead, he tugged her sleeve, saying, "Turn over."

Sara rolled over onto her back, and a smile played on his lips as he ran his finger along the half-open zipper of her skirt. "What did you have for dinner?"

She was too embarrassed to say so she just shook her head.

Jeffrey slid up her shirt and started to rub her stomach. "Better?"

She nodded.

"Your skin is so soft," he whispered, using the tips of his fingers. "Sometimes I think about it and I get this feeling in my heart like I'm flying." He smiled, as if a private memory was playing out in his head.

Several minutes passed before he said, "I heard Jimmy Powell's back in the hospital."

Sara closed her eyes, concentrating on his hand. She had been on the verge of crying most of the day, and his words made it harder to resist. Everything she had been through in the last forty-eight hours had tightened her up like a ball of string, but somehow his soft touch managed to unravel her.

She said, "This will be the last time," her throat tightening as she thought of the sick nine-year-old. Sara had known Jimmy all of his life, watched him grow from infant to child. His diagnosis had hit her almost as hard as it had his parents.

Jeffrey asked, "You want me to go to the hospital with you?"

"Please."

He lightened his touch. "And how about later?"

"Later?" she asked, feeling the urge to purr like a cat.

"Where am I sleeping?"

Sara took her time answering, wishing she could just snap her fingers and it was tomorrow and the decision had been made. What she finally did was gesture toward the boxes he had brought over from his house. "All of your stuff is here."

The smile he flashed didn't do a very good job of hiding his disappointment. "I guess that's as good a reason as any."

CHAPTER SEVEN

Jeffrey kept the radio down low as he drove out of Heartsdale. He realized he had been gritting his teeth when a sharp pain shot up the side of his jaw. Jeffrey heard an old man's sigh come from his chest, and felt like opening a vein. His shoulder hurt, and his right knee was acting up, not to mention his cut hand was still throbbing. Years of football had taught him to ignore aches and pains, but he had found as he got older that this was a harder trick to pull off. He felt really old today—not just old, but ancient. Getting shot in the shoulder a few months ago had been some kind of wake-up call that he wasn't going to live forever. There had been a time when he could trot out onto the football field and practically break every bone in his body, only to wake up feeling fine the next day. Now, his shoulder ached if he brushed his teeth too vigorously.

And now this hepatitis shit. Last week, when Jo had called to tell him, he had known it was her on the phone even before she said a word. She had a way of pausing before she spoke, hesitant, as if she was waiting for the other person to take the lead. That was one of the things he had liked about her, the fact that she let Jeffrey take charge. Jo refused to argue, and she had made an art out of being agreeable. There was something to be said for being with a woman who didn't have to think through every damn thing that came out of her mouth.

At least he wasn't going to be sleeping on the floor again tonight. He doubted Sara would welcome him into bed with open arms, but she appeared to be getting over some of her anger. Things had been going so well between them before Jo had called, and it was easy to blame someone else for his recent problems. The truth was that it was starting to seem like every day with Sara was one step forward and two steps back. The fact that he had asked her to marry him at least four times and each time been basically slapped in the face was beginning to grate as well. There was only so much he could take.

Jeffrey turned onto a gravel drive, thinking that between the farm and Dale Stanley's place, his Town Car was going to look like it had been through a war zone.

Jeffrey parked behind what looked like a fully restored Dodge Dart. "Damn," he whispered as he got out of his own car, unable to conceal his appreciation. The Dodge was cherry, dark blue with tinted windows, jacked up in the back. The bumper was seamless, bright chrome sparkling from the security light mounted to the garage.

"Hey, Chief." An extremely tall, skinny man wearing work coveralls came out of the garage. He was rubbing his hands on a dirty towel. "I think I met you at the picnic last year."

"Good to see you again, Dale." There weren't many men Jeffrey had to look up at, but Dale Stanley was practically a beanstalk. He looked a lot like his younger brother, if someone had grabbed Pat by the head and feet and stretched the young policeman a good twelve inches either way. Despite Dale's towering height, there was an easygoing air about the man, as if nothing in the world bothered him. Jeffrey put his age at around thirty.

"Sorry I had to ask you to come so late," Dale told him. "I didn't want to upset the kids. They get nervous when a cop pulls up." He glanced nervously back at the house. "I guess you know why."

"I understand," Jeffrey said, and Dale seemed to relax a bit. Patrolman Pat Stanley, Dale's little brother, had been involved in a pretty intense hostage situation a few months ago, barely escaping with his life. Jeffrey couldn't imagine what it was like to hear about something like that on the news, then wait for a police car to pull up to tell you that your brother was dead.

"They don't even like the sirens on TV," he said, and Jeffrey got the feeling Dale was the kind of guy who scooped up spiders and took them out of the house instead of just killing them.

Dale asked, "You got a brother?"

"Not that I know of," Jeffrey told him, and Dale threw back his head and laughed like a braying horse.

Jeffrey waited for him to finish before asking, "We're right on the county line, aren't we?"

"Yep," Dale agreed. "Catoogah's that way, Avondale's here. My kids'll go to the school up on Mason Mill."

Jeffrey looked around, trying to get his bearings. "Looks like you've got a nice place here."

"Thanks." He motioned toward the garage. "You wanna beer?"

"Sure." Jeffrey was unable to hide his admiration as they walked into the shop. Dale ran a tight ship. The floor was painted a light gray, not a drop of oil in sight. Tools were suspended on a pegboard, black outlines showing where everything belonged. Baby food jars containing bolts and screws hung from under the top cabinets like wine glasses in a bar. The whole place was lit up bright as day.

Jeffrey asked, "What exactly do you do here?"

"I'm restoring cars mostly," he said, indicating the Dart. "I've got a paint shed out back. The mechanicals are done in here. My wife does the upholstery."

"Terri?"

He tossed Jeffrey a look over his shoulder, probably impressed that Jeffrey remembered her name. "That's right."

"Sounds like a pretty good setup."

"Yeah, well," he said, opening a small refrigerator and taking out a Bud Light. "We'd be doing okay except for my oldest one. Tim sees your ex-wife more than he sees me. And now my sister is sick, had to quit her job over at the factory. Lot of stress on the family. Lot of stress on a man, trying to look after them."

"Sara mentioned Tim has asthma."

"Yeah, pretty bad." He twisted the top off the bottle and handed it to Jeffrey. "We've got to be real careful around him. I gave up smoking cold turkey the day the wife took him back from the doctor's. Tell you what, that liked to kill me. But, we do what we have to do for our kids. You don't have any, do you?" He laughed, adding, "I mean, not that you know of."

Jeffrey made himself laugh, though considering his circumstances it wasn't very funny. After an appropriate interval, he asked, "I thought you did metal plating."

"Still do," he said, picking up a piece of metal from his worktop. Jeffrey saw it was an old Porsche medallion, plated in shiny yellow gold. The set of fine-tipped paintbrushes beside it indicated Dale had been working on filling in the colors. "This is for the wife's brother. Sweet ride."

"Can you run me through the process?"

"Plating?" His eyes widened in surprise. "You came all the way out here for a chemistry lesson?"

"Can you humor me?"

Dale didn't stop to think it over. "Sure," he agreed, leading Jeffrey to a bench in the back of the shop. He seemed almost relieved to be in familiar territory as he explained, "It's called a three-step process, but there's more to it than that. Basically, you're just charging the metal with this." He pointed to a machine that looked like a battery charger. Attached were two metal electrodes, one with a black handle, the other with a red one. Beside the machine was another electrode with a yellow and red handle.

"Electricity runs positive from the red, negative from the black." Dale indicated a shallow pan. "First, you take what you want to plate and put it in here. Fill it with solution. You use the positive, clean it with the chrome stripper. Make it negative, activate the nickel."

"I thought it was gold."

"Nickel's underneath. Gold needs something to stick to. Activate the nickel with an acid solution, banana clip the negative to one side. Use a synthetic wrap on the end of the plating electrode, dip it into the gold solution, then bond the gold to the nickel. I'm leaving out all the sexy parts, but that's pretty much it."

"What's the solution?"

"Basic stuff I get from the supplier," he said, putting his hand on top of the metal cabinet above the plating area. He felt around and pulled out a key to unlock the door.

"Have you always kept that key up there?"

"Yep." He opened up the cabinet and took down the bottles one by one. "Kids can't reach it."

"Anybody ever come into the shop without your knowing it?"

"Not ever," he said, indicating the thousands of dollars worth of tools and equipment in the space. "This is my livelihood. Somebody gets in here and takes this stuff, I'm finished."

"You don't ever leave the door open?" Jeffrey asked, meaning the garage door. There were no windows or other openings in the garage. The only way in or out was through the metal roll-door. It looked strong enough to keep out a Mack truck.

"I only leave it open when I'm here," Dale assured him. "I close it up when I go into the house to take a piss."

Jeffrey bent down to read the labels on the bottles. "These look pretty toxic."

"I wear a mask and gloves when I use them," Dale told him. "There's worse stuff out there, but I stopped using it when Tim got sick."

"What kind of stuff?"

"Arsenic or cyanide, mostly. You pour it in with the acid. It's pretty volatile and being honest here, it scares the shit out of me. They've got some new stuff on the market that's still pretty nasty, but it can't kill you if you breathe it wrong." He pointed to one of the plastic bottles. "That's the solution."

Jeffrey read the label. "Cyanide free?"

"Yeah." He chuckled again. "Honest to God, I was looking for an excuse to change over. I'm just a big ol' pussy when it comes to dying."

Jeffrey looked at each bottle, not touching them as he read the labels. Any one of them looked like they could kill a horse.

Dale was rocking back on his heels, waiting. His expression seemed to say he was expecting some reciprocation for his patience so far.

Jeffrey asked, "You know that farm over in Catoogah?"

"Soy place?"

"That's it."

"Sure. Keep going that way," — he indicated the road heading southeast—"and you run right into it."

"You ever have anybody come over here from there?"

Dale started to put away the bottles. "Used to be they'd cut through the woods sometimes on their way to town. I got kind of nervous, though. Some'a them folks ain't exactly your upstanding types."

"Which folks?"

"The workers," he said, closing the cabinet. He locked it back and returned the key to its hiding place. "Hell, that family is a bunch of fucking idiots if you ask me, letting those people live with them and all."

Jeffrey prompted, "How's that?"

"Some of these folks they bring down from Atlanta are pretty bad off. Drugs, alcohol, whatever. It leads you to do certain things, desperate things. You lose your religion."

He asked, "Does that bother you?"

"Not really. I mean, I guess you could say it's a good thing. I just didn't like them coming on my property."

"You worried about being robbed?"

"They'd need a plasma torch to get into this place," he pointed out. "Either that or have to come through me."

"You keep a gun?"

"Damn straight."

"Can I see it?"

Dale walked across the room and reached up on top of another cabinet. He pulled down a Smith & Wesson revolver and offered it to Jeffrey.

"Nice gun," Jeffrey told him, checking the cylinder. He kept the weapon as meticulously clean as his shop, and fully loaded. "Looks ready for action," Jeffrey told him, handing back the gun.

"Careful now," Dale warned, almost jokingly. "She's got a hair trigger."

"That a fact?" Jeffrey asked, thinking the man was probably pleased with himself for setting up such a good alibi should he ever "accidentally" shoot an intruder.

"I'm not really worried about them robbing me," Dale explained, returning the weapon to its hiding place. "Like I told you, I'm real careful. It's just, they'd come through here and the dogs would go crazy, the wife would freak out, the kids would start crying, got me all het up and you *know* that ain't good." He paused, looking out at the driveway. "I hate to be this way, but we're not living in Mayberry. There are all kinds of bad people out there and I don't want my kids around them." He shook his head. "Hell, Chief, I don't have to tell you about that."

Jeffrey wondered if Abigail Bennett had used the cut-through. "Any of the people from the farm ever come to the house?"

"Never," he said. "I'm here all day. I would've seen them."

"You ever talk to any of them?"

"Just to tell them to get the fuck off my land," he said. "I'm not worried about the house. The dogs would tear them apart if they so much as knocked on the door."

"What'd you do?" Jeffrey asked. "I mean, to stop them from cutting through?"

"Put in a call to Two-Bit. Sheriff Pelham, I mean."

Jeffrey let Dale's comment slide. "Where'd that get you?"

"Same place as when I started out," Dale said, kicking his toe into the ground. "I didn't wanna bother Pat with it, so I just called up there myself. Talked to old Tom's son Lev. He's not bad for a Jesus freak. You met him?"

"Yeah."

"I explained the situation, said I didn't want his people on my property. He said okay."

"When was this?"

"Oh, about three, maybe four months ago," Dale answered. "He even came out here and we walked along the back property line. Said he'd put up a fence to stop them."

"Did he?"

"Yeah."

"You take him into the shop?"

"Sure." Dale looked almost bashful, a kid bragging about his toys. "Had a sixty-nine Mustang I was working on. Damn thing looked like it was breaking the law just sitting in the driveway."

"Lev's into cars?" Jeffrey asked, surprised by this detail.

"I don't know a man alive wouldn't be impressed by that car. Stripped it from the ground up—new engine, new suspension and exhaust—about the only thing original on that baby was the frame, and I chopped the pillars and dropped the top three inches."

Jeffrey was tempted to let him get sidetracked but knew he couldn't. He asked, "One more question?"

"Shoot."

"Do you have any cyanide around?"

Dale shook his head. "Not since I quit smoking. Too tempted to end it all." He laughed, then, seeing Jeffrey wasn't joining in, stopped. "Sure, I keep it back here," he said, returning to the cabinet over the metal plating area. Again, he found the key and unlocked the cabinet. He reached far into the back, his hand disappearing for a few moments into the recesses of the uppermost shelf. He pulled out a thick plastic bag that held a small glass bottle. The skull and crossbones on the front sent a shiver through Jeffrey's spine as he thought about what Abigail Bennett had been through.

Dale placed the bag on the counter, the glass bottle making a clink. "I don't even like touching this shit," he said. "I know it's stable, but it freaks me the fuck out."

"Do you ever leave the cabinet unlocked?"

"Not unless I'm using what's in there."

Jeffrey bent down to look at the bottle. "Can you tell if any salts are missing?"

Dale knelt, too, squinting at the clear glass. "Not that I can tell." He stood back up. " 'Course, it's not like I count it out."

"Did Lev seemed interested in what was inside this cabinet?"

"I doubt he even noticed it was there." He crossed his arms over his chest and asked, "There something I should be worried about?"

"No," Jeffrey told him, though he wasn't sure. "Can I talk to Terri?"

"She's with Sally," he said, then explained. "My sister. She's got this problem with her . . ." He indicated his lower regions. "Terri goes over when she has bad spells and helps her watch the kids."

"I need to talk to her," Jeffrey said. "Maybe she's seen someone around the garage who shouldn't be."

Dale stiffened, as if his honesty had been challenged. "Nobody comes into this place without me," he said, and Jeffrey believed him. The man wasn't keeping that gun around because it made him feel pretty.

Dale allowed, "She'll be back tomorrow morning. I'll tell her to come see you as soon as she gets back."

"Appreciate it." Jeffrey indicated the poison. "Do you mind if I take this?" he asked. "I want to dust it for fingerprints."

"Glad to have it out of here," Dale agreed. He opened one of his drawers and took out a latex glove. "You wanna use this?"

Jeffrey accepted the offer and slipped on a glove so that he could take the bag.

"I'm sorry I can't be specific with you, Dale. You've been really helpful, but I'd prefer if you didn't tell anybody I was over here asking about this."

"No problem." Dale's mood was almost exuberant now that the questioning was over. As Jeffrey was getting into his car, he offered, "You come on back sometime when you can sit a while. I took pictures of that sixty-nine 'Stang every step of the way."

❋ ❋ ❋

Lena was sitting on her front steps when Jeffrey pulled up in front of her house.

"Sorry I'm late," he told her as she got into the car.

"No problem."

"I was talking to Dale Stanley about plating."

She stopped in the middle of buckling her seat belt. "Anything?"

"Not much." He filled her in on Dale's operation and Lev's visit. "I dropped the cyanide by the station before I came to get you," he told her. "Brad is running it to Macon tonight to have one of their fingerprint guys take a look at it."

"Do you think you'll find anything?"

"The way this case has been going?" he asked. "I doubt it."

"Was Lev ever alone in the shop?"

"No." He had thrown out that question before leaving Dale's house. "I don't know how he would steal the salts, let alone transport them, but that's a pretty odd coincidence."

"I'll say," Lena agreed, settling down in her seat. She was drumming her fingers on the armrest, a nervous habit he'd seldom seen her employ.

He asked her, "Something wrong?"

She shook her head.

"You ever been to this place before?"

"The Pink Kitty?" She shook her head again. "I doubt they let women in unescorted."

"They'd better not."

"How do you want to do this?"

"It shouldn't be too busy on a Monday night," he said. "Let's show her picture around, see if anybody recognizes her."

"You think they'll tell us the truth?"

"I'm not sure," he admitted, "but I think we'll have a better chance of somebody talking to us if we go in soft instead of swinging our dicks around."

"I'll take the girls," she offered. "Nobody's gonna let you back into the dressing rooms."

"Sounds like a plan."

She flipped down the visor and slid open the mirror, checking her makeup, he guessed. He took another look at her. With her dark Latin coloring and perfect complexion, Lena probably didn't spend many nights alone, even if it was with that punk Ethan Green. Tonight, she wasn't wearing her usual suit and jacket, instead opting for some black jeans and a form-fitting red silk shirt that was open at the collar. She also wasn't wearing a bra that he could tell, and she was obviously cold.

Jeffrey shifted in his seat, turning off the air conditioning, hoping she hadn't seen him looking. Lena wasn't young enough to be his daughter, but she acted like it most of the time and he couldn't help but feel like a dirty old man for noticing her finer points.

She flipped the visor closed. "What?" She was staring at him again.

Jeffrey searched for something to say. "Is this a problem for you?"

"A problem how?"

He tried to think of a way to phrase it without pissing her off, then gave up. "I mean, you still drinking too much?"

She snapped, "You still fucking around on your wife?"

"She's not my wife," he shot back, knowing it was a lame retort even as the words left his mouth. "Look," he said, "it's a bar. If this is going to be too hard for you —"

"Nothing's too hard for me," she told him, effectively ending the conversation.

They drove the rest of the way in silence, Jeffrey staring ahead at the highway, wondering how he had become an expert at picking the most prickly women in the county to spend his time with. He also wondered what they would find at the bar tonight. There was no reason for a girl like Abigail Bennett to hide that book of matches in her Snoopy doll. She had carefully sewn it back up, and Jeffrey wouldn't have even known to look if he hadn't tugged on the end of a thread like pulling a loose string on a sweater.

A pink neon cat glowed in the distance, even though they were a good two miles from the bar. The closer they got, the more detail they could see, until the thirty-foot-tall feline in stilettos and a black leather bustier loomed in front of them.

Jeffrey parked the car close to the road. But for the sign, the building was nondescript, a windowless one-story structure with a pink metal roof and a parking lot big enough to hold about a hundred cars. This being a weeknight, there were only about a dozen spaces taken, mostly with trucks and SUVs. An eighteen-wheeler was parked long-ways in front of the back fence.

Even with the car windows up and the doors closed, Jeffrey could hear the music blaring from the club.

He reminded her, "We'll just take this slow."

Lena slid off her seat belt and got out of the car, obviously still pissed at him for asking about her drinking. He would put up with this kind of shit from Sara, but Jeffrey would be damned if he let himself get whipped by one of his subordinates.

"Hold up," he told her, and she stopped in place, keeping her back to him. "You check that attitude," he warned her. "I'm not putting up with any shit. You got that?"

She nodded, then resumed walking. He took his time, and she shortened her stride until they were walking shoulder to shoulder.

She stopped in front of the door, finally saying, "I'm okay." She looked him in the eye and repeated herself. "I'm really okay."

If Jeffrey hadn't had just about everybody he'd met today skillfully hide some vital piece of information about themselves while he stood around with his thumb up his ass, he probably would've let it slide. As it was, he told her, "I don't take lip from you, Lena."

"Yes, sir," she told him, not a trace of sarcasm in her tone.

"All right." He reached past her and opened the door. A fog of cigarette smoke hung like a curtain inside, and he had to force himself to enter. As Jeffrey walked toward the bar that lined the left side of the room, his back molars started to pulsate along with the heavy bass cranking out of the sound system. The space was dank and claustrophobic, the ceiling and floor painted a matte black, the chairs and booths scattered around the stage looking like something that had been pulled out of a Denny's fifty years ago. The odor of sweat, piss and something he didn't want to think about filled his nostrils.

The floor was sticky, especially around the stage that took up the center of the room.

About twelve guys in all ages, shapes and sizes were there, most of them elbowed up to the stage where a young girl danced in a barely visible thong and no top. Two men with their guts hanging over their jeans were propped up at the end of the bar, their eyes glued to the huge mirror behind it, half a dozen empty shot glasses in front of each of them. Jeffrey allowed himself a look, watching the reflected girl shimmy up and down a pole. She was boyishly thin with that gaze they all seemed to perfect when they were on stage: "I'm not here. I'm not really doing this." She had a father somewhere. Maybe he was the reason she was here. He had to think things at home were pretty bad if this was the kind of place a young girl ran to.

The bartender lifted his chin and Jeffrey returned the signal, holding up two fingers, saying, "Rolling Rock."

He had a name badge on his chest that said Chip, and he certainly acted like he had one on his shoulder as he pulled the tap. He slammed both glasses on the bar, foam dripping down the sides. The music changed, the words so loud that Jeffrey couldn't even hear how much the drinks were. He threw a ten on the bar, wondering if he'd get change.

Jeffrey turned around, looking out at what could politely be called a crowd. Back in Birmingham, he had visited his share of titty bars with other cops on the force. The strip joints were the only bars open when their shifts ended, and they had all filed into the clubs to wind down, talk a little, drink a lot and get the taste of the streets out of their mouths. The girls there had been fresher, not so young and malnourished that you could count their ribs from twenty feet away.

There was always an underlying tinge of desperation in these places, either from the guys looking up at the stage or the girls dancing on them. One of those late nights in Birmingham, Jeffrey had been in the bathroom taking a leak when a girl was attacked. He had broken down the door of the dressing room and pulled the man off her. The girl had this open disgust in her eyes — not just for her would-be attacker, but for Jeffrey, too. The other girls filed in, all of them half-dressed, all of them looking at him that same way. Their hostility, their razor-sharp hatred, had sliced into him like a knife. He had never gone back.

Lena had stayed at the front door, reading the notices on a bulletin board. As she walked across the room, every man watched her, whether in person or through one of the many mirrors. Even the girl on stage seemed curious, missing a beat as she swung around the pole, probably wondering if she had some competition. Lena ignored them, but Jeffrey saw their stares, their eyes tracing up and down her body in a visual rape. He felt his fists clench, but Lena, noticing, shook her head.

"I'll go in the back and check the girls."

Jeffrey nodded, turning around to get his beer. There was two dollars and some change on the bar, but Chip was nowhere in sight. Jeffrey drank from the mug, almost gagging at the lukewarm liquid. Either they were watering down their drinks with sewage here at the Pink Kitty or they had hooked up the taps to a bunch of horses they kept under the bar.

"Sorry," a stranger said, bumping into him. Jeffrey instinctively reached back to check his wallet, but it was still there.

"You from around here?" the guy asked.

Jeffrey disregarded the question, thinking this was a pretty stupid place to cruise for dates.

"I'm from around here," the guy said, listing slightly.

Jeffrey turned to look at him. He was about five six with stringy blond hair that looked like it hadn't been washed in weeks. Drunk out of his mind, he was clutching the bar with one hand, the other straight out from his side as if he needed it there to balance. His fingernails were edged with dirt, his skin a pale yellow.

Jeffrey asked, "You come here a lot?"

"Every night," he said, a snaggled tooth sticking out as he smiled.

Jeffrey took out a photo of Abigail Bennett. "You recognize her?"

The guy stared at the photo, licking his lips, still swaying back and forth. "She's pretty."

"She's dead."

He shrugged. "Don't stop her from being pretty." He nodded at the two mugs of beer. "You gonna drink that?"

"Help yourself," Jeffrey told him, moving down the bar to get away from him. The guy was probably just looking for his next drink. Jeffrey had dealt with that attitude before. He had seen it in his father every morning when Jimmy Tolliver dragged himself out of bed.

Lena made her way to the bar, her expression answering his question. "Just one girl in the back," she told him. "You ask me, she's a runaway. I left my card with her, but I doubt anything will come out of it." She looked behind the bar. "Where'd the bartender go?"

Jeffrey hazarded a guess. "To tell the manager a couple of cops are here."

"So much for coming in soft," she said.

Jeffrey had spotted a door beside the bar and assumed that's where Chip had scurried off to. Beside the door was a large mirror that had a darker tint than the others. He guessed someone, probably the manager or the owner, was on the other side, watching.

Jeffrey didn't bother knocking. The door was locked, but he managed to bust it open with a firm twist of the knob.

"Hey!" Chip said, backing into the wall with his hands up.

The man behind the desk was counting money, one hand going through the bills, the other tapping out numbers on an adding machine. "What do you want?" he asked, not bothering to look up. "I run a clean place. You ask anybody."

"I know you do," Jeffrey said, taking Abigail's photo out of his back pocket. "I need to know if you've seen this girl around here."

The man still didn't bother to look up. "Never seen her."

Lena said, "You wanna take a look and tell us again?"

He did look up, then. A smile spread out on his wet lips, and he took a cigar out of the ashtray at his elbow and chewed on it. His chair groaned like a seventy-year-old whore when he leaned back in it. "We don't usually have the pleasure of such fine company."

"Look at the picture," she told him, glancing down at the nameplate on his desk. "Mr. Fitzgerald."

"Albert," he told her, taking the Polaroid from Jeffrey. He studied the image, his smile dropping a bit before he stretched it back out. "This girl looks dead."

"Good call," Lena told him. "Where are you going?"

Jeffrey had been watching Chip edge toward another door, but Lena had caught him first.

Chip stuttered, "N-nowhere."

"Keep it that way," Jeffrey warned him. In the light of the office, the bartender was a scrawny guy, probably from a serious drug habit that kept him from eating too much. His hair was cut short over his ears and his face was clean shaven, but he still had the air of a derelict about him.

Albert said, "Wanna lookit this, Chippie?" He held out the photo, but the bartender didn't take it. Something was going on with him, though. Chip's eyes kept darting from Lena to Jeffrey to the picture then the door. He was still edging toward the exit, his back pressed to the wall as if he could sneak away while they were watching.

"What's your name?" Jeffrey asked.

Albert answered for him. "Donner, like the party. Mr. Charles Donner."

Chip kept sliding his feet across the floor. "I ain't done nothing."

"Stop right there," Lena told him. She took a step toward him, and he bolted, swinging open the door. Lunging, she caught the back of his shirt, spinning him around straight into Jeffrey's path. Jeffrey's reaction was slow, but he managed to catch the young man before he fell flat on his face. He couldn't keep the kid from banging into the metal desk, though.

"Shit," Chip cursed, holding his elbow.

"You're fine," Jeffrey told him, scooping him up by his collar.

He bent over at the waist, clutching his elbow. "Shit, that hurt."

"Shut up," Lena told him, picking up the Polaroid from the floor. "Just look at it, you pud."

"I don't know her," he said, still rubbing his elbow, and Jeffrey wasn't sure whether or not he was lying.

Lena asked, "Why'd you try to run?"

"I've got a record."

"No shit," Lena said. "Why'd you try to run?" When he didn't answer her, she popped the back of his head.

"Christ, lady." Chip rubbed his head, looking at Jeffrey, beseeching him for help. He was barely taller than Lena, and even though he had about ten pounds on her, she definitely had more muscle.

"Answer her question," Jeffrey told him.

"I don't wanna go back inside."

Jeffrey guessed, "You've got a warrant out on you?"

"I'm on parole," he said, still holding his arm.

"Look at the picture again," Jeffrey told him.

His jaw tightened, but Chip was obviously used to doing what he was told. He looked down at the Polaroid. He showed no visible recognition on his face, but Jeffrey saw his Adam's apple bob as if he was trying to stop his emotions.

"You know her, don't you?"

Chip glanced back at Lena as if he was afraid she'd hit him again. "If that's what you want me to say, yeah. Okay."

"I want you to tell me the truth," Jeffrey said, and when Chip looked up his pupils were as big as quarters. The guy was obviously high as a kite. "You know she was pregnant, Chip?"

He blinked several times. "I'm broke, man. I can barely feed myself."

Lena said, "We're not hitting you up for child support, you stupid fuck."

The door opened and the girl from the stage stood there, taking in the situation. "Y'all okay?" she asked.

Jeffrey had looked away when she opened the door, and Chip took advantage of the situation, sucker punching him square in the face.

"Chip!" the girl screamed as he pushed past her.

Jeffrey hit the floor so hard he literally saw an explosion of stars. The girl started screaming like a siren and she fought Lena tooth and nail, trying to keep her from chasing after Chip. Jeffrey blinked seeing double, then triple. He closed his eyes and didn't open them for what seemed like a long while.

※ ※ ※ ※

Jeffrey was feeling better by the time Lena dropped him off at Sara's. The stripper, Patty O'Ryan, had scraped a line of skin off the back of Lena's hand, but that was all she had managed to do before Lena twisted the girl's arm behind her back and slammed her to the floor. She had been cuffing the stripper when Jeffrey finally managed to open his eyes.

"I'm sorry," was the first thing Lena said, but it was somewhat drowned out by O'Ryan's brutal, "Fuck you, you fucking pigs!"

Meanwhile, Charles Wesley Donner had gotten away, but his boss had been helpful, and, with a little prompting, gave them everything but Chip's underwear size. The twenty-four-year-old had been working at the Pink Kitty for just under a year. He drove a 1980 Chevy

Nova and lived in a flophouse on Cromwell Road down in Avondale. Jeffrey had already called Donner's parole officer, who had been less than pleased to be awakened by a ringing phone in the middle of the night. She confirmed the address and Jeffrey had dispatched a cruiser to sit on it. An APB had gone out, but Donner had been in prison for six years on drug trafficking charges. He knew how to hide from the police.

Jeffrey eased open Sara's front door as gently as he could, trying not to wake her up. Chip wasn't strong, but he had landed his fist in the exact right place to bring Jeffrey down: under his left eye, just grazing the bridge of his nose. Jeffrey knew from experience the bruising would only get worse, and the swelling already made it hard to breathe. As usual, his nose had bled profusely, making it look a hell of a lot worse than it was. He had always bled like a faucet whenever he was hit on the bridge of his nose.

He turned on the under-counter lights in the kitchen, holding his breath, waiting for Sara to call out to him. When she didn't, he pried open the refrigerator and took out a bag of frozen peas. As quietly as he could, he broke up the freezer burn, separating the peas with his fingers. He clamped his teeth together and hissed out some air as he pressed the bag against his face, wondering again why it never hurt as much when you got injured as it did when you tried to fix it.

"Jeff?"

He jumped, dropping the peas.

Sara turned on the lights, the fluorescent tubes flickering above them. His head seemed to explode with it, a dull throbbing matching the flicker.

She frowned, taking in the shiner under his eye. "Where'd you get that?"

Jeffrey bent over to pick up the peas, all the blood rushing to his head. "The gettin' place."

"You have blood all over you." It sounded more like an accusation.

He looked down at his shirt, which was a lot easier to see in the bright lights of her kitchen than in the bathroom at the Pink Kitty.

"It's your blood?" she asked.

He shrugged, knowing where she was going with the question. She seemed to care more about the possibility of a stranger getting hepatitis from him than the fact that some stupid punk had nearly broken his nose.

He asked, "Where's the aspirin?"

"All I have is Tylenol, and you shouldn't take that until you know the results from your blood test."

"I've got a headache."

"You shouldn't be drinking, either."

The remark only served to annoy him. Jeffrey wasn't his father. He could certainly hold his liquor and one sip of a watered-down beer didn't qualify as drinking.

"Jeff."

"Just drop it, Sara."

She crossed her arms like an angry schoolteacher. "Why aren't you taking this seriously?"

The words came out before he anticipated the shitstorm they would kick up. "Why are you treating me like a fucking leper?"

"You could be carrying a dangerous disease. Do you know what that means?"

"Of course I know what it means," he insisted, his body feeling slack all of the sudden, like he couldn't take one more thing. How many times had they done this? How many arguments had they had in this same kitchen, both of them pushed to the edge? Jeffrey was always the one who brought them back, always the one to apologize, to make things better. He had been doing this all his life, from smoothing down his mother's drunken tempers to stepping in front of his father's fists. As a cop, he put himself in people's business every day, absorbing their pain and their rage, their apprehension and fear. He couldn't keep doing it. There had to be a time in his life when he got some peace.

Sara kept lecturing him. "You have to be cautious until we get the results from the lab."

"This is just another excuse, Sara."

"An excuse for what?"

"To push me away," he told her, his voice rising. He knew he should take a step back and calm down, but he was unable to see past this moment. "It's just another thing you're using to keep me at arm's length."

"I can't believe you really think that."

"What if I have it?" he asked. Again, he said the first thing that came to his mind. "Are you never going to touch me again? Is that what you're trying to tell me?"

"We don't know—"

"My blood, my saliva. Everything will be contaminated." He could hear himself yelling and didn't care.

"There are ways around—"

"Don't think I haven't noticed you pulling away."

"Pulling away?"

He gave a humorless laugh, so damn tired of this he didn't even have the energy to raise his voice again. "You won't even fucking tell me you love me. How do you think that makes me feel? How many times do I have to keep walking out on that tightrope before you let me come back in?"

She wrapped her arms around her waist.

"I know, Sara. And it's not that many more times." He looked out the window over the sink, his reflection staring back at him.

At least a full minute passed before she spoke. "Is that really how you feel?"

"It's how I feel," he told her, and he knew it was true. "I can't keep spending all my time wondering whether or not you're mad at me. I need to know . . ." he tried to finish, but found he didn't have the energy. What was the point?

It took some time, but her reflection joined his in the window. "You need to know what?"

"I need to know you're not going to leave me."

She turned on the faucet and took a paper towel off the roll. She said, "Take off your shirt."

"What?"

She wet the towel. "You've got blood on your neck."

"You want me to get you some gloves?"

She ignored the barb, lifting his shirt over his head, taking particular care not to bump his nose.

"I don't need your help," he told her.

"I know." She rubbed his neck with the paper towel, scrubbing at the dried blood. He looked at the top of her head as she cleaned him. Blood had dried in a trail down to his sternum, and she wiped this up before tossing the towel into the trash can.

She picked up the bottle of lotion she always kept by the sink and pumped some into the palm of her hand. "Your skin's dry."

Her hands were cold when she touched him and he made a noise that sounded like a yelp.

"Sorry," she apologized, rubbing together her hands to warm them. She tentatively placed her fingers on his chest. "Okay?"

He nodded, feeling better and wishing that she wasn't the reason why. It was the same old back and forth, and he was letting himself get pulled back in.

She continued to rub in the lotion in small circles, working her way out. She softened her touch, lingering around the pink scar on his shoulder. The wound had not completely healed yet, and he felt little electric tingles in the damaged skin.

"I didn't think you would make it," she said, and he knew she was thinking back to the day he had been shot. "I put my hands inside of you, but I didn't know if I could stop the bleeding."

"You saved my life."

"I could have lost you."

She kissed the scar, murmuring something he couldn't hear. She kept kissing him, her eyes closing. He felt his own eyes close as she kissed a slow pattern across his chest. After a while, she started to work her way down, unzipping his jeans. Jeffrey leaned back against the sink as she knelt in front of him. Her tongue was warm and firm as it traced the length of him, and he braced his hands on the countertop to keep his knees from buckling.

His whole body shook from wanting her, but he forced himself to put his hands on her shoulders and pull her back to standing. "No," he told her, thinking he'd rather die than risk giving her some awful disease. "No," he repeated, even though he wanted nothing more than to bury himself inside her.

She reached down, using her hand where her mouth had been. Jeffrey gasped as she cupped him with her other hand. He tried to hold back, but looking at her face only made it harder. Her eyes were barely open, a rush of red pinking her cheeks. She kept her mouth inches from his, teasing him with the promise of a kiss. He could feel her breath as she spoke, but again could not hear what she was saying. She started kissing him in earnest, her tongue so soft and gentle he could barely breathe. Her hands worked in tandem, and he nearly lost his restraint when she took his bottom lip between her teeth.

"Sara," he moaned.

She kissed his face, his neck, his mouth, and he finally heard what she was saying. "I love you," she whispered, stroking him until he could no longer hold back. "I love you."

TUESDAY

CHAPTER EIGHT

Lena heard Jeffrey yelling through his closed office door as soon as she walked into the squad room. She lingered near the coffee machine by his office, but couldn't make anything out.

Frank joined her, holding out his mug for a top-up even though it was already full.

She asked, "What's going on?"

"Marty Lam," Frank said, shrugging. "Was he supposed to be sitting on that house last night?"

"For Chip Donner?" Lena asked. Jeffrey had ordered a cruiser to wait outside Donner's house in case he showed up. "Yeah. Why?"

"Chief drove by on his way in this morning and nobody was there."

They both paused, trying to make out Jeffrey's words as his tone rose.

Frank said, "Chief is pretty pissed."

"You think?" Lena asked, her sarcasm thicker than the coffee.

"Watch it," Frank said. He had always thought that the almost thirty years he had on her should afford him some kind of deference.

Lena changed the subject. "You get that credit report back on the family?"

"Yeah," he said. "From what I could tell, the farm's running in the black."

"By a lot?"

"Not much," he said. "I'm trying to get a copy of their tax returns. It's not gonna be easy. The farm's privately held."

Lena stifled a yawn. She had slept about ten seconds last night. "What'd the shelters say about them?"

"That we should all thank God every day there are people like that on the planet," Frank said, but he didn't look ready to bow his head.

Jeffrey's door banged open, and Marty Lam walked out like an inmate doing the death row shuffle. He had his hat in his hands and his eyes on the floor.

"Frank," Jeffrey said, walking over. She could tell he was still angry, and could only imagine the reaming he had given Marty. The fact that he had a bruise under his eye the color of a ripe pomegranate probably hadn't done much to improve his disposition.

He asked Frank, "Did you get in touch with that jewelry supply company?"

"Got the list of customers who bought cyanide right here," Frank said, taking a sheet of paper out of his pocket. "They sold the salts to two stores up in Macon, one down along Seventy-Five. There's a metal plater over in Augusta, too. Took three bottles so far this year."

"I know it's a pain in the ass, but I want you to check them out personally. See if there's any Jesus stuff around that might connect them to the church or to Abby. I'm going to talk to the family later on today and try to find out if she ever left town on her own." He told Lena, "We didn't get prints on the bottle of cyanide from Dale Stanley's."

"None?" she asked.

"Dale always used gloves when he handled it," Jeffrey said. "Could be that's the reason."

"Could be someone wiped it down."

He told her, "I want you to go talk to O'Ryan. Buddy Conford called a few minutes ago. He's representing her."

She felt her nose wrinkle at the lawyer's name. "Who hired him?"

"Fuck if I know."

Lena asked, "He doesn't mind if we talk to her?"

Jeffrey was obviously not interested in being questioned. "Did I get it backward just then? You're my boss now?" He didn't let her answer. "Just get her in the fucking room before he shows up."

"Yes, sir," Lena said, knowing better than to push him. Frank raised his eyebrows as Lena left and she shrugged, not knowing what to say. There was no deciphering Jeffrey's mood over the last few days.

She pushed open the fire door to the back part of the station. Marty Lam was at the water fountain, not drinking, and she nodded

at him as she passed by. He looked like a deer caught in the headlights. She knew the feeling.

Lena punched the code into the lockbox outside the holding cells
and took out the keys. Patty O'Ryan was curled up on her bunk, her
knees almost touching her chin. Even though she was still dressed,
or rather half-dressed, in her stripper's outfit from last night, she
looked about twelve when she slept, an innocent tossed around by a
cruel world.

"O'Ryan!" Lena yelled, shaking the locked cell door. Metal
banged against metal, and the girl was so startled she fell onto the
floor.

"Rise and shine," Lena sang.

"Shut up, you stupid bitch," O'Ryan barked back, no longer looking twelve or innocent. She put her hands to her ears as Lena shook
the door again for good measure. The girl was obviously hungover,
the question was from what.

"Get up," Lena told her. "Turn around, put your hands behind
your back."

She knew the drill, and barely flinched when Lena put the cuffs
around her wrists. They were so thin and bony that Lena had to
ratchet the locking teeth to the last notch. Girls like O'Ryan rarely
ended up murdered. They were survivors. People like Abigail Bennett were the ones who needed to be looking over their shoulders.

Lena opened the cell door, taking the girl by the arm as she led her
down the hall. This close to her, Lena could smell the sweat and
chemicals pouring out of her body. Her mousy brown hair hadn't
been washed in a while, and it hung in chunks down to her waist. As
she moved, the hair shifted, and Lena saw a puncture mark on the
inside of the girl's left elbow.

"You like meth?" Lena guessed. Like most small towns all over
America, Grant had seen a thousandfold increase in meth trafficking
over the last five years.

"I know my rights," she hissed. "You don't have any call to keep
me here."

"Obstructing justice, attacking an officer, resisting arrest," Lena
listed. "You want to pee in a cup for me? I'm sure we can come up
with something else."

"Piss on you," she said, spitting on the floor.

"You're a real lady, O'Ryan."

"And you're a real cunt, you cocksucking bitch."

"Woops," Lena said, jerking the girl back by the arm so that she stumbled. O'Ryan gave a rewarding screech of pain. "In here," Lena ordered, pushing the girl into an interrogation room.

"Bitch," O'Ryan hissed as Lena forced her down into the most uncomfortable chair in the police station.

"Don't try anything," Lena warned, unlocking one of the cuffs and looping it through the ring Jeffrey had welded to the table. The table was bolted to the floor, which had proven to be a good idea on more than one occasion.

"You got no right to keep me here," O'Ryan said. "Chip didn't do nothing."

"Then why'd he run?"

"Because he knows you fuckers were gonna bang him up no matter what."

"How old are you?" Lena asked, sitting down across from her.

She tilted her chin up in defiance, saying, "Twenty-one," pretty much assuring Lena she was underage.

Lena told her, "You're not helping yourself here."

"I want a lawyer."

"You've got one on the way."

This took her by surprise. "Who?"

"Don't you know?"

"Fuck," she spat, her expression turning into a little girl's again.

"What's wrong?"

"I don't want a lawyer."

Lena sighed. There was nothing wrong with this girl that a good slapping wouldn't fix. "Why is that?"

"I just don't," she said. "Take me to jail. Charge me. Do whatever you want to do." She licked her lips coyly, giving Lena a once-over. "There something else you want to do?"

"Don't flatter yourself."

When the sexual offer didn't work, she turned back into the frightened little girl. Crocodile tears dribbled down her cheeks. "Just process me. I don't have anything to say."

"We've got some questions."

"Go fuck yourself with your questions," she said. "I know my rights. I don't have to say jack shit to you and you can't make me." Minus the expletives, she sounded very much like Albert, the owner of the Pink Kitty, when Jeffrey had asked him to come down to the station last night. Lena hated when people knew their rights. It made her job a hell of a lot harder.

Lena leaned across the table, saying, "Patty, you're not helping yourself."

"Fuck you with your helping myself. I can help myself fine just shutting the fuck up."

Spittle dotted the table, and Lena sat back, wondering what events had brought Patty O'Ryan to this kind of life. At some point, she had been someone's daughter, someone's friend. Now, she was like a leech, looking out for no one but herself.

Lena said, "Patty, you're not going anywhere. I can sit here all day."

"You can sit on a big fat cock up your ass, you cocksucking bitch."

There was a knock on the door and Jeffrey walked in, Buddy Conford behind him.

O'Ryan did an instant one eighty, bursting into tears like a lost child, wailing at Buddy, "Daddy, please get me out of here! I swear I didn't do anything!"

❋ ❋ ❋ ❋

Sitting in Jeffrey's office, Lena braced her foot against the bottom panel of his desk, leaning back in her chair. Buddy looked at her leg, and she didn't know if it was with interest or envy. As a teenager, a car accident had taken his right leg from the knee down. Buddy's left eye had been lost to cancer a few years later and more recently, an angry client had shot him point-blank range over the matter of a bill. Buddy had lost a kidney from that fiasco, but he still managed to get the charge of attempted murder against his client reduced to simple assault. When he said he was a defendant's advocate, he wasn't lying.

Buddy asked, "That boyfriend of yours staying out of trouble?"

"Let's not talk about it," Lena said, regretting yet again that she had involved Buddy Conford in Ethan's troubles. The problem was, when you were on the other side of the table and you needed a lawyer, you wanted the wiliest, most crooked one out there. It was the old proverb of lying down with dogs and waking up with fleas. Lena was still itching from it.

"You taking care of yourself?" Buddy pressed.

Lena turned around, trying to see what was keeping Jeffrey. He was talking to Frank, a sheet of paper in his hand. He patted Frank on the shoulder, then walked toward the office.

"Sorry," Jeffrey said. He shook his head once at Lena, indicating nothing had broken. He sat behind his desk, turning the paper face-down on the blotter.

"Nice shiner," Buddy said, indicating Jeffrey's eye.

Jeffrey obviously wasn't up for small talk. "Didn't know you had a daughter, Buddy."

"Stepdaughter," he corrected, looking as if he regretted having to admit it. "I married her mama last year. We've been dating off and on for pretty much the last ten years. She's just a handful of trouble."

"The mama or the daughter?" Jeffrey asked, and they shared one of their white-man chuckles.

Buddy sighed, gripping either side of the chair with his hands. He was wearing his prosthetic leg today, but he still had a cane. For some reason, the cane reminded Lena of Greg Mitchell. Despite her best intentions, she had found herself looking out for her old boyfriend this morning as she drove into work, hoping he was out for a walk. Not that she knew what she'd say to him.

"Patty's got a drug problem," Buddy told them. "We've had her in and out of treatment."

"Where's her father?"

Buddy held his hands out in a wide shrug. "Got me."

Lena asked, "Meth?"

"What else?" he said, dropping his hands. Buddy made a fine living from methamphetamine—not directly, but through representing clients who had been charged with trafficking in it.

He said, "She's seventeen years old. Her mama thinks she's been doing it for a while now. This shooting up is recent. I can't do anything to stop her."

"It's a hard drug to quit," Jeffrey allowed.

"Almost impossible," Buddy agreed. He should know. More than half of his clients were repeat offenders. "We finally had to kick her out of the house," he continued. "This was about six months back. She wasn't doing anything but staying out late, stumbling in high and sleeping till three in the afternoon. When she managed to wake up, it was mostly to curse her mama, curse me, curse the world—you know how it is, everybody's an asshole but you. She's got a mouth on her, too, some kind of voluntary Tourette's. What a mess." He tapped his leg with his fingers, a hollow, popping sound filling the room. "You do what you can to help people, but there's only so far you can go."

"Where'd she go when she moved out?"

"Mostly she crashed with friends—girlfriends, though I imagine she was entertaining some boys for pocket change. When she wore out her welcome, she started working at the Kitty." He stopped tapping. "Believe it or not, I thought that'd finally be the thing to straighten her out."

"How's that?" Lena asked.

"Only time you help yourself is when you hit rock bottom." He gave her a meaningful look that made her want to slap him. "I can't think of anything more rock bottom than taking off your clothes for a bunch of seedy-ass rednecks at the Pink Kitty."

Jeffrey asked, "She didn't happen to get mixed up with the farm over in Catoogah, did she?"

"Those Jesus freaks?" Buddy laughed. "I don't think they'd have her."

"But do you know?"

"You can ask her, but I doubt it. She's not exactly the religious type. If she goes anywhere, it's looking to score, seeing how she can work the system. They may be a bunch of Bible-thumping lunatics, but they're not stupid. They'd see right through her in a New York minute. She knows her audience. She wouldn't waste her time."

"You know this guy Chip Donner?"

"Yeah, I represented him a couple of times as a favor to Patty."

"He's not on my files," Jeffrey said, meaning Chip had never been busted by Grant County police.

"No, this was over in Catoogah." Buddy shifted in his seat. "He's not a bad guy, I have to say. Local boy, never been more than fifty miles from home. He's just stupid. Most of 'em are just stupid. Mix that with boredom and—"

"What about Abigail Bennett?" Jeffrey interrupted.

"Never heard of her. She work at the club?"

"She's the girl we found buried in the woods."

Buddy shuddered, like someone had walked over his grave. "Jesus, that's a horrible way to die. My daddy used to scare us when we'd go visit his mama at the cemetery. There was this preacher buried two plots over with a wire coming out of the dirt and going up to a telephone poll. Daddy told us they had a phone inside the coffin so he could call them in case he wasn't really dead." He chuckled. "One time, my mama brought a bell, one'a them bicycle bells, and we were all just standing around Granny's plot, trying to look solemn. She rang that bell and I liked to shit in my pants."

Jeffrey allowed a smile.

Buddy sighed, "You don't have me in here to tell old stories. What do you want from Patty?"

"We want to know what her connection is to Chip."

"I can tell you that," he said. "She had a crush on him. He wouldn't give her the time of day, but she was into him something horrible."

"Chip knows Abigail Bennett."

"How?"

"That's what we'd like to know," Jeffrey said. "We were hoping Patty could tell us."

Buddy licked his lips. Lena could see where this was going. "I hate to say this, Chief, but I don't hold any sway with her."

"We could work a deal," Jeffrey offered.

"No," he said, holding up his hand. "I'm not playing you. She hates my guts. Blames me for taking her mama from her, blames me for kicking her out of the house. I'm the bad guy here."

Lena suggested, "Maybe she doesn't hate you as much as she hates being in jail."

"Maybe," Buddy shrugged.

"So," Jeffrey said, obviously not pleased, "we let her sweat it out another day?"

"I think that'd be best," Buddy agreed. "I hate to sound hard about this, but she needs something more than common sense to persuade her." His lawyer side must have kicked in, because he quickly added, "And of course, we'll expect the assault and obstruction charges to disappear in exchange for her statement."

Lena couldn't help but grunt in disgust. "This is why people hate lawyers."

"Didn't seem to bother you when my services were needed," Buddy pointed out, cheerfully. Then, to Jeffrey, "Chief?"

Jeffrey sat back in his chair, his fingers steepled together. "She talks tomorrow morning or all bets are off."

"Deal," Buddy said, shooting out his hand so they could shake on it. "Give me a few minutes alone with her now. I'll try to paint the picture for her nice and pretty."

Jeffrey picked up the phone. "Brad? I need you to take Buddy back to talk to Patty O'Ryan." He slipped the receiver back in the cradle. "He's waiting in lockup."

"Thank you, sir," Buddy said, using his cane to stand. He gave Lena a wink before making his exit.

"Asshole," she said.

"He's just doing his job," Jeffrey told her, but she could see he felt the same. Jeffrey dealt with Buddy Conford on pretty much a weekly basis, and it usually worked to his benefit to cut deals, but Lena thought that O'Ryan would eventually talk on her own without any backdoor negotiations to save her ass from two years in prison. Not to mention Lena would've liked to have been consulted on whether or not to give the bitch a free pass considering she was the officer who had been assaulted.

Jeffrey was looking out into the parking lot. He said, "I told Dale Stanley to send his wife here first thing."

"You think she'll come?"

"Who the fuck knows." He sat back, breathing a sigh. "I want to talk to the family again."

"They're supposed to come tomorrow."

"I'll believe it when I see it."

"You think Lev will let you hook him up to a lie detector?"

"It'd tell us a hell of a lot either way," he said, looking out the window again. "There she is."

Lena followed his gaze as he stood, catching a small woman getting out of a classic Dodge. She had one kid in tow and another on her hip. A tall man walked beside her as they headed toward the station.

"She looks familiar."

"Police picnic," Jeffrey said, slipping on his jacket. "You mind keeping Dale busy?"

"Uh," Lena began, caught off guard by his suggestion. They usually did interviews together. "No," she said. "No problem."

"She might open up more without him around," Jeffrey explained. "He likes to talk."

"No problem," Lena repeated.

At the front desk, Marla squealed at the sight of the children, and she leapt up as she buzzed open the door, going straight to the baby on the mother's hip.

"Look at those adorable cheeks!" Marla screeched, her voice shrill enough to shatter glass. She pinched the baby's cheeks, and instead of crying, the kid laughed. Marla took him in her arms like she was his long-lost grandmother, stepping back out of the way. Lena felt her stomach drop about six inches as she finally saw Terri Stanley.

"Oh," Terri said, as if the breath had been knocked out of her.

"Thanks for coming in," Jeffrey told them, shaking Dale's hand. "This is Lena Adams . . ." His voice trailed off, and Lena forced herself to close her mouth, which had opened a couple of inches at the sight of Terri. Jeffrey looked at Lena, then Terri, saying, "Y'all remember each other from the picnic last year?"

Terri spoke, at least her mouth moved, but Lena could not hear what she said over the rush of blood pounding in her ears. Jeffrey need not have bothered with an introduction. Lena knew exactly who Terri Stanley was. The other woman was shorter than Lena and at least twenty pounds lighter. Her hair was pinned up into an old lady's bun though she was barely out of her twenties. Her lips were pale, almost blue and her eyes showed a flash of fear that seemed to mimic Lena's own. Lena had seen that fear before, a little over a week ago as she had waited for her name to be called so that she could leave the waiting room of the clinic.

Lena actually stuttered. "I-I . . ." She stopped, trying to calm herself.

Jeffrey was watching them both closely. Without warning, he changed his earlier strategy, saying, "Terri, do you mind if Lena asks you some questions?" Dale seemed about to protest, but Jeffrey asked, "Mind if I get another look at that Dart? She sure is sweet."

Dale didn't seem to like the suggestion, and Lena could see him trying to work out an excuse. He finally relented, picking up the toddler standing beside him. "All right."

"We'll be back in a minute," Jeffrey told Lena, giving her a meaningful look. He'd want an explanation, but Lena was at a loss for a story that did not incriminate herself.

Marla offered, "I'll take care of this one," holding up the baby, making him squeal.

Lena said, "We can talk in Jeffrey's office."

Terri only nodded. Lena could see a thin gold chain around her neck, a tiny cross hanging at the center. Terri picked at it, her fingers brushing the cross like a talisman. She looked as terrified as Lena felt.

"This way," Lena said. She moved first, straining to hear Terri's shuffling footsteps behind her as she walked toward Jeffrey's office. The squad room was almost empty, only a few cops in from patrol to fill out paperwork or just get in from the cold. Lena felt sweat pouring down her back by the time she got to Jeffrey's office. The walk had been one of the longest of her life.

Terri did not speak until Lena closed the door. "You were at the clinic."

Lena kept her back to the woman, looking out the window at Jeffrey and Dale as they walked around the car.

"I know it was you," Terri said, her voice tight in her throat.

"Yeah," Lena admitted, turning around. Terri was sitting in one of the chairs opposite Jeffrey's desk, her hands gripping the arms as if she could pull them off.

"Terri—"

"Dale will kill me if he finds out." She said this with such conviction that Lena had no doubt Dale would do it.

"He won't hear it from me."

"Who will he hear it from?" She was obviously terrified, and Lena felt her own panic drain away when she realized that they were both bound by their secret. Terri had seen her at the clinic, but Lena had seen Terri, too.

"He'll kill me," she repeated, her thin shoulders shaking.

"I won't tell him," Lena repeated, thinking she was stating the obvious.

"You damn well better not," Terri snapped. The words were meant as a threat, but she lacked the conviction to carry it off. She was almost panting for breath. Tears were in her eyes.

Lena sat down in the chair beside her. "What are you afraid of?"

"You did it, too," she insisted, her voice catching. "You're just as guilty as me. You murdered . . . you killed your . . . you killed . . ."

Again, Lena found her mouth moving but no words coming out.

Terri spat, "I may be going to hell for what I did, but don't forget I can take you with me."

"I know," Lena said. "Terri, I'm not going to tell anybody."

"Oh, God," she said, clutching her fist to her chest. "Please don't tell him."

"I promise," Lena vowed, feeling pity take over. "Terri, it's okay."

"He won't understand."

"I won't tell," she repeated, putting her hand over Terri's.

"It's so hard," she said, grabbing Lena's hand. "It's so hard."

Lena felt tears in her eyes, and she clenched her jaw, fighting the urge to let herself go. "Terri," she began. "Terri, calm down. You're safe here. I won't tell."

"I felt it . . ." she began, holding her stomach. "I felt it moving inside. I felt it kicking. I couldn't do it. I couldn't have another one. I couldn't take . . . I can't . . . I'm not strong enough . . . I can't take it anymore. I can't take it . . ."

"Shh," Lena hushed, smoothing back a wisp of hair that had fallen into Terri's eyes. The woman looked so young, almost like a teenager. For the first time in years, Lena felt the urge to comfort someone. She had been on the receiving end for so long that she had almost forgotten how to offer help. "Look at me," she said, steeling herself, fighting her own emotions. "You're safe, Terri. I won't tell. I won't tell anyone."

"I'm such a bad person," Terri said. "I'm so bad."

"You're not."

"I can't get clean," she confessed. "No matter how much I bathe, I can't get clean."

"I know," Lena said, feeling a weight lifting off her chest as she admitted this. "I know."

"I smell it on me," she said. "The anesthesia. The chemicals."

"I know," Lena said, fighting the urge to slip back into her grief. "Be strong, Terri. You have to be strong."

She nodded. Her shoulders were so slumped she looked as if she might fold in on herself. "He'll never forgive me for this."

Lena didn't know if she meant her husband or some higher power, but she nodded her head in agreement.

"He'll never forgive me."

Lena chanced a look outside the window. Dale was standing at the car but Jeffrey was to the side, talking to Sara Linton. He looked back at the station, throwing his hand out into the air as if he was angry. Sara said something, then Jeffrey nodded, taking what looked like an evidence bag from her. He walked back toward the station.

"Terri," Lena said, feeling the threat of Jeffrey's arrival breathing down her neck. "Listen," she began. "Dry your eyes. Look at me." Terri looked up. "You're okay," Lena said, more like an order than a question.

Terri nodded.

"You have to be okay, Terri." The woman nodded again, understanding Lena's urgency.

She saw Jeffrey in the squad room. He stopped to say something to Marla. "He's coming," she said, and Terri squared her shoulders, straightening up as if she were an actor taking a cue.

Jeffrey knocked on the door as he came into the office. He was obviously disturbed about something, but he held it back. The evidence bag Sara had given him in the parking lot was sticking out of his pocket, but Lena could not tell what it contained. He raised his eyebrows at her, a silent question, and she felt a lurch in her stomach as she realized she hadn't done the one thing he had told her to do.

Without pausing a beat, Lena lied. "Terri says she's never seen anyone at the garage but Dale."

"Yes," Terri said, nodding as she stood from the chair. She kept her eyes averted, and Lena was grateful Jeffrey seemed too preoccupied to notice the woman had been crying.

He didn't even thank her for coming in, instead dismissing her with, "Dale's waiting outside."

"Thank you," Terri said, chancing a look at Lena before she left. The young woman practically ran through the squad room, grabbing her kid from Marla as she made for the front door.

Jeffrey gave Lena the evidence bag, saying, "This was sent to Sara at the clinic."

There was a piece of lined notebook paper inside. Lena turned the bag over, reading the note. The four words were written in purple ink, all caps, taking up half the page. "ABBY WASN'T THE FIRST."

* * * *

Lena walked through the forest, her eyes scanning the ground, willing herself to concentrate. Her thoughts kept darting around like a pinball, one minute hitting against the possibility that there might be another girl buried out in these woods, the next colliding into the memory of the fear in Terri Stanley's voice as she begged Lena not to tell her secret. The woman had been terrified by the prospect of her husband finding out what she had done. Dale seemed harmless, hardly the type of man capable of Ethan's kind of rage, but she understood Terri's fear. She was a young woman who had probably never held a real job outside her home. If Dale left her and their two kids, she would be completely abandoned. Lena understood why she felt trapped, just as she understood Terri's fear of exposure.

All this time, Lena had been concerned about Ethan's reaction, but now she knew there was more to worry about than the threat of his violence. What if Jeffrey found out? God knew she had been through a lot of shit in the last three years — most of it of her own making — but Lena had no idea what would be the final line she crossed that made Jeffrey turn his back on her. His wife was a pediatrician and from what she had seen, he loved kids. It wasn't like they had political discussions all the time. She had no idea where he stood on abortion. She did know, however, that he would be pissed as hell if he found out Lena hadn't really interviewed Terri. They had been so tied up in their mutual fears Lena hadn't asked her about the garage, let alone if there had been any visitors Dale didn't know about. Lena had to find a way to get back in touch with her, to ask her about the cyanide, but she couldn't think how to do this without alerting Jeffrey.

Less than two feet away from her, he was muttering something under his breath. He had called in pretty much every cop on the force, ordering them to the woods to check for other gravesites. The search was exhausting, like combing the ocean for a particular grain of sand, and throughout the day, the temperature in the woods had kept going from one extreme to the other, the hot sun pouring through one minute, the cool shadows of the trees turning her sweat into a chill the next. As night was settling, it became even colder, but Lena had known better than to go back and get her jacket. Jeffrey was acting like a man possessed. She knew he was shouldering the blame for this, just like she knew there was nothing she could say that would help him.

"We should've done this Sunday," Jeffrey said, as if he could have miraculously guessed that one coffin in the forest meant there would be at least another. Lena didn't bother pointing this out; she had tried and failed several times before. Instead, she kept her eyes on the ground, the leaves and pine needles turning into a melted mess as her thoughts went elsewhere and her vision blurred with the threat of tears.

After nearly eight hours of searching and only getting through half of the more than two hundred acres, she doubted she would be able to find a neon sign with a big arrow pointing down, let alone a small metal pipe sticking out of the ground. Not to mention they were losing light fast. The sun was already dipping down low, threatening to disappear behind the horizon at any moment. They had pulled out their flashlights ten minutes ago, but the beams did little to aid the search.

Jeffrey looked up at the trees, rubbing his neck. They had taken one break around lunch, barely pausing to chew the sandwiches Frank had ordered from the local deli.

"Why would someone send that letter to Sara?" Jeffrey asked. "She doesn't have anything to do with this."

"Everyone knows y'all are together," Lena pointed out, wishing she could sit down somewhere. She wanted just ten minutes to herself, time enough to figure out how to get back in touch with Terri. There was the added problem of Dale. How would she explain why she needed to talk to his wife again?

"I don't like Sara mixed up in this," Jeffrey said, and she understood that one of the things driving his anger was the fact that Sara's involvement might put her in jeopardy. "The postmark was local," he said. "It's somebody in the county, in Grant."

"Could be someone from the farm knew better than to mail it from Catoogah," she pointed out, thinking anyone could've dropped a letter by the Grant post office.

"It was sent Monday," he said. "So whoever did it knew what was going on and wanted to warn us." His flashlight beam flickered and he shook it to no avail. "This is fucking ridiculous."

He held his portable radio to his hand, clicking the mic. "Frank?"

A few seconds passed before Frank asked, "Yeah?"

"We'll have to get lights out here," he said. "Call the hardware store and see if we can borrow anything."

"Will do."

Lena waited until Frank had signed off before trying to reason with Jeffrey. "There's no way we'll be able to cover the whole area tonight."

"You want to come out here tomorrow morning and realize some girl could have been saved tonight if we hadn't knocked off early?"

"It's late," she told him. "We could walk right past it and not even know."

"Or we could find it," he told her. "Whatever happens, we're back here tomorrow looking again. I don't care if we have to get bulldozers out here and dig up every fucking square inch. You got me?"

She looked down, continuing to hunt for something she wasn't even sure was there.

Jeffrey followed suit, but he didn't give up. "I should've done this Sunday. We should've been out in full force, gotten volunteers." Jeffrey stopped. "What was going on with you and Terri Stanley?"

Her attempt at a casual, "What do you mean?" sounded pathetic even to Lena.

"Don't dick me around," he warned. "Something's going on."

Lena licked her lips, feeling like a trapped animal. "She had too much to drink at the picnic last year," Lena lied. "I found her in the bathroom with her head in the toilet."

"She's an alcoholic?" Jeffrey asked, obviously ready to condemn the woman.

Lena knew this was one of his buttons, and not knowing what else to do, she pressed it hard. "Yeah," she said, thinking Terri Stanley could live with Jeffrey thinking she was a drunk as long as her husband didn't find out what she was doing in Atlanta last week.

Jeffrey asked, "You think she makes a habit of it?"

"Don't know."

"She was sick?" he asked. "Throwing up?"

Lena felt a cold sweat, forcing herself to lie, knowing even as she did it that she was making the best choice given the circumstances. "I told her she'd better straighten out," she said. "I think she's got it under control."

"I'll talk to Sara," he said, and her heart sank. "She'll call Child Services."

"No," Lena said, trying not to sound desperate. It was one thing to lie, quite another to get Terri into trouble. "I told you she's got it under control. She's going to meetings and everything." She racked her brain for some of Hank's AA talk, feeling like a spider caught in its own web. "Got her chip last month."

He narrowed his eyes, probably trying to decide if she was being honest or not.

"Chief?" his radio crackled. "West corner near the college. We've got something."

Jeffrey took off, and Lena found herself running after him, the beam from her flashlight bobbing as she pumped her arms. Jeffrey had at least ten years on her, but he was a hell of a lot faster than she was. When he made it to the crowd of uniformed patrolmen standing in the clearing, she was still a good twenty feet behind him.

By the time she caught up, Jeffrey was kneeling beside an indentation in the earth. A rusted metal pipe was sticking up about two inches into the air. Whoever had spotted the site must have done so out of sheer luck. Even knowing what to look for, Lena was having trouble keeping her focus on the pipe.

Brad Stephens came running from behind her. He was holding two shovels and a crowbar. Jeffrey grabbed one of the shovels and they both started digging. The night air was cool, but they were both sweating by the time the first shovel thumped against wood. The hollow sound stayed in Lena's ears as Jeffrey knelt down to brush away the last of the dirt with his hands. He must have done this same thing with Sara on Sunday. She couldn't imagine what the anticipation

had been like for him, the dread when he realized what he was un-
covering. Even now, Lena was having a hard time accepting that
someone in Grant was capable of doing such a horrible thing.

Brad jammed the crowbar into the edge of the box, and together
he and Jeffrey worked to pry away the wood. One slat came up,
flashlights shining eagerly into the opening. A foul odor escaped—
not of rotting flesh, but of mustiness and decay. Jeffrey put his
shoulder into the crowbar as he pried another board, the wood bending back on itself like a folded sheet of paper. The pulp was soaking
wet, dirt staining it a dark black. Obviously, the box had been buried
in the earth for a long time. In the crime scene photos of the grave by
the lake, the grave had looked new, the green pressure-treated wood
doing its job of holding back the elements even as it held in the girl.

Using his bare hands, Jeffrey pulled up the sixth board. Flashlights illuminated the interior of the stained box. He sat back on his
heels, his shoulders sagging either from relief or disappointment.
Lena felt her own mixture of both emotions.

The box was empty.

* * * *

Lena had stayed around the potential crime scene until the last sample was taken. The box had practically disintegrated over time, the
wood soaking into the ground. That the box was older than the first
they had found was obvious, just as it was obvious that the box had
been used for the same thing. Deep fingernail scratches gouged out
the top pieces Jeffrey had pried away. Dark stains riddled the bottom. Someone had bled in there, shit in there, maybe died in there.
When and why were just two more questions to add to the growing
list. Thankfully, Jeffrey had finally accepted that they couldn't continue looking for another box in the pitch dark. He had called off the
search and told a crew of ten to show back up at daybreak.

Back at the station, Lena had washed her hands, not bothering to
change into the spare outfit she kept in her locker, knowing nothing
but a long, hot shower could wash away some of the distress she was
feeling. Yet, when she came to the road that led into her neighborhood, she found herself downshifting the Celica, making an illegal

U-turn to bypass her street. She unlatched her seat belt and drove with her knees while she shrugged off her jacket. The windows slid down with the touch of a button, and she turned off the noise coming from the radio, wondering how long it had been since she had a moment to herself like this. Ethan thought she was still at work. Nan was probably getting ready for bed and Lena was totally alone with nothing but her own thoughts to keep her company.

She drove through downtown again, slowing as she passed the diner, thinking about Sibyl, the last time she had seen her. Lena had screwed up so many things since then. There was a time when no matter what, she didn't let her personal life interfere with her job. Being a cop was the one thing she was good at, the one thing Lena knew how to do. She had let her connection to Terri Stanley get in the way of her duties. Yet again, her emotions were jeopardizing the only thing in Lena's life that was a constant. What would Sibyl say about Lena now? How ashamed would her sister be at the kind of person Lena had become?

Main Street dead-ended at the entrance of the college, and Lena took a left into the children's clinic, turning around and heading back out of town. She rolled up the windows as the chill got to her and found herself fiddling with the dials on the radio, trying to find something soft to keep her company. She glanced up as she passed the Stop-N-Go, and recognized the black Dodge Dart parked beside one of the gas pumps.

Without thinking, Lena did a U-turn, pulling parallel to the Dart. She got out of her car, looking into the market for Terri Stanley. She was inside, paying the guy behind the register, and even from this distance, Lena could almost smell the defeat on her. Shoulders slumped, eyes cast down. Lena suppressed the urge to thank God she'd happened to run into her.

The Celica's gas tank was almost full, but Lena turned on the pump anyway, taking her time removing the gas cap and putting in the nozzle. By the first click of the pump, Terri had come out of the store. She was wearing a thin blue Member's Only jacket, and she pushed the sleeves up to her elbows as she walked across the brightly lit filling station. Terri was obviously preoccupied as she walked to her car, and Lena cleared her throat several times before the woman noticed her.

"Oh," Terri said, the same word she had uttered the first time she'd seen Lena at the police station.

"Hey." Lena's smile felt awkward on her face. "I need to ask you—"

"Are you following me?" Terri looked around as if she was scared someone would see them together.

"I was just getting gas." Lena took the nozzle out of the Celica, hoping Terri didn't notice she'd put in less than half a gallon. "I need to talk to you."

"Dale's waiting for me," she said, tugging down the sleeves of her jacket. Lena had seen something, though—something all too familiar. They both stood there for the longest minute of Lena's life, neither one knowing what to say.

"Terri . . ."

Her only answer was, "I need to go."

Lena felt words sticking in her throat like molasses. She heard a high-pitched noise in her ear, almost like a siren warning her away. She asked, "Does he hit you?"

Terri looked down at the oil-stained concrete, ashamed. Lena knew that shame, but on Terri it brought out anger in Lena like she hadn't known in a while.

"He hits you," Lena said, narrowing the space between them as if she needed to be close to be heard. "Come here," she said, grabbing Terri's arm. The woman winced from pain as Lena yanked up the sleeve. A black bruise snaked up her arm.

Terri didn't move away. "It's not like that."

"What's it like?"

"You don't understand."

"The hell I don't," she said, tightening her grip. "Is that why you did it?" she demanded, anger sparking like a brush fire. "Is that why you were in Atlanta?"

Terri tried to squirm away. "Please let me go."

Lena felt her rage becoming uncontrollable. "You're scared of him," she said. "That's why you did it, you coward."

"Please . . ."

"Please what?" Lena asked. "Please what?" Terri was crying in earnest now, trying so hard to pull away that she was almost on the ground. Lena let go, horrified when she saw a red mark on Terri's wrist working its way below the bruise Dale had made. "Terri—"

"Leave me alone."

"You don't have to do this."

She headed back to her car. "I'm going."

"I'm sorry," Lena said, following her.

"You sound like Dale."

A knife in her stomach would have been easier. Still, Lena tried, "Please. Let me help you."

"I don't need your help," she spat, yanking open the car door.

"Terri—"

"Leave me alone!" she screamed, slamming the door with a loud bang. She locked the door as if she was afraid Lena might pull her out of the car.

"Terri—" Lena tried again, but she had pulled away, tires burning rubber on the pavement, the hose from the gas pump stretching, then popping out of the Dart's gas tank. Lena stepped back quickly as gas splattered onto the ground.

"Hey!" the attendant called. "What's going on here?"

"Nothing," she told him, picking up the nozzle and replacing it on the pump. She dug into her pocket and tossed two dollars at the young man, saying, "Here. Go back inside." She climbed back into her car before he could yell anything else.

The Celica's tires caught against the pavement, the car fishtailing as she pulled away. She didn't realize she was speeding until she blew past a broken-down station wagon that had been parked on the side of the road for the last week. She forced her foot to back off on the accelerator, her heart still pounding in her chest. Terri had been terrified of Lena, looking at her like she was scared she'd be hurt. Maybe Lena would have hurt her. Maybe she would have turned violent, taking her rage out on that poor helpless woman just because she could. What the hell was wrong with her? Standing at the gas station, yelling at Terri, she had felt like she was yelling at herself. *She* was the coward. *She* was the one who was scared of what might be done to her if anyone found out.

The car had slowed to almost a crawl. She was on the outskirts of Heartsdale now, a good twenty minutes from home. The cemetery where Sibyl was buried was out this way, on a flat plain behind the

Baptist church. After her sister had died, Lena had gone there at least once, sometimes twice a week, to visit her grave. Over time, she had cut down on her visits, then stopped going altogether. With a shock, Lena realized she hadn't visited Sibyl in at least three months. She had been too busy, too wrapped up in doing her job and dealing with Ethan. Now, at the height of her shame, she could think of nothing more appropriate than going to the graveyard.

She parked at the front of the church, leaving her windows down and the doors unlocked as she walked toward the front gates of the memorial garden. The area was well-lit, overhead lights illuminating the grounds. She knew she had driven here for a reason. She knew what she needed to do.

Someone had planted a handful of pansies by the entrance to the cemetery, and they swayed in the breeze as Lena walked by. Sibyl's grave was to the side of the grounds that bordered the church, and Lena took her time walking through the grassy lawn, enjoying the solitude. She had spent almost twelve hours straight on her feet today, but something about being here, being close to Sibyl, made the walk less daunting. Sibyl would have approved of being buried here, Lena always thought. She had loved the outdoors.

The cement block Lena had upended and used for a bench was still on the ground beside Sibyl's marker, and Lena sat down, wrapping her arms around her knees. In the daytime, a huge pecan tree gave shade to the spot, tendrils of sunlight slipping through the leaves. The marble slab marking Sibyl's final resting place had been cleaned to a shine, and a quick look around at the other gravesites proved that this had been done by a visitor rather than the staff.

There weren't any flowers. Nan was allergic.

Like a faucet being turned on, Lena felt tears pool into her eyes. She was such a horrible person. As bad as Dale was to Terri, Lena had been worse. She was a cop, she had a duty to protect people, not scare the shit out of them, not grab their wrist so hard that she left a bruise. She was certainly in no position to call Terri Stanley a coward. If anything, Lena was the coward. She was the one who had scurried off to Atlanta under the cover of lies, paying some stranger to slice out her mistakes, hiding from the repercussions like a frightened child.

The altercation with Terri had brought back all the memories

Lena had tried to suppress, and she found herself back in Atlanta, re-living the whole ordeal again. She was in the car with Hank, his silence cutting like a knife. She was in the clinic, sitting across from Terri, avoiding her eyes, praying it would be over. She was taken back to the freezing operating room, her feet resting in the icy cold stirrups, her legs splayed for the doctor who spoke so calmly, so quietly, that Lena had felt herself being lulled into a sort of hypnotic state. Everything was going to be fine. Everything will be okay. Just relax. Just breathe. Take it slow. Relax. It's all over. Sit up. Here are your clothes. Call us if there are complications. You all right, darlin'? Do you have someone waiting for you? Just sit in the chair. We'll take you outside. Murderer. Baby killer. Butcher. Monster.

The protesters had been waiting outside the clinic, sitting in their lawn chairs, sipping from their thermoses of hot coffee, for all intents and purposes looking like tailgaters waiting for the big game. Lena's appearance had caused them all to stand in unison, to scream at her, waving signs with all sorts of graphic, bloody pictures. Obscenely, one even held up a jar, the implied contents obvious to anyone standing within ten feet of it. Still, it didn't look real, and she wondered at the man — of course it was a man — sitting at home, maybe at his kitchen table where his kids sat and had breakfast every morning, preparing the mixture in the jar just to torment frightened women who were making what Lena knew was the most difficult decision of their lives.

Now, sitting in the cemetery, staring at her sister's grave, Lena let herself wonder for the first time what the clinic did with the flesh and bone they had removed from her own body. Was it lying somewhere in an incinerator, waiting to ignite? Was it buried in the earth, an unmarked grave she would never see? She felt a clenching deep down in her gut, in her womb, as she thought of what she had done — what she had lost.

In her mind, she told Sibyl what had happened, the choices she had made that brought her here. She talked about Ethan, how something inside of her had died when she started seeing him, how she had let everything good about herself ebb away like sand being taken with the tide. She told her about Terri, the fear in her eyes. If only she could take it all back. If only she had never met Ethan, never seen Terri at the clinic. Everything was going from bad to worse. She

was telling lies to cover lies, burying herself in deceit. She couldn't
see a way out of it.

What Lena wanted most of all was to have her sister there, if only
for a moment, to tell her that everything was going to be okay. That
had been the nature of their relationship from the beginning of time:
Lena fucked up and Sibyl smoothed things over, talking it through
with her, making her see the other side. Without her guiding wisdom, it all seemed like such a lost cause. Lena was falling apart.
There was no way she could have given birth to Ethan's child. She
could barely take care of herself.

"Lee?"

She turned around, nearly falling off the narrow block. "Greg?"

He emerged from the darkness, the moon glowing behind him. He
was limping toward her, his cane in one hand, a bouquet of flowers in
the other.

She stood quickly, wiping her eyes, trying to hide her shock.
"What are you doing here?" she asked, rubbing grit off the back of
her pants.

He dropped the bouquet to his side. "I can come back when you're
finished."

"No," she told him, hoping the darkness hid the fact that she had
been crying. "I just . . . it's fine." She glanced back at the grave so
that she wouldn't have to look at him. She had a flash of Abigail Bennett, buried alive, and Lena felt an unreasonable panic fill her. For
just a split second she thought of her sister alive, begging for help,
trying to claw her way out of the casket.

She wiped her eyes before looking back at him, thinking she must
be losing her mind. She wanted to tell him everything that had happened—not just in Atlanta, but before then, back to that day she had
returned to the police station after running some samples to Macon,
only to have Jeffrey tell her that Sibyl was gone. She wanted to put
her head on his shoulder and feel his comfort. More than anything,
she wanted his absolution.

"Lee?" Greg asked.

She searched for a response. "I was just wondering why you're
here."

"I had to get Mama to bring me," he explained. "She's back in the
car."

Lena looked over his shoulder as if she could see the parking lot in front of the church. "It's kind of late."

"She tricked me," he said. "Made me go to her knitting circle with her."

Her tongue felt thick in her mouth, but she wanted nothing more than to keep hearing him talk. She had forgotten how soothing his voice could be, how gentle the sound. "Did she make you hold the yarn?"

He laughed. "Yeah. You'd think I'd quit falling for that."

Lena felt herself smile, knowing he hadn't been tricked. Greg would deny it at gunpoint, but he had always been a mama's boy.

"I brought these for Sibby," he said, holding up the flowers again. "I came yesterday and there weren't any, so I figured . . ." He smiled. In the moonlight, she saw he still hadn't managed to fix the tooth she had accidentally chipped during a game of Frisbee.

He said, "She loved daisies," handing Lena the flowers. For just a second, their hands brushed, and she felt as if she had touched a live wire.

For his part, Greg seemed unfazed. He started to leave, but Lena said, "Wait."

Slowly, he turned back around.

"Sit down," she told him, indicating the block.

"I don't want to take your seat."

"It's okay." She stepped back to place the flowers in front of Sibyl's marker. When she looked back up, Greg was leaning on his cane, watching her.

He asked, "You okay?"

Lena tried to think of something to say. She sniffed, wondering if her eyes were as red as they felt. "Allergies," she told him.

"Yeah."

Lena crossed her hands behind her back so she wouldn't wring them again. "How'd you hurt your leg, exactly?"

"Car accident," he told her, then smiled again. "Totally my fault. I was trying to find a CD and I took my eyes off the road for just a second."

"That's all it takes."

"Yeah," he said, then, "Mister Jingles died last year."

His cat. She had hated the thing, but for some reason she was sad to hear that he was gone. "I'm sorry."

The breeze picked up, the tree overhead shushing in the wind.

Greg squinted at the moon, then looked back at Lena. "When Mom told me about Sibyl . . ." His voice trailed off, and he dug his cane into the ground, pushing up some grass. She thought she saw tears in his eyes and made herself look away so that his sadness did not reignite her own.

He said, "I just couldn't believe it."

"I guess she told you about me, too."

He nodded, and he did something that not many people could do when they talked about rape: he looked her right in the eye. "She was upset."

Lena didn't try to hide her sarcasm. "I bet."

"No, really," Greg assured her, still looking at her, his clear blue eyes void of any guile. "My aunt Shelby—you remember her?" Lena nodded. "She was raped when they were in high school. It was pretty bad."

"I didn't know," Lena said. She had met Shelby a few times. As with Greg's mother, they hadn't exactly bonded. Lena would never have guessed the older woman had something like that in her life. She was very tightly wound, but most of the women in the Mitchell family were. The one thing Lena had been astounded by since her attack was that being raped had put her in what was not exactly an exclusive club.

"If I had known . . ." Greg began, but didn't finish.

"What?" she asked.

"I don't know." He reached down and picked up a pecan that had fallen off the tree. "I was really upset to hear it."

"It was pretty upsetting," Lena allowed, and surprise registered on his face. She asked, "What?"

"I don't know," he repeated, tossing the pecan into the wood. "You used to not say things like that."

"Like what?"

"Like feelings."

She forced out a laugh. Her whole life was a struggle with feelings. "What things did I used to say?"

He mulled it over. " 'That's life?' " he tried, mimicking her one-sided shrug. " 'Tough shit?' "

She knew he was right, but she couldn't begin to know how to explain it. "People change."

"Nan says you're seeing somebody."

"Yeah, well," was all she could say, but her heart had flipped in her chest at the thought of him bothering to ask. She was going to kill Nan for not telling her.

He said, "Nan looks good."

"She's had a hard time."

"I couldn't believe y'all were living together."

"She's a good person. I didn't really see that before." Hell, she didn't see a lot of things before. Lena had made an art out of fucking up anything remotely positive in her life. Greg was living proof of that.

For lack of something to do, she looked up at the tree. The leaves were ready to fall. Greg made to leave again and she asked, "What CD?"

"Huh?"

"Your accident," she pointed to his leg. "What CD were you looking for?"

"Heart," he said, a goofy grin breaking out on his face.

"*Bebe Le Strange*?" she asked, feeling herself grin back. Saturday had always been chore day when they lived together, and they had listened to that particular Heart album so many times that to this day Lena couldn't scrub a toilet without hearing "Even It Up" in her head.

"It was the new one," he told her.

"New one?"

"They came out with a new one about a year ago."

"That Lovemonger stuff?"

"No," he said, his excitement palpable. The only thing Greg loved more than listening to music was talking about it. "Kick-ass stuff. Back to the seventies Heart stuff. I can't believe you don't know about it. I was knocking on the door the first day it was out."

She realized then how long it had been since she had listened to music she really enjoyed. Ethan preferred punk rock, the kind of disaffected crap spoiled white boys screeched to. Lena didn't even know where her old CDs were.

"Lee?"

She had missed something he'd said. "Sorry, what?"

"I need to go," he told her. "Mama's waiting."

Suddenly, she felt like crying again. She forced her feet to stay on the ground and not do something foolish, like run toward him. God, she was turning into a sniveling idiot. She was like one of those stupid women in romance novels.

He said, "Take care of yourself."

"Yeah," she said, trying to think of something to keep him from going. "You, too."

She realized she was still holding the daisies, and she leaned down to put them on Sibyl's grave. When she looked back up, Greg was limping toward the parking lot. She kept staring, willing him to turn around. He didn't.

WEDNESDAY

CHAPTER NINE

Jeffrey leaned against the tile, letting the hot water from the shower blast his skin. He had bathed last night, but nothing could get rid of the feeling that he was covered in dirt. Not just dirt, but dirt from a grave. Opening that second box, smelling the musty scent of decay, had been almost as bad as finding Abby. The second box changed everything. One more girl was out there, one more family, one more death. At least he hoped it was just one girl. The lab wouldn't be able to come back with DNA until the end of the week. Between that and analyzing the letter Sara had been sent, the tests were costing him half his budget for the rest of the year, but Jeffrey didn't care. He would get another job down at the Texaco pumping gas if he had to. Meanwhile, some Georgia state representative was in Washington right now enjoying a two-hundred-dollar breakfast.

He forced himself to get out of the shower, still feeling like he needed another hour under the hot water. Sara had obviously come in at some point and put a cup of coffee on the shelf over the sink, but he hadn't heard her. Last night, he had called her from the scene, giving her the bare details of the find. After that, Jeffrey had driven what little evidence they found in the box to Macon himself, then gone back to the station and reviewed every note he had on the case. He made lists ten pages long of who he should talk to, what leads they should follow. By then, it was midnight, and he had found himself trying to decide whether or not to go to Sara's or his own home. He even drove by his house, too late remembering that the girls had already moved in. Around one in the morning, the lights were still on and he could hear music from the street as a party raged inside. He had been too tired to go in and tell them to turn it off.

Jeffrey slipped on a pair of jeans and walked into the kitchen, car-

191

rying his cup of coffee. Sara was at the couch, folding the blanket he had used last night.

He said, "I didn't want to wake you," and she nodded. He knew she didn't believe him, just like he knew that he was telling the truth. Like it or not, his nights had been spent alone for most of the last few years, and he hadn't known how to bring what he had found out there in the woods home to Sara. Even after what had happened in the kitchen two nights ago, getting in bed with her, climbing in between the fresh sheets, would have felt like a violation.

He saw her empty mug on the counter and asked, "You want some more coffee?"

She shook her head, smoothing down the blanket as she put it on the foot of the couch.

He poured the coffee anyway. When he turned around, Sara was sitting at the kitchen island, sorting through some mail.

"I'm sorry," he said.

"For what?"

"I feel like . . ." His voice trailed off. He didn't know what he felt like.

She flipped through a magazine, not touching the coffee he'd poured. When he didn't finish his thought, she looked up. "You don't have to explain it to me," she said, and he felt as if a great weight had been lifted.

Still, he tried, "It was a hard night."

She smiled at him, concern keeping the expression from reaching her eyes. "You know I understand."

Jeffrey still felt tension in the air, but he didn't know if it was from Sara or his own imagination. He reached out to touch her and she said, "You should wrap your hand."

He had taken off the bandage after digging in the forest. Jeffrey looked at the cut, which was bright red. As he thought about it, he felt the wound throb. "I think it's infected."

"Have you been taking the pills I gave you?"

"Yes."

She looked up from the magazine, calling him on the lie.

"Some," he said, wondering where he had put the damn things. "I took some. Two."

"That's even better," she said, returning to the magazine. "You can build up your resistance to antibiotics." She flipped through a few more pages.

He tried for humor. "The hepatitis will kill me anyway."

She looked up, and he saw tears well into her eyes at the suggestion. "That's not funny."

"No," he admitted. "I just . . . I needed to be alone. Last night."

She wiped her eyes. "I know."

Still, he had to ask, "You're not mad at me?"

"Of course not," she insisted, reaching out to take his uninjured hand. She squeezed it, then let go, returning to her magazine. He saw it was the *Lancet*, an overseas medical journal.

"I wouldn't have been much company anyway," he told her, remembering his sleepless night. "I kept thinking about it," he said. "It's worse finding it empty, not knowing what happened."

She finally closed the magazine and gave him her full attention. "Before, you'd said maybe someone came back for the bodies after they died."

"I know," he told her, and that was one of the things that had kept him from sleep. He had seen some pretty horrible things in his line of work, but someone who was sick enough to kill a girl, then remove her body for whatever reason, was a perpetrator he was unprepared to deal with. "What kind of person would do that?" he asked.

"A mentally ill person," she answered. Sara was a scientist at heart, and she thought there were concrete reasons that explained why people did things. She had never believed in evil, but then she had never knowingly sat across from someone who had murdered in cold blood or raped a child. Like most people, she had the luxury of philosophizing about it from behind her textbooks. Out in the field, he saw things very differently, and Jeffrey had to think that anyone capable of this crime had to have something fundamentally wrong with his soul.

Sara slid off the stool. "They should be able to do the blood types today," she told him, opening the cabinet beside the sink. She took out the sample packets of antibiotics and opened one, then another. "I called Ron Beard at the state lab while you were in the shower. He's going to run the tests first thing this morning. At least we'll have some idea how many victims there might have been."

Jeffrey took the pills and washed them down with some coffee.

She handed him two other sample packs. "Will you please take these after lunch?"

He would probably skip lunch, but he agreed anyway. "What do you think of Terri Stanley?"

She shrugged. "She seems nice. Overwhelmed, but who wouldn't be?"

"Do you think she drinks?"

"Alcohol?" Sara asked, surprised. "I've never smelled it on her. Why?"

"Lena said she saw her getting sick at the picnic last year."

"The police picnic?" she questioned. "I don't think Lena was there. Wasn't she on her hiatus then?"

Jeffrey let that settle in, ignoring the tone she gave "hiatus." He told her, "Lena said she saw her at the picnic."

"You can check your calendar," she said. "Maybe I'm wrong, but I don't think she was there."

Sara was never wrong about dates. Jeffrey felt a niggling question working its way through his brain. Why had Lena lied? What was she trying to hide this time?

"Maybe she meant the one before last?" Sara suggested. "I recall a lot of people drinking too much at that one." She chuckled. "Remember Frank kept singing the national anthem like he was Ethel Merman?"

"Yeah," he agreed, but Jeffrey knew that Lena had lied. He just couldn't figure out why. As far as he knew, she wasn't particularly close to Terri Stanley. Hell, as far as he knew, Lena wasn't close to anybody. She didn't even have a dog.

Sara asked, "What are you going to do today?"

He tried to get his mind back on track. "If Lev was telling the truth, I should have some people from the farm first thing. We'll see if he goes through with the polygraph. We're going to talk to them, see if anyone knows what happened to Abby." He added, "Don't worry, I'm not expecting a full confession."

"What about Chip Donner?"

"We've got an APB on him," Jeffrey said. "I don't know, Sara, I don't like him for this. He's just a stupid punk. I don't see him having the discipline to plan it out. And that second box was old. Maybe four, five years. Chip was in jail then. That's pretty much the only fact we know."

"Who do you think did it, then?"

"There's the foreman, Cole," Jeffrey began. "The brothers. The sisters. Abby's mother and father. Dale Stanley." He sighed. "Basically, everybody I've talked to since this whole damn thing started."

"But no one stands out?"

"Cole," he said.

"But only because he was yelling to those people about God?"

"Yes," he admitted, and coming from Sara it did sound like a weak connection. He had made an effort to back Lena off the religious angle, but he felt maybe he had picked up some of her prejudices. "I want to talk to the family again, maybe get them alone."

"Get the women alone," she suggested. "They might be more talkative without their brothers around."

"Good idea." He tried again, "I really don't want you mixed up with these people, Sara. I don't much like Tessa being involved, either."

"Why?"

"Because I've got a hunch," he said. "And my hunch tells me that they're up to something. I just don't know what."

"Being devout is hardly a crime," she said. "You'd have to arrest my mother if that were the case." Then added, "Actually, you'd have to arrest most of my family."

"I'm not saying it has anything to do with religion," Jeffrey said. "It's how they act."

"How do they act?"

"Like they've got something to hide."

Sara leaned against the counter. He could tell she wasn't going to give in. "Tessa asked me to do this for her."

"And I'm asking you not to."

She seemed surprised. "You want me to choose between you and my family?"

That was exactly what he had been asking, but Jeffrey knew better than to say it. He had lost that contest once before, but this time he was more familiar with the rules. "I just want you to be careful," he told her.

Sara opened her mouth to respond, but the phone rang. She spent a few seconds looking for the cordless receiver before finding it on the coffee table. "Hello?"

She listened a moment, then handed the phone to Jeffrey.

"Tolliver," he said, surprised to hear a woman's voice answer him.

"It's Esther Bennett," she said in a hoarse whisper. "Your card. The one you gave me. It had this number on it. I'm sorry, I—" Her voice broke into a sob.

Sara gave him a puzzled look and Jeffrey shook his head. "Esther," he said into the phone. "What's wrong?"

"It's Becca," she said, her voice shaking with grief. "She's missing."

* * * *

Jeffrey pulled his car into the parking lot of Dipsy's Diner, thinking he hadn't been to the joint since Joe Smith, Catoogah's previous sheriff, had been in office. When Jeffrey first started working in Grant County, the two men had met every couple of months for stale coffee and rubber pancakes. As time passed and meth started to be more of a problem for their small towns, their meetings became more serious and more regular. When Ed Pelham had taken over, Jeffrey hadn't even suggested a courtesy call, let alone a meal with the man. As far as he was concerned, Two-Bit couldn't fill a three-year-old girl's shoes, let alone the boots of a man like Joe Smith.

Jeffrey scanned the vacant parking lot, wondering how Esther Bennett knew about this place. He couldn't imagine the woman eating anything that didn't come from her own oven, picked from her own garden. If Dipsy's was her idea of a restaurant, she'd be better off eating cardboard at home.

May-Lynn Bledsoe was behind the counter when he walked into the diner, and she shot him a caustic look. "I's beginning to think you didn't love me no more."

"Couldn't be possible," he said, wondering why she was making an attempt at banter. He'd been in this diner maybe fifty times and she had never given him the time of day. He glanced around the room, noting it was empty.

"You beat the rush," she said, though he doubted people would be banging down the door anytime soon. Between May-Lynn's sour attitude and the tepid coffee, there wasn't much to recommend the

place. Joe Smith had been a fan of their cheese and onion home fries
and always asked for a triple order with his coffee. Jeffrey imagined
Joe's sudden heart attack at the age of fifty-six had put some people
off.

He saw a late-model Toyota pull into the parking lot and waited
for the driver to get out. The early morning wind was whipping up
dirt and sand in the gravel parking lot, and when Esther Bennett got
out of the car, the door caught back on her. Jeffrey went to help her,
but May-Lynn was in front of the door like she was afraid he'd
change his mind and leave. She was picking something out of her
back teeth that caused her to put her pinky finger into her mouth up
to the third knuckle as she asked, "You want the usual?"

"Just coffee, please," he said, watching Esther quickly take the
steps to the entrance, clutching her coat closed with both hands. The
bell over the door clanged as she walked in, and he stood to greet her.

"Chief Tolliver," Esther said, breathless. "I'm sorry I'm late."

"You're fine," he told her, indicating she should sit down. He tried
to take her coat, but she wouldn't let him.

"I'm sorry," she repeated, sliding into the booth, her sense of urgency as palpable as the smell of grilled onions in the air.

He sat across from her. "Tell me what's going on."

A long shadow was cast over the table, and he looked up to find
May-Lynn standing beside him, pad in her hand. Esther looked at
her, confused for a second before asking, "May I have some water,
please?"

The waitress twisted her lips to the side as if she'd just calculated
her tip. "Water."

Jeffrey waited for her to saunter back behind the counter before
asking Esther, "How long has she been missing?"

"Just since last night," Esther said, her lower lip trembling. "Lev and
Paul said I should wait a day to see if she comes back, but I can't . . ."

"It's okay," he said, wondering how anybody could look at this
panicked woman and tell her to wait. "When did you notice she was
gone?"

"I got up to check on her. With Abby—" she stopped, her throat
working. "I wanted to check on Becca, to make sure she was sleeping." She put her hand to her mouth. "I went into her room, and—"

"Water," May-Lynn said, sloshing a glass down in front of Esther.

Jeffrey's patience was up. "Give us a minute, okay?"

May-Lynn shrugged, as if he was in the wrong, before shuffling back to the counter.

Jeffrey took his turn with the apologies as he dabbed up the spilled water with a handful of flimsy paper napkins. "I'm sorry about that," he told Esther. "Business is kind of slow."

Esther watched his hands as if she had never seen anyone clean a table. Jeffrey thought it was more likely she'd never seen a man clean up after himself. He asked, "So, you saw last night that she was gone?"

"I called Rachel first. Becca stayed with my sister the night we realized Abby was missing. I didn't want her out in the dark with us while we searched. I needed to know where she was." Esther paused, taking a sip of water. Jeffrey saw that her hand trembled. "I thought she might have gone back there."

"But she hadn't?"

Esther shook her head. "I called Paul next," she said. "He told me not to worry." She made an almost disgusted sound. "Lev said the same thing. She's always come back, but with Abby . . ." She gulped in air as if she couldn't breathe. "With Abby gone . . ."

"Did she say anything before she left?" Jeffrey asked. "Maybe she was acting differently?"

Esther dug into the pocket of her coat and pulled out a piece of paper. "She left this."

Jeffrey took the folded note the woman offered, feeling a little like he had been tricked. The paper had a pink tint, the ink was black. A girlish scrawl read, "Mama, Don't worry about me. I'll be back."

Jeffrey stared at the note, not knowing what to say. The fact that the girl had left a note changed a lot of things. "This is her writing?"

"Yes."

"On Monday, you told my detective that Rebecca has run away before."

"Not like this," she insisted. "She's never left a note before."

Jeffrey thought in the scheme of things the girl was probably just trying to be considerate. "How many times has this happened?"

"In May and June of last year," she listed. "Then February this year."

"Do you know any reason why she might run away?"

"I don't understand."

Jeffrey tried to phrase his words carefully. "Girls don't usually just up and run away. Usually they're running away from something."

He could have slapped the woman in the face and got a better response. She folded the note and tucked it back into her pocket as she stood. "I'm sorry I wasted your time."

"Mrs. Bennett—"

She was halfway out the door, and he just missed catching her as she ran down the stairs.

"Mrs. Bennett," he said, following her into the parking lot. "Don't go like this."

"They said you'd say that."

"Who said?"

"My husband. My brothers." Her shoulders were shaking. She took out a tissue and wiped her nose. "They said you would blame us, that it was useless to even try to talk to you."

"I don't recall blaming anybody."

She shook her head as she turned around. "I know what you're thinking, Chief Tolliver."

"I doubt—"

"Paul said you'd be this way. Outsiders never understand. We've come to accept that. I don't know why I tried." She pressed her lips together, her resolve strengthened by anger. "You may not agree with my beliefs, but I am a mother. One of my daughters is dead and the other is missing. I know something is wrong. I know that Rebecca would never be so selfish as to leave me at a time like this unless she felt she had to."

Jeffrey thought she was answering his earlier question without admitting it to herself. He tried to be even more careful this time. "Why would she have to?"

Esther seemed to cast around for an answer, but didn't offer it to Jeffrey.

He tried again. "Why would she have to leave?"

"I know what you're thinking."

Again, he pressed, "Why would she leave?"

She said nothing.

"Mrs. Bennett?"

She gave up, tossing her hands into the air, crying, "I don't know!"

Jeffrey let Esther stand there, cold wind whipping up her collar. Her nose was red from crying, tears running down her cheeks. "She wouldn't do this," she sobbed. "She wouldn't do this unless she had to."

After a few more seconds, Jeffrey reached past her and opened the car door. He helped Esther inside, kneeling beside her so they could talk. He knew without looking that May-Lynn was standing at the window watching the show, and he wanted to do everything he could to protect Esther Bennett.

He hoped she heard his compassion when he asked her, "Tell me what she was running away from."

Esther dabbed at her eyes, then concentrated on the tissue in her hand, folding and unfolding it as if she could find the answer somewhere on the crumpled paper. "She's so different from Abby," she finally said. "So rebellious. Nothing like me at that age. Nothing like any of us." Despite her words, she insisted, "She's so precious. Such a powerful soul. My fierce little angel."

Jeffrey asked, "What was she rebelling against?"

"Rules," Esther said. "Everything she could find."

"When she ran away before," Jeffrey began. "Where did she go?"

"She said she camped in the woods."

Jeffrey felt his heart stop. "Which woods?"

"The Catoogah forest. When they were children, they camped there all the time."

"Not the state park in Grant?"

She shook her head. "How would she get there?" she asked. "It's miles from home."

Jeffrey didn't like the idea of Rebecca being in any forest, especially considering what had happened to her sister. "Was she seeing any boys?"

"I don't know," she confessed. "I don't know anything about her life. I thought I knew about Abby, but now . . ." She put her hand to her mouth. "I don't know anything."

Jeffrey's knee started to ache and he sat back on his heels to take off the pressure. "Rebecca didn't want to be in the church?" he guessed.

"We let them choose. We don't force them into the life. Mary's children chose . . ." She took a deep breath, letting it go slowly. "We let them choose when they're old enough to know their own minds. Lev went off to college. Paul strayed for a while. He came back, but I never stopped loving him. He never stopped being my brother." She threw her hands into the air. "I just don't understand. Why would she leave? Why would she do this now?"

Jeffrey had dealt with many missing-children cases over the years. Thankfully, most of them had resolved themselves fairly easily. The kid got cold or hungry and came back, realizing there were worse things than having to clean up your room or eat your peas. Something told him Rebecca Bennett wasn't running away from chores, but he felt the need to calm some of Esther's fears.

He spoke as gently as he could. "Becca's run away before."

"Yes."

"She always comes back in a day or two."

"She's always come back to her family—all of her family." She seemed almost defeated, as if Jeffrey wasn't understanding her. "We're not what you think."

He wasn't sure what he thought. He hated to admit it, but he was seeing why her brothers hadn't been as alarmed as Esther. If Rebecca made a habit of running away for a few days, scaring the crap out of everybody and then coming back, this could be just another cry for attention. The question was, why did she feel she needed attention? Was it some sort of teenage urge for attention? Or something more sinister?

"Ask your questions," Esther said, visibly bracing herself. "Go ahead."

"Mrs. Bennett," he began.

Some of her composure had returned. "I think if you're going to ask me if my daughters were being molested by my brothers, you should at least call me Esther."

"Is that what you're afraid of?"

"No," she said, her answer requiring no thought. "Monday, I was afraid of you telling me that my daughter was dead. Now, I am afraid of you telling me that there's no hope for Rebecca. The truth scares me, Chief Tolliver. I'm not afraid of conjecture."

"I need you to answer my question, Esther."

She took her time, as if it made her sick to even consider. "My brothers have never been inappropriate with my children. My husband has never been inappropriate with my children."

"What about Cole Connolly?"

She shook her head once. "Believe me when I tell you this," she assured him. "If anyone did harm to my children—not just my children, but any child—I would kill them with my bare hands and let God be my judge."

He stared at her for a beat. Her clear green eyes were sharp with conviction. He believed her, or at least he believed that she believed herself.

She asked him, "What are you going to do?"

"I can put out an APB and make some phone calls. I'll call the sheriff in Catoogah, but honestly, she has a history of running away and she left a note." He let that settle in, considering it himself. If Jeffrey had wanted to abduct Rebecca Bennett, he'd probably do it just like that: leave a note, let her history protect him for a few days.

"Do you think you'll find her?"

Jeffrey did not let himself dwell on the possibility of a fourteen-year-old somewhere in a shallow grave. "If I find her," he began. "I want to talk to her."

"You talked to her before."

"I want to talk to her alone," Jeffrey said, knowing he had no right to ask this, just as he knew Esther could always renounce her promise. "She's underage. Legally, I can't talk to her without the permission of at least one of her parents."

She took her time, obviously weighing the consequences. Finally, she nodded, "You have my permission."

"You know she's probably camping out somewhere," he told her, feeling guilty for taking advantage of her desperation, hoping to God he was right about the girl. "She'll probably come back on her own in a day or so."

She took the note back out of her pocket. "Find her," she said, pressing the page into his hand. "Please. Find her."

* * * *

When Jeffrey got back to the station, there was a large bus parked in the back of the lot, the words "Holy Grown Farms" stenciled on the side. Workers milled around outside despite the cold, and he could see the front lobby was packed with bodies. He suppressed a curse as he got out of his car, wondering if this was Lev Ward's idea of a joke.

Inside, he pushed his way through the smelliest bunch of derelicts he'd seen since the last time he'd driven through downtown Atlanta. He held his breath, waiting for Marla to buzz him in, thinking he might be sick if he stayed in the hot room for much longer.

"Hey there, Chief," Marla said, taking his coat. "I guess you know what this is all about."

Frank walked up, a sour look on his face. "They've been here for two hours. It's gonna take all day just getting their names."

Jeffrey asked, "Where's Lev Ward?"

"Connolly said he had to stay home with one of his sisters."

"Which one?"

"Hell if I know," Frank said, obviously over the experience of interviewing the great unwashed. "Said she had diabetes or something like that."

"Shit," Jeffrey cursed, thinking Ward really was jerking his chain. Not only was his absence wasting time, but it meant Mark McCallum, the polygraph expert the GBI had sent, would be spending another night in town courtesy of the Grant County Police Department.

Jeffrey took out his notepad and wrote down Rebecca Bennett's name and description. He slid a photograph out of his pocket, handing it to Frank. "Abby's sister," he said. "Put her details on the wire. She's been missing since ten o'clock last night."

"Shit."

"She's run away before," Jeffrey qualified, "but I don't like this coming so close to her sister's death."

"You think she knows something?"

"I think she's running away for a reason."

"Did you call Two-Bit?"

Jeffrey scowled. He had called Ed Pelham on his way back to the station. As predicted, the neighboring sheriff had pretty much laughed in his face. Jeffrey couldn't blame the man—the girl had a history of running away—but he had thought that Ed would take it more seriously, considering what had happened to Abigail Bennett.

He asked Frank, "Is Brad still searching the area around the lake?" Frank nodded. "Tell him to go home and get his backpack or camping gear or whatever. Get him and Hemming to go into the Catoogah state forest and start looking around. If anyone stops them, for God's sake, tell him to say they're out camping."

"All right."

Frank turned to leave but Jeffrey stopped him. "Update the APB on Donner to include the possibility he might be with a girl." Anticipating Frank's next question, he shrugged, saying, "Throw it at the wall and see what sticks."

"Will do," he said. "I put Connolly in interrogation one. You gonna get to him next?"

"I want him to stew," Jeffrey answered. "How long do you think it'll take to get through the rest of these interviews?"

"Five, maybe six hours."

"Anything interesting so far?"

"Not unless you count Lena threatening to backhand one of them if he didn't shut up about Jesus being Lord." He added, "I think this is wasting our fucking time."

"Have to agree with you," Jeffrey said. "I want you to go ahead and talk to the people on your list who bought cyanide salts from the dealer in Atlanta."

"I'll leave right after I talk to Brad and update the APB."

Jeffrey went to his office and picked up the phone before he even sat down. He called Lev Ward's number at Holy Grown and navigated his way through the switchboard. As he was on hold, Marla walked in and put a stack of messages on his desk. He thanked her just as Lev Ward's voice mail picked up.

"This is Chief Tolliver," he said. "I need you to call me as soon as possible." Jeffrey left his cell phone number, not wanting to give Lev the easy out of leaving a message. He rang off and picked up his notes from last night, unable to make any sense of the long lists he had made. There were questions for each family member, but in the cold light of day he realized that asking any one of them would get Paul Ward in the room so fast that his head would spin.

Legally, none of them had to talk to the police. He had no cause to force them to come in and he doubted very seriously if Lev Ward would deliver on his promise to take the lie detector test. Running their names through the computer hadn't brought up much information. Jeffrey had tried Cole Connolly's name, but without a middle initial or something more specific like a birth date or previous address, the search had returned about six hundred Cole Connollys in the southern United States. Opening it up to Coleman Connolly had added another three hundred.

Jeffrey looked at his hand, where the bandage had started to come off. Esther had gripped his hand before she left this morning, begging him again to find her daughter. He was convinced that if she knew anything, she'd be spilling her guts right now, doing whatever she could to get her only living child back in her home. She had defied her brothers and her husband by even talking to him, and when he had asked her if she was going to tell them whether or not they had spoken, she had cryptically answered, "If they ask me, I will tell them the truth." Jeffrey wondered if the men would even consider the possibility that Esther had done something on her own without their permission. The risk she had taken was indication enough that she was desperate for the truth. The problem was, Jeffrey didn't know where to begin to find it. The case was like a huge circle, and all he could do was keep going round and round until somebody made a mistake.

He skimmed through his messages, trying to focus his eyes long enough to read. He was exhausted and his hand was throbbing. Two calls from the mayor and a note that the Dew Drop Inn had called to discuss the bill for Mark McCallum, the polygraph expert he had ordered for Lev Ward, didn't help matters. Apparently, the young man liked room service.

Jeffrey rubbed his eyes, focusing on Buddy Conford's name. The lawyer had been called into court but would come to the station as soon as he could for the talk with his stepdaughter. Jeffrey had forgotten for a moment about Patty O'Ryan. He set the note aside and continued sorting through the stack.

His heart stopped in his chest when he recognized the name at the top of the next-to-last message. Sara's cousin Dr. Hareton Earnshaw, had called. In the note section, Marla had written, "He says everything is fine," then added her own question, "you okay?"

He picked up the phone, dialing Sara's number at the clinic. After listening to several minutes of the Chipmunks singing classic rock while on hold, she came onto the line.

"Hare called," he told her. "Everything's fine."

She let out a soft sigh. "That's good news."

"Yeah." He thought about the other night, the risk she took putting her mouth on him. A cold sweat came, followed by more relief than he had felt when he had first read Hare's message. He had sort of reconciled himself to dealing with bad news, but thinking about the possibility of taking Sara down with him was too painful to even fathom. He had caused enough hurt in her life already.

She asked, "What did Esther say?"

He caught her up on the missing child and Esther's fears. Sara was obviously skeptical. She asked, "She's always come back?"

"Yeah," he said. "I don't know that I would've even taken a report if not for the fact of Abby. I keep going back and forth between thinking she's just hiding somewhere for the attention and thinking she's hiding for a reason."

"The reason being Rebecca knows what happened to Abby?" Sara asked.

"Or something else," he said, still not sure what he believed. He voiced the thought he'd been trying to suppress since Esther's call this morning. "She could be somewhere, Sara. Somewhere like Abby."

Sara was quiet.

"I've got a team searching the forest. I've got Frank checking out jewelry stores. We've got a station full of ex-addicts and alcoholics from the farm, most of them smelling pretty ripe." He stopped, thinking he'd be talking for another hour or two if he kept listing dead leads.

Out of the blue, she said, "I told Tess I'd go to church with her tonight."

Jeffrey felt something in his gut squeeze. "I really wish you wouldn't."

"But you can't tell me why."

"No," he admitted. "It's a gut instinct, but I've got a pretty smart gut."

"I need to do this for Tess," she said. "And myself."

"You turning religious on me?"

"There's something I need to see for myself," she told him. "I can't talk about it now, but I'll tell you later."

He wondered if she was still mad at him for sleeping on the couch. "What's wrong?"

"Nothing's wrong—really. I just need to think some more before I can talk about it, she said. "Listen, I've got a patient waiting."

"All right."

"I love you."

Jeffrey felt his smile come back. "I'll see you later."

He slid the phone back on the hook, staring at the blinking lights. Somehow, he felt like he had gotten his second wind, and he thought now was as good a time as any to talk to Cole Connolly.

He found Lena in the hallway outside the bathroom. She was leaning against the wall, drinking a Coke, and she startled when he walked up, spilling soda down the front of her shirt.

"Shit," she muttered, brushing the liquid from her blouse.

"Sorry," he told her. "What's going on?"

"I needed to get some air," she said, and Jeffrey nodded. The Holy Grown workers had obviously spent the early hours of the morning toiling in the fields and had the body odor to prove it.

"Any progress?"

"Basically, all we've got is more of the same. She was a nice girl, praise the Lord. She did her best, Jesus loves you."

Jeffrey didn't acknowledge her sarcasm, though he wholeheartedly agreed with the sentiment. He was beginning to see that Lena's calling them a cult hadn't been that far off. They certainly acted as if they were brainwashed.

Lena sighed. "You know, actually, looking past all their bullshit, she seemed like a really nice girl." She pressed her lips together, and he was surprised to see this side of her. As quickly as it had appeared, it passed, though, and Lena said, "Oh, well. She must have had something to hide. Everybody does."

He caught a glint of guilt in her eye, but instead of asking about Terri Stanley and the police picnic, he told her, "Rebecca Bennett's missing."

Shock registered on her face. "Since when?"

"Last night," Jeffrey handed her the note Esther had pressed into his hand outside the diner. "She left this."

Lena read it, saying, "Something's not right," and he was glad that someone was taking this seriously. She asked, "Why would she run away this close to her sister dying? Even I wasn't that selfish when I was fourteen. Her mother must be going nuts."

"Her mother's the one who told me," Jeffrey said. "She called me at Sara's this morning. Her brothers didn't want her to report it."

"Why?" Lena asked, handing back the note. "What harm could it do?"

"They don't like the police involved."

"Yeah," Lena said. "Well, we'll see how they don't like the police involved when she doesn't come back." She asked, "Do you think she's been taken?"

"Abby didn't leave a note."

"No," she said, then, "I don't like this. I don't feel good about it."

"I don't either," he agreed, tucking the note back into his pocket. "I want you to take the lead with Connolly. I don't think he'll like his questions coming from a woman."

The smile on her face was brief, like a cat spotting a mouse. "You want me to piss him off?"

"Not on purpose."

"What are we looking for?"

"I just want a sense of him," he said. "Find out about his dealings with Abby. Float out Rebecca's name. See if he bites."

"All right."

"I want to talk to Patty O'Ryan again, too. We need to find out if Chip was seeing anybody."

"Anybody like Rebecca Bennett?"

Sometimes the way Lena's mind worked scared him. He just shrugged. "Buddy said he'd be here in a couple of hours."

She tossed her Coke into the garbage as she headed toward the interrogation room. "Looking forward to that."

＊ ＊ ＊

Jeffrey opened the door for her and watched Lena transform into the cop he knew she could be. Her gait was heavy, like she had brass balls hanging between her legs. She pulled out a chair and sat across from Cole Connolly without a word, legs parted, her chair a few feet back from the table. She rested her arm along the back of the empty chair beside her.

She said, "Hey."

Cole's eyes flashed to Jeffrey, then back to Lena. "Hey."

She reached into her back pocket, took out her notebook and slapped it on the table. "I'm detective Lena Adams. This is Chief Jeffrey Tolliver. Could you give us your full name?"

"Cletus Lester Connolly, ma'am." There was a pen and a few pieces of paper in front of him alongside a well-worn Bible. Connolly straightened the papers as Jeffrey leaned against the wall, arms crossed over his chest. He was at least sixty-five if he was a day, but Connolly was still a fastidious man, his white T-shirt crisp and clean, sharp creases ironed into his jeans. His time in the fields had kept his body trim, his chest well-developed, his biceps bulging from his sleeves. Wiry white hair jutted up all over his body, sticking out from the collar of his T-shirt, sprouting from his ears, carpeting his arms. He was pretty much covered in it on every place but for his bald head.

Lena asked, "Why do they call you Cole?"

"That was my father's name," he explained, his eyes wandering back to Jeffrey. "Got tired of being beat up for being named Cletus. Lester's not much better, so I took my daddy's name when I was fifteen."

Jeffrey thought that at the very least this explained why the man hadn't come up on any computer checks. There was no doubt that he had been in the system for a while, though. He had that alertness about him that came from being in prison. He was always on guard, always looking for his escape.

"What happened to your hand?" Lena asked, and Jeffrey noticed that there was a thin, one-inch cut on the back of Connolly's right index finger. It wasn't anything significant—certainly not a fingernail scratch or defensive wound. It looked more like the kind of injury that happened when you were working with your hands and stopped paying attention for a split second.

"Working in the fields," Connolly admitted, looking at the cut. "Guess I should put a Band-Aid on it."

Lena asked, "How long were you in the service?"

He seemed surprised, but she indicated the tattoo on his arm.

Jeffrey recognized it as a military insignia, but he wasn't sure which branch. He also recognized the crude tattoo below it as of the prison variety. At some point, Connolly had pricked his skin with a needle, using the ink from a ballpoint pen to stain the words "Jesus Saves" indelibly into his flesh.

"I was in twelve years before they kicked me out," Connolly answered. Then, as if he knew where this was going, he added, "They told me I could either go into treatment or get booted." He smacked his palms together, a plane leaving the ground. "Dishonorable discharge."

"That must've been hard."

"Sure was," he agreed, placing his hand on the Bible. Jeffrey doubted this meant the man was going to tell the truth, but it painted a pretty picture. Cole obviously knew how to answer a question without giving away too much. He was a textbook study in evasion, maintaining eye contact, keeping his shoulders back and adding in a non sequitur to the equation. "But not as hard as living life on the outside."

Lena gave him a little rope. "How's that?"

He kept his hand on the Bible as he explained, "I got banged up for boosting a car when I was seventeen. Judge told me I could go into the army or go to jail. I went right from my mama's tit to Uncle Sam's, excuse the language." He had a sparkle in his eye as he said this. It took a few minutes for a man to let down his guard with Lena, then he started to treat her as one of the boys. Right before their eyes, Cole Connolly had turned into a helpful old man, eager to answer their questions—at least the ones he deemed safe.

Connolly continued, "I didn't know how to fend for myself in the real world. Once I got out, I met up with some buddies who thought it'd be easy to rip off the local convenience store."

Jeffrey wished he had a dollar for every man on death row who had gotten his start robbing convenience stores.

"One of 'em ratted us out before we got there—cut a deal for a reduction on a drug charge. I was cuffed before I even walked through the front door." Connolly laughed, a sparkle in his eyes. If he regretted being ratted out, there didn't seem to be a whole lot of bitterness left in him. "Prison was great, just like being in the army. Three squares a day, people telling me when to eat, when to sleep, when to take a crap. Got so when parole came around, I didn't want to leave it."

"You served your full term?"

"That's right," he said, his chest puffing out. "Ticked off the judge with my attitude. Had me quite a temper once I was inside and the guards didn't like that, either."

"I don't imagine they did."

"Had my fair share of those," he indicated Jeffrey's bruised eye, probably more to let him know he was aware that the other man was in the room.

"You fight a lot inside?"

"About as much as you'd expect," he admitted. He was watching Lena carefully, sizing her up. Jeffrey knew she was aware of this, just like he knew that Cole Connolly was going to be a very difficult interview.

"So," she said, "you found Jesus inside? Funny how he hangs around prisons like that."

Connolly visibly struggled with her words, his fists clenching, his upper body tightening into a solid brick wall. Her tone had been just right, and Jeffrey got a fleeting glimpse of the man from the field, the man who didn't tolerate weakness.

Lena pressed a little more gently. "Jail gives a man a lot of time to think about himself."

Connolly gave a tight nod, coiled like a snake ready to strike. For her part, Lena was still casually laid back in the chair, her arm hanging over the back. Jeffrey saw under the table that she had moved her other hand closer to her weapon, and he knew that she had sensed the danger as well as he had.

She kept her tone light, though, trying some of Connolly's own rhetoric. "Being in prison is a trying time for a man. It can either make you strong or make you weak."

"True enough."

"Some men succumb to it. There's a lot of drugs inside."

"Yes, ma'am. Easier to get 'em there than it is on the outside."

"Lots of time to sit around getting stoned."

His jaw was still tight. Jeffrey wondered if she had pushed him too far, but knew better than to interfere.

"I did my share of drugs." Connolly spoke in a clipped tone. "I've never denied it. Evil things. They get inside you, make you do things you shouldn't. You have to be strong to fight it." He looked up at

Lena, his passion replacing his anger as quickly as oil displaces water. "I was a weak man, but I saw the light. I prayed to the Lord for salvation and He reached down and held out His hand." He held up his own hand as if in illustration. "I took it and I said, 'Yes, Lord. Help me rise up. Help me be born again.' "

"That's quite a transformation," she pointed out. "What made you decide to change your ways?"

"My last year there, Thomas started making the rounds. He is the Lord's conduit. Working through him, the Lord showed me a better way."

Lena clarified, "This is Lev's father?"

"He was part of the prison outreach program," Connolly explained. "Us old cons, we liked to keep things quiet. You go to church, you attend the Bible meetings, you're less likely to find yourself in a position where your temper might be sparked by some young gun looking to make a name for himself." He laughed at the situation, returning to the genial old man he had been before his outburst. "Never thought I'd end up being one of those Bible-toters myself. There are folks who are either for Jesus or against him, and I took against him. The wages of my sin would have surely been a horrible, lonely death."

"But then you met Thomas Ward?"

"He's been sick lately, had a stroke, but then he was like a lion, God bless him. Thomas saved my soul. Gave me a place to go to when I got out of prison."

"Gave you three squares a day?" Lena suggested, referring to Connolly's earlier statement about the military and then prison taking care of him.

"Ha!" the old man laughed, slapping his hand on the table, amused at the connection. The papers had ruffled and he smoothed them back down, making the edges neat. "I guess that's as good a way of putting it as any. I'm still an old soldier at heart, but now I'm a soldier for the Lord."

Lena asked, "You notice anything suspicious around the farm lately?"

"Not really."

"No one acting strange?"

"I don't mean to be flip," he cautioned, "but you gotta think about the sort of people we've got in and out of that place. They're all a little strange. They wouldn't be there if they weren't."

"Point taken," she allowed. "I mean to say, any of them acting suspicious? Like they might be involved in something bad?"

"They've all been in something bad, and some of them are still in it at the farm."

"Meaning?"

"They're sitting in a shelter up in Atlanta feeling all sorry for themselves, looking for a change of scenery, thinking that'll be the final thing that makes them change."

"But it's not?"

"For some of them it is," Connolly admitted, "but for a lot more of them, they get down here and realize that the thing that got them into the drugs and the alcohol and the bad ways is the thing that keeps them there." He didn't wait for Lena to prompt him. "Weakness, young lady. Weakness of soul, weakness of spirit. We do what we can to help them, but they first have to be strong enough to help themselves."

Lena said, "We were told that some petty cash was stolen."

"That'd be several months back," he confirmed. "We never caught who did it."

"Any suspects?"

"Around two hundred," he laughed, and Jeffrey assumed that working with a bunch of alcoholics and junkies didn't exactly foster a lot of trust in the workplace.

Lena asked, "No one more interested in Abby than they should be?"

"She was a real pretty girl," he said. "Lots of the boys looked at her, but I made it clear she was off-limits."

"Anyone in particular you had to tell this to?"

"Not that I can recall." Jail habits were hard to break, and Connolly had the con's inability to give a yes or no answer.

Lena asked, "You didn't notice her hanging around anybody? Maybe spending time with someone she shouldn't?"

He shook his head. "Believe you me, I have been racking my brain since this happened, trying to think of anybody who might mean that sweet little girl some harm. I can't think of nobody, and this is going back some years."

"She drove a lot by herself," Lena recalled.

"I taught her to drive Mary's old Buick when she was fifteen years old."

"You were close?"

"Abigail was like my own granddaughter." He blinked to clear his tears. "You get to be my age, you think nothing can shock you. Lots of your friends start getting sick. Threw me for a loop when Thomas had his stroke last year. I was the one what found him. I can tell you it came as a hard reckoning seeing that man humbled." He wiped his eyes with the back of his hand. Jeffrey could see Lena nodding, like she understood.

Connolly continued, "But, Thomas was an old man. You can't expect it to happen, but you can't be surprised, either. Abby was just a good little girl, missy. Just a good little girl. Had her whole life ahead of her. Ain't nobody deserves to die that way, but her especially."

"From what we've gathered, she was a remarkable young woman."

"That's the truth," he agreed. "She was an angel. Pure and sweet as the driven snow. I would've laid down my life for her."

"Do you know a young man named Chip Donner?"

Again, Connolly seemed to think about it. "I don't recall. We get a lot in and out. Some of them stay a week, some a day. The lucky ones stay a lifetime." He scratched his chin. "That last name sounds familiar, though I don't know why."

"How about Patty O'Ryan?"

"Nope."

"I guess you know Rebecca Bennett."

"Becca?" he asked. "Of course I do."

"She's been missing since last night."

Connolly nodded; obviously this wasn't news. "She's a strong-headed one, that child. Runs off, gives her mama a scare, comes back and it's all love and happiness."

"We know she's run away before."

"At least she had the decency to leave word this time."

"Do you know where she might have gone?"

He shrugged. "Usually camps in the woods. I used to take the kids out when I was younger. Show 'em how to get by using the tools God gave us. Teaches them a respect for His kindness."

"Is there any particular spot you used to take them?"

He nodded as she spoke, anticipating the question. "I was out there first thing this morning. Campsite hasn't been used in years. I've got no idea where that girl might've gone off to." He added, "Wish I did—I'd take a switch to her bottom for doing this to her mother right now."

Marla knocked on the door, opening it at the same time. "Sorry to bother you, Chief," she said, handing Jeffrey a folded piece of paper.

Jeffrey took it as Lena asked Connolly, "How long have you been with the church?"

"Going on twenty-one years," he answered. "I was there when Thomas inherited the land from his father. Looked like a wilderness to me, but Moses started out with a wilderness, too."

Jeffrey kept studying the man, trying to see if there was a tell to his act. Most people had a bad habit that came out when they were lying. Some people scratched their noses, some fidgeted. Connolly was completely still, eyes straight ahead. He was either a born liar or an honest man. Jeffrey wasn't about to lay down bets on either.

Connolly continued the story of the birth of Holy Grown. "We had about twenty folks with us at the time. Of course, Thomas's children were pretty young then, not much help, especially Paul. He was always the lazy one. Wanted to sit back while everybody else did the work so he could reap the rewards. Just like a lawyer." Lena nodded. "We started out with a hundred acres of soy. Never used any chemicals or pesticides. People thought we were crazy, but now this organic thing's all the rage. Our time has really come. I just wish Thomas was able to recognize it. He was our Moses, literally our Moses. He led us out of slavery—slavery to drugs, to alcohol, to the wanton ways. He was our savior."

Lena cut off the sermon. "He's still not well?"

Connolly turned more solemn. "The Lord will take care of him."

Jeffrey opened Marla's note, glancing at it, then doing a double take. He suppressed a curse, asking Connolly, "Is there anything else you can add?"

He seemed surprised by Jeffrey's abruptness. "Not that I can think of."

Jeffrey didn't need to motion Lena. She stood, and Connolly followed her. Jeffrey told him, "I'd like to follow up with you tomorrow if that's possible. Say in the morning?"

Connolly looked trapped for a second, but recovered. "Not a problem," he said, his smile so forced Jeffrey thought his teeth might break. "Abby's service is tomorrow. Maybe after that?"

"We should be talking to Lev first thing in the morning," Jeffrey told him, hoping this information would get back to Lev Ward. "Why don't you come in with him?"

"We'll see," Connolly said, not committing to anything.

Jeffrey opened the door. "I appreciate you coming in and bringing everybody."

Connolly was still confused, and seemed more than a little nervous about the note in Jeffrey's hand, as if he very much wanted to know what it said. Jeffrey couldn't tell if this was habitual thinking from his criminal days or just natural curiosity.

Jeffrey said, "You can go ahead and take back everybody else. I'm sure there's work to do. We don't want to waste any more of your time."

"No problem," Connolly repeated, jutting out his hand. "Let me know if there's anything else you need."

"Appreciate it," Jeffrey said, feeling the bones in his hand crunch as Connolly shook it. "I'll see you in the morning with Lev."

Connolly got the threat behind his words. He had dropped the helpful old man act. "Right."

Lena started to follow him out, but Jeffrey held her back. He showed her the note Marla had given him, making sure Connolly couldn't see the secretary's neat, grade-school teacher's cursive: "Call from 25 Cromwell Road. Landlady reports 'suspicious smell.' "

They had found Chip Donner.

＊　＊　＊　＊

Twenty-five Cromwell Road was a nice home for a well-to-do family living back in the thirties. Over the years, the large front parlors had been divided into rooms, the upper floors sectioned up for renters who didn't mind sharing the one bathroom in the house. There were not many places an ex-con could go to when he got out of prison. If he was on parole, he had a finite amount of time to establish residency and get a job in order to keep his parole officer from throwing him back inside. The fifty bucks the state gave him on the way out the door didn't stretch that far, and houses like the one on Cromwell catered to this particular need.

If anything, Jeffrey figured this case was opening up his olfactory sense to all different kinds of new experiences. The Cromwell house smelled like sweat and fried chicken, with a disturbing undertone of rotting meat courtesy of the room at the top of the stairs.

The landlady greeted him at the door with a handkerchief over her nose and mouth. She was a large woman with ample folds of skin hanging down from her arms. Jeffrey tried not to watch them sway back and forth as she talked.

"We never had no trouble from him at all," she assured Jeffrey as she led him into the house. Deep green carpet on the floor had once been a nice shag but was now flattened down from years of wear and what looked like motor oil. The walls probably hadn't been painted since Nixon was in the White House and there were black scuff marks on every baseboard and corner. The woodwork had been stunning at one time, but several coats of paint obscured the carvings on the molding. Incongruously, a beautiful cut-glass chandelier that was probably original to the house hung in the entranceway.

"Did you hear anything last night?" Jeffrey asked, trying to breathe through his mouth without looking like a panting dog.

"Not a peep," she said, then added, "Except for the TV Mr. Harris keeps on next door to Chip." She indicated the stairs. "He's gone deaf over the last few years, but he's been here longer than any of them. I always tell new boys if they can't take the noise, then find somewhere else."

Jeffrey glanced out the front door to the street, wondering what was keeping Lena. He had sent her to get Brad Stephens so that he could help process the scene. Along with half the rest of the force, he was still out in the woods, searching for anything suspicious.

He asked, "Is there a rear entrance?"

"Through the kitchen." She pointed to the back of the house. "Chip parked his car under the carport," she explained. "There's an alley cuts through the backyard takes you straight in from Sanders."

"Sanders is the street that runs parallel to Cromwell?" Jeffrey verified, thinking that even if Marty Lam had been sitting on the front door like he was supposed to, he wouldn't have seen Chip come in. Maybe Marty would think about that while he sat at home on his ass during his week-long suspension.

The woman said, "Broderick turns into Sanders when it crosses McDougall."

"He ever have any visitors?"

"Oh, no, he kept himself to himself."

"Phone calls?"

"There's a pay phone in the hall. They're not allowed to use the house line. It doesn't ring much."

"No particular lady friends came by?"

She giggled as if he had embarrassed her. "We don't allow female visitors in the house. I'm the only lady allowed."

"Well," Jeffrey said. He had been postponing the inevitable. He asked the woman, "Which room is his?"

"First on the left." She pointed up the stairs, her arm wagging. "Hope you don't mind if I stay here."

"Have you looked in the room?"

"Goodness, no," she said, shaking her head. "We've had a couple of these happen. I know what it looks like plain enough without the reminder."

"A couple?" Jeffrey asked.

"Well, they didn't die here," she clarified. "No, wait, one did. I think his name was Rutherford. Rather?" She waved her hand. "Anyway, the one the ambulance picked up, he was the last. This was about eight, ten years ago. Had a needle in his arm. I went up there because of the smell." She lowered her voice. "He had defecated himself."

"Uh huh."

"I thought he was gone, but then the paramedics came and toted him off to the hospital, said he still had a chance."

"What about the other one?"

"Oh, Mr. Schwartz," she remembered. "Very sweet old man. I believe he was Jewish, bless him. Died in his sleep."

"When was this?"

"Mother was still alive, so it must have been nineteen . . ." she thought about it, "nineteen eighty-six, I'd guess."

"You go to church?"

"Primitive Baptist," she told him. "Have I seen you there?"

"Maybe," he said, thinking the only time he'd been in a church in the last ten years was to catch a glimpse of Sara. Cathy's culinary arts gave her great sway with her girls during Christmas and Easter, and Sara generally let herself get talked into going to church services on these days in order to reap the benefits of a big meal afterward.

Jeffrey glanced up the steep stairs, not relishing what was ahead of him. He told the woman, "My partner should be here soon. Tell her to come up when she gets here."

"Of course." She put her hand down the front of her dress and rooted around, seconds later producing a key.

Jeffrey forced himself to take the warm, somewhat moist key, then started up the stairs. The railing was wobbly, torn from the wall in several places, an oily sheen to the unpainted wood.

The smell got worse the closer he got to the top, and even without directions he could've found the room with his nose.

The door was locked from the outside with a padlock and hasp. He put on some latex gloves, wishing like hell he'd donned them before taking the key from the landlady. The lock was rusty, and he tried to hold it by the edges so he wouldn't smudge any fingerprints. He forced the key, hoping it wouldn't break in the lock. Several seconds of praying and sweating in the dank heat of the house yielded a satisfying click as the padlock opened. Touching only the edges of the metal, he opened the hasp, then turned the handle of the door.

The room was pretty much what you would expect after seeing the front hall of the house. The same filthy green carpet was on the floor. A cheap roller shade was in the window, the edges pinned down with blue masking tape to keep the sunlight from streaming in. There wasn't a bed, but a sleeper couch was halfway open as if someone had been interrupted during the process of unfolding the mattress. All the drawers of the one dresser in the room were open, their contents spilling out onto the rug. A brush and comb along with a glass bowl that contained about a thousand pennies were in the corner, the bowl shattered in two, the pennies flooding out. Two table lamps without shades were on the floor, intact. There wasn't a closet in the room, but someone had nailed a length of clothesline along the wall to hang shirts on. The shirts, still on hangers, littered the floor. One end of the clothesline was still nailed to the wall. Chip Donner held the other end in his lifeless hand.

Behind Jeffrey, Lena dropped her crime scene toolbox on the floor with a thud. "Guess it was the maid's day off."

Jeffrey had heard Lena's tread on the stairs, but he couldn't take his eyes off the body. Chip's face looked like a raw piece of meat. His lower lip had been nearly ripped off and was resting on his left cheek as if someone had just brushed it aside. Several broken teeth dotted his chin, the pieces piercing the flesh. What was left of his lower jaw hung at a slant. One eye socket was completely concave, the other empty, the eyeball hanging down the side of his cheek by what looked like a couple of bloody threads. Donner's shirt was off, his white skin almost glowing in the light from the hall. His upper body had about thirty thin, red slashes crisscrossed all around it in a pattern that Jeffrey didn't recognize. From this distance, it looked like somebody had taken a red Magic Marker and drawn perfectly straight lines all over Donner's torso.

"Brass knuckles," Lena guessed, pointing to the chest and belly. "There was a trainer at the police academy who had the same thing right here on his neck. Perp popped out from behind a trash can and laid into him before he could pull his piece."

"I can't even tell if he still has a neck."

Lena asked, "What the hell is sticking out of his side?"

Jeffrey squatted down for a better view, still standing just shy the doorway. He squinted, trying to figure out what he was seeing. "I think those are his ribs."

"Christ," Lena said. "Who the hell did he piss off?"

CHAPTER TEN

Sara shifted her weight, feeling dead on her feet. She had started the autopsy of Charles Donner over three hours ago and still hadn't found anything conclusive.

She tapped the Dictaphone back on, saying, "Extraperitoneal rupture of the bladder caused by downward blunt force trauma. No pelvic fracture is visible." She told Jeffrey, "His bladder was empty, that's the only reason it didn't rupture. He may have gone to the bathroom before going to his room."

Jeffrey wrote something down in his notebook. Like Sara and Carlos, he was wearing a mask and safety goggles. When Sara had first entered the house on Cromwell, she had nearly gagged at the smell. Donner had obviously died very recently, but there was a scientific explanation for the odor. His intestines and stomach had been ruptured, bile and feces filling his abdominal cavity and leaking out through the punctures on his side. The heat of his cramped bedroom had gone to work on the viscera, fermenting them in his torso like a festering sore. His abdomen was so swollen with bacteria that by the time Sara had gotten him back to the morgue and opened him up, matter had sloshed over the sides of the autopsy table, splattering onto the floor.

"Transverse fracture to the sternum, bilateral rib fractures, ruptured pulmonary parenchyma, superficial capsular lacerations to the kidneys and spleen," she stopped, feeling like she was going through a grocery list. "The left lobe of the liver has been amputated and crushed between the anterior abdominal wall and the vertebral column."

Jeffrey asked, "You think this took two people?"

"I don't know," she said. "There aren't any defensive wounds on his arms or hands, but that could just mean that he was taken by surprise."

"How could one person do this to somebody?"

She knew he wasn't asking a philosophical question. "The abdominal wall is slack and compressible. Normally, when something hits it, it readily transmits the force to the abdominal viscera. It's like slapping your palm against a puddle of water. Depending on the force, hollow organs like the stomach and intestines can burst, the spleen is lacerated, the liver is damaged."

"Houdini died like that," Jeffrey told her, and despite the circumstances, Sara smiled at his love of mundane history. "He had an open challenge to anyone in the world to hit him in the stomach as hard as they could. Some kid caught him off guard and ended up killing him."

"Right," Sara agreed. "If you tighten your abdominal muscles, you can disperse the impact. If not, you can get yourself killed. I doubt Donner had time to think about it."

"Can you make a guess about what killed him yet?"

Sara looked at the body, what was left of the head and neck. "If you told me this kid had been in a car crash, I would absolutely believe you. I've never seen this much blunt force trauma in my life." She pointed to the flaps of skin that had been rubbed off the body from sheer impact. "These avulsive injuries, the lacerations, the abdominal injuries— " She shook her head at the mess. "He was punched so hard in the chest that the back of his heart was bruised by his spinal column."

"You sure this happened last night?"

"At least in the last twelve hours."

"He died in the room?"

"Definitely." Donner's body had festered in his intestinal juices as they dripped down from the open wound in his side. Stomach acids had eaten black holes in the shag. When Sara and Carlos had tried to move the body, they had found the corpse was stuck to the green carpet. They had been forced to slice off his jeans and cut out the section of the rug they had been glued to in order to remove him from the scene.

Jeffrey asked, "So, what killed him?"

"Take a number," she said. "A dislocation at the atlanto-occipital

junction could have transected the spinal cord. He could've had a
subdural hematoma caused by rotational acceleration." She counted
off the possibilities on her hand, "Cardiac arrhythmia, transected
aorta, traumatic asphyxia, pulmonary hemorrhage." She gave up
counting. "Or, it could have been just plain old shock. Too much
pain, too much trauma, and the body just shuts down."

"You think Lena was right about the brass knuckles?"

"It makes sense," she allowed. "I've never seen anything like these
marks. They're the right width, and it would explain how someone
could do this with their fists. External damage would be minimal,
just whatever the force of the metal against the skin would do, but in-
ternally"—she indicated the mess of viscera she had found inside the
body—"This is exactly what I would expect to find."

"What a nasty way to die."

She asked, "Did you find anything in the apartment?"

"No fingerprints but Donner's and the landlady's," he said, flipping back through his notes and reading, "Couple of bags—probably
heroin—and some needles hidden in the stuffing on the underside of
the couch. Around a hundred bucks in cash tucked into the base of a
lamp. A couple of porn mags in the closet."

"Sounds about right," she said, wondering when she had stopped
being surprised at the amount of pornography men consumed. It was
getting so that if a man didn't have some sort of pornography at his
disposal, she was instantly suspicious.

Jeffrey said, "He had a gun, a nine-mil."

"He was on parole?" Sara asked, knowing the gun violation would
have sent Donner back to jail before he could open his mouth to explain.

Jeffrey didn't seem bothered by it. "I'd have a gun if I lived in that
neighborhood, too."

"No sign of Rebecca Bennett?"

"No, no sign of any girl, for that matter. Like I said, there were
only the two sets of fingerprints in the room."

"That could be suspicious in and of itself."

"Exactly."

"Did you find the wallet?" After they'd cut the pants off, Sara had
noticed that Donner's pockets were empty.

"We found some loose change and a receipt from the grocery store for some cereal behind the dresser," Jeffrey told her. "No wallet, though."

"He probably emptied his pockets when he got home, went to the bathroom and then his room, where he was blindsided."

"By who, though?" Jeffrey asked, more of himself than Sara. "It could be some dealer he screwed over. A friend who knew he had the baggies, but not where he kept them. A thief from the neighborhood looking for some cash."

"I would assume a bartender kept cash around."

"He wasn't beaten for information," Jeffrey said.

Sara agreed. No one had stopped in the middle of attacking Chip Donner to ask him where he kept his valuables.

Jeffrey seemed frustrated. "It could be somebody connected to Abigail Bennett. It could be somebody who never met her. We don't even know if the two of them are connected."

"It didn't look as if there were signs of a struggle," Sara said. "The place looked ransacked."

"It didn't look that ransacked," Jeffrey disagreed. "Whoever was looking for something wasn't doing a very good job."

"A junkie can't exactly maintain focus." She contradicted herself by saying, "Of course, anyone that strung out wouldn't be coordinated enough for this kind of attack."

"Not even with PCP?"

"I hadn't thought of that," Sara admitted. PCP was a volatile drug and had been known to give users unusual strength as well as vivid hallucinations. When she had worked in Atlanta's Grady Hospital, she'd admitted a patient to the ER one night who had broken the weld on the metal bedrail he was handcuffed to and threatened one of the staff with it.

She allowed, "It's possible."

He said, "Maybe whoever killed him messed up the room so it'd look like a robbery."

"Then it would have to be a person who came there specifically to kill him."

"I don't understand why he doesn't have any defensive wounds," Jeffrey said. "He just laid down and took the beating?"

"He has a high transverse fracture of the maxilla, a LeFort III. I've only seen that in textbooks."

"You've got to speak English for me."

"The flesh of his face was nearly beaten off his skull," she said. "If I had to guess what happened, I would say someone took him completely by surprise, punched him in the face and knocked him out."

"One punch?"

"He's a small guy," she pointed out. "The first hit could've been the one that snapped his spinal cord in two. His head jerks around, that's it."

"He was holding on to the laundry line," he reminded her. "It was wrapped around his hand."

"He could've reflexively grabbed it as he fell," she countered. "But there's no way at this point to tell which injury is ante- and what's post-mortem. I think what we'll find is that whoever did this knew how to put a beating on somebody, and they did it quickly and methodically, then got out of there."

"Maybe he knew his attacker."

"It's possible." She asked, "What about his next door neighbor?"

"Around ninety years old and deaf as a board," Jeffrey said. "Tell you the truth, from the way the room smelled, I don't even think the old man leaves it to go to the bathroom."

Sara thought that could be true about all the occupants of the house. After being in Donner's room for just half an hour, she felt filthy. "Was anybody else in the house last night?"

"Landlady was downstairs, but she keeps the TV up loud. Two other guys were living there—both alibied out."

"You sure?"

"They were arrested for drunk and disorderly an hour before it happened. They slept it off courtesy of your tax dollars in the Grant County Jail."

"I'm glad I can give something back to the community." Sara snapped off her gloves.

As usual, Carlos had been standing quietly by, and she asked, "Can you go ahead and stitch him up?"

"Yes, ma'am," he said, going to the cabinet to get the proper materials.

Sara took off her safety glasses and head covering, relishing the feel of fresh air. She slipped off her gown and dropped it in the laundry bag as she headed back to her office.

Jeffrey did the same as he followed her, saying, "I guess it's too late to go to church with Tessa tonight."

She glanced at her watch as she sat down. "Not really. I've got time to run home and take a shower."

"I don't want you to go," he said, leaning against her desk. "I don't like how any of these people are looking."

"Do you have a connection between the church and Donner?"

"Does tenuous count?"

"Is there anyone in particular you think might have done this?"

"Cole Connolly's been in prison. He'd know how to put a beating on somebody."

"I thought you said he was an old man."

"He's in better shape than I am," Jeffrey said. "He didn't lie about his jail-time, though. His records are pretty old, but they show twenty-two years of hard time in the Atlanta pen. The car boost from when he was seventeen probably happened in the fifties. It wasn't even on the computer, but he mentioned it anyway."

"Why would he kill Chip, though? Or Abby, for that matter? And what's his connection to the cyanide? Where would he get it?"

"If I could answer those questions, we probably wouldn't be here," he admitted. "What do you need to see for yourself?"

She remembered her phrase from earlier on the phone and felt like kicking herself for saying anything at all. "It's just something stupid."

"Stupid how?"

Sara stood up and closed the door, even though Carlos was probably the most discreet person she had ever met.

She sat back down, her hands clasped in front of her on the desk. "It's just something stupid that popped into my head."

"You never have stupid things pop into your head."

She thought to correct him, the most recent example being her risky behavior the other night, but instead said, "I don't want to talk about it right now."

He stared at the back wall, making a clicking noise with his tongue, and she could tell he was upset.

"Jeff." She took his hand in both of hers, holding it to her chest. "I promise I'll tell you, okay? After tonight, I'll tell you why I need to do this, and we'll both laugh about it."

"Are you still mad at me about sleeping on the couch?"

She shook her head, wondering why he wouldn't let that go. She had been hurt to find him on the couch, not mad. Obviously she wasn't as good an actress as she liked to think. "Why would I be mad at you about that?"

"I just don't understand why you're so hell-bent on getting involved with these people. Considering the way Abigail Bennett was killed and the fact that another girl connected with this case is missing, I'd think you'd be doing your damned best to keep Tessa away from them."

"I can't explain it right now," she told him. "It doesn't have anything to do with you or him"—she gestured toward the exam room— "Or this case, or some religious conversion on my part. I promise you that. I swear."

"I don't like being left out of your life like this."

"I know you don't," she told him. "And I know it's not fair. I just need you to trust me, okay? Just give me a little room." She wanted to add that she needed the same room she had given him last night, but didn't want to bring up the subject again. "Just trust me."

He stared at her hands around his. "You're making me really nervous, Sara. These could be very dangerous people."

"Are you going to forbid me to do it?" She tried teasing, "I don't see a ring on my finger, Mr. Tolliver."

"Actually," he said, sliding open her desk drawer. She always took off her jewelry and left it in her office before performing a procedure. His Auburn class ring was sitting beside the pair of diamond earrings he had given her for Christmas last year.

He picked up the ring, and she held out her hand so that he could slide it onto her finger. She thought he would ask her not to go again, but instead he told her, "Be careful."

❋ ❋ ❋ ❋

Sara parked her car in front of her parents' house, surprised to see her cousin Hare leaning against his convertible Jaguar, decked out like a model in *GQ*.

He tossed out a "Hey, Carrot," before she had time to close her car door.

Sara looked at her watch. She was five minutes late picking up Tessa. "What are you doing here?"

"I've got a date with Bella," he told her, taking off his sunglasses as he walked over to meet her. "Why's the front door locked?"

She shrugged. "Where are Mama and Daddy?"

He patted his pockets, pretending to look for them. Sara loved her cousin, she really did, but his inability to take anything seriously made her want to strangle him sometimes.

She glanced at the apartment over the garage. "Is Tessa home?"

"She's wearing her invisible suit if she is," Hare told her, slipping back on his sunglasses as he leaned against her car. He was wearing white slacks and Sara wished for just a moment that her father hadn't washed her car.

She told him, "We're supposed to go somewhere." Not wanting to endure the ridicule, Sara didn't tell him where. She looked at her watch again, thinking she would give Tessa ten more minutes, then go home. She wasn't particularly excited about going to church, and the more she thought about Jeffrey's concerns, the more she was beginning to believe this was a bad idea.

Hare slid down his glasses, batting his eyelashes as he asked, "Aren't you going to tell me I look pretty?"

Sara was unable to stop herself from rolling her eyes. The thing she detested most about Hare was that he wasn't content to be silly by himself. He always managed to bring out the juvenile in others.

He offered, "I'll tell you if you tell me. You go first."

Sara had dressed for church, but she wasn't going to take the bait. "I talked to Jeffrey," she said, crossing her arms over her chest.

"Y'all married yet?"

"You know we're not."

"Don't forget I want to be a bridesmaid."

"Hare—"

"I told you that story, didn't I? About the cow getting the milk for free?"

"Cows don't drink milk," she returned. "Why didn't you tell me he'd been exposed?"

"There was some oath they made me take after medical school," he told her. "Something that rhymes with step-o-matic . . ."

"Hare—"

"Super-matic . . ."

"Hare." Sara sighed.

"Hippocratic!" he exclaimed, snapping his fingers. "I wondered why we all had to stand around in robes eating canapés, but you know I never pass up an opportunity to wear a dress."

"Since when did you develop scruples?"

"They dropped around the time I was thirteen." He winked at her. "Remember how you used to try to grab them when we took baths together?"

"We were two years old when I did that," she reminded, giving a disparaging downward glance. "And the phrase 'needle in a haystack' comes to mind."

"Oh!" he gasped, putting his hands to his mouth.

"Hey," Tessa called. She was walking down the street, Bella at her side. "Sorry I'm late."

"That's okay," Sara told her, relieved and disappointed at the same time.

Tessa kissed Hare's cheek. "You look so pretty!"

Hare and Sara said, "Thank you," at the same time.

"Let's go up to the house," Bella told them. "Hare, fetch me a Cocola, will you?" She dug around in her pocket and pulled out a key. "And get my shawl off the back of my chair."

"Yes, ma'am," he said, sprinting toward the house.

Sara told Tessa, "We're running late. Maybe we should—"

"Give me a minute to change," Tessa said, darting up the stairs to her apartment before Sara could bow out gracefully.

Bella put her arm around Sara's shoulder. "You look about ready to collapse."

"I was hoping Tess would notice."

"She probably did, but she's too excited about you coming along to let that get in the way." Bella leaned on the railing as she sat on the front steps.

Sara joined her aunt, saying, "I don't understand why she wants me to go."

"This is a new thing for her," Bella said. "She wants to share it."

Sara sat back on her elbows, wishing Tessa had found something more interesting to share. The theater downtown was running a Hitchcock retrospective, for instance. Or they could always learn needlepoint.

"Bella," Sara asked. "Why are you here?"

Bella leaned back beside her niece. "I made a fool of myself for love."

Sara would have laughed if anyone else had said it, but she knew her aunt Bella was particularly sensitive where romance was concerned.

"He was fifty-two," she said. "Young enough to be my son!"

Sara raised her eyebrows at the scandal.

"Left me for a forty-one-year-old chippie," Bella said sadly. "A redhead." Sara's expression must have shown some sort of solidarity, because Bella added, "Not like you." Then, putting a finer point on it, "Carpet didn't exactly match the drapes." She stared out at the road, wistful. "He was some kind of man, though. Very charming. Dapper."

"I'm sorry you lost him."

"The bad part is that I threw myself at his feet," she confided. "It's one thing to be dumped, quite another to beg for a second chance and have your face slapped."

"He didn't—"

"Oh, good Lord no," she laughed. "I pity the wayward soul who tries to raise his hand to your aunt Bella."

Sara smiled.

"You should take that as a lesson, though," the older woman warned. "You can only be rebuffed so many times."

Sara chewed her bottom lip, thinking she was getting really tired of people telling her she should marry Jeffrey.

"You get to be my age," Bella continued, "and different things matter than they did when you were young and fancy-free."

"Like what?"

"Like companionship. Like talking about literature and plays and current events. Like having someone around who understands you, has gone through the things you have and come out at the other end that much the wiser for it."

Sara could sense her aunt's sadness, but didn't know how to alleviate it. "I'm sorry, Bella."

"Well," she patted Sara's leg. "Don't worry about your aunt Bella. She's been through worse, I'll tell you that. Tossed around like a used box of crayons"— she winked— "but I've managed to maintain the same vibrant colors." Bella pursed her lips, studying Sara as if she had just noticed her for the first time. "What's on your mind, pumpkin?"

Sara knew better than to try to lie. "Where's Mama?"

"League of Women Voters," Bella said. "I don't know where that father of yours got off to. Probably down at the Waffle House talking politics with the other old men."

Sara took a deep breath and let it go, thinking now was as good a time as any. "Can I ask you something?"

"Shoot."

Sara turned to face her, lowering her voice in case Tessa had her windows open or Hare was about to sneak up on them. "You mentioned before about Daddy forgiving Mama when she cheated."

Bella cast a wary glance. "That's their business."

"I know," Sara agreed. "I just . . ." She decided to come out and say it. "It was Thomas Ward, wasn't it? She was interested in Thomas Ward."

Bella took her time before giving a single nod. To Sara's surprise, she provided, "He was your father's best friend since they were in school together."

Sara couldn't remember Eddie ever mentioning the man's name, though considering the circumstances, it made sense.

"He lost his best friend because of it. I think that hurt him almost as much as the possibility of losing your mother."

"Thomas Ward is the man who runs this church Tessa is so excited about."

Again, she nodded. "I was aware."

"The thing is," Sara began, wondering again how to phrase her words. "He has a son."

"I believe he has a couple of them. Some daughters, too."

"Tessa says he looks like me."

Bella's eyebrows shot up. "What are you saying?"

"I'm afraid to say anything."

Above them, Tessa's door opened and slammed shut. Her footsteps were quick on the stairs. Sara could almost feel her excitement.

"Honey," Bella said, putting her hand on Sara's knee. "Just because you're sitting in the henhouse, that don't make you a chicken."

"Bella—"

Tessa asked, "Ready?"

"Y'all have fun," Bella said, pressing her hand into Sara's shoulder as she stood. "I'll leave the light on."

❈ ❈ ❈ ❈

The church was not what Sara had been expecting. Located on the outskirts of the farm, the building resembled pictures of old Southern churches Sara had seen in storybooks as a child. Instead of the huge, ornate structures gracing Main Street in Heartsdale, their stained glass windows coloring the very heart of the town, the Church for the Greater Good was little more than a clapboard house, the exterior painted a high white, the front door very similar to the front door of Sara's own house. She would not have been surprised if the place was still lit by candles.

Inside was another story. Red carpet lined a large center aisle and Shaker-style wooden pews stood sentry on either side. The wood was unstained, and Sara could see the cutmarks in the scrolled backs where the pews had been carved by hand. Overhead were several large chandeliers. The pulpit was mahogany, an impressive looking piece of furniture, and the cross behind the baptismal area looked like it had been taken down from Mt. Sinai. Still, Sara had seen more elaborate churches with more riches openly displayed. There was something almost comforting in the spare design of the room, as if the architect had wanted to make sure the focus stayed on what happened inside the building rather than the building itself.

Tessa took Sara's hand as they entered the church. "Nice, huh?"

Sara nodded.

"I'm so glad you're here."

"I hope I don't disappoint you."

Tessa squeezed her hand. "How could you disappoint me?" she asked, leading Sara to the door behind the pulpit. She explained, "It starts in the fellowship hall, then we come in here for the service."

Tessa opened the door, revealing a large, brightly lit hall. There was a long table down the center with enough chairs to seat at least fifty people. Candelabras were lit, their flames gently flickering. A handful of people were sitting at the table, but most were standing around the roaring fire at the back of the room. There was a coffee urn on a card table under a bank of large windows along with what looked like the infamous honey buns Tessa had mentioned.

Getting ready for tonight, Sara had made the grand concession of wearing panty hose, some long ago admonishment from her mother about the connection between bare legs in church and burning in hell coming into her mind as she picked out something to wear. She saw from the crowd that she could have saved herself the trouble. Most of them were in jeans. A few of the women wore skirts, but they were of the homespun kind she had seen on Abigail Bennett.

"Come meet Thomas," Tessa said, dragging her over to the front of the table. An old man was sitting in a wheelchair, two women on either side of him.

"Thomas," Tessa told him, bending down, putting her hand over his. "This is my sister, Sara."

His face was slackened on one side, lips slightly parted, but there was a spark of pleasure in his eyes when he looked up at Sara. His mouth moved laboriously as he spoke, but Sara couldn't understand a word he said.

One of the women translated, "He says you have your mother's eyes."

Sara wasn't under the impression she had her mother's anything, but she smiled politely. "You know my mother?"

Thomas smiled back, and the woman said, "Cathy was here just yesterday with the most wonderful chocolate cake." She patted his hand like he was a child. "Wasn't she, Papa?"

"Oh," was all Sara could say. If Tessa was surprised, she didn't show it. She told Sara, "There's Lev. I'll be right back."

Sara stood with her hands clasped in front of her, wondering what in the hell she had thought she could accomplish by coming here.

"I'm Mary," the woman who had spoken first told her. "This is my sister Esther."

"Mrs. Bennett," she said, addressing Esther. "I'm so sorry for your loss."

"You found our Abby," the woman realized. She wasn't exactly looking at Sara, rather somewhere over her shoulder. After a few seconds, she seemed to focus back in. "Thank you for taking care of her."

"I'm sorry there wasn't more I could do."

Esther's lower lip trembled. Not that they looked anything alike, but the woman reminded Sara of her own mother. She had Cathy's quietness about her, the resolute calm that came from unquestioning spirituality.

Esther said, "You and your husband have been very kind."

"Jeffrey's doing everything he can," Sara said, knowing not to mention Rebecca or the meeting at the diner.

"Thank you," a tall, well-dressed man interrupted. He had sidled up to Sara without her knowing. "I'm Paul Ward," he told Sara, and she would have known he was a lawyer even if Jeffrey hadn't told her. "I'm Abby's uncle. One of them, that is."

"Nice to meet you," Sara told him, thinking he stuck out like a sore thumb. She didn't know much about fashion, but she could tell the suit Paul was wearing had set him back a bit. It hung on him like a second skin.

"Cole Connolly," the man beside him said. He was much shorter than Paul and probably thirty years older, but he had an energetic vibe, and Sara was reminded of what her mother had always called being filled with the spirit of the Lord. She was also reminded of what Jeffrey said about the man. Connolly looked harmless enough, but Jeffrey was seldom wrong about people.

Paul asked Esther, "Would you mind checking on Rachel?"

Esther seemed to hesitate, but she agreed, telling Sara, "Thank you again, Doctor," before she left.

Apropos of nothing, Paul told Sara, "My wife, Lesley, couldn't make it tonight. She's staying home with one of our boys."

"I hope he's not ill."

"Usual stuff," he said. "I'm sure you know what I'm talking about."

"Yes," she answered, wondering why she felt as if she needed to keep her guard up around this man. For all intents and purposes he looked like a deacon at the church—which he probably was—but Sara hadn't liked the familiar way he spoke to her, as if by knowing her job, he knew something about her.

Putting a finer point on it, Paul asked Sara, "You're the county coroner?"

"Yes."

"The service for Abby is tomorrow." He lowered his voice. "There's the matter of the death certificate."

Sara felt a bit shocked that he had been forward enough to ask her, but she told him, "I can have copies sent to the funeral home tomorrow."

"It's Brock's," he told her, naming Grant's undertaker. "I'd appreciate it if you would."

Connolly cleared his throat uncomfortably. Mary whispered, "Paul," indicating their father. Obviously, the old man was troubled by this talk. He had shifted in his chair, his head turned to the side. Sara could not tell whether there were tears in his eyes.

"Just a bit of business out of the way," Paul covered. He changed the subject quickly. "You know, Dr. Linton, I've voted for you several times." The coroner's job was an elected position, though Sara was hardly flattered, considering she had run uncontested for the last twelve years.

She asked him, "You live in Grant County?"

"Papa used to," he said, putting his hand on the old man's shoulder. "On the lake."

Sara felt a lump in her throat. Close to her parents.

Paul said, "My family moved out here several years ago. I never bothered to change my registration."

"You know," Mary said, "I don't think Ken has, either." She told Sara, "Ken is Rachel's husband. He's around here somewhere." She pointed to a round-looking Santa Claus of a man who was talking to a group of teenagers. "There."

"Oh," was all Sara could say. The teens around him were mostly girls, all dressed as Abby had been, all around Abby's age. She scanned the rest of the room, thinking that there were a lot of young women here. She studiously avoided Cole Connolly, but she was keenly aware of his presence. He seemed normal enough, but then what did a man who could bury and poison a young girl—perhaps several young girls—look like? It wasn't as if he'd have horns and fangs.

Thomas said something, and Sara forced her attention back to the conversation.

Mary translated again, "He says he's voted for you, too. Good Lord, Papa. I can't believe none of y'all have changed your registrations. That must be illegal. Cole, you need to get onto them about that."

Connolly looked apologetic. "Mine is in Catoogah."

Mary asked, "Is yours still over in Grant, Lev?"

Sara turned around, bumping into a large man who was holding a small child in his arms.

"Whoa," Lev said, taking her elbow. He was taller than she was, but they shared the same green eyes and dark red hair.

"You're Lev," was all she could say.

"Guilty," he told her, beaming a smile that showed perfect white teeth.

Sara was not normally a vindictive person, but she wanted to take the smile off his face. She chose probably the most inappropriate way in the world to do it. "I'm sorry about your niece."

His smile dropped immediately. "Thank you." His eyes moistened, he smiled at his son, and just as quickly as the emotions had come, he had pushed them away. "Tonight we're here to celebrate life," he said. "We're here to raise up our voices and show our joy in the Lord."

"Amen," Mary said, patting the railing of her father's wheelchair for emphasis.

Lev told Sara, "This is my son, Zeke."

Sara smiled at the child, thinking that Tessa was right, he was just about the most adorable boy she had ever seen. He was on the small side for five, but she could tell from his big hands and feet that he was due for a growth spurt soon. She said, "Nice to meet you, Zeke."

Under his father's watchful eye, the boy reached out his hand for Sara to shake. She took his tiny fingers in her larger ones, feeling an instant connection.

Lev rubbed his back, saying, "My pride and joy," an indisputable look of happiness on his face.

Sara could only nod. Zeke's mouth opened in a yawn that showed his tonsils.

"Are you sleepy?" she asked.

"Yes, ma'am."

"He's pretty wiped out," Lev excused. He set Zeke down on the floor, saying, "Go find your aunt Esther and tell her you're ready for bed." Lev kissed the top of his head, then patted his bottom to get him moving.

"It's been a hard couple of days for all of us," Lev told Sara. She could feel his grief, but part of her wondered if he was putting on a show for her benefit, knowing she would report back to Jeffrey.

Mary said, "We take comfort in knowing she's in a better place."

Lev's brow furrowed as if he didn't understand, but he recovered quickly, saying, "Yes, yes. That's true." Sara could tell from his reaction that he had been taken off guard by his sister's words. She wondered if he had been talking about Rebecca instead of Abby, but there was no way to ask without revealing what Esther had done.

Sara saw Tessa across the room. She was unwrapping a honey bun as she talked to a plainly dressed young man who had his long hair pulled back into a ponytail. Tessa saw Sara looking and excused herself, walking over. Her hand trailed along Zeke's head as she passed the boy. Sara had never been so happy to see her sister in all her life—until she opened her mouth.

She pointed to Sara and Lev. "Y'all look more alike than we do."

They laughed, and Sara did her best to join in. Both Lev and Paul were taller than Sara, Mary and Esther easily matching her own five eleven. For once, Tessa was the one whose height made her look out of place. Sara could think of few other times when she had felt more uncomfortable.

Lev asked Sara, "You don't remember me, do you?"

Sara looked around the room, feeling embarrassed that she didn't remember a boy she had met over thirty years ago. "I'm sorry, I don't."

"Sunday school," he said. "Was it Mrs. Dugdale, Papa?" Thomas nodded, the right side of his face going up into a smile. "You kept asking all these questions," Lev told Sara. "I wanted to tape your mouth shut because we were supposed to get Kool-Aid after we did our Bible verses and you'd keep holding up your hand and asking all sorts of things."

"Sounds about right," Tessa said. She was eating a honey bun, acting as if she hadn't a care in the world, as if her mother hadn't had an affair with the man sitting in a wheelchair beside her, the man who had fathered a child who looked almost identical to Sara.

Lev told his father, "There was this storybook with a drawing of Adam and Eve, and she kept saying, 'Mrs. Dugdale, if God created Adam and Eve, why do they have belly buttons?' "

Thomas whooped an unmistakable laugh, and his son joined in. Sara must have been getting used to Thomas's speech, because she understood him perfectly when he said, "It's a good question."

Lev said, "I don't know why she didn't just tell you it was an artistic rendering, not actual footage."

Sara remembered very little of Mrs. Dugdale other than her constant cheerfulness, but she did recall, "I think her response was that you had to have faith."

"Ah," Lev said, thoughtful. "I detect a scientist's disdain for religion."

"I'm sorry," Sara apologized. She had certainly not come here to insult anyone.

" 'Religion without science is blind,' " Lev quoted.

"You're forgetting the first part," she reminded him. "Einstein also said that science without religion is lame."

Lev's eyebrows shot up.

Unable to stop her smart mouth, Sara added, "And he also said that we should look for what is, not what we think should be."

"All theories, by their nature, are unproven ideas."

Thomas laughed again, obviously enjoying himself. Sara felt embarrassed, as if she had been caught showing off.

Lev tried to keep her going. "It's an interesting dichotomy, isn't it?"

"I don't know," Sara mumbled. She wasn't about to get into a philosophical argument with the man in front of his own family, standing in the back room of the church his father had probably built with his own two hands. Sara was also mindful that she did not want to make things bad for Tessa.

Lev seemed oblivious. "Chicken or the egg?" he asked. "Did God create man, or did man create God?"

Trying not to get pulled in, Sara decided to say something she thought he wanted to hear. "Religion plays an important role in society."

"Oh, yes," he agreed, and she couldn't tell if he was teasing her or baiting her. Either way, she was annoyed.

She said, "Religion gives a common bond. It creates groups, families, who form societies with common values and goals. These societies tend to thrive more than groups without a religious influence. They pass on this imperative to their children, the children pass it on to theirs, and so on."

"The God gene," he provided.

"I suppose," she allowed, really wishing she hadn't let herself get roped into this.

Suddenly, Connolly spoke up, angrier than Sara could have imagined. "Young lady, you are either at the right hand of God or you are not."

Sara blushed crimson at his tone. "I just—"

"You are either the faithful or the faithless," Connolly insisted. There was a Bible on the table and he picked it up, raising his voice. "I pity the faithless, for they inherit an eternity in the fiery pits of hell."

"Amen," Mary murmured, but Sara kept her eyes on Connolly. In the blink of an eye, he had changed into the man Jeffrey had warned her about, and she quickly tried to appease him. "I'm sorry if I—"

"Now, Cole," Lev interrupted, his tone teasing as if Connolly were a tiger without the teeth. "We're just joshing around here."

"Religion is nothing to play around with," Connolly countered, the veins standing out in his neck. "You, young lady, you don't play with people's lives! We're talking about salvation here. Life and death!"

Tessa said, "Cole, come on," trying to diffuse the situation. Sara could certainly take care of herself, but she was glad to have her sister's support, especially considering she had no idea what Connolly was capable of.

"We have a guest, Cole." Lev's tone was still polite, but there was a definite edge to it—not exactly threatening but asserting whatever authority he had in this place. "A guest who is entitled to her own opinions, much as you are."

Thomas Ward spoke, but Sara could only make out a few words. She gathered he said something about God blessing man with the freedom to choose.

Connolly was visibly biting back his anger when he said, "I should go see if Rachel needs help." He stormed away, his fists clenched at his sides. Sara noticed his broad shoulders and muscular back. She found herself thinking that despite his age, Cole Connolly could easily take on half the men in this room without breaking a sweat.

Lev watched him go. She didn't know the preacher well enough to tell if he was amused or irritated, but he seemed genuine when he told her, "I do apologize for that."

Tessa asked, "What on earth was that all about? I've never seen him so upset."

"Abby has been a great loss to us," Lev answered. "We all deal with grief in our own way."

Sara took a second to find her voice. "I'm sorry I upset him."

"You have no need to apologize," Lev told Sara, and from his chair, Thomas made a noise of agreement.

Lev continued, "Cole's from a different generation. He's not one for introspection." He gave an open smile. " 'Old age should burn and rave at close of day . . . ' "

Tessa finished, " 'Rage, rage against the dying of the light.' "

Sara didn't know what shocked her more, Connolly's flash of anger or Tessa quoting Dylan Thomas. Her sister had a twinkle in her eye, and Sara finally understood Tessa's sudden religious conversion. She had a crush on the pastor.

Lev told Sara, "I'm sorry he upset you."

"I'm not upset," Sara lied. She tried to sound convincing, but Lev looked troubled that his guest had been insulted.

"The problem with religion," Lev began, "is that you always get to that point where the questions can't be answered."

"Faith," Sara heard herself saying.

"Yes." He smiled, and she didn't know if he was agreeing with her or not. "Faith." He raised an eyebrow at his father. "Faith is a tricky proposition."

Sara must have looked as angry as she felt, because Paul said, "Brother, it's a wonder you never managed to marry a second time, the way you have with women."

Thomas was laughing again, a trail of spittle dribbling down his chin, which Mary quickly wiped off. He spoke, an obvious effort as what he had to say was not brief, but again Sara couldn't make out a word of it.

Instead of translating, Mary chastised, "Papa."

Lev told Sara, "He said if you were a foot shorter and a hair more annoyed, you'd be the spitting image of your mother."

Tessa laughed with him. "It's nice to have that put on somebody else for a change." She told Thomas, "People are always saying I look like my mama and Sara looks like the milkman."

Sara wasn't certain, but she thought there was something reserved about Thomas's smile.

Lev said, "Unfortunately, the only thing I inherited from Papa is his bull-headedness."

The family laughed good-naturedly.

Lev glanced at his watch. "We'll be starting in a few minutes. Sara, do you mind joining me out front?"

"Of course not," she said, hoping he didn't want to finish their discussion.

Lev held open the door to the sanctuary for her, closing it softly behind them. He kept his hand on the knob as if he wanted to make sure no one followed them.

"Listen," he said, "I'm sorry if I pushed your buttons in there."

"You didn't," she replied.

"I miss my theological debates with my father," he explained. "He can't talk very well, as you can see, and I just . . . well, I might have gotten a little carried away in there. I want to apologize."

"I'm not offended," she told him.

"Cole can get a little prickly," he continued. "He sees things in black and white."

"I gathered."

"There are just certain kinds of people." Lev showed his teeth as he smiled. "I was in the academic world for a few years. Psychology." He seemed almost embarrassed. "There's a trend among the highly educated to assume anyone who believes in God is either stupid or deluded."

"It was never my intention to give you that impression."

He got the dig, and put in one of his own. "I understand Cathy is a very religious person."

"She is," Sara said, thinking she never wanted this man to even think about her mother, let alone mention her name. "She's one of the most intelligent people I know."

"My own mother passed away shortly after I was born. I never had the pleasure of knowing her."

"I'm sorry to hear that," Sara told him.

Lev was staring at her, then he nodded as if he had made up his mind about something. If they hadn't been in a church and if he hadn't had a gold cross pinned to his lapel, she could have sworn he was flirting with her. He said, "Your husband is a very lucky man."

Instead of correcting him, Sara told him, "Thank you."

❈ ❈ ❈ ❈

Jeffrey was lying in bed reading *Andersonville* when Sara got home. She was so glad to have him there that for a moment she didn't trust herself to speak.

He closed the book, using his finger to mark his place. "How'd it go?"

She shrugged, unbuttoning her blouse. "Tessa was happy."

"That's good," he said. "She needs to be happy."

She unzipped her skirt. Her panty hose were on the floor of the car, where she had taken them off on the way home.

"Did you see the moon?" he asked, and she had to think a minute to understand what he meant.

"Oh." She looked out the bedroom windows, where the lake was reflecting the full moon almost perfectly. "It's gorgeous."

"Still no word on Rebecca Bennett."

"I talked to her mother tonight," Sara said. "She's very worried."

"I am, too."

"Do you think she's in danger?"

"I think I'm not going to sleep well until we find out where she is."

"Nothing on the search in the woods?"

"Nothing," he confirmed. "Frank didn't find anything at the jewelry stores. We still haven't heard back from the lab on blood typing from the second box."

"Ron must have gotten tied up," she said, thinking it was odd for the pathologist not to do something he had promised to do. "They could've gotten in a rush or something."

He gave her a careful look. "Anything happen tonight?"

"In particular?" she asked. The confrontation with Cole Connolly came to mind, but Sara was still upset about the discussion. She didn't quite know how to articulate her feelings to Jeffrey, and the more she thought about it, the more she considered Lev's interpretation of Connolly's behavior might be correct. She was also a little embarrassed by her own behavior and wasn't completely sure she hadn't baited the old man into the altercation.

She told Jeffrey, "The brother Paul asked me for a copy of Abby's death certificate."

"That's odd," Jeffrey commented. "I wonder why?"

"Maybe there's a will or a trust?" Sara unfastened her bra as she walked into the bathroom.

"He's a lawyer," Jeffrey told her. "I'm sure there's some legal wrangling behind it." He put the book on his bedside table and sat up.

"Anything else?"

"I met Lev's son," she said, wondering why she was bringing it up. The child had the longest, prettiest eyelashes she had ever seen, and just the thought of the way he had yawned, his mouth widening with the kind of abandon only a child can show, opened up a space in her heart that she had tried to close a long time ago.

"Zeke?" Jeffrey asked. "He's a cute kid."

"Yeah," she agreed, checking the clothes basket for a T-shirt that was clean enough to sleep in.

"What else happened?"

"I let myself get into a religious discussion with Lev." Sara found one of Jeffrey's shirts and put it on. When she stood up, she noticed his toothbrush in the cup beside hers. His shaving cream and razor were lined up beside each other, his deodorant next to hers on the shelf.

"Who won?" he asked.

"Neither," she managed, squirting toothpaste onto her toothbrush. She closed her eyes as she brushed her teeth, feeling dead tired.

"You didn't let anybody talk you into getting baptized, did you?"

She felt too tired to laugh. "No. They're all very nice. I can see why Tessa likes going there."

"They didn't handle snakes or speak in tongues?"

"They sang 'Amazing Grace' and talked about good works." She rinsed her mouth and dropped her toothbrush back into the cup. "They're a lot more fun than Mama's church, I can tell you that."

"Really?"

"Uh huh," she said, climbing into bed, relishing the feel of clean sheets. The fact that Jeffrey did the laundry was reason enough to forgive him for most if not all of his ills.

He slid down beside her, leaning up on his elbow. "Fun how?"

"No fire and brimstone, as Bella would say." Remembering, she asked, "Did you tell them I'm your wife?"

He had the grace to look embarrassed. "It might have slipped out."

She lightly punched him in the chest and he fell over on his back as if she had really hit him.

She said, "They're a tight bunch."

"The family?"

"I didn't notice anything particularly weird about them. Well, no more weird than my family, and before you open your mouth, Mr. Tolliver, remember I've met your mother."

He accepted defeat with a slight nod of his head. "Was Mary there?"

"Yes."

"She's the other sister. Lev's excuse for not coming in was that she was ill."

"She didn't look sick to me," Sara told him. "But I didn't exactly give her an exam."

"What about the others?"

She thought for a moment. "Rachel wasn't around much. That Paul certainly likes to control things."

"Lev does, too."

"He said my husband is a lucky man." She smiled, knowing this would annoy him.

Jeffrey worked his jaw. "That so?"

She laughed as she put her head on his chest. "I told him I was the lucky one to have such an honest husband." She said "husband" in the grand Southern tradition, drawing out the word as "huuuz-bun."

She smoothed down his chest hair because it was tickling her nose. Jeffrey traced his finger along his Auburn class ring, which she was still wearing. She closed her eyes, waiting for him to say something, to ask her the same question he had been asking her for the last six months, but he didn't.

Instead, he said, "What did you need to see for yourself tonight?"

Knowing she couldn't postpone the inevitable much longer, she told him, "Mama had an affair."

His body tensed. "*Your* mother? Cathy?" He was as disbelieving as Sara had been.

"She told me a few years ago," Sara said. "She said it wasn't a sexual affair, but she moved out of the house and left Daddy."

"That doesn't sound like her at all."

"I'm not supposed to tell anybody."

"I won't tell," he agreed. "God, who would believe me?"

Sara closed her eyes again, wishing her mother had never told her in the first place. At the time, Cathy had been trying to help Sara see that she could work things out with Jeffrey if she really wanted to, but now, the information was about as welcome as a theological discussion with Cole Connolly.

She told him, "It was with this guy who founded the church. Thomas Ward."

Jeffrey waited a beat. "And?"

"And I don't know what happened, but obviously Mama and Daddy got back together." She looked up at Jeffrey. "She told me they got together because she was pregnant with me."

He took a second to respond. "That's not the only reason she went back to him."

"Children change things," Sara said, coming as close to talking about their own inability to have children as she had ever dared. "A child is a bond between two people. It ties you together for life."

"So does love," he told her, putting his hand to her cheek. "Love ties you together. Experiences. Sharing your lives. Watching each other grow old."

Sara laid her head back down.

"All I know," Jeffrey continued, as if they hadn't been talking about themselves, "is that your mother loves your father."

Sara braced herself. "You said Lev has my hair and my eyes."

Jeffrey didn't breathe for a full twenty seconds. "Christ," he whispered, disbelieving. "You don't think that—" He stopped. "I know I was teasing you, but—" Even he couldn't say it out loud.

Sara kept her head on his chest as she looked up at his chin. He had shaved, probably expecting some kind of celebration tonight in light of the good news about his blood test.

She asked him, "Are you tired?"

"Are you?"

She twirled her fingers in his hair. "I might be open to persuasion."

"How open?"

Sara laid back, taking him with her. "Why don't you feel for yourself?"

He took her up on the offer, giving her a slow, soft kiss.

She told him, "I'm so happy."

"I'm happy you're happy."

"No," she put her hands to his face. "I'm happy you're okay."

He kissed her again, taking his time, teasing her lips. Sara felt herself start to relax as he pressed his body into hers. She loved the weight of him on top of her, the way he knew how to touch her in all the right places. If making love was an art, Jeffrey was a master, and as his mouth worked its way down her neck, she turned her head, eyes partly closed, enjoying the sensation of him until her peripheral vision caught an unusual flash of light across the lake.

Sara narrowed her eyes, wondering if it was a trick of the moon against the water or something else.

"What?" Jeffrey asked, sensing her mind was elsewhere.

"Shh," she told him, watching the lake. She saw the flash again, and pressed against Jeffrey's chest, saying, "Get up."

He did as he was told, asking, "What's going on?"

"Are they still searching the forest?"

"Not in the dark," he said. "What—"

Sara snapped off the bedside light as she got out of bed. Her eyes took a moment to adjust, and she kept her hands in front of her, feeling her way to the window. "I saw something," she told him. "Come here."

Jeffrey got out of bed, standing beside her, staring across the lake. "I don't see—" He stopped.

The flash had come again. It was definitely a light. Someone was across the lake with a flashlight. The spot was almost exactly where they had found Abby.

"Rebecca."

Jeffrey moved as if a gun had been fired. He'd thrown on his jeans before Sara even managed to find her clothes. She could hear his footsteps cracking the pine needles in the backyard as she slipped on a pair of sneakers and took out after him.

The full moon illuminated the path around the lake, and Sara kept pace with Jeffrey from several yards behind. He hadn't put on a shirt, and she knew that he wasn't wearing shoes because she had put on his. The heel of the right sneaker was pushed down, and Sara made herself stop for a few seconds in order to slip it on properly. This cost her precious time, and she pushed herself even harder as she ran, feeling her heart pound in her throat. She ran this same route most mornings, but now she felt as if it was taking forever to get to the other side of the lake.

Jeffrey was a sprinter while Sara was better suited for long-distance running. When she finally passed her parents' house, her second wind kicked in and in a few minutes, she had caught up with him. They both slowed their pace as they approached the forest, finally coming full stop as a flashlight beam crossed the path in front of them.

Sara felt herself being yanked down by Jeffrey as he crouched out of sight. Her own breathing matched his, and she thought that the noise alone would give them away.

They watched as the flashlight went toward the woods, further in to the spot where Jeffrey and Sara had found Abigail just three days ago. Sara had a moment of panic. Perhaps the killer came back later for the bodies. Perhaps there was a third box that all their searching had not turned up and the abductor had returned to perform another part of the ritual.

Jeffrey's mouth was close to her ear. He whispered, "Stay here," walking off in a crouch before she could stop him. She remembered he was barefooted, and wondered if he was even thinking through his actions. His gun was back at the house. No one knew they were out here.

Sara followed him, keeping well behind, desperately trying not to step on anything that would make a noise. Ahead, she could see the flashlight had stilled, pointing down at the ground, probably at the empty hole where Abby had been.

A high-pitched scream echoed in the woods, and Sara froze.

A laugh—more like a cackle—followed, and she was more frightened by this than the scream.

Jeffrey kept his voice firm, authoritative, as he told the person holding the light, "Stay exactly where you are," and the girl screamed again. The flashlight went up, and Jeffrey said, "Get that thing out of my face." Whoever was on the other end obeyed, and Sara took another step forward.

He said, "What the fuck do you two think you're doing out here?"

Sara could see them all now—a teenage boy and girl standing in front of Jeffrey. Even though he was wearing nothing but a pair of jeans, he looked threatening.

The girl screamed again when Sara accidentally stepped on a twig.

"Jesus," Jeffrey hissed, still out of breath from the run. He asked the young couple, "Do you know what happened out here?"

The kid was about fifteen and almost as scared as the girl beside him. "I-I was just showing her . . ." His voice cracked, though he was well beyond that embarrassing stage. "We were just having fun."

"You think this is fun?" Jeffrey snarled. "A woman died out here. She was buried alive."

The girl started crying. Sara recognized her immediately. She cried just about every time she was at the clinic, whether she was getting an injection or not.

Sara asked, "Liddy?"

The girl startled, though she had seen Sara standing there seconds ago. "Dr. Linton?"

"It's okay."

Jeffrey snapped, "It's not okay."

"You're scaring them to death," Sara told Jeffrey, then asked the kids, "What are you two doing out here this late?"

"Roger wanted to show me . . . to show me . . . the place . . ." She sniveled, "I'm sorry!"

Roger joined in, "I'm sorry, too. We were just messing around. I'm sorry." He was speaking fast now, probably realizing Sara had the power to get him out of this. "I'm sorry, Dr. Linton. We didn't mean anything bad. We were just—"

"It's late," Sara interrupted, suppressing the desire to throttle

them. Her side ached from the run and she felt the chill in the air.
"You both need to go home now."

"Yes, ma'am," Roger said. He grabbed Liddy by the arm and practically dragged her toward the road.

"Stupid kids," Jeffrey muttered.

"Are you okay?"

He sat down on a rock, muttering a low curse, still breathing hard.
"I cut my damn foot."

Sara joined him, aware that she was out of breath herself. "Are
you just determined not to get through one day this week without in-
juring yourself?"

"You'd think," he allowed. "Christ. They scared the shit out of
me."

"At least it wasn't . . ." She didn't finish the sentence. They both
knew what it could have been.

"I've got to find out who did this to her," Jeffrey said. "I owe that
to her mother. She needs to know why this happened."

Sara looked across the lake, trying to find her house—their house.
The floodlights had been tripped when they ran outside, and as Sara
watched they blinked off.

She asked, "How's your foot?"

"Throbbing." His chest heaved in a sigh. "Jesus, I'm falling
apart."

She rubbed his back. "You're fine."

"My knee, my shoulder." He lifted his leg. "My foot."

"You left out your eye," she reminded him, wrapping her arm
around his waist, trying to comfort him.

"I'm turning into an old man."

"There are worse things you can turn into," she pointed out, though
from his silence she could tell he wasn't in the mood for teasing.

"This case is getting to me."

All of his cases got to him; it was one of the many things she loved
about him. "I know," she said, admitting, "I'd feel a lot better if we
knew where Rebecca was."

"There's something I'm missing," he said. He took her hand in his.
"There has to be something I'm missing."

Sara looked out at the lake, the moon glinting against the waves as
they lapped against the shore. Was this the last thing Abby had seen

before she'd been buried alive? Was this the last thing Rebecca had seen?

She said, "I need to tell you something."

"More about your parents?"

"No," she said, feeling like kicking herself for not telling him this before. "It's about Cole Connolly. I'm sure it's nothing, but—"

"Tell me," he interrupted. "I'll decide whether it's nothing or not."

THURSDAY

CHAPTER ELEVEN

Lena sat at the kitchen table, staring at her cell phone. She had to call Terri Stanley. There was no way of getting around it. She had to apologize, to tell her she would do everything she could to help her. What she would do beyond that was a mystery. How could she help her? What could she do to save Terri when there was nothing Lena could do to save herself?

In the hall, Nan shut the bathroom door with a click. Lena waited until she heard the shower running, then Nan's pained rendition of some pop song that was playing on every radio station, before she flipped the phone open and dialed the Stanleys' number.

Since the altercation at the gas station, Lena's mind had turned the number into a mantra, so that as her fingers worked the buttons, she had a sense of déjà vu.

She put the phone to her ear, counting six rings before the phone was picked up. Her heart stopped mid-beat as she prayed that the person on the other end wasn't Dale.

Obviously, Lena's name showed up on the Stanleys' caller ID. "What do you want?" Terri hissed, her voice little more than a whisper.

"I want to apologize," Lena said. "I want to help you."

"You can help me by leaving me alone," she replied, her voice still low.

"Where's Dale?"

"He's outside." Terri sounded increasingly frightened. "He'll be back any minute. He'll see your number on the phone."

"Tell him I called to thank you for coming in."

"He's not going to believe that."

"Terri, listen to me —"

"It's not like I've got a choice."

"I shouldn't have hurt you."

"I've heard that before."

Lena winced at the implication. "You need to get out of there."

She was quiet for a second. "What makes you think I want to?"

"Because I know," Lena said, tears coming into her eyes. "Jesus, Terri. I know, okay? Trust me."

Terri was silent for so long that Lena thought she had hung up. "Terri?"

"How do you know?"

Lena's heart was thumping hard enough to press against her ribs. She had never admitted anything about Ethan to another person, and she still found herself unable to come right out and say it. She could only tell Terri, "I know about it the same way you do."

Again, the younger woman was quiet. Terri asked, "You ever try to get away?"

Lena thought about all the times she had tried to make a break: not answering the phone, avoiding the gym, hiding out at work. He always found her. He always found a way back in.

"You think you can help me?" Terri asked. An almost hysterical note was threaded through the question.

"I'm a cop."

"Sister, you ain't nothin'," she said, harshly. "We're both drowning in the same ocean."

Lena felt her words pierce like daggers. She tried to speak, but there was a soft click on the line, then nothing. Lena waited, holding out hope, until the recorded voice of the operator bleated through the receiver, advising her to hang up and try the number again.

Nan came into the kitchen, her natty pink robe tied around her waist, a towel wrapped around her head. "You going to be home for dinner tonight?"

"Yes," Lena said. Then, "No. I don't know. Why?"

"I thought it would be nice to talk," she said, putting the kettle on the stove. "See how you're doing. I haven't talked to you since you got back from Hank's."

"I'm doing okay," Lena assured her.

Nan turned to look at her closely. "You look upset."

"It's been a rough week."

"I saw Ethan riding his bike up the driveway just now."

Lena stood so quick she was dizzy. "I should get to work."

"Why don't you invite him in?" Nan offered. "I'll make some more tea."

"No," Lena muttered. "I'm running late." She was always nervous when Ethan was around Nan. He was too volatile, and she was too ashamed to let Nan see the kind of man she had ended up with.

Lena said, "I'll see you later," tucking her cell phone into her jacket. She practically ran out the front door, stopping short when she saw Ethan standing at her car. He was pulling off something that had been taped to the driver's side window.

She walked down the steps as if her heart wasn't in her throat.

"What's this?" Ethan asked, holding up a mailing envelope. She recognized Greg's handwriting from ten feet away. "Who else calls you Lee?"

She grabbed it from him before he could stop her. "Just about everybody who knows me," she told him. "What are you doing here?"

"I thought I'd come by to see you before work."

She looked at her watch. "You're going to be late."

"It's okay."

"Your parole officer told you that if you were late again, she'd write you up."

"That dyke can kiss my ass."

"She can send you back to jail is what she can do, Ethan."

"Chill out, okay?" He made a grab for the envelope, but again she was too quick. He frowned and asked, "What is it?"

Lena saw she wasn't going to get out of the driveway until she opened the envelope. She turned it over, pulling the tape carefully like she was an old lady trying to save the wrapping paper on a present.

"What is it?" Ethan repeated.

She opened the envelope, praying to God there wasn't something inside that would cause a problem. She slid out a CD with a blank white label on it. "It's a CD," she said.

"A CD of what?"

"Ethan," Lena began, looking back at the house. She could see Nan peering through the front window. "Get in the car," she told him.

"Why?"

She popped the hatch so he could stow his bike. "Because you're going to be late for work."

"What's the CD?"

"I don't know." She started to pick up his bike, but he took over, the muscles on his arms flexing against his long-sleeved T-shirt. Back in his skinhead days, he had tattooed himself all over with Aryan Nazi symbols, and now he seldom wore anything that would expose them—especially at his job bussing tables at the university coffee shop.

She got into the car, waiting for him to secure the bike and get in. Lena tucked the CD over the visor, hoping he would forget about it. Ethan pulled it out as soon as he settled into the seat.

"Who sent you this?"

"Just a friend." She told him, "Put on your seat belt."

"Why was it taped to your car?"

"Maybe he didn't want to come in."

Lena realized she had said "he" about a second after the word left her mouth. She tried to act like it hadn't happened, putting the car into reverse and backing out of the driveway. As she turned back around, she chanced a look at Ethan. His jaw was so tight she was surprised his teeth didn't start cracking.

Without saying anything, he turned on her radio and pressed the eject button. His Radiohead CD slid out. He held it by the edges, forcing in Greg's CD as if it was a pill he wanted to shove down somebody's throat.

Lena felt herself tense as guitar was strummed, followed by some feedback. The intro took a few seconds, heavy guitar and drums leading up to the unmistakable voice of Ann Wilson.

Ethan wrinkled his nose like there was a bad smell. "What's this shit?"

"Heart," she said, trying to keep her emotions flat. Her own heart was beating so fast she was sure he could hear it over the music.

He kept scowling. "I've never heard this song before."

"It's a new album."

"A new album?" he repeated, and even though she kept her eyes on the road she could still feel him staring a hole into her. "Aren't they the ones who were fucking each other?"

"They're sisters," Lena said, disgusted that old rumor was still around. Heart had made a huge impact on the rock scene, and invariably, the boys in charge had felt threatened enough to spread nasty rumors. Being a twin, Lena had heard every filthy male fantasy about sisters there was. The thought of it made her sick.

Ethan turned up the volume a notch as she coasted through a stop sign. "It's not bad," he said, probably testing her. "Is this the fat one singing?"

"She's not fat."

Ethan barked a laugh.

"She can lose weight, Ethan. You'll always be a stupid bastard." When he just laughed again, she added, "Like Kurt Cobain was so hot."

"I didn't like that faggot."

"Why is it," Lena asked, "that every woman who doesn't want to fuck you is a dyke and every guy who isn't cool enough to be you is a faggot?"

"I never said—"

"My sister happened to be a lesbian," Lena reminded him.

"I know that."

"My best friend is a lesbian," Lena said, even though she had never given much thought to Nan being her best friend.

"What the fuck is wrong with you?"

"What's wrong with me?" she echoed, slamming on the brakes so hard his head nearly banged into the dashboard. "I told you to put on your fucking seat belt."

"All right," he said, giving her a look that said she was being an unreasonable bitch.

"Forget it," she told him, taking off her own seat belt.

"What are you doing?" he asked as she reached over to open his door. "Jesus Christ, what—"

"Get out," she ordered.

"What the fuck?"

She pushed him harder, screaming, "Get the fuck out of my car!"

"All right!" he screamed back, getting out of the car. "You're god-damn crazy, you know that?"

She pressed the gas pedal to the floorboard, making his door slam from the momentum. She drove maybe fifty feet before hitting the brakes so hard the tires squealed. When she got out of the car, Ethan was walking up the road, his body vibrating with rage. She could see his fists were clenched and spit flew from his mouth as he yelled, "Don't you ever drive away from me again, you stupid bitch!"

Lena felt amazingly calm as she pulled his bike out of the back of the car and dropped it on the road. Ethan started running to catch up with her. He was still running when she glanced up in her rearview mirror as she turned the corner.

❖ ❖ ❖ ❖

"What are you smiling about?" Jeffrey asked as soon as she walked into the squad room. He was standing by the coffee machine, and she wondered if he was waiting for her.

"Nothing," she told him.

He poured her a cup of coffee and handed it to her.

She took it, feeling cautious, saying, "Thanks."

"You want to tell me about Terri Stanley?"

Lena felt her stomach drop.

He topped off his own cup before saying, "In my office."

Lena led the way, sweat dripping down her back, wondering if this was finally the last straw for him. The only job she had ever known was being a cop. There was nothing else she could do. Her hiatus last year had proven as much.

He leaned on his desk, waiting for her to take a seat.

He said, "You weren't at the picnic last year."

"No," she agreed, clutching the arms on the chair much as Terri Stanley had done two days before.

"What's going on, Lena?"

"I thought . . ." Lena began, not able to finish her sentence. What did she think? What could she tell Jeffrey without revealing too much about herself?

"Is it the alcohol?" he asked, and for a moment she had no idea what he was talking about.

"No," she said. Then, "I made that up."

He didn't seem surprised. "Really?"

"Yeah," she admitted. She let some of the truth come out, a thin stream of air escaping from a balloon. "Dale hits her."

Jeffrey had been about to take a sip of coffee, but his cup stopped midair.

"I saw bruises on her arm." She nodded her head, like she was confirming it to herself. "I recognized them. I know what they look like."

Jeffrey put down his cup.

"I told her I'd help her get away."

He guessed, "She didn't want to go."

Lena shook her head.

He shifted, crossing his arms over his chest. "You think you're the right person to help her?"

Lena felt the heat of his stare. This was the closest they had come to talking about Ethan since she had started seeing him last year.

"I know he uses his hands on you," Jeffrey said. "I've seen the marks. I've seen you coming in with makeup covering the bruises under your eye. I've seen the way you cringe when you breathe because he's hit you so hard in the gut you can barely stand up straight." He added, "You work in a police station, Lena. You didn't think a bunch of cops would notice?"

"Which cops?" she asked, feeling panicked, exposed.

"This cop," he said, and that was all she really needed to hear.

Lena looked at the floor, shame pulsing through every inch of her body.

"My dad used to hit my mom," he said, and though she had guessed this a long time ago, Lena was surprised that he was confiding in her. Jeffrey seldom talked about anything from his personal life that didn't connect directly to a case. "I used to get in between them," he said. "I figured if he was beating on me, he'd have less for her later."

Lena traced her tongue along the inside of her lip, feeling the deep scars from the many times Ethan had busted the skin. He had broken a tooth six months ago. Two months after that, he had slapped her so hard on the side of the head that she still had trouble hearing things out of her right ear.

"Never worked that way," Jeffrey said. "He'd get mad at me, beat me to the floor, then he'd haul off on her just as hard. Used to be I'd think he was trying to kill her." He paused, but Lena refused to look up. "Till one day I figured it out." He paused again. "She wanted him to," he said, no trace of emotion in his voice. He was matter-of-fact about it, as if he had realized a long time ago that there was nothing he could do.

He continued, "She wanted him to end it. She didn't see any other way out."

Lena felt herself nodding. She wasn't getting out. This morning was just part of an act she used to convince herself she wasn't completely lost. Ethan would be back. He was always back. She would only be free when he was finished with her.

Jeffrey said, "Even with him dead, part of me still thinks she's waiting for it. Waiting for that one hit that knocks the life out of her." Almost to himself, he added, "Not that there's much life left."

Lena cleared her throat. "Yeah," she said. "I guess that's how Terri feels."

Jeffrey was obviously disappointed. "Terri, huh?"

She nodded, making herself look up, willing tears not to come into her eyes. She felt so raw that it was a struggle to even move. With anyone else, she would be breaking down, telling them everything. Not Jeffrey, though. She couldn't let him see her like this. No matter what, she couldn't let him see how weak she was.

She said, "I don't think Pat knows."

"No," Jeffrey agreed. "Pat would haul Dale in if he knew. Even if they are brothers."

"So, what are we going to do?"

"You know how it is." He shrugged. "You've been on the job long enough to know how it works. We can bring a case, but it won't stick unless Terri steps up to the plate. She's got to testify against him."

"She won't do that," Lena said, remembering how she had called the woman a coward. Called herself a coward. Could Lena stand up in court and point out Ethan? Would she have the will to accuse him, to send him away? The thought of confronting him sent a tingle of fear straight up her spine.

"Something I learned from my mama," Jeffrey said, "is that you can't help people who don't want to be helped."

"No," she agreed.

"Statistically, an abused woman is most likely to be murdered when she leaves her abuser."

"Right," she said, flashing on Ethan again, the way he had chased after her car this morning. Had she thought it would be that easy? Had she really thought he would let it go at that? He was probably planning his revenge right now, thinking of all kinds of pain he could bring down on her to punish her for even thinking she could get away.

He repeated, "You can't help people who don't want to be helped."

Lena nodded. "You're right."

He stared at her for another moment. "I'll check in with Pat when he's back, tell him what's up."

"You think he'll do anything?"

"I think he'll try," Jeffrey answered. "He loves his brother. That's the thing people don't understand."

"What people?"

"People who aren't in it," he said, taking his time to explain. "It's hard to hate somebody you love."

She nodded, chewing her lip, unable to speak.

He stood. "Buddy's here." He asked, "We okay?"

"Uh," Lena began. "Yeah."

"Good," he said, all business as he opened the door. He walked out of the office and Lena followed, still not knowing what to say. Jeffrey was acting as if nothing had happened between them, flirting with Marla, saying something about her new dress, as he leaned down to buzz Buddy into the squad room.

The lawyer hobbled in on a single crutch, his prosthetic leg nowhere to be seen.

Jeffrey's tone seemed forced to Lena, like he was trying his damnedest to pretend everything was right in the world. He joked with Buddy, "Wife take your leg again?"

Buddy wasn't his usual avuncular self. "Let's just get this over with."

Jeffrey stood back, letting Buddy go ahead of him. As they started to walk, Lena saw that Jeffrey was limping almost in exact time with Buddy. Buddy noticed this, too, and gave a sharp look.

Jeffrey seemed embarrassed. "I cut my foot last night."

Buddy raised his eyebrows. "Don't let it get infected." He tapped his stump to reinforce the warning. Jeffrey's face turned almost completely white.

He said, "I had Brad put Patty in the back room."

Lena took the lead, walking back to the interrogation room, trying not to think about what Jeffrey had said in his office. She forced herself to focus instead on his conversation with Buddy about the high school football team. The Rebels were looking at a tough season, and the men recited statistics like preachers reading from the Bible.

She heard Patty O'Ryan before she even opened the door. The girl was screaming like a banshee in heat.

"Get me the fuck out of here! Get these fucking chains the fuck off me, you goddamn motherfuckers!"

Lena stood outside the door as she waited for the others to catch up. She had to section off the part of her brain that kept going over Jeffrey's words. She had to stop letting her feelings get in the way of her job. She had already fucked up the interview with Terri Stanley. There was no way she could screw up again. She wouldn't be able to face herself.

As if sensing her thoughts, Jeffrey raised an eyebrow at Lena, asking if she was ready to do this. Lena gave him a curt nod, and he looked through the window in the door, telling Buddy, "She's having a little problem with withdrawal this morning."

"Get me the fuck out of here!" O'Ryan screeched at the top of her lungs. At least, Lena hoped that was the loudest the girl was capable of screaming. As it was, the glass was shaking in the door.

Jeffrey offered to Buddy, "You wanna go in there and talk to her alone before we start this?"

"Hell no," he said, shocked by the suggestion. "Don't you dare leave me alone in there with her."

Jeffrey opened the door, holding it for Buddy and Lena.

"Daddy," O'Ryan said, her voice husky from yelling so much. "I've got to get out of here. I've got an appointment. I've got a job interview. I need to go or I'm gonna be late."

"You might want to go home and change first," Lena suggested, noting that O'Ryan had torn her skimpy stripper attire.

"You," O'Ryan said, focusing all her rage on Lena. "You just shut the fuck up you spic bitch."

"Settle down," Jeffrey told her, sitting across from her at the table. Buddy's spot was normally on the other side with the defendant, but he sat in the chair by Jeffrey. Lena would be damned if she would put herself within the girl's reach again, so she stood by the mirror, arms crossed, to watch the proceedings.

Jeffrey said, "Tell me about Chip."

"What about Chip?"

"He your boyfriend?"

She looked at Buddy for the answer. To his credit, he didn't give her an inch.

O'Ryan told Jeffrey, "We had a thing." She jerked her head back to get her hair out of her eyes. Under the table, her foot was bobbing up and down like a rabbit in heat. Every muscle in her body was tensed, and Lena guessed from all this that the girl was jonesing for a fix. She had seen enough junkies going through withdrawal in the cells to know that it must hurt like a motherfucker. If O'Ryan wasn't such a bitch, she might feel sorry for her.

"What's a 'thing'?" Jeffrey asked. "That mean you slept with him some, maybe got high together?"

She kept her focus on Buddy, as if she wanted to punish him. "Something like that."

"Do you know Rebecca Bennett?"

"Who?"

"What about Abigail Bennett?"

She gave a disgusted snort that made her nostrils flair. "She's a Jesus freak from over at that farm."

"Did Chip have a relationship with her?"

She shrugged, the handcuff around her wrist banging into the metal ring on the table.

Jeffrey repeated, "Did Chip have a relationship with her?"

She didn't answer. Instead, she kept tapping the handcuff against the ring.

Jeffrey sat back with a sigh, like he didn't want to do what he was about to have to do. Buddy obviously recognized the play, and though he braced himself, he didn't do anything to stop it.

"Recognize Chip?" Jeffrey asked, dropping a Polaroid on the table.

Lena craned her neck, trying to see which of the crime scene photos from Chip Donner's room he had led with. They were all bad, but this one in particular—the close-up of the face showing where the lips had been practically ripped off—was horrendous.

O'Ryan smirked at Jeffrey. "That's not Chip."

He tossed down another photo. "Is this him?"

She glanced down, then looked away. Lena saw Buddy was staring at the only door in the room, probably wishing he could hop the hell out of here.

"How about this one?" Jeffrey asked, tossing down another.

O'Ryan was beginning to understand. Lena saw her bottom lip start to tremble. The girl had cried plenty of times since being taken into custody, but this was the first time Lena thought her tears were real.

Her body had stilled. She whispered, "What happened?"

"Obviously," Jeffrey began, dropping the rest of the Polaroids on the table, "he pissed somebody off."

She pulled up her legs on the chair, holding them against her chest. "Chip," she whispered, rocking back and forth. Lena had seen suspects do this often. It was a way they had of soothing themselves, as if over the years they had realized no one was going to do it for them, so they had to adapt.

Jeffrey asked, "Was somebody after him?"

She shook her head. "Everybody liked Chip."

"I'd guess from these pictures there's somebody out there who wouldn't agree with you." Jeffrey let that sink in. "Who would do this to him, Patty?"

"He was trying to do better," she said, her voice still low. "He was trying to clean up."

"He wanted to get off drugs?"

She was staring at the Polaroids, not touching them, and Jeffrey stacked them together, putting them back in his pocket. "Talk to me, Patty."

Her body gave a great shudder. "They met on the farm."

"The soy farm in Catoogah?" Jeffrey clarified. "Chip was there?"

"Yeah," she said. "Everybody knows you can hang there for a couple of weeks if you need to. You go to church on Sundays, pick a couple of beans, and they give you food, give you a place to sleep. You pretend to pray and shit and they give you a safe place to stay."

"Did Chip need a safe place to stay?"

She shook her head.

Jeffrey's tone was conciliatory. "Tell me about Abby."

"He met her on the farm. She was a kid. He thought she was funny. Next thing you know, he's busted for holding. Goes up a few years. When he comes back, Abby's all grown." She wiped a tear from her eye. "She was just this goody-two-shoes bitch, and he fell for it. Fell for all of it."

"Tell me what happened."

"She'd come to the Kitty. Can you believe that?" She laughed at the absurdity. "She'd be in her ugly, plain clothes and Mary Janes and she'd say, 'Come on, Chip, come on to church with me. Come pray with me.' And he'd go right with her without even telling me good-bye."

"Were they sexually involved?"

She snorted a laugh. "There's not a crowbar been invented could pull those knees apart."

"She was pregnant."

O'Ryan's head snapped up.

"Do you think Chip was the father?"

She didn't even hear the question. Lena could see the anger building in her like a kettle about to boil over. She was like Cole Connolly in that they shared the same quick temper, but for some reason, Lena felt more of a threat from the girl being out of control than the older man.

"Stupid bitch," she hissed through her teeth. She was clanging the handcuff against the metal ring again, rapping out noise like a snare drum. "He probably took her to the fucking woods. That was our fucking spot."

"The woods over in Heartsdale? The forest?"

"Stupid cunt," she spat, oblivious to the connection he was trying to make. "We used to go there and get high when we were in school."

"You went to school with Chip?"

She indicated Buddy. "Till that fucker kicked me out," she said. "Threw me on the streets. I had to fend for myself." Buddy didn't stir. "I told him to stay away from her. That whole fucking family is crazy."

"What family?"

"The Wards," she said. "Don't think she's the only one'a them been to the Kitty."

"Who else has been?"

"All of them. All the brothers."

"Which ones?"

"All of them!" she screamed, slamming her fist into the table so hard that Buddy's crutch clattered to the floor.

Lena uncrossed her arms, ready to respond if O'Ryan tried to do something stupid.

"They pretend to be so high and mighty, but they're just as disgusting as the rest of them." Again, she snorted, this time sounding more like a pig. "That one had an itty-bitty cock, too. He'd come in about three seconds, then start to fucking cry like a girl." She used a whiney tone, " 'Oh, Lord, I'm going to hell, oh, Lord, I'm gonna burn with Satan.' Fucking made me sick. Bastard didn't care about hell when he was grabbing my head, forcing me to swallow it."

Buddy paled, his jaw slack.

Jeffrey asked, "Which brother, Patty?"

"The short one," she said, scratching her arm so hard she left red streaks. "The one with the spiked up hair."

Lena tried to think which one she meant. Both Paul and Lev had been as tall as Jeffrey, both with a full head of hair.

O'Ryan kept scratching her arm. Soon, she would draw blood. "He'd give Chip whatever he wanted. Smack, coke, weed."

"He was dealing?"

"He was giving it away."

"He was giving away drugs?"

"Not to me," she snapped angrily. She looked down at her arm, tracing the red streaks. Her leg started bobbing under the table again, and Lena guessed the girl was going to lose her shit if she didn't get a needle in her arm soon.

O'Ryan said, "Just to Chip. He'd never give anything to me. I even offered him cash, but he told me to fuck off. Like his shit don't smell."

"Do you remember his name?"

"No," she said. "He was always up there, though. Sometimes he'd just sit at the end of the bar and watch Chip. Probably wanted to fuck him."

"Did he have red hair?"

"No," she answered, like he was stupid.

"Did he have dark hair?"

"I don't remember the color, okay?" Her eyes flashed, more like an animal needing to feed. "I'm done talking." She told Buddy, "Get me out of here."

Jeffrey said, "Hold on there."

"I've got a job interview."

"Right," Jeffrey said.

"Get me out of here!" she yelled, leaning over the table as far as she could to get into Buddy's face. "Now, goddamnit!"

Buddy's mouth smacked when he opened it. "I don't think you're done answering questions."

She mimicked him like a petulant three-year-old. "I don't think you're done answering questions."

"Settle down," Buddy warned.

"You settle down, you one-legged piece of shit," she screamed back. Her body was shaking again, vibrating from the need. "Get me the fuck out of here. Now!"

Buddy picked up his crutch off the floor. He wisely waited until he got to the door to say, "Chief, do whatever you want with her. I'm washing my hands."

"You fucking cocksucking coward!" O'Ryan screeched, lunging for Buddy. She had forgotten she was still chained to the table and she was yanked back like a dog on a short leash. "Bastard!" she screamed, going into full meltdown. Her chair had been upturned in the scuffle and she kicked it across the room, then yelped from the pain in her foot. "I'll sue you, you fucking bastards!" she yelled, clutching her foot. "Motherless fucks!"

"Patty?" Jeffrey asked. "Patty?"

Lena fought the urge to put her hands over her ears as the girl wailed like a siren. Jeffrey was scowling when he stood, sticking to the periphery of the room as he made his exit. Lena quickly followed him into the hall, keeping her eyes on O'Ryan until there was a solid door between them.

Jeffrey shook his head, like he couldn't believe a human being was capable of acting that way. "This is the first time in my life I actually feel sorry for the bastard," he said, meaning Buddy. He walked down the hall to get away from the noise. "Do you think there's another Ward brother?"

"There has to be."

"Black sheep?"

Lena remembered their conversation with the family two days ago. "That's Paul's job, I thought."

"What?"

"Paul said he was the black sheep of the family."

Jeffrey opened the fire door into the squad room for her. She could see Mark McCallum, the GBI polygraph expert, sitting in Jeffrey's office. Across from him sat Lev Ward.

She asked, "How the hell did you manage that?"

"Got me," Jeffrey told her, looking around the squad room, probably for Cole Connolly. Marla was at her desk, and he asked her, "Did Lev Ward come in alone?"

She glanced out through the lobby window. "Far as I can tell."

"When did he get here?"

"About ten minutes ago." She smiled helpfully. "I figured you'd want me to go ahead and call Mark over here to get started before lunch."

"Thanks," he told her, walking back toward his office.

Lena offered, "You want me to get Brad and go fetch Cole?"

"Let's hold off on that," Jeffrey said, knocking on his office door.

Mark waved them in. "Just getting set up," he told them.

"Thanks for staying in town, Mark." Jeffrey shook the man's hand. "I hear you've been enjoying the room service over at the Dew Drop."

Mark cleared his throat and went back to twisting some knobs on his machine.

"Chief," Lev said, looking as comfortable as anyone can with their body wired to a polygraph machine. "I got your message this morning. I'm sorry I couldn't make it yesterday."

"Thanks for coming in," Jeffrey said, taking out his notebook. He wrote as he talked. "I appreciate you taking the time to do this."

"The family is getting together at the church in a few hours to pay tribute to Abby." He turned to Lena. "Good morning, Detective," he said quietly, then focused back on Jeffrey. "I'd like as much time as I can to prepare my remarks. This is a very difficult time for us all."

Jeffrey didn't look up from his writing. "I was expecting Cole Connolly to come with you."

"I'm sorry," Lev said. "Cole didn't mention anything to me. He'll be at the tribute. I'll tell him to come by directly after."

He kept writing on the pad. "You're not having a funeral?"

"Unfortunately, the body had to be cremated. We're just doing a small fellowship with the family to talk about her life and how much we all loved her. We like to do things simply."

Jeffrey finished writing. "Outsiders aren't welcome?"

"Well, it's not a regular service, more a family gathering. Listen—"

Jeffrey tore off the sheet of paper and handed it to Mark. "We'll get you out of here as quickly as possible."

Lev eyed the note, not hiding his curiosity. "I appreciate that." He sat back in the chair. "Paul was against my coming here, but I've always believed it's better to cooperate."

"Mark?" Jeffrey asked as he sat down behind his desk. "It's not too cramped with all of us in here, is it?"

"Uh . . ."Mark hesitated for a split second. Normally, he was alone in the room with the subject, but it wasn't as if polygraphs were admissible in court and Ward hadn't been arrested. Lena suspected that more than anything else, lie detector machines were just meant to scare the crap out of people. She wouldn't be surprised to open one up and find mice inside scurrying on wheels.

"Sure," Mark said. "No problem." He fiddled with more dials, then uncapped his pen. "Reverend Ward, are you ready to begin?"

"Lev, please."

"All right." Mark had a notebook beside the polygraph that was hidden from Lev by the bulk of the machine. He opened it up, tucking Jeffrey's note into the pocket. "I'd like to remind you to stick to yes or no answers, if you could. We don't need you to elaborate on anything at this point. Anything you feel needs an explanation can be discussed with Chief Tolliver later. The machine will only register yes and no responses."

Lev glanced at the blood pressure cuff on his arm. "I understand."

Mark flipped on a switch and paper slowly scrolled from the machine. "Please try to relax and stare straight ahead."

The colored needles on the page twitched as Lev said, "All right."

Mark kept his tone flat as he read from the questions. "Your name is Thomas Leviticus Ward?"

"Yes."

Mark made a notation on the paper. "You live at sixty-three Plymouth Road?"

"Yes."

Another notation. "You are forty-eight years of age?"

"Yes."

And another. "You have a son, Ezekiel?"

"Yes."

"Your wife is deceased?"

"Yes."

The questioning continued through the mundane details of Lev's life to establish a baseline for the veracity of his answers. Lena had no idea what the bouncing needles signified, and Mark's marks were hieroglyphics to her. She found herself zoning out until they got to the important parts.

Mark's voice remained flat and disinterested, as if he was still asking about Lev's educational background. "Do you know of anyone in your niece Abigail's life who might wish her harm?"

"No."

"Has anyone to your knowledge ever expressed sexual interest in her?"

"No."

"Did you kill your niece Abigail?"

"No."

"Has she ever expressed interest in someone you might find inappropriate?"

"No."

"Were you ever angry at your niece?"

"Yes."

"Did you ever strike her?"

"Once on the bottom. I mean, yes." He smiled nervously. "Sorry."

Mark ignored the interruption. "Did you kill Abigail?"

"No."

"Did you ever have sexual contact with her?"

"Never. I mean, no."

"Did you ever have any inappropriate contact with her?"

"No."

"Have you met a man named Dale Stanley?"

Lev seemed surprised. "Yes."

"Did you go into his garage with him?"

"Yes."

"Do you have a brother named Paul Ward?"

"Yes."

"Do you have any other brothers?"

"No."

"Do you know where your niece Rebecca Bennett is?"

Lev gave Jeffrey a surprised look.

Mark repeated, "Do you know where your niece Rebecca Bennett is?"

Lev returned his focus straight ahead, answering, "No."

"Was there anything in Dale Stanley's garage that you took away with you?"

"No."

"Did you bury Abigail in the woods?"

"No."

"Do you have any knowledge of anyone who might mean to do harm to your niece?"

"No."

"Have you ever been to the Pink Kitty?"

His lips frowned in confusion. "No."

"Did you ever find your niece sexually attractive?"

He hesitated, then, "Yes, but—"

Mark stopped him. "Yes or no, please."

For the first time, Lev seemed to lose some of his composure. He shook his head, as if to admonish himself for his answer. "I need to explain myself." He looked at Jeffrey. "Could we please stop this?" He didn't wait for response before tugging the pads off his chest and fingers.

Mark offered, "Let me," obviously wanting to protect his equipment.

Lev said, "I'm sorry. I just . . . This is just too much."

Jeffrey indicated that Mark should let Lev unhook himself from the machine.

"I was trying to be honest," Lev said. "Good Lord, what a mess."

Mark closed his notebook. Jeffrey told Lev, "We'll be back in a second."

Lena moved out of their way, taking Jeffrey's chair as the two men walked out to talk.

"I would never hurt Abby," Lev told her. "What a mess. What a mess."

"Don't worry about it," Lena said, leaning back in the chair. She hoped she didn't look as smug as she felt. Something in her gut had told her Lev was involved. It would only be a matter of time before Jeffrey cracked him.

Lev clasped his hands between his knees and bent over. He stayed that way until Jeffrey came back into the room. He started talking before Jeffrey could take Mark's seat. "I was trying to be honest. I didn't want some foolish lie to make you . . . Oh, good Lord. I'm sorry. I've made such a mess here."

Jeffrey shrugged like it was a simple misunderstanding. "Explain it to me."

"She was . . ." He covered his face with his hands. "She was an attractive girl."

"Looked a lot like your sister," Lena remembered.

"Oh, no," Lev said, his voice shaking. "I have never been inappropriate with either my sister or my niece. Any of my nieces." His tone almost begged them to believe him. "There was one time — one time — Abby was walking through the office. I didn't know it was her. I just saw her from behind and my reaction was . . ." He directed his words toward Jeffrey. "You know how it is."

"I don't have any pretty little nieces," he answered.

"Oh, Lord." Lev sighed. "Paul told me I would regret this." He sat back up, clearly troubled. "Listen, I've read my share of true crime stories. I know how this works. You always look at family members first. I wanted to rule that out. I wanted to be as honest as I could." He rolled his eyes up at the ceiling, as if hoping for an intervention from on high. "It was one time. She was walking down the aisle by the photocopier, and I didn't recognize her from behind, and when she turned around, I almost fell on the floor. It's not that — " He stopped, then continued, treading carefully. "It's not that I was thinking it through, let alone considering it. I was just staring into space, and I thought, 'Well, there's a nice looking woman,' and then

I saw it was Abby and, I promise you, I couldn't even talk to her for a month afterward. I have never felt so ashamed about anything in my life."

Lev held out his hands. "When the officer asked that question, that's the first thing that popped into my mind—that day. I knew he'd be able to tell if I was lying."

Jeffrey took his sweet time revealing, "The test was inconclusive."

All the air seemed to go out of Lev. "I've messed things up by trying to make them right."

"Why didn't you want to report the fact that your other niece is missing?"

"It seemed—" He stopped, as if he couldn't find the answer. "I didn't want to waste your time. Becca runs off a lot. She's very melodramatic."

Jeffrey asked, "Did you ever touch Abigail?"

"Never."

"Did she ever spend time alone with you?"

"Yes, of course. I'm her uncle. I'm her minister."

Lena asked, "Did she ever confess anything to you?"

"That's not how it works," Lev said. "We would just talk. Abby loved reading the Bible. She and I would parse the scriptures. We played Scrabble. I do this with all my nieces and nephews."

Jeffrey told him, "You can see why this sounds strange to us."

"I am so sorry," Lev said. "I've not helped this along one bit."

"No," Jeffrey agreed. "What were you doing on the Stanley place?"

He took a moment to shift his train of thought. "Dale called about some of our people using his property as a cut-through. I spoke to him, walked the property line and agreed to put up a fence."

"Odd that you did this personally," Jeffrey suggested. "You're pretty much in charge of the farm, aren't you?"

"Not really," he answered. "We all run our various areas."

"That wasn't my impression," Jeffrey said. "You seem like the man in charge to me."

Lev seemed reluctant to admit, "I'm responsible for the day-to-day operations."

"It's a pretty large place."

"Yes, it is."

"Walking Dale's property line, talking about building a fence, that wasn't something you'd delegate?"

"My father is constantly on me to do just that. I'm afraid I'm a bit of a control freak. It's something I should work on."

"Dale's a big guy," Jeffrey said. "It didn't bother you to go out there alone?"

"Cole was with me. He's the foreman on our farm. I don't know if you had time to get into that yesterday. He's one of the original success stories at Holy Grown. My father ministered to him in prison. Over two decades later, Cole's still with us."

Jeffrey said, "He was convicted of armed robbery."

Lev nodded, saying, "That's right. He was going to rob a convenience store. Someone turned him in. The judge didn't take kindly to him. I'm sure Cole made his bed, just as I'm sure he laid in it for twentysome years. He's a very different man from the one who helped plan that robbery."

Jeffrey moved him along. "Did you go into Dale's shop?"

"I'm sorry?"

"Dale Stanley. Did you go into his shop when you went out there to talk about the fence?"

"Yes. I'm not normally into cars—that's not my thing—but it seemed polite to oblige."

Lena asked, "Where was Cole during all of this?"

"He stayed in the car," Lev told her. "I didn't bring him for intimidation. I just wanted to make sure Dale knew I wasn't alone."

"Cole stayed in the car the whole time?" Jeffrey asked.

"Yes."

"Even when you walked back across the fence line between your property and Dale's?"

"It's the church's property, but yes."

Jeffrey asked, "Have you ever used Cole for intimidation?"

Lev looked uncomfortable. He took his time answering. "Yes."

"In what way?"

"Sometimes we have people who want to take advantage of the system. Cole talks to them. He takes it personally when people try to exploit the church. The family, really. He has an extraordinary loyalty to my father."

"Does he ever get physical with them, these people who try to take advantage?"

"No," Lev insisted. "Absolutely not."

"Why are you so certain?"

"Because he's aware of his problem."

"What does that mean?"

"He has—had—a very bad temper." Lev seemed to be remembering something. "I'm sure your wife told you about his outburst last night. Believe me, it's simply a matter of him being passionate about his beliefs. I'll be the first to admit that he went a little overboard, but I would have handled the situation if the need arose."

Lena wondered what the hell he was talking about, but she knew better than to interrupt.

For his part, Jeffrey skipped it completely, asking, "How bad was Cole's temper? You said he *had* a bad temper. How bad was it?"

"He used to get physical. Not when Papa knew him, but before." Lev added, "He's a very strong man. Very powerful."

Jeffrey fished out some line. "I'm not trying to contradict you, Lev, but I had him in here yesterday. He looks like a pretty harmless guy to me."

"He *is* harmless," Lev said. "Now."

"Now?"

"He was special ops in the army. He did a lot of bad things. You don't start using a thousand dollars worth of heroin a week because you're happy with your life." He seemed to sense Jeffrey's impatience. "The armed robbery," Lev added. "He probably would have gotten a lighter sentence—he didn't even make it into the store—but he resisted arrest. An officer was badly beaten, almost lost an eye." Lev seemed troubled by the image. "Cole used his hands on him."

Jeffrey sat up. "That wasn't on his record."

"I can't tell you why," Lev said. "I've never seen his records, of course, but he isn't ashamed about admitting his past transgressions. He's talked about it in front of the congregation as part of his Testament."

Jeffrey was still on the edge of his seat. "You said he used his hands?"

"His fists," Lev elaborated. "He made money from bare-knuckle boxing before he was thrown in jail. He did some serious damage to some people. It's a part of his life he's not proud of."

Jeffrey took a moment to process that. "Cole Connolly's head is shaved."

Lev's change in posture showed that was the last thing he was expecting. "Yes," he said. "He shaved it last week. He used to keep it in a military cut."

"Spiky?"

"I guess you could say that. Sometimes the sweat would dry and it stuck up a bit." He smiled sadly. "Abby used to tease him about it."

Jeffrey crossed his arms. "How would you describe Cole's relationship with Abby?"

"Protective. Honorable. He's good to all the kids on the farm. I would hardly say he singled Abby out for attention." He added, "He watches Zeke for me all the time. I trust him completely."

"Do you know a Chip Donner?"

Lev seemed surprised by the name. "He worked on the farm off and on for a few years. Cole told me he stole some money from petty cash. We asked him to leave."

"You didn't call the police?"

"We don't normally involve the police in our affairs. I know that sounds bad—"

"Stop worrying about how things sound, Reverend Ward, and just tell us what happened."

"Cole asked the Donner boy to leave. The next day he was gone."

"Do you know where Cole is right now?"

"We all took the morning off because of Abby's tribute. I imagine he's in his apartment over the barn, getting ready." Lev tried again, "Chief Tolliver, believe me, all of this is in his past. Cole is a gentle man. He's like a brother to me. To all of us."

"Like you said, Reverend Ward, we need to eliminate family first."

CHAPTER TWELVE

Jeffrey could feel Lena's excitement matching his own as they pulled up in front of the equipment barn where Cole Connolly lived. If solving a case was like a roller coaster, they were on the back end of the incline, heading ninety miles an hour toward the next loop. Lev Ward happened to carry a photograph of his family in his wallet. Patty O'Ryan had been her usual colorful self when she'd pointed out Cole Connolly as the cocksucking motherfucker who visited Chip at the Pink Kitty.

"The cut on his finger," Lena said.

"What's that?" Jeffrey asked, but then understood. Connolly had said the cut on his right index finger had come from working in the fields.

"You'd think that he'd have more than a little cut on the back of his hand, considering what Chip Donner looked like." She allowed, "Of course, O. J. just had a cut on the back of his finger."

"So did Jeffrey McDonald."

"Who's that?"

"Viciously stabbed his whole family to death—two kids and his pregnant wife." He told her, "The only wound he didn't give himself was a cut on the back of his finger."

"Nice guy," Lena remarked, then, "You think Cole took Rebecca?"

"I think we're going to find out," Jeffrey told her, hoping to God the girl had just run away, that she was somewhere safe and not buried underground, taking her last breaths as she prayed for someone to find her.

He turned the car onto the gravel drive they had taken to the farm last Monday. They had followed Lev Ward's ancient Ford Festiva as the preacher closely observed the speed limit. Jeffrey had a feeling he would do this even without a cop following him. When Lev pulled into the drive to the barn, he actually used his turn signal.

Jeffrey put the car into park. "Here we go," he told Lena as they both got out of the car.

Lev pointed to a stairway inside the barn. "He lives up there."

Jeffrey glanced up, glad there were no windows at the front of the barn to give Connolly a warning. He told Lena, "Stay here," making his way inside the barn. Lev started to follow but Jeffrey stopped him. "I need you to stay down here."

Lev seemed ready to protest, but he said, "I think you're way off base here, Chief Tolliver. Cole loved Abby. He's not the sort of man to do something like this. I don't know what kind of animal is capable, but Cole is not—"

Jeffrey told Lena, "Make sure no one interrupts me." To Lev, he said, "I'd appreciate it if you stayed here until I came down."

"I have to prepare my remarks," the preacher said. "We're putting Abby to rest today. The family is waiting on me."

Jeffrey knew the family included a pretty sharp lawyer, and he sure as shit didn't want Paul Ward barging in on his conversation with Connolly. The ex-con was sharp, and Jeffrey was going to have a hard enough time cracking him without Paul shutting things down.

Jeffrey wasn't in his jurisdiction, he didn't have an arrest warrant and the only probable cause he had to talk to Connolly came from the word of a stripper who would kill her own mother for a fix. All he could tell Lev was, "Do what you have to do."

Lena tucked her hands into her pockets as the pastor drove away. "He's going straight to his brother."

"I don't care if you have to hog-tie them," Jeffrey told her. "Keep them away from that apartment."

"Yes, sir."

Quietly, Jeffrey walked up the steep set of stairs to Connolly's apartment. At the top of the landing, he looked through the window in the door and saw Connolly standing in front of the sink. His back was to Jeffrey, and when he turned around, Jeffrey could see he had been filling a kettle with water. He didn't seem startled to find someone looking through his window.

"Come on in," he called, putting the kettle on the stove. There was a series of clicks as the gas caught.

"Mr. Connolly," Jeffrey began, not sure how he should approach this.

"Cole," the old man corrected. "I was just making some coffee." He smiled at Jeffrey, his eyes sparkling the same way they had the day before.

Connolly offered, "You want a cup?"

Jeffrey saw a jar of Folgers instant coffee on the countertop and suppressed a feeling of revulsion. His father had sworn by the power of Folgers crystals, claiming it was the best curative for a hangover.

As far as Jeffrey was concerned, he'd rather drink out of the toilet, but he answered, "Yeah, that'd be great."

Connolly took down another cup out of the cabinet. Jeffrey could see there were only two.

"Have a seat," Connolly said, measuring out two heaping spoonfuls of grainy black coffee into the mugs.

Jeffrey pulled out a chair at the table, taking in Connolly's apartment, which was a single room with a kitchen on one side and the bedroom on the other. The bed had white sheets and a simple spread, all tucked in with military corners. The man lived a Spartan existence. Except for a cross hanging over the bed and a religious poster taped to one of the white-washed walls, there was nothing that would reveal anything about the man who called this place his home.

Jeffrey asked, "You live here long?"

"Oh," Connolly seemed to think about it. "I guess going on fifteen years now. We all moved onto the farm some time back. I used to be in the house, but then the grandkids started growing, wanting their own rooms, their own space. You know how kids are."

"Yeah," he said, "You've got a nice place here."

"Built it out myself," Connolly said proudly. "Rachel offered me a place in her house, but I saw this room up here and knew I'd be able to do something with it."

"You're quite a carpenter," Jeffrey said, taking in the room more carefully. The box they had found Abby in had precision mitered joints as did the other. The man who had built those boxes was meticulous, taking time to do things right.

"Measure twice, cut once." Connolly sat at the table, putting a cup in front of Jeffrey and keeping one for himself. There was a Bible between them, holding down a stack of napkins. "What brings you here?"

"I have some more questions," Jeffrey said. "Hope you don't mind."

Connolly shook his head, as if he had nothing to hide. "Of course not. Anything that I can do to help. Fire away."

Jeffrey got a whiff of the instant coffee in front of him, and had to move the cup out of the way before he could speak. He decided to begin with Chip Donner. O'Ryan had given them a concrete connection. The tie to Abby was more tenuous, and Connolly wasn't the type to hang himself with his own rope. "Have you ever heard of a bar called the Pink Kitty?"

Connolly kept his gaze steady, watching Jeffrey. "It's a strip club out on the highway."

"That's right."

Connolly moved his mug a quarter of an inch to the left, centering it in front of the Bible.

"You ever been there, Cole?"

"That's a funny question to be asking a Christian."

"There's a stripper says you were there."

He rubbed the top of his bald head, wiping away sweat. "Warm in here," he said, walking over to the window. They were on the second level and the window was small, but Jeffrey tensed in case Connolly tried to make a break for it.

Connolly turned back to him. "I wouldn't much trust the word of a whore."

"No," Jeffrey allowed. "They tend to tell you what they think you want to hear."

"True enough," he agreed, putting up the jar of Folgers. He went to the sink and washed the spoon, using a well-worn towel to dry it before returning it to the drawer. The kettle started to whistle, and he used the towel to take it off the eye of the stove.

"Hand those over," he asked Jeffrey, and Jeffrey slid the cups across the table.

"When I was in the army," Cole said, pouring boiling water into the cups, "there wasn't a titty bar around we didn't hit one time or another. Dens of iniquity, one and all." He put the kettle back on the stove and took out the spoon he had just washed to stir the coffee. "I was a weak man then. A weak man."

"What was Abby doing at the Pink Kitty, Cole?"

Connolly kept stirring, turning the clear liquid into an unnatural black. "Abby wanted to help people," he said, going back to the sink. "She didn't know she was walking into the lion's den. She was an honest soul."

Jeffrey watched Cole wash the spoon again. He put it in the drawer, then sat down across from Jeffrey.

Jeffrey asked, "Was she trying to help Chip Donner?"

"He wasn't worth helping," Cole replied, putting the cup to his lips. Steam rose, and he blew on the liquid before setting it back down. "Too hot."

Jeffrey sat back in his chair to get away from the smell. "Why wasn't he worth helping?"

"Lev and them don't see it, but some of these people just want to work the system." He pointed a finger at Jeffrey. "You and I know how these people are. It's my job to get them off the farm. They're just taking up space where somebody else might be—somebody who wants to do better. Somebody who's strong in the Lord."

Jeffrey took the opening. "These bad people just want to work it to their advantage. Take what they can and get out."

"That's exactly right," Cole agreed. "It's my job to get them out fast."

"Before they ruin it for everybody."

"Exactly," he said.

"What did Chip do with Abby?"

"He took her out to the woods. She was just an innocent. An innocent."

"You saw him take her out into the woods?" Jeffrey asked, thinking it was pretty odd for a seventy-two-year-old man to be following around a young girl.

"I wanted to make sure she was okay," Connolly explained. "I don't mind telling you that I was worried for her soul."

"You feel a responsibility for the family?"

"With Thomas like he is, I had to look after her."

"I see it all the time," Jeffrey encouraged. "All it takes is one bad apple."

"That is the truth, sir." Connolly blew on the coffee again, chancing a sip. He grimaced as his tongue was singed. "I tried to reason with her. She was going to leave town with that boy. She was packing her bag, heading right down the road to wickedness. I could not let that happen. For Thomas's sake, for the sake of the family, I could not let them lose another soul."

Jeffrey nodded, the pieces falling into place. He could see Abigail Bennett packing her bags, thinking she was going to start a new life, until Cole Connolly came in and changed everything. What must have been going through Abby's mind as he led her into the forest? The girl had to have been terrified.

Jeffrey said, "I don't see that you wanted her to die."

Connolly's head snapped up. He stared at Jeffrey for a beat.

"You built that box, Cole." He indicated the apartment. "You do things right. Your workmanship gives you away." Jeffrey tried to ease him into it. "I don't think you meant for her to die."

Connolly didn't answer.

"It's her mama I worry about," Jeffrey said. "Esther's a good woman."

"That's the truth."

"She needs to know what happened to her daughter, Cole. When I was in her house, looking at Abby's things, trying to find out what happened to her, Esther begged me. She grabbed my arm, Cole. She had tears in her eyes." He paused. "Esther needs to know what happened to her baby, Cole. She needs it for her peace of mind."

Connolly just nodded.

"I'm getting to this point, Cole," Jeffrey said. "Where I'm going to have to start bringing people in. I'm gonna have to start throwing things against the wall, seeing if they stick."

Connolly sat back in his chair, his lips pressed tightly together.

"I'll bring in Mary first, then Rachel."

"I doubt Paul will let that happen."

"I can keep them for twenty-four hours without making a charge." He added, still trying to find the right pressure point, "It's my opinion Mary and Rachel might be material witnesses."

"Do what you want." He shrugged.

"It's Thomas who's going to be the hard one," Jeffrey persisted, keeping his eyes trained on Connolly, trying to judge how far to push the old man. At the mention of his mentor's name, Connolly's body tensed, and Jeffrey continued, "We'll do everything we can to keep him comfortable. Those cells doors are pretty narrow, but I'm sure we can carry him in if his wheelchair won't fit."

The sink faucet had a small leak, and in the silence that followed, Jeffrey could hear the dripping water echo in the small room. He kept his eyes on Connolly, watched the man's expression change as he struggled with the image of Jeffrey's threat.

Jeffrey saw his leverage and pressed even harder. "I'll keep him in jail, Cole. I'll do whatever it takes to find out what happened. Don't think I won't."

Connolly's grip on the coffee cup was tight, but it slackened as he seemed to make up his mind. He said, "You'll leave Thomas alone?"

"You have my word."

Connolly nodded. Still, he took his time continuing. Jeffrey was about to prompt him when the old man said, "None of 'em ever passed before."

Jeffrey felt a surge of adrenaline, but did his best not to break the rhythm of the conversation. No one came out and admitted they'd done something horrible. They always came around it the back way, easing into the admission, convincing themselves that they were actually good people who had momentarily slipped and done a bad thing.

Connolly repeated, "None of 'em ever passed."

Jeffrey tried to keep the accusation out of his tone. "Who else did you do this to, Cole?"

He slowly shook his head.

"What about Rebecca?"

"She'll turn up."

"Turn up like Abby?"

"Like a bad penny," he said. "Nothing I did to that girl ever got through. She never listened to anything I said." Connolly stared into his coffee, but there wasn't a trace of remorse about him. "Abby was in the family way."

"She told you that?" Jeffrey asked, and he could imagine Abby trying to use the information for leverage, thinking it would talk the crazy old man out of putting her in the box.

"Liked to broke my heart," he said. "But it also gave me the conviction to do what had to be done."

"So you buried her out by the lake. In the same spot Chip had taken her to for sex."

"She was going to run away with him," Connolly repeated. "I went to pray with her, and she was packing, getting ready to run off with that trash, raise their baby in sin."

"You couldn't let her do that," Jeffrey encouraged.

"She was just an innocent. She needed that time alone to contemplate what she had allowed that boy to do. She was soiled. She needed to rise and be born again."

"That's what it's about?" Jeffrey asked. "You bury them so that they can be born again?" Connolly didn't answer, and he asked, "Did you bury Rebecca, Cole? Is that where she is now?"

He put his hand on the Bible, quoting, " 'Let the sinners be consumed out of the earth . . . let the wicked be no more.' "

"Cole, where's Rebecca?"

"I told you, son, I don't know."

Jeffrey kept at him. "Was Abby a sinner?"

"I put it into the Lord's hands," the other man countered. "He tells me to give them time for prayer, for contemplation. He gives me the mission, and I give the girls the opportunity to change their lives." Again, he quoted, " 'The Lord preserveth all them that love Him, but all the wicked will be destroyed.' "

Jeffrey asked, "Abby didn't love the Lord?"

The man seemed genuinely sad, as if he had played no part in her terrible death. "The Lord chose to take her." He wiped his eyes. "I was merely following His orders."

"Did He tell you to beat Chip to death?" Jeffrey asked.

"That boy was doing no good to the world."

Jeffrey took that as an admission of guilt. "Why did you kill Abby, Cole?"

"It was the Lord's decision to take her." His grief was genuine. "She just run out of air," he said. "Poor little thing."

"You put her in that box."

He gave a curt nod, and Jeffrey could feel Cole's anger revving up. "I did."

Jeffrey pressed a little more. "You killed her."

" 'I have no pleasure in the death of the wicked,' " he recited. "I'm just an old soldier. I told you that. I'm a conduit through which He speaks."

"That so?"

"Yes, that's so," Connolly snapped at his sarcasm, banging his fist against the table, anger flaring in his eyes. He took a second to get it back under control, and Jeffrey remembered Chip Donner, the way his guts had been pulverized by those fists. Instinctively, Jeffrey pressed his back against the chair, reassured by the pressure of his gun.

Connolly took another sip of coffee. "With Thomas like he is . . ." He put his hand to his stomach, an acrid-sounding belch slipping out. "Excuse me," he apologized. "Indigestion. I know I shouldn't drink the stuff. Mary and Rachel are onto me all the time, but caffeine is the one addiction I cannot give up."

"With Thomas like he is?" Jeffrey prompted.

Connolly put down the cup. "Someone has to step up. Someone has to take charge of the family or everything we've worked for will go to the wayside." He told Jeffrey, "We're all just soldiers. We need a general."

Jeffrey remembered O'Ryan telling them that the man at the Kitty gave Chip Donner drugs. "It's hard to say no when someone's waving it in front of your face." He asked, "Why were you giving Chip drugs?"

Connolly moved in his chair, like he was trying to get comfortable. "The snake tempted Eve, and she partook. Chip was just like the others. None of them ever resist for long."

"I bet."

"God warned Adam and Eve not to partake of the tree, yet they did." Cole slid a napkin from under the Bible and used it to wipe his forehead. "You are either strong or you are weak. That boy was weak." He added sadly, "I guess in the end our Abigail was, too. The Lord works in His own way. It's not our job to question."

"Abby was poisoned, Cole. God didn't decide to take her. Somebody murdered her."

Connolly studied Jeffrey, coffee cup paused before his mouth. He took his time answering, taking a drink from the mug, setting it down in front of the Bible again. "You're forgetting who you're talking to, boy," he warned, menace underlying his quiet tone. "I'm not just an old man, I'm an old con. You can't trick me with your lies."

"I'm not lying to you."

"Well, sir, you'll excuse me if I don't believe you."

"She was poisoned with cyanide."

He shook his head, still disbelieving. "If you want to arrest me, I think you should go ahead. I have nothing else to say."

"Who else did you do this to, Cole? Where's Rebecca?"

He shook his head, laughing. "You think I'm some kind of rat, don't you? Gonna flip on a dime just to save my own ass." He pointed his finger at Jeffrey. "Let me tell you something, son. I—" He put his hand to his mouth, coughing. "I never—" He coughed again. The coughing turned into gagging. Jeffrey jumped from his chair as a dark string of vomit emptied from the man's mouth.

"Cole?"

Connolly started breathing hard, then panting. Soon, he was clawing at his neck, his fingernails ripping into the flesh. "No!" he gasped, his eyes locking onto Jeffrey's in terror. "No! No!" His body convulsed so violently that he was thrown to the floor.

"Cole?" Jeffrey repeated, rooted where he stood as he watched the old man's face fix into a horrible mask of agony and fear. His legs bucked, kicking the chair so hard that it splintered against the wall. He soiled his pants, smearing excrement across the floor as he crawled toward the door. Suddenly, he stopped, his body still seizing, eyes rolling back in his head. His legs trembled so hard that one of his shoes kicked off.

In less than a minute, he was dead.

❊ ❊ ❊ ❊

Lena was pacing beside Jeffrey's Town Car when he made his way down the stairs. Jeffrey took out his handkerchief, wiping the sweat off his brow, remembering how Connolly had done the same thing moments before he'd died.

He reached in through the open car window to get his cell phone. He felt sick from bending over, and took a deep breath as he straightened.

"You okay?"

Jeffrey took off his suit jacket and tossed it into the car. He dialed Sara's office number, telling Lena, "He's dead."

"What?"

"We don't have long," he told her, then asked Sara's receptionist, "Can you get her? This is an emergency."

Lena asked, "What happened?" She lowered her voice. "Did he try something?"

He was only faintly surprised that she could suspect him of killing a suspect in custody. Considering all they had been through, he hadn't exactly set a great example.

Sara came onto the phone. "Jeff?"

"I need you to come to the Ward farm."

"What's up?"

"Cole Connolly is dead. He was drinking coffee. I think it must have had cyanide in it. He just . . ." Jeffrey didn't want to think about what he had just seen. "He died right in front of me."

"Jeffrey, are you okay?"

He knew Lena was listening, so he just left it at, "It was pretty bad."

"Baby," Sara said, and he looked past his car, like he was checking to make sure no one was coming, so Lena wouldn't read the emotion in his face. Cole Connolly was a disgusting man, a sick bastard who twisted the Bible to justify his horrible actions, but he was still a human being. Jeffrey could think of few people who deserved that kind of death, and while Connolly was up there on the list, Jeffrey didn't like being a spectator to the man's suffering.

He told Sara, "I need you to get over here fast. I want you to look at him before we have to call the sheriff in." For Lena's benefit, he added, "This isn't exactly my jurisdiction."

"I'm on my way."

He snapped the phone closed, tucking it into his pocket as he leaned against the car. His stomach was still rolling, and he kept panicking, thinking he had taken a drink of coffee when he knew for a fact he hadn't. This was the only time in his life that his father's miserable habits had actually benefited Jeffrey instead of kicking him in the ass. He said a silent prayer to Jimmy Tolliver to thank him, even though he knew if there was a heaven, Jimmy wouldn't make it past the door.

"Chief?" Lena asked. She'd obviously been speaking. "I asked about Rebecca Bennett. Did he say anything about her?"

"He said he didn't know where she was."

"Right." Lena glanced around the farm, asking, "What do we do now?"

Jeffrey didn't want to be in charge right now. He just wanted to lean against the car, try to breathe and wait for Sara. If only he had that option.

"When Sara gets here," he told her, "I want you to fetch Two-Bit. Tell him your phone wouldn't work out here. Take your time getting there, okay?"

She nodded.

He looked into the dark barn, the narrow flight of stairs looking like something Dante would've written about.

Lena asked, "He admitted to doing this to other girls?"

"Yes," he said. "He said that none of them had ever died before."

"Do you believe him?"

"Yeah," he answered. "Somebody wrote that note to Sara. Somebody out there survived this."

"Rebecca," she guessed.

"It wasn't the same handwriting," he told her, remembering the note Esther had given him.

"You think one of the aunts wrote it? Maybe the mother?"

"There's no way Esther knew," he said. "She would've told us. She loved her daughter."

"Esther's loyal to her family," Lena reminded him. "She defers to her brothers."

"Not all the time," he countered.

"Lev," she said. "I don't know about him. I can't pin him down."

He nodded, not trusting himself to answer.

Lena crossed her arms and fell silent. Jeffrey looked up the road again, closing his eyes as he tried to regain control over his sour stomach. It was more than queasiness, though. He felt dizzy, almost like he might pass out. Was he sure that he hadn't tasted the coffee? He'd even drunk some of that bitter lemonade the other day. Was it possible he had swallowed some cyanide?

Lena started pacing back and forth, and when she went into the barn, he didn't stop her. She came back out a few minutes later, looking at her watch. "I hope Lev doesn't come back."

"How long has it been?"

"Less than an hour," she told him. "If Paul gets here before Sara does—"

"Let's go," he said, pushing himself away from the car.

Lena followed him back through the building, for once keeping quiet. She didn't ask him anything until they were inside the kitchen and she saw the two cups of coffee on the table. "Do you think he took it on purpose?"

"No," Jeffrey said, never so certain of anything in his life. Cole Connolly had looked horrified when he'd realized what was happening to him. Jeffrey suspected Connolly even knew who had done it. The panic in his eyes told Jeffrey he knew exactly what had happened. What's more, he knew that he had been betrayed.

Lena walked carefully past the body. Jeffrey wondered if the room was hazardous, what precautions they should take, but his mind wouldn't stay on any one thing for very long. He kept thinking about that cup of coffee. No matter what the circumstances, he always accepted an offer of a drink from someone if he was trying to get information out of them. It was cop 101 to set the other party at ease, make them think they were doing something for you. Make them think you were their friends.

"Look at this." Lena was standing at the closet, pointing to the clothes neatly hanging on the rod. "Same as Abby's. Remember? Her closet was like this. I swear you could've put a ruler to it. They were the same width apart." She indicated the shoes. "Same here, too."

"Cole must have put them back," Jeffrey provided, loosening his tie so that he could breathe. "He came in on her when she was packing to leave town."

"Old habits die hard." Lena reached into the back of the closet, pulling out a pink suitcase. "This doesn't look like his," she said, setting the plastic case on the bed and opening it.

Jeffrey's brain told his feet to move so that he could go over, but they refused. He had actually stepped back, almost to the door.

Lena didn't seem to notice. She was pulling at the lining of the suitcase, trying to see if anything was hidden. She unzipped the outer pocket. "Bingo."

"What is it?"

She turned the case upside down and shook it. A brown wallet dropped out onto the bed. Touching only the edges, she opened it and read, "Charles Wesley Donner."

Jeffrey tugged at his tie again. Even with the window open, the room was turning into a sauna. "Anything else?"

Lena used the tips of her fingers to slip something out of the lining. "A bus ticket to Savannah," she told him. "Dated four days before she went missing."

"Is there a name on it?"

"Abigail Bennett."

"Hold on to that."

Lena tucked the ticket into her pocket as she walked over to the bureau. She opened the top drawer. "Just like Abby's," she said. "The underwear's all folded the same way hers was." She opened the next drawer, then the next, "Socks, shirts, everything. Looks identical."

Jeffrey pressed his back against the wall, his gut clenching. He was having trouble catching his breath. "Cole said she was going to leave with Chip."

Lena went to the kitchen cabinets, and Jeffrey told her, "Don't touch anything," sounding like a panicked woman.

She gave him a look, walking back across the room. She stood in front of the poster, hands on her hips. A large set of hands was pictured cradling a cross. Fire radiated out from the cross like bolts of lightning. She smoothed her hand over the poster like she was brushing something off it.

"What is it?" Jeffrey managed, not wanting to see for himself.

"Hold on." Lena picked at the corner of the poster, trying not to rip the taped edge. Slowly, she peeled back the paper. The wall behind it had been cut out, several shelves nailed into the studs.

Jeffrey forced himself to take a step forward. There were baggies on the shelves. He could've guessed what was in them, but Lena brought them over anyway.

"Look," she said, handing him one of the clear bags. He recognized the contents, but the more interesting part was the fact that there was a label on it with someone's name.

He asked, "Who's Gerald?"

"Who's Bailey?" She handed him another bag, then another. "Who's Kat? Who's Barbara?"

Jeffrey held the bags, thinking he was holding a couple thousand dollars worth of dope.

Lena said, "Some of these names sound familiar."

"How so?"

"The people from the farm that we interviewed." Lena went back to the cutout. "Meth, coke, weed. He's got a little bit of everything here."

Jeffrey looked at the body without thinking, then found himself unable to look away.

Lena suggested, "He was giving Chip drugs. Maybe he was giving these other people drugs, too?"

"The snake tempted Eve," Jeffrey said, quoting Connolly.

Footsteps echoed behind him, and he turned to see Sara walking up the stairs.

"I'm sorry it took so long," she told him, though she had gotten there in record time. "What happened?"

He stepped out onto the landing, telling Lena, "Cover that up," meaning the poster. He slipped the baggies into his pocket so he could process them without having to wait for Ed Pelham to take his sweet time. He told Sara, "Thanks for coming."

"It's fine," she told him.

Lena joined him on the landing. He told her, "Go get Two-Bit," knowing there was nothing else they would find. He had put off bringing in the Catoogah County sheriff long enough.

Sara took his hand as soon as Lena had left.

Jeffrey told her, "He was just sitting there drinking coffee."

She looked into the room, then back at him. "Did you have any?"

He swallowed, feeling like he had glass in his throat. That was probably how it had started for Cole, a feeling in his throat. He had started coughing, then gagging, then the pain had ripped him nearly in two.

"Jeffrey?"

He could only shake his head.

Sara kept holding his hand. "You're cold," she told him.

"I'm a little upset."

"You saw the whole thing?"

He nodded. "I just stood there, Sara. I just stood there watching him die."

"There was nothing you could do," she told him.

"Maybe there was —"

"It killed him too quickly," she said. When he did not respond, she put her arms around him, holding him. She whispered, "It's okay," into his neck.

Jeffrey let his eyes close again, resting his head on her shoulder. Sara smelled like soap and lavender lotion and shampoo and everything clean. He inhaled deeply, needing her scent to wash away the death he had been breathing for the last thirty minutes.

"I have to talk to Terri Stanley," he said. "The cyanide is the key. Lena didn't —"

"Let's go," she interrupted.

He didn't move at first. "Do you want to see —"

"I've seen enough," she told him, tugging his hand to get him moving. "There's nothing I can do right now. He's a biohazard. Everything in there is." She added, "You shouldn't have even been in there. Did Lena touch anything?"

"There was a poster," he said, then, "He had drugs hidden behind it."

"He was using?"

"I don't think so," he answered. "He was offering them to other people, seeing if they would take it."

The Catoogah County sheriff's sedan pulled up, dust swirling in a cloud behind it. Jeffrey couldn't see how the man had gotten here so quickly. Lena hadn't even had time to drive to the sheriff's office.

"What the hell is going on here?" Pelham demanded, jumping out of the car so fast he didn't even bother to shut the door.

"There's been a murder," Jeffrey told him.

"And you just happened to be here?"

"Did you speak to my detective?"

"I passed her on the road and she waved me down. You better be goddamn glad I was already out this way."

Jeffrey didn't have the strength to tell him where he could stick his threat. He walked toward Sara's car, wanting to get as far away from Cole Connolly as he could.

Pelham demanded, "You wanna tell me what the fuck you're doing in my jurisdiction without clearing it with me first?"

"Leaving," Jeffrey told him, as if that wasn't obvious.

"You don't walk away from me," Pelham ordered. "Get the hell back here."

"You gonna arrest me?" Jeffrey asked, opening the car door.

Sara was right behind him. She told Pelham, "Ed, you might want to call in the GBI for this one."

He puffed his chest out like an otter. "We can handle our own crime scenes, thank you very much."

"I know you can," she assured him, employing that sweetly polite tone she used when she was about to cut someone in two. "But as I suspect the man upstairs has been poisoned with cyanide, and as it only takes a concentration of three hundred parts per million of air to kill a human being, I would suggest you call in someone who might be better equipped to handle hazardous crime scenes."

Pelham adjusted his gunbelt. "You figure it's dangerous?"

Sara told him, "I don't think Jim's going to want to handle this one." Jim Ellers was the Catoogah coroner. Now in his late sixties, he had owned one of the more successful funeral homes before he retired, but had kept the job as coroner for pocket money. He wasn't a trained doctor, rather someone who didn't mind performing autopsies to help pay his greens fees.

"Shit!" Pelham spat at the ground. "Do you know how much this is gonna cost?" He didn't wait for an answer as he stomped back to his car and pulled out his CB.

Jeffrey climbed into the car and Sara followed.

"What an ass," she mumbled, starting the car.

He asked, "Give me a lift to the church?"

"Sure," she agreed, backing away from the barn. "Where's your car?"

"I guess Lena's still in it." He looked at his watch. "She should be here soon."

"Are you going to be okay?"

"I'm going to need a stiff drink," he told her.

"I'll have it waiting when you get home."

He smiled despite the circumstances. "I'm sorry I wasted your time bringing you out here."

"It's not a waste of time," she told him, pulling up in front of a white building.

"This is the church?"

"Yes."

He got out of the car, looking up at the small, unassuming structure. He told Sara, "I'll be home later."

She leaned over and squeezed his hand. "Be careful."

He watched her pull away, waiting until he couldn't see her car any longer before walking up the steps to the church. He thought about knocking, but changed his mind, opening the door and entering the chapel.

The large room was empty, but Jeffrey could hear voices from the back. There was a door behind the pulpit, and this time he did knock.

Paul Ward answered the door, shock registering on his face. "Can I help you?"

He was blocking the doorway, but Jeffrey could see the family assembled at a long table behind him. Mary, Rachel and Esther were on one side while Paul, Ephraim and Lev were on the other. At the head of the table was an older man in a wheelchair. In front of him was a metal urn that probably contained Abby's ashes.

Lev stood, telling Jeffrey, "Please come in."

Paul took his time moving out of Jeffrey's way, obviously not happy to have him in the room.

"I'm sorry to interrupt," Jeffrey began.

Esther asked, "Have you found something?"

Jeffrey told her, "There's been a new development." He went to the man in the wheelchair. "I don't think we've met, Mr. Ward."

The man's mouth moved awkwardly, and he said something that Jeffrey took for "Thomas."

"Thomas," Jeffrey repeated. "I'm sorry to meet under these circumstances."

Paul asked, "What circumstances?" and Jeffrey looked to the man's brother.

"I didn't tell them anything," Lev said defensively. "I gave you my word."

"What word?" Paul demanded. "Lev, what the hell have you gotten yourself into?" Thomas made a calming motion with a shaking hand, but Paul told him, "Papa, this is serious. If I'm going to be counsel for the family, they need to listen to me."

Surprisingly, Rachel barked, "You're not in charge of us, Paul."

"Paul," Lev interceded. "Please sit down. I don't think I've gotten myself into any trouble."

Jeffrey wasn't too sure about that, but he said, "Cole Connolly is dead."

There was a collective gasp around the room, and Jeffrey suddenly felt like he was in some kind of Agatha Christie story.

"My Lord," Esther said, hand to her heart. "What happened?"

"He was poisoned."

Esther looked at her husband, then to her oldest brother. "I don't understand."

"Poisoned?" Lev asked, sinking down into a chair. "What on earth?"

"I'm pretty sure it was cyanide," Jeffrey told them. "The same cyanide that killed Abby."

"But . . ." Esther began, shaking her head. "You said she suffocated."

"Cyanide is an asphyxiant," he told her, as if he hadn't purposefully hidden the truth from them. "Someone probably put the salts in water and poured it down the pipe —"

"Pipe?" Mary asked. It was the first time she had spoken and Jeffrey saw that her face had turned milk white. "What pipe?"

"The pipe that was attached to the box," he explained. "The cyanide reacted —"

"Box?" Mary echoed, as if this was the first time she had heard it. Maybe it was, Jeffrey thought. The other day, she had run from the room when he'd started to explain what had happened to Abby.

Perhaps the menfolk had kept this particular piece of news from her delicate ears.

"Cole told me he'd done this before," Jeffrey said, looking at each of the sisters in turn. "Did he punish the other kids this way when they were growing up?" He looked at Esther. "Did he ever punish Rebecca this way?"

Esther seemed to be having trouble breathing. "Why on earth would he—"

Paul cut her off. "Chief Tolliver, I think we need to be alone right now."

"I've got some more questions," Jeffrey said.

Paul replied, "I'm sure you do, but we're—"

"Actually," Jeffrey interrupted, "one of them is for you."

Paul blinked. "Me?"

"Did Abby come see you a few days before she went missing?"

"Well . . ." he thought about it. "Yes, I think so."

Rachel said, "She took those papers to you, Paul. The ones for the tractor."

"Right," Paul remembered. "I left them here in my briefcase." He explained, "There were some legal documents that had to be signed and sent off by close of business."

"She couldn't fax them?"

"They had to be the originals," he explained. "It was a quick trip, down and back up. Abby did that a lot."

"Not a lot," Esther contradicted. "Maybe once or twice a month."

"Semantics," Lev said. "She would run down papers for Paul so he didn't have to take four hours out of his day on the road."

"She took the bus," Jeffrey said. "Why didn't she drive herself?"

"Abby didn't like driving on the interstate," Lev answered. "Is there a problem? Do you think she met someone on the bus?"

Jeffrey asked Paul, "Were you in Savannah the week she disappeared?"

"Yes," the lawyer replied. "I told you that before. I spend every other week there. It's just me handling all the legal business for the farm. It's very time-consuming." He took a small notebook out of his pocket and scribbled something down. "This is my Savannah office number," he said, tearing off the sheet of paper. "You can call my secretary there—Barbara. She can verify where I was."

"What about at night?"

"Are you asking me for an alibi?" he demanded, incredulous.

Lev said, "Paul—"

"Listen here," Paul said, getting into Jeffrey's face. "You've interrupted my niece's funeral. I understand you have to do your job, but this is not the time."

Jeffrey stood his ground. "Take your finger out of my face."

"I've had just about enough—"

"Take your finger out of my face," Jeffrey repeated, and, after a moment, the man had the good sense to drop his hand. Jeffrey looked at the sisters, then at Thomas, sitting at the end of the table. "Someone murdered Abbey," he told them, feeling a barely controlled sense of rage burning deep inside of him. "She was buried in that box by Cole Connolly. She stayed in there for several days and nights until someone— someone who knew she was buried out there—came along and poured cyanide into her throat."

Esther put her hand to her mouth, tears springing into her eyes.

"I've just watched a man die that death," he told them. "I watched him writhe on the floor, gasping for air, knowing full well that he was going to die, probably begging God to go ahead and take him just to release him from the pain."

Esther dropped her head, crying in earnest. The rest of the family seemed shocked, and as Jeffrey glanced around the room, no one but Lev would look him in the eye. The preacher seemed about to speak, but Paul put his hand on his brother's shoulder, stopping him.

"Rebecca's still missing," Jeffrey reminded them.

"Do you think . . ." Esther began. Her question trailed off as the implications hit her full force.

Jeffrey watched Lev, trying to read his blank stare. Paul's jaw had tightened, but Jeffrey didn't know if this was from anger or concern.

It was Rachel who finally asked the question, her voice quavering at the thought of her niece in danger. "Do you think Rebecca's been taken?"

"I think somebody in this room knows exactly what's been going on—is probably a part of it." Jeffrey tossed a handful of business cards down on the table. "These have all my numbers," he told them. "Call me when you're ready to find out the truth."

FRIDAY

CHAPTER THIRTEEN

Sara lay in bed on her side, looking out the window. She could hear Jeffrey in the kitchen, knocking pans around. Around five this morning, he had scared the shit out of her, jumping around in the dark as he put on his running shorts, looking like an ax murderer in the shadows cast by the moon. An hour later, he had wakened her again, cursing like a sailor when he accidentally stepped on Bob. Displaced from the bed by Jeffrey, the greyhound had taken to sleeping in the bathtub and was just as indignant as Jeffrey to find them both simultaneously in the tub.

Still, she was somewhat comforted by Jeffrey's presence in the house. She liked rolling over in the middle of the night and feeling the warmth of his body. She liked the sound of his voice and the smell of the oatmeal lotion he used on his hands when he thought she wasn't looking. She especially liked that he cooked breakfast for her.

"Get your ass out of bed and come scramble the eggs," Jeffrey yelled from the kitchen.

Sara muttered something she would be ashamed for her mother to hear as she dragged herself out from under the covers. The house was freezing cold even though the sun was beating down on the lake, waves sending coppery glints of light through the back windows. She grabbed Jeffrey's robe and wrapped it around herself before padding down the hallway.

Jeffrey stood at the stove, frying bacon. He was wearing sweatpants and a black T-shirt, which set off his bruised eye nicely in the morning sun.

He said, "I figured you were awake."

"Third time's a charm," she told him, petting Billy as he leaned up against her. Bob was splayed on the couch with his feet in the air.

She could see Bubba, her erstwhile cat, stalking something in the backyard.

Jeffrey had already gotten out the eggs and sat the carton beside a bowl for her. Sara cracked them open, trying not to drip the whites all over the counter. Jeffrey saw the mess she was making and took over, saying, "Sit down."

Sara sank into the stool at the kitchen island, watching him clean up her mess.

She asked the obvious. "You couldn't sleep?"

"No," he told her, tossing the rag into the sink.

He was worried about the case, but she also knew that he was almost as troubled about Lena. Their entire relationship, Jeffrey had been in some state of concern for Lena Adams. In the beginning it was because she was too hot-headed on the street, too aggressive with her arrests. From there, Jeffrey had been worried about her competitiveness, her yearning to be the best on the squad no matter what shortcuts she felt she had to take. He had trained her carefully as a detective, partnering her with Frank but taking her under his wing, grooming her for something — something Sara thought the other woman would never get. Lena was too single-minded to lead, too selfish to follow. Twelve years ago, Sara could have predicted he would still be worrying over Lena today. That she was mixed up with that Nazi skinhead Ethan Green was really the only thing that had ever surprised her about the other woman.

Sara asked, "Are you going to try to talk to Lena?"

Jeffrey didn't answer her question. "She's too smart for this."

"I don't think abuse has anything to do with intelligence or lack thereof," Sara said.

"That's the reason I don't think Cole went after Rebecca," Jeffrey told her. "She's too willful. He wouldn't pick someone who would fight back too much."

"Is Brad still looking over in Catoogah?"

"Yeah," he said, not sounding hopeful that the search would yield anything. He skipped on to Cole Connolly as if he had been having a different conversation in his head. "Rebecca would've told her mother what was going on and Esther . . . Esther would have ripped out Cole's throat." Using his good hand, he broke the eggs one by one into the bowl. "Cole wouldn't have risked it."

"Predators have an innate ability to choose their victims," Sara agreed, thinking again about Lena. Somehow, the circumstances of her damaged life had taken over, making her an easy target for someone like Ethan. Sara completely understood how this happened. It was all logical, yet knowing Lena, she was still having trouble accepting it.

"I kept seeing him last night, the panic in his eyes when he realized what was happening. Jesus, what a horrible way to die."

"It's the same thing that happened to Abby," she reminded him. "Only she was alone in the dark and had no idea what was happening to her."

"I think he knew," Jeffrey said. "At least, I think he figured it out in the end." There were two mugs in front of the coffeemaker and he filled them, handing Sara one. She saw him hesitate before taking a sip, and wondered if there would ever be a time when he could drink coffee without thinking about Cole Connolly. In the scheme of things, Sara had a much easier job than Jeffrey did. He was out there on the front line. He saw the bodies first, told the parents and loved ones, felt the weight of their desperation to find out who had taken away their child or mother or lover. It was no wonder that cops had one of the highest suicide rates of any profession.

She asked, "What's your gut feeling?"

"I don't know," he answered, mixing the eggs with a fork. "Lev admitted that he was attracted to Abby."

"But that's normal," she said, then backed up, "Well, normal if it happened the way he said it did."

"Paul says he was in Savannah. I'm going to check that out, but that still doesn't account for his evenings."

"That could just as easily point to his innocence," Sara reminded him. She had learned from Jeffrey a long time ago that someone who had a pat alibi was generally a person to look at closely. Sara herself couldn't come up with a witness who could swear Sara had been at home alone all night when Abigail Bennett had been murdered.

"No news on the letter you were sent yet," he said. "I doubt the lab will find anything anyway." He frowned. "It's costing a fucking fortune."

"Why do it?"

"Because I don't like the idea of somebody contacting you about a case," he told her, and she could hear resentment in his tone. "You're not a cop. You're not involved in this."

"They could have sent it to me knowing that I would tell you."

"Why not just send it to the station?"

"My address is in the phone book," she said. "Whoever sent it might have worried that a letter would get lost at the station." She asked, "Do you think it was one of the sisters?"

"They don't even know you."

"You told them I was your wife."

"I still don't like it," he said, dividing the eggs between two plates and adding a couple of slices of toast to each. He veered back to the original subject. "The cyanide is what's hard to connect." He offered her the plate of bacon and she took two pieces. "The more we look into it, the more it seems like Dale is the only possible source." Jeffrey added, "But Dale swears he keeps the garage locked at all times."

"Do you believe him?"

"He may beat his wife," Jeffrey began, "but I think he was telling me the truth. Those tools are his bread and butter. He's not going to leave that door open, especially with people coming through from the farm." He took out the jelly and passed it to her.

"Is it possible he's involved?"

"I don't see how," Jeffrey told her. "He's got no connection to Abby, no reason to poison her or Cole." He suggested, "I should just run the whole family in, split them up and see who breaks first."

"I doubt Paul would allow that."

"Maybe I'll tag the old man."

"Oh, Jeffrey," she said, feeling protective of Thomas Ward for some unknown reason. "Don't. He's just a helpless old man."

"Nobody's helpless in that family." He paused. "Not even Rebecca."

Sara weighed his words. "You think she's involved?"

"I think she's hiding. I think she knows something." He sat beside her at the counter, picking at his eyebrow, obviously mulling over the niggling details that had kept him up all night.

Sara rubbed his back. "Something will break. You just need to start back at square one."

"You're right." He looked up at her. "It keeps going back to the cyanide. That's the key. I want to talk to Terri Stanley. I need to get her away from Dale and see what she says."

"She's got an appointment at the clinic today," Sara told him. "I had to fit her in during lunch."

"What's wrong?"

"Her youngest hasn't gotten any better."

"Are you going to talk to her about the bruises?"

"I'm in the same boat as you," she said. "It's not like I can back her into a corner and get her to tell me what's going on. If it were that easy, you'd be out of a job."

Sara had experienced her own guilt last night, wondering how she had seen Terri Stanley all these years and never guessed what was happening at home.

She continued, "I can't really betray Lena's confidence and for all I know, it'll scare her off. Her kids are sick. She needs the clinic. It's a safe place for her." Sara assured him, "If I ever see so much as a hair disturbed on those kids, you'd better believe I'll say something about it. She'd never leave the building with them."

He asked, "Does she ever bring Dale with her when she comes to the clinic?"

"Not that I've seen."

"Mind if I stop in to talk to her?"

"I don't know if I'm comfortable with that," she said, not liking the idea of her clinic being used as a second police station.

He told her, "Dale has a loaded gun in his shop, and something tells me he doesn't like cops talking to his wife."

"Oh," was all she could say. That changed things.

"Why don't I just wait around in the parking lot for her to come out?" he suggested. "Then I'll take her to the station."

Sara knew this would be a lot safer, but she still didn't relish the thought of being involved in setting up Terri Stanley for a surprise attack. "She'll have her son with her."

"Marla loves children."

"I don't feel good about this."

"I'm sure Abby Bennett didn't feel good about being put in that box, either."

He had a point, but she still didn't like it. Despite her better judgment, Sara relented, "She's scheduled to come in at twelve fifteen."

※ ※ ※ ※

Brock's funeral home was housed in a Victorian mansion that had been built in the early 1900s by the man who had run the railroad maintenance depot over in Avondale. Unfortunately, he had dipped into the railroad's coffers in order to finance the construction and when he had been caught, the place had been sold at auction. John Brock had purchased the mansion for a ridiculously low sum and turned it into one of the nicest funeral homes this side of Atlanta.

When John died, he passed the business on to his only son. Sara had gone to school with Dan Brock and the funeral home had been on her bus route. The family lived above the business, and every weekday morning, she had cringed as the bus pulled up in front of the Brocks' house — not because she was squeamish, but because Brock's mother insisted on waiting outside with her son, rain or shine, so that she could kiss him good-bye. After this embarrassing farewell, Dan would clamber onto the bus, where all the boys would make smooching noises at him.

More often than not, he ended up sitting beside Sara. She hadn't been part of the popular crowd or the drug crowd or even the geeks. Most times, she had her head in a book and didn't notice who was sitting beside her unless Brock plopped himself down. He was chatty even then, and more than a bit strange. Sara had always felt sorry for him, and that hadn't changed in the thirty plus years since they had ridden to school together. A confirmed bachelor who sang in the church choir, Brock still lived with his mother.

"Hello?" Sara called, opening the door onto the grand hall that went the full length of the house. Audra Brock hadn't changed much in the way of decorating since her husband had bought the mansion, and the heavy carpeting and drapes still fit the Victorian period. Chairs were scattered down the hall, tables with Kleenex boxes discreetly hidden beside flower arrangements offering respite for mourners.

"Brock?" she asked, setting down her briefcase on one of the chairs so that she could dig out Abigail Bennett's death certificate. She had promised Paul Ward she would have the paperwork to Brock yesterday, but she'd been too busy to get to it. Carlos had taken a rare day off, and Sara didn't want to keep the family waiting one more day.

"Brock?" she tried again, looking at her watch, wondering where he was. She was going to be late getting to the clinic.

"Hello?" There hadn't been any cars parked outside, so Sara assumed there wasn't a funeral taking place. She walked down the hallway, peering into each of the viewing parlors. She found Brock in the farthest one. He was a tall, gangly man, but he had managed to lean the entire upper part of his body into a casket, the lid resting on his back. A woman's leg, bent at the knee stuck up beside him, a dainty, high-heel clad foot dangling outside the casket. Sara would have suspected something obscene if she didn't know him better.

"Brock?"

He jumped, smacking his head against the lid. "Lord a'mighty," he laughed, clutching his heart as the lid slammed down. "You near about scared me to death."

"Sorry."

"Guess I'm in the right place for it!" he joked, slapping his thigh.

Sara made herself laugh. Brock's sense of humor matched his social skills.

He ran his hand along the shiny edge of the bright yellow casket. "Special order. Nice, huh?"

"Uh, yeah," she agreed, not knowing what else to say.

"Georgia Tech fan," he told her, indicating the black pinstriping along the lid. "Say," he said, beaming a smile. "I hate to ask, but can you give me a hand with her?"

"What's wrong?"

He opened the lid again, showing her the body of a cherubic woman who was probably around eighty. Her gray hair was styled into a bun, her cheeks slightly rouged to give her a healthy glow. She looked like she belonged in Madame Tussauds instead of a lemon-yellow casket. One of the problems Sara had with embalming was the artifice involved; the blush and mascara, the chemicals that pickled the body to keep it from rotting. She did not relish the thought of dying and having someone—worse yet, Dan Brock—shoving cotton into her various orifices so that she wouldn't leak embalming fluid.

"I was trying to pull it down," Brock told her, indicating the woman's jacket, which was bunched up around her shoulders. "She's kind of husky. If you could hold up her legs and I could pull . . ."

She heard herself saying, "Sure," even though this was the last thing she wanted to do with her morning. She lifted the woman's legs at the ankles and Brock made quick work pulling down the suit jacket, talking all the while. "I didn't want to have to tote her back downstairs to the pulley and Mama's just not up to helping with this kind of thing anymore."

Sara lowered the legs. "Is she okay?"

"Sciatica," he whispered, as if his mother might be embarrassed by the affliction. "It's terrible when they start getting old. Anyway." He tucked his hand around the coffin, straightening the silk lining. When he was finished, he rubbed his palms together as if to wash his hands of the task. "Thanks for helping me with that. What can I do you for?"

"Oh," Sara had almost forgotten why she came. She walked back to the front row of chairs where she had put Abby's paperwork. "I told Paul Ward I'd bring the death certificate over to you by Thursday, but I got tied up."

"I'm sure that won't be a problem," Brock said, flashing a smile. "I don't even have Chip back from the crematorium yet."

"Chip?"

"Charles," he said. "Sorry, Paul called him Chip, but I guess that can't be his real name."

"Why would Paul want Charles Donner's death certificate?"

Brock shrugged, as if the request was the most natural thing in the world. "He always gets the death certificates when people from the farm pass."

Sara leaned her hand against the back of the chair, feeling the need to grab onto something solid. "How many people die on the farm?"

"No," Brock laughed, though she didn't see what was funny. "I'm sorry I gave you the wrong impression. Not a lot. Two earlier this year—Chip makes three. I guess there were a couple last year."

"That seems like a lot to me," Sara told him, thinking he had left out Abigail, which would bring the tally to four this year alone.

"Well, I suppose," Brock said slowly, as if the peculiarity of the circumstances had just occurred to him. "But you have to think

about the types of folks they've got over there. Derelicts, mostly. I
think it's real Christian of the family to pick up the handling costs."

"What did they die of?"

"Let's see," Brock began, tapping his finger against his chin. "All
natural causes, I can tell you that. If you can call drinking and drug-
ging yourself to death natural causes. One of 'em, this guy, was so
full of liquor it took less than three hours to render his cremains.
Came with his own accelerant. Skinny guy, too. Not a lot of fat."

Sara knew fat burned more easily than muscle, but she didn't like
being reminded of it so soon after breakfast. "And the others?"

"I've got copies of the certificates in the office."

"They came from Jim Ellers?" Sara asked, meaning Catoogah's
county coroner.

"Yep," Brock said, waving her back toward the hall.

Sara followed, feeling uneasy. Jim Ellers was a nice man, but like
Brock he was a funeral director, not a physician. Jim always sent his
more difficult cases to Sara or the state lab. She couldn't recall anything other than a gunshot wound and a stabbing that had been
transferred to her office from Catoogah over the last eight years. Jim
must have thought the deaths at the farm were pretty standard.
Maybe they were. Brock had a point about the workers being derelicts. Alcoholism and drug addiction were hard diseases to manage,
and left untreated, they generally led to catastrophic health problems
and eventual death.

Brock opened a set of large wooden pocket doors to the room
where the kitchen had once been. The space was now his office, and
a massive desk was in the center, paperwork heaped in the in-box.

He apologized, "Mama's been a little too poorly to straighten up."

"It's okay."

Brock went over to the row of filing cabinets along the back of the
room. He put his fingers to his chin again, tapping, not opening any
drawers.

"Something wrong?"

"I might need a minute to try to think of their names." He grinned
apologetically. "Mama's so much better at remembering these things
than I am."

"Brock, this is important," she told him. "Go get your mother."

CHAPTER FOURTEEN

"Yes, ma'am," Jeffrey said into the telephone, rolling his eyes at Lena. She could tell that Barbara, Paul Ward's secretary, was giving him everything but her social security number. The woman's tinny voice was so loud that Lena could hear it from five feet away.

"That's good," he said. "Yes, ma'am." He leaned his head against his hand. "Oh, excuse me—excuse—" he tried, then, "I've got another call. Thank you." He hung up, Barbara's cackling coming out of the earpiece even as he dropped the receiver back on the hook.

"Jesus Christ," he said, rubbing his ear. "Literally."

"She try to save your soul?"

"Let's just say she's really happy to be involved with the church."

"So, she'd say anything she could to cover for Paul?"

"Probably," he agreed, sitting back in his chair. He looked down at his notes, which consisted of three words. "She confirms what Paul said about being in Savannah. She even remembered working late with him the night Abby died."

Lena knew that pinpointing time of death wasn't an exact science. "All night?"

"That's a point," he allowed. "She also said Abby came by with some papers a couple of days before she went missing."

"Did she seem okay?"

"Said she was a little ray of sunshine, as usual. Paul signed some papers, they went to lunch and he took her back to the bus station."

"They could've had some kind of altercation during lunch."

"True," he agreed. "But why would he kill his niece?"

"It could be his baby she was carrying," Lena suggested. "It wouldn't be the first time."

Jeffrey rubbed his jaw. "Yeah," he admitted, and she could tell the

310

thought left a bad taste in his mouth. "But Cole Connolly was pretty sure it was Chip's."

"Are you sure Cole didn't poison her?"

"As close to sure as I can be," he told her. "Maybe we need to separate out the two, forget worrying about who killed Abby. Who killed Cole? Who would want him dead?"

Lena wasn't entirely convinced of Connolly's truthfulness about Abby's death. Jeffrey had been pretty shaken up after watching the man die. She wondered if his conviction of Cole's innocence was influenced by what had to have been a truly grotesque experience.

She suggested, "Maybe somebody who knew Cole had poisoned Abby decided to get revenge, wanted him to suffer the same way Abby had."

"I didn't tell anyone in the family that she was poisoned until after Cole was dead," he reminded her. "On the other hand, whoever did it knew he drank coffee every morning. He told me the sisters were always on him, trying to get him to quit."

Lena took it a step further. "Rebecca might know, too."

Jeffrey nodded. "There's a reason she's staying away." He added, "At least I hope she's choosing to stay away."

Lena had been thinking this same thing. "You're sure Cole didn't put her somewhere? To punish her for something?"

"I know you think I shouldn't take him at his word," Jeffrey began, "but I don't think he took her. People like Cole know who to choose." He leaned across his desk, hands clasped in front of him, as if he was saying something vital to the case. "They pick the ones they know won't talk. It's the same way with Dale picking Terri. These guys know who they can push around—who will shut up and take it and who won't."

Lena felt her cheeks burning. "Rebecca seemed pretty defiant. We only saw her that once, but I got the feeling she didn't let anybody push her around." She shrugged. "The thing is, you never know, do you?"

"No," he said, giving her a careful look. "For all we know, Rebecca's the one behind all of this."

Frank stood in the doorway with a stack of papers in his hand. He said something neither one of them had considered. "Poisoning is a woman's crime."

"Rebecca was scared when she talked to us," Lena said. "She didn't want her family to know. Then again, maybe she didn't want them to know because she was playing us."

Jeffrey asked, "Did she seem like the type?"

"No," she admitted. "Lev and Paul, maybe. Rachel's pretty sturdy, too."

Frank said, "What's the brother doing living in Savannah, anyway?"

"It's a port city," Jeffrey reminded him. "Lots of trade still goes on down there." He indicated the papers in Frank's hand. "What've you got?"

"The rest of the credit reports," he said, handing them over.

"Anything jump out at you?"

Frank shook his head as Marla's voice crackled over the intercom. "Chief, Sara's on line three."

Jeffrey picked up the phone. "Hey."

Lena made to leave in order to give him some privacy, but Jeffrey waved her back down in her chair. He took out his pen, saying into the phone, "Spell that," as he wrote. Then, "Okay. Next."

Lena read upside down as he wrote a series of names, all men.

"This is good," Jeffrey told Sara. "I'll call you later." He hung up the telephone, not even pausing for a breath before saying, "Sara's at Brock's. She says that nine people have died on the farm in the last two years."

"Nine?" Lena was sure she'd heard wrong.

"Brock got four of the bodies. Richard Cable got the rest."

Lena knew Cable ran one of the funeral homes in Catoogah County. She asked, "What was the cause of death?"

Jeffrey ripped the sheet of paper off his pad. "Alcohol poisoning, drug overdoses. One had a heart attack. Jim Ellers over in Catoogah did the autopsies. He ruled them all natural causes."

Lena was skeptical, not of what Jeffrey was saying, but of Ellers's competence. "He said nine people in two years, living on the same place, died from natural causes?"

Jeffrey said, "Cole Connolly had a lot of drugs hidden in his room."

"You think he helped them along?" Frank asked.

"That's what he did with Chip," Jeffrey said. "Cole told me that himself. Said he was tempting him with the apple, something like that."

"So," Lena surmised, "Cole was picking out the 'weak' ones, dangling drugs or whatever in front of their faces, seeing if they would take them and prove him right."

"And the ones who took them ended up going to their maker," Jeffrey said, but she could tell from his crocodile smile he had more.

She asked, "What?"

He told her, "The Church for the Greater Good paid for all the cremations."

"Cremations," Frank repeated. "So, we can't exhume the bodies."

Lena knew there was more to it than that. She asked, "What am I missing?"

Jeffrey told them, "Paul Ward got all their death certificates."

Stupidly, Lena began, "Why would he need—" but answered her own question before she finished. "Life insurance."

"Bingo," Jeffrey said, handing Frank the paper with the names. "Get Hemming and go through the phone book. Do we have one for Savannah?" Frank nodded. "Find the big insurance companies. We'll start there first. Don't call the local agents, call the corporate national fraud hotlines. The local agents might be involved."

Lena asked, "Will they give out that information over the phone?"

"They will if they think they've been cheated out of some dough," Frank said. "I'll get right on it."

As Frank left the room, Jeffrey pointed his finger at Lena. "I knew this had to be about money. It had to be about something concrete."

She had to admit, "You were right."

"We found our general," he told her. "Cole said he was just an old soldier, but he needed a general to tell him what to do."

"Abby was in Savannah a few days before she died. Maybe she found out about the life insurance policies."

"How?" Jeffrey asked.

"Her mother said she worked in the office for a while. That she was good with numbers."

"Lev saw her in the office once at the photocopier. Maybe she saw something she wasn't meant to." He paused, mulling over the possibilities. "Rachel said Abby went to Savannah before she died because Paul had left some papers behind in his briefcase. Maybe Abby saw the policies."

She asked, "So, you think Abby confronted him in Savannah?"

Jeffrey nodded. "And Paul called Cole to prod him on to punish her."

"Or he called Lev."

"Or Lev," he agreed.

"Cole already knew about Chip. He followed him and Abby out into the woods." She had to say, "I don't know, though. It's strange. Paul didn't strike me as the overly religious type."

"Why would he have to be?"

"Telling Cole to bury his niece in a coffin in the woods?" she asked. "Lev seems more like your general to me." She added, "Plus, Paul was never in Dale's garage. If that's where the cyanide came from, then it points straight back to Lev, because he's the only one we can connect to the garage." She paused a moment. "Or Cole."

"I don't think it was Cole," Jeffrey insisted. "Did you ever have a real conversation with Terri Stanley about that?"

She felt her blush come back, this time from shame. "No."

His lips pressed into a tight line, but he didn't say the obvious. If she had talked to Terri before, maybe they wouldn't be sitting here right now. Maybe Rebecca would be safe at home, Cole Connolly would still be alive, and they would be back in the interrogation room, talking to the person who had killed Abigail Bennett.

"I fucked up," she said.

"Yeah, you did." He waited a few seconds before saying, "You don't listen to me, Lena. I need to be able to trust you to do what I say." He paused as if he expected her to interrupt him. She didn't, and he continued, "You can be a good cop, a smart cop. That's why I made you detective." She looked down, unable to take the compliment, knowing what was coming next. "Everything that happens in this town is my responsibility, and if somebody gets hurt or worse because you can't follow my orders, then it's all on me."

"I know. I'm sorry."

"Sorry isn't good enough this time. Sorry means you understand what I'm saying and you're not going to do it again." He let that sink in. "I've heard sorry one too many times now. I need to see actions, not hear empty words."

His quiet tone was worse than if he had yelled at her. Lena looked down at the floor, wondering how many times he was going to let her screw things up before he finally cut her loose.

He stood quickly, taking her by surprise. Lena flinched, gripped by an inexplicable panic that he was going to hit her.

Jeffrey was shocked, looking at her as if he had never seen her in his life.

"I just—" she couldn't find the words to say. "You scared me."

Jeffrey leaned out the door, telling Marla, "Send back the woman who's about to walk in." He told Lena, "Mary Ward is here. I just saw her pull up into the parking lot."

Lena tried to regain her composure. "I thought she didn't like to drive."

"Guess she made an exception," Jeffrey answered, still looking at her like she was a book he couldn't read. "Are you going to be able to do this?"

"Of course," she said, pushing herself out of the chair. She tucked in her shirt, feeling fidgety and out of place.

He took her hand in both of his, and she felt another shock. He never touched her like that. It wasn't something he did.

He said, "I need you to be on your game right now."

"You've got me," she assured him, pulling back her hand to tuck in her shirt again even though it was already tight. "Let's go."

Lena didn't wait for him. She squared her shoulders and walked across the squad room with purposeful strides. Marla's hand was on the buzzer as Lena opened the door.

Mary Ward stood in the lobby, her purse clutched to her chest.

"Chief Tolliver," she said, as if Lena wasn't right in front of her. She had a ratty old black and red scarf around her shoulders, looking more like a little old lady now than the first time they had seen her. The woman was probably only ten years older than Lena. She was either putting on an act or was truly one of the most pathetic people walking the face of the earth.

"Why don't you come back to my office," Jeffrey offered, putting his hand at Mary's elbow, guiding her through the open doorway before she could change her mind. He said, "You remember Detective Adams?"

"Lena," Lena supplied, ever helpful. "Can I get you some coffee or something?"

"I don't drink caffeine," the woman replied, her voice still strained, as if she had been screaming and had made herself hoarse. Lena could see she had a balled tissue up her sleeve and assumed she'd been crying.

Jeffrey sat Mary at one of the desks outside his office, probably wanting to keep her off guard. He waited for her to sit, then took the chair beside her. Lena hung back behind them, thinking Mary would be more comfortable talking to Jeffrey.

He asked, "What can I help you with, Mary?"

She took her time, her breathing audible in the small room as they waited for her to speak. "You said my niece was in a box, Chief Tolliver."

"Yes."

"That Cole had buried her in a box."

"That's right," he confirmed. "Cole admitted it to me before he died."

"And you found her there? You found Abby yourself?"

"My wife and I were in the woods. We found the metal pipe in the ground. We dug her out ourselves."

Mary took the tissue from her sleeve and wiped her nose. "Several years ago," she began, then, "I guess I should back up."

"Take your time."

She seemed to do exactly that, and Lena pressed her lips together, fighting the urge to shake it out of her.

"I have two sons," Mary said. "William and Peter. They live out west."

"I remember you telling us that," Jeffrey said, though Lena didn't.

"They chose to leave the church." She blew her nose in the tissue. "It was very hard for me to lose my children. Not that we turned our backs on them. Everyone makes their own decisions. We don't exclude people because they . . ." She let her voice trail off. "My sons turned their backs on us. On me."

Jeffrey waited, the only sign of his impatience his hand gripping the arm of the chair.

"Cole was very hard on them," she said. "He disciplined them."

"Did he abuse them?"

"He punished them when they were bad," was all she would admit. "My husband had passed away a year before. I was grateful for Cole's help. I thought they needed a strong man in their lives." She sniffed, wiping her nose. "These were different times."

"I understand," Jeffrey told her.

"Cole has—had—very firm ideas about right and wrong. I trusted him. My father trusted him. He was first and foremost a man of God."

"Did anything happen to change that?"

She seemed overcome by sadness. "No. I believed everything he said. At the cost of my own children, I believed in him. I turned my back on my daughter."

Lena felt her eyebrows shoot up.

"You have a daughter?"

She nodded. "Genie."

Jeffrey sat back in the chair, though his body remained tense.

"She told me," Mary continued. "Genie told me what he had done to her." She paused. "The box in the woods."

"He buried her there?"

"They were camping," Mary explained. "He took the children camping all the time."

Lena knew Jeffrey was thinking about Rebecca, how she had run away to the woods before. He asked, "What did your daughter say happened?"

"She said Cole tricked her, that he told her he was going to take her for a walk in the woods." She stopped, then willed herself to go on. "He left her there for five days."

"What did you do when she told you about this?"

"I asked Cole about it." She shook her head at her own stupidity. "He told me that he couldn't stay on the farm if I believed Genie over him. He felt that strongly about it."

"But he didn't deny it?"

"No," she told Jeffrey. "I never realized it until last night. He never denied it. He told me that I should pray about it, let the Lord tell me whom to believe—Genie or him. I trusted in him. He has such a strict sense of right and wrong. I took him for a God-fearing man."

"Did anyone else in the family know about this?"

She shook her head again. "I was ashamed. She lied." Mary corrected, "She lied about some things. I see that now, but at the time, it was harder to see. Genie was a very rebellious young girl. She used drugs. She ran around with boys. She turned away from the church. She turned away from the family."

"What did you tell them about Genie's disappearance?"

"I sought my brother's counsel. He told me to tell them she had run away with a boy. It was a believable story. I thought it saved us all the embarrassment of the truth, and neither of us wanted to upset Cole." She dabbed the tissue at the corner of her eye. "He was so valuable to us then. My brothers were both away at school. None of us girls were capable of taking care of the farm. Cole ran everything along with my father. He was critical to the operation."

The fire door banged open and Frank came in, stopping in his tracks when he saw Jeffrey and Mary Ward sitting at the desk. He walked over and put his hand on Jeffrey's shoulder, handing him a folder. Jeffrey opened the file, obviously knowing Frank would not have interrupted unless it was important. Lena could tell that he was looking at several faxed pages. The station was run on a tight budget and the machine was about ten years old, using thermal rolls instead of plain paper. Jeffrey smoothed out the pages as he scanned them. When he looked up, Lena couldn't tell if he had read good news or bad.

"Mary," Jeffrey said. "I've been calling you Ms. Ward this whole time. Is your married name Morgan?"

Her surprise registered on her face. "Yes," she said. "Why?"

"And your daughter is named Teresa Eugenia Morgan?"

"Yes."

Jeffrey gave her a minute to collect herself. "Mary," he began. "Did Abby ever meet your daughter?"

"Of course," she said. "Genie was ten when Abby was born. She treated her like her own little baby. Abby was devastated when Genie left. They were both devastated."

"Could Abby have visited your daughter that day she went to Savannah?"

"Savannah?"

He took out one of the faxed pages. "We have Genie's address listed as 241 Sandon Square, Savannah."

"Well, no," she said, a bit troubled. "My daughter lives here in town, Chief Tolliver. Her married name is Stanley."

❈ ❈ ❈ ❈

Lena drove to the Stanley place while Jeffrey talked on his cell phone to Frank. He kept his spiral notepad balanced on his knee as he wrote down whatever Frank was telling him, giving the occasional grunt to confirm he'd heard what was being said.

Lena glanced in her rearview mirror to make sure Brad Stephens was behind them. He was following in his cruiser, and for once, Lena was glad to have the junior patrolman around. Brad was goofy, but he had been working out lately and had the muscle to show for it. Jeffrey had told them about the loaded revolver Dale Stanley kept on top of one of the cabinets in the garage. She wasn't looking forward to confronting Terri's husband, but part of her was hoping he tried something so that Jeffrey and Brad had an excuse to show him what it felt like for someone larger and stronger than you to bring down a world of pain on your ass.

Jeffrey told Frank, "No, don't put her in a cell. Give her some milk and cookies if you have to. Just keep her away from the phone and her brothers." Lena knew he was talking about Mary Morgan. The woman had been startled when Jeffrey had told her she wasn't to leave the police station but, like most law-abiding citizens, she was so scared of going to jail that she had just sat there, nodding, agreeing with everything he said.

"Good work, Frank." Jeffrey told him, "Let me know what else you come up with," and rang off. He started scribbling on his pad again, not speaking.

Lena didn't have the patience to wait for him to finish with his notes. "What did he say?"

"They've found six policies so far," he told her, still writing. "Lev and Terri are listed as beneficiaries for both Abby and Chip. Mary Morgan is on two, Esther Bennett is on two others."

"What'd Mary say about that?"

"She said she had no idea what Frank was talking about. Paul handles all the accounts for the family."

"Did Frank believe her?"

"He's not sure," Jeffrey said. "Hell, I'm not sure and I talked to her for half an hour."

"I wouldn't guess they're living high on the hog."

"Sara says they make their own clothes."

"Paul doesn't," she pointed out. "How much were the policies worth?"

"Around fifty thousand each. They were greedy, but they weren't stupid."

Lena knew that anything exorbitant would have raised suspicion with the insurance agencies. As it was, the family had managed to collect nearly half a million dollars over the last two years, all of it tax free.

"What about the house?" Lena asked. The policies had listed each beneficiary as living at the same address in Savannah. A quick call to the Chatham County courthouse had revealed that the house on Sandon Square was purchased by a Stephanie Linder five years ago. Either there was another Ward sibling Jeffrey didn't know about or someone was playing a nasty joke on the family.

Lena asked, "You think Dale is involved in this, too?"

"Frank ran a credit check," he said. "Dale and Terri are both in debt up to their eyeballs—credit cards, mortgage, two car payments. They've got three medical collections against them. Sara says the kid's been in the hospital a couple of times. They're hurting for money."

"You think Terri killed her?" Lena asked. Frank was right when he said poisoning was generally a woman's crime.

"Why would she do it?"

"She knew what Cole did. She could've been following him."

"But why kill Abby?"

"Maybe she didn't," Lena tried. "Maybe Cole killed Abby and Terri decided to give him some of his own medicine."

He shook his head. "I don't think Cole killed Abby. He was genuinely sad that she was dead."

Lena let it go, but in her mind, she thought he was giving a large benefit of the doubt to one of the sickest fucks she'd ever run into.

Jeffrey opened his cell phone and dialed a number. Someone obviously answered on the other end, and he said, "Hey, Molly. Can you give a message to Sara for me?" He paused a beat. "Tell her we're heading out to the Stanley place right now. Thanks." He hung up, telling Lena, "Terri had an appointment with Sara around lunchtime."

It was half past ten. Lena thought about the gun in Dale's garage. "Why didn't we just pick her up then?"

"Because Sara's office is out of bounds."

Lena thought this was a pretty lame excuse, but she knew better than to push him on it. Jeffrey was the best cop she had ever known, but he was like a whipped puppy as far as Sara Linton was concerned. The fact that she jerked him around so much would have been embarrassing to any other man, but he seemed to take pride in it.

Jeffrey must have sensed her thoughts — at least some of them — because he said, "I don't know what Terri's capable of. I sure as hell don't want her going ballistic in an office full of little kids."

He pointed to a black mailbox jutting up beside the road. "It's up here on the right."

Lena slowed, turning into the Stanley driveway, Brad right behind her. She saw Dale working in the garage and felt her breath catch. She had met him once, years ago, at another police picnic when his brother, Pat, had just joined the force. Lena had forgotten how large he was. Not just large, but strong.

Jeffrey got out of the car, but Lena found herself hesitating. She made her hand move to the handle on the door, made herself open it and get out. She heard Brad's door shut behind her, but didn't want to take her eyes off Dale for a second. He stood just inside the doorway of the garage, hefting a heavy-looking wrench in his meaty hands. The cabinet with the gun was a few feet away. Like Jeffrey, he had a dark bruise under his eye.

"Hey, Dale," Jeffrey said. "How'd you get the shiner?"

"Ran into a door," he quipped, and Lena wondered how he'd really gotten it. Terri would need to stand on a chair to reach his head. Dale weighed about a hundred pounds more than she did and was at least two feet taller. Lena looked at his hands, thinking one was large enough to wrap around her throat. He could strangle her without giving it a second thought. She hated that feeling, hated the sensation of her lungs shaking in her chest, her eyes rolling back, everything starting to disappear as she willed herself not to pass out.

Jeffrey stepped forward, Brad and Lena on either side of him. He told Dale, "I need you to come out of the garage."

Dale tightened his hand around the wrench. "What's going on?" His lips twitched in a quick smile. "Terri call you?"

"Why would she call us?"

"No reason," he shrugged, but the wrench in his hand said he had something to worry about. Lena glanced at the house, trying to see Terri. If Dale had a bruised eye, Terri probably had something ten times worse.

Jeffrey was obviously thinking the same. Still, he told the man, "You're not in trouble."

Dale was smarter than he looked. "Don't seem that way to me."

"Come out of the garage, Dale."

"Man's home is his castle," Dale said. "You got no right coming in here. I want you off my property right now."

"We want to talk to Terri."

"Nobody talks to Terri unless I say so, and I ain't saying so, so . . ."

Jeffrey stopped about four feet from Dale, and Lena moved to his left, thinking she could get to the gun before Dale. She suppressed a curse when she realized that the cabinet was well out of her reach. Brad should have taken this side. He was at least a foot taller than she was. By the time Lena dragged over a stool to retrieve the gun, Dale would be on his way to Mexico.

Jeffrey said, "Put the wrench down."

Dale's eyes darted to Lena, then Brad. "Maybe ya'll should back up a step or two."

"You're not in charge here, Dale," Jeffrey told him. Lena wanted to put her hand on her gun, but knew that she should take her signals from Jeffrey. He had his arms at his sides, probably thinking he could talk Dale down. She wasn't convinced.

"Y'all are crowdin' me," Dale said. "I don't like that." He lifted the wrench to chest level, resting the end in his palm. Lena knew the man wasn't an idiot. The wrench could do a lot of damage, but not to three people at the same time, especially considering the three people had guns on their belts. She watched Dale closely, knowing in her gut that he would make a try for the gun.

"You don't want to do this," Jeffrey told him. "We just want to talk to Terri."

Dale moved swiftly for a man his size, but Jeffrey was faster. He yanked the baton from Brad's belt and slammed it into the back of Dale's knees as the taller man lunged for the gun. Dale dropped to the floor like a stack of bricks.

Lena felt nothing but shock as she watched the normally docile Brad jam his knee into Dale's back, pressing him into the ground as he cuffed him. One swipe to the back of the knees and he had fallen. He wasn't even putting up a fight as Brad jerked back his hands, using two sets of cuffs to keep his wrists bound behind his back.

Jeffrey told Dale, "I warned you not to do this."

Dale yelped like a dog when Brad pulled him up to his knees. "Jesus, watch it," he complained, rolling his shoulders like he was afraid they'd been popped out of the sockets. "I want to call my lawyer."

"You can do that later." Jeffrey handed the baton back to Brad, saying, "Put him in the back of the car."

"Yes, sir," Brad said, pulling Dale up to standing, eliciting another yelp.

The big man shuffled his feet on the way to the car, a storm of dust kicking up behind him.

Just so Lena could hear, Jeffrey said, "Not such a tough guy, huh? I bet it makes him feel real good beating on his little wife."

Lena felt a bead of sweat roll down her back. Jeffrey swiped some dust off the leg of his pants before heading toward the house. He reminded Lena, "There are two kids in there."

Lena cast around for something to say. "Do you think she'll resist?"

"I don't know what she'll do."

The door opened before they reached the front porch. Terri Stanley stood inside, a sleeping baby on her hip. At her side was another kid, probably about two. He was rubbing his little fists into his eyes as if he'd just woken up. Terri's cheeks were sunken, dark circles rimmed her eyes. Her lip was busted open, a fresh, bluish-yellow bruise traced along her jaw, and angry red welts wrapped around her neck. Lena understood why Dale hadn't wanted them to talk to his wife. He'd beaten the shit out of her. Lena couldn't see how the woman was still standing.

Terri watched her husband being led to the squad car, studiously avoiding Jeffrey and Lena's eyes as she told them in a flat voice, "I'm not going to press charges. You might as well let him go."

Jeffrey looked back at the car. "We're just gonna let him stew there for a while."

"Y'all are just making it worse." She spoke carefully, obviously trying not to crack the lip back open. Lena knew the trick just as she knew it was hell on your throat, making you strain your voice just so your words could be understood. "He never hit me like this before. Not in the face." Her voice wavered. She was trapped, overwhelmed. "My kids've gotta see this."

"Terri . . ." Jeffrey began, but obviously didn't know how to finish it.

"He'll kill me if I leave him." Her drawl was exaggerated by her swollen lip.

"Terri—"

"I'm not gonna press charges."

"We're not asking you to."

She faltered, as if that hadn't been the response she was expecting.

Jeffrey said, "We need to talk to you."

"About what?"

He pulled an old cop's trick. "You know about what."

She looked at her husband, who was sitting in the back of Brad's cruiser.

"He's not going to hurt you."

She gave him a wary look, as if he'd told a really bad joke.

Jeffrey said, "We're not going anywhere until we talk to you."

"I guess come on in," she finally relented, stepping back from the open door. "Tim, Mama needs to talk to these people." She took the boy's hand, leading him into a den that had a large TV as the focal point. Lena and Jeffrey waited in the large entrance foyer at the base of the stairs while she put a DVD into the player.

Lena looked up at the high ceiling, which opened onto the upstairs hall. Where a chandelier should be hanging there were only a few stray wires jutting out of the Sheetrock. There were scuff marks on the walls by the stairs, and someone had kicked a small hole at the top. The spindles holding up the railing on the other side looked almost bent, several cracked or broken toward the landing at the top. Terri, she bet, picturing Dale dragging the woman up the stairs, her legs kicking wildly behind her. There were twelve steps in all, twice as many spindles to grab onto as she tried to stop the inevitable.

The shrill voice of Spongebob Squarepants echoed off the cold tiles in the foyer, and Terri came out, still holding her youngest son on her hip.

Jeffrey asked her, "Where can we talk?"

"Let me put him down," she said, meaning the baby. "The kitchen's through the back." She started up the stairs and Jeffrey motioned for Lena to follow her.

The house was larger than it looked from the outside, the landing at the top of the stairs leading to a long hallway and what looked like three bedrooms and a bath. Terri stopped at the first room and Lena paused, not following her in. Instead, she stood at the door to the nursery, watching Terri lay the sleeping baby in the crib. The room was brightly decorated, clouds on the ceiling, a pastoral scene on the walls showing happy sheep and cows. Over the crib was a mobile with more sheep. Lena couldn't see the kid while his mother stroked his head, but his little legs stretched out when Terri took off the crocheted booties. Lena hadn't realized that baby feet were so small, their toes little nubs, their arches curling like a banana peel as they pulled their knees to their chest.

Terri was staring intently at Lena over her shoulder. "You got kids?" She made a hoarse noise that Lena took as an attempt at a laugh. "I mean other than the one you left in Atlanta."

Lena knew she was trying to threaten her, using her words to remind Lena that they had both been in that clinic for the same thing, but Terri Stanley wasn't the type of woman who could carry this off. When the mother turned around, all Lena could do was feel sorry for her. The light was bright in the room, sunlight illuminating the bruise along Terri's jaw as if it were in Technicolor. Her lip had cracked, a sliver of blood seeping out onto her chin. Lena realized that six months ago, she could have been looking at a mirror.

"You'd do anything for them," Terri said with a tone of sadness. "You'd put up with anything."

"Anything?"

Terri swallowed, wincing from the pain. Dale had obviously choked her. The bruises weren't out yet, but they would come soon enough, looking like a dark necklace around her throat. Heavy concealer would take care of it, but she would feel stiff all week, turning her head carefully, trying not to wince when she swallowed, biding her time as she waited for the muscles to relax, the pain to go away.

She said, "I can't explain—"

Lena was in no position to lecture her. "You know you don't have to."

"Yeah," Terri agreed, turning back around, pulling a light blue blanket up around the baby's chin. Lena stared at her back, wondering if Terri was capable of murder. She would be the type to poison if she did anything. There was no way Terri could see someone face-to-face and kill them. Of course, she had obviously gotten her own back with Dale. He didn't get the bruise on his eye from shaving.

"Looks like you got him one good," Lena said.

Terri turned around, confused. "What?"

"Dale," she said, indicating her own eye.

Terri smiled a genuine smile, and her whole face changed. Lena got a glimpse of the woman she had been before all this happened, before Dale started beating her, before life became something to endure instead of enjoy. She was beautiful.

"I paid for it," Terri said, "but it felt so good."

Lena smiled, too, knowing how good it felt to fight back. You paid for it in the end, but it was so fucking fantastic when you were doing it. It was almost like a high.

Terri took a deep breath and let it go. "Let's get this over with."

Lena followed her back down the stairs, their footsteps echoing on the wooden boards. There were no rugs on the main floor and the noise sounded like a horse clattering around. Dale had probably done this on purpose, making sure he knew exactly where his wife was at all times.

They walked into the kitchen where Jeffrey was looking at the photographs and children's colorings on the refrigerator. On the drawings, Lena could see where Terri had written the names of the animals they were supposed to represent. Lion, Tiger, Bear. She dotted her i's with an open circle the way girls did in high school.

"Have a seat," Terri said, taking a chair at the table. Jeffrey remained standing, but Lena sat opposite Terri. The kitchen was neat for this time of morning. Plates and silverware from breakfast were drying in the rack and the counters were wiped clean. Lena wondered if Terri was naturally fastidious or if Dale had beat it into her.

Terri stared at her hands, which were clasped in front of her on the table. She was a small woman, but the way she held herself made her seem even smaller. Sadness radiated off her like an aura. Lena couldn't imagine how Dale managed to hit her without breaking her in two.

Terri offered, "Y'all want something to drink?"

Lena and Jeffrey answered no at the same time. After what happened with Cole Connolly, Lena doubted she'd ever take anything from anyone again.

Terri sat back in her chair, and Lena looked at her closely. She realized that they were about the same height, the same build. Terri was about ten pounds lighter, maybe an inch or two shorter, but there wasn't that much different about them.

Terri asked, "Y'all aren't here to talk about Dale?"

"No."

She picked at the cuticle on her thumb. Dried blood showed where she had done this before. "I guess I should've known you guys would come eventually."

"Why's that?" Jeffrey asked.

"The note I sent to Dr. Linton," she told him. "I guess I wasn't real smart about it."

Again, Jeffrey showed no reaction. "Why is that?"

"Well, I know y'all can get all kinds of evidence from it."

Lena nodded like this was true, thinking the girl had watched too many crime shows on TV, where lab techs ran around in Armani suits and high heels, plucking a miniscule piece of somebody's cuticle from a rose thorn then trotting back to their labs where through the miracle of science they discovered that the attacker was a right-handed albino who collected stamps and lived with his mother.

Setting aside the fact that no crime lab in the world could afford the zillions of dollars worth of equipment they showed, the fact was that DNA broke down. Outside factors could compromise the strand, or sometimes there wasn't enough for a sample. Fingerprints were subject to interpretation and it was very rare there were enough points for comparison to hold up in court.

Jeffrey asked, "Why did you send the letter to Dr. Linton?"

"I knew she'd do something about it," Terri said, then added quickly, "Not that y'all wouldn't, but Dr. Linton, she takes care of people. She really looks after them. I knew she'd understand." She shrugged. "I knew she'd tell you."

"Why not just tell her in person?" Jeffrey asked. "You saw me Monday morning at the clinic. Why didn't you tell me then?"

She gave a humorless laugh. "Dale'd kill me if he knew I'd gotten messed up in all of this. He hates the church. He hates everything about them. It's just . . ." Her voice trailed off. "When I heard what happened to Abby, I thought y'all should know he's done it before."

"Who's done it before?"

Her throat worked as she struggled to say the name. "Cole."

"He put you in a box out in the state forest?" Jeffrey asked.

She nodded, her hair falling into her eyes. "We were supposed to be camping. He took me out for a walk." She swallowed. "He brought me to this clearing. There was this hole in the ground. A rectangle. There was a box inside."

Lena asked, "What did you do?"

"I don't remember," she answered. "I don't think I even had time to scream. He hit me real hard, pushed me in. I cut my knee open, scraped my hand. I started yelling but he got on top of me and raised his fist, like he was going to beat me." She paused, trying to keep her composure as she told the story. "So, I just laid there. I just laid there while he put the boards on top of me, nailing them in one by one . . ."

Lena looked at her own hands, thinking about the nails that had been driven in, the metallic sound of the hammer hitting the metal spike, the unfathomable fear as she laid there, helpless to do anything to save herself.

"He was praying the whole time," Terri said. "Saying stuff about God giving him the strength, that he was just a vessel for the Lord." She closed her eyes, tears slipping out. "The next thing I know, I'm looking up at these black slats. Sunlight was coming through them, I guess, but it felt like a lighter shade of dark. It was so dark in there." She shuddered at the memory. "I heard the dirt coming down, not fast but slow, like he had all the time in the world. And he kept praying, louder, like he wanted to make sure I could hear him."

She stopped, and Lena asked, "What did you do?"

Again, Terri's throat worked as she swallowed. "I started screaming, and it just echoed in the box. It hurt my ears. I couldn't see anything. I could barely move. I still hear it sometimes," she said. "At night, when I'm trying to sleep, I'll hear the thud of the dirt hitting the box. The grit coming through, getting stuck in my throat." She had started to cry harder at the memory. "He was such a bad man."

Jeffrey said, "And that is why you left home."

Terri seemed surprised that he asked this.

He explained, "Your mother told us what happened, Terri."

She laughed, a hollow-sounding noise devoid of any humor. "My mother?"

"She came into the station this morning."

More tears sprang into her eyes, her lower lip started quivering. "She told you?" she asked. "Mama told you what Cole did?"

"Yes."

"She didn't believe me," Terri said, her voice no more than a murmur. "I told her what he did, and she said I was making it up. She told me I was going to go to hell." She looked around the kitchen, her life. "I guess she was right."

Lena asked, "Where did you go when you left?"

"Atlanta," she answered. "I was with this boy—Adam. He was just a way to get out of here. I couldn't stay, not with them not believing me." She sniffed, wiping her nose with her hand. "I was so scared Cole was gonna get me again. I couldn't sleep. I couldn't eat. I just kept waiting for him to take me."

"Why'd you come back?"

"I just . . ." she let her voice trail off. "I grew up here. And then I met Dale . . ." Again, she didn't finish the thought. "He was a good man when I met him. So sweet. He wasn't always the way he is now. The kids being sick puts a lot of pressure on him."

Jeffrey didn't let her continue along that track. "How long have y'all been married?"

"Eight years," she answered. Eight years of having the shit beaten out of her. Eight years of making excuses, covering his tracks, convincing herself that this time was different, this time he would change. Eight years of knowing deep in her gut that she was lying to herself, but not being able to do anything about it.

Lena would be dead in eight years if she had to endure that.

Terri said, "When Dale met me, I was clean, but I was still messed up. Didn't think much of myself." Lena could hear the regret in her voice. She wasn't wallowing in self-pity. She was looking back on her life and seeing how the hole she had dug for herself wasn't much different from the one Cole Connolly had put her in.

Terri told them, "Before that, I was into speed, shooting up. I did some really bad things. I think Tim's the one who's paid for it most." She added, "His asthma is really bad. Who knows how long those drugs stay in your system? Who knows what it does to your insides?"

He asked, "When did you clean up?"

"When I was twenty-one," she answered. "I just stopped. I knew I wouldn't see twenty-five if I didn't."

"Have you had any contact with your family since then?"

She started picking at her cuticle again. "I asked my uncle for some money a while back," she admitted. "I needed it for . . ." Her throat moved again as she swallowed. Lena knew what she needed the money for. Terri didn't have a job. Dale probably kept every dime that came into the house. She had to pay the clinic somehow, and borrowing money from her uncle had been the only way.

Terri told Jeffrey, "Dr. Linton's been real nice, but we had to pay her something for all she's been doing. Tim's medication isn't covered by his insurance." Suddenly, she looked up, fear lighting her eyes. "Don't tell Dale," she pleaded, talking to Lena. "Please don't tell him I asked for money. He's proud. He doesn't like me begging."

Lena knew he would want to know where the money went. She asked, "Did you ever see Abby?"

Her lips quivered as she tried not to cry. "Yes," she answered. "Sometimes, she used to come by during the day to check on me and the kids. She'd bring us food, candy for the kids."

"You knew she was pregnant?"

Terri nodded, and Lena wondered if Jeffrey felt the sadness coming off her. She was probably thinking about the child she had lost, the one in Atlanta. Lena felt herself thinking the same thing. For some reason, the image of the baby upstairs came to her mind, his little feet curling in the air, the way Terri tucked the blanket under his soft chin. Lena had to look down so that Jeffrey wouldn't see the tears stinging her eyes.

She could feel Terri looking at her. The mother had an abused woman's sense of other people, an instinctive recognition of changing emotions that came from years of trying not to say or do the wrong thing.

Jeffrey was oblivious to all of this as he asked, "What did you say to Abby when she told you about the baby?"

"I should have known what was going to happen," she said. "I should have warned her."

"Warned her about what?"

"About Cole, about what he did to me."

"Why didn't you tell her?"

"My own mother wouldn't believe me," she said bluntly. "I don't know . . . Over the years, I thought maybe I was making it up. I did so many drugs then, lots of bad stuff. I wasn't thinking straight. It was easier to just think that I made it up."

Lena knew what she was talking about. You lied to yourself in degrees just so you could get through the day.

Jeffrey asked, "Did Abby tell you she was seeing somebody?"

Terri nodded, saying, "Chip," with some regret. "I told her not to get mixed up with him. You've got to understand, girls don't know much growing up on the Holy Grown farm. They keep us secluded, like they're protecting us, but what it really does is make it easier for all the men." She gave another humorless laugh. "I never even knew what sex was until I was having it."

"When did Abby tell you she was leaving?"

"She came by on her way to Savannah about a week before she died," Terri said. "She told me she was going to leave with Chip when Aunt Esther and Uncle Eph went into Atlanta in a couple of days."

"Did she seem upset?"

She considered the question. "She seemed preoccupied. That's not like Abby. There was a lot on her mind, though. She was . . . she was distracted."

"Distracted how?"

Terri looked down, obviously trying to conceal her reaction. "Just with stuff."

Jeffrey said, "Terri, we need to know what stuff."

She spoke. "We were here in the kitchen," she began. She indicated Lena's chair. "She was sitting right there. She had Paul's briefcase in her lap, holding it like she couldn't let go. I remember thinking I could sell that thing and feed my kids for a month."

"It's a nice briefcase?" Jeffrey asked, and Lena knew he was thinking exactly the same thing she was. Abby had looked in the briefcase and found something Paul didn't want her to see.

She said, "He probably paid a thousand dollars for it. He spends money like it's water. I just don't understand."

Jeffrey asked, "What did Abby say?"

"That she had to go see Paul, then when she came back, she was leaving with Chip." She sniffed. "She wanted me to tell her mama and daddy that she loved them with all her heart." She started to cry again. "I need to tell them that. I owe Esther that at least."

"Do you think she told Paul she was pregnant?"

Terri shook her head. "I don't know. She could've gone to Savannah to get some help."

Lena asked, "Help getting rid of the baby?"

"God no," she said, shocked. "Abby would never kill her baby."

Lena felt her mouth working, but her voice was caught somewhere in her throat.

Jeffrey asked, "What do you think she wanted from Paul?"

"Maybe she asked him for some money?" Terri guessed. "I told her she'd need some money if she was going off with Chip. She doesn't understand how the real world works. She gets hungry and there's food on the table. She's cold and there's the thermostat. She's never had to fend for herself. I warned her she'd need money of her own, and to hide it from Chip, to keep something back for herself, in case he left her somewhere. I didn't want her to make the same mistakes I had." She wiped her nose. "She was such a sweet, sweet girl."

A sweet girl who was trying to bribe her uncle into paying her off with blood money, Lena thought. She asked, "You think Paul gave her the money?"

"I don't know," she admitted. "That was the last time I saw her.

She was supposed to leave with Chip after that. I really thought she had until I heard . . . until you found her on Sunday."

"Where were you last Saturday night?"

Terri used the back of her hand to wipe her nose. "Here," she told them. "With Dale and the kids."

"Can anyone else verify that?"

She bit her bottom lip, thinking. "Well, Paul dropped by," she told them. "Just for a minute."

"Saturday night?" Jeffrey verified, glancing at Lena. Paul had insisted several times that he was in Savannah the night his niece died. His chatty secretary had even backed him up. He said he had driven to the farm on Sunday evening to help look for Abby.

Jeffrey asked, "Why was Paul here?"

"He brought Dale that thing for one of his cars."

Jeffrey asked, "What thing?"

"That Porsche thing," she answered. "Paul loves flashy cars—hell, he loves flashy anything. He tries to hide it from Papa and them, but he likes to have his toys."

"What kind of toys?"

"He brings in old beaters he finds at auctions and Dale fixes them up for a discount. At least Dale says he's giving a discount. I don't know what he charges, but it's gotta be cheaper to do it here than it is in Savannah."

"How often does Paul bring in cars?"

"Two, three times that I can think of." Terri shrugged. "You'd have to ask Dale. I'm in the back mostly, working on the upholstery."

"Dale didn't mention Paul came by when I saw him the other night."

"I doubt he would," Terri said. "Paul pays him in cash. He don't report it on the taxes." She tried to defend his actions. "We've got collections after us. The hospital's already garnishing Dale's wages from when Tim went in last year. The bank reports back everything that goes in and out. We'd lose the house if we didn't have that extra cash."

"I don't work for the IRS," Jeffrey told her. "All I care about is Saturday night. You're sure Paul came by Saturday?"

She nodded. "You can ask Dale," she said. "They stayed in the garage for about ten minutes, then he was gone. I just saw him through the front window. Paul doesn't really talk to me."

"Why is that?"

"I'm a fallen woman," she said, absent any sarcasm.

"Terri," Jeffrey began, "was Paul ever in the garage alone?"

She shrugged. "Sure."

"How many times?" he pushed.

"I don't know. A lot."

Jeffrey wasn't so conciliatory anymore. He pressed her harder. "How about in the last three months or so? Was he here then?"

"I guess," she repeated, agitated. "Why does it matter if Paul was in the garage?"

"I'm just trying to figure out if he had time to take something that was out there."

She snorted a laugh at the suggestion. "Dale would've wrung his neck."

"What about the insurance policies?" he asked.

"What policies?"

Jeffrey took out a folded sheet of fax paper and put it on the table in front of her.

Terri's brow furrowed as she read the document. "I don't understand."

"It's a fifty-thousand-dollar life insurance policy with you as the beneficiary."

"Where did you find this?"

"You don't get to ask the questions," Jeffrey told her, dropping his understanding tone. "Tell us what's going on, Terri."

"I thought—" she began, then stopped, shaking her head.

Lena asked, "You thought what?"

Terri shook her head, picking at the cuticle on her thumb.

"Terri?" Lena prodded, not wanting Jeffrey to be too hard on her. She obviously had something to say; now was not the time to be impatient.

Jeffrey adjusted his tone. "Terri, we need your help here. We know Cole put her in that box, just like he did with you, only Abby never got out. We need you to help us find out who killed her."

"I don't . . ." Terri let her voice trail off.

Jeffrey said, "Terri, Rebecca is still missing."

She said something under her breath that sounded like a word or two of encouragement. Without warning, she stood, saying, "I'll be back."

"Hold on a minute." Jeffrey caught her by the arm as she started to leave the kitchen but Terri flinched and he let go.

"Sorry," she apologized, rubbing her arm where Dale had bruised her. Lena could see tears from the pain well into the other woman's eyes. Still, Terri repeated, "I'll be right back."

Jeffrey didn't touch her again, but he said, "We'll go with you," in a tone that said it wasn't just a friendly suggestion.

Terri hesitated, then gave him a curt nod. She looked down the hallway as if to make sure no one was there. Lena knew she was looking for Dale. Even though he was handcuffed in the squad car, she was still terrified he could get to her.

She opened the back door, giving another furtive glance, this time to make sure Lena and Jeffrey were following. She told Jeffrey, "Leave it open a crack in case Tim needs me," meaning the door. He caught the screen so it wouldn't slam, playing along with her paranoia.

Together, the three of them walked into the backyard. The dogs were all mutts, probably rescued from the pound. They whined quietly, jumping up at Terri, trying to get her attention. She absently stroked their heads as she passed, edging around the garage. She stopped at the corner and Lena could see an outbuilding behind it. If Dale was looking this way, he would be able to see them go to the building.

Jeffrey realized this about the same time Lena did. He was offering, "I can—" when Terri took a deep breath and walked out into the open yard.

Lena followed her, not looking at the squad car, feeling the heat of Dale's stare anyway.

"He's not looking," Jeffrey said, but both Lena and Terri were too frightened to look.

Terri took a key out of her pocket and slid it into the locked shed door. She turned on the lights as she went into the cramped room. A sewing machine was in the center, bolts of dark leather stacked against the walls, harsh light overhead. This must be where Terri sewed upholstery for the cars Dale rebuilt. The room was dank, musty. It was little more than a sweatshop and must have felt like hell itself in the dead of winter.

Terri turned around, finally looking out the window. Lena followed her gaze and saw the dark silhouette of Dale Stanley sitting in the back of the squad car. Terri said, "He's gonna kill me when he finds out about this." She told Lena, "What's one more thing, huh?"

Lena said, "We can protect you, Terri. We can take him to jail right now and he'll never see the light of day again."

"He'll get out," she said.

"No," Lena told her, because she knew there were ways to make sure prisoners didn't get out. If you put them in the right cell with the right person, you could fuck up their lives forever. She said, "We can make sure," and from the look Terri gave her, Lena knew the other woman understood.

Jeffrey had been listening to all of this as he walked around the small room. Suddenly, he pulled a couple of bolts of material away from the wall. There was a noise from behind them, almost like a scurrying mouse. He pulled away another bolt, holding out his hand to the girl crouched against the wall.

He had found Rebecca Bennett.

CHAPTER FIFTEEN

Jeffrey watched Lena with Rebecca Bennett, thinking that even after all these years, if someone asked him to explain what made Lena tick, he would be at a loss for words. Five minutes ago, she had sat in this same kitchen as he talked with Terri Stanley, barely speaking, acting as if she was a scared child. Yet, with the Bennett girl, she was in charge, being the cop she could be instead of the abused woman she was.

"Tell me what happened, Rebecca," she said, her voice strong even as she took the girl's hands in hers, balancing authority with empathy. Lena had done this a million times before, but still the transformation was hard to believe.

Rebecca hesitated, still a frightened child. She was obviously exhausted, the time spent hiding from her uncle wearing away at her like the constant flow of water over a river rock. Her shoulders were turned in, her head bowed as if all she wanted in the world was to disappear.

"After you guys left," Rebecca began, "I went to my room."

"This was Monday?"

Rebecca nodded. "Mama told me to lie down."

"What happened?"

"I got cold, and I pulled back my sheets and found some papers there."

"What papers did you find?" Lena asked.

Rebecca looked at Terri, and the older woman gave a small nod, indicating it was okay. Rebecca paused, her eyes on her cousin. Then she tucked her hand into the front pocket of her dress and pulled out a neatly folded stack of papers. Lena glanced at them, then handed them to Jeffrey. He saw that they were originals of the insurance policies Frank had already pulled.

Lena sat back in her chair, studying the girl. "Why didn't you find them Sunday?"

Rebecca glanced at Terri again. "I stayed at my aunt Rachel's Sunday night. Mama didn't want me out looking for Abby."

Jeffrey remembered Esther had said much the same thing at the diner. He looked up from the documents just in time to catch an exchanged glance between the two cousins.

Lena had obviously seen this, too. She placed her hand palm down on the table. "What else, Becca? What else did you find?"

Terri started chewing her lip again while Rebecca stared at Lena's hand on the table.

"Abby trusted you to do the right thing with what she left," Lena said, keeping her tone even. "Don't betray that trust."

Rebecca kept staring at Lena's hand so long Jeffrey wondered if the girl was in a trance. Finally, she looked up at Terri and nodded. Without speaking, Terri walked over to the refrigerator and pulled the magnets holding some of the kids' drawings. There were several layers before she got to the metal surface.

She said, "Dale never looks here," sliding out a folded sheet of ledger paper from behind a child's stick rendering of the crucifixion. Instead of handing it to Jeffrey or Lena, she gave the page to Rebecca. Slowly, the girl unfolded the paper, then slid it across the table to Lena.

"You found this in your bed, too?" Lena asked, reading the page. Jeffrey leaned over her shoulder, seeing a list of names, recognizing some of them as workers on the farm. The columns were broken out into dollar amounts and dates, some already passed, some in the future. Jeffrey mentally compared the dates to the policies. With a jolt, he realized that this was some kind of income projection, a tally of who had what policy and when they could be expected to cash out.

"Abby left it for me," Rebecca said. "She wanted me to have it for some reason."

"Why didn't you show it to anybody?" Lena asked. "Why did you run away?"

Terri answered for her cousin, speaking quietly as if she was afraid she would get into trouble for doing so. "Paul," she said. "That's his handwriting."

Rebecca had tears in her eyes. She nodded to Lena's silent question, and Jeffrey felt the tension ratchet up at the revelation, the exact opposite of what he had been expecting when they finally told the truth. The girls were obviously terrified of what they held in their hands, yet giving it to the police did not bring them any relief.

Lena asked, "Are you afraid of Paul?"

Rebecca nodded, as did Terri.

Lena studied the paper again, though Jeffrey was sure she understood every word on the page. "So, you found this on Monday, and you knew that this was Paul's handwriting."

Rebecca did not respond, but Terri provided, "She came here that night sick with worry. Dale was passed out on the couch. I hid her in the shed until we could figure out what to do." She shook her head. "Not that there's ever anything we can do."

"You sent that warning to Sara," Jeffrey reminded her.

Terri shrugged with one shoulder, as if acknowledging that the letter had been a cowardly way of revealing the truth.

Lena was gentle when she asked Terri, "Why didn't you tell your family about this? Why not show them the documents?"

"Paul's their golden boy. They don't see him for what he really is."

"What is he?"

"A monster," Terri answered. Her eyes filled with tears. "He acts like you can trust him, like he's your best friend, and then he turns around and stabs you in the back."

"He's bad," Rebecca mumbled in agreement.

Terri's tone was stronger as she continued, but there were still tears in her eyes. "He acts all cool, like he's on your side. You wanna know where my first hit came from?" She pressed her lips together, looking at Rebecca, probably wondering if she should say this in front of the girl. "Him," she said. "Paul gave me my first line of coke. We were in his office and he said it was okay. I didn't even know what it was—could've been aspirin." She was angry now. "He got me hooked."

"Why would he do that?"

"Because he could," Terri said. "That's what he really gets off on, corrupting us. Controlling everybody while he sits back and watches our lives crumble."

"Corrupting you how?" Lena asked, and Jeffrey knew where she was going.

"Not like that," Terri said. "Jesus, it'd be easier if he screwed us." Rebecca stiffened at her language, and Terri moderated her words. "He likes to bring us down," she said. "He can't stand girls—hates all of us, thinks we're stupid." Her tears started to fall, and Jeffrey could see that her anger came from a burning sense of betrayal. "Mama and them think he walks on water. I told her about Cole and she went to Paul and Paul said I was making it up, so she believed him." She gave a snort of disgust. "He's such a bastard. He acts all friendly, like you can trust him, and then you do and he punishes you for it."

"Not him," Rebecca said, though quietly. Jeffrey could see that the girl was having a hard time admitting that her uncle was capable of such evil. Still, she continued, "He gets Cole to do it. And then he acts like he doesn't know what's going on."

Terri wiped her eyes, her hands shaking as she acknowledged the pattern.

Lena waited a few seconds before asking, "Rebecca—did he ever bury you?"

She shook her head slowly. Then she said, "Abby told me he did it to her."

"How many times?"

"Twice." She added, "And then this last time . . ."

"Oh, God," Terri breathed. "I could've stopped it. I could've said something—"

"There was nothing you could do," Lena told her, though Jeffrey didn't know if this was true.

"That box . . ." Terri began, squeezing her eyes shut at the memory. "He comes back every day, praying. You can hear him through the pipe. Sometimes he yells so loud, and you cringe, but you're just so happy to know someone is out there, that you're not completely alone." She used her fist to wipe her eyes, a mixture of sadness and anger in her words. "The first time he did it to me, I went to Paul, and Paul promised he'd talk to him. I was so stupid. It took me so long to figure out it was Paul telling him to do it. There's no way Cole could've known all that stuff about me, what I was doing, who I was with. It all came from Paul."

Rebecca was sobbing now. "Nothing we did was ever right. He was always riding Abby, trying to get her to mess up. He kept telling her it was only a matter of time before some man came along and gave her what she deserved."

"Chip," Terri spat out the name. "He did the same thing with me. Put Adam in my way."

Jeffrey asked, "Paul set up Abby with Chip?"

"All he had to do was make sure they were together a lot. Men are stupid that way." She blushed, as if remembering that Jeffrey was a man. "I mean—"

"It's okay," Jeffrey told her, not pointing out that women could be just as stupid. He would be out of a job if they weren't.

Terri said, "He just liked to see bad things happen. He likes to control things, set people up and then take them down hard." She chewed her bottom lip, a trickle of blood coming from the broken skin. Obviously, the years that had passed hadn't lessened her anger. "Nobody ever questions him. They all just assume he's telling the truth. They worship him."

Rebecca had been quiet, but Terri's words seemed to be making her stronger. She looked up and said, "Uncle Paul put Chip in the office with Abby. Chip didn't know anything about that kind of work, but Paul made sure they were together enough so that things happened."

"What kind of things?" Lena asked.

Terri said, "What do you think? She was going to have a baby."

Rebecca gasped at this, turning stunned eyes to her cousin.

Terri apologized quickly. "I'm sorry, Becca. I shouldn't have told you."

"The baby," Rebecca whispered, hand clutched to her chest. "Her baby is dead." Tears came streaming down her cheeks. "Oh, my Lord. He murdered her baby, too."

Lena went deadly quiet, and Jeffrey watched her closely, wondering why Rebecca's words had such an impact on her. Terri had gone just as blank, staring at the refrigerator, the colorful drawings her children had made. *Lion. Tiger. Bear.* Predators, all of them. Like Paul.

Jeffrey didn't know what the hell was going on, but he did know that Lena had dropped a serious question. He stepped in, asking, "Who killed her baby?"

Rebecca looked up at Terri, and they both looked at Jeffrey.

"Cole," Terri said, as if it was obvious. "Cole killed her."

Jeffrey clarified, "He poisoned Abby?"

"Poison?" Terri echoed, mystified. "She suffocated."

"No she didn't, Terri. Abby was poisoned." Jeffrey explained, "Someone gave her cyanide."

Terri sank back in her chair, her expression revealing she finally understood what had happened. "Dale has cyanide in his garage."

"That's right," Jeffrey agreed.

"Paul was in there," she said. "He was in there all the time."

Jeffrey kept his attention on Terri, hoping to God Lena saw how much she had fucked this up by not getting Terri to answer this simple question two days ago. He asked it now. "Did Paul know about the cyanide?"

She nodded. "I walked in on them once. Dale was plating some chrome for one of Paul's cars."

"When was this?"

"Four, five months ago," she said. "His mama called and I went out to tell him. Dale got mad at me because I wasn't supposed to be in there. Paul didn't like me there. Didn't even like to look at me." Her expression darkened, and Jeffrey could tell she didn't want to say all of this in front of her cousin. "Dale made some joke about the cyanide. Just showing off to Paul, letting him know how stupid I was."

Jeffrey could imagine, but he needed to hear it. "What did Paul say, Terri?"

She gnawed her lip, and a fresh trickle of blood appeared. "Dale told me he was going to put the cyanide in my coffee one of these days, that I wouldn't even know it until it hit my stomach and the acids activated the poison." Her lip quivered, but this time it was from disgust. "He told me it'd kill me slow, that I'd know exactly what was happening, and he'd just watch me there, thrashing on the floor, shitting in my pants. He told me he'd look me in the eye till the last minute so I'd know he was the one who did it to me."

Jeffrey asked, "What did Paul do when Dale said this?"

Terri looked at Rebecca, reached over to stroke her hair. She was still having trouble saying bad things about Dale, and Jeffrey wondered what she was trying to protect the young girl from.

Jeffrey asked his question again. "What did Paul do when he said that, Terri?"

Terri dropped her hand to Rebecca's shoulder. "Nothing," she said. "I thought he would laugh, but he did absolutely nothing."

❈ ❈ ❈ ❈

Jeffrey looked at his watch for the third time, then back up at the secretary posted sentinel in front of Paul's office at the farm. She was less chatty than the one in Savannah, but just as protective of her boss. The door behind her was open, and Jeffrey could see rich leather chairs and two huge chunks of marble with a glass top that served for a desk. Shelves lined the room, leather law books and golfing memorabilia scattered around. Terri Stanley was right, her uncle certainly liked to have his toys.

Paul's secretary looked up from her computer, saying, "Paul should be back soon."

"I could wait inside the office," Jeffrey suggested, thinking he could go through Paul's things.

The secretary chuckled at the idea. "Paul doesn't even like me in there when he's gone," she said, still typing on her computer. "Better you should wait out here. He'll be back in a jiff."

Jeffrey crossed his arms, sitting back in the chair. He had only been waiting five minutes, but he was beginning to think he should go find the lawyer himself. The secretary hadn't called her boss to announce the fact that the chief of police was here, but his white Town Car with government plates was pretty easy to pick out in a crowd. Jeffrey had parked it right in front of the building's main doors.

He looked at his watch again, marking another minute gone by. He had left Lena at the Stanley place so she could keep an eye on the two women. He didn't want Terri's guilt to make her do something stupid, like call her aunt Esther or worse, her uncle Lev. Jeffrey had told them Lena was there to protect them, and neither of the girls had questioned this. Brad had run Dale in on a resisting charge, but that wouldn't stick more than a day. Jeffrey doubted very seriously Terri would help with the prosecution. She was barely thirty, trapped with two sick kids and no discernable job skills. The best thing he could do was call Pat Stanley and tell him to get his brother's house in order. If it were up to Jeffrey, Dale would be lying at the bottom of a quarry right now.

The secretary said, "Reverend Ward?" and Lev stuck his head in the room. "Do you know where Paul is? He has a visitor."

"Chief Tolliver," Lev said, entering the room. He was drying his hands on a paper towel and Jeffrey assumed he'd been in the bathroom. "Is something wrong?"

Jeffrey sized up the man, still not completely certain Lev didn't know exactly what was going on. Rebecca and Terri had insisted he was oblivious, but it was clear to Jeffrey that Lev Ward was the leader of this family. He couldn't imagine Paul getting away with this kind of thing right under his older brother's nose.

Jeffrey said, "I'm looking for your brother."

Lev looked at his watch. "We've got a meeting in twenty minutes. I don't imagine he's gone far."

"I need to talk to him now."

Lev offered, "May I help you with something?"

Jeffrey was glad he was making this easy. He said, "Let's go to your office."

"Is this about Abby?" Lev asked, walking down the hallway toward the back of the building. He was wearing faded jeans, a flannel shirt, and scuffed cowboy boots that looked as if the soles had been replaced about a dozen times since they were made. Clipped onto his belt was a leather sheath containing a retractable carpet knife.

"You laying carpet?" Jeffrey asked, wary of the tool, which held an extremely sharp safety razor capable of cutting through just about anything.

Lev seemed confused. "Oh," he said, looking down at his side as if he was surprised to find the sheath there. "Opening boxes," he explained. "Deliveries always come on Fridays." He stopped in front of an open door. "Here we are."

Jeffrey read the sign on the door, which read, "Praise the Lord and come on in!"

"My humble abode," Lev told him, indicating the room.

In contrast to his brother, Lev did not have a secretary guarding his space. As a matter of fact, his office was small, almost as small as Jeffrey's. A metal desk stood in the center of the room, a rolling chair without arms behind it. Two folding chairs were in front and books were stacked around the floor in neat piles. Child's colorings, probably Zeke's, were pinned to the walls with thumbtacks.

"Sorry about the mess," Lev apologized. "My father says a cluttered office is a sign of a cluttered mind." He laughed. "I guess he's right."

"Your brother's office is a little . . . more grand."

Lev laughed again. "Papa used to get onto him all the time when we were little, but Paul's a grown man now, a little old to be taken over the knee." He turned serious. "Vanity is a sin, but we all have our weaknesses."

Jeffrey glanced back out into the hall. There was a short corridor opposite the office that held a Xerox machine. He asked, "What's your weakness?"

Lev seemed to really give it some thought. "My son."

"Who's Stephanie Linder?"

Lev seemed puzzled. "Why would you ask that?"

"Answer my question."

"She was my wife. She died five years ago."

"Are you sure about that?"

He turned indignant. "I think I know whether or not my wife is dead."

"I'm just curious," Jeffrey said. "You see, your sister Mary came in today and told me she has a daughter. I don't remember anyone mentioning that before."

Lev had the wisdom to look contrite. "Yes, that's right. She does have a daughter."

"A daughter who ran away from her family."

"Genie—Terri—that's what she likes to go by now—was a very difficult teenager. She had a very troubled life."

"I'd still say it's a bit troubled. Wouldn't you?"

"She's straightened up," he defended. "But she's a proud girl. I still have hopes for a reconciliation with the family."

"Her husband beats her."

Lev's mouth opened in surprise. "Dale?"

"Cole put her in a box, too, just like Abby. She was about Rebecca's age when he did it. Did Mary ever tell you that?"

Lev put his hand on his desk as if he needed help standing. "Why would . . ." His voice trailed off as he obviously began to realize what Cole Connolly had actually been doing all these years. "My God," he whispered.

"Three times, Lev. Cole put Abby in that box three times. The last time, she didn't come out."

Lev looked up at the ceiling, but Jeffrey was relieved to see it was to try to staunch the tears in his eyes instead of to break into spontaneous prayer. Jeffrey gave the man some space, letting him wrestle with his emotions.

Finally, Lev asked, "Who? Who else did he do this to?" Jeffrey didn't answer, but he was glad to hear the fury in Lev's tone. "Mary told us Genie ran away to Atlanta to have an abortion." Obviously, he thought he could anticipate Jeffrey's next remark, because he said, "My father has strong feelings about life, Chief Tolliver, as do I. Still . . ." He paused, as if needing a moment to collect himself. "We would never have turned our backs on her. Never. We all do things that God does not approve of. That doesn't necessarily mean we're bad people. Our Genie—Terri—wasn't a bad girl. She was just a teenager who did a bad thing—a very bad thing. We looked for her. I looked for her. She didn't want to be found." He shook his head. "If I had known . . ."

"Somebody knew," Jeffrey said.

"No," Lev insisted. "If any of us had known what Cole was up to, there would've been stern repercussions. I would have called the police myself."

"You don't seem to like getting the police involved in anything."

"I want to protect our workers."

"Seems to me you've put your family in jeopardy while you were trying to save a bunch of strangers."

Lev's jaw tightened. "I can see why you view it that way."

"Why didn't you want to report that Rebecca was missing?"

"She always comes back," he said. "You must understand, she's very head-strong. There's nothing we can do to . . ." He didn't finish his sentence. "You don't think . . ." He faltered. "Cole . . . ?"

"Did Cole bury Becca like he buried the other girls?" Jeffrey finished his question for him, watching Lev closely, trying to figure out what was going on in the other man's head. "What do you think, Reverend Ward?"

Lev exhaled slowly, like he was having trouble absorbing all of this. "We need to find her. She always goes into the woods—my God, the woods—" He made to go, but Jeffrey stopped him.

"She's safe," Jeffrey said.

"Where?" Lev asked. "Take me to her. Esther's beside herself."

"She's safe," was all Jeffrey would tell him. "I'm not finished talking to you."

Lev saw that the only way out the door was past Jeffrey. Though he would certainly win that fight, Jeffrey was glad the bigger man didn't push it.

Lev asked, "Will you at least call her mother?"

"I already did," Jeffrey lied. "Esther was very relieved to hear she was safe."

Lev settled back down, relieved but still obviously conflicted. "This is a lot to absorb." He had the habit of biting his bottom lip, the same as his niece. "Why did you ask about my wife?"

"Did she ever own a house in Savannah?"

"Of course not," he replied. "Stephanie lived here all of her life. I don't even think she'd ever been to Savannah."

"How long has Paul worked there?"

"About six years, give or take."

"Why Savannah?"

"We have a lot of vendors and buyers in the area. It's easier for him to do business with them face to face." He seemed a bit guilty when he added, "The farm is a slow pace for Paul. He likes to be in the city sometimes."

"His wife doesn't go with him?"

"He has six kids," Lev pointed out. "He's obviously home a great deal of time."

Jeffrey noticed he misinterpreted the question, but perhaps in this family it was normal for husbands to leave their wives alone with the kids every other week. Jeffrey couldn't think of a man out there who wouldn't be happy with this kind of arrangement, but he was hard-pressed to think of any woman who would be.

He asked, "Have you ever been to his house in Savannah?"

"Quite often," Lev answered. "He lives in an apartment over the office."

"He doesn't live in a house on Sandon Square?"

Lev roared a laugh. "Hardly," he said. "That's one of the wealthiest streets in the city."

"And your wife never visited there?"

Lev shook his head again, sounding slightly irritated when he said, "I've been answering all of your questions to the best of my abilities. Is there ever going to come a point when you can tell me what this is all about?"

Jeffrey decided it was his turn to give a little. He took out the original insurance policies from his pocket and handed them to Lev. "Abby left these for Rebecca."

Lev took the pages, unfolding them and spreading them flat on his desk. "Left them how?"

Jeffrey didn't answer, but Lev didn't notice. He was leaning over his desk, tracing his finger down each page as he read. Jeffrey noticed the set to his jaw, the anger in his stance.

Lev straightened up. "These people lived on our farm."

"That's right."

"This one." He held up one of the pages. "Larry ran off. Cole told us he ran off."

"He's dead."

Lev stared at him, his eyes moving back and forth across Jeffrey's face as if to read where this was going.

Jeffrey took out his notepad, telling him, "Larry Fowler died from alcohol poisoning on July twenty-eighth of last year. He was removed from the farm by the Catoogah county coroner at nine fifty P.M."

Lev stared another second, not quite believing. "And this one?" he asked, lifting the page. "Mike Morrow. He drove the tractor last season. He had a daughter in Wisconsin. Cole said he went to live with her."

"Drug overdose. August thirteenth, twelve forty P.M."

Lev asked, "Why would he tell us they ran off when they died?"

"I guess it'd be a little hard to explain why so many people have died on your farm in the last two years."

He looked at the policies again, scanning the pages. "You think . . . you think they . . ."

"Your brother paid for nine bodies to be cremated."

Lev's face was already pasty, but his face turned completely white as he absorbed the implication behind Jeffrey's words. "These signatures," he began, studying the documents again. "That's not mine," he said, stabbing his finger at one of the pages. "This," he said, "that's not Mary's signature; she's left-handed. That's certainly not Rachel's. Why would she have an insurance policy on a man she never even knew?"

"You tell me."

"This is wrong," he said, wadding up the pages in his fist. "Who would do this?"

Jeffrey repeated, "You tell me."

A vein was throbbing in Lev's temple. His teeth were clenched as he thumbed back through the papers. "Did he have a policy on my wife?"

Jeffrey answered honestly. "I don't know."

"Where did you get her name?"

"All of the policies are registered to a house on Sandon Square. The owner is listed as Stephanie Linder."

"He . . . used . . ." Lev was so livid he was having trouble speaking. "He used my . . . my wife's name . . . for *this*?"

In his line of work, Jeffrey had seen plenty of grown men reduced to tears, but usually they were crying because they had lost a loved one or—more often than not—because they realized they were going to jail and felt sorry for themselves. Lev Ward's tears were from sheer rage.

"Hold on," Jeffrey said as Lev pushed past him. "Where are you going?"

Lev ran up the hall to Paul's office. "Where is he?" Lev demanded.

Jeffrey heard the secretary say, "I don't—"

Lev was already running toward the front doors, Jeffrey close behind him. The preacher didn't look particularly fit, but he had a long stride. By the time Jeffrey made it to the parking lot, Lev was already at his car. Instead of getting in, the man stood there, frozen.

Jeffrey trotted over to him. "Lev?"

"Where is he?" he snarled. "Give me ten minutes with him. Just ten minutes."

Jeffrey wouldn't have thought the mild-mannered preacher had it in him. "Lev, you need to go back inside."

"How could he do this to us?" he asked. "How could he ... " Lev seemed to be working out all the implications. He turned to Jeffrey. "He killed my niece? He killed Abby? And Cole, too?"

"I think so," Jeffrey said. "He had access to the cyanide. He knew how to use it."

"My God," he said, not just an expression but a genuine entreaty. "Why?" he pleaded. "Why would he do this? What did Abby ever do to anyone?"

Jeffrey didn't try to answer his questions. "We need to find your brother, Lev. Where is he?"

Lev was too angry to speak. He shook his head tightly from side to side.

"We need to find him," Jeffrey repeated, just as his phone chirped from his pocket. He glanced at the caller ID, seeing it was Lena. He stepped back to answer the phone, snapping it open, saying, "What is it?"

Lena was whispering, but he heard her loud and clear. "He's here," she said. "Paul's car just pulled into the driveway."

CHAPTER SIXTEEN

Lena's heart thumped in her throat, a constant pulse that made it hard to speak.

"Don't do anything until I get there," Jeffrey ordered. "Hide Rebecca. Don't let him see her."

"What if—"

"No fucking what-ifs, detective. Do as I say."

Lena glanced at Rebecca, saw the terror in the girl's eyes. She could end this right now—throw Paul to the floor, take the bastard into custody. Then what? They'd never get a confession out of the lawyer. He's be laughing all the way to the grand jury, where they'd dismiss the case for lack of evidence.

Jeffrey said, "Am I being clear?"

"Yes, sir."

"Keep Rebecca safe," he ordered. "She's our only witness. That's your job right now, Lena. Don't fuck this up." The phone clicked loudly as he disconnected.

Terri was at the front window, calling out Paul's movements. "He's in the garage," she whispered. "He's in the garage."

Lena grabbed Rebecca by the arm, pulling her into the foyer. "Go upstairs," she ordered, but the frightened girl wouldn't budge.

Terri said, "He's going around the back. Oh, God, hurry!" She ran down the hall so that she could follow his progress.

"Rebecca," Lena said, willing the girl to move. "We need to go upstairs."

"What if he . . ." Rebecca began. "I can't . . ."

"He's in the shed," Terri called. "Becca, please! Go!"

"He'll be so mad," Rebecca whimpered. "Oh, Lord, please . . ."

Terri's voice trilled. "He's coming toward the house!"

"Rebecca," Lena tried again.

Terri ran back into the hall, pushing Rebecca as Lena tugged the girl toward the stairs.

"Mommy!" Tim grabbed onto his mother, wrapping his arms around her leg.

Terri's voice was stern when she told her son, "Go upstairs now." She spanked Tim on the bottom when he didn't move quickly enough.

The back door opened and they all froze as Paul called, "Terri?"

Tim was at the top of the stairs, but Rebecca stood frozen in fear, breathing like a wounded animal.

"Terri?" Paul repeated. "Where the hell are you?" Slowly, his footsteps traveled through the kitchen. "Christ, this place is a mess."

Using all her strength, Lena picked up Rebecca, half carrying, half dragging the girl up the stairs. By the time she reached the top, she was out of breath, her insides feeling like they had been ripped in two.

"I'm here!" Terri called to her uncle, her shoes making clicking noises across the tile foyer as she walked back to the kitchen. Lena heard muffled voices as she pushed Rebecca and Tim into the closest room. Too late she realized they were in the nursery.

In the crib, the baby gurgled. Lena waited for him to wake up and cry. What seemed like an hour passed before the child turned his head away and settled back to sleep.

"Oh, Lord," Rebecca whispered, praying.

Lena put her hand over the girl's mouth, carefully walking her toward the closet with Tim in tow. For the first time, Rebecca seemed to understand, and she slowly opened the door, her eyes squeezed shut as she waited for a noise that would alert Paul to their presence. Nothing came, and she slid to the floor, grabbing Tim in her arms and hiding behind a stack of winter blankets.

Softly, Lena clicked the door closed, holding her breath, waiting for Paul to come rushing in. She could barely hear him speaking over the pounding of her own heart, but suddenly his heavy footsteps echoed up the stairs.

"This place is a pigsty," Paul said, and she could hear him knocking things over as he went through the house. Lena knew the house was spotless, just like she knew Paul was being an asshole. "Jesus

Christ, Terri, you back on coke again? Look at this mess. How can you raise your children here?"

Terri mumbled a reply, and Paul screamed, "Don't back talk me!" He was in the tiled foyer now, his voice booming up the stairs like a roll of thunder. Carefully, Lena tiptoed to the wall opposite the nursery, flattening herself against it, listening to Paul yell at Terri. Lena waited another beat, then slid to her left, edging toward the stair landing so she could peer downstairs and see what was going on. Jeffrey had told her to wait, to hide Rebecca until he got there. She should stay back in the room, keep the kids quiet, make sure they were safe.

Lena held her breath, inching closer to the stairs, chancing a look.

Paul's back was to her. Terri stood directly in front of him.

Lena slid back behind the corner, her heart beating so hard she could feel the artery thumping in the side of her neck.

"When's he going to be back?" Paul demanded.

"I don't know."

"Where's my medallion?"

"I don't know."

She had given him this same answer to all of his questions, and Paul finally snapped, "What *do* you know, Terri?"

She was silent, and Lena looked downstairs again to make sure she was still there.

"He'll be back soon," Terri said, her eyes flicking up to Lena. "You can wait for him in the garage."

"You want me out of the house?" he asked. Lena quickly pulled back as Paul turned around. "Why's that?"

Lena put her hand to her chest, willing her heart to slow. Men like Paul had an almost animal instinct. They could hear through walls, see everything that went on. She looked at her watch, trying to calculate how much time had passed since she had called Jeffrey. He was at least fifteen minutes away, even if he came with lights and siren blaring.

Paul said, "What's going on, Terri? Where's Dale?"

"Out."

"Don't get smart with me." Lena heard a loud popping noise, flesh against flesh. Her heart stopped in her chest.

Terri said, "Please. Just wait in the garage."

Paul's tone was conversational. "Why don't you want me in the house, Terri?"

Again, there was the popping noise. Lena did not have to look to know what was happening. She knew the sickening sound, knew it was an open-handed smack, just as she knew exactly what it felt like on your face.

There was a sound from the nursery, Rebecca or Tim shifting in the closet, and a floorboard creaked. Lena closed her eyes, frozen. Jeffrey had ordered her to wait, to protect Rebecca. He hadn't given her any instructions on what to do if Paul found them.

Lena opened her eyes. She knew exactly what she would do. Carefully, she slid her gun out of its holster, aiming it at the space above the open landing. Paul was a big man. All Lena had in her favor was the element of surprise, and she wasn't going to give that up for anything. She could almost taste the triumph she'd feel when Paul turned that corner, expecting to see a frightened child but finding a Glock shoved in his smug face.

"It's just Tim," Terri insisted, downstairs.

Paul said nothing, but Lena heard footsteps on the wooden stairs. Slow, careful footsteps.

"It's Tim," Terri repeated. The footsteps stopped. "He's sick."

"Your whole family's sick," Paul taunted, pounding his shoe onto the next stair; his Gucci loafer that could pay the mortgage on this small house for a month. "It's because of you, Terri. All those drugs you did, all that fucking around. All those blow jobs, all those ass fuckings. I bet the jism's rotting you from the inside out."

"Stop it."

Lena cupped the gun in her hand, holding it straight out in front of her, pointing it at the open landing as she waited for him to get to the top so she could shut him the fuck up.

"One of these days," he began, taking another step. "One of these days, I'm going to have to tell Dale."

"Paul—"

"How do you think he's going to feel knowing he's put his dick in all that?" Paul asked. "All that come just swirling around inside you."

"I was sixteen!" she sobbed. "What was I going to do? I didn't have a choice!"

"And now your kids are sick," he said, obviously pleased by her distress. "Sick with what you did. Sick with all that disease and filth inside you." His tone made Lena's stomach tighten with hate. She felt the urge to make some kind of noise that would get him up here faster. The gun felt hot in her hand, ready to explode as soon as he passed into her line of vision.

He continued to climb the stairs, saying, "You were nothing but a fucking whore."

Terri did not respond.

"And you're still turning tricks?" he said, coming closer. Just another few steps and he would be there. His words were so hateful, so familiar. He could be Ethan talking to Lena. Ethan coming up the stairs to beat the shit out of her.

"You think I don't know what you needed that money for?" Paul demanded. He had stopped about two steps from the top, so close that Lena could smell his flowery cologne. "Three hundred fifty bucks," he said, slapping the stair railing as if he was telling some kind of joke. "That's a lot of money, Ter. What'd you use all that money for?"

"I said I'd pay you back."

"Pay me back when you can," he said, as if he was her old friend instead of tormentor. "Tell me what it was for, Genie. I was only trying to help you."

Lena gritted her teeth, watching his shadow linger on the landing. Terri had asked Paul for the money to pay the clinic. He must have made her grovel for it, then kicked her in the teeth before she left.

"What'd you need it for?" Paul asked, his steps receding down the stairs now that he had found an easier prey. In her head, Lena was screaming for him to come back, but a few seconds later she heard his shoes hit the tile in the foyer with a loud bang as if he had jumped down the last steps in glee. "What'd you need it for, whore?" Terri didn't respond and he slapped her again, the noise pounding in Lena's ears. "Answer me, whore."

Terri's voice was weak. "I used it to pay the hospital bills."

"You used it to carve out that baby inside you."

Terri made a wheezing noise. Lena dropped the gun to her side, her eyes squeezing shut at the sound of the other woman's grief.

"Abby told me," he said. "She told me everything."

"No."

"She was real worried about her cousin Terri," he continued. "Didn't want her to go to hell for what she was going to do. I promised her I'd talk to you about it." Terri said something and Paul laughed. Lena pivoted around the corner, gun raised, aiming at Paul's back as he struck Terri across the cheek again, this time so hard that she fell to the floor. He grabbed her up, spinning her around just as Lena hid herself back behind the corner.

Lena closed her eyes again, her head playing back in slow motion what she had just seen. He had reached down to grab Terri, yanking her up as he spun toward the stairs. There was a bulge under his jacket. Was he carrying a gun? Did he have a weapon on him?

Paul's tone was one of disgust. "Get up, you whore."

"You killed her," Terri accused. "I know you killed Abby."

"Watch your mouth," he warned.

"Why?" Terri begged. "Why would you hurt Abby?"

"She did it to herself," he said. "Y'all should know better by now than to piss off ol' Cole." Lena waited for Terri to say something, to tell him that he was worse than Cole, that he had directed everything, put the idea in Cole's head that the girls needed to be punished.

Terri was silent, though, and the only thing Lena heard was the refrigerator kicking on in the kitchen. She peered around the corner just as Terri found her voice.

"I know what you did to her," she said, and Lena cursed the woman's brazenness. Of all the times for Terri to develop a backbone, this was not it. Jeffrey would be here soon, maybe in another five minutes.

Terri said, "I know you gave her the cyanide. Dale told you how to use it."

"So?"

"Why?" Terri asked. "Why would you kill Abby? She never did anything to you. All she ever did was love you."

"She was a bad girl," he said, as if that was reason enough. "Cole knew that."

"You told Cole," Terri said. "Don't think I don't know how that works."

"How what works?"

"How you tell him we're bad," she said. "You put all these terrible ideas into his head, and he goes out and punishes us." Her laugh was caustic. "Funny how God never tells him to punish the boys. You ever been in that box, Paul? You ever get buried for seeing your whores in Savannah and snorting your coke?"

Paul's tone was a snarl. " 'Go, see now this cursed woman and bury her—' "

"Don't you dare throw the scriptures at me."

" 'She hath rebelled against her God,' " he quoted. " 'They shall fall by the sword.' "

Terri obviously knew the verse. Her anger curdled the air. "Shut up, Paul."

" 'Their infants shall be dashed in pieces . . . Their women with child shall be ripped up.' "

" 'Even the Devil can quote scripture for his cause.' "

He laughed, as if she had scored a point off him.

She said, "You lost your religion a million years ago."

"You're one to talk."

"I don't go around pretending it ain't true," she retorted, her tone getting stronger, sharper. This was the woman who had hit Dale back. This was the woman who had dared to defend herself. "Why did you kill her, Paul?" She waited, then asked, "Was it because of the insurance policies?"

Paul's back stiffened. He hadn't been threatened by Terri's mention of the cyanide, but Lena guessed that the insurance policies added a whole new level to the equation.

He asked, "What do you know about that?"

"Abby told me about them, Paul. The police know."

"What do they know?" He grabbed her arm, twisting it. Lena felt her body tense. She raised her Glock again, waiting for the right moment. "What did you tell them, you little idiot?"

"Let go of me."

"I'll take your head off, you stupid bitch. Tell me what you told the police."

Lena startled as Tim came out of nowhere, running past her, nearly tumbling down the stairs to get to his mother. Lena reached for the boy and missed, pulling herself back at the last minute so that Paul wouldn't see her.

"Mama!" the child screamed.

Terri made a surprised sound, then Lena heard her say, "Tim, go back upstairs. Mama's talking to Uncle Paul."

"Come here, Tim," Paul said, and Lena's stomach lurched as his little feet tapped their way down the stairs.

"No—" Terri protested, then, "Tim, come away from him."

"Come on, big guy," Paul said, and Lena chanced a quick look. Paul was holding Tim in his arms, the child's legs wrapped around his waist. Lena pulled back, knowing if Paul turned around he would see her. She mouthed, Fuck, cursing herself for not taking the shot when she could. Across the hall, she glimpsed Rebecca in the nursery, reaching out to pull the closet door shut. In Lena's mind, she cursed even harder, damning the girl for her inability to hold on to the boy.

Lena glanced into the foyer, trying to assess the situation. Paul's back was still to her, but Tim clung tight to him, his spindly little arm hooked around Paul's shoulders as he watched his mother. At this distance, there was no telling what kind of damage her nine-millimeter would do. The bullet could rip through Paul's body and go right into Tim's. She could kill the child instantly.

"Please," Terri said, and Paul could have been holding her own life in his hands the way she was acting. "Let him go."

"Tell me what you told the police," Paul said.

"Nothing. I didn't tell them anything."

Paul didn't buy it. "Did Abby leave those policies with you, Terri? Is that what she did?"

"Yes," Terri said, her voice trembling. "I'll give them to you. Please, just let him go."

"You get them now and then we'll talk."

"Please, Paul. Let him go."

"Go get the policies."

Terri was obviously not a practiced liar. When she said, "They're in the garage," Lena knew Paul saw right through her. Still, he said, "Go get them. I'll watch Tim."

Terri must have hesitated, because Paul raised his voice, saying, "Now!" so loudly that Terri screamed. When he spoke again, his tone was back to normal, and somehow to Lena it was more frightening. "You've got thirty seconds, Terri."

"I don't—"

"Twenty-nine . . . twenty-eight . . ."

The front door slammed open and she was gone. Lena stood utterly still, her heart thumping like a drum.

Downstairs, Paul spoke as if he was talking to Tim, but made sure his voice was loud enough to carry. "You think your aunt Rebecca's upstairs, Tim?" he asked, cheerful, almost teasing. "Why don't we go see if your aunt Rebecca's up there, huh? See if she's hiding out like the little rat she is . . ."

Tim made a noise Lena couldn't understand.

"That's right, Tim," Paul said, like they were playing a game. "We'll go up and talk to her, and then we'll beat her face. You like that, Tim? We'll beat her face until her bones crack. We'll make sure Aunt Becca's pretty little face is so broken that no one ever wants to look at it again."

Lena listened, waiting for him to climb the stairs so that she could blow his head off his shoulders. He did not. Obviously, this taunting was part of the game for him. Even knowing this, the dread that filled her at the sound of his voice could not be stopped. She wanted so badly to hurt him, to shut him up forever. No one should ever have to hear him again.

The door opened and slammed shut. Terri was out of breath, her words tumbling over one another. "I couldn't find them," she said. "I looked—"

Fuck, Lena thought. Dale's gun. No.

Paul said, "You'll forgive me if I'm not surprised."

"What are you going to do?" Terri's voice was still shaking, but there was something underneath the fear, some hidden knowledge that gave her power. She must have gotten the revolver. She must have thought she could do something to stop him.

Tim said something and Paul laughed. "That's right," he agreed, then told Terri, "Tim thinks his aunt Rebecca is up there."

Lena heard another sound, this time a click. She recognized it instantly—a hammer being pulled back on a gun.

Paul was surprised, but hardly alarmed. "Where'd you get that?"

"It's Dale's," she said, and Lena felt her gut clench. "I know how to use it."

Paul laughed as if the gun was made of plastic. Lena peered over the top of the stairs, watching him walk toward Terri. She had missed her chance. He had the kid now. She should have confronted him on the stairs. She should have taken him then. Why the fuck had she listened to Jeffrey? She should've just swung around the corner and emptied her gun into the bastard's chest.

Paul said, "There's a big difference between knowing how to use a gun and actually using it," and Lena felt the cut to his words, hating herself for her indecision. Goddamn Jeffrey and his orders. She knew how to handle herself. She should've listened to her gut in the first place.

Terri said, "Just get out, Paul."

"You gonna use that thing?" he asked. "Maybe you'll hit Tim?" He was teasing her like it was a game. "Come on. See what kind of shot you are." Lena could see him clearly, closing the space between him and Terri, Tim in his arms. He was actually jostling the child, goading his niece. "Come on, Genie, let's see you do it. Shoot your own baby. You've already killed one, right? What's another?"

Terri's hands were shaking. She had the gun up in front of her, legs spread apart, palm supporting the butt of the revolver. Her determination seemed to falter more with every step he took closer.

"You stupid whore," he taunted. "Go on, shoot me." He was only a foot away from her. "Pull the trigger, little girl. Show me how tough you are. Stand up for yourself for once in your pathetic little life." Finally, he reached out and grabbed the gun from her, saying, "You stupid bitch."

"Let him go," she pleaded. "Just let him go and leave."

"Where are those papers?"

"I burned them."

"You lying slut!" He slammed the revolver into her left cheek. Terri fell to the floor, blood sloshing out of her mouth.

Lena felt her own teeth start to ache as if Paul had hit her and not Terri. She had to do something. She had to stop this. Without thinking, she went to her knees, then flattened her chest to the floor. Procedure said she should identify herself, give Paul the opportunity to drop the gun. She knew there was no chance he would surrender. Men like Paul didn't give up if they thought there was a chance of escape. Right now, he had two chances: one on his hip, the other on the floor.

Lena angled her body across the hall, placing herself at the top of the landing, gripping her gun in both hands, resting the butt on the edge of the stair.

"Now, now," Paul said. His back was to Lena as he stood over Terri, Tim's legs wrapped around his waist. She couldn't tell where the boy's body was, could not line up the shot and know with 100 percent certainty that she would not hit the child, too.

"You're upsetting your son here." Tim was silent. He had probably watched his mother get the shit beaten out of her so many times before that it no longer penetrated.

Paul said, "What did you tell the police?"

Terri had her hands out in front of her as once more Paul lifted his foot to kick her. "No!" she screamed as his Italian loafer came down on her face. Again, she slammed into the floor, the air going out of her with a painful groan that cut Lena to the core.

Again, Lena sighted the gun, her hands steady as she tried to line up the shot. If Paul would just stop moving. If Tim would just slide down a little bit more, she could end all of this now. He had no idea Lena was at the top of the stairs. Paul would be on the ground before he knew what hit him.

Paul said, "Come on, Terri." Even though Terri made no move to rise, he picked up his foot again and smashed it into her back. Terri's mouth opened, breath groaning out.

"What did you tell them?" he repeated, his mantra. Lena saw him move the revolver to Tim's head and she lowered her own gun, knowing she could not take the risk. "You know I'll shoot him. You know I will blow his little brains all over this house."

Terri struggled to her knees. She clasped her hands in front of her, a supplicant, praying, "Please, please. Let him go. Please."

"What did you tell them?"

"Nothing," she said. "Nothing!"

Tim had started to cry, and Paul shushed him, saying, "Be quiet now, Tim. Be a strong man for Uncle Paul."

"Please," Terri begged.

Lena saw a movement out of the corner of her eye. Rebecca stood in the doorway of the nursery, poised on the threshold. Lena shook her head once, then, when the girl did not move, she hardened her expression, waving her back in forceful pantomime.

When Lena turned back to the foyer, she saw that Tim had buried his face in the crook of Paul's shoulder. The boy's body stiffened as he looked up and saw Lena at the top of the stairs, her gun pointing down. Their eyes locked.

Without warning, Paul whirled around, revolver raised, and fired a shot that went straight toward her head.

Terri screamed at the explosion, and Lena rolled to the side, hoping to God she was out of the line of fire as another shot rang through the house. There was a splintering of wood as the front door burst open, followed by Jeffrey's "Don't move!" but Lena heard it as if from a great distance, the sound of the bullet ringing in her ear. She wasn't sure whether it was sweat or blood that dribbled down the side of her cheek as she looked back over the stairs. Jeffrey was standing in the foyer, his gun pointed at the lawyer. Paul still held Tim tight to his chest, the revolver trained at the boy's temple.

"Let him go," Jeffrey ordered, his eyes darting up to Lena.

Lena raised her hand to her head, recognized the sticky feel of blood. Her ear was covered in it, but she couldn't feel any pain.

Terri was crying, keening, as she held her hands to her stomach, begging Paul to release her child. She sounded as if she was praying.

Jeffrey told Paul, "Lower your gun."

"Not going to happen," he quipped.

"You've got nowhere to go," Jeffrey said, again looking up at Lena. "We've got you surrounded."

Paul let his gaze follow Jeffrey's. Lena made an attempt to stand, but vertigo got the best of her. She settled back onto her knees, her gun down at her side. She couldn't keep her eyes focused.

Paul said calmly, "Looks like she needs help."

"Please," Terri pleaded, almost in her own world. "Please, just let him go. Please."

"There's no way out of this for you," Jeffrey said. "Drop the gun."

Lena tasted something metallic in her mouth. She put her hand to her head again, testing her scalp. She didn't feel anything alarming, but her ear started to throb. Gently, she tested the cartilage until she found out what was causing the blood. The top part of her earlobe was missing, maybe a quarter of an inch. The bullet must have grazed her.

She sat up on her knees, blinking, trying to clear her vision. Terri was looking at her, almost drilling a hole into her, eyes begging Lena to do something to stop this.

"Help him," she implored. "Please help my baby."

Lena wiped a trickle of blood out of her eye, finally seeing what the bulge under Paul's jacket was. A cell phone. The bastard had a cell phone clipped to his belt.

"Please," Terri begged. "Lena, please."

Lena pointed her gun at Paul's head, feeling a searing hatred burn her throat as she told him, "Drop it."

Paul swung around, taking Tim with him. He looked up at Lena, gauging the situation. She could tell part of him didn't believe a woman could actually threaten him, and this made her hate him even more.

She made her voice a deadly threat. "Drop it, you bastard."

For the first time, he looked nervous.

"Drop the gun," Lena repeated, keeping her hand steady as she rose to her feet. If she could have been sure of her shot, she would've killed him there and then, unloaded her magazine into his head until there was nothing but a stump of spine sticking out.

Jeffrey said, "Do it, Paul. Drop the gun."

Slowly, Paul lowered his gun, but instead of letting it fall to the ground, he trained it on Terri's head. He knew they wouldn't shoot him as long as he had Tim as a shield. Pointing the gun at Terri was just one more way to assert his control over the situation.

He said, "I think y'all should take your own advice."

Terri sat there on the floor, her hands reaching out to her son. She pleaded, "Don't hurt him, Paul." Tim tried to go to his mother but Paul held him tight. "Please don't hurt him."

Paul backed toward the front door, saying, "Put down your guns. Now."

Jeffrey watched him, not doing anything for several beats. Finally, he put his weapon on the floor and held up his hands, showing they were empty. "Backup's on the way."

"Not fast enough," he guessed.

Jeffrey said, "Don't do this, Paul. Just leave him here."

"So you can follow me?" Paul sneered, shifting Tim on his hip. The child had realized what was going on and his breath was coming hard, like he was having trouble getting air. Paul kept moving closer to the door, oblivious to the boy's pain. "I don't think so." He looked up at Lena. "Your turn, *Detective*."

Lena waited for Jeffrey's nod before crouching down to place her gun on the floor. She stayed low, keeping close to the weapon.

Tim's breathing was more labored, and he started making a whooping sound as he struggled to inhale.

"It's okay," Terri whispered, inching toward him, crawling on her knees. "Just breathe, baby. Just try to breathe."

Paul edged toward the front door, keeping his eye on Jeffrey, thinking he was the real threat. Lena took a few steps down the stairs, not knowing what she would do if she reached the bottom. She wanted to tear him apart with her hands, hear him scream with agony as she ripped into him.

"It's okay, baby," Terri crooned, crawling on her knees toward them. She reached out, touching her son's foot with the tips of her fingers. The boy was gasping in earnest now, his thin chest heaving. "Just breathe."

Paul was almost out the door. He told Jeffrey, "Don't try to follow me."

Jeffrey said, "You're not going to take that kid."

"Watch me."

He made to leave, but Terri held Tim's foot in the palm of her hand, keeping them both in place. Paul pressed the gun to her forehead. "Get back," Paul warned, and Lena froze on the stair, unsure who he was talking to. She took another step as Paul warned Terri, "Move away."

"His asthma—"

"I don't care," Paul barked. "Move away."

"Mama loves you," Terri whispered over and over, oblivious to Paul's threat as she clung to Tim's foot. "Mama loves you so much—"

"Shut up," Paul hissed. He tried to pull away, but Terri held on tight, wrapping her hand around Tim's leg to get a better grip. Paul raised the revolver, slamming the butt of it down on her head.

Jeffrey grabbed up his gun in one fluid motion, pointing it at Paul's chest. "Stop right there."

"Baby," Terri said. She had staggered, but remained on her knees, holding on to Tim's leg. "Mama's here, baby. Mama's here."

Tim was turning blue, his teeth chattering as if he was cold. Paul tried to pull him away from his mother, but she held on, telling her son, " '. . . my grace is sufficient for thee . . .' "

"Let go." Paul tried to jerk him back, but still she would not release her son. "Terri— " Paul looked panicked, as if some kind of rabid animal had clamped on to him. "Terri, I mean it."

" '. . . my strength is made perfect in weakness . . .' "

"Let go, goddamnit!" Again, Paul raised the gun, striking her even more savagely. Terri fell back, but she reached out with her other hand, grabbing on to Paul's shirt, pulling it as she struggled to stay upright.

Jeffrey had his gun on Paul, but even this close, he couldn't risk a shot. The boy was in the way. His problem was the same as Lena's. An inch too far and he'd end up killing him.

"Terri," Lena tried, as if she could somehow help. She had reached the bottom stair, but all she could do was watch as Terri held on to Tim, her bleeding forehead pressed to his leg. The boy's eyelids flickered. His lips were blue, his face a ghostly white as his lungs strained for air.

Jeffrey warned, "Stop right there, Paul."

" 'When I am weak,' " Terri whispered, " 'then am I strong.' "

Paul struggled to pull away, but Terri maintained her hold, clutching on to the waist of his pants. Paul raised the gun higher and brought it down, but Terri tilted her head up at the last minute. The gun glanced off her cheek, hitting her collarbone, slipping in Paul's hand. A single bullet fired straight up into Terri's face. The woman staggered again, somehow keeping herself upright as she held on to Paul and her boy. There was a gaping hole in her jaw, fragmented bone hanging down. Blood poured out of the open wound, splattering onto the tiled floor, and the injured woman reflexively tightened her grip on Paul's shirt, bloody handprints streaking the white.

"No," Paul said, stumbling back, trying to get away from her. He was horrified at what he was seeing, his expression showing a mixture of fear and revulsion. In shock, he let go of the gun and almost dropped Tim as he fell against the porch railing.

Terri kept her tight grip on Paul, using all her remaining strength to hold on. Blood wicked into his shirt as she pulled him down to the ground, falling on top of him. She kept pulling at his shirt, pulling herself up toward her son. Tim's skin was deadly white, his eyes closed. Terri put her head on Tim's back, the pulverized side of her face turned away from her son.

Jeffrey kicked the revolver away from Paul's hand, then slid the child out from under his mother. He laid Tim flat on the ground and started to give him CPR. "Lena," he said, then yelled, "Lena!"

She startled out of her trance, her body working on autopilot as she snapped open her phone and called an ambulance. She knelt beside Terri, putting her fingers to the woman's neck. There was a faint pulse, and Lena smoothed back her hair from her shattered face, saying, "You're going to be okay."

Paul tried to move out from under her, but Lena snarled, "If you so much as breathe, I'll kill you."

Paul nodded, his lips trembling as he looked down in horror at Terri's head in his lap. He had never killed this close before, had always shielded himself from the dirty reality of his deeds. The bullet had torn through the side of Terri's face, exiting out of the base of her neck. Black dots burned into the skin from the powder burns. Her left cheek was shredded, her tongue visible through the damage. Fractured bone mingled with blood and gray matter. Fragments of her back molars were stuck in her hair.

Lena put her face close to Terri's, saying, "Terri? Terri, just hang on."

Terri's eyes fluttered open. She took shallow breaths, struggling to speak.

"Terri?"

Lena could see her tongue moving inside her mouth, the white bone shaking from the effort.

"It's okay," Lena soothed. "Help is on the way. Just hang on."

Her jaw worked slowly, labored with the desperate effort of speaking. She couldn't enunciate, her mouth would not cooperate. It seemed to take everything out of her to say, "I . . . did it."

"You did it," Lena assured her, grabbing her hand, careful not to jostle her. Spinal injuries were tricky, the higher up the more damage. She didn't even know if Terri could feel her, but she had to hold on to something.

Lena said, "I've got your hand, Terri. Don't let go."

Jeffrey muttered, "Come on, Tim," and she heard him counting, pressing the boy's chest, trying to make his heart beat.

Terri's breathing slowed. Her eyelids flickered again. "I . . . did . . . it."

"Terri?" Lena asked. "Terri?"

"Breathe, Tim," Jeffrey urged. He took a breath of his own and forced it into the boy's slackened mouth.

Bubbles of bright red blood popped on Terri's wet lips. There was a gurgling sound in her chest, a fluid look to her features.

"Terri?" Lena begged, holding on to her hand, trying to press life back into her. She heard a siren in the distance, calling like a beacon. Lena knew it was backup; the ambulance couldn't get there this quickly. Still, she lied.

"Hear that?" Lena asked, gripping Terri's hand as tightly as she could. "The ambulance is on the way, Terri."

"Come on, Tim," Jeffrey coaxed. "Come on."

Terri blinked, and Lena knew she could hear the wail of the siren, knew help was coming. She exhaled sharply. "I . . . did . . ."

"One-one-thousand, two-one-thousand," Jeffrey said, counting the compressions.

"I . . . di . . ."

"Terri, talk to me," Lena pleaded. "Come on, girl. What did you do? Tell me what you did."

She struggled to speak, giving a weak cough, spraying a fine mist of blood into Lena's face. Lena stayed there, stayed close to her, tried to keep eye contact so that she would not go.

"Tell me," Lena said, searching her eyes for something, some sign that she would be okay. She just needed to keep her talking, keep her holding on. "Tell me what you did."

"I—"

"You what?"

"I—"

"Come on, Terri. Don't let go. Don't give up now." Lena heard the cruiser screech to a halt in the drive. "Tell me what you did."

"I . . ." Terri began. "I . . . got . . ."

"What did you get?" Lena felt hot tears on her cheeks as Terri's grip slackened around her own. "Don't let go, Terri. Tell me what you got."

Her lip curled, a spasm; almost, as if she wanted to smile but no longer knew how.

"What did you get, Terri? What did you get?"

"I . . . got . . ." She coughed out another spray of blood. " . . . away."

"That's it," Jeffrey said as Tim gasped, taking his first breath of air. "That's great, Tim. Just breathe."

A stream of blood flowed from the corner of Terri's mouth, forming a solid line down her cheek like a child's bright crayon trailing across a page. What was left of her jaw went slack. Her eyes were glassy.

She was gone.

❋ ❋ ❋ ❋

Lena left the police station around nine that evening, feeling like she hadn't been home in weeks. Her body felt weak, every muscle sore as if she'd run a thousand miles. Her ear was still numb from the shot they had given her at the hospital so they could suture up the damage Paul's bullet had done. Her hair would cover the missing bit, but Lena knew that every time she looked in a mirror, every time she touched the scar, she would remember Terri Stanley, the look on her face, that almost-smile as she slipped away.

Even though there wasn't a visible sign of it, Lena felt like she still had some of Terri's blood on her—in her hair, under her fingernails. No matter what she did, she could still smell it, taste it, feel it. It was heavy, like guilt, and tasted of bitter defeat. She had not helped the woman. She had done nothing to protect her. Terri had been right— they were both drowning in the same ocean.

Her cell phone rang as she turned into her neighborhood, and Lena checked the caller ID, praying like hell Jeffrey didn't need her back at the station. She squinted at the number, not recognizing it. Lena let the phone ring a few more times before it suddenly came to her. Lu Mitchell's number. She had almost forgotten it after all these years.

She nearly dropped the phone trying to open it, then cursed as she put it up to her injured ear. Lena switched it around, saying, "Hello?" There was no response, and her heart dropped, thinking the call had gone to her voice mail.

She was about to end the connection when Greg said, "Lee?"

"Yeah," she said, trying not to sound breathless. "Hey. How's it going?"

"I heard on the news about the woman," he said. "Were you there?"

"Yeah," she told him, wondering how long it had been since someone asked her about work. Ethan was too self-centered and Nan was too squeamish.

"Are you okay?"

"I watched her die," Lena told him. "I just held her hand and watched her die."

She heard his breathing over the line and thought about Terri, the way her last breaths had sounded.

He told her, "It's good that she had you there."

"I don't know about that."

"No," he disagreed. "It's good that she had someone with her."

Before she could stop herself, she said, "I'm not a very good person, Greg."

Again, all she could hear was his breathing.

"I've made some really bad mistakes."

"Everybody has."

"Not like me," she said. "Not the ones I have."

"Do you want to talk about it?"

She wanted more than anything else to talk about it, to tell him everything that had happened, to shock him with the ugly details. She couldn't, though. She needed him too badly, needed to know he was just down the street, holding his mama's yarn while Lu knitted him another ugly scarf.

"So," Greg said, and Lena strained to fill the silence.

"I'm enjoying the CD."

His tone went up. "You got it?"

"Yeah," she told him, forcing some cheer into her voice. "I really like that second song."

"It's called 'Oldest Story in the World.'"

"I'd know that if you'd written down the titles."

"That's why you go out and buy the CD for yourself, you goof." She had forgotten what it was like to be teased, and Lena felt some of the weight that had been on her chest start to lighten.

He continued, "The liner notes are great. Lots of pictures of the girls. Ann looks so damn hot." He gave a self-deprecating chuckle. "I wouldn't kick Nancy out of bed, either, but you know I like dark-haired women."

"Yeah." She felt herself smiling, too, and wished that they could talk like this forever, that she wouldn't have to think about Terri dying in front of her, or of Terri's children being abandoned by the one person in the world who could protect them. Now, all they would have was Dale—Dale and the fear of being killed like their mama.

She forced this out of her brain, saying, "The twelfth song is good, too."

"That's 'Down the Nile,' " he told her. "Since when do you like ballads?"

"Since . . ." She didn't know since when. "I don't know. I just like it." She had pulled into the driveway behind Nan's Toyota.

" 'Move On' is cool," Greg was saying, but she didn't really follow. The porch light had turned on. Ethan's bike was leaned against the front stairs.

"Lee?"

Her smile was gone. "Yeah?"

"You okay?"

"Yeah," she breathed, her mind reeling. What was Ethan doing in the house? What was he doing with Nan?

"Lee?"

She swallowed hard, making herself speak. "I need to go, Greg. Okay?"

"Is something wrong?"

"No," she lied, feeling like her heart might explode in her chest. "Everything's fine. I just can't talk now." She hung up before he could respond, dropping the phone in the seat beside her, opening the door with a hand that refused to be steady.

Lena wasn't sure how she made it up the steps, but she found herself with her hand on the doorknob, her palms slick and sweaty. She took a breath, opening the door.

"Hi!" Nan popped up from the chair where she had been sitting, moving behind it as if she needed a shield. Her eyes were wide, her voice unnaturally high. "We were just waiting for you. Oh, my God! Your ear!" She put her hand to her mouth.

"It's better than it looks."

Ethan was on the couch, his arm across the back, his legs open in a hostile stance that managed to take up the entire room. He didn't speak, but he didn't have to. The threat of him seeped out of every pore.

"Are you okay?" Nan insisted. "Lena? What happened?"

Lena said, "There was a situation," keeping her eyes on Ethan.

"They didn't say much of anything on the news," Nan said. She was edging toward the kitchen, almost giddy from stress. Ethan stayed where he was, his jaw in a tight line, his muscles flexed. Lena saw his book bag beside his feet and wondered what he had in there. Something heavy, probably. Something to beat her with.

Nan offered, "Would you like some tea?"

"That's okay," Lena told her, then said to Ethan, "Let's go to my room."

"We could play some cards, Lee." Nan's voice wavered. She was obviously alarmed, and she stood her ground. "Why don't we all play some cards?"

"That's okay," Lena answered, knowing she had to do everything in her power to keep Nan out of harm's way. Lena had brought this on herself, but Nan would not be hurt because of it. She owed that to Sibyl. She owed that to herself.

Nan tried, "Lee?"

"It's okay, Nan." Again, she told Ethan, "Let's go to my room."

He didn't move at first, letting her know he was in charge of the situation. When he got up, he took his time, stretching his arms in front of him, faking a yawn.

Lena turned her back to him, ignoring the show. She went into her room and sat on the bed, waiting, praying that he would leave Nan alone.

Ethan sauntered into her bedroom, eyeing her suspiciously. "Where you been?" he asked, shutting the door with a soft click. He gripped his book bag in one hand, keeping his arms at his side.

She shrugged. "Work."

He dropped the bag with a solid clunk onto the floor. "I've been waiting for you."

"You shouldn't come here," she told him.

"That so?"

"I would've called you." She lied, "I was going to come by later."

"You bent the rim on my front tire," he said. "It cost me eighty bucks to get a new one."

She stood, going to the bureau. "I'll pay you back," she said, opening the top drawer. She kept her money in an old cigar box. Beside it was a black plastic case that held a Mini-Glock. Nan's father was a cop and after Sibyl had been murdered, he had insisted his daughter take the gun. Nan had given it to Lena, and Lena had put it in the drawer as a backup. At night, her service weapon was always on the bedside table, but knowing the other Glock was in the drawer, sitting in the unlocked plastic case, was the only reason she was able to go to sleep.

She could take the gun now. She could take it and use it and finally get Ethan out of her life.

"What are you doing?" he demanded.

Lena took out the cigar box and slid the drawer closed. She put the box on top of the dresser and opened the lid. Ethan's large hand reached in front of her, closing back the lid.

He was standing behind her, his body barely touching hers. She felt the whisper of his breath on the back of her neck when he said, "I don't want your money."

She cleared her throat so that she could speak. "What do you want?"

He took another step closer. "You know what I want."

She could feel his cock harden as he pressed it against her ass. He put his hands on either side of her, resting them on top of the dresser, trapping her.

He said, "Nan wouldn't tell me who CD-boy is."

Lena bit her lip, feeling the sting as she drew blood. She thought about Terri Stanley when they had knocked on her door this morning, the way she had held her jaw rigid as she talked to keep her lip from breaking open. Terri would never have to do that again. She would never again lie awake at night, wondering what Dale was going to do next. She would never have to be afraid.

Ethan started rubbing against her. The sensation made her feel sick. "Me and Nan had a real good talk."

"Leave Nan alone."

"You want me to leave her alone?" His hand snaked around, grabbing her breast so hard she had to sink her teeth into the flesh of her lip to keep from crying out. "This is mine," he reminded her. "You hear me?"

"Yes."

"Nobody touches you but me."

Lena closed her eyes, willing herself not to scream as his lips brushed against her neck.

"I'll kill anybody who touches you." He tightened his fist around her breast as if he wanted to rip it off. "One more dead body don't mean shit to me," he hissed. "You hear?"

"Yes." Her heart thudded once in her chest, then she could no longer feel it beating. She had felt numb with fear, but just as suddenly, she felt nothing.

Slowly, Lena turned around. She saw her hands come up, not to slap him but to tenderly cup his face. She felt light-headed, dizzy, as if she were somewhere else in the room, watching herself with Ethan. When her lips met his, she felt nothing. His tongue had no taste. His calloused fingers as he pushed his hand down the front of her pants brought no sensation.

On the bed, he was rougher than ever before, pinning her down, somehow more angry that she wasn't resisting. Through it all, Lena still felt apart from herself, even as he pushed into her like a blade slicing through her insides. She was aware of the pain as she was aware of her breathing; a fact, an uncontrollable process through which her body survived.

Ethan finished quickly and Lena lay there feeling like she had been marked by a dog. He rolled onto his back, breathing hard, satisfied with himself. It wasn't until she heard the steady low snore of his sleep that Lena felt her senses slowly begin to return. The smell of his sweat. The taste of his tongue. The sticky wetness between her legs.

He hadn't used a condom.

Lena carefully rolled onto her side, feeling what he had left drain out of her. She watched the clock slowly mark the time, first minutes, then hours. One hour. Two. She waited until three hours had passed before she rose from the bed. She held her breath, listening for a change in the cadence of Ethan's breathing as she crouched to the floor.

She moved slowly, as if through water, sliding open the top drawer of her bureau, taking out the black plastic case. She sat on the floor, her back to Ethan, holding her breath as she unsnapped the lock. The noise filled the room like a gunshot. She tried not to gasp as Ethan shifted in bed. Lena closed her eyes, fighting panic as she waited for his hand on her back, his fingers wrapped around her throat. She turned her head, looking over her shoulder.

He was on his side, facing away from her.

The weapon was loaded, a round from the magazine already chambered. She cradled the gun in her hands, feeling it grow heavier and heavier until she let her hands drift to her lap. A smaller version of her service weapon, the mini could do just as much damage up close. Lena closed her eyes again, feeling the mist of blood Terri had sprayed into her face, hearing her last words, almost triumphant: *I got away.*

Lena stared at the gun, the black metal cold against her hands. She turned to make sure Ethan was still sleeping.

His book bag was on the floor where he had dropped it. She gritted her teeth as she opened the zipper, the sound reverberating in her chest. The bag was a nice one, Swiss Army, with several large pockets and plenty of storage. Ethan kept everything in the bag—his wallet, his books for school, even some gym clothes. He wouldn't notice a couple of extra pounds.

Lena reached into the bag, unzipping the large rear compartment that snaked around the inside of the bag. There were pencils in there, some pens, but nothing else. She hid the gun inside and pulled the zip closed, leaving the bag on the floor.

Moving backward, she crawled to the bed, using her hands to lift herself up, then inch-by-inch lowering herself down beside Ethan.

He exhaled, almost a snort, and rolled over, his arm flopping across her chest. Lena turned her head to see the clock, counting away the minutes until the alarm would go off, until Ethan would be out of her life forever.

SATURDAY

CHAPTER SEVENTEEN

Sara tightened her hand on Bob's leash as his nose jerked toward the field on the side of the road. Being a sight hound, Bob had no control over his urge to chase anything that ran, and Sara knew if she let go of the leash, she would probably never see the dog again.

Jeffrey, who was holding just as tightly to Billy's leash, glanced into the field, too. "Rabbit?"

"Chipmunk," she guessed, steering Bob to the other side of the road. He gave in easily, laziness being just as much of a genetic imperative for greyhounds, and loped down the road, his slim hiney shifting with each step.

Jeffrey slipped his arm around Sara's waist. "You cold?"

"Uh-uh," she said, closing her eyes against the sun. They had both cursed loudly when the phone had awakened them at five till seven this morning, but Cathy's offer of a pancake breakfast had persuaded them to roll out of bed. They both had a lot of work to catch up on this weekend, but Sara reasoned they would be better prepared on a full stomach.

"I've been thinking," Jeffrey said. "Maybe we should get another dog."

She gave him a sideways glance. Bob had just about died of a heart attack this morning when Jeffrey turned on the shower without first checking to make sure the dog wasn't sleeping in his usual spot.

"Or a cat?"

She laughed out loud. "You don't even like the one we have now."

"Well," he shrugged. "Maybe a new one, one we both picked out."

Sara leaned her head back on his shoulder. Despite what Jeffrey believed, she couldn't always read his mind, but right now Sara knew exactly what he really wanted. The way he had talked about

Terri and her son last night had made Sara realize something that she had never even considered. For years, she had only thought of her inability to have children as a personal loss, but now she could see that it was Jeffrey's loss as well. She couldn't exactly explain why, but somehow, knowing he had this need as deeply as she did made it feel less like a failure and more like something to overcome.

"I'm gonna keep an eye on those kids," he said, and she knew he meant Terri's two children. "Pat's going to come down pretty hard on him."

Sara doubted the man's brother held any sway in the matter, and asked, "Will Dale keep custody?"

"I don't know," he said. "When I was pushing on his chest . . ." Jeffrey began, and she knew that he felt sick about the fact that he had cracked two of Tim Stanley's ribs while giving the boy CPR. "They're so little. His bones are like toothpicks."

"It beats letting him die," Sara said. Then, realizing how hard her words must sound to him, she added, "Cracked ribs heal, Jeffrey. You saved Tim's life. You did everything right."

"I was glad to see that ambulance."

"He'll be out of the hospital in a few days," she assured him, rubbing his back to soothe his worries. "You did everything right."

"It made me think about Jared," he said, and her hand stopped moving of its own accord. Jared, the boy he had thought of as a sort of nephew all these years, only to find out recently that he was actually a son.

He said, "I remember when he was little, I'd throw him up in the air and catch him. God, he loved that. He'd laugh so hard he'd get the hiccups."

"I'm sure Nell wanted to kill you," Sara said, thinking Jared's mother had probably held her breath the entire time.

"I could feel his ribs pressing against my hands when I caught him. He's got such a great laugh. He loved being up in the air." He gave a half-smile, thinking out loud, "Maybe he'll be a pilot one day."

They walked, both of them silent, their footsteps and the jingle of the dogs' metal ID tags the only sound. Sara pressed her head against Jeffrey's shoulder, wanting more than anything to just be there in the moment. He tightened his arm around her, and she looked at the dogs, wondering what it would feel like to be pushing a stroller instead of holding on to a leash.

At the age of six, Sara had quite conceitedly told her mother that one day she would have two children, a boy and a girl, and that the boy would have blond hair and the girl would have brown. Cathy had teased her about this early show of single-mindedness well into Sara's twenties. Through college, then medical school, then finally her internship, it had been a long-standing family joke, especially considering the fact that Sara's dating life was sparse to say the least. They had mocked her relentlessly about her precociousness for years, then the teasing had abruptly stopped. At twenty-six, Sara had lost her ability to ever have a child. At twenty-six, she had lost her childhood belief that just wanting something badly enough made it possible.

Walking along the street, her head on Jeffrey's shoulder, Sara let herself play that dangerous game, the one where she wondered what their children would have looked like. Jared had Jeffrey's dark coloring, his mother's intense blue eyes. Would their baby have red hair, a shock of auburn that grew like springs? Or would he have Jeffrey's black, almost blue, mane, thick and wavy, the sort of hair you couldn't stop running your fingers through? Would he be kind and gentle like his father, growing into the sort of man who would one day make some woman happier than she'd ever thought she could possibly be?

Jeffrey's chest rose and fell as he took a deep breath and let it go.

Sara wiped her eyes, hoping he didn't see how silly she was being. She asked, "How's Lena?"

"I gave her the day off." Jeffrey rubbed his eyes, too, but she couldn't look up at him. "She deserves a medal for finally following orders."

"The first time is always special."

His acknowledged the joke with a wry chuckle. "God, she's such a mess."

She squeezed her arm around his waist, thinking that the two of them weren't in much better shape themselves. "You know you can't straighten her out, right?"

He gave another heavy sigh. "Yeah."

She looked up at him, saw that his eyes were as moist as hers.

After a few seconds, he clicked his tongue at Billy, getting him back on the road. "Anyway."

"Anyway," she echoed.

He cleared his throat several times before he could tell her, "Paul's lawyer should be here around noon today."

"Where's he coming from?"

"Atlanta," Jeffrey said, all his disgust for the city resting on that one word.

Sara sniffed, trying to get her composure back. "Do you really think Paul Ward is going to confess to anything?"

"No," he admitted, tugging on Billy's leash as the dog stopped to investigate some weeds. "He shut his mouth as soon as we pulled Terri off him."

Sara paused, thinking about the woman's sacrifice. "Do you think the charges will stick?"

"The attempted kidnapping and shooting we've got down easy," he answered. "You can't argue with two cops as witnesses." He shook his head. "Who knows which way it'll go? I sure as shit could argue premeditated; I was right there. There's no telling with a jury . . ." He let his voice trail off. "Your shoe's untied." He handed her Billy's leash and knelt in front of her to tie the lace. "They've got him for murder during the commission of a felony, attempted murder with Lena. There has to be something in there that keeps him behind bars for a long time."

"And Abby?" Sara asked, watching his hands. She remembered the first time he had tied her shoe for her. They had been in the woods, and she hadn't been sure how she felt about him until that very moment when he had knelt down in front of her. Watching him now, all she could wonder was how she had ever not known how much she needed him in her life.

"Get back," Jeffrey shooed Billy and Bob as the dogs tried to catch the moving laces. Jeffrey finished the double knot then straightened, taking the leash. "I don't know about Abby. Terri's evidence put the cyanide in his hands, but she's not here to tell the tale. Dale's not exactly gonna brag about how he told Paul to use the salts." He put his arm back around her waist, pulling her closer as they continued walking. "Rebecca's shaky. Esther told me I could talk to her tomorrow."

"Do you think she'll give you anything useful?"

"No," he admitted. "All she can say is that she found some papers Abby left. Hell, she can't even say for sure whether or not Abby left them. She didn't hear what happened with Terri because she was in the closet the whole time and she can't testify about the burials because it's hearsay. Even if a judge let it in, Cole was the one who put the girls in the boxes. Paul kept his hands clean." He admitted, "He covered his tracks pretty well."

Sara said, "I don't imagine even a slick lawyer from Atlanta will be able to put a good spin on the fact that his client's entire family is willing to testify against him." Oddly, that was the real threat to Paul Ward. Not only had he forged his family's signatures on the policies, he had cashed checks written out to them and pocketed the money. The fraud alone could keep him in prison until he was an old man.

"His secretary's recanted, too," Jeffrey told her. "She says Paul didn't work late that night after all."

"What about the people on the farm who died? The workers Paul had policies on?"

"Could be they just died and Paul lucked out," he said, though she knew he didn't believe that. Even if he wanted to prosecute, there was nothing Jeffrey could do to find any evidence of foul play. The nine bodies had been cremated and their families—if they had any— had given up on them long ago.

He told her, "Cole's murder is the same story. There weren't any prints but his on the coffee jar. Paul's fingerprints were in the apartment, but so were everybody else's."

"I think Cole got his own justice," she said, aware that she was being harsh. In her years before Jeffrey, Sara had had the luxury of seeing the law in very black-and-white terms. She had trusted the courts to do their jobs, jurors to take their oaths seriously. Living with a cop had made her do a sharp about-face.

"You did a good job," she told him.

"I'll feel like that's true when Paul Ward's sitting on death row."

Sara would rather see the man live out the rest of his natural life behind bars, but she wasn't about to start a death penalty discussion with Jeffrey. This was the one thing that he couldn't change her mind on, no matter how hard he tried.

They had reached the Linton house, and Sara saw her father kneeling in front of her mother's white Buick. He was washing the car, using a toothbrush to clean out the spokes on the tire rims.

"Hey, Daddy," Sara said, kissing the top of his head.

"Your mother was out at that farm," Eddie grumbled, dipping the toothbrush into some soapy water. He was obviously bothered that Cathy had paid her old boyfriend a visit, but had decided to take it out on the car instead. "I told her to take my truck, but does she ever listen to me?"

Sara was aware that as usual her father had not bothered to acknowledge Jeffrey's presence. She said, "Daddy?"

"Huh?" he grumbled.

"I wanted to tell you . . ." She waited for him to look up. "Jeffrey and I are living together."

"No shit," Eddie said, returning to the tire.

"We're thinking of getting another dog."

"Congratulations," he answered, his tone far from celebratory.

"And getting married," she added.

The toothbrush paused, and beside her, Jeffrey actually gasped.

Eddie brushed at a speck of tar with the toothbrush. He looked up at Sara, then at Jeffrey. "Here," he said, holding the toothbrush out to Jeffrey. "If you're going to be part of this family again, you've got to take your share of responsibilities."

Sara took Billy's leash from Jeffrey so that he could take off his jacket. He handed it to her, saying, "Thanks."

She gave him her sweetest smile. "My pleasure."

Jeffrey took the brush and knelt beside her father, going at the spokes in earnest.

This obviously wasn't good enough for Eddie. He instructed, "Put some elbow grease into it. My girls can do a better job than that."

Sara put her hand to her mouth so that they wouldn't see her smile.

She left them alone to either bond or kill each other, tying the dogs' leashes around the railing on the front porch. Inside, there was a burst of laughter from the kitchen, and Sara walked down the hall, thinking that it felt like years had passed instead of six days since the last time she had made this trip.

Cathy and Bella were almost in the exact place as before, Bella sitting at the kitchen table with a newspaper, Cathy working at the stove.

"What's going on?" Sara asked, kissing her mother's cheek as she stole a piece of bacon off the plate.

"I'm leaving," Bella told her. "This is my farewell breakfast."

"I'm sorry to hear that," Sara answered. "I feel like I haven't even seen you."

"Because you haven't," Bella pointed out. She waved off Sara's apology. "You've been tied up with your work stuff."

"Where are you going to go?"

"Atlanta," Bella said, then gave her a wink. "Take a long nap before you come see me."

Sara rolled her eyes.

"I mean it, sugar," Bella told her. "Come see me."

"I might be a little busy for a while," Sara began, not quite knowing how to deliver her news. She felt a foolish grin on her lips as she waited for their undivided attention.

"What is it?" her mother asked.

"I've decided to marry Jeffrey."

Cathy turned back to the stove, saying, "Well, that took long enough. It's a wonder he still wants you."

"Thanks a lot," Sara answered, wondering why she even bothered.

"Don't mind your mama, darling," Bella said, rising from the table. She hugged Sara hard, saying, "Congratulations."

"Thank you," Sara responded in a pointed tone, mostly for her mother's benefit. Cathy seemed oblivious.

Bella folded the paper and tucked it under her arm. "I'll leave y'all to talk," she told them. "Don't say anything bad about me unless I can hear it."

Sara watched her mother's back, wondering why she wasn't speaking. Finally, Sara couldn't stand the silence, and said, "I thought you'd be happy for me."

"I'm happy for Jeffrey," Cathy told her. "You took your own damn sweet time."

Sara folded Jeffrey's jacket over the back of Bella's chair and sat

down. She was ready for a lecture on her own failings, so was surprised at Cathy's next words.

"Bella told me you went to that church with your sister."

Sara wondered what else her aunt had told her mother. "Yes,
ma'am."

"You met Thomas Ward?"

"Yes," Sara repeated, dropping the ma'am. "He seems like a very
nice man."

Cathy tapped her fork on the side of the skillet before turning
around. She folded her arms over her chest. "Do you have a question
to ask me, or would you rather take the cowardly route and filter it
through your aunt Bella again?"

Sara felt a flush work its way up her neck to her face. She hadn't
thought it through at the time, but her mother was right. Sara had
mentioned her fears to Bella because she knew her aunt would take
it back to her mother.

She took a breath, screwing up her courage. "Was he the one?"

"Yes."

"Lev is . . ." Sara searched for the words, wishing she *could* do this
through her aunt Bella. Her mother's eyes pierced her like needles.
"Lev has red hair."

"Are you a doctor?" Cathy asked sharply.

"Well, ye—"

"Did you go to medical school?"

"Yes."

"Then you should know something about genetics." Cathy was angrier than Sara had seen her mother in a long time. "Did you even
stop to think how your father would feel if he thought you thought
even for a minute—" She stopped, obviously trying to control her
fury. "I told you at the time, Sara. I told you it was purely emotional.
It was never physical."

"I know."

"Have I ever lied to you in my life?"

"No, Mama."

"It would break your father's heart if he knew . . ." She had been
pointing her finger at Sara, but she dropped her hand. "Sometimes I
wonder if you have a brain in your head." She turned back around to
the stove, picking up the fork.

Sara took the rebuff as well as she could, keenly aware that her mother had not really answered her question. Unable to stop herself, she repeated, "Lev has red hair."

Cathy dropped the fork, turning back around. "So did his mother, you idiot!"

Tessa entered the kitchen, a thick book in her hands. "Whose mother?"

Cathy reined herself in. "Never you mind."

"Are you making pancakes?" Tessa asked, dropping the book on the table. Sara read the title, *The Complete Works of Dylan Thomas*.

"No," Cathy mocked. "I'm turning water into wine."

Tessa shot a look at Sara. Sara shrugged, as if she wasn't the cause of her mother's fury.

"Breakfast will be ready in a few minutes," Cathy informed them. "Set the table."

Tessa stood in place. "I actually had plans this morning."

"Plans to do what?" Cathy asked.

"I told Lev I'd come by the church," she said, and Sara bit her tongue not to say anything.

Tessa saw the effort and defended, "This is a hard time for all of them."

Sara nodded, but Cathy's back was straight as an arrow, her disapproval as obvious as a flashing light.

Tessa tried to tread carefully. "They're not all bad people just because of what Paul did."

"I didn't say they were." Cathy provided, "Thomas Ward is one of the most upstanding men I have ever met." She glared at Sara, daring her to say something.

Tessa apologized, "I'm sorry I'm not going to your church, I just—"

Cathy snapped, "I know exactly why you're going over there, missy."

Tessa raised her eyebrows at Sara, but Sara could only shrug again, glad her mother was taking up the fight.

"That is a house of worship." Cathy pointed her finger at Tessa this time. "Church is not just another place to get laid."

Tessa barked a laugh, then stopped when she saw that her mother was serious. "It's not that," she defended. "I like being there."

"You *like* Leviticus Ward."

"Well," Tessa allowed, a smile curling her lips. "Yeah, but I like being at the church, too."

Cathy tucked her hands into her hips, looking back and forth between her two daughters as if she didn't know what to do with them.

Tessa said, "I'm serious, Mama. I want to be there. Not just for Lev. For me."

Despite her feelings on the subject, Sara backed her up. "She's telling the truth."

Cathy pressed her lips together, and for a moment Sara thought she might cry. She had always known that religion was important to her mother, but Cathy had never forced it down their throats. She wanted her children to choose spirituality of their own accord, and Sara could see now how happy she was that Tessa had come around. For a brief moment, Sara felt jealous that she couldn't do the same.

"Breakfast ready?" Eddie bellowed, the front door slamming behind him.

Cathy's grin turned into a scowl as she turned back to the stove. "Your father thinks I'm running a damn Waffle House."

Eddie padded into the room, his toes sticking out of his socks. Jeffrey was behind him with the dogs, who promptly came to the table and settled on the floor, waiting for scraps.

Eddie looked at his wife's stiff back, then at his daughters, obviously sensing the tension. "Car's cleaned," Eddie offered. He seemed to be waiting for something and Sara thought if he was looking for a medal, he had picked the wrong morning.

Cathy cleared her throat, flipping a pancake in the skillet. "Thank you, Eddie."

Sara realized she hadn't told her sister the news. She turned to Tessa. "Jeffrey and I are getting married."

Tessa put her finger in her mouth and used it to make a popping noise. The woo-hoo she uttered was far from ecstatic.

Sara sat back in her chair, resting her feet on Bob's belly. As much crap as she had gotten from her family over the last three years, she thought she at least deserved a hearty handshake.

Cathy asked Jeffrey, "Did you enjoy the chocolate cake I sent you the other night?"

Sara stared down at Bob as if the meaning of life was writ large on his abdomen.

Jeffrey drew out the word, "Ye-ah," giving Sara a cutting look that she felt without having to see. "Best yet."

"I've got more in the fridge if you want it."

"That's great," he told her, his tone sickly sweet. "Thank you."

Sara heard a trilling sound, and it took her a moment to realize Jeffrey's cell phone was ringing. She dug around in his jacket pocket and pulled out the phone, handing it to him.

"Tolliver," he said. He looked confused for a second, then his expression went dark. He walked back into the hall for some privacy. Sara could still hear what he was saying, but there weren't many clues from his side of the conversation. "When did he leave?" he asked. Then, "Are you sure you want to do this?" There was a slight pause before he said, "You're doing the right thing."

Jeffrey returned to the kitchen, making his apologies. "I have to go," he said. "Eddie, do you mind if I borrow your truck?"

Much to Sara's surprise, her father answered, "Keys are by the front door," as if he hadn't spent the last five years hating every bone in Jeffrey's body.

Jeffrey asked, "Sara?"

She grabbed his jacket and walked with him down the hall. "What's going on?"

"That was Lena," he said, excited. "She said Ethan stole a gun from Nan Thomas last night."

"Nan has a gun?" Sara asked. She couldn't imagine the librarian having anything more lethal than a set of pinking shears.

"She said it's in his book bag." Jeffrey took Eddie's keys off the hook by the front door. "He left for work five minutes ago."

She handed him his jacket. "Why is she telling you this?"

"He's still on parole," Jeffrey reminded her, barely able to control his elation. "He'll have to serve his full term—ten more years in jail."

Sara didn't trust any of this. "I don't understand why she called you."

"It doesn't matter why," he said, opening the door. "What matters is he's going back to jail."

Sara felt a stab of fear as he walked down the front steps. "Jeffrey." She waited for him to turn around. All she could think to say was, "Be careful."

He winked at her, as if it was no big deal. "I'll be back in an hour."

"He has a gun."

"So do I," he reminded her, walking toward her father's truck. He waved, as if to shoo her away. "Go on. I'll be back before you know it."

The truck door squeaked open and with great reluctance, she turned to go back inside.

Jeffrey stopped her again, calling, "Mrs. Tolliver?"

Sara turned around, her foolish heart fluttering at the name.

He gave her a crooked smile. "Save me some cake."

ACKNOWLEDGMENTS

At this stage in my career, it'd take a 3,000-page book to thank everyone who has supported me along the way. At the top of any list has to be Victoria Sanders and Kate Elton, who I hope aren't both sick of me by now. I am so grateful to all my friends at Random House here and around the world. Working with Kate Miciak, Nita Taublib and Irwyn Applebaum has been such joy. I feel like the luckiest writer on earth to have these folks on my team and I am so happy that Bantam is my new home. The highest praise I can think to give them is they are people who are passionate about reading.

In the UK, Ron Beard, Richard Cable, Susan Sandon, Mark Mc-Callum, Rob Waddington, Faye Brewster, Georgina Hawtrey-Woore and Gail Rebuck (and everyone in between) continue to be much-loved champions. Rina Gill is the best bossy Sheila a girl could ask for. Wendy Grisham whipped out a Bible in the middle of the night, thus saving everyone in this novel from being named "thingy."

I had the unbelievable experience of going Down Under this past year and I'd like to thank the folks at RH Australia and RH New Zealand for helping make this the trip of a lifetime. You guys made me feel so welcome even though I was a zillion miles from home. I am especially grateful to Jane Alexander for showing me the kangaroos and not warning me until after the fact that sometimes koalas poo when you hold them (photos can be seen at www.karinslaughter.com/australia). Margie Seale and Michael Moynahan deserve high praise indeed. I am humbled by their energetic support.

Further thanks for their support over the years go to Meaghan Dowling, Brian Grogan, Juliette Shapland and Virginia Stanley. Rebecca Keiper, Kim Gombar and Colleen Winters are the cat's pajamas, and I'm so glad for our continued friendship.

Yet again, David Harper, MD, provided me medical information to make Sara sound like she knows what she's doing. Any mistakes are either because I didn't listen to him or because it's just really boring when a doctor does something the right way. On a personal note, I'd like to thank BT, EC, EM, MG and CL for their daily company. FM and JH have been there in a pinch. ML and BB-W loaned me their names (sorry, guys!). Patty O'Ryan was the unfortunate winner of a "Get your name in a Grant County book!" raffle. Ha! That'll teach you to gamble! Benee Knauer has been as solid as a rock. Renny Gonzalez deserves special commendation for his sweet heart. Ann and Nancy Wilson have taken the sting out of getting older — y'all still rock me. My father made me soup when I went to the mountains to write. When I came home, DA was there — as always, you are my heart.